W
E

Nipigon Lodge
Windlass for pulling boats
The Hollow
Montgomery's Tavern
Barricade
THE BUSH
YONGE ST.
Gallows Hill
Davenport Rd.
Don R.
Toll gate
BLOOR ST.
COLLEGE PARK
Sharp House
Jarvis' Picket
Elmsley Estate
Trafalgar Lodge
COLLEGE AVE
LIBERTIES
CITY LIMITS
Toll gate
QUEEN ST.
to Kingston
DUCHESS ST.
Jail & Court h.
St. James
DUKE ST.
YONGE ST.
CHURCH ST.
JARVIS ST.
KING ST.
Coffin Block
Goderham's Mill
Don R.
McDonald's Pier
RIO

BRIGHT TO THE WANDERER

BRIGHT TO THE WANDERER

BY BRUCE LANCASTER

AN ATLANTIC MONTHLY PRESS BOOK

LITTLE, BROWN AND COMPANY · BOSTON

1942

CL

PRINTED IN THE UNITED STATES OF AMERICA

For My Wife

JESSIE PAYNE LANCASTER

to whom both book and author owe a debt far beyond the limits of words

Foreword and Acknowledgment

THE whole story of the Upper Canada Rebellion of 1837 may not be told in a single volume. This book attempts to set out only those things which a given family in Toronto — the Stensroods — might conceivably have experienced in those days when the future of all Canada — and indirectly of all North America — was cast. Readers, particularly those in Canada, will realize that many facets exist which could not be touched upon. A family or an individual, living in the Huron Tract, about Niagara, or near the Thousand Islands, while caught up in the same stream, would have been subjected to different influences and been reacted on by different forces than those which are set forth here as peculiar to one group or one locality.

The main course of events, as set down in the chronicles of the times, has been closely followed, although minor liberties have been taken with certain movements of historical characters. As to the interpretation of events, that is a matter of opinion. This work was undertaken without any preconceived ideas or theories and its completion reflects the impression left on me by the writings of the times and later studies.

There are many acknowledgments to be made. The principal one, which can only be an understatement no matter how often it may be made, or at what length, will be found in the dedication.

North of our border, there are many people to whose thought, understanding, and co-operation this book owes much.

William Arthur Deacon, of Toronto, first suggested the setting, gave unstintingly from his own wide knowledge, recommended sources, put us in touch with other authorities on Canadian history, life, and lore.

Charles W. Jefferys, Royal Canadian Academy, of York Mills, Ontario, gifted artist and tireless scholar, put at our disposal his great knowledge, unwritten, written, painted, and sketched. When we returned to Cambridge, he sent, in answer to my incessant questions, a stream of notes, suggestions, and observations.

Charles R. Sanderson, Chief Librarian of the Toronto Public Library, was unsparing of his time, thought, and encouragement. His fine staff was co-operative and helpful.

I am also indebted to Professor W. B. Kerr, of the University of Buffalo, for much material generously sent me out of his valuable researches, and to Professor Fred Landon and Mr. J. J. Talman of the University of Western Ontario for data which I could not otherwise have found.

On our own side of the border, the Harvard College Library has provided a rich source of Canadiana and has always been ready with suggestions and recommendations.

The title of this book I owe to Melville Fuller Weston, of Cambridge, who allowed me to borrow the line from one of his fine poems.

And to Chester Kerr, Director of the Atlantic Monthly Press, is due a special tribute for constant encouragement during the writing and for the ablest of editorial guidance when the completed draft was presented.

B. L.

Cambridge, Massachusetts
January, 1942

CONTENTS

BRIGHT TO THE WANDERER

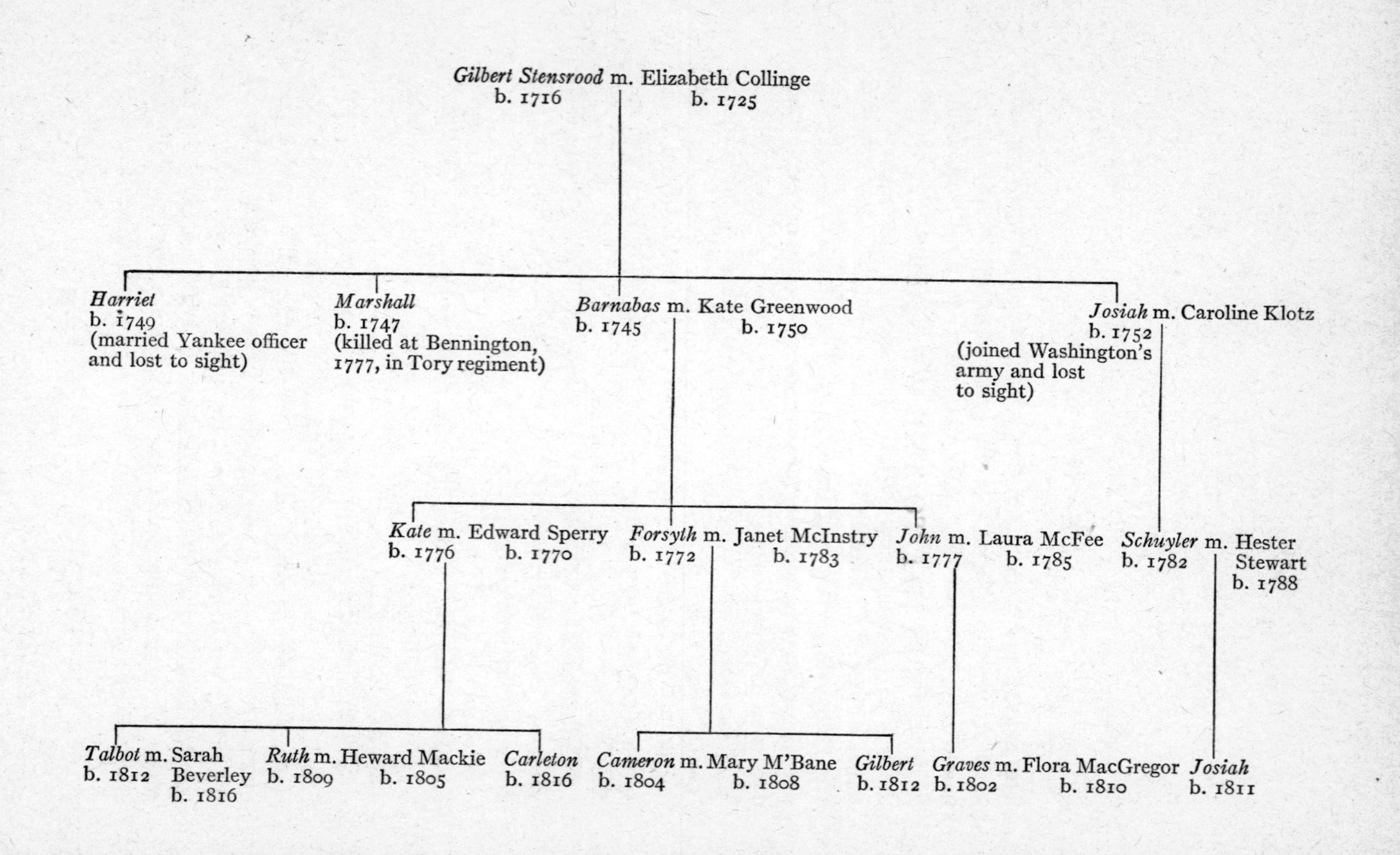

Gilbert Stensrood m. Elizabeth Collinge
b. 1716 b. 1725
Harriet
b. 1749
(married Yankee officer and lost to sight)
Marshall
b. 1747
(killed at Bennington, 1777, in Tory regiment)
Barnabas m. Kate Greenwood
b. 1745 b. 1750
Josiah m. Caroline Klotz
b. 1752
(joined Washington's army and lost to sight)
Kate m. Edward Sperry
b. 1776 b. 1770
Forsyth m. Janet McInstry
b. 1772 b. 1783
John m. Laura McFee
b. 1777 b. 1785
Schuyler m. Hester Stewart
b. 1782 b. 1788
Talbot m. Sarah Beverley
b. 1812 b. 1816
Ruth m. Heward Mackie
b. 1809 b. 1805
Carleton
b. 1816
Cameron m. Mary M'Bane
b. 1804 b. 1808
Gilbert
b. 1812
Graves m. Flora MacGregor
b. 1802 b. 1810
Josiah
b. 1811

I

Flight — 1781

THE gale seemed to pause for breath and falling snow eddied aimlessly among the wet boles of the forest. Then it struck with renewed fury, drove the sharp flakes whistling out of the west, drilled them against the black trees, spread them in a hard powder over the ruts of the wilderness trail, whirled them spattering over the sullen waters of Champlain that tossed dully, lead under a leaden sky. Gilbert Stensrood bent his gray head to the blast, gripped his staff tighter in mittened fingers, and tried to spread the slack of his coat over the shoulders of his wife, who plodded painfully beside him. She looked up, wan face wet with snow, and forced a smile. "Don't, Gil. You need it. I'm warm in my shawl. And the bundle — " she moved her elbows under the green and red plaid and a shapeless mass shifted — "the bundle helps keep out the cold."

He frowned, heavy eyebrows snow-crusted, started to protest. Then her slight body wavered and she stumbled against him. He threw an arm about her. "Here, here! Time to rest."

Gray eyes looked up at him, compressed lips quivered. She shook her head. "We *must* keep going. We must."

His arm tightened. "We can't keep going if we don't rest. Beth, your lips are blue."

"I'm all right. If I could just catch my breath. If — "

But Gilbert was already striding away through the ankle-deep snow, solid legs sturdy in gray wool stockings. The capes of his green coat flapped and heaved to the gale as he tore branches in splintering wreckage from a low pine and threw them hissing onto the dry snow, banked others against the lichened shelter of a great rock. "Sit here in the lee, Beth." His voice echoed flatly in the shifting white curtain. "That's it. Pull your shawl tighter."

He knelt by her, slid the cords of the bundle from her shoulders, rubbed her thin hands, frail in their wool coverings, blanketed her snugly in the heavy folds of the shawl. She leaned back against a padding of boughs, her feet, huge in their burlap wrappings, black against the snow. "Oooh! It's good! Just to rest my back against something." She threw back the cowl of her plaid, brushed snow from her mass of soft dark hair, gray-streaked. Then she closed her eyes.

Gilbert ducked through a sling that held an oblong leather box about his neck. His burden thudded solidly on the boughs as he studied his wife, steel-blue eyes troubled. "Beth, you'd better try my boots again. That sacking's nearly — "

Eyes still closed, she shook her head. "No good. They gave me blisters. Not healed yet." She huddled the shawl closer about her. "Any sign of the others?"

He peered south down the vista of broken snow and pitiless, naked trees. "Trail's empty. They can't be far behind, though. We'll wait till they catch up." He turned his hawklike nose toward his wife. "Feeling better?"

She nodded. "My legs feel as if they were melting. But they don't get stiff the way they did." She drew her delicately marked eyebrows together. "Gil — how much food have we left?"

He scrabbled in the snow with his staff. "Two — maybe three days, if we're careful." Then the lines about his firm mouth and chin softened. "But we won't need that much, I'm sure. We're bound to come on a post any time now. Might even run onto one today." He drew a deep breath. "*Then* we'll be all right." His staff prodded again, struck against a buried log. "H'm, more corduroy. We must be walking on one of the roads that Burgoyne built in '77."

She opened her eyes, then closed them wearily. "If he *only* had — "

There was a short nod. "If — but we're not talking about that."

She rode over his interruption. "Then it wouldn't have happened." Her voice quivered. "Oh, Gil, *why* did they have to do it? You didn't deserve it. You've always been — "

Gently he stroked her hand, brushed snow from her knees. "Just as soon as we reach a post, it'll be all over — all over. Just — " He raised his head, the motion sending a thin cascade of snow from his cocked hat. "Listen!"

Through the weaving pall of white came a slow, measured clop-clop-clop, storm-muffled. He struggled stiffly to his feet. "A sleigh, or we'd hear the wheels bumping."

In the half-light a bulk showed in irresolute outlines, grew solid, grew larger. He made out a plodding horse, a high-piled sleigh, a hunched figure scuffing by it. He held up his hand as the shapes drew nearer and a man, his battered hat bound down by a dirty cloth, stared through storm-reddened eyes and growled: "What you want?"

"Have you seen — "

There was a gasp from under the sodden felt. "God damn! It's the Judge!" A torn mitten jabbed at the ragged hat brim. "My duty to you, sir. Ain't seen you good in this light an' anyways wasn't expectin' — " Then pent-up amazement burst through respect. "What you doin' way up here, sir? An' your lady!" He jabbed at his hat again. "Settin' in the snow! What — what you *doin'* here?"

The other smiled wryly. "The same thing you are."

Mittened hands worked in perplexity. "But you! Everybody knowed Judge Stensrood! Ain't you got that carriage? Where's the black man that used to drive you to Albany?"

Again the wry smile. "Where's your big wagon? Where are those bays you bought last year?" With his staff Gilbert pointed at the rickety sleigh with its roof of canvas, at the wheezing, bony horse that slumped in the shafts, head down to the storm.

Red eyes stared, a wide mouth gaped. "Well — so that's a fac'! So that's a fac'! I wouldn't a believed it if I ain't seen it. No, sir! That I wouldn't."

"Hmph. You and I've seen a lot of things in the past five years we wouldn't have believed without seeing." He turned toward the rock. "Beth, my dear, you remember Tom Fulton? From Glens Falls way?" Fulton bobbed his head. "Tom, you didn't see my son on the trail, did you?"

"Mister Barnabas? That I didn't. No one but some poor folk. The man was pullin' a hand sled an' his woman was carryin' a bundle an' they had one shaver ridin' on the sled an' two walkin'."

Gilbert spoke quickly. "That was Barnabas. Our food and bedding are on the sled."

"Food? For the seven of you? An' beddin'?" Fulton dove at the tattered canvas that stretched over the splintery sides of the sleigh.

There were subdued clucks and squawks that were suddenly cut through by the cry of an awakening baby and the muffled, angry voice of a woman. Then broken boots treaded the air as Fulton's ample posterior hunched backward from under the canvas. Stifled words sifted out into the bitter air: "But I tell you it's him. Him an' his lady. Ain't he saved our farm for us?" There was a tired assent and Fulton tramped proudly back, a sacking-wrapped bundle in his arms.

"We're movin' faster'n you an' you *ain't* got enough for seven. No, you ain't. I got ample. Just me an' Samanthy an' little Tom." He thrust the bundle at the Judge. "No, I ain't wantin' thanks. An' I'd be proud could I ask you to ride with us. But the missus is ailin' an' everything we've got's heaped on the sleigh an' the horse about beat. I'd be proud. You done things for poor folks all your life an' now poor folks got a chance to do something for you, an' high time, I say." He ducked his head to Beth, shouted to his horse, who, with twitching ears, flopped his flat hoofs on through the snow in unfathomable indifference. By a bend in the trail, Fulton turned, called: "I'll speak the first post I come to. Likely they'll send horses for folk like you."

Gilbert watched the sleigh work out of sight, then pitched the sacking onto the snow. "Bacon! That much more for the children." He sat down beside his wife. "There goes another good man."

She opened her eyes. "Why did he give it to you?"

"Because he's a good man." His mouth set. "Yes, a good man. I watched him take bad land and make a good farm out of it." He shrugged. "Well — *he's* gone."

"I don't remember him."

"No reason why you should. Back in '68 — no, it was '70 — I helped him prove his title against forged papers and a good deal of undue influence. He kept the farm. Now — " He shrugged again, stared at the fresh ruts that cut away to the north.

She made a helpless gesture. "You did so much good in the Valley. How could Valley men have — " She started, stared south through the flakes that were driving less fiercely now. Two black figures wavered and shifted. She leaned forward eagerly. "There they are!"

Through the thinning fall the figures drew nearer — a tall, wide-shouldered man in a long, caped overcoat, straining at the tongue of a hand sled, a slimmer figure by his side, back bowed by a sagging bundle while one free hand steadied a little form perched on the high-piled sled. Behind, two children wrapped beyond recognition stumbled dully on, heads jerking and hands clutching at cords fastened to the load.

Gilbert clumped heavily to meet them. The toiling man looked up unsmiling, then ducked his head and increased his pace, clots of snow flying before him. His labored voice sounded thin in the forest hush. "Hello, Father. You and Mother rested? I want to push on."

A shrill treble cry broke out. The child slid from the load, ran on stumpy legs calling: "It's Grampa!" The two behind the sled, a thin boy and his round-faced sister, dropped their cords and shuffled stiffly to him, looking up in mute, bewildered inquiry. Shrilly the smallest piped: "We almost home? Want to feed my rabbits."

Gilbert's mouth softened. He picked him up and set him on his shoulder. "Almost home, John." Then he gravely studied the shawled woman, noting the dark-circled eyes, cheeks grayish under the false flush of the cold. "Sure you don't want to rest, Kate?"

She shook her head, pretty in spite of weariness. "I don't dare. When I stop, my feet ache so. We gave the children a long rest at noon." She settled a wool scarf about the neck of the child on Gilbert's shoulder. "And John's been riding most of the way. Oh — " her voice grew solicitous as Beth crunched toward them over the snow — "you ought to have rested till we caught up. You were so tired yesterday."

Beth laughed. "I had to come and see my little man." She held out her arms and John wriggled to her from Gilbert's shoulder, sturdily shod feet drumming against her bundle.

Barnabas, panting, narrowed his deep-set gray eyes. "Mother — not John and all that load."

She rubbed her cheek against the boy's. "I'd carry two of him." She looked down at the other children. "Forsyth, you've been watching little Kate?"

Forsyth frowned at his sister from the immeasurable height of his nine years. "She wants to walk all the time. Just because she's a year older than John she thinks she's too big to ride."

A snub nose wrinkled over the edge of a fur collar. "I *am* too big.

Father can't pull John *and* me." She tossed her head and a sodden doll whose arms were tied about her neck bobbed wildly. "An' besides we're almost home, aren't we, Grampa?"

From Beth's arms John chorused, "Almost home. Want to feed my rabbits."

His mother cut in quickly. "Grampa knows when we'll get there. Just you keep warm and don't worry about home." Her mouth tightened. She found Forsyth's eyes on her in troubled query. Gilbert coughed, then said shortly, "Better move. Day's getting on."

Barnabas nodded, tugged at the tongue, arms straining out behind his back. Gilbert plodded to the rock, caught up the leather box and Tom Fulton's bacon, wedged them under the canvas cover. "There. Want me to haul, Barney?"

"I'm in the swing of it." His face, a younger replica of his father's save for the eyes, jutted into the storm as his neck and shoulders settled to the pull of the sled. Gilbert fell into step with him. Slowly they padded on, talk scant and sparing.

"See Tom Fulton? He passed you back there."

"A sleigh went by. Didn't look up."

"Gave us a slab of bacon."

"That'll help."

"A lot. How did you catch up with us so quickly?"

"Hitched onto a sleigh back there."

"Whose?"

"Don't know. Took us a few miles, then turned off on that west trail."

"H'm, not sure that's safe, trusting yourself to a stranger. We've come a long way, what with that cart and the sloop up the lake. But you can't tell, even up here. If that man spread the word and people took after us, mounted—" The wrinkles deepened about his mouth.

"Had to take the chance. Worried about Kate. Hasn't enough clothes."

"Only the children have. Thank God, they'll be able to keep warm. I still don't see how you got through with their extra things, even to little Kate's doll. Wood keeping dry?"

"Have to watch. And the bedding. Snow cakes on the runners. Works up under the canvas. Why couldn't that damned sloop have taken us right up the Richelieu instead of dumping us by Valcour Island?"

"Glad we got as far as we did. That much nearer a post."

"Can't understand why we haven't met one by now. Well, let's not talk. Need my breath."

In the white silence of the forest they worked north. The snow thinned out, died away, and a cutting wind blew dry and bitter. The trail twisted on by the sullen lake, now slanting down a harsh ravine, now lying flat under the numbing quiet of the trees. Beth and Kate walked on either side of the sled, to whose load they had added little Kate, while Forsyth, trying desperately to master hunger, cold, and nameless fear, tramped on behind, crying quietly to himself.

The trees spaced wider, closed in again. The forest slowly dimmed about them. Suddenly Barnabas raised his head, sniffed, then called hoarsely, "A fire!" His voice dropped almost reverently. "The post!"

Gilbert stared and the mask of worry and fatigue slipped from his face. His lungs worked spasmodically. He flung up his hand. "Beth! Kate! The post!"

Like a sob their answer came to him. "The post! We've won through!" Beth laughed shakily as Barnabas shouted: "Hallo! The post!" Then she and Kate began ordering the children's thick wrappings, talking swiftly, bright-eyed. Gilbert dropped back, chuckled at John, and shoved at the rear of the sled. On the load John blinked, stirred. "We home now?"

"Home?" Gilbert's voice rang happily. "Home—under His Majesty's colors. That's it, Fors, shove with me. Home at last."

"There's smoke! In a hut!" Barnabas's voice was unsteady.

There was movement by the huddled shack under the trees, a man slouched out toward the trail and stood facing south, heavy musket held easily across his thighs. Soon Gilbert could make out a skullcap, brass-fronted, worn red facings on a green jacket, leather leggings, moccasins. He ran ahead, holding up his hand. "Where's your officer? We're King's people. We want to push on to Sorel or Verchères."

The thin face was impassive. The tight mouth opened slightly. "You can't."

Gilbert stared. "We *can't!*" His eyes narrowed. "I know that uniform. You're a Johnson Ranger. I knew Sir William and Sir John."

The man spat. "Maybe you knew 'em. But you ain't goin' north."

Rage swelled in Gilbert's chest. "Barney! You hear that?"

Panting, Barnabas nodded, checked the sled. The women drew up on either side. He wiped his forehead. "See here, my man. This is a mistake. This is my father, a Crown Judge. We're King's people."

The heavy musket shifted in mittened hands. "No one can't go north."

Beth tossed back the shawl from her handsome head, smiled at the gaunt man. "Of course you've orders. But call your officer. I know he'll let us through."

The leather cap shook. "I'm in charge."

Gilbert shook his head in exasperation. "But who gave you those orders?"

"*I'm* givin' 'em to you. But if you want to know, they're General Haldimand's."

A curtain of ice settled over the Stensroods. Gilbert stammered. "But General Haldimand—I *know* him. If he heard, he'd—Good God, man, what are we going to do?"

The Ranger dropped the butt of his musket in the snow, cupped his hands over the muzzle. "I know what you *could* a done. You ain't too old to a fit." Cold eyes rested on Barnabas. "Sure God *you* ain't. Now when it's gettin' over, you ask *me* what to do. I ain't had to ask no one what to do when it started." He leaned on his musket. "I'll tell you something. General gave them orders 'cause they's too many folks like you that wouldn't fight when you c'd a, a-comin' to us now. Major Nairne's got so many like you to the head of the Richelieu that he can't ration 'em, can't bed 'em. No more goes till Haldimand says so. Now I'll tell you something else. What you can do. You can go back where you came from—if you dast. Or you can turn an' hit for the trail that runs west 'bout two mile back. Follow it an' mebbe you'll find a post that'll let you by. But you won't never get to the Richelieu."

Barnabas dropped the tongue of the sled. "You've got to let us by. Damn it, can't you see we've women and children with us?"

"I see 'em."

Gilbert checked Barnabas's forward stride. "That's no use. He's got his orders." He rallied himself. "At least you'll let the women and children spend the night in the hut. It's getting late."

"No room. I bed down five Rangers there. No orders 'bout you."

Barnabas's voice was thick, his face a flushed mask of anger. "But I tell you, my father was a Crown Judge. *You* can't talk to him like— "

The man spat again. "He *was* a Judge. Mebbe. Don't look like one now." His eyes were scornful on travel-stained clothes, on Beth's wrapped feet. "Better get movin' or you'll miss the turn in the dark. An' I'm watchin' here to see you ain't doublin' back past me."

Wearily Gilbert tugged at the sled, headed it around south. Barnabas made a wild gesture, then snatched the tongue of the sled from his father and stamped off through the snow, the others trailing after him in silence. From the load a thin voice called fretfully, "Almost home?"

Beth's arm slipped about the little shoulders, her wrapped fingers soothed the round, puckered cheeks. "Almost home. That man —that man just told us a better way to go." Her voice hung in the cold air, gentle and reassuring. "He's helping us, so we'll be home much sooner."

To the quiet rhythm of her tone, the trampling feet suddenly found a surer tread, beat resolute and crisp into the crust as, ahead of them, thickening dusk flowed pitilessly onto the trail. Gilbert's eyes turned back to the sled where John, already nodding, rested his head confidently against his grandmother's supporting arm.

They found the western trail, followed it until Barnabas could no longer see the guiding ruts. Then they hacked pine boughs, built a shelter against the night. With a miserly hand Gilbert drew out precious dry wood from the sled. Meager bits of salt pork were cooked, eaten in silence. Then exhaustion mercifully settled over them and their bodies slept. Only Barnabas kept watch, skillfully nursing the fire with an eye always on the dark mouth of the shelter, quick to tuck in a blanket tossed off by restless arm or leg.

Bodies slept, but minds gnawed and worried at memories which waking moments barred fiercely. Beth Stensrood stirred, moaned, as tragic pictures rose before her, pictures that showed a ruddy glare over the black shoulder of a hill, telling of the fiery torment of the broad house by the Hudson where she had come as a bride, where she had borne her children. Now the home was gone, with all the children save Barnabas. Marshall, savagely for the King, lay somewhere along the Walloomsac, caught up in the red wreck of Baum's dragoons. Harriet, only daughter, was lost in sullen devotion to her husband, one of Stark's men. And Josiah, petted imp of the family, had run away to join that man Washington and was, no doubt, part of the army that had shut down on Cornwallis at Yorktown. She sighed, turned in her sleep; saw polished floors; saw a figured box where a cherished India shawl lay in bright folds; saw a deep cradle by a sunny window. Then her mind filled with shadowy clouds of red uniforms, moving to bring the aegis of the King between her and past torments.

The elder Kate, too, was deep in vision-filled sleep. The same flames, the distant yelling of a mob, the crash of axes, possessed her mind. Sharp was the memory of her shivering children, bewildered in a winter midnight. She flinched from the picture of the frightened, furtive man who had rapped on the window at night, warning them to go, go at once. Then a scene of flame surging back pitilessly until she could hear the vicious crackle as heat played over the smooth sheen of the piano in the wide room.

Outside, the watch fire waxed and waned, shot long tongues of light up among the cold branches that netted overhead, drew back in haste as though baffled by the down-pressing darkness. Barnabas, staring into the coals, raised his head sharply as something stirred in the night. Then he nodded, moved over as his father crept out of the shelter, hair as neatly clubbed as on court days.

"All asleep?" asked Barnabas.

"Seem to be. Go in. I'll watch."

"Can't sleep. Look here, what did you think of that Ranger?"

Gilbert rubbed his chin. "Well, he wasn't very mannerly. And of course he looked down on us as noncombatants. It'll be different when we meet a real King's officer."

Barnabas kicked savagely at an ember. "I've been thinking all along that as soon as we reached a King's post, we'd be all right. I want Mother and Kate looked after properly. They've come so far with so little. I don't know how they managed to laugh so the children wouldn't know what had happened. I couldn't have done it. I felt sick. Actually sick."

Gilbert smiled quietly. "Kate's a fine girl. And I've always been prejudiced in favor of your mother."

"They were wonderful. But—this trail to the west. It'll take us to the St. Lawrence way above the mouth of the Richelieu. We can't tell how far we'll have to go to reach another post. I tell you, I'm worried about Mother and Kate. They aren't dressed for it, fed for it." He studied the fire somberly. "I'm beginning to think you were right. We ought to have gone to New York when we had the chance. Then we could have taken passage for England."

"No. You were right in holding out then. Here's where we belong. If the Crown makes peace with the rebels, we'll be looked after, we who stayed by the King."

"Hope so." Barnabas carefully slid another log onto the fire. "Father, this is about the first chance we've had to talk since we started. What do you think set the mob off? Yorktown?"

"H'm—yes. I'd say so. It looked like the end and so there was nothing to hold the ultras in check. The moderates never wanted to bother us, but those others!" He puffed out his cheeks. "They wanted our property. I guess Nat Ogilby'll bid it in. And he'll be very severe with the leaders for letting the house burn. Nat always envied us that house."

Barnabas sprang to his feet. "God damn him! *He* stirred up the mob. He—"

Gilbert reached up, pulled him back by the skirts of his coat. "Remember, Barney, Nat and his like can't beat us. But we can whip ourselves if we think back into the past. We agreed—"

"I know. I know." Barnabas crouched by the blaze again. "We've got to look ahead—ahead only." He leaned his chin on his knees, scowling. "We'd planned to take stock of things when we got to Nairne's camp at Verchères. We're not going there, now. It changes—"

Gilbert stretched his legs to the fire. "You know, in a way I'm rather grateful to that Ranger. There'd have been a lot of people like us, probably people we know, at Verchères, but that's in Lower Canada where all the French are. That would have been hard. They've their own society, language, laws, church, officials, and so on. But Upper Canada, the Ontario country, will be different. There aren't many people there. Trained men ought to be at a premium. I'm sure my old judgeship will place me. You stood high at the New York bar. Maybe they'll make you a judge out of hand. Thirty-six is none too young in a new country." He rubbed his knees gently. "Yes, as soon as we're under the Crown again, everything'll be all right." He rose, stamped about in the snow, sniffing. "H'm, smells like a thaw."

"God forbid. We might have to leave the sled and break up the load into bundles. That sled's about saved our lives. And yet the man at Fort Miller who gave it to us is a red-hot rebel."

Gilbert stretched. "If there'd been three of him, he'd have raised the countryside against us. Being alone, he dared to be human. Now go to bed. I'll mind the fire."

The thaw ended abruptly during the noon halt of the second day and a needle-sharp wind turned the whitish slop into a treacherous pavement that made walking a torment. At first, feet broke through the knifelike skin that cut leg and ankle. Then it grew more solid and the party staggered and slipped, panting and sweating under a coppery, heatless sun. There was little talk around the sled where Gilbert, harnessed with cords, struggled on with Barnabas. Like the men, the women and Forsyth concentrated on the secure placing of each foot while little Kate and John stared in wonder from their perch. Once they passed two women and a man, resting under the lip of a low cliff, heads bowed and eyes on the cruel ground, heedless of Gilbert's weary hail. By a brook, whose snow-smothered bridge of logs tricked feet and runners with almost human malevolence, they saw traces of other runners, wheels, found discarded sacking that Gilbert seized and bound over the worn rags on his wife's feet. Now and again black smudges showed where others before them had camped or rested. At such spots Forsyth was sent to scuff about in search of some jettisoned bit that might ease the journey. But those who traveled the western trail had been frugal and the trampled snow gave back only the unclean litter of hasty camp or uneasy rest.

The afternoon wore on and clouds began to bank in the west. By a gray rock ledge, Barnabas suddenly stopped, held up his hand. Gilbert looked at him in weary surprise. The women, grateful for the halt, leaned against the sled. Through stiff, chilled lips Gilbert muttered: "What is it?"

Barnabas tilted his head. "Listen. It echoes."

"Echoes? What echoes?" Gilbert seemed impatient.

"Hear it? Off this ledge. Kate, Mother—please keep still."

Then through the ageless hush of the forest they heard it—a faint, ghostly pattering that seemed to well out of the wet rocks. Gilbert nodded. "Yes—I've got it. Rain? Can't be."

Beth whispered: "Deer! I've heard them run like that through the woods by the Batten Kill. Venison! If you only had your musket!"

Barnabas shook his head. "No. No. Listen again. There's a rhythm. It's—"

Gilbert's eyes narrowed. His voice, strangled, forced out the word: "Drums!"

"Drums!" Barnabas waved his arms. "Drums! Off there to the right! Echoing back from the rocks. Drums! No damned Rangers! King's troops!"

The women stared at him, unbelieving. Then Beth sat quietly on the sled, an arm about John, gently stroking his head as she looked north, trying to pierce through the thick wall of trees that hemmed them in. Across the load, Kate crooned wordlessly to her daughter, settled her hair under its fur cap, folded and refolded the scarf about the child's plump throat, unseeing. From the rear Forsyth tramped up to join the men, planted his feet wide apart and stared along the trail in cool appraisal, leaving the emotions of the moment to the women and children.

Then Gilbert drew a long breath. "Can't be far, Barney." He caught his son's eye, chuckled.

Barnabas answered the laughter. "Not far. We're through." He rested one hand on Gilbert's shoulder, the other on Forsyth's. "The Stensrood men and women, eh?"

"That's it." Gilbert chuckled again. "Here we are." He squared his shoulders, settled them into the galling harness. His voice rang under the bare boughs. "Beth! Kate! Here go the Stensroods."

There was a deep hollow, a killing grade. Then a twisting track that skirted wet, oozing rocks and finally led out onto the bare shoulder of a hill where they stopped, staring at the slip and toss of the wide St. Lawrence, bright in the dying day, at the tight blockhouse by the shore and at the men in red who filed away through a narrow gate like a bloody sword slowly sheathing. Over all fluttered the King's colors, fluttered and snapped to the voice of the muttering drums.

Gilbert's face worked. He tried to speak, then grimly set his strength against the weight of the sled. Barnabas smeared his cuff across his eyes, matched his father's pace. Behind, he heard his wife's voice, oddly muffled. "Look, John. The flag! We're home!"

The clearing outside the stockade was a welter of trampled snow and mud, stiff-frozen, between scattered stumps, as Gilbert and Barnabas dragged the sled out of the last patch of woods. Before them the blockhouse loomed, and beyond it ran the broad ruffle of the St. Lawrence, stretching away to the lift of the pines on the distant northern shore. Gilbert panted, "We'll find the commandant."

Barnabas jerked his head toward a file of light infantrymen, green facings on their red jackets, who wheeled into line before neat huts. "Sergeant in charge. Going to dismiss the men. Ask him as soon as he's through. Look — this hut's empty. The others can sit there until we find where to go."

The sled swung to the left, grated over the frozen mud, and halted before the hut. Barnabas ducked through the low door, then his voice floated out. "Clean and tight." Gilbert slid out of the harness, peered into the dim shelter. "Lucky! Room for all. I'll — "

Outside a voice rasped: "Here, you men can't go in there! Sergeant Gratton! What d'you mean, letting these people muck about in my huts?"

Gilbert flushed, backed out, Barnabas at his elbow. They found a bony, long-faced man in red staring with distaste at the group about the sled. A thin-lipped, twisted mouth opened. "I said, you can't go in there!"

Gilbert eyed the tarnished lace of the cocked hat, saw the bulge of the shoulder knot under the red cloak. "Captain? Or is it Major? I was merely going to shelter my family here until I could find you. I'm Gilbert Stensrood, a Crown Judge, and I — "

Hard lines about the eyes smoothed away. "Judge, eh? His

Majesty's Courts? You're well away, sir. Stensrood? From Lincolnshire?"

Relief settled over Gilbert. "Nottinghamshire, originally. But my people have been settled near Albany for a long time."

The lines etched over the long face again. "Ho! Colonial, are you? Well, you can't use my huts."

"This is scarcely the tone I expected from one of His Majesty's officers. We're King's people, driven from Albany. It's been a long road."

Two dim shadows fell across the ground. Beth and Kate, each carrying a child, drew up by Gilbert and the glowering man. Beth spoke. "The children have been sleeping in the snow ever since we started out."

Irritable eyebrows flicked up, impatient. Then hard eyes turned on Gilbert. "Now look here. This is His Majesty's post. I'm responsible for it. I've got no orders about you people. I have about the post and the men. That's all I know."

Gilbert stared. "No orders? But all we want—"

"All you want is for me to move the men out into the woods and turn their rations over to you. I know. I've got nearly thirty of you Colonials begging around my door. You all want the same. Give you an inch and you'll yell for the whole damned continent. You—"

"Just a moment, Major." Gilbert's voice was edged.

"Captain. Captain Manson of the Thirty-fourth."

"Well, Captain, then. As King's people we call on you to help us. We do need food. We do need shelter. You refuse. I suppose you've got your orders. Very well, you're in command here. What shall we do?"

"Do? Do? What you been doing. Just keep it up. Herd your lot in the woods over there with the other runaways. It's off the limits of the post and I'll thank you to stay off. Can't have civilians interfering with troops. Can't—" The clopping of hoofs muffled his words, shouts echoed, and a familiar voice cried, "You can't take him. I need him." The din drew nearer. From a gap between two huts a soldier trotted a gaunt horse while a ragged countryman ran after him. "I need him, I tells you. I—here's the Cap'n. *He* won't let you do that!"

Gilbert stared. "Tom—Tom Fulton! Here—what's the matter?"

Fulton gave a little cluck of relief and ran toward him, battered hat in hand. "The soldiers, sir. They've took my horse. I'd take it kindly if you'd make 'em give him back."

Gilbert's chest tightened, he felt blood pounding back of his eyes. "Is this necessary, Captain? I'd like to know your authority. How—"

Manson turned a red shoulder on the Judge. "You—with the horse! Take him to the sheds. Yes, give the fellow a receipt for him." He swung back to Gilbert. "Now I tell you again I've nothing for you. And you've got to get off the limits of the post. There'll be boats to take you across the river. No, I don't know when and I don't know what you'll do till they do come. The only orders I've got are to embark as many of you people as the boats will hold. Stay in the woods until you're sent for and keep away from the post. Now I'm going to my dinner." He lurched off, flicking angrily at the dirty snow with a switch.

The woods that crowded in on the stumps of the clearing were sharp with the sour reek of wet, lichened rocks and the moldy smell of rotten, trampled moss hung like a thick veil close to the ground. In the shelter of a rude lean-to, cobbled together by some earlier Loyalist, the children slept heavily. Outside, the night woods stirred to the uneasy comings and goings of other refugees, and at the north the St. Lawrence lapped and muttered among the rocks of the shore.

By a dull-flamed fire of wet wood, whose acrid, choking smoke rose in thick wreaths, Gilbert and Barnabas took stock of the remaining supplies. Beth, by her husband's elbow, watched fearfully. Kate, seated on the sled, frowned as she ripped one of the capes from Barnabas's coat to make extra wrappings for John.

Gilbert straightened his back. "About two pounds of pork. How much of Tom's bacon's left?"

"Nearly gone." Beth rubbed her finger tips against her temples. "He tried to give me more when I went to see his wife. He's not got much."

Barnabas fingered a jagged rent in his stocking. "Say half a pound. Then we've some dried apples in that bag. Kate, did all the bread mold?"

She looked up from her ripping. "Yes. The children couldn't eat it."

"Well, if that's all, that's all." Gilbert spread out his hands. "We'll have to — "

Barnabas sprang to his feet. "It's not what *we*'ve got to do. It's that red fool at the fort. He's got plenty of stores. I saw them when I went to the river for water. *He*'s the one who's got to do something." He picked up his sodden hat. "If he won't give, he'll sell. Father — it's time to open the leather box."

Gilbert's head shook. "I went to him when you were at the river. Wouldn't even see me. Shouted his answers to an orderly."

Barnabas's voice rose. "Then by God I'll shake it out of him. I'll — "

"Shake it out of a man with seventy bayonets back of him? And did you see the cells? On the north side and below the level of the river."

Beth's hands were busy with the food. "We'll get through. I don't need as much as I've been eating."

Kate shook out the rank coat. "I'm sure *I* don't. The — the walking keeps me from getting hungry." She raised her head. "Someone's coming."

Through the dark trunks, feet crunched. A shape was silhouetted against a distant fire. Gilbert raised his hand. "If it's Tom Fulton, *don't* let him give — "

The shape drew nearer, a muted voice called, "Ho! You astir?"

Barnabas leaned forward, scowling. "Who's there?"

Weak flames glinted on a brass-fronted cap, lit up a red jacket, played on a sergeant's shoulder knot as a squat man clumped up to the shelter, a heavy kettle swinging from scarred hands. A thick, savory steam seeped into the cold air, its richness almost painful to starved nostrils as the kettle thudded to the ground. The sergeant wiped his hands on his leather breeches, ducked his head to the women. " 'Pears you might need a mossel of this."

Four heads lifted eagerly. Gilbert moistened his lips. "Did — did Captain Manson send this? I couldn't believe he'd not — "

A wooden ladle stirred noisily in the greasy depths. Lumps of meat, solid potatoes, swirled madly to its touch. "You got bowls?"

Kate burrowed in a dark corner, brought out a round, fat pot in trembling hands. "For the children. I've got a cover for it."

The square face lightened. "Nippers? Wake 'em up. Stuff 'em."

Beth shook her head. "They ate before they went to sleep. This will be for morning. Stew! The first food they've had except salt pork and bacon since we left." Her eyes were bright.

"Aye, that'll do for 'em. The dawn ration." His ladle slopped and splashed.

Barnabas eyed the filling pot. "That's it!" He spoke in an eager whisper. "Right up to the brim. Like to wake 'em up now, just to see 'em tuck into it. Eh? Our bowls? That's our only one. We traveled light."

"Most does as comes this way." He shoved the kettle toward Beth, gave her the ladle. "Allus tastes better out a common pot."

Beth put out her hand. "You first, Kate. You've the children — "

Kate shook her head. "I've seen you and Father pretend to eat when you were putting bits aside for them."

Barnabas nodded in silent approval while the sergeant squatted by the fire, watching with grave interest. Gilbert wiped his forehead. "Makes me feel weak, just the smell of it. No, Kate, I'll come after you. Sergeant, I asked you if Captain Manson sent this."

A flat nose wrinkled scornfully. "Not him. The lads to the mess seen you — "

"The soldiers!" Barnabas stared. "Father, they've got to be paid for this. They'll — "

"They won't take nothin'." The broad chin jutted. "Some says as how we're rough. Some says we're hard. I ain't sayin' no to that. But we been seein' a lot of folks comin' in here, folks in rags, folks with holler bellies. So, in the mess we says: 'Maybe we're rough an' maybe we're hard. But so long's rations is issued us, they ain't goin' to be no hungry folk in these woods.' They ain't a man as ain't stowin' away a bit each day out of what's issued him. We lumps what we gets an' we takes it to the woods. Mostly I takes it. If Cap'n heard, it'd only mean my shoulder knot. For the others, it'd be floggin'."

Gilbert leaned his chin in his cupped hand, studied the sergeant's hard face. "They go without so these people won't starve?"

The man scratched his ear, frowning. "It ain't so much, out of seventy-seven men. An' young Ensign Parham, he's down by the river giving rum to sick folks. He does what he can for all he's gentry. But mostly it takes poor folk to look a'ter poor folk. Not as you allus been poor, but you ain't got much to give away now, if you takes my meanin'."

Beth sighed, handed the ladle to Kate. "Your turn, my dear. Sergeant, I still don't see why you *have* to do this, if there are plenty of stores."

"I don't either," frowned Gilbert. "I know enough law to tell you that the captain has full authority to issue Crown stores to needy subjects so long as the troops don't go short."

"He's got enough to vittle a regiment," growled the sergeant.

"Then what's the matter with him?" asked Barnabas angrily.

"Matter? It's 'cause he is what he is. And that's scared."

"Scared?"

"Look at him. Been twenty year a captain. Never a step up in that time. Been a long time in America and always shoved out into the bush, livin' in posts like this. Ain't got friends on the Staff. Ain't got influence. He's sour and he's scared. Sure he could issue stores. But then he'd have to 'count for 'em on paper. Where'd that paper go? To headquarters where he ain't got no friends. No tellin' what might happen to them papers. Might be used to cover somebody on Staff that needed coverin'. Then where'd Manson be? Maybe the cost of the stores stopped out of his pay. Maybe he'd face a court-martial."

Gilbert nodded. "I see. And the law says he *can* issue stores, not that he must. But at least he could have given us shelter."

The sergeant raised his eyebrows. "He don't like civilians. An' with maybe fifty swarmin' round the post, how does he know when there may be damage done to Crown prop'ty? Every time a run-away crosses the clearin', he sweats for fear something'll happen he'll have to pay for." He wagged his head. "No, sir. He'll do for you what he *has* to and that's all."

Gilbert wiped his lips on his sleeve, pushed the kettle to Barnabas. "When I get across the river — "

A scarred forefinger pointed. "When you gets across the river, you'll be tellin' your story to another soldier. Now maybe that soldier don't like Manson, or just don't care. All the same, it'll be civilian against soldier. It'll be Colonial against Britisher, so far's he'll be able to see. An' another thing — if Manson sees anything he wants, he'll take it, same's he done to that feller's horse today. Course, he'll give a bit of paper for it, but let him who's got the paper try to get rations with it across the river! But the post books'll show Cap'n's picked up another horse 'thout costin' the Crown nothin' an' inspectin' officers likes to see such. No, they ain't nothin' you can do. Just—" He stared out into the dark, then jumped to his feet. "That's him now." He pointed to a distant lantern that waved and flickered among the trees. "Out seein' what folks has got that he wants. He ain't findin' *me* here." He snatched the kettle away from Barnabas. "Don't dast let you finish. Dump some stew into some bark or something. Come tomorrow night, me or one of my mates." He slid out of the shelter, melted away in the dark.

Beth wiped her eyes. "Gil, we *can* do something for him and the others."

Gilbert rose, set the covered pot out of the reach of clumsy feet. "We'll find a way. Now everyone to bed. No need to tend the fire, Barney. Perhaps we'll cross in the morning."

Wearily they huddled under their scant covers. The muted clatter of the camp died slowly out, giving way to the steady hiss of the wind in the bare branches. The stars swung up the sky, hard and clear. Then away by the toss and murmur of the great river, a woman's voice soared in sad invocation. Beth stirred, shook her head, tried to shut out the sound that was cracking the web of sleep about her. Far but full the tones hummed in the treetops, piteous and insistent. She raised herself on her elbow, listening, striving to catch the words that melted away, half heard, in the night. The wind died and in the wilderness hush the distant voice seemed to gather strength. The tattered words took shape, were whole and living as though welling up like a mist from the sleeping woods.

"Who watcheth over all, whose eye is never sleeping,
God make the dark night bright to the wanderer!"

The last notes died away and the world was still again. Beth sank back in her blankets, wide-eyed, her throat tight. She looked at her husband by her side, muttering and shifting in his sleep, at the huddle of blankets beyond where Barnabas lay motionless, with John pillowed on his shoulder. "Bright to the wanderer," she thought. "Bright to all wanderers wherever they may be." She lifted a hand to her wet cheeks. "I'm *not* going to think back. I can't. But—oh, Jos—Josiah—where are you?" She drew the blanket about her head, lay silent.

Later Barnabas stirred, drew up his knees. Through the black swathings of his mind a voice bored incessantly. Something tugged at his feet. He growled, shook his head, trying to evade the sound that drew him back to cold and weariness. The voice grew stronger. He roused himself angrily, found the words "Boats is here" beating against his brain. He tumbled from his blankets, wrapping them securely about John, crept to the edge of the shelter, where he saw the sergeant, lantern held high, with two privates shivering close at his elbow. "Huh? What's that? What?"

"The boats. Cap'n gives you fifteen minutes to get to the river."

"Boats? Why, can't be. Not morning yet."

"Mornin'! Ain't gone midnight. But they're here."

Barnabas shook his head. "Wait till tomorrow. Too tired now."

"No, you won't wait till tomorrer. Cap'n writ your names on the list. If you don't go now, you'll wait a long time afore you gets another chance. Hurry. Fifteen minutes ain't long."

Barnabas swore helplessly, crept over, and shook his father as the sergeant growled on. "Course 'e knowed it. Course 'e c'd a told you. But not 'im. 'E'd rather think of you beddin' down and then routin' you out. Hurry. I'm callin' the others as is goin'." He tramped off, lantern swinging.

Gilbert sat up, dazed, as Barnabas gently roused the women. John, frightened by the darkness and the sudden stir, began to cry, dully, monotonously. Barnabas settled the wrappings about him, turned to Gilbert. "It's not far to the river. Will you take the tongue? I'll get into your harness. I'll have my hands free." Gilbert nodded, fumbled for his boots with stiff fingers. John cried on, rigid and shivering. Barnabas hunched into the harness, talking softly. "There, that's the little man. Slip your arm around my neck. How's that? Now hold on. Know where we're going? Father and his big man? We're going out on a boat, just the way we went that time on the Hudson, spearing fish with all the torches. Couldn't go without you, could I, John? Remember? You sat by me and held the big spear for me. There, that's it, that's my man. Now, Father — ready?"

By the lift and ruffle of the great river two wide bateaux nosed at a log landing while wiry French oarsmen thrashed their arms and stamped about under a curtain of stars. Far on the opposite shore a pin point of light glowed steadily against the black loom of unseen pines. The Stensroods, last of a thin trickle of fugitives moving out from the rocking trees, felt the logs of the wharf under their feet, blinked in the flare of grimy lanterns as Manson's voice rasped over the water. "Move, you men! Think I want to stay up all night? Can't be kept waiting like this. You, there! You can't get in that boat. Full now. *I* say it's full and I don't care if your wife *is* in it. Get in the other boat or you'll bloody well swim. Sergeant, shove him into that boat!"

Gilbert muttered, "Barney! Keep quiet and do exactly as he says. Don't argue. Beth, Kate! Keep close to us. Forsyth, hold your mother's cape." He raised his voice. "Thank you, Captain. We're ready."

Lanterns threw blotches of shifting red on the uniform that moved toward them, picked out stained gold on the hat. "Ready? You're ready as soon as I say so. Now—leave that sled. Don't load it."

"The sled?" Barnabas, heedless of the now sleeping John, burst out in a rage. "There's plenty of room for it. We'll need it on the other side."

Manson's mouth tightened. "I need it on *this* side. You boatmen! Don't load that sled." He motioned roughly to Gilbert. "Get on board."

With unsteady knees they climbed into the wide, flat-bottomed boat while Barnabas, swearing under his breath, passed John to his mother and began unloading the sled, stowing the scanty goods under the plank seat. "There," he muttered. "All away, Father. Damn that captain. We could take ten more people in these boats. Dozens still on shore. See Fulton?"

"Shh! No. Other boat perhaps. Now—we'll be off!"

In the darkness huddled shapes sat drooping and silent, looked apprehensively over their shoulders. There was a sharp bark from Manson and the first bateau pushed out, hung in the current, then nosed upstream as six oars cut whitely into the water. In the second craft the headman uttered a weird cry. Oars bit deep into the heavy drift of the stream and the blunt bow edged out. The boat shivered as it met the full force of the current, then turned west in the wake of its mate.

A hoarse howl boomed from the landing. Something scraped and bumped over the logs, fell with a muffled smack into the river.

Manson's wrath spattered over the waves. "The sled! God damn it, you've got my sled!"

The headman, stern oar under his arm, shrugged. "Wot 'e talk 'bout *traîneau,* eh? 'Bout sled? I not know wot 'e say." He spat. "*Sacré voleur anglais! Sacré capitaine!*" He turned his back to the wake of the boat where a taut line hissed and something flat and dark bobbed along, half submerged.

Barnabas gripped Gilbert's arm. "Hear that? The Frenchman — he saved the sled!"

Gilbert nodded. "I didn't dare believe it. But there it is." He tucked Beth's shawl tighter about her. "All right, my dear?"

Eyes closed, she nodded, gave to the slow rock of the bateau as the waves, beating on the thick boards, seemed to mark the rhythm of the words that flowed through her mind: "God make the dark night bright to the wanderer."

Gilbert, mouth grimly set, stared at the reflections of the pines of the known land as they shimmered and flickered in the dull belt of water that widened and widened to the lurch of the river. Then he sighed, turned his eyes toward the cold black belt, blacker than the night, where, strange and comfortless, the towering lift of the trees of the north loomed, menacing. Over their ragged crests a single bright star danced and wavered.

II

Toronto — 1835

The Stensroods settled in the vast tract of English-speaking Canada — Upper Canada — that stretched from the Ottawa River to the utmost rim of western exploration.

This new land was governed in accordance with the usual British system, representative of the people and responsible to the people — in theory. In practice, it reflected a narrower, darker day. There was a Lieutenant Governor sent out from England, selected without regard for the wishes of the people. To advise him, he could appoint an Executive Council of local notables. For the machinery of government, there were the two houses of time-honored pattern, the Legislative Council and the Legislative Assembly. But, as the wheels turned, enlightened theory was transformed into vicious practice. The Executive Council was responsible only to the Lieutenant Governor. The Legislative Council, the higher body, was appointed by that same officer — and for life. The Assembly, chosen by a wide electorate, had few powers and its measures were subject to veto by the irresponsible upper house, by the Lieutenant Governor or the Crown.

Under this system, as the years rolled by, symptoms which the Stensroods and other steady Liberals watched with alarm grew into a disease that swept all Upper Canada. For, with no responsibility, the power and control of this great region passed into the hands of a small group — a clique, ring, which became known as the Family Compact.

Under Compact rule, the key offices of the Province were denied to all save loyal Compact adherents. The courts, thus staffed, rendered decisions favorable to the Compact. Schools were operated primarily for the benefit of Compact sons. The

Church of England, largely unrepresented, allied itself with the Compact and fought all other sects savagely. It also claimed for its endowment one seventh of all the lands of Upper Canada.

To protest against this regime was treason, often bitterly punished. Freedom of speech and of the press was dead.

The public lands, including the huge tracts claimed by the Church of England and known as the Clergy Reserves, were in Compact hands, a condition which encouraged speculation by those in power and choked off immigration.

Among the Family Compact there were many who sincerely believed that such rigid, narrow control was best for the country—that it was a regime divinely ordained. Others, greedy for power, for wealth, fought viciously against any change or enlightenment. And, well- or ill-intentioned, they filled the country with their creatures of whom they asked only loyalty to the Compact. Such loyalty was rewarded from public funds or public lands, for of course the Compact held it was none of the people's business how their money was spent.

So, through the Province, the names of the Compact clans were either bitterly cursed or timidly revered—the Strachans, the Robinsons, the Hagermans, the Powells, the Boultons, the Sherwoods, the Elmsleys, and so on—families whose highest aim seemed the perpetuation of a tight, reactionary aristocracy which would, without benevolent or malevolent despotism, guide the destinies of the land.

All shades of liberal opinion were aligned against the Compact, the most violent opposition being led by a little Scot, William Lyon Mackenzie,[1] *an Ontario Samuel Adams.*

So the years bowled along in Upper Canada and, with each year that passed, ominous undertones emerged, undertones that strongly suggested an earlier turmoil, south of the border, in the 1770's.

FAR out on the broad sweep of Ontario, a wind stirred in the pearly belt that joined lake and sky. Gently it crept over the water, bearing a reminder of departed summer to the new city of Toronto that sprawled like a long, narrow grid on the northern shore.

[1] Grandfather of the present premier, William Lyon Mackenzie King.

Rolling across the wooded island that shut in the bay, it pushed oily ripples against the beached boats by the Fish Market, rustled among the piles of Brown's Pier and then broke up into lazy whirls to carry its warming message inland. In King Street a stray eddy sailed west from Yonge Street, swung along the brick fronts of the buildings — Laurie and Company, the Surrogate's office, Northcote's with its tang of ginger root. Sinking to the rutted surface of the street, it caught up a light cloud of chaff and dust, tossed it aloft to settle over a narrow door where the number "197½" showed harsh by the weathered sign, "The Law Offices of Stensrood and Stensrood."

In the big room at the head of the stairs, three black-coated clerks wrote languidly under the cold eye of a goat-faced man who clawed sternly at scant white whiskers as he copied a long document in beautiful fragile characters. From time to time his glance fell on the two closed doors beyond the worn railing, on the black letters nearest him — "Mr. Forsyth Stensrood," and beyond, "Mr. Cameron Stensrood."

Behind the first door, Forsyth Stensrood drew down his black eyebrows, startling against his lean, ruddy face; tossed back his mane of iron-gray hair. He flattened out a thick document, its folds crackling under his hands, seized a pen fiercely from the silver inkstand, and plunged it into the ink. Then he yawned, flipped the pen back onto the desk, and stretched his long body luxuriously. "Hi, hum, *huddy!* Summer's back, it seems." He worried at his stock, ran a rueful finger along the high edge of his collar. With a guilty glance at his littered desk he rose, walked to the window, and threw it open.

The breeze fluttered among the papers, through piled books and pamphlets on the glass-fronted secretary. Forsyth studied the scene before him as though it were something novel — the huddle of old wagons, chests, ironware, crates, in the yard back of Capreol's auction rooms; the rippling roofs that stretched away to the bay, broken only by the narrow ravine of Melinda Street and the broader one of Wellington.

The dormer windows seemed to lift sleepy eyes at him and he yawned in sympathy, looked west to the burst of gold and scarlet leaves that welled above the big houses on Front Street — the Powells', the Boultons', and the cold reserve of Archdeacon

Strachan's. His forehead wrinkled and he turned back to the still reaches of Toronto Bay, to the wide toss of Ontario beyond Gibraltar Point, face relaxing as though the soft blue of the water pleased him more than the thoughts called up by the sight of the sheltered wealth of Front Street.

The stern-faced clock above his desk struck sharply, three times. He turned, glared at it, then meekly resumed his seat, signed his name wearily to several sets of papers and picked up a thick file marked "*The King* vs. *George Innis*." His lassitude dropped slowly from him. He sat forward, intent on the neat script. The clock ticked on. Page after page was turned off onto the smooth wood of the desk. From time to time his hands moved to a stack of newspapers, uniformly headed "*The Ontario Aegis*—Geo. Innis, Pub'r." His heavy eyebrows knotted as he compared marked columns of type with the flowing handwriting.

Then a strong voice rang in the outer office. "Afternoon, Finchley. Any messages for me?"

The thin quaver of the old clerk leaked through the door. "Your father would be glad if you'd step into his office, sir."

Forsyth pushed back the sheets, smiled up at his eldest son, short and wiry. "Well, Cam? Any luck?"

Cameron Stensrood laid his pot hat on a pile of paper, flipped up the tails of his blue coat, and sat down, smoothing his reddish hair. His wide-set eyes were worried. "Father, it's getting worse."

Forsyth laughed shortly. "Been getting worse ever since Grandfather met the first patrol by Champlain. What have they done now? Raised Innis's bail?"

Cameron's underlip pushed out slightly. "There's to be no bail. And they've got him in the Criminal Cells."

His father stared, a whitish tinge creeping over his face. "Cells? For Innis?"

Cameron rubbed the back of one hand across the palm of the other. "The Compact doesn't want it known. But I found out. It's true."

Forsyth leaped from his chair, slammed down the window. "Wind's round to the east." He took his seat again, chin in his hands. "This is worse than the Gourlay case. Trump up a libel charge and throw him in the cells." He jerked back in his chair. "There's no more libel in Innis's *Aegis* than there is in the New

Testament." He rubbed his long fingers across his chin, then snatched the topmost newspaper from the pile. "The Compact can't call *this* libel!"

Cameron jammed his hands into his pockets. "Read it again—and I'll tell you another interpretation they've put on it."

Forsyth unfolded the sheet, began. "Here it is. 'If the editor of one of our journals' (that *Patriot*—damned Compact rag) 'persists in publishing vicious attacks on reputable citizens of Toronto, he will fast find himself losing the respect and confidence of people in high places and humble.' Libel!" He snorted, flung the sheet back on his desk. "What new have they read into that?"

Cameron carefully turned back his wristbands. "Well, they say now that that particular copy of the *Patriot* had a speech by our esteemed ruler, Sir John Colborne, blasting out at Will Mackenzie and Marsh Bidwell. Therefore, the attack in the *Aegis* isn't against the *Patriot* and its kept editors. It's against Sir John, who represents the Crown, and hence against the Crown."

"H'm," said Forsyth, eyes on the ceiling. "Can't see that that makes much difference. Just shifts the application of the libel."

Cameron edged his chair closer. "Don't you see? Our benevolent Solicitor General, Kit Hagerman, is trying to twist in a treason charge and Colborne's backing him to the limit."

Bleak lines settled about Forsyth's firm mouth. He whispered: "Treason." Then: "They can't do it. But—but—if they could exile Gourlay just for asking questions . . . I'll have to have a talk with John Robinson."

Cameron made a gesture of disgust. "I saw him. Our impeccable Chief Justice was gracious enough to tell me that he really hadn't followed the case. It was in the very capable hands of Handsome Kit Hagerman and why hadn't he seen more of us lately?"

"That's bad. That's bad." Forsyth shook his head slowly. "Hagerman's a born hangman. But why the cells? Why?"

Cameron sneered. "Public safety. There've been rumors—started by the Compact, of course—of indignation meetings as far away as Stormont over Innis's arrest. The Compact calls them gatherings of republicans, separationists, atheists, Yankees. You see? Yankee annexationists hand in glove with our radicals." He shrugged. "I gather the Compact doesn't like our client."

His father turned to the window, looked out on the darkening lake, at the slanting rays of the sun that were gilding roof and shingle below him. Far out on the water, beyond Gibraltar Point, a single white sail glowed, then faded. On the horizon a steamer trailed an iridescent plume of smoke against the purpling haze. He cleared his throat. "They'll be after us soon. Cam—I think you're better off out of this."

Head bent over the smeared pages, Cameron grunted absently, "I'm staying."

"But there's no telling how far the Compact'll go in this case. They can't hurt me—much. But you're young. You're winning a rare name at the bar. They'll stop at nothing to trip anyone connected with Innis."

Still bent over the papers, Cameron shrugged. "Think I'd drop out of this and leave you alone? Why, even if I wanted to, Mary'd take the youngsters and leave me. I swear she would." He rose, crossed quickly to his father and laid a hand on his shoulder. "Damn it, what can the Compact *do?* We'll show 'em that that game can be played two ways. We'll have a Family Compact of our own. They'll find out that Stensroods are damned tough."

Forsyth turned abruptly, gripped his son's hand, and then stamped off to a narrow closet, where he pulled out a long-skirted coat, a tall beaver, a stout stick. "Am I dropping you at your house?"

Cameron grinned. "Course you are. You don't expect your eldest son to walk two miles out Yonge Street just because his wife is using the family carriage, do you?" He sniffed. "H'm, our neighbor's certainly busy with his ginger-beer making. When I came in I thought he'd stored some of his roots under your desk. Reminds me of the times when we lived on Queen Street and you used to take me through the mud on Saturdays for ginger beer at Northcote's. My cubs sniff at anything less than ice cream at Rossi's. These youngsters don't know what the old days were like."

"You don't either," grinned Forsyth. "I remember when we landed near Kingston in 1781 and your grandmother traded a little pork to an Indian for some maple sugar. Ginger beer! Ice cream!"

Cameron picked up his hat. "Well, this isn't getting home. How many are coming down for Grandfather's celebration next week?"

Forsyth chuckled. "Every last soul—unless the roads are too bad. Your Uncle John's coming down from Simcoe with all his tribe. Hope they get through. Damnation, if they'd take just 10 per cent of the money we pay on Compact sinecures and put it into roads, we'd be able to move about the way they do in New York State. Yes, they'll all be there. Kate's bringing all her people — worse luck." He hunched himself into his coat. "To think of a sister of mine marrying into the Compact and then her daughter doing just the same. It's enough — oh, confound it, I forgot to stow those Innis papers away." He lunged at his desk, began stuffing the sheets into pigeonholes and drawers. "You'll be there, and Mary. Gil too, of course, and — " He turned a key in a heavy lock. "There! Now if *you're* through footling about — "

They crossed the outer office, bowing gravely to Finchley and his pale clerks, creaked down the narrow stairs into the chilling air, and turned east along King Street with its glitter of small panes and glow of brick, feet ringing on the wooden sidewalk. All about them eddied the late afternoon life of Toronto. People clopped along, peering in windows, making quick sallies across the rutted street to the walkless north side: well-dressed townsmen in glossy beavers and long overcoats; threadbare, anxious-looking women from flimsy houses far off by the Garrison or down by the Fish Market; staring country people in thick homespun; mechanics in vizored caps; a redcoat or two, polished shako bright with its regimental crest; the loose, easy gait and quick grin of an occasional Negro.

Cameron pointed to a fat woman, buried in shawls, who fought her way through the mud to the opposite side, wooden pattens clinking against hidden stones. "Look at that! It's a damned disgrace. A city of ten thousand and just one sidewalk. Did you use undue influence when Will Mackenzie was Mayor to have it laid on our side of the street? Bah! The only one in town. Look at Albany!"

They stepped off the boards, crossed the deep ruts of Yonge Street where heavy teams struggled north, the drivers nursing their horses along, husbanding their strength against the killing grades by Hogg's Hollow and the Blue Hill far beyond the edge of the city. Safe on the opposite corner, Forsyth stopped to watch. A heavy brewery cart toiled by, the name "John Doel" bright on its dark sides; then a jolting quartermaster's cart, red-coated driver lolling on the seat. Crashing hoofs and popping whips brought on a long line of straining horses in whose wake a sharp-prowed Durham boat rocked and creaked in its heavy cradle as it started on its journey that would take it twenty miles out Yonge Street to Holland Landing. There it would be launched again to cut through the waters of Lake Simcoe, the River Severn, and the isle-studded sweep of Georgian Bay.

Forsyth shook his head. "The old days! I told you you didn't know anything about them. When I watch this corner I always think back to the time when you couldn't get a gig north of Queen Street. Now look at it! Damn Albany and its sidewalks. It's an older city anyway. And if you want to get competitive, they have far finer and bigger municipal scandals than we do."

Cameron shrugged, eyes on the high stern of the Durham boat. "You mean Albany airs its scandals. We perpetuate ours. Now if Mackenzie had been re-elected Mayor last spring—"

"*If* he'd been re-elected, it might have kept him out of mischief, though I doubt it."

Cameron shook his head. "I've got a better opinion of him than you have. He's damned able."

"Able? Of course he is. But he's too hot. He doesn't do anything except infuriate the Compact and that means that every Reformer suffers. He gets the farmers restless. He makes the extreme radicals think they've got a chance to start a real demonstration. No, I'm afraid of Will Mackenzie. He's so right in his heart and so wrong in his head."

"His head? Why, if he didn't blast out—"

"If he didn't blast out, he wouldn't always be serving notice on the Compact that they've got violent opposition. Whenever Will lets go, it gives the Compact a chance to say: 'See—we told you so! The country *can't* govern itself.' Some day he may give them grounds for real repressive measures."

"That's no way—" Cameron burst out angrily. Then he laughed suddenly, linked arms with his father. "History may not repeat, but the Stensroods do. You told me that when you were younger Grandfather used to tone you down when you got too violent. Now you're doing it to me. And just this morning I was throwing cold water on that cub brother of mine. Why, do you know what Gil was saying?"

Forsyth chuckled, waved his stick. "Repeat? Damned if we

don't. When I was young, I ran with all the Compact boys. So did you until I made you sit through the Gourlay trial and see for yourself what the Compact could do to an innocent man who had crossed them. And now Gil—why, not so long ago he was beginning to look down on me because I worked. His mouth was always full of what a gentleman was and wasn't." He snorted mildly. "But *I* knew he'd lose the Compact poison he sucked up at the Blue School. Since he started studying medicine with Richland, going about with him to all parts of the Home District, he's been seeing what the Compact's doing to the country."

Cameron drew down the corners of his mouth. "Been seeing too much, if you ask me. He'll end up wilder than Mackenzie. He—" Then he caught a quizzical glint in his father's eye and grinned in spite of himself. "Bet you're thinking that some day Gil'll be worrying about *his* son's wild ideas. And yet—" His face grew serious again as he looked across to the high-shouldered bulk of the jail and the matching courthouse. "Yet—I don't know. Look over there. We've got a client down in the coldest cells when he ought to be sitting at his desk. And beyond"—he pointed to the blunt, towerless façade of St. James's Church—"Innis'll be flayed from the pulpit next Sunday for trying to carry out what Strachan's creed is supposed to teach. I swear sometimes I feel like joining Mac and his Canadian Alliance."

His father nodded. "So do I—sometimes. But remedies can be worse than the disease." They turned down Church Street, picking their way carefully in the pale light of scattered bracket lamps. "You know, what I always come back to is—Hi! What the devil's that?"

At the narrow mouth of Blenheim Lane, where it cut its way west, a knot of men shouted and waved their arms. From the deep brick throat of the alley came a dull roar, the sharp, splintery smash of wood, the fading scream of shattered glass. Forsyth gripped his stick. "Come on. Sounds like—" A man lurched past them, cannoned into Forsyth, pelted on shouting: "The traitor! The God-damn traitor!"

Forsyth started after him, rubbing his arm. Cameron called: "Father! Stay here. I'll have a look!"

"The devil you will! We'll go together." He plunged on.

The alley boiled, seethed with waving arms, echoed to hoarse shouts. Cameron suddenly exploded. "By God! It's the *Aegis!* They can't do that!" He twisted past his father, tried to force his way into the lane. From opposite sides of the mouth, two roughly dressed men shouldered against him, forced him back. Cameron tried to shake them off. "Let me by, damn it! Let me by! I've a right—"

"You ain't got no right to go nowhere we don't want you." Four heavy arms shoved him aside.

Cameron's hat flew off as he struggled with them. "I'm going in there, I tell you!"

"Goin' in, huh?" A club, short and knotty, whistled through the air. "Goin' in? You're goin' *out*—or you're goin' into the lake. Grab him, Taffy!"

Cameron suddenly staggered as Forsyth's hand fell on his collar, jerked him away. The two men grunted, slid back into the alley. Then Forsyth's voice sounded low and stern: "Are you crazy, Cam? *You* can't do anything. They'll—"

Cameron, face livid, struggled in his father's grasp. "Let me go! They can't—"

"Cam! Remember Pat Burns? Stabbed in sight of fifty people and the Compact had alibis by the bushel for everyone there." He bent, scooped up his son's beaver. "Here, set this on your head. It'll help keep you cool."

Angrily, Cameron jammed the tall hat on the back of his head. "At any rate, I can see." He sprang onto a mounting-block, neck craned.

Down the choked alley he saw a long, black board ripped from dingy brick walls, saw the words *Ontario Aegis* leap out as strong light played along it. Upraised hands whirled the plank about, sent it smashing through the last glazed window. A huddle of men struggled out of a low door, staggering and shuffling under the weight of some massive bulk. A scream rose to meet them. "The presses! Smash 'em! To the bay with 'em!" Then, higher: "Tom! Tom! Dump the type into the sacks. Swing that sledge on the plates!" A light flared in a black window and Cameron caught a glimpse of an old woman, terror-stricken, crouched in a corner behind a low table. He jumped down, feet clacking on loose stones. "I'm going to find *someone!* Where's the Sheriff?"

Forsyth, eyes grave, said tersely: "Not here."

"I'll find him! I'll find the Mayor!" He ran off up Church Street, elbowing his way through a growing crowd, turned onto King. Then he stopped, stared at a shiny carriage that bowled and rocked as it swung north. He waved his arm, shouted: "Mr. Sullivan! Damn it, Mr. Mayor! Mayor Sullivan!"

The carriage slowed down to a walk, a glossy hat showed in the window, then ducked back quickly. Cameron ran on. "Mr. Sullivan! The mob! They're at the *Aegis!* It's a riot! It's — "

The hat reappeared cautiously, a hand lifted in salute. "Oh — Stensrood. Didn't recognize you. Good evening to you." The horses quickened their pace. Cameron shouted again: "The mob! The mob!"

"Eh? Yes. Has been warm. Deucedly warm." The words blurred past the whirling spokes. " 'Member me to your father."

"Damn it, I say it's a riot!"

"Can't hear you. Come see me. Any time — glad — see you. And your father." The horse broke into a sharp trot and the carriage bobbed and swayed out of earshot.

Cameron snarled a curse under his breath, turned back to Church Street where he found his father eying the dwindling mob stonily. "Come on, Father. Let's get out of here. Listen, I saw Sullivan. I called to him. He heard me perfectly and made the coachman whip up."

"Course he did. If you hadn't been in New York in '26, you'd have seen the same thing when they wrecked Mackenzie's paper. The old story again. It's — " He caught his breath sharply, nudged his son. "Look there — by the Market."

Angrily, Cameron turned, saw a little man, bulbous forehead shaded by an enormous pot hat, a little man who stood in the shadow of the Market pillars, trembling. "Come on. It's Will Mackenzie," said Forsyth. "I want to speak to him." Together they worked their way across the street. Forsyth raised the head of his stick to his hat brim. "Bad business, Mac."

The pot hat tilted back, deep-set blue eyes looked up. "I've seen worse." Tight-pressed lips worked incessantly, small hands were restless on the head of a heavy cane. "This is nothing new. I've seen the sons of at least three Councilors there in the alley. Sons of your colleagues." He snarled. "The next time you dine with your Compact friends you can tell 'em about it." He raised his big head, glared down toward the waterfront. "Hah! There go the presses. There goes the type. Hear 'em splash?"

"It's an outrage," growled Forsyth, while Cameron nodded angrily.

"Don't waste your indignation on me," grunted Mackenzie. "Next time you hear service in St. James's, tell Strachan that his noble mob took a shop by storm while he and the rest kept the owner in jail. Tell 'em the shop had a heavy garrison—one old woman. Bah! At least, when they wrecked my paper, they did it in broad daylight. Tell Strachan, tell Robinson, tell Hagerman, tell Denison, that their rats don't dare come out in the sun any more. Stensrood, you disgrace yourself every time you speak to those men. Speak? By God, you dine with 'em, have 'em in your house. Reformer! You and Bidwell and Baldwin!" He snorted, seized his stick, and hurried away with quick, nervous steps.

Forsyth looked after him. "Wonder what he'll do now. Hope he'll keep out of the country districts. He might stir up a blaze that'd be hard to stop."

"Damned if I don't think he's right. Give the Compact a taste of its own medicine."

"And have martial law—under the Compact? Have troops in? Every known Reformer marked as a traitor? How'd you like *that?* Well, come along or Barnard'll have put our horses back in their stalls."

In the warm reek of Barnard's Market Street stables, close by the high-pillared front of Ontario House, two sleek bays shifted their feet impatiently, fretted at their bits. A diminutive Negro by their heads grinned as Forsyth and Cameron clumped over the scarred boards. From a dingy, lamplit cave the immense girth of Barnard waddled out. "Evenin', Judge. Evenin', Mist' Cameron. Want as Tobey should drive you?"

"I'll drive," said Cameron, taking the reins. "Get in, Father. Spread that rug over us, Tobey. Getting colder."

Barnard tilted about on splay feet, hand on the polished side of the carriage. "S'pose you heard the row to Blenheim Lane, Judge?"

"Saw it."

Barnard's big head shook. "Cruel bad. And Mr. Innis in jail for libel. Why, you'll hear more libel in this stable of a Sunday a'ternoon when folks begin to drop in than you'll find in a year of the

Aegis." He teetered back and forth, veined cheeks bulging. "Wanted to tell you, Judge—I've gone and joined the Canadian Alliance."

Cameron grunted. "Don't you stable Strachan's horses sometimes? And Powell's? And Boulton's? They'd not be pleased."

Watery eyes hardened. "That's as may be. But they's a sight to be said and it hits me the Alliance is a good way of sayin' it. Mr. Mackenzie's workin' in all the counties and gettin' solid folk, folk that just want to work hard and be let alone."

Forsyth frowned. "Could be dangerous. Remember, Barnard, violence is the worst cure in the world."

"That it is." Barnard slapped the side of the carriage emphatically. "But we *got* to do something. Can't have goin's-on like just now's." He stepped back. Cameron gathered the horses, swung them expertly out onto Market Street, headed them toward Yonge.

Forsyth tucked the robe tighter about him. "Is it really getting colder? Or is it just the day I've had? A caller came in that I want to tell you about later. Young Englishman, fretted by the Land Office. Thinking of what he faces rather chills me. Then Innis in the cells. Then the *Aegis*. Then Mackenzie. Or is it just old age? Nothing new about this. Lived with it all my life."

He settled back in the seat. The carriage rolled over the uneven surface of Yonge Street, which began its slow climb out of the city. Clusters of lights winked, black fences slipped silently past, were replaced by dense belts of the original forest. Now and then big houses loomed, far off the road, tree-lined crescents leading up to them, bland windows glowing beyond networks of branches.

The bar of the Bloor Street tollgate lifted, clacked behind them. Forsyth folded his hands under the robe. "You know, Cam, it's hard to be certain in the dark, but I think that one of those voices whooping in Blenheim Lane belonged to your cousin Carleton Sperry—yes, I'm almost sure of it."

III

The Compact Branch — 1835

TALL and gray-haired, Kate Sperry stood by the coal fire and watched approvingly as the tight-faced English maid spread the tea things with dry efficiency on a low table. Then she strolled slowly across to the long windows of the drawing room, wide gray skirts rustling over the carpet and tight stays creaking slightly under the pointed basque. Dusk blurred the broad sweep of Spadina Avenue outside and choked the flaming maples over by the Boultons' great house. To the north Kate could see nothing but broken fields and thick woods, and without looking she could count the few houses that lay between her and distant Queen Street.

Absently she toyed with the cords of the heavy curtains, wondering vaguely how she had ever consented to move from the snug brick house on Bay Street to this waste. That had been when Edward had been taken into the Bank of Upper Canada, appointed to the Clergy Reserve Offices and made a Legislative Councilor all in the same week. She still glowed with the memory of that first big step. After all, with a carriage it didn't matter so much and people began calling at once — not just old friends of her family, but people like Mrs. Robinson and Mrs. Strachan and — Well, her card tray had always been full and Edward had gone on and on. She was very proud of her husband, even if she didn't quite understand all his activities.

She parted the curtains a little wider as hoofs plopped dully on the soft surface of the avenue. It might be one of the children, looking in for tea. Quickly she closed them. Just a dray, loaded with barrels. Still, they might drop in — Talbot or his wife Sarah; or perhaps Ruth. She turned back to the tea table, sat in a deep chair by the fire as the maid lit a tall lamp by the door, its shaft carved in the shape of a heron's leg, then another on a solid slab of mahogany by the sofa. The soft light glowed on carved, polished wood, on heavy framed prints on the high walls.

Left alone, Kate idly picked up a small stack of white squares, leafed through them. Bills, invitations, acceptances, regrets. Then her face brightened as she slipped out a stiff card, crested, which announced in rigid script that His Excellency the Lieutenant Governor and Lady Colborne requested the pleasure of the presence of Mr. and Mrs. Edward Sperry . . . She sipped her tea, eyes complacent on crest. This, of course, was for one of the larger affairs. But some day His Excellency would command their presence at some of his more intimate gatherings. It had taken years to get a card like this one, but now with Edward being appreciated—

The maid's voice from the wide door broke in on her musings. "Mrs. Heward Mackie, mum."

Kate's face lightened as a slim girl, brittlely pretty face framed by a deep bonnet, swept into the room in a wide billow of skirts, beaver muff held correctly high. "Ruth! My dear! Do come in. And why do you always make Stearns announce you?"

"I saw the lights and just thought I'd look in, Mother." She untied her bonnet strings, slipped out of her coat with its fringe of capes, and handed both to the maid. "Hang 'em up in the closet, Stearns, and look sharp about it." Her voice was rather high and piercing. She kissed her mother mechanically, then strolled to the mantel, dabbing at her fluffy blonde hair, small mouth tight as the wide mirror above showed a ringlet out of place, a wisp of hair loose by her neck. Then she smiled as she saw the flawless white of her shoulders, the low, sweeping cut of her basque. To herself she said: "There's not another woman in Toronto who can wear a basque like this—not any that's had two children, anyway." Aware of her mother's voice, she left the mirror and its fascinations reluctantly.

"I was just saying, Ruth, that I *don't* see why you make the servants announce you in your own mother's house."

Ruth hitched her rather sharp chin. "All the people we know do it. And besides, it keeps the servants up to the mark." She bent over the tea table. "What's all this? Cakes from Rossi's? And all by yourself?"

Kate deftly filled a cup for her. "I always hope that you or Talbot or Sarah will look in."

"Let me know when they do, so I'll miss 'em." Ruth carefully selected a small pink cake, nibbled it daintily.

"Ruth! Your own brother and—"

She nibbled on. "Tal's right enough. But Sarah! What a muff! Do you know that she pads out the front of her bodice with cotton?" She surveyed her own curving basque complacently. "And she told me that she never let Tal as much as kiss her until they were married." She sniffed, then explored the silver plate of cakes.

"Sarah's a very nice girl. And her father got Tal that nice berth with the Canada Company." Kate spoke with approving firmness. Then she eyed her daughter more closely. "My dear, that dress! I really didn't see in this light until just now."

"Dress?" said Ruth over the edge of her teacup. "What about it?"

"Heward's meeting you and you're going somewhere? Is that it?" Kate's eyebrows arched encouragingly.

Ruth shook her head. "Probably won't see him. I had some shopping to do and then I left a few cards. Had to have something decent on in case people were at home, didn't I?"

"But—but it's so—so low. It's—"

Ruth dismissed the matter with a wave. "All the people we know are wearing this style now. You ought to see Maude Jennison, if you think *this* is low. She's always just about to fall out of hers." She smiled to herself. "She did, once. It was at the Squire's tea and—"

Perplexity and concern lined Kate's forehead. "Do you think you and Heward are *quite* wise to see so much of those people? I hear they're—"

"They're all right," said Ruth tersely. She cocked her head as light wheels drilled along in the dark beyond the windows, then relaxed as they faded away.

Kate folded her hands in her lap. "I'm sure they're amusing and all that. But I have heard that the women drink brandy at table with the men. They stay right on after dinner. And when the Bradys gave that dance last spring—"

"I was there. It was all right." Ruth dismissed the matter with a curt wave. "Is Carleton at home?"

Kate leaned forward. "I'm serious, Ruth. I've been meaning to speak to you about this for a long time and—"

Ruth leaned sulkily back. "Why should you worry? They're my friends, not yours."

"Why should I worry? They're your friends and they're getting talked about all the time." She dropped her voice. "So are you."

Ruth's eyelids drooped slightly. Her chin puckered. "By whom?"

"Oh, Ruth, I don't mean that *I* think there's any cause. But if your friends are conspicuous, they make you conspicuous, too."

Ruth's voice hardened. "Conspicuous in what way?"

Kate hesitated. "Well, you're with Jennie Brady a lot and last spring she was seen on the Hamilton boat with that Englishman who was visiting the Laughlins." She paused. "Mr. Brady wasn't there."

"Don't believe it," said Ruth curtly.

Her mother's lips tightened. "Well, perhaps you'll believe this, then. At the dance at the Marklands', *you* were seen — "

"Doing what?" asked Ruth sharply.

"You were seen kissing — yes, kissing, that rake of a Powell Colter. Now, what do you say to that? What — "

Ruth suddenly buried her face in her hands, her shoulders shaking. Kate slipped quickly to her side, stroked her shoulder gently. "I hadn't meant to tell you that, dear, but I *am* so worried about you and — "

Ruth suddenly dropped her hands, threw back her head, shrieked with laughter. Kate fumbled at her girdle. "Here — Ruth — my salts — there, there — it's all right — it's — "

Tears rolling down her cheeks, Ruth blindly pushed her mother's hand away. "Oh — oh — oh! No, I'm *not* hysterical! Really. It's — it's just so funny, that's all. Oh, oh, oh." She rocked back and forth, hand to her throat. "You see — you see — Powell wasn't *at* the Marklands'. He was in bed with gout and — " Her laughter died away suddenly. Her chin set again. "And anyway, I didn't kiss anyone at the Marklands'. I — I wasn't feeling well. I went home early. I — "

Kate sank back in her chair, eyes grave on her daughter. Ruth threw back her head, defiant. "And anyway, what if I did — which I didn't? What if — "

"You don't know what you're saying." Kate's voice was low, full. "If you don't think of yourself, at least there's Heward."

"There's Heward," mimicked Ruth. "That's something nice to tie to, isn't it?"

"Ruth! Your husband!"

Ruth's feet drummed lightly on the carpet. "And someone might tell him I'm his wife." She sat up, erect, tense, hands pressed deep into the cushions. "When I was so sick after Robbie was born, I found a note in his pocket from that nasty little American actress at the Theater Royal. And when I showed it to him he just laughed and said that she was more fun in bed than I was. He— "

"Ruth!" Kate's face was white. "You mustn't say— "

"And since he's been given that berth in Customs, he's set up that red-haired trollop of a Grace Lane in that house on Duchess Street and— "

Kate stretched out a hand. "My dear! And you've never told me. Why didn't you? I might have helped. I might— "

Ruth shook her head. "I don't want sympathy. This is my own affair. I'll run it. I'm the only one who can."

"I just can't understand it. I just can't." Kate stared somberly into the fire.

"Oh, heavens, Mother, you must have guessed *some*thing. You've seen Heward and me together enough. This has been going on a long time."

"You always seemed just like other people to me. And Heward's always *so* courteous to you."

"In public," snapped Ruth.

"You don't love him any more?" asked Kate sadly.

"*Love* him?" Ruth's voice was cutting. "I married him just—just to *get* married. Lots of girls do, only they won't admit it."

"Your father— " began Kate.

"We'll keep this just to ourselves, thank you. And don't worry about me. I'll be all right. I'll— " She paused as Stearns's white apron and black skirts showed beyond the portieres.

Kate drew a deep breath, turned an easy smile on the maid. "Yes, Stearns?"

"Captain Blagden, mum, of the Fifteenth."

Ruth's eyes half closed, a slight smile played at the corners of her full lips as her mother nodded to the prim maid. Then wide red shoulders filled the doorway, a big, black-haired man, shako in the crook of his arm, bowed easily, murmuring, "So good of you to receive me, Mrs. Sperry. And— " another bow— "bless my soul, what luck! Mrs. Mackie." Ruth's smile deepened as her mother called for more hot water and cakes.

Blagden perched himself on the edge of a small chair that creaked to his bulk and chattered on to Kate of town and garrison matters. Ruth sank farther back on the sofa, idly amusing herself by counting the brass buttons on the white-lined tails of his coat, on the high, choking collar. The ruddy, handsome face rarely turned to her, being bent deferentially toward Kate, who, pleased, listened to his tale of what the entree to such a home meant to an exile like himself. Then the talk swung to more personal matters, to the hat worn by Mrs. Lieutenant Fagan of the Engineers, to the probable successors to the Fifteenth, to the whereabouts of officers who had been stationed at old Fort York over the past five years. The conversation grew animated as Blagden and Kate gaily wrangled over a Major Hunter, the captain claiming that he had been gazetted to Gibraltar.

Kate threw back her head laughing. "That shows how much you soldiers know. He's still in Quebec."

Thick eyebrows raised, Blagden turned to Ruth, smiling. "It's a pity, isn't it, to take such an advantage? Why, Mrs. Sperry, I've a copy of the orders in my quarters. I'll send it to you if I may."

Kate rose. "No need of that. I saw it myself in the *U.C. Gazette*. It's right over here on the table." She crossed the room quickly, muttering to herself, "It's right here. It's right here."

The captain coughed, let his hand fall by his red-striped leg. Quickly Ruth's fingers curled about it. She tilted her head toward him. "Hello, Blaggy," she whispered.

"Hello, chit. Took a little doing, but here I am." He slowly released her hand, strode across the room to join Kate by the table. "Perhaps I may help— Ah—sure enough. There it is. My dear Mrs. Sperry, I'm overwhelmed. Ha-ha! With that I must beat a retreat—I hope in good order."

Ruth rose languidly. "I've a carriage, Captain Blagden. May I offer you a seat?"

He bowed, the braid on his jacket wrinkling across his broad chest. "Too good of you. Just going on to Bay Street. My orderly'll take the horses back and—By Jove, though, it would be a convenience. Yes, I'd be delighted to accept." He picked up his shako. "Mrs. Sperry, this has been a real pleasure—even—ah—including my defeat. May I hope—"

Kate watched the red shoulders towering over Ruth as the two walked sedately out of the room, then went slowly back to her chair, face grave. The fire chuckled in the grate. Later, Stearns came in to take away the tea things and still she sat, brooding.

The front door banged and she heard her husband's thick voice calling. "Stearns! Your mistress in? Very good." She looked up to see Edward Sperry's thin, rather foxy face at the door, his lean body immaculate in bottle-green coat and fawn trousers.

"Well, Edward?" Her tone was weary.

"Well, my dear?" He rubbed his hands pontifically and took up his stand on the hearthrug. "Been at the British Coffee House. Saw Beverley Robinson in the street today. Bowed to the Archdeacon on my way to Parliament. Had a word with Kit Hagerman. H'm. H'm. Busy times. That confounded Marshall Bidwell's yelping about the Clergy Reserves again and damned if John Rolph isn't backing him. H'm. H'm. Carleton home yet?"

"Not yet. Ah—Ruth was here."

Sperry's eyebrows lifted. "So? Like to have seen her. What she have to say?"

"Oh—" Kate passed her fingers over her temples. "Nothing much, I guess."

"Nothing much? Said something, didn't she?"

"It was just the usual—" She sat up. "Here's Carleton. I know his slam at the door."

Sperry strode pompously to the door, called, "Carleton? That you?"

A young voice replied, "Who else?" Feet banged along the corridor and Carleton Sperry swaggered into the room, self-consciously smoothing his light hair. "Evening, Mother." He bent over her chair, the tails of his sky-blue coat swinging, brass buttons gleaming. Then he studied his face in the mirror, rubbing at a dark smear along his heavy chin. His father joined him, said in a low tone, "How'd it go?"

Carleton swung his shoulders a little. "The way I said it would."

"How much did it cost?"

"Had to give away about fifty shillings, first and last."

"Who else d'you have?"

"Chaps I knew at school. You know most of their fathers."

Sperry hooked an elbow over the edge of the mantel. "Sure everything was all right?"

There was a short nod. "Saw to it myself." He held out his hands. A long scrape ran over the back of each. "Did that getting the presses out."

"Good work. Good work." He laid a hand on his son's shoulder. "No trouble?"

"No chance for it. Tell you one thing though. One of the men we picked up down on Princes Street, one of the toughs, told me that Uncle Fors and Cam came by. They must have seen it. But they didn't get into the Lane."

"The watch — I mean, the constables — didn't interfere?"

"I told you there was no chance. Jarvis Soule saw to that."

Edward Sperry drew a deep breath. "Well, that's all right, then. It's just another unfortunate disturbance caused by loyal people being driven to the point of madness by the threats of the radicals. It'll have a good effect when it gets into the papers. Warn those damned trouble-mongers off." He sat on the sofa across from Kate. "Yes, everyone'll be pleased. Ah — Kate, my dear, you remember talking to me about ordering a special carriage from New York? I think you may consider that done. Ye-e-es. I'll order it at once." He rose slowly. "Time to change for dinner. Come along, Carleton. You need a bit of sprucing up."

As he walked toward the door, he threw an arm over his son's shoulder. "Happened to hear — course there's no harm in it — that you'd signed a note at the Bank of U.C. That right?"

Carleton flushed. "Just had to get hold of — "

"I said it was all right. No harm. And I think that you can forget about that note, now. And they'll be glad to oblige you in the future."

Kate, by the fire, heard their steps climbing the stairs, their voices a muffled blur. Slowly her chin sank forward into her hand. "I must find some way to help Ruth."

IV

The Country Branch — 1835

John Stensrood halted by the towering maple on the hill trail and looked north through the gathering gloom. Plow land and pasture land rolled away, gray and brown, to the timeless belt of black and green where the pines edged his fields. He pushed his low-crowned beaver onto the back of his head and fumbled in the pockets of his short homespun coat for pipe, tobacco, and tinder, then sat on a limestone slab and watched the blue smoke curl up to melt away among the fading glory of the scarlet leaves.

His keen gray eyes, bright in his lined, shaven face, roved from field to forest, from rock to swift brook, traced the well-loved trail that Stensrood feet had worn from the lower pastures up over the hill to his maple. Then his memory choked the long swells of loam and rock with giant trees, filled the valleys and ravines with branch and trunk, erased stone wall and path until the land lay as it had when he had first seen it, more than thirty years ago. He smoked on, eyes now far off on a point where a bare hill sloped sharply away to the northwest, his head slightly cocked as though waiting for something.

Then he drew a deep breath as gold suddenly flamed beyond the far hill. He rose, intent on the arm of Lake Simcoe touched with a last, blazing stab from the dying sun. The glow deepened, slowly faded. John nodded to himself, muttered: "That's it. See it only about twice a year. Sun angles on that cleft in the west and lights up the arm. Did it the first time I ever saw this land." He raised his hand to his hat brim in unconscious reverence, turned, and followed the worn old trail south by a brook that raged and foamed over slaty stone, then west along a great outcropping of rock. As he topped the last rise, the solid buildings of his farm were soft in the twilight haze, orange windows glowing from the rambling house.

Somewhere in the dusk, cowbells clanked in mellow dissonance. From the house, a furious barking rose and a whitish blur shot toward him. John chuckled, called: "Steady, Brock, steady. Think I'm a Compacter, do you?"

The great collie, silken coat tossed in the light breeze, leaped about him, smothering ecstatic barks. John caught him by the collar, pulled his ears in rough sport. A widening bar of orange glowed against the dark front of the house, was cut by a woman's figure. A voice that carried a musical trace of a Scots burr floated out. "That you, Father?"

"And Brock. He thought I was the Reverend Strachan and wanted to get me by the throat. Supper about ready?"

"Just needs you and that man of mine. He's late."

"Didn't expect him any sooner. I'll go out and have a look at the barns and—"

"No need. I did it myself. Bedded the oxen and fed them. The milking—"

"Fed 'em, did you?" John's voice was sharp in the dusk. "Where's Murphy? Where's Delaney and Vulmea?"

"Took their pay and went to Holland Landing. They'll be fighting or in the gutter by now. I warned 'em not to show their flat faces around here again, as soon as I saw they were going to go lushing."

"Good for you, Flora," said John tersely. He stepped up onto the shallow porch that joined the original log cabin to the newer frame-and-rough-cast farmhouse. "Well, the last of the apples are in. All barreled in the north orchard and ready for market. My paper come?"

Flora stepped aside. "Come in by the stove. I've got your slippers laid out. There's your paper."

John's high boots rang on the broad boards of the wide room that was kitchen, dining room, and living room in one. Then the wooden armchair by the stove creaked to his weight as he struggled out of his boots and scuffed his feet into deerskin slippers with little grunts of relief. He stretched out his legs, puffed at the last embers of his pipe as he eyed the shiny stove with benevolent affection. "Like it, Flora?"

She carried a lamp to a table beyond, bent over a high-piled basket of mending. "H'm, it's all right. Sometimes I go back to the old fireplace oven, though." She shifted the lamp closer to John and the long shadows of dried fruits and vegetables that hung like bats from the rafters danced wildly across the floor.

John frowned judicially. "It's a good stove. Aren't more'n two or three outside Toronto. Why, even Sam Lount over at Holland Landing hasn't got one yet. One, two, three pots on top and—" he sniffed—"something in the oven, too. Hard to do all that at the hearth."

His daughter-in-law deftly threaded a needle, the lamplight brightening up the neat mass of sun-bleached hair, bringing out the freckles on her clear healthy skin. "Maybe it's too easy. Makes me feel sinful." She grinned suddenly. "Same way I'd feel if I had babies without any trouble." Her gray-green eyes danced. "Maybe that's why Will always acts worse 'n a kelpie. Having *him* was no trouble."

John smothered a grin, then pulled out a pair of bent spectacles and began turning over the pages of the *Correspondent and Advocate,* muttering to himself and mumbling at the stem of his now cold pipe. Somewhere back in the shadows, beyond the high churn, an American clock ticked loudly. The fire snapped and hissed in the stove. From time to time Flora dropped her mending, hovered over the pots or stooped by rattling crocks, moving about the big kitchen with effortless efficiency, tall, deep-bosomed, strong.

Over fresh mending—a homespun skirt with a jagged rent in the hem—she talked easily about doings in the farmhouse. How little George Washington Stensrood had thrown rotten apples at his sister, Martha Washington. How the youngest, sturdy little William Lyon Mackenzie Stensrood, had, in intervals of unadulterated deviltry, actually walked the whole length of the kitchen. Oh, and the youngest ox had a cracked hoof and the new dasher for the churn simply made butter without being touched. It had been a full day, what with those Irish running off to get drunk, but times would be pretty easy as soon as Will was able to look after himself, and it would mean less changing him.

John nodded from time to time, pleasantly aware of the easy flow of talk that did not interfere with his rather sleepy perusal of his paper. Suddenly he snorted with amusement, then broke out into a bellow of laughter that showed his white, even teeth. Flora looked up, corners of her mouth quirking in anticipatory pleasure. "What is it?"

John bellowed, coughed, pounded his thigh. "This—this—in the *Correspondent*. It's—it's—" He bent double, whipped off his spectacles, then clapped them back across his high-bridged nose. "It's—it's about that—that, well, that Hagerman. Listen. 'The *tout ensemble* [French, I guess] of this prodigy of oratory, whilst dwelling on this point of his subject, was peculiarly illustrative of the workings of his polished mind.

> One eye half closed, half out his slavering tongue,
> His twisted nose from nature's post half wrung—

But we will not pursue the description, lest it may prove too flattering to his vanity.'" John whooped again, waved the paper. "Too flattering! Hagerman! Handsome Kit! And oh! This—this! 'It was said to his beard and will be said again that his moral courage failed him when he advanced toward the battlefield [that means back in '12, my dear] and that the moment he saw the Yankees' shining steel, the Yankees saw his back.' That's one for Kit Hagerman, I tell you. That's—"

Flora suddenly dropped her work, head atilt. "Someone in the yard. Coming up from the barns. It's—"

There was a heavy tread on the porch outside, the door opened slowly. A beaver hat scraped the lintel of the door as Graves Stensrood, bulky in a short topcoat, edged his wide shoulders into the room.

Flora took a keen look at the troubled gray eyes, the slight droop to the mouth, and ran to him. "Well, Graves! Home so late that you forgot to kiss your wife." There was a hearty smack. "Like that!" Graves's face lightened; he flipped his hat onto a low chest by the window, rubbed his cheek against Flora's as he rumpled her reddish hair. "Glad you reminded me, Flo. Supper on? I'm hungry as the devil. Father, you didn't have to wait for me. I told you—"

John folded his paper. "Flora and I've been having such a good time here we forgot all about you and supper too." He smiled, but his eyes sought his son's in mute inquiry.

Flora slipped from Graves's arms. "You two sit down and not a word until we're done eating." Pots rattled, kettles scraped and shifted, then a heaping platter and smoking bowls appeared on the table. Graves pulled out a chair for her with a flourish, sat silent while his father muttered a deep-voiced grace, then turned his attention to the stew, which was rich with lumps of beef and potatoes and bore an added savor of kidneys, fine cut, swimming in its depths. A great white pitcher of buttermilk slowly emptied; a vast plate of golden scones, bright with butter, dwindled to the last crumb; a deep apple tart sank in its bowl in a welter of juice and last flakes of pastry. At last John pushed back his plate. "Well, Flora, that was *good!*"

Furtively running her pink tongue along a big spoon, Flora mumbled, "Like the tart? Mother Stensrood taught me that the first year Graves and I were married." She deftly cleared a space on the table. "Now, Graves, let's hear about your day."

Frowning, Graves filled a short pipe, face somber again. "Let's hear about yours, first. Mine's a long story." He turned to his father. "Are Gibbon and his son going to work for us?"

John shook his head as he stuffed stringy tobacco into his pipe. "Told him he could have the cabin above the brook. Told him we'd share on all crops. Told him I'd help him clear that bit of land he's got up near the lake."

Graves stared. "And still he wouldn't?"

"Willing enough to until I told him no liquor or spirits ever came onto this farm."

Flora, broad chin resting on her hands, raised her eyebrows. "He'd let that keep him off?"

"Nothing less. Told me I'd be trying to say what he ate, next. Got nasty about it. Called me a water-drinking Yankee and went away."

Flora sighed. "That means it'll be another two-three years before we can get that upper land under crops."

"At least," said John, clicking his pipestem against his teeth. "Now for you, Graves." He leaned forward.

Graves shook his head as though to clear away unpleasant thoughts. "Well, I saw McLennan. He's — well, I can hardly believe it. He says he's closing the old Squaw Trail."

John's jaw dropped. "He's — he's what?"

Graves nodded dully. "Closing it. For good."

John looked at Flora across the littered table. So the old Squaw

Trail, originally an Indian thoroughfare, running through the Stensrood acres across heavy forest to Yonge Street, the great military road from Holland Landing to Toronto and the lake, was to be no more. From the time when John had felled his first tree, he had used it as a vital link to the only important market. Time and again the tract had changed hands, but year in and year out, the Stensrood horses, wagons, sleighs, had threaded through the dense growth of pine, to turn south to Toronto. If this were blocked—

John's rather slow voice broke through the silence. "But he can't close it. Why—why—" he began to laugh quietly—"why, as a matter of law, we've established a right-of-way over it. It's good English law."

Flora drew a deep breath. "Of course! When we lived down in Glengarry, before I met Graves, my Uncle Shamus established a path right slap across those big grounds that old McQuarrie tried to lay out like a laird's park." Dimples began to show in her full cheeks. "Go back and tell him that, Graves." She laid a hand over his.

Graves stared morosely at the table. "Course I told him that. He said I'd better not go to court with it. Showed me a lot of affidavits from people saying the Trail hadn't been used for years."

John's fist smashed on the table to the jarring of crockery and glass. "But we can show—"

Graves raised his eyebrows. "Show a Compact court?" He ruffled his dark hair, forehead creased. "No, I'm afraid he can do it. If he does—why, we'll have to skirt the north end of his tract, and that's almost at the point where the Holland River joins Lake Simcoe. Then we'll have to float our goods down to Holland Landing and hire carts there to take our things into Toronto."

Flora's eyes began to snap. "And that we'll do. I'll carry potatoes on my back sooner'n knuckle under to McLennan. We'll show him! He's no proper Scot, for all he wears a tartan on voting days. He's Low Country and—"

John scratched his chin, elbows on the table. "Well, that extra carry'd be mighty hard, Graves. Think we could do it?"

Graves opened his calloused hands. "Oh—we could do it. But when we'd sold our goods, we'd find a big loss instead of a decent profit."

Flora leaned forward, her rounded breasts soft against the table edge. "If I know that McLennan, he did that to bargain with you. What did he want?"

John looked respectfully at Flora. "Take a Scot to catch a Scot. What was it, Graves?"

"Why, we can buy him out—the whole tract. At five dollars an acre."

Flora winced. "Five dollars an acre! My grandfather MacGregor, the closest man in Ayrshire, 'd roll in his grave. It's not worth—"

"Not worth fifty cents an acre," snapped John. "Anything else?"

Graves studied the grain of his pipe. "Ye-e-es. He let me know that he'd be glad to open the Trail again and—uh—lose the affidavits if—" He paused.

"If what?" asked Flora sharply.

"*If* we'd vote with the Compact—and he'd keep it open as long as we voted with 'em."

John sat tense, eyes hot. "What did you do?"

"Got out before I hit him."

"Shame on you!" cried Flora, her slight accent thickening. "He'd need of a good Scots clout pit tae the side o' his thick head. He'd—"

"Yes. He'd have liked that. He's just been made a magistrate." He suddenly hammered on the table, eyes blazing. "I tell you, it's getting too much. We fight frosts and swamps and stumps and blights. That's enough, without having to fight the damned Compact. Look at us! All the land we want. Good land. We're good farmers. But as soon as we really get where we can take a deep breath, the Compact steps in with some of its stinking work. Remember how you lost your first farm, Father? Remember when you sat in the Assembly and tried to get more roads leading into Yonge Street and went to Maitland about it? What did he tell you? Chucked your report back at you and told you to 'leave such matters in wiser hands.'"

His father nodded. "I remember. Called me a yokel, too. Or rather that aide of his did."

Graves shook his heavy fist. "I'm getting sick of it. Look, there'll be no school this fall or winter or spring. The farmers can't afford a teacher. We've got our youngsters growing up here with just what you and I and Flora can teach them. God knows how long before they'll be able to read or write—Martha and Will, that is. And it's not just us. It's a whole province, growing up illiterate—illiterate, I tell you. There's money for education and that damned Strachan's got it all for the Church of England Colleges—for children whose people can afford to have private tutors or private schools until they're in their teens."

Flora folded her hands quietly. "And what are we going to do about the Trail?"

"I don't know," sighed John. "Buying's out of the question."

"Wouldn't Uncle Fors help?" she asked.

John's mouth set obstinately. "He would. Gladly. But—" he rapped his knuckles sharply on the table—"I've never gone to him for a penny—bad times or good. He wanted to do this and that for us. Father's offered a dozen times. We're not taking anything but what we earn."

Flora nodded approvingly. "I didn't mean money help. But Uncle Fors is a lawyer."

Graves laughed grimly. "By the time he's through defending Innis, he'll have trouble getting a hearing in any court in U.C."

"Well," said John slowly, "he might be able to suggest something. We'll see him next week when we go down for Father's dinner."

Graves threw himself back in his chair. "I tell you, I'm getting sick of it." He turned to Flora. "What would you think of selling our land and moving to town?"

Slowly she shook her head. "I wouldn't like it here alone. And that's how I'd be." She clenched her fists. "I'll stay and fight, if I have to cut my way through the Trail." She raised her eyes to the space over the front door where an ancient claymore hung across the barrel of a rusty Tower musket.

John laughed suddenly, patted her on the shoulder. "We're all staying. And I'll tell you another thing. I had word that Will Mackenzie'll be by before long to look at his namesake. We'll talk to him." He rose, yawning and stretching. "Well, I'm for bed. Have to be stirring early now that the Paddies have run away from us. And the Lord knows what we'll do with the apples." He picked up a candle, lit it with a spill, and shuffled off to his room, his deerskin slippers hissing over the boards.

Flora leaned her elbows on the table, eyes on the deep shadows beyond the stove. Graves stroked her hair gently. "What are you plotting?" he asked.

She drew a deep breath. "Just heard something today. Set me thinking."

"What was it?"

"Mrs. Kirk looked by. Mr. Kirk's sold his place."

Graves stared. "Sold? Kirk sold his land?"

"So she said. He's going to settle in Michigan. He's joining some cousins who're selling their farm near Mimico."

Graves blinked. "But—but what the devil for?"

"Kirk says he's in trouble with the Compact. You know, about asking so many questions in the Assembly. Why does Strachan hold so many offices—with pay? Why does Hagerman's young cousin draw pay on the Welland Canal and live in Toronto?"

"Kirk's a fool. Why, one day we'll get a Reformer from England as Lieutenant Governor and then everything'll be all right. We'll have responsible government for good. We'll—"

She raised her eyebrows. "When will that be? And will he open up the Squaw Trail for us? In time?"

He blew out his cheeks. "It's just a question of waiting." Then his face grew solemn. "If it never happened—"

"Well?" asked Flora.

"Damned if I don't think I'd join Kirk."

"And what'll you do while you're waiting for this Reformer?"

He laughed, sprang from his chair. "Help you clear things up. Then we're going to open the big chest and see about our town clothes. Got to look right for Grandfather next week. Sure you don't want to get a new dress?"

She pushed back from the table, rose in scorn. "Pay out good silver for a new dress? The one I've got's all right. I've only had it eight years." She eyed him sharply as he bent over the table. "No—the small things first—that's it. Now start handing them to me and—"

A reek of hot water filled the kitchen as they worked in silence, both minds reckoning distances, hauling costs, as they sought ways of avoiding that long swing to the mouth of the Holland River.

V

Young Gilbert (I) — 1835

A PLAIN-FACED nurse in somber gray was looking in wistful admiration at the wide shoulders and well-set head bent over the desk in the entry of the Toronto General Hospital. She watched long fingers drive a pen over the neat pages of the register, smiled uncertainly as a deep, pleasant voice intoned the written lines with mock solemnity. "'Patrick Cumnor — St. George's Ward — fracture of left tibia — admitted per order David Richland, M.D. — attended by same and by Gilbert Stensrood, M.D., almost.' How does that sound, Hartley? Professional?"

The plain head bent. "It does that, sir. But — uh — have you put in the date? And the time?"

Gilbert Stensrood looked up, and the overhead lamp shone on a square chin, a wide mouth that grinned amicably, a high-bridged nose and wide-set gray eyes. "Ho! The date? Of course!" He snatched up the pen, wrote rapidly. "See — 'October 7, 1835, at a quarter to six in the evening.' Oh — and Dr. Richland wants you to look in on the case before you go off duty, so don't go slipping away early to meet your beau."

Nurse Hartley, pleased, twisted her hands. "Oh, Mr. Stensrood! I always go to my sister's when I'm off."

He frowned at her. "You do, do you? It's downright cruel to the boys. Hi! Look at that clock. Way after seven." He swung toward the wide white door with an easy stride.

The nurse raised a timid hand. "You — you could have a chop and some ale in the steward's quarters. I — I'd get it for you."

Gilbert waved a vizored cap. "Thanks, Hartley. You'd better be spending your time with tibiae and not feeding apprentice medics. And besides — " his voice dropped — "I'm not going home. I'm going — " he leaned forward — "I'm going to sleep in the dissection shed tonight. In the shed, with all the livers and spleens and legs. If anyone wants me, I'll be on the top shelf, just beyond the brine tanks." He clicked the heavy brass latch and swung out into the night, his head nearly brushing the lintel of the door.

The autumn air was rich with the scent of wood smoke and fallen leaves as he strode past the low buildings of Upper Canada College. An occasional horseman clopped by, hoofs echoing flatly in the crisping air. From the doorway of a big house a voice hailed: "Oh, Gil! That you, Gil? Where you going?"

He hurried on, calling over his shoulder. "On a call for Doc. See you later."

The voice followed him. "Ensign Weston's bet he'll ride his horse into the British Coffee House. Loser treats the crowd! Come on!"

"Maybe. Later." Gilbert pulled his cap farther over his eyes, quickened his pace. "What the devil do I want to see Weston make a fool out of himself for? And they'll lush till sunup."

On Bay Street he hurried past a trim, hip-roofed house, skirted a high fence, and paused by a solid gate. Hand on the latch, he looked cautiously about. "If those damned loafers have followed me—" Then he saw that the street was empty, pushed open the gate, and stepped into a blackness that was mellow with the smell of hops and malt, walked cautiously toward the half-seen bulk of a long, low shed, hands fumbling before him. He found a dangling bell cord, tugged sharply at it twice. A crack of light appeared in the end of the building, widened into a door, was reflected back onto a big sign where the words "John Doel—Brewer" wavered in the dull glow. A head showed in the gap. "Who's there?"

Gilbert pushed through the door. "Who's asking?"

A little man barred the way, then grinned. "Should have known when I saw that topknot of yours up in the branches. Come on in."

From the high rafters, lanterns shone down on rows of great vats, on a long space of floor where planks and kegs made uneasy perches for some thirty men. At the far end a candle burned on a low table where four figures bent in earnest talk. Gilbert crammed his cap into his pocket. "Who's there, Steve? Lesslie, Dutcher—yes, Doel and—who's the big one?"

"Peter Perry. Better get a seat. Lesslie's got something to say."

Gilbert made his way toward the rough benches, eying the crowd—earnest faces, eager faces, sullen faces. He nodded to big Dr.

Morrison, to John Armstrong, shook his head smilingly at their gestures toward a seat, and edged in along a bench crowded with younger men — axe makers from Armstrong's plant, hands from Dutcher's foundry, a foreman from Freeman's soap works down by the lake. They made room for him with uncertain grins, glancing at his well-cut brown coat, his shepherd's-plaid trousers. He turned to the man on his left, a sallow-faced foundryman whose hands were streaked with soot and iron filings. "What's it for tonight?"

"Don't know. Someone came to the foundry about three and gave the word." He screwed his long neck around as the bell jangled by the far door. "More folks. Uh — think Mist' Doel'll tap a keg for us?" His prominent eyes played hopefully on the great vats. "I ain't never been to a meetin' here before."

Gilbert grinned. "Always does." He leaned forward, touched a fat-faced man on the knee. "Tim, Joe was asking about beer. Do we ever leave here dry?"

There was a chuckle. "Had to swim last time. Gil an' me, we had 'bout forty mugs. Ain't we, Gil? An' say, Gil, 'member Iz Steeple, tryin' to get out where they wa'n't no door?"

Gil nodded, shutting his ears to whispers farther down the bench. "Him — know *him?* How — " . . . "Ain't his folks got the big place t'other side Hogg's Hollow? Sure, that's him an' — " . . . "What his people do?" . . . "Father used to be a jedge. Told Governor Maitland to go to hell and went back to law. That's — "

A sudden hush fell over the long room. Tall and thin, James Lesslie rose behind the table, holding up his hand. "I guess everyone's here so we might as well start. Now of course this isn't a regular meeting of the Canadian Alliance, and we don't usually have to meet secretly like this. But with all the excitement about George Innis and the demonstrations they've had for him all over the Province, we thought it wiser to come quietly here instead of meeting at the rooms."

A voice from the benches broke in belligerently. "To hell with 'em. Meet where we want and let 'em come. We can outfight the damn Compact any day."

Lesslie smiled. "It wouldn't have helped. And it might have hurt Innis's case. We'd planned today to present a resolution to Government House about Innis. But something's happened. Most of you know it now. The Compact wrecked Innis's plant about an hour or so ago. I talked the matter over with Will Mackenzie and we decided the best thing to do was to keep quiet as possible." There was a discontented buzz. Lesslie shook his head. "I know it's hard. But we can't tell what the Compact'll do. We do know they'll make capital out of the least thing we do, write, or say. We want to avoid anything that may hurt Innis. So we're asking you to keep that in mind, to pass it on to all Alliance members you meet and to all people who feel as we do. The case is in the most competent hands in Upper Canada. Mr. Forsyth Stensrood and his son are defending Innis, as you probably know." He looked about. "Didn't I see Gil Stensrood stalking about here? Oh, yes. Know anything new about the case, Gil?"

Gil shook his head. "Haven't seen Father or Cam for a couple of days. I get up before Father does and come home after he's asleep, usually."

Someone snickered. "So that's why Gil wants to be a sawbones. Can stay out with the gals as long's he wants an'—"

Lesslie waved his arms. "Let's get back to business. We'll do nothing about Innis—for the moment. But here's something we *can* do. We've learned that Robert Baldwin's going to England soon."

There was a growl from the front of the hall. "What's that got to do with the Canadian Alliance? *He* ain't nothin' to us."

"Easy, easy," cautioned Lesslie. "There's no better Reformer in Upper Canada than Rob Baldwin. He doesn't see the road to Reform the way we do, but I guess there isn't a man here that doesn't trust him and respect him."

A low murmur of assent rippled over the packed heads.

"So Baldwin's going to England," went on Lesslie. "He's going to see Lord Glenelg, the Colonial Secretary. He's going to *tell* him and every soul that'll listen what's wrong here. Writing's done no good, so he's going to try talking."

Someone chuckled dryly. "Going to tell 'em what's wrong here? Expects to be gone a spell, doesn't he?"

Lesslie coughed. "Well—he's paying his own way, of course. The Baldwins are rich and he can do it. Now, before he goes, Will Mackenzie and I want to send him a statement of what the Alliance thinks is wrong. I'm signing it as President and Mac as Secretary. So we've written out here what we think's wrong—"

The foundryman nudged Gil. "Why not say what's right? It'd take less time."

Gil snorted. "What's wrong? Put it in one word. Compact."

Lesslie's voice droned on. "Some of the members want to put down their own particular grievances. We feel that's a waste of time. If we get what we want from England, the grievances'll take care of themselves. Here's what we've set down." He slid a pair of steel spectacles over his nose, cleared his throat, and began to read. "Neglect of the Constitution — taxation without representation — no liberty of the press or speech — waste of public revenues among swarms of officials from England — total want of responsibility — corruption in the courts — " The list trailed on.

An axe maker near Gil shifted uneasily. "Huh! Baldwin knows that 's well 's we do."

Gil raised his hand slightly. "Won't do any harm to let him know we know it too."

From a near-by bench a lean, hard-faced man sprang up, the lamplight playing on the weathered skin of face and neck. "That ain't enough. It ain't hot enough. And what good'll Baldwin do, goin' over an' givin' 'em that? Mackenzie went in '32, got to talk to a lot of folks. And what happened?"

A voice answered, "He got Hagerman and Boulton kicked out."

The man turned. "But they ain't stayed kicked. Hagerman's back in his job and Boulton's Governor of Nova Scotia. Now Jim, I ain't sayin' that what you got there ain't true. I'm sayin' it ain't hot enough. We got to demand our rights. Look at me. Fifteen year a government surveyor and lost my job. Why? Not that I ain't a good surveyor, but that I voted for Mackenzie and — "

"And me!" A man stood up behind Gilbert. "Lived on my land since '20. Improved it. Made a good farm out of it. Tried to sue a feller for money he'd owed me five year. He had the money, too. Could a paid easy. But he had a brother that known a sheriff, and the first thing I knowed I was throwed off my land. They'd been to the Land Office and changed the records. That bastard that owed me the money's got my farm now and I ain't got anything. Had the land since — "

The big room exploded. Men sprang to their feet, shouting, shaking their fists. Voices rocketed to the ceiling, shattered, eddied about.

Lesslie waved his arms. "Quiet! *Please!* Quiet!" His voice flared out. "There isn't a man here that hasn't got a case against the Compact. But if we get what we demand — "

The storm broke again. "*How* we goin' to get it? We've writ and we've talked. We've got to do more'n that. We've got to — "

Lesslie leaned forward, eyes glaring. "What — got to *what?*" There was a silence. "Well, I don't hear any answer, do I?"

A single voice trumpeted. "We've gotto fight!"

"Damn it!" shouted Lesslie. "We *are* fighting. We're — "

"I mean *fight!* I mean — " A wild shout of "Treason" welled up, shook the sides of the building. Lesslie waved his arms, trying to control the storm. Suddenly Gilbert found himself on his feet, towering above the heads before him. He felt a strange tightness in his chest, knew that his hands were trembling. The room seemed to dance before his eyes and his own voice rang strangely in his ears.

"Where's treason in that? By God, you're afraid of your own shadows. The Crown says we've got certain rights. The Compact takes 'em away from us. If we fight, it's *for* the Crown and *against* the Compact. We've got to — " A bench overturned, there was a surge toward Gil, shouts of encouragement, howls of disapproval. "He's right! He's right!" clashed in the air against "Stop his dirty mouth. Treason!"

A door behind the speaker's table slammed open and a little man, vast pot hat pushed back from a domelike forehead, entered the room. He banged his hat on the table. There was a wild yell of: "Mac! Mac! You're just in time to set these fools straight!"

Mackenzie's ice-blue eyes glared, firm chin jutted. His restless hands flew from lapels to pockets, whirled in the air. "You're splitting again. Splitting! You can't do it. That's how Reform always goes on the rocks. Get three Reformers together and one says 'Yes!' and another says 'Perhaps' and a third says 'No!' We've *got* to stand solid. When we fail, it's because we don't. Now we're going to keep quiet about Innis — for the moment. We're going to let Baldwin take our protests to England. We're going to stand together and vote the biggest Reform majority in history into the Legislature."

"What for?" asked a dull voice.

"To let England know what's doing here in Upper Canada. The Crown doesn't know it, but the calendar here in Upper Canada's being turned back—it's being turned back—" he leaned forward over the table, dropped his voice—"back to 1770."

There were shouts of "No! No! We ain't rebels. We—"

Mackenzie's fists drummed. "I wish every man in this room would read Stedman's *American Revolution!*" He set his chin, glared. "Like causes produce like effects. We want to tell those in power that if they follow the example of 1775, no matter what *we* do, they'll bring about a day when there won't be a single British colony in North America for the Compact to hide in. And it'll be their doing—not ours. England's got to be warned." The restless mouth tightened. "If she won't take the warning—"

"What then?" a single voice snapped.

Mackenzie smiled grimly. "Read history." He suddenly whirled about. "I can't stay longer. Sorry." He snatched up his hat. "Keep working. Keep together." The door banged behind him.

Gil's mechanic neighbor looked dubiously about as Lesslie adjourned the meeting. "Well—what'd you think of that?"

Gil laughed. "I think I want some beer after that. Come on. Doel's men are starting some kegs over there."

They joined a shuffling line that edged its way beyond the vats. Gil found himself beside Dr. Morrison, who growled, "You went too far, Gil. But I was glad to see you on your feet."

"Went too far, did I?" laughed Gil. "I suppose when you're Mayor, you'll have the meetings watched for sedition."

"Elect me and find out."

"We'll do it," said Gil tersely. "What do you hear from Lower Canada?"

Morrison shrugged. "Same as here. The Château Clique at Quebec's as bad as the Compact. Papineau's as strong there as Mac is here. But Holy Church won't back him. I hear that the priests are losing control of the Frenchies. Might help us some if things blew off down there. It'd—look—someone's calling you."

Far off by the end of the vats, a voice called: "Gil! Hi! Gil!"

Gil craned his neck. "More'n one Gilbert in the world, I guess."

Morrison nodded, then slapped the rounded side of a keg. "Hey, John Doel, is your keg dry?"

Doel looked up, grinning. "Ontario'll go dry before my kegs do.

Here, take a mug." He pushed one forward from a solid platoon arranged on a plank. "Hold it under the spiggot. Now—good God, Gil! Where do you put it so fast? I filled your mug a minute ago."

Gil's hand shoved forward. "Not mine. I've just come up with Dr. Morrison."

Doel straightened, frowned. "Now I filled your mug just before Morrison asked me if the keg was dry. You had your overcoat on and shoved your arm between the barrels right here."

Gil laughed. "You've been having more than beer. I've just come and anyway I didn't wear an overcoat. Isn't that so?" He appealed to Morrison.

"That's right, John. We were talking about Papineau."

Doel made a scornful gesture. "What you two rigging up here? Gil was over there at the left and stuck his arm—" He suddenly clutched the edge of the keg. "God above, Doc! Look!" He pointed to a small knot of men talking heatedly under a flickering lantern.

Morrison stared, saw uncertain light fall on wide-set eyes, a high-bridged nose, a wide mouth and strong chin. He spun about on Gil. "Do you see that?"

"See what?" Gil's nose was buried in his mug.

"That—that—damned if I didn't think it *was* you."

"Thought who was who?"

"There. Beyond the third keg."

Gil frowned. "That fellow? Damn it, he looks more like Jonas Jones's horse than he does like me. He's—"

"You're not looking at the right one. Hi! He's coming this way! McIntosh's got him in tow."

There was a deep rumble from the short, heavy-chested man who was urging the stranger back toward the barrel. "John, we want more beer. We—" The pair moved into the full glare of the lantern. Gil's jaw dropped, he took a step forward. Doel bellowed: "What in hell am I lookin' at?"

Gil and the stranger said simultaneously, "Who the devil—" and stared harder. Then the stranger laughed uncertainly. "Uh—my name's Stensrood."

Gil stiffened. "Are you trying to make a joke of this?"

The other flushed. "Damned for a joke. Who are you, if you think my name's so funny?"

The crowd about the barrel stared, speechless. Gil's jaw set. "*My* name happens to be Stensrood. Gilbert Stensrood. Any comments?"

"Gilbert — but that was my great-grandfather's name. He was a judge, near Albany."

Gil blinked. "So — so was mine."

Doel's roar set the barrel staves humming. "Cousins! By God, they're cousins!"

The young men stared at each other, then looked away, grinning sheepishly. Gil set his mug on the barrel. "Where are you from? England?"

"England!" The other's voice was scornful. "Not a chance. From Albany, New York."

"New *York?* I didn't know we had any kin in the States."

"And I didn't know we had any in Canada. I only know about old Gilbert because I had to go over some family papers. He was a Tory. I thought he went back to England."

Gil rubbed the back of his hand across his forehead. "In the States — in the States." His frown deepened. "Wait a minute. Grandfather had a brother — no, he was killed. He was a Tory, anyway. Ha!" He slapped the top of the barrel. "I've got it. There was another. He ran away from home to join the rebels and — "

"Wait a minute." The interruption was edged. "You mean to join General Washington, don't you?"

"Huh? Oh, of course. General Washington. His name was — name was — "

"Josiah Stensrood."

"That's it."

"So's mine. I was named for him. He ended up a major of artillery."

Gil sat heavily on an upended keg. "Damned funny. Makes me dizzy. And what the devil are *you* doing at an Alliance meeting?"

Josiah blew carefully at the froth on his mug. "Came to Toronto on business. Had a letter to Dr. John Rolph. Rolph knew I was interested in shipping, so he sent me to Mr. McIntosh. Mr. McIntosh thought I might be interested in coming here, being from the States."

McIntosh rumbled, "Rolph vouched for him. So'll I. Had dinner with him at Jordan's. He's sound and he'll keep his mouth shut."

"Nobody questioned your bringing him?" asked Doel.

McIntosh shook his head. "Tom Carberry was on the door when we came in. We were late. Stood in the back of the hall."

"And everyone who saw him thought he was Gil." Morrison nodded wisely. He turned to Josiah. "What's your business here?"

"I'm with my father. Buying, selling, shipping. We may want to open here in Toronto."

"What do you deal in?" asked Gil.

"Anything from tallow and corn to cocoanuts and horses."

McIntosh leaned forward. "How about rifles? Powder and shot?"

Josiah grinned. "Thanks. I've seen the tariff list. I'm not going to touch stuff that's barred. If I get a license, I want it to last."

"That's wise," said Doel grimly. "I wouldn't give a farthing for your chances in court if Colborne hauled you up for smuggling arms."

"Where are you going now?" asked Gil.

"Back to Ontario House. I've got to catch the stage for Hamilton tomorrow."

"Tomorrow? Not leaving for good, are you?"

"Not I. Coming back in a day or two. How do I get to the hotel? Down to the lake and—"

"I'll go with you," said Gil. "I've got a horse waiting near there." Josiah nodded and they walked south down Bay Street, Gil's cap bobbing along beside Josiah's beaver. Gil went on: "It's been damned amusing, running into you like this."

Josiah chuckled. "Wasn't it? I'd been wondering why so many people tried to speak to me. Interesting, that meeting. It reminds me of something—I can't quite put my finger on it—something I've heard or—" He snapped his fingers. "Got it! It reminds me of what I read in history about Boston just before the Revolution. That tall spook who was reading something—"

"That's the President of the Alliance," said Gil.

"Well, all that stuff—courts, taxation without representation, no responsibility, and so on. Yes sir, that's it." He looked with grave approval on Gil. "They seemed to think a lot of you there. If we do open up here, I'll ask you to give me a lecture on politics. And then, perhaps we could do some business together."

"Hope you won't do business with me," laughed Gil. "I'm studying medicine."

Josiah whistled. "Takes a long time, doesn't it? I'd go crazy, just waiting like that. Got to be *do*ing something."

Gil grunted. "You're doing plenty, studying medicine. Most of our family are lawyers, but the idea of sitting about a law office — " He made a gesture of disgust.

"Law or medicine would kill me off. I took a year at Columbia to please the family. But I got sick of it and came into the firm. Wish I'd done it earlier."

Gil smothered a yawn. "Sometimes I wish I'd gone into business or the army or something. Not often, though. Soon as Doc Richland starts talking to me about healing, I forget the nights when I don't get home till long after midnight."

"Live near here?" asked Josiah.

"Out Yonge Street with my father and mother — a long way out. Grandfather built the place in '16. It's called Nipigon Lodge. He lives in one of the wings."

Josiah tilted his hat onto the back of his head. "Can't get over it. Your father's my uncle and — "

"Uncle!" said Gil. "Damned if he is. He's a kind of cousin to you."

Josiah waved in a magnificent sweep. "I'm claiming him as uncle. That's settled. He's my uncle and your mother's my aunt and I never heard of them until just now. I've gone and got myself a whole new set of relatives."

"You've just started," laughed Gil. "I've a brother. Likewise an uncle up near Lake Simcoe and an aunt in town. And *they*'ve all got families."

"Well, my father wanted to do things wholesale if we opened up here. I'm doing it with relatives if nothing else. You ought to have 'em put up in cases so the whole lot can be seen at once."

"Well, they'll all be in town next Friday for Grandfather's birthday. It's his ninetieth."

"His ninetieth? Next Friday?" Josiah seemed pleased. "Why, of course I'll come. Wouldn't miss it for anything."

Gil stared. "But — but this is a family party."

Josiah nodded. "*My* great-uncle's birthday. What time is it?"

"Well — look here — I mean — that is, *I*'d be glad to have you. But — well — take Mother. She doesn't like Yankees."

"She will. Is it full dress?"

"Oh, I don't mean you. Just Yankees in general. You see, you burned her father's house in '12. It was down by the Garrison. She had a bad time getting away."

Josiah waved again. "And *you* burned our President's house in Washington. That's much more serious. But *I'd* never hold it against you—against any Canadian."

Gil frowned, then began to grin. "All right. You're coming. And I've got an idea." Josiah listened, nodding from time to time, until they reached the great three-story pillars of Ontario House.

By the broad low steps of the hotel they paused, looked out over the bay where a late moon struggled through filmy streamers of cloud. "That's agreed, then?" asked Gil.

Josiah rubbed his chin reflectively. "Well—it'll be like shoving me into a lion's den, but—sure—I'll do it. Ought to be fun—for you."

"That's what I'm counting on," laughed Gil. "Drop me a note at the Hospital when you get back. Know where you get your coach? Right over there by the Coffin Block and remember that Weller won't wait if you're late." He watched his cousin disappear through the broad doors of the hotel, then walked rapidly to Barnard's, where a sleepy groom, yawning and sniffling, saddled his raw-boned gray.

The hoofbeats were ghostly as he rode up Church Street past scattered, darkened houses, past the headless trunk of St. James and the high-shouldered mass of the courthouse. By the corner of Queen Street he dismounted, led the gray into a copse that grew close by the roadside, slipped the bridle over his arm, and perched on a high stone. North of him stretched a mile-long tract where houseless streets were hopefully slashed through brush and meadow, dark save for the western edge where the long sweep of Yonge Street showed itself in a broken chain of lights, remote, impersonal.

He looked at his watch, turning the dial to catch the faint sheen of the moon, then peered along Queen Street. "Not much past ten. Can't have gone by yet," he muttered. "Still early—" He raised his head quickly as wheels and hoofs beat a slow tempo somewhere in the darkness to the west. He half rose, then slumped back in disgust as a country cart, bound for the valley of the Don, limped by, the rough-coated horse swinging its long neck like a clumsy camel. He glared at the watch again, jammed it back in his pocket, jiggled his foot impatiently against the rock. Beyond him, the gray snuffled and snorted among dead grasses, tossed her head with a sharp jangle of metal.

Then a steady patter of hoofs sounded, the roll and thump of solid wheels. He stepped cautiously to the edge of the road, saw, beyond Yonge Street, a pair of lights that dipped and swayed, grew larger. Quickly he led the gray to the edge of the road and with deft fingers unbuckled the nigh stirrup leather. The mare swung her long head toward him in mild surprise, then resumed her calm champing.

The wheels jarred louder on the rough surface, the glare of the carriage lights were in Gil's eyes. With one free hand he jabbed the gray in the ribs, made her waltz in puzzled alarm across the road. The two blacks that tugged at the carriage came to a clopping halt, the lean man on the box clawed at the reins and cursed under his breath.

The window of the carriage dropped, a tiptilted nose and full blue eyes, startled, showed in the glow of the lamps. A clear voice called: "What is it, Timms? Why—Gil Stensrood." The young face vanished from the window, bent toward a massive turbaned head. "It's Mr. Stensrood, Aunt Clara." Then the smooth forehead, marked by eyebrows whose outer ends slanted oddly downward, showed again. "What on earth are you doing here, Gil? And you remember Aunt Clara—from Kingston?"

Gil ducked his head to the forbidding shape in the shadows, then smiled at the blue eyes. "Hope I didn't scare you, Sandra. Those fools at Barnard's shortened my stirrup. Just found it out now."

She eyed the dangling stirrup leather speculatively. "H'm. So you rode all the way before—well, I'm glad you chose this place to fix it."

He beamed. "So'm I. Hadn't seen you in weeks, Sandra. What've you been doing?"

She cocked her head. "Why haven't you come to find out? Why, last Sunday Boulton Gray and Tom Robinson and your cousin Carleton and—oh, I don't know how many others—rode out. We had such fun." She settled herself against the padded seat, watching him from under long lashes.

Gil kicked at a loose stone. "Oh, *that* lot. They haven't anything better to do and—"

"What!" She sat up very straight. "Do you call coming out to see me 'not having anything better to do'?"

He reddened. "Oh, no! Didn't mean that. Only Doc gives me such a lot of work."

"Don't scowl like that. You look like Dr. Strachan when he's preaching."

"Well, it is serious." He bent toward the window. "Do you know, Doc let me set a leg tonight. All by myself. I tell you, it felt fine when I heard the ends of the bone grate."

"Gil!" She clapped her hands over her ears, the plumes of her deep bonnet dancing. "Ugh! Makes me feel as if someone had poured minnows down my back! You're — "

The dark form in the carriage stirred impatiently. "Alexandra Kingscote! I promised your father I'd bring you straight back. And there's cold air coming through the window and I can't hear what you say and you're keeping Mr. Stensrood standing about."

Gil leaned forward eagerly. "It's my fault, Mrs. Mayo. I — I shouldn't — "

"What? What? I can't hear. Alexandra! Do tell Timms to drive on. I — "

A whip cracked. A white hand fluttered from the window as the wheels rolled away, a clear voice calling, "Do come and see me, Gil!"

Gil watched the carriage work on toward the huddle of inn and tollgate by the bridge over the Don, then remounted and started on the long ride out Yonge Street to Nipigon Lodge. Eyes half-closed, he let the past hours flow back through his mind, saw again the echoing flare of Doel's brewery, heard the measured tones of James Lesslie, the staccato whiplash of Mackenzie's voice. But he found the whole scene overlaid by the memory of blue eyes, a tip-tilted nose, and delicate eyebrows that slanted so oddly down toward rounded cheeks.

VI

Young Gilbert (II) — 1835

Oblivious of the growing trickle of people who hurried or loitered along King Street in the early morning, of the creaking of farm carts and lumbering drays that rocked toward the waterfront or the Dundas Street tollgates, Forsyth Stensrood made his way slowly to his office, frowning. Thoughts as swift as the waves in the bay danced about in his mind. "What the devil are they trying to do? At first it looked as though they just wanted to frighten Innis out of the field. But now — *is* Mackenzie right? Are they *trying* to stir up trouble so they can put it down heavily and then grab more power? Damn it, I'm getting discouraged. Jesse Ketchum's talking about moving to Buffalo. Maybe it's better there. No, by God, it isn't. I'm a Canadian. I'll keep on fighting. After the trial — Wonder how Janet'd like Buffalo?"

He raised his eyes to look at a towering elm that was a living torch of bright gold leaves against the infinite blue of the sky. Light striking across his face brought out hidden lines, showed him weary, sick at heart. Then he saw a tall form swing out of the wide doors of the British Coffee House. Fatigue became as light as the crimson leaves fluttering idly down from the maples. He waved his stick. "Morning, Gil. You must have left Nipigon before sunrise."

Gil checked his stride, grinned. "Yes, had to go clear out to Etobicoke with Doc. Turned out to be a case of bastard pleurisy. But I learned a lot. On the way back, Doc let me lance a boil on old Mrs. Follet's neck." He shook his head professionally. "Never saw so much pus."

His father smiled gently. "When I see that gleam in your eye, it makes me wish I'd taken up medicine instead of law. Coming to mean a lot to you, isn't it?"

Gil looked surprised. "A lot? Why — I hadn't thought about

it. Yes — guess it does." He eyed Forsyth gravely. "You feeling all right? Look a bit done in."

Forsyth shook his head. "A good doctor never practises on his own family. I'm all right."

"H'm — didn't I hear that they won't let you see Innis?"

Forsyth started. "Who told you that?"

"It's around town. But I knew they couldn't do that."

"They have." He shuddered at the thought of the last time he'd been allowed to see the editor in the dank, underground cells, to talk to him through a small slide in the door while a guard listened to everything that was said. The guard could hear everything. Yes, everything, even to the chattering of Innis's teeth. Could the guard see the bluish tinge to Innis's lips as he talked hoarsely through the slit? No matter. The Rector of York's study was bright with the crackle of a wood fire. Handsome Kit Hagerman basked in front of a fine bed of coals. He was suddenly aware of Gil's hand on his arm, of concern in the young eyes.

"I say, there *is* something wrong with you. Dashed white about the muzzle."

Forsyth shook himself. "Just worried about this case, I guess."

"Well, stop worrying. I was starting to tell you an idea *I* had. I'll get Doc Richland to certify that Innis's cell is unfit for human habitation. I know damn well it is. That'll get him into better quarters, at least. Then we'll find some way for you to see him."

A faint smile struggled over Forsyth's face. "I know you would if you could, Gil. But the Compact's ahead of us there. One of their tame doctors has certified that the cells are as healthy as Strachan's palace."

Gil exploded. "But damn it, they aren't! He'll take a consumption there if nothing worse. Let me set Doc onto it. Then we'll have his certificate against the Compact's."

"Against the Compact's, Gil? And remember, Richland's a Yankee and — "

Gil tugged at his vizor. "And he's also the best doctor in Upper Canada. Everyone knows that. Look here, how many people have heard what's happening to Innis? I'm going to talk to — "

A hand fell on his arm. "Gil, let me handle this. You lance your medical boils and I'll do my best with the legal ones. And Gil — " He looked gravely at his son. "You get about a lot. I'm afraid you'll hear a lot of explosive stuff as this case goes on. You've always had a steady head. Hold onto it, no matter what blows. Hot heads may bring us far worse times than we've ever seen. Just try to douse all the cold water you can on any hotheads you meet."

Gil scowled. "But to sit still and — "

"Sometimes it's the best way. Sometimes it's the only way. You'll remember? Good. Now, where are you going?"

"To Lesslie's. He ordered a book for me. William Buchan's *Domestic Medicine*. John Coffin's notes. It may have come in by last night's packet. I'll walk as far as your office with you."

Side by side they clumped along the narrow boards of King Street, Gil pouring out an unbroken stream of new-won medical lore and his father listening contentedly. At 197½ they parted and Forsyth slowly climbed the stairs. "Did me good, seeing Gil. Now — what the devil, what the devil can I do about Innis?"

He entered his office, closed the door, then stared at the white square on his desk, at the thick script of the address. Cautiously he opened the letter, read slowly while incredulity struggled with faint relief across his face. His eyes ran again and again along the prim lines: ". . . and can guess what you want to see me about without being told. The Innis case is entirely in Kit Hagerman's hands. It would be most improper for me to interfere. But I can give you assurance on one point which I've heard is bothering you — though I can see no reason why it should. That is, that the jury will be drawn openly. I greatly regret that you oppose Government in this case, but feel sure that you'll come to our side as the trial develops. With every assurance of friendship and esteem, your friend, John Beverley Robinson."

Forsyth carefully folded the note. "I hadn't dared hope. I really hadn't. Now — now there's a chance the jury won't be packed. It can't be — 'drawn openly.' We've a chance."

Gil Stensrood leaned against the wedge-shaped façade of the Coffin Block close by the waterfront and watched Weller's clumsy stage fill slowly for its daily run to Hamilton. A pair of tight-faced lawyers, a hulking countryman, a nun, white-coifed and bursting with Gallic volubility, an ensign of the Fifteenth immaculate in scarlet and blue, two severe-browed women shepherding a tremulous girl. The stage door clacked, the wheels bowled away to a pounding of hoofs and the brittle smack of the driver's whip.

Thin wheels grated out of the west along Front Street. Gil saw a shaggy, ewe-necked horse dragging a light chaise that rocked and pitched in the wake of uncertain-gaited hoofs. From the depths of the hood, a gaunt, big-boned man shouted unintelligibly above the clatter, made an abrupt gesture with a lean, scarred hand. Gil jumped across the street, swung himself onto the worn leather of the seat. A lined face turned to him. "Morning," said Dr. Richland.

Gil flapped a hand. "Morning. Didn't keep you waiting, did I?"

The doctor rubbed an unshaven chin. "No. But you kept yourself. C'd see you a quarter-mile down the street, gaping and scratching your back against the Coffin Block."

"What would you have said if I'd kept *you* waiting?" laughed Gil.

"Nothing. Just wouldn't a waited. I told you—Hi! God damn it! Where's my black bag?"

"Did you take it out of the chaise last night?"

"Course I didn't."

"Then it's between your feet, where I always put it."

The doctor's shapeless shoes flopped about on the floor. There was a sigh of relief. "Damned if it ain't." He smacked the reins. "Huddup!"

The chaise spun along past the scattered houses of King Street, east. To the south the great wings of Gooderham's windmill flashed gold and silver in the climbing sun. Then the planks of the Don bridge rattled under the wheels. The river was a winding ripple of blue, shade-flecked. Gil looked upstream, savoring the dance and sparkle of the water. He turned to Richland. "Where are we going today, Doc?"

The lined face contracted in thought. "Well, first we're going to see old Mrs. Bemis. Nothing wrong with her but a long, hot summer and weak bowels. Then we're going east through the woods to look at Hi Gregg. Team bolted when he was stumping a field and dragged him over some rocks. Got a gash in the leg. Cracked nose, too, I guess. Well, that won't do any hurt. Hi was homely as a moose to start with. Then they's Karl Lester with his busted leg out of falling from a loft, the clumsy fool. Then—oh, hell,

I can't call 'em all to mind without digging out my list and it's buttoned away so's it's too much trouble to get at."

He swung the chaise expertly north along a track that forked from the Kingston Road, headed the bay through a sun-dappled tunnel where occasional tight cottages crouched among trees or clung to the steep bluffs of the east bank. "Gil, you brought back my *Anatomy* yet?"

"Want to keep it a little longer. Hoped I'd be through with it by now. But I've been—uh, been out late a few nights and then Nipigon's all upset getting ready for Grandfather's ninetieth."

The doctor wagged his head sadly over his greasy stock. "That man! His ninetieth. I'd give a hundred dollars to get a look at him when he's done. Be 'bout the most interesting cadaver I ever did see." He rubbed his chin slowly. "Kind of hinted 'bout it to him once. He damned my eyes and told me he'd live to see mine. Then he gave me a glass of prime brandy. Uh—you don't suppose—" he peered hopefully at his young assistant—"you don't suppose perhaps if *you* spoke to him—being one of the family, see? Might look different to him? Um? Well, no, don't suppose it would." He sighed, then shook himself. "How you ever expect to get to be a doctor if you don't know your anatomy? Just sitting here jabbering! If I'd done that—now just you sit back and give me a whole lot of muscles. Start at the shoulder and work down." He waved the frazzled willow switch that served him as a whip.

Gil settled his cap, began to intone. "*Platysma, deltoid, biceps flexor cubiti, triceps extensor cubiti, brachialis anticus*—"

Richland, nodding, shifted his probing from bones to arteries. The road wound on, twisted among trees that shone softly in dense yellow halos or blazed like dusty embers. Above, the sky was gentian-blue. Black against it, crow sentinels, high among bright leaves, looked down on the laboring horse and shot cawing away to meet the thin, dark clouds that rose from the rare plowed fields. To the left, where the trunks broke from time to time, the young city of Toronto showed, its hunched roofs and few spires seeming to march down the long, gentle slope to bay and lake.

Gil broke off suddenly in the midst of a description of the thorax. "Doc, there's a meeting of the Canadian Alliance next week."

Thick eyebrows were impassive. "Is there, now?"

"Heard that some of the people'd be glad to see you there."
"H'mph. Would they? Bessie! Pick up your damned feet."
"Well — " Gil's forehead wrinkled. "What do you think of it?"
Richland shook the reins. "Don't think. And let me give you a lesson. Politics and medicine don't mix, no more'n bush whiskey and old brandy. Look at John Rolph. He don't know whether he's a doctor or a lawyer or a politician. Bet he gives his patients Reform speeches and hands out calomel to political meetings. And speaking of calomel, Gil — meant to tell you. Go light on it."
"Go light? Thought you said — "
"Go light. There's some that don't give anything else. But it makes the spit come faster'n God meant it to. Oh, yes." He waved his switch testily. "Talk like the books if you want and call it increased salivation. But spit's easier to say and it don't take so long. Yep, go light. Why, during the war I saw a feller that's face was rotted clean away from too much calomel. Just ain't had any cheeks left. Use it wise and use it light."
"I see," said Gil absently. He leaned his forearms on his knees, giving easily to the lurch of the chaise. "But this Alliance, Doc. It's fighting the kind of things I've heard you swear about. Why, yesterday you swore so hard about Innis that you made Bessie shy. Damn it, what you've said about the Compact'd kill a bear at fifty paces."
"Well, I guess the Compact's got a lot to answer for. But, Lord, take Grub Holly. Grub'd be lazy and shiftless if he lived on the edge of God's own green footstool. No — if the Compact busts folks up or they bust each other up, I'll patch 'em best I can." He flicked his switch. "But politics and medicine don't mix. 'Specially for me, being born in the States."
"How'd you happen to come up here?" asked Gil.
"Didn't come. Was brought."
"Brought?"
"Sure. Back in '12. When Ike Brock fooled Hull at Detroit. I got took prisoner along with the others. Got treated so good I began to like the folks here and it come to me one night I might's well stay. So I did. And then — " he nodded wisely to himself — "and then, New York State was lousy with doctors. Upper Canada wasn't — and ain't." He turned a bony shoulder toward Gil. "Hey!

What you trying to do? Been fidgeting since a half a mile back. What—Oh, God! I might a known."

The woods on the left of the road opened suddenly, gave way to a smooth, grassy slope, high brick walls and a slanting drive. Far up the reach of gravel, a two-story house spread graceful roof lines, showed a deep verandah where dry, grayish vines coiled thickly. Gil peered out. "Trafalgar Lodge! Wonder if—"

Richland's weather-beaten face set. "Keep your mind on old lady Bemis's bowels and forget about Trafalgar. Let me tell you another thing. There's plenty besides politics that don't mix with medicine. Old lady Bemis is more important than—" His fingers played about his tough old chin. "Wonder if I dast give her a drop of that essence I got the last time I was to Buffalo. Sure'd like to see what it'd do to her. Now it might—it might—Hey! You want to fall out?"

He clutched Gil's shoulder as the latter leaned far out, one hand raised uncertainly. Then a door slammed briskly somewhere in the solid brick stables, a slight figure, blue-caped, swung lightly into view, walked quickly up the drive toward the house. Gil's arm flew up. "Sandra! Oh, Sandra!"

Red lining flashed as the figure spun about, a white hand twinkled. "Gil! Pull up! I'll come to the gate," called a clear voice.

Gil waved again. "Can't wait. Be back later. Just wanted to say—Ouch!" Richland had flicked the old horse, set its stiff legs into a trot. "Just wanted to say—"

"What? What? I can't hear you." Her voice was high but smooth.

Gil clutched the hood of the chaise, leaned perilously out. "Be—back—this—way—later!"

Slim hands cupped about the round face. "*Where* did you say you were going? I can't—" The drum of the wheels swallowed up her call, then a turn in the road hid her. Gil jounced back in the seat, frowning. "Why the devil couldn't we have stopped—just for a minute?"

Richland sniffed. "Told you there's other things than politics that don't mix with medicine. Stopping and talking to Sandra Kingscote's one of 'em." His eyebrows lifted tolerantly. "Course, I could let you out now. And you could walk back to town afterwards, 'cause I'd not bother to stop for you."

Gil sighed. "Guess you're right, Doc. Guess there are a lot of things you can't do when you're learning to be a doctor." Richland purred approvingly. "Oh, there was something I started to tell you back there only — "

"Only you were hanging on the wheels trying to see if that Kingscote snip was mooning around the gates."

"Well, anyway, it's that I got my copy of Buchan this morning. Came in from Boston and — "

"Good! Now I want you to start right in and see what he says about putrid fevers. And when you get through that — "

The lecture trailed on, was broken at a solid brick house and again at a sag-shouldered cottage. After each halt the doctor's talk flowed like a stream that, checked by log jams, gathers strength and rushes on in full spate. Gil, silent, nodded and frowned. Then, in the late afternoon on the way home, as Richland changed from his pharmacopoeia to a discussion of a bran box for fractures, he waved impatiently. "Look here, Doc. That's an awful lot to remember. Why don't you let me sit in your office while you tell me things? I could take notes and — "

"Notes!" Richland thumped his beaver back off his forehead. "I've told you before. Look here, Gil, when you tackle medicine, it ain't what goes onto paper that counts. It's what goes into that thick head of yours. Damn it, into your heart. Notes! I want to teach doctors, not God-damned apothecary's clerks. You've got your books to keep you steady. If you forget anything, there you are. But when *I* talk to you, I'm making you live the years when I was learning and there ain't a man that can put them onto paper. He's got to soak 'em up, make 'em part of him. Course, if you *want* a mess of poll-parrot paper, why, I guess Grant Russell'd oblige. Or Hornby. And your father can get back the fee he paid me for wiping you back of the ears. I'll give it to him! With interest!"

Gil shoved his hands into his pockets. "How deep do you make the bran box?"

Richland reined in, grinning. "Never mind 'bout that now. Gil, you ain't done bad today. And I'll tell you something else. We drove clear past Trafalgar Lodge without your noticing it." He chuckled. "It's 'bout a quarter of a mile back there. Now get out. Don't want to see you until tomorrow. Be at Yonge and Wellington at seven sharp and I'll show you the God-damnedest case of jaundice in Upper Canada."

Gil stared. "Huh? Jaundice? Trafalgar? Why—" He jumped to the ground. "See you tomorrow." He twitched at his cap, settled his stock, and then broke into a run, dusting futilely at his checked trousers.

The great gate by the stables gaped wide, and he walked rapidly up the slanting drive where the air was heavy with the soft smell of burning leaves. Then his feet rang on the clear boards of the verandah, firm tread masking the nervousness of his hesitant glance at the wide door and curtained windows. He cleared his throat, reached for the brass knocker. Swiftly it slid from his moist fingers as the door fanned open, and Sandra, eyebrows raised, looked at him in mild surprise. "Why—Gil! I didn't expect you!"

He stared. "But—but I told you this morning that I'd stop in and—"

Her hands played about the golden crown of her hair. "Oh—so you did. Of course. But it got late and I'd really forgotten, and then I saw you drive by with that messy old Richland. I thought—"

"Saw me? How could you have seen me? The carriage was hidden by the wall."

"I was upstairs at the hall dormer."

"At the—" Gil began to grin. "Sister Anne—Sister Anne—"

Her nose lifted coldly. "Of course not. It was just—well, Timms is burning leaves and I wanted to see that he didn't rake too close to the hollyhocks so—"

Gil threw back his head. "Hollyhocks! They're behind the house." He caught her hands, drew her out onto the verandah. "You were watching the road. Well, we did go by, but Doc was talking so fast that I couldn't make him stop until we'd rounded the bend." He shook his head sadly. "If you knew how I had to yell to make him stop."

Dimples flicked across her smooth cheeks. "Well, perhaps I was watching. With part of an eye. That's all." She stepped back through the door. "Let's go in by the fire."

He followed into a broad hall where a deep stone fireplace yawned in the shelter of graceful stairs. Gil tossed his cap onto a carved settle, grinning. "'Member the time Stafford and I shut you up in that settle?"

"You were pigs, both of you. You wanted to go fishing in the Don—"

"And you were messing about underfoot and we told you that if you got inside the settle and counted ten, you'd find a big chunk of maple sugar on the hearth."

"I've never believed you since. And then I couldn't lift the cover and had to stay there for hours."

"How could I know you couldn't lift it? Besides, it was your brother's idea. Blame Staff and not me." He sat beside her on the settle, watching the play of firelight on the ringlets that framed her face, on the curve of cheek and neck. "Like the way—like the way that blue looks in the firelight."

"Do you?" She spread out her wide skirts. "Oh, Gil! Isn't it wonderful about Government House! We got our cards today. And I've got a new flowered silk to wear. It came all the way from New York."

He rubbed his nose. "Wish it wasn't Government House. Too many d—uh, uniforms."

"Don't be an idiot. And anyway, you could have a uniform if you wanted it. Why don't you study with Dr. Russell? He'd get you appointed as militia surgeon right away. I never could see why you had to tag along after Richland."

Gil rested his chin in his hand, studied the fire. "He's the best doctor in Upper Canada."

"Ye-es, that's what people say. But he can't *do* anything for you."

"Do anything? Why, he'll teach me better than anyone else."

She shook her head impatiently. "I don't mean that. I mean—well, look at his patients."

"Been doing it—all day," murmured Gil.

"Oh, yes! In little cabins and huts and I don't know what! But he hasn't got a good practice. That's what your cousin, Ruth Mackie, was saying just the other day. If you were with someone who'd speak to the right people, you'd be appointed to a regiment or get a berth with the Canada Company or with that new insurance thing that Dr. Strachan's interested in. You know that any good doctor'd jump at the chance to get your name to use with his."

"Then what? Look at the people I was with at the Blue School, at U.C. College. Powell Allan! He's got something to do at the Bank of U.C. But not much. Clerks do all the work and he gets paid ten times what they do. Denison Alvord—never worked in school or college and now he's a surveyor—who doesn't survey. He's only a land spy for his uncle, but paid by the people. Same with Jarvis Eames. He knows about as much law as Doc's horse. He spends most of his time getting false witnesses when his relatives need them."

Her eyes were wide, shocked. "Gil! They're all your friends. You can't talk like that about them. I know them, too. Perhaps better than you do. And I know their sisters."

"Friends of mine? Well, we grew up together. Mind you, I like them. Amusing, most of them. But—well, I've seen a lot, going round with Doc. Now—" he rapped his knuckles into his open palm—"now most of my old friends are getting paid by the country for nothing—just about nothing. Some of my own family are. Uncle Sperry for one. And look at Heward Mackie. Major in the militia and doesn't know a rifle from a musket. He gets paid by the Canada Company and the Bank of U.C. Told me once he'd never been inside the Bank except once and then he was drunk."

She looked at him, puzzled. "But that's all *politics*. Those people are your kind."

"*My* kind? Heward Mackie my kind, for example?"

Sandra's firm mouth set. "Don't turn up your nose like that."

"Confound it, Sandra, look at Ed Sperry. His father was a hospital sergeant with the Eighth. He bought up land from discharged German soldiers. Sometimes he gave a gallon of rum for twenty acres to men who couldn't speak English, who didn't know what they were doing. He got Ed into the Land Office later. Ed doesn't know anything about land except that a Government office is a fine place to speculate from."

"Gil! You ought to be ashamed of yourself!"

"It's true. And that's why I don't want to be *given* a license to practise medicine or a nice berth with a bank or company."

She shook her head. "I never heard anything like this before! Never!" She looked severely at him. "Gil, you're just posing again. It's like your wearing that ridiculous mechanic's cap instead of a beaver like everyone else. Or are you just doing it to tease me? Aren't you ever sensible?"

"Sensible!" Gil started to answer sharply, then found his seriousness suddenly melted by the smiling curves of Sandra's lips, by the sparkle of her eyes. "Sensible? I'm sensible enough. See what you think of this. It's one of the reasons why I wanted to see you today. Look. Next month, Mother's giving a ball at Nipigon. Just a small one. I asked Cam and Mary and they said you could stay with them. It'll be the fifteenth. You'll come?"

"At Nipigon?" Her eyes danced. "Of course."

"And you'll come a day or so before? We'll have some riding. You see, I'll be free then because Doc's going over into the States. Mary'll send you a note and—"

She jumped up, spun lightly on the wide hearth, blue skirts flaring, petal-like. "Next month? I'll pack now. Who'll be there?"

"Oh, mostly people you know. Martha Russell, Laura Boulton, Sheila Baldwin—" he paused—"and, of course, Molly Allan."

Her eyebrows flew up. "Oh—Molly Allan. Well—" She sat down on a small stool by the fire. "Well—I hope she has a good time. I'm sure *I* shan't do anything to interfere with her—" Her red lips set, she whirled up from the stool. "Gil!" She seized his brown lapels, shook him. "Molly sailed for England last week and you know it. What *is* the matter with you today? First you tell me that there isn't a respectable person in Upper Canada. Then you—oh, I could—"

Laughing, he reached for her. She slid deftly out of range, stood on the last step of the staircase, hands clasped about the tall newel-post. "I hope you get cholera, Gil." She rested her chin on her clasped hands. "Tell me—who else?"

He rattled off some names as she nodded. Then, in the depths of the hall, a tall clock struck five. Gil started. "Five!" He shifted his feet reluctantly. "Well—getting late. Got to—hope I'll see you—"

Still leaning on the post, she put out her hand. "Come again soon, Gil. And—oh, don't you want to speak to Father? He always likes to see you."

Gil turned his cap in his hands. "Oh—he's always so busy and—"

"Come on," she said firmly, skipping down from her perch.

He followed her across a wide drawing room where heavy oak furniture shone dark in the glow of an American lamp and in the fading light that sifted through small, leaded panes. Then he halted as she drummed on a broad panel. The massive door swung open, and Gil looked past Sandra into a thick reek of tobacco smoke that hung over deep chairs and circled about a hazy fire. Then he saw the squat, broad figure of George Kingscote rising from a chair, heard his deep rumble: "Something for me, Sandra? I was just—oh, bless my soul. Didn't see you, Gil. Come in, come in."

Sandra perched on the arm of her father's chair, rumpled his thick, grizzled hair. "Gil's been out cutting off heads and legs and things. He stopped in on his way home."

Kingscote smiled up at his daughter. "Glad you brought him in, my dear. Don't see you very often, Gil. How's your family? And your mother?" He sighed. "She was such a close friend of Mrs. Kingscote. You probably don't remember Sandra's mother very well but—And your grandfather? Amazing man. Please give 'em all my regards." He smacked the ashes out of his pipe. "Well, Gil. Been hearing mighty funny stories about you."

"I could tell you funnier ones," said Sandra.

Kingscote patted her hand affectionately. "Perhaps I didn't mean funny in that way. Gil, they say you're dropping all your old friends. Joe Dewhurst told me that he saw you eating your dinner out of a box with some of the hands at Armstrong's foundry. Another man told me that you go into Doel's brewery a lot." He chuckled. "Not that there's anything wrong in that. Doel's beer's good. But they say you go in there to talk to the brewers themselves."

"Why not?" asked Gil, eyebrows raised. "They're all Canadians, aren't they?"

"Oh, yes, yes. I suppose so," said Kingscote rather testily. "May do you good professionally to get to know 'em. But I tell you, Gil, there's more to life than that. All those people grovel to Mackenzie."

Sandra, swinging her feet from the arm of the chair, broke in: "You can't talk to him, Father. Just now he was raving against all the people we know, the people we grew up with. He said—"

"I just said they'd sold themselves to the Compact," cried Gil. "You know as much about 'em as I do. Haven't people like—"

Kingscote waved his empty pipe. "Hold on, now! The Compact's a disgrace. I agree with you utterly there. But there's a wide difference between disapproving of the Compact and inciting sedition the way Mackenzie does."

"You mean, it's inciting sedition to say that the Compact's denied all the rights that the Crown says we should have as British subjects?" said Gil hotly.

Sandra laughed. "See, Father? It's no use. And he wouldn't go to that ball at the Boultons' because he said they'd stolen land that belonged to the people. He said—"

Kingscote rumpled his hair. "Confound it, though. There's a lot in what he says. But see here, Gil—I'm an older man than you and I want to tell you that there are a few things you're forgetting. In the first place, that's bad stuff to be handing about. Gets the people restless. In the second, when you talk about Strachan and Robinson and Hagerman, you're talking against the legal government." His eyes widened. "Why, that Mackenzie and his lot— they'd cut away from the Crown. They'd let the Yankees in here to run us. They'd—"

"They'd do no such thing," said Gil shortly. "What they want is a *real* Parliament."

Kingscote flapped a thick hand. "There, there, Gil. Cool down. There's nothing wrong with what they want. It's—it's the way they go at it."

"Their way's better than just sitting by and saying you don't like the Compact," argued Gil.

Kingscote blew out his cheeks. "Well, Gil," he said slowly, "doesn't do any good to go against the Crown. You think over what I said just now." He rose, held out his hand. "Glad you came in. Timms will saddle a horse for you. Just leave it at Barnard's and—Good-bye. Good-bye. Glad you came in."

Gil and Sandra walked slowly toward the door. "Don't bother about Timms," he said. "There are always carts going into town at this time and I'll hop on one of 'em."

She shook his elbow. "Farm carts and brewers' carts and fish carts! Gil, didn't you learn anything from what Father said? He's right, you know. That Mac—Mackenzie—he doesn't care about the people here. He just wants revenge on the Compact."

He laughed shortly. "Well—didn't you listen to me? Didn't I tell you that—"

She looked up at him as though he were an intractable small

boy. "You'll get over it. Upper Canada isn't like that. And the people we know aren't either. Now stop being serious. You're very nice when you're not. Are you going to be serious at Nipigon?"

He smiled at her. "Only about you."

She tossed her head. "Keep that for Molly Allan." Then dimples began to play over her cheeks. "It'll be fun, Gil. What'll the music be?"

"Part of the band of the Fifteenth, I guess. Uh — Sandra — "

"H'm?"

"You look awful pretty tonight."

She nodded gravely. "That's being serious in the right way. Coming out again soon?"

He sighed. "I don't know. Tomorrow I've got to go out beyond Grenadier Pond. Out beyond Eglinton the next day. Then — "

She held the door open. "Make it soon." Her hand fluttered and he walked down the long drive to the road.

In the dusk behind him, wheels ground steadily, grew louder. Gil stepped to the side of the road. A farm cart — a belated dray — he'd be sure of a place in either. Then he saw a light chaise, its side lights winking on the nodding bushes by the road. He held up his hand, called, "Got room for — "

The chaise halted abruptly. From the shadows under the hood, Gil saw a vast pot hat, heard a voice snap, "Get in. Going right to town."

Gil clambered in, then stared as the little man made room for him. "Didn't — didn't realize it was you, Mr. Mackenzie. I'd been — "

Reins slapped smartly, the lean horse started. "You're young Stensrood, aren't you? Saw you at the meeting the other night. Heard you had the sense to get up on your feet when you wanted to say something."

Gil, still amazed, stammered, "I — I was there. But I didn't know that you — "

"I know a lot of people," said Mackenzie shortly. "Know your Uncle John up near Holland Landing. Why doesn't he talk to your father? He could tell him a lot of things. Your father, Baldwin, Bidwell, Rolph — some of the best men in Canada. They're all too damn timid." Mackenzie's hands were restless on the reins.

Gil, eying him sidewise, could see that his tight-pressed lips were perpetually working. He went on: "Need more like you. No one seems to care what the Compact's doing. It's all very well to talk about the next elections. We just talk and let the Compact act. They're trying intimidation up in the Gwillimburys — there's bribery. There's even talk of calling out the militia to keep Reformers away from the polls. What does your father say to things like that?"

"He's defending Innis," said Gil, quietly.

"And that's a fine thing," said Mackenzie vehemently. "But he ought to go farther. He ought — "

Gil stirred uneasily. "You see, one thing they're afraid of — a lot of people are afraid of. You said that things now are like they were in the Colonies, back in the '70s. They're afraid — "

"Then they're afraid of the wrong thing," Mackenzie burst out. "What I'm afraid of is that the Compact'll make things so bad that history'll keep on repeating." He raised a nervous hand. "At bottom the questions are pretty much the same. Only down there, *both* sides lost their heads and it turned into a damned piece of treason, a rising against the Crown. We'll never have that here. We'll never have violence." He talked on, spoke of the rising Liberalism in England, of how sure he was that it would find its reflection in Upper Canada before things got too bad.

Gil listened, intent, the fierce staccato beat of the little Scotchman's words strong in his ears, while the wheels of the chaise seemed to grind out an undertone: "We'll-never-have-violence-never-have-violence-never-have-violence."

VII

Nipigon Lodge — 1835

By the curve of the great staircase that swept into the hall of Nipigon Lodge with a flourish of white and mahogany, Primula, amorphous wife of the black butler, cautiously set a tray across the arms of a chair. She stole a glance at the portieres that masked the clattering drawing room. Then her black fingers, like blunt-nosed turtles' heads, poked carefully in among the bright glasses, edged the carafe of sherry aside, closed about the squat bottle of rum. The cork came out with a slight smack that set big eyes rolling in momentary fright. Sleek rum slid into the glass hidden back of the alabaster Dying Gladiator. The woolly head tipped back and the glass was nudged gently back behind the eternally expiring warrior.

Primula wagged her head at the white mass. "Boy, did you take a taste of this, you'd feel 'bout's good's I do. Yes*suh!*" She picked up the tray, started gravely for the drawing room, eyes content and pink tongue playing furtively about the corners of her mouth.

Suddenly the subdued buzz behind the portieres swelled. Primula paused, noncommittal, head cocked. She heard Forsyth speaking to her mistress. "Here he is, Janet. Told you he wouldn't be late." Then Janet's clear tones. "Yes, Kate — there at the window. He usually raps there before he comes in."

A higher, rather fretful voice cried: "Janet! What are you talking about? He's at *this* window — here on this side of the room. See — he's — "

Primula heard a buzz of voices. "John Stensrood! Do you mean you can't — " . . . "Yes. There he is. Just where Aunt Kate said." . . . "Are you trying to tell *me* there's a living man who can run fast enough to get from that window to this, just while I've been watching? Look! I told you. You just saw the reflection. You women always — " . . . "Ed Sperry! I looked right up from here and — " . . . "Eeek! He's at *both* windows. At once. I'm going to — "

Primula drew a long breath. "Nev' heard of white folks seein' haints before. Was they colored, I'd sure know something'd happened to poor Mist' Gilbert."

There was a rattle at the broad front door opposite the stairs. The hinges creaked wearily. Primula's face became a decorous, respectful mask. "Good evenin', Mist' Gilbert," she said.

From the passage behind her a voice answered. "Why, good evening, Primula."

She swung about, then stared from one tall man to the other. Slowly her face faded from ebony to tan to gray. Gripping the tray firmly, she sank to the bottom step, black skirts flaring out. "Whuff!" she said.

By the door, Josiah inclined his head. "In a nutshell." Then he tossed his vizored cap onto a chair, joined Gil by the portieres. Gil raised his hand. "Ready? Now!"

The portieres rattled back on their wooden rings. Two voices said in unison: "Did I hear someone call me?"

A dead hush settled over the room. Suddenly Flora's fresh laugh rang out. "Go back and do it again, Gil. I still don't believe it."

From the fireplace, Janet Stensrood came quickly to them, gray silk rustling. "A friend of Gil's is always welcome. And you've a special right to be here tonight." Her calm eyes glanced toward the portrait of old Gilbert over the mantel, the severity of his judicial robes softened by a faint but unmistakable twinkle in the deep-set eyes, the suggestion of a lift that ran from nose to mouth.

By her elbow Forsyth said: "You couldn't have picked a better time to come." He inclined his head gravely. Then his eyes struggled against a pucker, his mouth against a grin. "And *why* did you young scamps have to make a Roman entry like this? It's — it's — "

Josiah flushed uncomfortably, eyes darting about this room that was crowded with his unknown kin. "Why — I hope we didn't startle — it was my idea and — "

"Your idea be — blowed," cut in Gil. He slipped an arm about his mother's slight shoulders. "Father, I wish you could have seen Primula when we came in. She — "

Janet smothered a laugh. "There was enough to see right here. "Now — " She smiled up at Josiah, eyebrows raised.

"Oh, of course. Why, Gil usually calls me 'you,' but my — "

"I'm doing this," said Gil. "Mother, Father — this is your long-lost cousin, Josiah Stensrood. Of Albany, New York."

Forsyth's eyes narrowed. "Josiah — of course." He recovered himself. "My father'll be very glad to see his brother's grandson." He smiled down on Janet's silvery hair. "My dear, I think Josiah'll like to meet the others. I know they're anxious — "

Gil watched his mother and Josiah move off across the soft rugs, saw Edward Sperry's eyes narrow in quick speculation, saw Kate's feathered turban bend stiffly.

Gil whispered to his father, "Watch Uncle Ed. Trying to see what he can get out of Jos."

"Hush!" frowned Forsyth. "You're probably too close to the mark for good manners." He watched the wide blue shoulders move down the room. "Quite a shock, seeing him. He's a Stensrood. No doubt of that."

Gil grinned. "Watch Tal and Sarah. They don't know just what to make of him. Carleton, too. And — " His eyebrows jumped as he caught Ruth's restless glance searching the newcomer with hard appraisal while her husband, Heward Mackie, was being bluff and cordial in a most condescending way.

Forsyth drew a deep breath. "Well, Gil, between the two of you you've made this a night to remember. So that's Josiah's grandson." His eyes wandered back to the portrait of the old Judge. "Too bad *he* isn't here tonight. But he is. He is. Broken down into his component parts. Tory, middle-of-the-road, radical, and republican. Family Compact, Reformer, Mackenzie-ite, and Yankee." He looked at the slight pucker about the painted eyes. "Looking for someone else, eh? He'll be here. He'll be here."

Gil glanced at the heavy carved chair, thronelike by the fire. "Gives you a funny feeling, doesn't it? Idea of something unbroken."

Forsyth nodded. "And in a few years, the children'll be grown and coming to these evenings. Cam's, Talbot's, Graves's."

Suddenly the portiere rings rattled, the heavy hangings slid back under Primula's masterful grasp. All heads turned toward the door.

Out of sight up the stairs, a cane rapped, two treads sounded, slow but firm. Then a tall old man, gold-headed stick tapping crisply, came gravely down. The lamplight was soft on the cloud of white hair about his clean-shaven face, on the trim white of his linen and the rich wine of his coat. A lean, loose-jointed Negro, capped in gray wool, face lined and seamed like old leather, walked by him, a wrinkled black hand on his elbow. A soft Negro voice drifted into the room. "Just you watch that last step, Mist' Barnabas!"

The old man raised his stick as the room seemed to rise to meet him. "No, no!" His voice was husky, but strong. "No need to hop up like a lot of jack-in-the-boxes." His strong mouth crooked at the corners. "I like it, though. Damned if I don't. But sit down! I'm going to, soon's I get to my chair. Ha-ha! All here but the great-grandchildren." He chuckled. "Saw most of them this afternoon. Disgraceful noisy pack. Wish they'd come oftener!"

He tapped on down the room. "Kate, you're too young to wear brown. Tell her so, Ed. Mary, did you put on that blue just to please me? Gil, you young rascal, you've got to hurry up and get your license. Then you can look after me if I ever get sick. Never have been, but there's always time." He neared his throne-like chair, back a little bent, but features firm and eyes bright. "There you all are. Talbot, Sarah — " He paused by his chair. "And — " The white head snapped back. "What the — "

Janet, her arm slipped through Josiah's, stood before him. "Father, here's another Stensrood who's come a long way to be here tonight. Your grandnephew, Josiah."

The old veined hands slowly met on the bright top of the stick. He leaned forward, keen-eyed. Josiah met his gaze steadily. Barnabas Stensrood's voice was hushed. "You're like him. You're damnably like him." Almost to himself, he said: "My brother, Josiah. Would run away and join Washington." His eyes narrowed again. "Hotheaded fool, wasn't he?"

The answer was level, quiet. "I don't think so, sir."

Barnabas's stick rapped on the floor. "Confound it, neither do I." A gasp fluttered about the room. "Thought he was doing right.

Talked to me the night before he went. Knew he was seeing the last of his family, but go he would." The white head shook. "You know—he liked us, too. Cost him a lot to do what he thought he ought to." There was a slow nod. "Like him. Devilish like him." He chuckled suddenly. "Damn it, you're like *us*. You're a Stensrood." He put out a worn hand. "Josiah, you're welcome."

The old Negro touched his elbow. "Chair's ready, Mist' Barnabas."

"Eh? What? Of course." He added confidentially to Josiah: "Insist on cosseting me. I've given up. Take my advice and don't *you* ever let a pack of children hound you about." He sat down carefully. "Thomas, I don't want that footstool." He shook his stick. "Tonight I'll have both feet on the ground, right on the ground."

Thomas's face split in a white-toothed grin as he whisked the stool away. "Yes *sir!*" He bowed, stepped down the room, elbows loose and knees high.

Barnabas's eye played about the room. "John, the sight of you and your brood, just splitting you're so healthy, makes me want to get out of the city and join you on the farm. That's *life!* And look at this fine Scotch lassie. Just made for it."

Eyes kindly, indifferent, jealous, turned on Flora. Unabashed and quite at ease in her ancient dress with its wide stripes, she moved toward the great chair. "Come out and stay with Graves and me."

He rapped on the floor with his stick. "By George, I'd like to."

Gil smiled sympathetically, then heard Ruth whisper to Heward, "Wouldn't he! Think of those children! Those names! George Washington! William Mackenzie!" Her hard eyes played over Josiah, who stood easily beside Graves.

Barnabas went on, "Any more children?"

Flora shook her sun-bleached head, then her eyes twinkled. "But the Lord knows we try hard enough."

Ruth snorted audibly and Sarah, flushing, turned on Talbot as a safe refuge. Barnabas stared, then chuckled. "You're like a wind off a hayfield, Flora. You—you're out of Chaucer. Nothing I hate like a leer and a snicker." His glance shot toward Carleton. He rubbed his hands, a look of deep content on his worn face. "All here, eh, Janet? Isn't it time—" He threw back his head. "What the devil's that?"

Primula was rolling out a long strip of brown carpeting that reached from the door to the foot of the old man's chair. A hush fell over the room. There was a shuffling in the hall, a soft scraping, and Thomas toiled through the door, dragging behind him something low and broad, heaped with white packages. Barnabas stared, rose slowly to his feet, found John by his side, eyes wide. Forsyth stifled an exclamation and Kate, unbelieving, pressed her hands to her cheeks. Slowly Thomas padded down the long room, drawing his load easily. At Barnabas's feet he turned, deftly spun the battered hand sled about, placed the iron-looped tongue in Barnabas's hand. His face was solemn. "Miss Janet she say mebbe you 'member this. This here on top's presents."

The old man still stared, fingers playing over the rough iron of the hand grip. Then he moistened his lips. "The sled!"

Kate moved to her father while John and Forsyth muttered together. Then Barnabas sat slowly down. "That's it. The very sled." He looked up at the portrait. "*You* remember this, eh?" His fingers ran over the battered tongue. "That nick nearly broke it, loading it onto the sloop at Ticonderoga. That dent—I remember it. A soldier on the landing on the St. Lawrence swung his musket butt against it." He drew out his handkerchief, blew his nose fiercely, blinked, stared defiantly about the crowded room. "Most of you young people don't know about this. If it hadn't been for this sled—well, we wouldn't be here now."

Fascinated, Gil edged closer, found Josiah's shoulder against his. Barnabas went on. "John, you remember this?"

The weather-beaten face softened. "Some. It was cold, riding on top of it."

"You, Kate?"

"Father, of course I do. But where—"

"How about you, Fors?"

Forsyth nodded. "Not likely to forget it." Gil knelt, fingered the worn edges of the boards. His father smiled gently. "See those notches, Gil? I walked behind it to keep the load from falling off—or to pick up your Uncle John if he rolled. Or Aunt Kate. I used to bark my shins against those boards. Sharp, they were."

Barnabas nodded shortly. "Your great-grandfather and I hauled it all the way from Albany."

Josiah looked thoughtful. "And you could have stayed if you'd pretended to think like the others?"

Barnabas's chin set. "And my brother Josiah could have stayed with us. We all left the old home because it was the only way we could live with ourselves. He left for one reason, we for another. And we were all of us right."

Sarah Sperry murmured to Talbot, "Why *must* they dig all that up?" Gil looked sharply at her, then caught a swift exchange of glances between Sperry and Mackie, a shrug that said, faintly tolerant: "These people from the Colonies, eh?"

Unexpectedly, Ruth's brittle voice broke in. "I think I'd like to have been with you."

Pleasure smoothed the deep lines from Barnabas's face. "Would you, my dear?" He looked keenly at her. "It would have done you good. And us." He turned back to the sled as Heward Mackie pinched his wife's shoulder. "Well, well," the old man went on. "What do you think of it, Thomas?"

"Me? What I think of it?" The black face glowed. "I'd a been mighty proud to a pulled it, Mist' Barnabas."

Barnabas smiled. "This is worth being ninety. Where the devil did you find it?"

Janet smoothed her soft hair. "It was in the barn. Do you remember when you moved from Kingston to Toronto?"

"Course I do. Only they called it York then. It was in '92."

"You left a lot of things in a warehouse. They were sent here later and stowed in the barn. The sled was with them and I found it last summer."

Barnabas nodded gravely. "It *would* take you to find it, Janet."

Kate edged closer to the sled. "And now aren't you going to open your presents?"

His eyebrows ruffled. "What? And have all you gaping at me like a lot of hyenas? Devil a bit. I'll have 'em taken to my wing. Then Thomas and I'll open 'em by ourselves. Won't we, Thomas?"

Thomas grinned. "Yes *sir!*"

"Then I'll find some way of thanking each of you. I know there's thought in every package." He stooped, peering. "Don't know *that* writing, though. Next to Gil's." He straightened, glanced at Josiah. "I'm a fool. Course I know it." Out of the corner of his eye he saw Carleton smothering a yawn, back half-turned on the group. "I'll say this for the States, Carleton. They teach penmanship there. Yours is like a half-witted child turned loose in a coal scuttle."

Sarah edged closer to Gil, her colorless hair tickling his cheek. "Wish he'd open 'em. There's a real silk scarf in ours. And Carleton found a beautiful pair of slippers at McKay's. I wish he'd wave ours in front of that Flora and Graves. What do you suppose *they* sent? Homespun?"

Carleton, lounging near by, snickered. "More likely hayseed. The difference between theirs and ours is—"

"Is that theirs is paid for," snapped Gil.

"Have to be. They couldn't get credit. Not in those clothes. Here—the old boy's talking again." Carleton looked covertly at his watch.

The strong, husky tones flowed easily under the dark rafters. ". . . And so, thank you all—and most grateful and happy—and—and—Damn it, Janet, do I starve on my ninetieth birthday?"

In slow procession the family wound across the print-hung hall. Gil and Josiah closed in on Forsyth. "You look as pleased as if this were your day," said Josiah.

"I've reason to be pleased."

Josiah laughed. "I should think you'd have plenty." He indicated the chattering wave that preceded them.

"It's more than that. It's something beyond the family, even. Josiah, this won't mean anything to you, but I want to tell Gil. Gil, I had a note from Hagerman. There's no doubt of the jury."

Gil nodded. "Rather expected that, though, after Robinson saying so, didn't you?"

"Oh, there's more than that. We're to have a quick trial. And still more, I'm to be allowed to see Innis from tomorrow on." He turned to Josiah. "There—that's all. Sorry."

"Don't be sorry," said Josiah. "And you're wrong about it's not meaning anything to me. I've heard a lot. Here, in Hamilton, in Dundas—" He waved his hand. "I think I can see why you're so pleased. What does the rest of the Compact say?"

Forsyth raised his eyebrows. "You *have* been learning. Why, I've heard that some of the more violent ones are furious. But we'll talk about that later."

The broad dining room opened before them, firelight and candles shining on the massive table with its gleam of bright glass, damask, and silver. Beyond it a carved sideboard twinkled with crystal and plate. Forsyth touched Josiah's elbow. "You'll sit across there between my wife and my sister Kate."

Gil found himself between Sarah and Ruth. Beyond Ruth's strained prettiness he saw John Stensrood's weather-beaten chin and stringy neck. Ruth smiled at Gil. "Won't he ask a blessing?" She turned to John. "It's such a nice custom. *We* always do."

"Blessing on what?" said Gil to himself. Then he grinned at John's rumbling answer. "Nice when you've got time. Mostly when we have supper we're too tired for anything but food. Guess it's different in the city." Under her cold gaze he slowly turned down his cluster of wineglasses. "No, when you've been stumping a field or haying or plowing, food and sleep's all you want."

Ruth's eyebrows rose lazily. "How interesting." She turned a smooth white shoulder on him, smiled at Gil. "So you're going to be a doctor? We-e-ell." Her lids fluttered. "Gil, you'll have all the women in Toronto turning into *per*manent *in*valids. Who are you studying with? Dr. Powell? Or that fascinating Dr. Sewell?"

Mildly amused he answered, "I thought you knew. Dr. Richland."

She screamed faintly. "A *Yan*kee! Gil! I heard that but I never really believed it. You can't— " She hitched her shoulders as a procession of black faces paraded in from the kitchen, steaming plates held high.

Gil seized his spoon. "Been with Doc going on two years. How often do you have to hear a thing to believe it?"

She bent her head, ringlets swinging. "Now Gil, I'm going to advise you. I'm really a *lot* more experienced than you are."

"Yes, I know," said Gil, busy with a thick pea soup.

Her thin mouth tightened. "You— " She bit her lip. "What I mean is, I can advise you. I want to see you get on in the world. You don't want to be just a—a— " she dropped her voice—"a peasant. Later on you'll want to know people like Dr. Strachan and Judge Jones and that wonderful Alan MacNab and— "

"I do know 'em." Gil laid down his spoon. "That's one reason I went with Richland."

She shook her head at him. "I could shake you. You're so blind. Running about after this Yankee and heaven knows where *he* came from, when you might be with these people from really fine old English families like— "

Gil sampled his sherry appreciatively. "Like Strachan? His father was a laborer in a quarry. Our revered Rector of York came out here as a Scotchbyterian dominie. Then he saw there was more money in Church of England, so he changed. Hear he's working on a coat of arms now and trying to tie up to Alfred the Great."

Stony-faced, Ruth folded her hands in her lap. If she had *only* been seated next to Josiah. He was fun, even if he was a Yankee. She puckered her forehead as she saw him laughing easily with Janet and her mother. Gil, chuckling inwardly, went back to his soup.

Sarah's low tones roused him. "I was saying, Gil, what do you think of that? On his right hand!" She nodded gently toward the head of the table where Barnabas devoted himself to Flora, whose sturdy sunburned arms were dark against the sleek tablecloth.

Gil nodded. "Don't they get on, though. Does him a lot of good. Wish she'd come down oftener."

Stung from her placidity, Sarah curled her lip. "If you want *my* opinion, she's after the estate."

Gil grunted. "Not Flora! And anyway, don't you know we've got primogeniture here? Estate's got to go to the eldest son. That means Father, then Cam."

Sarah shook her head. "*She*'ll find a way. Gil, all she ever thinks about is money. And money's *not* important. The most important thing in the world is *breeding*."

Her words tumbled out into a sudden hush. Flora looked up eagerly. "I agree with you, Sarah. I'm always telling Graves he puts too much into crops. Breeding! Not that that isn't trouble, too. Lord, when I think of spring coming on and all the cows and mares in heat and the nearest bull eight miles away across a Clergy Reserve strip! And as for a stallion!" She shook her head sadly.

Sarah gasped while Barnabas, catching Flora's gleaming eye, chuckled over his soup. "That's it, my dear. Fill up the country with good stock, two-legged and four, and the rest'll take care of itself." He grew serious again. "Go on, I want to hear about brushing out that road. Hard work. Did it myself in the old days. So'd Forsyth. Now, where do you start? Head of Pefferlaw Brook? Bless me, I know the brook. Then — "

Sarah leaned across Gil, saw John absorbed in Mary's talk, said to Ruth, "If I were Grandfather, I'd buy Uncle John and Graves out. Bring 'em to the city."

"And put 'em into the Land Office?" muttered Gil.

Ruth's eyes widened. "Oh — that'd *never* do. They haven't the — the style — "

"You mean they're too honest, don't you?" said Gil.

Sarah frowned. "Gil, you can be *so* disagreeable. What I mean is, they haven't got any money and it isn't good for the family to — "

"Don't talk so loud," warned Gil. "Uncle John's a fine farmer and so's Graves. They've had land troubles, but they've never taken a penny from Grandfather. He's tried to help them time and again, but they always say they're all right, thank you, and please don't do it again."

Ruth's chin set. "They ought to be *made* to." She picked daintily at the turtle, spiced and served in its shell, that followed the soup. "To think that dear Lady Simcoe invented this dish!"

Gil nodded. "Dear Lady Simcoe! Friend of yours?"

She laid down her fork. "There you are, Gil. You're always talking about education as if you had all there was in U.C. But — " she shrugged — "you don't even know that Lady Simcoe was here before I was born. Colonel Simcoe was Governor and won the War of 1812."

"Stout man," said Gil. "The memorial to him says he left U.C. in 1796 and died in England in 1808."

Ruth mentally erased him, and engaged Sarah in a long discussion of the shortcomings of most of the women of Toronto which lasted through the great roasts of beef and ham that black hands eased gently onto the table.

Gil devoted himself to food, watched Josiah good-humoredly parry Edward Sperry's bantering thrusts about life south of the border, was surprised to see Talbot's usually empty face light up as the new cousin told of a trip west to the Mississippi and up to Chicago. Then he looked toward the head of the table, saw Flora's sun-bleached hair bending closer to Barnabas's white shock, heard the old voice pleading: "But there's plenty in the family to make it easier for all of you. Make 'em sell out. I'll give Graves that strip along the Don."

Flora looked startled. "Sell *out?* And with this grand fight with

McLennan on our hands? And in ten years more, our farm'll be the best in the county and—"

"It's too hard work. I know what I'm talking about."

Flora looked wonderingly at him. "What's hard about it? And I don't *want* more help. Think I want strange people poking about in my house, or looking after the cows when they're dropping calves? Why—Graves and I have got *everything*. We—"

Barnabas was looking at her quizzically. "So you've got everything. H'm. Don't know that I've heard more than three people say that in the last ninety years. Most people—" Gil saw the old eyes wander down the table. "Well, I guess just you and—" He looked up at the black face of Thomas, watchful above the high, carved chair. "Just you and Thomas and me, eh? But remember, Flora, I'm always here, always here." He raised his wineglass, squinted through its rich depths.

Gil sighed, watched Wedgwood replace Limoges on the bright cloth as ice cream from Rossi's was proudly borne in. Sarah forgot her gossip, forgot her irritation with Gil, as the particolored block steamed lightly on its platter. "Rossi's," she murmured. "There never was such ice cream. Gil, I've heard people who've been in England say that it's even better than the ice cream at Grange's." Her eyes shone. Heedless of the clatter of talk, she bent to her plate.

Janet skillfully gathered the women with her eyes, and led them back to the drawing room in rustling parade; ruddy port circled the table. The men hunched their chairs nearer to Barnabas, who slowly spun his glass in a fragile hand. "Ha! Glad we got those confounded toasts over early. Not that I mind drinking to His Majesty—" he inclined his head slightly—"but, damn it, a glass was made to talk over. Here, Carleton, pull your chair up closer. Haven't heard a word out of you yet. Seems to me I don't know a thing about you."

"Very busy, Grandfather," mumbled Carleton as he gulped his port, eyes hopefully on the decanter.

"Busy? Busy? I never hear of it. When are you going to get married?"

Edward Sperry delicately cracked a walnut, smiled to himself. "Don't worry about Carleton. He's fitting himself to take his place in Toronto. The way Talbot and Ruth have taken theirs."

John pushed his unstained glass farther from him. "What sort of a place, Ed?"

Gil caught Josiah's eye across the table.

Sperry went on, rather loftily, "The sort of place one of our family deserves." He turned to Forsyth. "I was telling Kate just the other night that we're the only ones who do anything to keep up a position. You others make it damned hard for us. Talbot does his part. So do Heward and Carleton. But the rest of you! Fors, you and Cam are almost in trade. And there's no need of it. It's bad for the family. Why, if I dropped the word—" he made an expansive gesture—"say, to Kit Hagerman, he'd make a place for Cam where he wouldn't have to scrape like a greengrocer. I *know* Kit'd do it in a minute—for me. And there's no reason, Fors, why *you* shouldn't sit on boards with men like John Strachan and Bev Robinson and—"

"Yes, there is," smiled Forsyth.

Edward Sperry waved magnificently. "Nonsense! You're too modest. They'd be glad to have you, I'm sure. And, of course, we could find something appropriate for John and Graves. Not in the city, of course."

Graves, his broad face quietly amused, clasped his hands on the table. "Appropriate for us? You must be mighty powerful, Uncle Ed."

Sperry swelled. "Oh, it's just in knowing the right people, Graves."

Still smiling, Graves said, "We think we know the right people. And we're quite happy where we are." His father nodded in silent approval.

Talbot rattled walnut shells about. "You don't know how you hurt yourself, Cam. You're just an ordinary lawyer. Uncle Fors gave up his judgeship. Uncle John and Graves actually *work* their own farms. And as for Gil! Going about the country with a Yank—a doctor, visiting people you wouldn't even hire, let alone dine with."

Edward Sperry broke in again. "Damn it all, Tal and I are right. You put it very well, Tal. You people *are* in trade. Why aren't you asked to dine at the Margetts'? At the Gilmours'?"

Gil flushed, started to speak, then caught Cameron's eye. His brother said: "Let's stay in trade. You know how Margett made his start? Came here from New York State with a prison record. Then he married the woman who ran the Frontenac Arms, a filthy stews down in the Devil's Quarter-Acre. Then he learned something to the disadvantage of—well, Father knows—and to keep him quiet, he was put into the Clergy Reserve Offices."

Gil leaned over the table. "Gilmour? Shipped out from England because his family couldn't stand him. He borrowed some money, married, and turned his house into a bordello, no less, and staffed with his new family. That landed him in the Welland Canal business."

Mackie stared coldly at him. "I suppose you got that from that damned horse doctor of yours." He turned to Forsyth. "See what he gets into? You oughtn't to let him—"

Edward Sperry raised his hand. "That's just what I'm talking about. Here we are, sitting over good port, and all of you talk like men in trade. If you'd only know the right people!" He suddenly pushed back his chair, frowned at his watch. "I'm afraid our carriage is here now." His fox face smiled toward Barnabas. "Yes, it's sure to be."

Barnabas stared. "God bless my soul! Not going? Why, damn it, the evening's just begun!"

The pointed face wagged importantly. "Be a pleasure. Be a pleasure. But if you knew what it means to sit on so many boards." He sighed, a martyr to duty. "Got to see Sir John. Got to see—oh, well, a lot of people tomorrow. Got to—Ready, Hew? Ready, Tal?" Chairs scraped hastily on the floor. "No, no. You others just sit here. We'll collect our wives and say good-night to Janet and Mary. Oh—and of course to Flora. Here, Carleton, here. Wait and say good-night before you leave the room. That's it, and tell Grandfather we'll *all* be back for his ninety-first birthday." He frowned at his watch again, bowed, and shepherded his flock out of the room.

Barnabas's eyebrows jumped. "All be back for my ninety-first? He's an optimist."

John's neck craned. "Optimist? Why, you've never been sick in your life, Father."

Barnabas smiled slowly. "Oh—*I'll* be here. Now don't let the decanter fall asleep. John, I can't see why you and Graves have to follow the cold-water Methodists. You don't know what you're missing."

"Live up in the Bush and you'll see what we're missing. Bad whiskey at sixpence a quart's done more harm than the whole Compact—almost." John scowled at his empty glass. "I've seen whole families lying drunk among the stumps and work needing to be done."

Gil nodded. "I've seen it too. And no farther away than the valley of the Don. Anything like that in the States, Jos?"

"Pretty bad out in the settlements." He set down his glass carefully. "What was that you were saying about the Welland Canal, Gil?"

"How did you hear about that?" asked Cam.

"There was a lot in our papers. Didn't say what happened to the people who got caught."

John smiled grimly. "Nothing happened. The courts said, 'Well, now isn't that too bad!' And that was all."

Josiah looked puzzled. "No sentences?"

Graves shook his head sourly. "How could there be? There never are for the Compact. Look at Peter Robinson."

"Who's he?" asked Josiah.

"Brother of John Beverley, the Chief Justice," put in Forsyth. "He's a very good case in point, Peter is. It's been proved that he, as Commissioner of Crown Lands, is short several thousand pounds of public moneys. That's all. Just proved. He's still Commissioner. As for Merritt, who was head of the whole Canal business, just read Mackenzie's report on *him*."

Josiah frowned. "I've been hearing about this Mackenzie ever since I landed. Just who is he?"

"The greatest man in Canada," said Graves shortly.

Forsyth smiled indulgently. "Well, he's the busiest. You see, Jos, this Mackenzie's probably the happiest man in the world. He's a born agitator—and he lives in Upper Canada. I can't think of another part of the world where he'd have such a field. The Compact gives him so much fuel that he's living his rather demagogic life right to the hilt. Every second."

Gil flushed. "But Father—"

John cut in shortly. "I don't agree with you, Fors. He's no demagogue. He's a patriot to his finger tips." He turned to Jos.

"He was born desperately poor in Scotland, tried shopkeeping, didn't like it. Saved a little money and came out here. He and John Lesslie — "

"Brother to James. You remember," murmured Gil to Josiah.

"And John Lesslie," went on John, "started a shop and did very well with it. Mackenzie drifted into politics, and before you could turn around founded the Reform Party — or was one of the founders. He dropped business — and he was making a pretty penny, too — and started a paper. Ever since, he's been the one real champion of Reform."

"And when they turned the town of York into the city of Toronto last year, Mackenzie was elected the first Mayor," put in Graves.

"Those are the facts," said Cameron. "But as to Mac's intentions — well, I honestly don't think he has any. If a Reform Government came in from top to bottom, he'd be lost. Nothing to agitate against. Could be dangerous, I think."

"Dangerous!" shouted John. "Look at the courts. I'll go farther than Mackenzie. I say if we can't get Englishman's justice in an Englishman's court, then we're justified in — "

"In what, John?" asked Forsyth quickly.

Gil slapped his hand on the table. "We're justified in violence. That's what Uncle John means."

Graves nodded approvingly. "Well, so you're learning something, if the others aren't."

John nodded grimly. "That's what it's like, Jos. Now mind you, there's no one in Upper Canada more loyal to the King than I am, but — "

Barnabas emptied his glass, got up, Thomas attentive by his elbow. He chuckled. " 'No one more loyal to the King than I, but — ' Damn it, I heard those very words along the Hudson, John, back in the '70's. Heard 'em from Phil Schuyler and he meant 'em, too. Know who Phil was? Ha! Jos knows! Great friend of my father." He chuckled again. "He became a rebel general. Old Phil! Ha! Thomas, you and I are going to join the ladies. The rest of you cubs better come along before John starts raising — what did they use to call 'em in the old days? — Minutemen — that's it. Now, Thomas — "

They followed him slowly across the hall. As they entered the living room, Barnabas waved his stick at Flora, who stood with her back toward the fire. "Don't you stir, Flora. Plenty of room for both of us."

Gil, trailing in the rear, saw her grin, toss back her head. "Just getting it warm for once. As soon as winter comes, I'll be sitting in puddles most of the time."

The old man settled himself in his chair, looked down benignly on the old sled. "Gil, I wish you'd just move this a little nearer me. Good." His fragile hand reached out, closed around the iron handle. "You don't know how this brings back the old years. This—and the talk around the table. Same old story. Bah! What a pack of fumblers we are!" His keen eyes swung suddenly to Josiah, who sat on a low bench between Cam and Mary. "Aren't we, Jos?"

Josiah, startled from his contemplation of a print of some forgotten sea fight on the wall above him, looked down. "What? Well, I don't know. Plenty of bad things going on in the States."

Barnabas looked at him severely. "Now I must say that's beautifully tolerant of you." His stick drummed on the floor. "Did you think I meant *just* Toronto? Or *just* U.C.? Damn it, I meant all of us. Fumbling and mumbling. You thought you'd found the right way to live. Well, you're not shaken down yet. Maybe you never will be. We thought we'd found it, those of us who stayed by the King. And look at us!"

"I think we were right," said Forsyth quietly.

Barnabas leaned slowly forward. "Yes? And when does the Innis trial come off?"

Janet, serene face alert, smiled at him. "Father, are you working around for a chance to say that the Compact's right?"

"I think he's heading toward Will Mackenzie," said Gil.

"Heading? Heading?" The old voice was sharp. "*I* don't have to head anywhere. Not at ninety. And if I did, I wouldn't know where. Webster? Jackson? I don't think so. Strachan? Robinson? Or Baldwin and Fors? Or Mackenzie? I don't know. We're all fumblers. If we weren't, we'd know by now who's right."

"Aren't you a little hard on us who have to choose?" asked Mary, busy with a bit of embroidery.

"No! I'm easy. Fumblers. H'm, perhaps I am. Fumblers isn't the word. I think I know it. It's—it's—" His eyes seemed suddenly far away. "The woods by the St. Lawrence. We were waiting. We'd been bitterly disappointed. Someone sang in the woods, at night—in the snow. A woman. What—what was it?"

Suddenly Janet's clear tones sounded softly:—

> "Who watcheth over all, whose eye is never sleeping,
> God make the dark night bright to the wanderer."

Barnabas started. "Ha! That's it. 'Bright to the wanderer.' Wanderers, not fumblers. Wanderers, the whole lot. Compacters, moderates, Mackenzie-ites."

Gil, on the sofa between John and Flora, wrinkled his forehead, tried to catch the air. "Funny—I've heard that—and yet I haven't. Is it English, Mother?"

Janet shook her head. "I don't know."

Barnabas stared at her. "Then where did you learn it?"

She bit off a piece of thread. "From a very beautiful lady. From Mrs. Barnabas Stensrood. I used to sing Gil to sleep with it."

The old hands closed over the iron handle. "That's it. Kate heard it, too. Odd how you remember things. She sang it when she was in the bateau, starting across the St. Lawrence. She was trying to cover little Kate and John, here, with her cloak. Across the St. Lawrence! Ha! What we thought we were coming to then. John Simcoe! He'd planned an aristocracy based on land. Coronets! Respectful peasants in the hedgerows, touching their forelocks! The damned idiot! Titles! In Upper Canada!"

Flora was delighted. "Titles? Graves, you'd be Duke of Muckheap and Father'd be Earl of Lower Hayfield. Gil, what'd you be? Count of Calomel? Or—" She stopped, wrinkled her nose, staring at the heavy curtains of the east windows. "Burning rubbish this time of night?" She sniffed again. "There is *some*thing." She crossed to the window. "Look! It *is* fire. Out on the drive. What—"

The others crowded to her side, peered out onto a dull, mounting flare that swelled in the night, at a vague, shifting mass of people, aimless in the wavering light. Mary caught Cameron's arm. "Look—it must be the people from around York Mills. They've—why, they've come to set up an illumination for Grandfather. Oh!" She slipped an arm about Janet's shoulder. "All those people! Grandfather!" She beckoned. "It's for you! It's—"

"For me? Bless my soul! Thomas, you leave me alone. You go out to the buttery and tell that pack out there to roll out a barrel of beer for 'em. Roll out two! Let 'em wallow in it. Damn it, I hope there won't be a clear head on Yonge Street from the bay to Lake Simcoe by sunrise. Roll 'em out." He waved his stick. "Damn these curtains. Nail 'em back if you have to. Want to see 'em! Ha! Good folk, every soul there. They—"

The press flowed closer through the night, turned the bend of the drive and spilled over onto the sere grass. The sullen flare broke up into knots of spluttering torches, shone on waving arms, on tall hats and flat caps, glinted feebly on a crude wagon that bumped along the gravel, something tall and spidery rearing up from it against the star-flecked sky. John nudged Forsyth. "This'll please him. Deserves it, too. Done a lot for the country." He nodded to himself, looked quickly away as he saw Mary's fingers slip to her eyes, then drop. "They've got—Good God! What's that?"

The wagon was swiftly trundled broadside to the house. Above its clumsy frame, two uprights and a crossbeam made a square, inverted U. From the beam three dark masses swung and dangled. More torches flamed and flared. The mob, the battered cart, seemed to leap out of the night, and sharp and clear were the placards that hung from the limp effigies, the painted sign harsh over the beam.

The voice of the crowd welled up, heavy sticks pointed to placard and sign, hammered on the board where "Traitor" was a hard parade of black letters against white wood, rapped on the placards that bore the names "F. Stensrood," "Innis," "C. Stensrood." An arm swung in the murky flare. Somewhere in the dark, glass splintered in a cold whine.

Flora's strong arms swept in a swift arc as the curtains blotted out the mob and the voice of the mob. Eyes hard and bright, she faced the others, who stared, stunned and white. Her voice was thick in her throat. Her tones struggled out, blurred with the forgotten tang of the Highlands. "Nae gangrel bodies c'n pit a slight tae a hoose whaur a MacGreegor's made welcome!"

Outside the clamor swelled. More glass shattered and a broken shout of "traitors" rocketed up. Flora swung away from the window. "I'll gae oot an' cowp their dirty wee bit cart an'—"

Forsyth caught her arm. "Flora! Stay here! Janet, you better take the girls into the back passage. John, you and Graves and—Gil! Josiah! Come back here! Drop those sticks. John, you take Father and—"

John's face was streaked with anger. "Let me go! I'd like a brush with that lot. Graves! Stay here! I order you." Other voices joined in: "You stay here with—" . . . "I'm youngest! I'm going to—" . . . "Gil! Once more, put—down—that—stick!"

Something pounded on the floor. Barnabas trumpeted: "Silence! You cubs keep quiet. Thomas! Take my arm!" He walked stiffly down the room. "*I* shall attend to this."

Darkness seemed to pour into the hall as Barnabas flung the door open and stepped out onto the broad porch where a dim lantern shone softly on his erect white head. He glared out into the night, then cocked his ear. He heard a key grate in the lock, muttered: "Sure that's turned, Thomas? Can't have that pack stamping out and interfering with us."

There was a murmur from the shadowy bodies about the burning effigies, a sudden sway toward the porch, a thick mutter. "It's the old man. We wasn't told nothin' 'bout him."

Barnabas raised his stick, threw back his head chuckling. "Well, well, well!"

Feet shifted uneasily on the trampled grass. Barnabas tucked his stick under his arm, rubbed his hands. "Now this is devilish kind of you. It's—it's—damn it, it's neighborly and I can't think of a better thing for a man or woman to be." He lifted his hand. "I've been neighbor to most of you for more years than a man's got a right to count. Been a neighbor to *some*one in U.C. since seventeen hundred and eighty-one." He rolled out the words, savoring them. "Long time, isn't it? But there's nothing in those years to match what my Yonge Street neighbors have done tonight."

There was a puzzled murmur, half-angry, from the torchlit grass. Barnabas waved his hand, went on. "Now—I don't see very well, can't see little things. But I *can* see that you've gone to work and made an illumination for a neighbor on a night that means a lot to him. And I can't hear too well, but I know that what you're shouting is as warm and as friendly as what I'm saying to you now."

Slowly rough-shod feet crept nearer. The firm, husky voice went on. "You've done something to make an old man happy, damn it. I want you to do something else. Now, this is my ninetieth birthday. Don't need to tell you that. You know it or you wouldn't be here." He chuckled richly. "Well, I've never had a ninetieth birthday before." Reluctant laughter welled up from the crowd. "So I've told my people to roll out two barrels of beer and I want you to knock the bungs out and drink until the foam runs out of your ears. And if two barrels aren't enough, by God, we'll roll out two more! Now I've talked too long. I'm getting cold. But before I go in, I want you to join me in three cheers for His Majesty, King William the Fourth."

There was an instant of pause and then the night rocked to the outburst. Barnabas waved his stick. "Damned if I don't think he could have heard that clear in London. Now, here comes the beer round the side of the house. Good night and thank you! Thomas, turn the key."

The door jarred open and he stalked into the soft inner warmth, eyes fierce and lips compressed, marched to the chair by the fire under the wondering disapproval of his family. Janet threw a shawl over his knees while Mary stirred up the fire. Flora, white-faced and hands working, sat silently on the sofa.

There was a moment's pause, then Forsyth broke out, "You should *not* have done that."

Barnabas glared at him. "I'll not be told what I should have done and what I should not have done. Not by any of you! It worked, didn't it?"

"And you locked the door," growled John.

"Of course I did! At least you had the sense to quit tugging at it as soon as you heard the crowd quiet down." His fierce eyes swept over the room. "Where's Gil? Where's Josiah?"

The others looked about. Graves frowned. "They were both here. I saw them when — " Footsteps beat softly in the corridor beyond the living room, padded cautiously on into the hall. A tousled head, a muddy shoulder, ducked swiftly past the door, started up the stairs.

The stick pounded on the floor. "Gilbert! Josiah! Come to me!"

The footsteps crept unwillingly back. Gil, face discolored, shirt torn and coat over his arm, stood in the doorway. Beside him, Josiah alternately swept a handkerchief over his muddy forehead and dabbed at a bleeding lip. Barnabas stretched out a lean old hand, sharp forefinger pointing. "I ordered you to stay inside. *Where were you?*"

Gil threw back his head defiantly. "Went out."

Josiah, dabbing, mumbled, "By the side door."

"Ha! You did! But you *heard* me! Don't they teach English in the schools? Or in the States? *What* did you do?"

Gil's chin set. "Went out." He examined skinned knuckles. "We found that damned Parry Allan there. He was egging 'em on."

"Eh? He was? What did you do?"

Gil looked rueful. "Nothing. Jos got to him first. Knocked him clear across Yonge Street."

Flora, color returned, got up and stood by the fire. "That's what they needed!" With lingering relish she asked, "Any others?"

Barnabas tapped her foot with his stick. "I'm doing this, Flora. Josiah, what about you?"

"Well, there was a sort of a fight after that. Gil pulled someone off my neck and—"

The crown of white hair shook. "That was the worst thing you could have done. I was calming them at the front. If they had any idea that I was being a decoy—well, we might have seen the fire spread from the cart to the roof of Nipigon. It was hare-brained! It was idiotic! It was damned foolishness! It was disobedience! It was—it was, damn it, it was just what I'd a done at your age. Thomas! We all want brandy. Old, rich brandy!" He began to chuckle. "Flora, I'd give a lot to see you stirred up again. Always told Graves he had a fine girl." His eyes fell on the bedraggled pair. "You two! Go upstairs and try to get civilized again! Primula'll bring you hot water—and your brandy. But—ah—don't get *too* civilized." He chuckled again.

Side by side Gil and Josiah trotted up the broad staircase, shaking their heads.

They swung down a long, paneled corridor into Gil's room where a wide four-poster mounted guard. By the window a tall secretary showed a tangle of books and specimen bottles behind its glass doors. They limped to the bed, sat down heavily. Then Josiah began to laugh. "I'd rather face that whole mob than my great-uncle."

Gil fingered a rising welt on his forehead. "Grandfather's quite a buck."

Downstairs by the fire, Barnabas closed his eyes as he sipped his brandy, seeking refuge in a fatigue he did not feel to hide his thoughts from his family. "Traitors—because they defend an innocent man against the Compact!" He sighed, shook his head. "Wouldn't tell these cubs here for a pot of gold. But—it's getting worse. I swear it's getting worse. And it was bad enough before." The haunting air of the old hymn began to play through his mind. "God make the dark night bright to the wanderer."

He drank again, then lifted his eyes to the portrait of old Gilbert Stensrood. Suddenly his glass jarred on the arm of his chair. "What did *you* think, seeing Josiah here tonight? Don't grin at me like that. Damn it, you *must* know it now. Father, we backed the wrong horse."

VIII

Justice — 1835

"THERE's your father. Cam's with him," said Josiah.

"Where?" Gil looked along the slow press that choked King Street, surging in a dull shuffle toward the high-shouldered courthouse and its brick twin, the jail.

"See his hat? Over on the other side, just beyond the two men on horseback."

"Got him," said Gil tersely, giving to the sway of the crowd. "Let's get over there." Sidewise, he began to work his way against the drift, Josiah edging after him. "Keep working left, Jos. Getting closer." He craned his neck. "Hi! What's that?"

Away by the open space between courthouse and jail, a belt of red, hard in the sun of the winter morning, flared among the dark coats of the civilians; shakos shone and glittered.

"By God! They've called troops out. A whole company of the Fifteenth."

"I'll be damned!" panted Jos. "Bayonets fixed, too. See 'em shine. Must be a guard in our honor."

Gil shrugged grimly. "You'll see. Hoy! Watch out!"

The sway of the crowd carried them against the end of a low cart. Boots grated in the dust, cloth ground and rasped against cloth as they worked free again. Then a voice bellowed, "Clear a way! Clear a way!" The crowd shook, broke slowly to left and right as a red-faced officer drove a nervous horse along the street. "Clear a way! You people have got to leave a passage here." The press shivered, closed in behind him, thicker than ever.

Gil lunged, wriggled on, threw out a hand. "How does it look, Father?"

Forsyth turned, smiled mechanically. "Hoped you'd get here, Gil. You too, Jos. Here they are, Cam."

Cameron nodded, his stock awry and lapels crushed. "Devil of a mess, isn't it?" He suddenly drove both arms, palms open, against a heavy man in front of him. "No you don't, m'lad!" The man scowled, edged away. "Fourth time they've tried that," said Cam.

"Tried what?" asked Gil.

"Roughs tried to get us in a knot and run us down to the bay."

Josiah looked grimly pleased. "Did they? Come on, Gil. You link with Uncle Fors and I'll hook up with Cam." His vast shoulders heaved ahead, looming above the crowd.

Gil shuffled along by his father. "Bad, eh?"

"I'm afraid so, Gil. Our carriage was stoned, coming down Yonge Street. That's why we're walking. They don't dare throw stones now for fear of hitting a Compact nose."

"You didn't tell me how the case looks."

Forsyth's forehead wrinkled. "Wish I knew. The Compact hangers-on are so damned ugly, it almost makes me hopeful." He dropped his voice. "If we do get Innis off, I want you and Jos to get out quick. Go right out to Nipigon. It won't be safe for a Stensrood to — "

Gil stared. "*We* mouse off and leave you and Cam?"

"They'll have to give us a guard of troops."

"Huh! We'll talk about that when the time comes. Think you may get him off?"

"Gil, I can't see more than one move ahead. The Compact promises one thing, then goes back on it, promises something else. For instance, I've never been able to see Innis alone. And they never moved him to another cell. He's better, though."

"Better?"

"He was in bad shape. But he's quite brisk, now. He wants to defend himself, so we wrote out a defense together. If there's any fairness at all, it ought to do him good. Then, in case of an adverse decision, we drew up a plea for him to present after the verdict. He'll have it in his pocket."

"He's going to defend *himself?*"

"He's had law experience. It'll produce a fine effect, I think. I'd only be saying the same — Here, here! Jos! I don't want *two* trials on my hands."

Josiah looked apologetically over his shoulder. "But he *looked* as if he was going to start something, didn't he, Cam?"

The crowd was thinning out a little as they shuffled past the high walls of the jail and the stockade that joined it to the court.

"Well, Cam and I are slipping off here," said Forsyth. "See you later."

Gil gripped his hand. "Good luck, Father." Then he worked up beside Josiah. "Got your pass, Jos? They'll take up the passes inside."

They tramped on by a line of wooden-faced infantry, bayonets bright. The bulk of the crowd stopped in the street, ready for its long wait for the verdict. In the open triangle formed by the steps and the two lines of troops, little knots of men stood, watching. Their hands were jammed into their coat pockets from which jutted heavy clubs. A dozen paces in front of Gil, a thickset man started for the steps on sturdy bowlegs. A man detached himself from one of the knots, called, "Let me see your pass."

The man looked mildly surprised. "I got it all right."

One of the knots edged toward him. The leader said again, "Let me see your pass."

Bowlegs braced themselves securely. "Well, by God! By what authority?"

"That's my business." A powerful hand stretched out.

The stocky man grinned, brought out a strip of paper. "Just to keep you happy, if you really want to see it."

The paper was snatched from him, torn in shreds.

"I'll be God damned!" The bowlegs slid to one side, capable fists shot out. The leader dodged, shouted, "Get him." A club thwacked on broad shoulders, a foot moved swiftly, and the stocky man rolled on the frozen ground. Hands seized him, hustled him off, shouting for help.

Josiah ducked his head, started in pursuit. Gil wrenched at his collar, pulled him back. "It's no use. You'd only get a broken head. Look at 'em all."

Josiah stamped with rage. "But they didn't give him a chance. And all those damned soldiers looking on and — "

"It's no use, I tell you."

Josiah growled. "Seems to me you've been saying 'It's no use' too damned long up here."

"We have," muttered Gil. "Now — up the steps with you."

They started up the stone slabs. Then a hand fell on Josiah's shoulder. "Let's have a look at — "

Josiah's big arms whirled. "Get out of my way." The man spun dizzily, crashed against the side of the building. From the ground below a man shouted, "Let 'em alone! Let 'em go in." Gil caught Josiah's arm. "For God's sake, will you get inside?" He shoved and hustled his cousin through the doors.

Josiah chafed his hands. "Is that all? Aren't they coming after us?"

"Won't dare. Now come along."

Josiah trotted obediently by his side. "Hell! I was hoping I'd really get a shot at someone."

"Day isn't over yet," growled Gil.

At the foot of the shallow stairs, a watery-eyed man mildly took up their passes. Josiah said to him gently, "There are men outside who didn't want us to behold the majesty of the law."

"Eh?" said the man, blinking.

"They tried to take our passes away."

"Dear, dear, dear." The sigh was profound. "Court day is often rough. But we can't afford proper police. It would make for high taxes, it would."

"How much do you suppose it cost to have those gangs out there?" asked Josiah.

Gil tugged at his elbow. "Come along, Jos. That won't do any good." He ran upstairs, Josiah at his elbow, pushed open a door marked "Visitors."

The little balcony was packed. Men and women jammed into the seats, crouched by the railing, sat in the short aisles. Gil looked about. "Get that space at the back, Jos. We'll have to stand, but we can see better." They slid behind the last row of seats, leaned against the wall.

The opposite balcony was even fuller, but the great pit of the court itself was bare. Gil felt an inner quaking as he eyed the cold dignity of the judge's bench, the jury box, the prisoner's pen, the tables where the opposing counsel would sit. Even the Royal Arms back of the bench seemed menacing, hostile. His hands felt moist, cold, his knees weak. He thought: "Father and Cam — they've got to walk out there — and save Innis. Kit Hagerman's prosecuting the case. He'll — "

He started, aware that Josiah was prodding him. "Huh? What?"

"Over there. Opposite side, near the front. Damned pretty girl. Know her?"

A dull pain swept over Gil. He nodded shortly. "Yes. Lives out the Don." He tried to keep his eyes off the lifted face under the gray bonnet, off the mass of soft hair that fell to the shoulders in ringlets, the laughing mouth. It had all happened at the ball at Nipigon. Stung by the thoughtless jokes of some of the guests, by a reference to William Lyon MacFalstaff and his Alliance army, he had found relief from the hot rage which, under his own roof, he had to hide, in whispering to Sandra, at every chance, lurid details of the rise of some of the Compact families, of their present activities. Shocked at first, she too had shown a flare of temper, seeing in his remarks only an attack on friends of her father and of herself, on people with whom she had grown up. She had faced him, saying that they were her friends; that if Gil held such opinions of them he must think the same of her and her family. Thereafter she had carefully avoided him. And now she sat in the opposite balcony, laughing, in a knot of Compact matrons and young men who had come to see justice done to a traitor. He shut his ears to Josiah's rhapsody, coldly took note of the three Sperrys laughing and bowing as though they were at a theater, saw Heward Mackie being deferential to a judge's son. The honest red face of Colonel Fitzgibbon, hero of the War of 1812 and Commander of the Militia, shone out like clean sunlight through a miasmic fog.

Then footsteps sounded in the pit below. A court official, sword by his side, walked slowly and pompously through a wide door, a vast glass bowl in his arms. Through its bright sides, tight rolls of paper showed.

Josiah paused in his inspection of the bonnets in the opposite balcony, whispered: "What's the matter? Is he going to take a bath?"

Gil shook his head impatiently. "It's the jury rolls. The Compact's made a great play of honest drawing in this case. No chance of packing, they say. One of the reasons we feel hopeful." He squinted at the bowl. "Looks all right to me."

"H'm." Josiah rubbed his chin slowly. "Does it?"

Gil shrugged. "There are the rolls. A deputy'll stick his hand in. We can see through the glass."

The bowl thudded down onto a table in the center of the room. The official dusted off his hands, looked up to the balconies as though expecting applause, and stalked slowly out. The arched ceiling echoed back a low buzzing, a few laughs. Then more attendants swarmed onto the floor, arranged chairs in scuffling lines for latecomers who couldn't find room in the balconies. The buzz grew, suddenly died away.

Another door opened and five men filed into the room. Gil started. "They're going to draw now. Right away. That man with the big sword — Deputy Sheriff Mason."

"Compacter?"

"Of course."

A black staff rapped on the floor. A lean, elderly man with a turkey-like wattle gabbled off a string of unintelligible words in a high, reedy voice. Mason walked gravely to the table. The balconies seemed to sway toward him.

Josiah nudged Gil. "Quick. See the rolls?"

Gil nodded impatiently.

"Twelve men to a jury?"

"That's it."

"Well, from where I am, there's a little stack of rolls apart from the others. See it — toward the front of the bowl. I'd say just about twelve. I'd — "

Gil turned pale, gripped the back of the chair ahead of him.

Mason raised his hand solemnly, then plunged it among the papers. Josiah clutched Gil's shoulder, fingers clawlike. "He's got 'em. God damn it, he's got 'em!"

Heads turned in the balcony. From the floor a deep voice rumbled: "At the least sign of disorder, I shall clear the court."

A dead hush followed. Then the voice went on. "The jury for the case of *The King* versus *George Innis* has been drawn. Michael Cuniffe, Ralph Comer . . ."

As the names rolled out, a line of men passed from a door close by the bench, took their places in the jury box.

Gil ground his teeth. "Had 'em all ready. Had 'em right there. Every damned one of 'em *known* as paid by the Compact." He shivered.

"Couldn't do this at home," growled Josiah.

"Couldn't? How about New York? And anyway, you're not at home now."

"Think you have to tell me? This makes me so damned mad I'd like to wreck the place."

"No concern of yours."

"Oh, isn't it? Isn't this against *my* uncle? They—" He stopped, stared.

The hush was intense as a door by the bench opened again and Forsyth, head held high, walked coolly to the table by the right of the room. Cameron, face expressionless but eyes alert, followed him. After them came the clerk of courts, a short, sad-faced man, then a troop of minor officials. Forsyth and Cameron seated themselves, began to talk in low tones.

Gil watched them, felt all his muscles straining as though from the high balcony he could pour his own young strength down to the aid of his father and his brother, for them and the man they were defending.

Another door banged aggressively and Kit Hagerman stamped out onto the floor, an obsequious train following him, slammed down at the table opposite Forsyth and turned his swarthy face and broken nose in a fierce scowl at the jury.

Josiah gasped. "My God! What a pirate! Is *he* prosecuting?"

Gil, mouth dry, nodded.

The staff rapped again. In a flutter of black robes, the Judge climbed briskly to the bench, faced the court, his long, impassive face unchanging.

Gil gnawed at his knuckles. "This is worse yet. We thought Robinson might hear the case. Bad enough, but—that man—"

"Who is he?"

"D'Arcy Blaine. Cousin of the Boultons. God, Jos, this is bad."

The clerk's sad face bobbed up. "May it please Your Honor—the case of *The Crown* versus *George Innis*."

Cold as a splinter of glass, the voice from the bench answered: "Let the accused be brought in."

A tense ripple flowed over the packed balconies. "He's coming." Josiah's voice was strained.

Gil gulped, nodded. "One thing in our favor. Innis always makes a good appearance. Big, hearty, got an easy manner. Keen as mustard but never loses his head."

The murmuring snapped short as though giant fingers had closed on a hundred throats. Out into the courtroom, hemmed in by four heavy guards, there stepped a bent, shrunken old man. An old, old man of forty whose clothes hung in bags and wrinkles from his sagging shoulders, flapped loosely about shrunken legs. Aimless hands wandered vaguely to a shock of white hair, played about slack lips. Hesitant uncertain eyes blinked, lifted in mild, uncomprehending surprise to the balconies, to the close-packed chairs on the floor. His feet shuffled. A not unkindly push guided him to the prisoner's box, where he stood, hands resting loosely on the rail.

The room blurred before Gil's eyes. He felt his throat contract.

Josiah leaned forward. "Where's Innis, Gil?"

Dumbly, Gil pointed.

"But you said he was — "

Gil swallowed hard. "Right. He *was*."

Josiah settled back against the wall, his mouth a slash above his square chin, his eyes cold.

A shiver ran down Gil's spine as the chill voice knifed out from the bench. "George Innis, you are charged with being a seditious and ill-disposed person. You have contrived and maliciously intended the peace and tranquillity of our lord, the King, within the Province of Upper Canada, to disquiet and disturb. You have plotted to incite discontent, unrest, sedition — "

Josiah seized Gil's arm. "He can't do that! He's stated the charge and then gone ahead as though it was proved. He — "

"You tell him about it," said Gil shortly.

" — and to drive the liege subjects of His Majesty in this Province to treason. To treason against the person of His Majesty. You have plotted and planned to drench the Province in blood — and then to sell it for thirty pieces of silver to the barbarians south of the border. You have — "

In the prisoner's box, the accused swayed gently back and forth, a meaningless smile on his face. A shaft of sunlight fell across his hands as they lay loosely on the rail before him. He smiled tremulously as though the bright flecks pleased him, as though they were something warm and friendly, something that formed a sure bar between him and the voice from the bench.

Then Blaine reared back in his chair, swung suddenly on the vaguely smiling man in the prisoner's box. "How say you, George Innis, are you guilty or not guilty?"

The smile faded from the gray lips and shriveled cheeks, faded into utter vacuity. The watery eyes roved along the wide planks of the floor, rested for a moment on a bright-colored neckcloth across the room, blinked slowly.

Again the voice from the bench. "Guilty or not guilty?"

A hand jogged Innis's elbow. He started. Then split reedy tones wavered out into the hush of the court. "Eh? Oh — not guilty, Your Honor." His hands plucked at his chin. "Really, I'm quite sure I'm not guilty of — of anything." A grayness settled over him again.

Blaine folded his arms. "George Innis — are you ready for trial?"

Strange pipings trickled out of Innis's stringy throat as he ran loose-fingered hands along the rail in quest of the bar of sunlight.

"The prisoner states that he is ready for trial."

Josiah shook Gil's shoulder. "Ready for trial! He's ready for — "

His words were drowned in a shout and clatter as Forsyth sprang to his feet. His voice pounded against the walls. "My Lord, I object!"

A gavel whacked. "Objection disallowed!"

Gil saw his father take a step forward, Cameron by his side. "I *must* object! No opportunity has been given for challenging the jury. And my client is *not* ready for trial. My Lord, look at him — "

Again the gavel battered down. "Every opportunity was allowed for challenge. If defense did not take advantage of it, that is no concern of the court. And the prisoner has stated that he is ready for trial."

"My Lord!"

Blaine laid down the gavel, spoke in a hard, level tone. "If counsel for the accused persists in interfering with the progress of the trial, I shall be compelled to cite him in contempt."

Gil, mopping his forehead, muttered, "This is hell."

Josiah suddenly turned away. "I've got to get out of here. Got to get out or I'll get into trouble."

Gil caught his arm. "For God's sake, don't leave me. I'll go crazy. Look — he's calling the prosecution now."

"Why do they bother?" growled Josiah. "Look at that broken-nosed bastard." Malevolently he eyed Hagerman, who leaned on his table, while a long-faced, bat-eared assistant fussed about with stacks of papers. A dead hush settled over the court. Hagerman turned his dark face toward Innis, stared hard at him.

"What'll they say about this in England?" asked Josiah.

"Nothing. Any report they get'll be from Colborne. And he'll get *his* report from the Compact."

Hagerman's arm shot out. "Gentlemen of the jury! Look at that man! He stands before you self-convicted! I appeal to you, as loyal subjects of the King and as loyal Canadians, to do your duty. Innis! Swaggering there in the prisoner's box. Did you see how his contemptible arrogance showed as he disregarded, sneered at, the questions put him from the bench? But of course you did! His contempt for one of His Majesty's Judges."

The voice roared on. Gil's head spun under the merciless whiplash of sound. Broken phrases beat into his brain . . . "And I submit for the consideration of the gentlemen of the jury this passage from that foul rag the *Aegis*. Listen to me — and judge for yourselves. 'And when such unrest should be promptly followed by a swift inrush of United States troops — ' I ask you, *what* unrest? The unrest that that republican jackal leering from the prisoner's box hoped to stir up, the unrest that — "

"Did he really write that?" asked Josiah.

Gil shook his head dully. "Saw it at Father's office. It was in the *Aegis* back in '25 before Innis had ever heard of the paper. And it referred to Texas, not Ontario."

The din crashed on. Time and again Gil saw his father leap to his feet, heard his shout of "I object," that was always followed by the smash of the gavel, the stark words: "Objection overruled."

Gil turned his eyes from the bench to the prisoner's box, saw Innis smiling gently and vacantly at Hagerman, who suddenly raised his hand. "And now, gentlemen, I'm going to ask the prisoner a question. A question for him to answer — if he dares." The swarthy face loomed over Innis. "On the twenty-ninth of December, eighteen hundred and thirty-four, why, George Innis, did you go to Lambton? Do you dare tell the court whom you saw there — and *what* you discussed?"

Innis looked vaguely at him, carefully pleating a loose fold of his sleeve in restless fingers. "What? I don't think I hear very well." He smiled up at Blaine's cold face. "I've been ill, you know. I must have been ill. I — I think — "

Hagerman's big hand flew up again. "I asked you about Lambton."

Polite perplexity spread over Innis's face. "Eh? Oh — lambs. Lambs. Dear me, yes. Back in Wiltshire. In the spring. They used to play up and down the slope by the river. That's where my daughter was buried, you know. She used to love them so. Yes, yes. I understand your question now. It's always warm in Wiltshire. The rooms are light. They're warm, too." Slowly his empty smile faded. "But—but I'm not in Wiltshire now. I can't be. My room's cold. It's dark. I'm—why, I'm in Canada. I—"

From the balcony across from Gil, a snicker broke out. Gil heard Josiah snarl. "Let me out of here. I'll—"

Gil shook his head blindly.

Josiah settled back against the wall, then grunted: "At least someone over there's got some decency. Looks as if they'd chucked out the fool that laughed."

Gil looked dully across, saw a slight stir of people weaving and shifting. Then his eyes snapped back to the floor. "Look—Jos!" He pointed. Erect and cool, Forsyth was facing the bench. Gil ducked his head. "Oh God, Father, get him off, get him off."

There were quick footsteps in the corridor behind the balcony. The door flew open. Gil, amazed, stared down at a sleek fur bonnet. A hand clutched at his. "Gil—I'm a fool!" She leaned against him, fingers locked in his, head down. "Just let me stand here, Gil."

Gil's arm fell about her shoulders, drew her toward him in silence. The cheek against his sleeve was wet. They faced the court together while Josiah alternately stared at Sandra and cursed Hagerman in muttered syllables.

On the floor, all eyes were turned on Innis, who stood patient and bewildered. Forsyth kept making significant motions toward his own breast pocket. Politely Innis looked at him, then back at the shaft of light that crept slowly across the room. Once his hand twitched upward toward his pocket, then fell purposeless by his side.

"My Lord." Forsyth's voice was strangely vibrant. "My client wished to plead his own case. Now it appears that he has changed his mind. If it pleases the court, I shall open the defense."

He exchanged a few low words with Cameron, then turned to the jury.

Slowly, almost casually, he spoke to them of the ideal that all men had for Upper Canada, for the life that free British subjects should expect within its borders; sketched how Innis, throughout his course, had spoken for everyone who held such ideals. Deftly, skillfully, he drew the whole courtroom into his picture, every soul in it, wove a harmonious pattern so that Innis seemed to have spoken for every juror, even for Hagerman, scowling uneasily at his table below the bench. Devotion to the Crown, devotion to the Province, to all Canadians, high and low — such were the mainsprings of George Innis. Innis had written, had fought, had thought, for all Canadians, for one country.

The jury began to stir uneasily. Blaine, high on the bench, sat motionless, frigid, while Hagerman leaned on thick forearms like a beast ready to spring.

Then Forsyth turned to the prosecution, took the first charge, deftly drew its sting and tossed it back, useless and harmless. But Hagerman's growl rumbled out: "My Lord — objection."

The gavel smashed down. "Objection sustained. Clerk is directed to strike defense counsel's remarks from the record."

Gil winced. A small voice said shakily, "Handkerchief, please."

He looked down at Sandra. "You took mine."

"Oh — I forgot. Gil — I was such a fool."

"No you weren't."

"I was. It's worse than you said." She ducked her head. "I just can't look at him. That poor, poor man. And over there, they're all laughing at him. Even Staff is." She leaned her head against his arm again.

Gently he patted her shoulder, eyes still on the floor below. Point after point he heard his father bring up, ridicule, demolish, only to be met with the sullen "Objection!" while the shattering smash of the gavel sustained the murmured words that directed the clerk to strike out the argument.

At last Forsyth had to rest his case. Blaine's chill glance turned toward the twelve men. "The jury will now retire to consider its verdict."

A tall, hard-faced man in sleek black rose from the box. "Your Honor, the jury *has* considered its verdict. The jury finds the defendant guilty."

Gil slumped against the wall. "I knew it. But I didn't know it would be so hard." His face was pale. "Father and Cam — they did their best. They — "

Two small hands seized his. From the other side a heavy arm fell across his shoulders. He barely heard the expressionless voice of Blaine intone a citation from the statutes: " — And you, George Innis, shall quit forever the Province of Upper Canada within twenty-four hours, said time to be reckoned from this very moment. Your goods and chattels shall from this moment revert to the Crown. Should you venture to disobey the ruling of this, His Majesty's court, should you ever attempt to return to Upper Canada again, you are liable under the law to suffer death without benefit of clergy, to be hanged by the neck until dead."

In the sudden clatter that greeted the sentence, Forsyth sprang to his feet crying: "We appeal! We appeal!"

The gavel crashed. "Order! There is no appeal."

"Then the defendant has the right of protest on grounds of illegal arrest and illegal trial."

Gil saw his father again make the gestures toward his pocket, saw Innis frown vaguely, then smile in utter noncomprehension. Blaine leaned from the bench. "Does the prisoner wish to protest?"

Innis passed his hand over his white hair. "I — I — there was *some*thing I was going to do." Then he smiled confidingly at the Judge. "It can't have been very important. It — " He frowned. "But — yes — there was. What could it have been? I've been ill, you know, and — " His eye fell on Forsyth, who looked pleadingly at him. "Why, there's a man I know. Perhaps he can — "

Forsyth stepped forward. "My Lord, on behalf of my client, I protest arrest and trial. I — "

Blaine's eye was on the prisoner. "Do you wish to protest against the ruling of His Majesty's courts or don't you?" His tone was an icy threat.

Terror streaked Innis's worn face. "Against the court? Oh, no! Not against His Majesty's courts. No. That would be — I couldn't — You see, I believe in — "

Blaine's voice slashed through Innis's stammering. "The prisoner does not wish to protest. I hereby declare this court to be adjourned." Above him, the royal arms hung dull.

By Gil's elbow, a low voice spoke. "Gil — get me out of here. I want to get out."

Gil turned quickly. "Yes. Now. Jos, take her other arm."

They forced their way through the door, went heavily down the stairs, Sandra's heels clicking dispiritedly. Out in the bright noon, the waiting crowd had begun to break up, some drifting off sullenly, others rushing about in a tornado of whoops and cheers. Isolated fights broke out along King Street. Fanned along the courthouse steps, the shako'd infantry looked on, some impassive, some bored.

Josiah checked Sandra. "Here — where do you think you and Gil are going? Want to get in the middle of that?" He nodded toward struggling groups of men. "Keep your head up, Gil. Want to get us all killed? Come this way."

He butted suddenly between two startled infantrymen, jostled his way through the red lines, dragging Sandra and Gil after him. As they turned up Church Street, Gil protested. "I want to get back there to Father and Cam."

"Don't be a fool. They'll be tied up for another two hours. Steady." He straightened Sandra's bonnet, which had been knocked askew in pushing past the soldiers. "There. That's it. Now Gil, stiffen your back. Won't help Innis by moping. You've got to keep on fighting for him."

Gil threw back his shoulders, drew a deep breath. "Right." His steps suddenly rang surer as the three struck up Church Street, then turned past the high tower of the fire station where bright brass and polished leather glowed in a cavernous shed.

Gil stared down at Sandra as though suddenly aware of her. Under her deep bonnet he could see a long golden ringlet. Warmth began to steal over him. He bent his head. "Where do you want to go?"

She clutched his arm tighter. "I want to go home. Gil, please take me home."

Slowly, almost shamefully, he became aware of an elation that welled up within him, that overlaid for the moment the agony of the courtroom. "Sandra — about that night at Nipigon — "

She turned a woebegone face to him. "Stop, Gil. I don't even want to think about it. I told you I was a fool. Isn't that enough?"

Josiah coughed loudly. "Look here, you two. I think I'd better go down and have a swim off the King's Pier."

"Shut up," said Gil. "You stay with us. We'll go to Barnard's and get the carriage. You can drop me where I've got to meet Doc. Then you two go on and get Father and Cam."

She shook her head. "Gil, I just want to go home." Her voice was unsteady. "Take me home."

Gil stood irresolute. "I ought to get to work."

Her eyes turned up to him, pleading. "Our carriage is at Barnard's too. It can take you right back. Please."

Josiah shook him by the shoulders. "Don't potter. Go."

"All right," said Gil suddenly. "Look, Jos, Doc's up at Stoyel's. Go tell him I'll be late. Have him leave word at Barnard's where I can find him." He held out his arm, his voice gentle. "Come along, Sandra."

Head bowed, she hurried along by his side. "Let's get there quick, Gil. I don't want to see anyone. Don't want to speak to anyone."

He patted her arm. "Trust me. I know every alley between here and the Garrison. Now tell me about Trafalgar. How does it seem to have Staff back? How— "

She seemed to shudder away from the thought of home. "It's been awful, Gil. Father's been frightened—really frightened about something. He won't say what. But a letter came from Dr. Strachan and he's been so odd ever since. And Staff!"

Gil forced a reassuring laugh. "Staff'll help. Don't you worry. I want to see him as soon as I can and— "

Her bonnet shook. "Gil, he's changed. So changed. And the friends he brings home! He—he told me he didn't want to see you. I told him—I told him that you were making a fool of yourself and that I wasn't seeing you any more. He was pleased. And at the trial! He was betting with Tom D'Arcy that Hagerman'd make Mr. Innis cry or faint." She shivered. "What *can* have happened to him?"

Gil listened incredulously. Then he swung his shoulders confidently. "He'll be all right. You always used to be able to manage him, even if you were younger. He thinks an awful lot of you, Sandra."

She dabbed at her face with a handkerchief. "He won't now. Gil, he's gone over to the Compact even worse than Heward Mackie. A letter came to Father from Mr. Baldwin. Staff got hold of it and tore it up. I told Father and he just looked scared and said he wasn't interested in what Baldwin had to say. Robert Baldwin! And Staff gave the ugliest laugh. And Gil—I've been as bad as they. I—I just went to the trial to see what they'd do to Mr. Innis. I hoped they'd hurt him because that would hurt you." Her arm tightened on his.

Gil struggled against a glow of elation. "Just forget about all that. You and I'll get hold of Staff and straighten him out. We—"

Alone on the bleak stretch of Adelaide Street, Josiah watched the two figures vanish down an alley. Then he scratched his head. "H'm—looks as if I was going to get *another* cousin. Now why the hell do I *always* come in at *this* stage when it's someone as pretty as she is?" He shrugged, walked rapidly off toward Stoyel's. At the corner of March Street he stopped, bowed with elaborate courtesy to a carriage that bowled slowly along, a scarlet-coated officer bending from the saddle on one side, a blue-coated gunner on the other. In the low seat, smiling over a coquettishly held muff, Ruth Mackie seemed unaware of the greeting.

Josiah's eyebrows jumped. Then his face hardened and his mouth grew tight as he remembered the swarthy face and broken nose of Hagerman. He strode on, wishing that Handsome Kit had had two noses—one intact as yet.

IX

Betrothal — 1836

The news, received in the early winter of 1835, that Sir John Colborne, Lieutenant Governor of Upper Canada, had been recalled, brought at first no particular stir. Both Compact and Reform had been expecting it, not only because the conventional term of service had expired, but also because, egged on by the Compact, he had actually defied the Colonial Office in a case where its wishes ran counter to those of the Compact. The reigning clique shrugged, wondered what particular old soldier might be sent out as their next cat's-paw. Reformers, looking for no improvement at Government House, thought of the Reform majority in the Legislative Assembly, a body that might in time win the powers that British constitutional practice granted. That majority was their only comfort.

As a final act, Colborne, in defiance of instructions, broke up the Clergy Reserves, established fifty-seven Church of England Rectories in a land where that body was close to nonexistent. The Compact, chuckling, benefited.

Then strange rumors began to drift over from England. A Reformer was to be sent out to take Colborne's place, said the first whisper. The next knew his name — Sir Francis Bond Head. A third christened him "The Tried Reformer," spoke of a lifetime of concern with schools, roads, finance, representation. Ultra-Compact men grew suddenly sullen, suspicious. Reformers, moderate and radical, shouted their joy at the dawning of a new era. To their shouts were joined those of the more moderate of the Compact and men who had supported it because, in their mind, it was the Government and the Crown.

The last line of red-coated troopers swept off toward King Street at a sharp trot, the great crowd which had waited all day along the

Don closing in on their heels in a shouting, cheering torrent. Wide canvas banners danced high in air—"Welcome to the Tried Reformer!", "For the King and Reform!", "Welcome to Sir Francis and True Reform." Scattered knots of fifers and drummers, all formation lost, brayed and thumped in meaningless discord.

Gil, standing with Sandra on the front seat of the sleigh, waved his fur cap, shouted and cheered, his voice lost in the tumult. Suddenly he was aware of a tug at his arm, saw Sandra, cheeks flushed and eyes bright, dancing with excitement. He bent toward her. "What? What? I can't hear!"

"I said go on. Let's go on to Government House. I want to see the crowd there."

Gil eyed the choked, snowy street that led into the city, shook his head. "We'd never get ten yards. Look at that. Jammed from house to house. We'd—"

Sandra shook her mittened fists at him. "But I want to see him again." She whirled about, called to Mary in the rear seat. "Make him go. I'll—"

Gil gathered the reins. "All right. I'll try it." The horses danced, shied as running men jostled their sleek flanks. Then they stopped of their own accord. "No use. King Street's jammed. So's Queen."

Sandra waved her mittens in the air. "You're just toast and water. I wish Josiah were here. He'd get through somehow!"

"Of course he would," agreed Gil. "Only he'd get into about four fights on the way and forget where he was going."

Mary suddenly sprang into the snow, soft furs flying. "If you two want to get mauled in that mob, now's your chance. But if you'll get into the back seat, I'll drive you out to Nipigon for tea. It's a much better idea."

Gil held his breath as Sandra hesitated. She said, "But—about getting back—"

Mary smiled in the depths of her gray fur bonnet. "When you have to go, we'll just drive to York Mills and take you home on the Don. It's been frozen for days. You'll be back in time for dinner."

Gil leaped out, bundled Sandra among the thick robes of the back seat. "Let's not give her time to say no, Mary. Hurry before she changes her mind."

Mary gathered the horses, threaded them expertly through the dwindling press of Queen Street. Excited voices floated past the sleigh as one group after another was left behind. "And we'll get schools, now, out in the country." . . . "And roads. Can maybe get a road through from—" . . . "No more damned Compact." . . . "Wait till he gets after Hagerman and Strachan and Robinson and—" . . . "Hey! Everybody down to Government House and cheer him some more!"

Mary, sitting resolutely square in the front seat, sent the sleigh past the open sweeps where the Jarvis and Allan mansions crouched sullenly, curtains drawn and chimneys barely smoking. Gil crowed. "Look at 'em! Same all over town. Every Compact house looks like —Hi! Watch out!"

A battered sleigh shot out of Jarvis Street. A frayed willow switch waved and a deplorable beaver tipped to Mary and Sandra. Richland's rusty runners whined on beside the shiny sleigh. The doctor leaned from a welter of moth-eaten robes. "Knew Gil was plumb crazy, but I didn't think you two'd be here."

Sandra laughed, waved a deep seal muff. "Did you *see* him? Did you see Sir Francis?"

Richland shook his head. "Been sitting with old Parshal Goosetray."

Gil shouted. "Goosetray! But he's been out of his head for the last ten years."

"Uh-huh," grunted Richland. "Been nice and peaceful, setting with old Goosetray." He pointed down Church Street with his whip at a shouting, singing column of men, banners high over their heads. "Had a mighty quiet time."

"Well, you missed something big," called Mary. "It was—it was like seeing history being made."

Sandra nodded. "It was wonderful."

"More'n wonderful," roared Richland. "Did you notice—"

"Ho!" shouted Gil. "Listen to him. Been with Goosetray all afternoon, has he? How'd you know what to notice, Doc?"

Richland rubbed a thick thumb over his chin. "Well, you see Parshal took kind of a nap and I sneaked off down the alley to King Street. Figured someone might get hurt in the jam. When you get a lot of fools hollering and stamping, most anything's apt to happen."

"Then he *did* see our Reformer," said Mary.

Gil chuckled. "Knew he'd get there somehow."

Richland leaned out toward them again. "I never saw anything in my life like the expression on Sir Francis's bonded head when he saw those banners calling him a Reformer. No, sir. I never did. You could a knocked him over with a bee's whisker. Guess after that he just got downright numb. Huddup, Bessie!" The willow swished through the air and the unspeakably shaggy Bessie rocketed off down Upper George Street.

Sandra stared. "What did he mean?"

"Oh—that's just Doc," said Gil.

"Of *course* Sir Francis looked surprised," said Mary. "He can't know what it's been like here. A man like that would take Reform as a matter of course. Naturally the banners and all surprised him."

Sandra nestled closer to Gil. "I can't make the doctor out. Sometimes he's nice as he can be. But most of the time he treats me as if I had the mind of a child of three."

Gil waved loftily. "Oh—of course—Doc's a flatterer, like all Yankees."

She sat up very straight. "Oh, he is, is he? Well, what he said about you was—" She suddenly slid into his arms as Mary cut sharply onto Yonge Street, the sleigh tilting crazily. She recovered herself. "I thought you said you could drive, Mary."

Gil crowed. "She can. Do it again."

Mary reined in as a long procession of sleighs and cutters filed slowly down the long drive from the somber MacCaulay mansion, flowed out into the street.

Gil stared. "What the—"

In the first sleigh, well muffled in furs, sat the Chief Justice, who spoke gravely to the Rector of York, his restraint in marked contrast to the flaming wrath on the churchman's face. After them came Hagerman, scowling and satanic, Jonas Jones, then a long line of Boultons, Powells, Denisons, Cruikshanks, Allans, Campbells—mournful, angry, frightened, or sullen.

Sandra eyed the gloomy procession in wonder. "What is it?"

Gil shook his head. "Looks like a Compact funeral." He craned his neck. "That's just what it is. Look—all those men on foot—up in the grounds. Dickson and all his Orangemen. Lot of waterfront toughs at sixpence a head. And the niggers! That's Campbell's militia company." He started. "By God, do you suppose—"

"Suppose what?"

"That they'll try to kidnap Sir Francis?"

Mary shook her head. "They wouldn't have looked so glum. I think you're right about your funeral, Gil." She pointed her whip toward the uneven lines of men who began to shuffle down through the snow to Yonge Street. "Well, this isn't getting to Nipigon." The horses started smoothly off, then shied suddenly as a tall man jumped a snowbank, caught at the reins.

Mary reined in quickly. Sandra cried, "Why, it's Staff! What on earth are you trying to do?"

Stafford's fresh, handsome face was blank with surprise. "Sandra! I thought you were at—Oh, afternoon, Mary. Didn't recognize you. Sandra, I thought you were at the McDonalds'. I—"

"I was. And don't you see Gil?"

Stafford nodded, a little sheepish. "Meant to come and see you. But—well, anyway, you're in time. I'll hold up the head of the column here and you can catch up with the last sleigh, Mary." He stepped back.

Mary laughed. "We're off for Nipigon."

Stafford leaned on the dashboard. "But don't you see? You're just in time." His smile was persuasive, contagious.

"In time for what, Staff?" asked Gil.

"Don't you know? Sir John's got to move out of Government House because that blasted Reformer's come. We're going to escort him to the Ontario House. He'll stay there until it's time for him to go."

Sandra leaned from the sleigh, ruffled his dark hair. "He'll have to get on without us. Come along out to Nipigon."

Stafford looked bewildered. "But—but it's Sir John and—"

Gil hooted with laughter. "Think we'd go and see that old battle-axe to his hotel? What do you want us to do? Tuck him into bed?"

Stafford flushed, swallowed a sharp answer. "Oh, I've heard about your frolicking with the Alliance. But anyway—this is different. It's not just Sir John. It's a courtesy toward the old Lieutenant Governor." He dropped his voice. "And if Strachan saw you and Mary there, he'd know it was because of me. I'd tell him."

Sandra leaned forward. "Staff, you're making us late. You're—"

Stafford's face became covertly threatening. "Mary, it might be good for Cam if you were seen—"

She gathered the reins. "And it wouldn't be good for me if he heard about it." She made room on the seat. "Come on along with us. We're — "

Stafford exploded. "Go on, then. But you're making a big mistake." He laid a hand on his sister's arm. "Come with me, Sandra!"

She shrank back.

"Come on. I've a cutter up there. Don't argue. I'm telling you to."

Gil's hand shot out, wrenched Stafford's fingers away. "Better keep your paws out of the sleigh."

"Be careful, Gil. This is no affair of yours. Do what you damn please. But Sandra's been seen riding about with you. Do you think I'm going to let it be said that I've got a sister that's disloyal? By God, you're going to ride with me and — "

Mary tightened her reins with a deft turn of the wrist. "Stand clear, Staff. We're going."

Stafford jumped back to the horses' heads. "Not yet. Mary, you better get out of that sleigh." He waved to the men who were filing past. "Here, you! Get that man out of the sleigh. If he won't get out, tip it over. Sandra, Mary! Get out before you're hurt."

Gil stood up. "If Sandra and Mary weren't here, I'd tell you to try it, Staff." He looked at the men who were drifting uncertainly toward the sleigh. "I know most of you. Tom Keenan, Mart Smith, Joe Egan — if you start any trouble here, remember this: courts are going to be different now, with a Reform governor. No one coming up and swearing that you were in Montreal or Oswego or Buffalo. No judge that'll wink at the jury when he makes the charge."

Grumbling, the men fell back. Stafford turned on them. "You damned cowards. We'll get you out if anything happens. We'll — "

A hoarse voice said, "Ain't lookin' much like that now. And I ain't touchin' that feller." He pointed at Gil. "Him and that Yankee doctor, they nussed my woman when she was down with a flux and ain't asked a cent for it."

Flushed and furious, Stafford swung on Sandra. "All right! Go with your traitor friends." He raised his voice. "People know that the *rest* of our family's loyal."

The sleigh started smoothly off up Yonge Street. Gil looked back on the slouching files that trailed off to the south in the wake of the procession. "Huh! Let 'em kiss Sir John good-bye if they want to. They won't be seeing *his* like again, thank God. Staff's an idiot. But he'll see — Sandra, you want to tell him that he'll — " He turned to her, saw her face was buried in her muff, saw her shoulders shaking. Quietly he slipped an arm about her. In the front seat, Mary glanced over her shoulder, then switched about abruptly, eyes on the road.

When they had passed the roofed tollgate at Bloor Street, passed the Potter's Field and the massed buildings of Bloor's great brewery, Sandra carefully dried her eyes, linked arms with Gil. Her voice was husky, muffled. "Gil — "

"Uh-huh?"

"Staff isn't *really* like that."

"Of course he isn't. Always was hotheaded. But he's got that same old grin and — "

"We've always been so close. We were always together after Mother died. We always looked after each other."

"I remember," said Gil, gruffly. "When he fell in the Don, you fell in too, trying to grab him by the kilts. 'Bout four or five, you were then."

"He never used to tease me, either. Not the way Talbot Sperry used to tease Ruth or — "

"H'm," said Gil. "Guess he didn't — much — "

"Gil! He *never* — and then people just don't understand him. When he'd get in trouble at the Blue School, he'd always come and tell me everything and — And all the time he was in New York, he used to ask my advice. He sometimes needed — And — and then when he came back here — "

Gil patted her hand. "Staff's all right. He's just been away a long time and naturally he took up with the same people he'd been at school with. Give him time. You and I'll work him over until he'll be joining the Canadian Alliance and voting for Mackenzie. Anyway, the Compact's dead now."

She raised her muff to her quivering chin. "It'd been such a wonderful day, Gil. And then — "

"Forget about it."

"Oh, Gil — *why* did he talk like that? I really thought he wasn't serious at first." She lifted her eyes to the thick trees that crowded in on the white ribbon of Yonge Street, stared at them as though they were closing in on her.

Without turning, Mary called back. "I can't hear what you're saying back there, but if you're worrying about Staff, don't. By tomorrow he'll have such a fit of remorse that he'll be just groveling and you'll have your work cut out trying to cheer him up."

As though to herself Sandra murmured, "I don't know what I'll do. I don't. He's changed so — "

Gil slipped his arm about her shoulders again. "Look, Sandra, it'll be different now. I mean — about my license. Doc says I can get it next year and we won't have to worry about the Compact refusing it now."

She sat silent, eyes on the snowy trees.

"And — uh — you see — why then it'd be all right and I — I mean I could start right in to practise and — " He suddenly swept her into his arms. "Oh, confound it, can't you see — "

Slowly she turned, raised her hands gently to his face. "I can, Gil dear. I — " Then her fur-clad arms were tight about his neck. The runners hissed smoothly along to the brisk chatter of sleigh-bells.

Sandra started as Mary's voice sounded in her ears. "Well — here's Montgomery's farm already — not to mention his tavern."

She drew quickly away from Gil, settling her bonnet. On either side of the road, the trees had fallen away, showing long stretches of cleared land, and in the middle distance a big red building, with a great sign that dangled out over the snow. She leaned her head back against Gil's shoulder, reached up and touched his glowing cheek. "Gil dear," she whispered. "You're so sweet. Tell your family when we get to Nipigon?"

He shook his head. "Not going to wait." He prodded Mary's shoulder. "Mary! Got a surprise for you. I — "

"I'm bowled over," said Mary as she pulled the horses up in front of Montgomery's. "What do you suppose I sat alone for? What do you suppose I shouted about Montgomery's for?" She turned in the seat, reached over and took Sandra's hand, eyes bright. "And I'm very happy, Sandra. Now you've got to behave for a minute. Look at all the people at the tavern."

"Do they *have* to be there?" growled Gil. Then his face brightened. "There's John Montgomery himself." He waved to a big, red-faced man, half country and half town, who stood on the little porch. "Why aren't you in town, John?"

A heavy hand waved. "Had to look after the boys around here." He ducked his head awkwardly to Mary and Sandra, came heavily down the steps. "You ladies ought to be more careful. Don't you know you're riding with a dangerous radical?" He chuckled hoarsely.

Sandra cocked her chin. "So is he. And he knows it."

"And we're talking with a worse," said Mary, smiling. "How many Alliance meetings have you had out here, Mr. Montgomery?"

He smiled comfortably. "Won't have to have 'em much more. Ah — um — will you take something?" Without waiting for an answer, he waved to an aproned boy who thumped along the porch, tray in hand. "Bring those glasses down here. Port, it is. Won't harm a kitten." He distributed glasses, raised his own. "Well, here's to Reform and a new life!"

Over the top of his glass, Gil met Sandra's eyes, smiling. "To the new life," he echoed.

"Hear! Hear!" said Mary.

Montgomery rumbled on. "Been a big day, a mighty big day."

"Hasn't it!" said Sandra fervently.

There was an approving nod. "That's what I like to see. Now in my day, a pretty girl'd no more think about a new Governor than — well, I don't know what." He nodded again, then stared at his glass in alarm. "Here! What I been doing! Putting port on top of whiskey. Oh, my liver! Oh, my head! Have to put a double dose right on top of that now." He snatched at the tray and galloped back into the tavern.

The horses jogged easily along. Gil drew a deep breath. "We've had our first toast. The new life."

Sandra nodded. "I'll never forget Montgomery's Tavern or Montgomery's farm as long as I live."

Gil grinned exultantly. "Guess I knew it was going to be you, Sandra. I — I've never paid much attention to other girls."

She blew out her cheeks. "Gil, you're the most notorious flirt in Upper Canada. You know you are. How about Molly Allan? How about Beth Mace?" She settled closer to him. "You know, Gil, I shouldn't tell you this, but I used to be terribly jealous of Molly Allan — "

"Molly?" His voice was high in denial. "Why — I *liked* her all right, but — well — *her* eyebrows didn't slant down at the corners or — Know the first time I ever saw you? Mother drove out to call on your mother at Trafalgar. I was in kilts and you were in a sort of basket thing."

She smiled up at him. "Did you like me?"

He wrinkled his forehead in thought. "H'm, yes. I guess so. You had—you had a cloth Indian to play with and you kept waving it and gurgling at me."

She looked quickly about. "Know what I was trying to say?" She slipped her arms around his neck, then subsided decorously, hands folded in front of her.

"And I—" began Gil.

"Sh!" She laid a hand on his, indicated another sleigh coming toward them. Then they both braced their feet as the horses began their slow zigzag down the killing slope of Hogg's Hollow, rested at the bottom and then began the heartbreaking climb up the other side, Mary taking cunning advantage of each turnout, each widening of the road, to vary the monotony of the endless, vicious grade.

At the crest, close by the old capstans that hauled the great boats up the slope, Mary let the horses stand. Gil unhooked the checkreins, rubbed their cracking nostrils, then climbed quickly back by Sandra.

Mary sat sidewise in the seat, smiled on the glowing pair. "Aren't I a perfect duenna? Sandra, your bonnet's all askew."

"*I'd* say you were perfect," said Sandra. "Don't know what Father'd say."

Mary nodded, reminiscently. "I'm generous by nature. And I remember when Cam and I thought of being engaged at the same time. Though I always think I had something to do with putting it in his head. It was at a dance at the Boultons' Grange. And we drove home with my Aunt Cora afterwards. She sat between us. She must have weighed twenty stone and I couldn't even *see* Cam."

"You made up for it afterwards," grinned Gil. "You used to come out to Nipigon with your mother. *I* thought you and Cam were peculiarly revolting."

She sniffed. "Sandra, if you only knew what a revolting little animal *he* was. Grubby and— Well, better start. Hook up the checkreins, Gil. We'll have to make a triumphant entry to Nipigon." The runners cut crisply on. "Have you two thought where you're going to live?"

Gil looked owlish. "There's a little house on Bathurst Street.

I went through it the other day. Some ensigns and lieutenants living out of barracks have it now, but they'll be transferred within the year."

Sandra looked loftily at him. "Weren't you taking a good deal for granted, Mr. Stensrood?"

He nodded solemnly. "Yes, I was."

"Did you ever hear anything like that, Mary? Looking before—"

"I certainly was," Gil went on. "It's just a block from Doc's and there's a little ell that I could fit up for a dispensary and the rooms are big and it gets a lot of sun."

She settled back against his shoulder. "Take me to see it? Is it pretty?"

He waved his arm. "It's wonderful. Why, at least four people could sit in the dispensary while I was looking at a fifth, and—uh—Sandra, we shan't have very much at first."

"Don't care. I've been managing Trafalgar long enough to know how to keep *you* in order. I want a lot of flowers and I want a cat. I want—"

Gravely she ticked off a list of essentials through her mittens. Gil listened happily. At last the sprawling bulk of Nipigon Lodge showed warm and mellow across the snow, the two brick wings of later years glowing against the sturdy rough-cast of the original house that Barnabas had built in 1816. The horses swung easily up the drive. Gil drew a deep breath. "Never knew a day could be like this. Look at—at everything."

From the clustered chimneys of Nipigon, blue smoke curled into the air, floated lazily away toward the high-shouldered lift of the barns. North, south, and east, elm, oak, and maple were delicate traceries of black against the sky whose thin clouds were scattering, opening deep belts of dusky blue. Far in the west the sun burned red through a cloud bank, flooded the snowy fields below with a warm-tinted stream.

Mary checked the sleigh by the door and the three climbed stiffly out. Gil clanged the great knocker as Mary asked: "Who's going to bubble over first with the news?"

Sandra moved closer to Gil. "I'm scared."

"No you're not," said Gil. "I am."

"Well—" Mary's eyebrows lifted.

"Let's—let's not say anything—just at first," said Sandra.

"That's it! That's it!" agreed Gil hastily. He slammed the knocker again. "Now — "

The door was snatched from his grasp and Primula's bulging eyes looked out, her white apron ruffling in the wind. "For de Lord's sake, Mist' Gilbert! Skeered someone was tryin' to bust down de door an' — " Decorum swept over her in a cloud. Gravely she drew back. "Miss Mary. Miss Kingscote. Jes' give me them things and I'll rest 'em right here. Folks is to the living room."

As Primula struggled with snow boots and wraps, Janet's clear voice floated through the portieres. "Is that you, Gil? You're just in time for tea. Grandfather's waiting — "

Another voice drowned her out. "Grandfather's waiting to hear what this latest damned fool from England looks like. Come in here and tell me."

Sandra hung back. Mary slipped an arm about her as Gil threw back the portieres. "Well, we're here and we've seen him and seen everything — "

In the chair by the fire, old Barnabas's white mane flew back. Janet looked up, lips parted, from the silver-loaded tea table. Then she smiled. "Sandra, my dear, what a pretty shade of blue. Come and sit by me. We want to hear all about it. Mary, your favorite corner of the sofa's waiting for you." Under her smooth hair, calm eyes smiled again on Sandra. "You look so much like your mother. She was such a friend of mine. Seeing you here is like having her back again. That's it. Sit right here."

Barnabas chuckled hoarsely. "Don't go spoiling Janet. Come sit by me." He smiled like a friendly old lion as Sandra dropped easily to a cricket, bright head close by his elbow. "Now let's hear about the new wonder-worker. You saw him? How'd he look? Were a lot of people out? Did he bring a wife with him? Is she pretty? Now the rest of you keep quiet, I want to hear what Sandra thinks of him."

Gil leaned back on the sofa beside Mary, watched Sandra, her face animated and expressive as she brought to life again the snowy bluffs by the Don, the tramping lines and columns of men, the flutter of banners. As he watched, Sandra became part of Nipigon. She belonged just where she was, close by old Barnabas, close by his mother. He'd seen her in the very room many times, but now, by some mysterious alchemy, she was one of them, had always been there, must always be.

At last Barnabas leaned back in his chair. "That's well told, my dear." His keen old eyes played rapidly from face to face. Then he laid his hand gently on Sandra's head. "I'm very glad. Very." He sat up straight, rapped on the floor. "You know, the Stensroods always *did* marry pretty women."

Janet gasped. "Father!"

He chuckled again, smiled down at Sandra. "Saved you and Gil a lot of trouble, haven't I? Been fretting and wondering all the way out Yonge Street, wondering just how you'd say it and who'd say it, haven't you?"

Janet dropped her hands in her lap, gentle face wondering. "Is — is it true, Sandra?"

Barnabas trumpeted: "Of course it's true. Didn't you see 'em as they came through the door? Why, all *I* had to do was to look at Mary. She was saying it for 'em. Plain as a pikestaff."

Quickly Janet rose, kissed Sandra. "I'm very glad," she said simply. Then she began to smile happily. "Now tell me everything. When did all this happen? When did you make up your minds? Have you — "

Mary waved her teacup. "I can tell you everything. It happened just opposite Potter's Field. They're going to — "

Barnabas raised his stick. "Let 'em alone, Mary. When Cam brought you out here the first time, you just peeked out from behind his shoulder and stammered every time you spoke."

"I didn't stammer," said Mary. "I just didn't talk and I didn't talk because you'd given me some port and I'd never had any before. I didn't dare do anything but nod."

Sandra laughed. "Well, I've had port this afternoon. It was at Montgomery's. I can talk, though. It happened coming out here. That's when we settled on it. Or Gil did."

Barnabas frowned at his grandson. "What did you wait so long for? You're twenty-four and more."

Sandra smiled. "That's what *I* was wondering, why did he wait?"

Gil grinned. "Doc says I'm not very bright. Guess he's right or I'd have done it sooner. But how'd I know she'd say yes?"

"I could have told you," said Sandra.

"Of course," went on Gil, "I'd been worrying about my license as a doctor. I heard after the Innis trial that the Compact'd just laugh at my application. But now Sir Francis has come — "

Janet laid down her cup. "What a day! Sir Francis safe at Government House and now you two capping it with your news. And Mary, I think Forsyth will go back to the bench and Cam'll get a judgeship of his own."

"Well, you people mark a new era, you and Gil." Barnabas spoke slowly. "For the first time in generations, a Stensrood'll marry under a clear sky. Lord, when I went down the Hudson to ask old Major Greenwood for his consent, the French wars weren't long over and the other trouble was riding high on the horizon. That was in 1771. Janet, when you and Fors married, things looked pretty black here. Simcoe'd gone, the Compact was getting into the saddle. We didn't know what was going to happen. It was even worse for Mary and Cam. Didn't seem a chance for an honest man from the Bay of Quinté to the St. Clair. But now — "

He raised his eyes to the portrait above him. "Well, Father, maybe I was wrong about backing horses. Guess we were right. Wish you were here to see it. Gil and Sandra'll be starting off in the kind of country we thought we were coming to when we hauled the old sled through York State." He nodded to himself. "Looks to me as if the wanderers had come home at last." He smiled down at Sandra. "Know how lucky you and Gil are? Why, you'll have just what those fools back in the Colonies got themselves killed for. All Canada'll have it. It's taken a long time, but we've got it. And no bloodshed."

Gil nodded. "And see that sunset flaring up for us!" He and Sandra moved to the window. She slipped her arm through his, looked across the snowy fields. The sun was a solid band of gold that poured soft color across the country. Then Sandra felt a touch on her arm, found Barnabas standing beside her. "Look at it. You'll live up to your luck under *that* — not under a storm of fire and guns and blood."

On the distant ridge beyond Hogg's Hollow, the shallow roof of Montgomery's Tavern was black against the sky. Slowly the warm glow of the sun faded as a belt of cloud, menacing, ominous, veiled it in a murky haze. The gold died in the last blaze and the fields about Montgomery's farm were stained — blood-red.

X

The Tried Reformer — 1836

Josiah shook a mound of snow from the crown of his beaver and plunged through the doors of the British Coffee House. A tall figure turned from a table by the fire, called: "Get lost or something, Jos?"

Josiah grinned as a waiter hurriedly stripped the heavy coat from his shoulders. "Maybe. Don't know yet. What you got there? Whiskey punch? Same for me, waiter. Well, how've you been, Gil? How's Sandra?"

"Fine as ever," smiled Gil.

"When are you going to treat the town to the good news? I'm just waiting for a chance to give a dinner here."

Gil frowned. "Not just yet. Her old gentleman's been in a rage since Head came. I think that damned Staff's egging him on. We'll give him a chance to cool down first."

Josiah buried his nose in his steaming glass. "Better chuck Staff in the bay."

"Damn it, Jos, he used to be my closest friend. And Sandra's always been wrapped up in him. She can't forget that — but he can. I tell you, it's damned uncomfortable when I go out there. To hear him talk, she and I carried a Yankee flag the day Head came. Well, it'll work out somehow."

"I still say chuck him in the bay," growled Josiah.

"Forget him," said Gil shortly. "You all in order?"

"Every bit. Rented an office in the Coffin Block; taken warehouse space from Hincks. Got all my licenses and papers." He smiled sardonically. "You've got no idea what a moral town this is now. Not a suggestion of greasing palms, no hints that for twenty pounds the customs men'll wink."

"Corn going to come through all right?"

"Got options on enough of next summer's crop to keep Fisher's mill up the Humber going day and night. That's what I went back to the States for." He held up his empty glass, caught the waiter's eye. "Of course, there's good money in that but it won't last forever. But it will last until you get enough roads here so you bring your own corn to your own mills. Damned silly, isn't it? I bring corn eight hundred miles cheaper than you can bring your own fifty."

"That's the Compact again. Too much land tied up in speculation. Hence no roads. Hence not enough land cleared to give us the crops we ought to have. Well, that'll be over now. What were you doing this afternoon?"

"Had tea with our cousin Ruth." He set down his glass. "I tell you, Gil, the Compact's in a panic."

"Panic? They're mad as the devil but — "

"No. It's a panic, I tell you." He dropped his voice. "There were other people for tea. They were talking about leaving for the States. Said U.C.'d be no place for a gentleman to live. Though I doubt if the man who said that has much first-hand information on the subject."

"Who was it?"

"Man named Margett. Your Uncle Sperry was speaking of him at Nipigon."

"*Our* Uncle Sperry?"

"N-no. I don't think it's right for me to claim *him*. Margett's wife was with him." He shook his head. "She ought to be in a museum. Thin, but the most obvious mammal I ever saw."

Gil grinned. "She's his second. People refer to her as 'Mrs. Margett — not the first but the udder one.' So they were talking treason, were they?"

"Not only that but no one made any nasty remarks about Americans — except one swine of a captain from the Fifteenth. In fact, I was rather courted. Seems they'd known all along that the neighbor to the south was the finest country on earth. Guess they just hadn't mentioned it to me before. Margett even made a little speech and said he didn't care how soon they chucked out the Crown and set up a republic here — or joined another republic which he wouldn't name."

Gil whistled. "He said *that?* Well, it means just one thing: some-one higher up said it first or he wouldn't dare. I'd heard rumors that people were saying that high up in the Compact but—"

"Guess you can believe 'em," said Josiah. "And young Carleton Sperry came in and was almost reverent to me. Amusing young devil. Ruth was badgering him about not paying attention to the Compact girls and he said he couldn't stand 'em. Said: 'They toil not, neither do they sin.'"

Gil laughed, then grew grave. "Tell me more that they said about Head."

"That's about all," said Josiah. "They're all scared, it seems, of what'll happen when a Reform government begins looking into the past. And they're more than slightly scared." He did not add that Edward Sperry had sought him out, cursing Head's advent and asking Josiah to keep an eye out for a berth which he—Sperry—might fill in the States if—

"No sympathy from me," said Gil. "When things really start, there'll be a rush across the border that'll make Boney's retreat from Moscow look like a review of the Coldstreams."

Josiah chuckled. "I'll hang on their flanks like the Cossacks." He sloshed punch about in his glass. "Let's go to Jordan's for dinner. Then we might look in at the Theater Royal. They're playing the *Golden Farmer* tonight."

Gil shook his head. "Going back to the Hospital."

"Then why the devil did you ask me to meet you here? I thought we'd have a night of it."

"Oh, I just wanted you to buy me a drink," said Gil.

"No novelty in that. Now, if you were going to buy *me* one, that'd—"

"Well, I did have another reason. Father's coming in. I thought we ought to have a small celebration until I go back to my spleens and pancreases." He dropped his voice. "You see, he's been asked to sit on the Executive Council."

"The Council? No!" Josiah stared.

"True, though. Head's forming a new one. And there's not a Compacter on it. Not a Powell, not a Strachan, not a Robinson, not a Sherwood. But Rob Baldwin's been invited, too. Rolph. Perhaps Bidwell."

Josiah narrowed his eyes. "A clean sweep, by God. And the best of Reform. H'm. Have to get a letter off to Father and the partners. I think they may want to increase their investment here." He blew out his cheeks. "Well, this is a proud day for me. *My* uncle an Executive Councilor. Now I know everything'll be all right. I was doubtful about Head at first, but — "

"You were? Why?"

"I heard he'd been at Waterloo, just like Colborne and Maitland and the rest. Waterloo veterans have ruined this country."

Gil snorted. "He was on the campaign, but not at the battle. He was wounded a few days before. At Fleurus or some such place. That doesn't count."

"I'm relieved," said Josiah. "Doubly so. No Waterloo and my uncle on the Council." A gust of wind whirled through the long room as the big door slowly opened. "Hi! Here he is now. Who's old Mooseface with him?"

"Shut up," said Gil, eying the purplish, pendulous cheeks that stumped along beside his father through a cloud of obsequious waiters. "That's Sherwood Crane."

"Ought to mount his head and stick it up over the fireplace. Is he going to be a Councilor too?"

"No chance," said Gil, dropping his voice. "Even his toenails are Compact."

"What's my uncle doing with him, then?"

"Nothing wrong with Crane. Just believes the people don't know what's good for 'em and that what he calls their betters do. Honest as the devil but — " He rose, Josiah clattering up after him. "Hello, Father. Evening, Mr. Crane."

Forsyth nodded, smiling faintly. "Good to see you both. Sherwood, this is my nephew from the States."

Mr. Crane's long face bobbed slightly to Gil. Josiah's hand was ignored. A wheezy voice said: "I tell you, Forsyth, you've *got* to reconsider. The Church *and* the State must govern. What's a country without an established Church? A damned, barbaric democracy, that's what it is. I don't approve of a lot of things Strachan's done, but damn it, he *is* the Church. He's got a *right* to say how the country'll be run. You'd rather let a lot of farmers do it. No! If you deny the absolute control of Church and State, you deny the rights of the Crown."

Forsyth shook his head wearily. "I told you before that the Crown will be stronger. The country's got to be run by a Lieutenant Governor who's responsible to an elected assembly that's responsible to the people. No use going over all that again. Well—sit here between Gil and me. We'll—"

The long face shook. "Forsyth, I told you my creed as we were walking over here. There's another tenet I didn't mention—everlasting hatred to the United States of America and every one of their subjects!" He swung about on his heel, tramped off down the smoky room.

Forsyth sat down dispiritedly. "Don't take that to heart, Jos. He—"

Josiah laughed. "I don't. Why, I know people at home that end up every dinner by drinking to the damnation of the British Crown. Besides, I could even stand Handsome Kit Hagerman tonight. My congratulations, Uncle Fors."

Gil signaled a waiter, ordered more punch. "Come on now, Father, I've been letting twelve patients die at the Hospital just to hear about it. How was he? What did he say? Are the others coming in with you? What does he say about schools? How many judges is he going to move? Has he signed warrants to hang Strachan and Hagerman yet?"

Forsyth sipped his punch slowly. Gil watched him. "Looks as if he'd been wrestling with bears, doesn't he, Jos?"

Josiah frowned as he noticed the pallor of the usually ruddy face, the deep lines about the eyes, the almost haggard glance. "Been a long session, Uncle Fors? Well, just take Gil's questions one by one."

Forsyth sipped again, set down his glass carefully. "He's—he's a child!"

Gil laughed. "What did you expect? Someone like Grandfather? You've been saying for a long time we needed young men. Now we've got a young Reformer. Come on. What about him?"

Forsyth's voice was hollow. "I said—he's a child." His head seemed to settle between his shoulders, an almost frightened look spread over his face. "A handsome, weak-mouthed, amiable child—that's what he is. Reformer!" He gulped down more punch, turned his tired gaze on Gil. "When I first went in I tried to tell him something of the situation here. He laughed. Actually laughed—the way a child would if you mentioned trigonometry. He said—these are his words as closely as I can remember them: 'My dear Mr. Stensrood, *I* don't know any more about *pol*itics than—than the horses that brought me here.' Seemed to think it amusing. 'I've never attended a political meeting in my life. I've never belonged to any party. I've never even voted.'" Forsyth rested his head in his hand. "The Tried Reformer!"

Gil felt a cold chill contract his stomach. "He's never — "

Josiah broke in eagerly. "All the better for you, Uncle Fors. You and Baldwin and the others — you can guide him along. Why, he might have come out here with a whole set of theories of his own that'd knock yours galley-west. It's — "

Without looking up, Forsyth shook his head. "No such luck. He was only interested in finding out which people up here are 'agreeable dogs at a dinner' — or something like that. Oh, he knows all about our troubles. Glenelg gave him a copy of 'The Report of the Committee on Grievances' that Mackenzie wrote. He's read it, is going to settle everything at once and have statues put up to him all over Canada."

Josiah leaned forward. "But don't you see — the Executive Council can see he does it in the right way. Why, you and Baldwin — "

Forsyth gestured wearily. "Don't you realize that the Executive Council has no duties, except as the Lieutenant Governor may prescribe? And he's not going to prescribe any." He drew a long, uncertain breath. "You've seen those big plaster cakes in Rossi's window? Well, that's what we're supposed to be. Pretty to look at but not for use." He passed his hand over his eyes. "I wish you could have seen him — or rather, I'm glad you didn't. He jumps from idea to idea. Gets the most fatuous grin that you ever saw. His eyebrows jump up and that weak little mouth widens as he tells you how there aren't going to be any more poor. Yes, yes, we'll fix that. And the wicked Yankees shan't come over and rob us. That's another idea and another imbecile beam. And the farmers are going to get what they like for their crops and at the same time no one's going to pay high prices. He's found another toy. And oh, yes! He's thought a lot about the churches. They're all going to share alike. Scottish, C. of E., Methodists, Quakers, Baptists. No discrimination. And of course, the C. of E. must be supreme and we can't encourage the Methodists too much on account of the Yankee connection. It's going to be a lot of fun, setting things in order. Bah! I almost regret Colborne."

Josiah rapped on the table. "Don't look so sick. You'll be near him. You can influence — "

Forsyth turned sad eyes on him. "How long, Josiah, do you suppose it'll be before the Compact finds out what he is? I'd say by eight o'clock tonight. Perhaps sooner." He waved impatiently. "I know the Compact's been blasting away at him in both houses. But — they'll eat their words. They will pack Government House with a lot of agreeable dogs for his dinners. Strachan, Robinson, Hagerman, Boulton, Sherwood — they'll tie him in knots."

"I'll bet on you and Baldwin to keep 'em off him," said Josiah.

Forsyth looked somberly at him. "You'd lose. I'm not going to be there."

"What?" said Gil. "Not going to be there?"

"Not I." Forsyth was emphatic. "I can do no earthly good there. I might do a great deal of harm. For one thing, my word still has some weight in Reform circles. I'll lose it if I become a puppet for Head."

"Look here, Uncle Fors," said Josiah. "The very fact that you and Baldwin are in the Council will be an enormous help to trade — to your import and export trade. Why, if I write to Father and the partners that Head is really rather a dim lamp, but that he has you and — "

"How long would that last? Head can name the Twelve Apostles if he wants. They'd be just as effective. No, I'm not accepting. That was what Crane was arguing about as we came in. What it amounts to is that he wants my seal of approval on the Compact and its new trained monkey." His eyes grew cold. "Good God, it's — it's going to be worse than ever."

"And you're going to sit by?" asked Josiah.

"Of course he isn't," flared Gil. "He's going — "

"I'm going to devote every minute to keeping Reform in order. That's what I'm going to do. It may take the rest of my life. But it's got to be done."

"Keep it in *order?*" exclaimed Gil.

"Can't you see? It's going to be far worse than it ever was before. And Reform — I mean the radical side, Mackenzie's side — has just had a glimpse of the moon. Now it's snatched away from them. The whole Province'll boil. It mustn't boil over. What we've got to do is stamp down the Compact on one side and Mackenzie and his lot on the other." He shivered slightly.

Josiah looked surprised. "Seems to me that Mackenzie's just the man who's needed now."

"No! No! No! You don't understand him. He knows what's wrong here. He fights it. But—he doesn't know where he's going."

"You're wrong, Father," said Gil shortly. "He does know where he's going."

"He can't know. He'll run the country into bloodshed, I tell you. He'll set Reform back twenty, thirty years. He'll divide the Province so that every house'll be a battleground. Think of the hundreds, thousands of people who hate the Compact, but who'd oppose revolt through loyalty to the Crown. And oppose it with arms."

Gil set his chin. "But revolt—of course, *I* don't think it'd ever come to that—revolt'd be *for* the Crown."

"How do you feel, Jos?" asked Forsyth suddenly.

"H'm—hard to say. I'm not a Canadian. From my own standpoint, I'd rather have things quiet. A fight would kill trade for a long time. I guess you're right, Uncle Fors." He scowled. "No, by God, if I were a Canadian, I'd want action and I'd want it quick."

Forsyth smiled wanly. "I see that my job keeping things quiet starts right here. At least, I'll have Cam on my side." He turned to his son. "We're coming into very serious times, Gil. Perhaps you can help. You know how I feel. The best thing to do is take it easy—take it easy. *Don't* help stir things up. And the same advice to you, Jos. You've got your business to think of. You've made a good start. Don't hurt it." He rose slowly. "Well, nothing's happened yet, at least. And Strachan may have a stroke and Hagerman may slip and break his neck." He hunched his shoulders as a solemn waiter held his heavy coat for him.

"Going clear to Nipigon?" asked Josiah. "In this storm?"

"My motto is, take it easy. I can't go back on my own advice, can I? No, I'm putting up with Cam and Mary. Save five miles of Yonge Street. Can I take either of you anywhere?"

"I've got to go to the Hospital," said Gil.

"I'm going to sit here and drink punch and hate Strachan," put in Josiah. He looked at the departing figure of his uncle. "Sense in what he said, Gil. No point in my chucking rocks at my business. And"—he beckoned to a waiter—"it just occurs to me that if you go around snorting sparks and offering little Mac a kingly crown, it won't make it any easier for Sandra out at Trafalgar."

Gil jumped up. "Damn it, things are in a mess. I can't think straight. I'm going to the Hospital now." He snatched his cap and coat, shouldered his way out into the storm.

His feet kicked out little puffs of dry snow as he turned into King Street, fighting his way along. He shook snow from his vizor. "Can't believe it. Can't believe it. The—everything looked so perfect the day Sandra came to Nipigon. We thought Head—I've got to see her again. Can't go on like this. When'll there be a chance? Who'll help?"

Sleighbells jangled through the flatness of the storm. He raised his head as a big sleigh swung importantly into the driveway of Judge Jones's house. By the glowing door, he saw other sleighs drawn up, their horses shivering under heavy blankets, the coachmen stamping about, flapping their arms. Every window in the great pile was ablaze. From within, the thin voice of a violin drifted out, blended with the subdued sweep of a piano, then faded into the silence that hung over the city.

Gil stamped on harder. "The agreeable dogs are gathering," he snarled to himself. "Dogs! Sons of bitches. Damn the lot of 'em. Oh, God *damn* them." He waded on to the Hospital; dove through its arched doors as though into a sanctuary.

XI

Hospital — 1836

A BRISK wind off the bay whipped the budding branches that spread over Front Street as Gil, clutching his tall hat, hurried along in the shelter of the Coffin Block, dodging the frantic latecomers who pelted on down to Brown's Wharf where the steamer *Transit,* Hamilton-bound, was hooting hoarsely. He collided with an irate major, sidestepped a racing carpenter, and then charged through a door under the sign "North American Trading Company."

A lone clerk, eyes squinting behind spectacles, gaped at him from a high desk. "Mr. Stensrood here?" asked Gil shortly.

The clerk made jabbing motions over his shoulder with a quill. "In the sample room. Heard him — "

Gil flung open a wide door, peered into a cavernous space where flickering lanterns joined their glow to the trickle of light from two small windows. "Jos! Oh, Jos!"

A heavy shape loomed in the semidarkness of a sack-piled corner, came toward him, a smaller figure shuffling in his wake. "Who — Oh, Gil. Come on in." Josiah jerked a thumb at the bent man beside him, who thrust forward a bald head, sharp elbows jerking out behind him. "This is Ogle Ketchipaw, Gil. Best head clerk on the Lakes. My cousin, Ogle. Give him the run of the place anytime."

Gil nodded to the peering Ketchipaw. "Just stopped by to — "

"Hoping you would. Haven't seen us in working order, have you?" He snatched a dangling lantern, flashed it about the trimly stacked room. "Look at that!" The lanternlight danced and skipped along, melting the gloom. "Just a few of everything. One bar of iron. One pig of iron. One chunk of pummice. And see those jars? Corn — seed corn — calomel — flaxseed — honey — almonds. All the buyer has to do is look at just one sample. God! Ever been to

Murray and Newbigging's? Or Bugg and Snarr's? Break your shins over everything. Look at a ton of hay to buy a bale. *Our* bulk's at the warehouse. This is *modern* selling, it is. Want rice?" He snatched up a jar, shook the white grains at Gil. "That's what we carry. No need to look at a cartload, is there?" He snapped the jar back on its shelf. "And for you and Doc — " He swept his arm toward the wall. "Manna, spirits of Mindereus, salt of hartshorn, jalap, Seneca rattlesnake root, scammony. Great, isn't it, Ogle?"

Mr. Ketchipaw scraped his shaven chin. "I like bulk," he said in a high voice. "Like to see it. Like to feel it. Lose them little jars and snippets in the dark."

Josiah threw back his head. "Go down to the warehouse and fumble all you like. And I'm going to have bigger windows punched here. Won't need lanterns. Ogle, you finish up in the last bay. I'll be back later. Come on into the office, Gil."

"Can't stop long, Jos. I just wanted to leave my black bag with you."

Josiah led the way past the gaping clerk, pushed Gil into a small office where a low fire chuckled and muttered beyond a battered desk and two stiff chairs. He threw open a cupboard. "Here — shove it in there. Help yourself to a cigar from that box on the desk. They're — Hey! What have you been doing to yourself?"

"Doing?" asked Gil.

"Where's your grave digger's cap? Look at the new blue coat. Look at the fawn breeches. Boots from London. A real beaver. Going to vet Strachan?"

Gil shook his head, leaned against the window. "Going up to see Jesse Ketchum. The Alliance has a petition."

"Going to petition the Tired Reformer? What about?"

Gil teetered his chair on two legs. "While you were away in April, Rob Baldwin and Rolph quit the Executive Council. Shows Father was right in not accepting. Head filled it up with solid Compact — Sullivan, Elmsley, and so on. But he's not taking advice from them — any more than he would from the first lot. Strachan and Robinson are telling him what to do. They write letters, he signs 'em. They read his mail and tell him what to answer." He got up and walked to the window, stood looking out across to the peninsula where the bent trees were a haze of green against the warm blue of the sky. "The petition's telling Head first that he should have worked with Baldwin and the rest. Then it kicks at his putting in Compact people whom no one trusts. Not that that simpering fool at Government House'll pay any attention to it. It's just a matter of serving notice officially on him." He left the window, stood staring into the fire.

Josiah, big hands clasped behind his neck, studied him. "You better let Doc have a look at you. You've dropped about ten pounds. You're talking down in your boots. You look as if you'd been on the randan for a week. You've eaten most of your cigar and you forgot to light it. In general, you look like a professional mourner."

Gil burst out, "Damn it, everything's wrong."

Josiah sat up quickly. "Can I help?"

"Guess not. It's—oh hell, for one thing I had word—not officially—that I'd do well not to go before the Medical Board for my license."

Josiah spluttered: "The Board? Why, I saw the make-up in the *U.C. Gazette*. Dr. Baldwin's on it. So are Rolph, Duncombe, Morrison. Don't tell me Head could scare *them!*"

Gil drummed on the shallow mantel. "He couldn't. But *they* won't be drawn to examine *me*."

"Will you sit down and quit stamping around? How can I think with you—" He blew wavery smoke rings at the ceiling. "Uh—think Doc's grounded you pretty well?"

"Pass any test that's fair." Gil sat on the edge of his chair, fingers busy about his waistcoat pockets.

"H'mmm. How about this? Father knows a lot of doctors and people in Albany. Why not go down there and qualify?"

"No!" Gil's mouth snapped shut. "I'm Canadian. I'm going to qualify in Canada. And besides, if I left the country for that, the Compact'd probably say a New York license wasn't good in Ontario."

Josiah sat up. "Not good? A New York license? Where'd Doc get his training? Where'd Stoyel? Where'd—"

Gil bit nervously at his thumb, eyes on the fire. "This is now."

Josiah tilted back again, stared at the ceiling. "Well, then, let's see." He absently spattered a lump of ash on the floor. "Now—oh—I meant to ask you. Notice Ogle's voice? Told me he'd had the branks. That isn't—"

Gil laughed shortly. "No—it isn't. Branks is North British for mumps."

Josiah appeared relieved. "Oh—I see. They do say mumps'll do it. Well—let's get back. That license. Wouldn't hurt you to *try* New York State."

"Wouldn't help. Might hurt, too. If I cross the border, the Compact'll say I've gone to plot with Daniel Webster and Jackson."

"Let 'em. You'll have your license. And—look here, one of the reasons you wanted to get your license was so's you could look at Sandra across a breakfast table, wasn't it? What'd *she* think of New York?"

Gil pitched his unsmoked cigar in among the coals. "That's the worst of it."

"What is? Worst of what?" said Josiah, leaning forward.

"Polite note from Mr. Kingscote. Requests that I discontinue my attentions to his daughter."

Josiah made a gesture of disgust. "What's the matter with the old bastard?"

"Compact's got him scared about something. And that damned Staff eggs him on. Talks about loyalty—which means doing just what the Compact says." He waved his arm. "Of course! Let Strachan and the rest run the country. It's no one else's business. It's treason if you even think it is." He kicked viciously at a coal that snapped from the low fire.

Josiah's feet banged to the floor. "I've got it. I'll drive out and have a talk with the old man. I'll—"

Gil laughed scornfully. "He'd set the dogs on you. If he's afraid to have a Reformer seen about the place, how about a Yankee?" He rumpled his brown hair.

"Pah! With the highest respect, I think you're a lot of inchworms up here. The Compact's got you scared and—"

Gil flushed. "Scared? You saw what they did to Innis, didn't you?"

"Well—here's something else—"

There was a discreet rap at the door. "What is it, Ogle?" asked Josiah impatiently.

Mr. Ketchipaw's flute tones sang through the office. "What'll I do with that carboy of emetic salts?"

Josiah swept him away with a flourish. "Take 'em!" He clasped his hands behind his neck again. "Another idea. Sandra comes into town, doesn't she? Sometimes? Of course she does! Simple! Find out when she does and marry her!" He turned up his hands in triumph.

"Then what?" growled Gil. "The Compact'd have the marriage annulled before the service was over."

"Oh, hell! They wouldn't do *that*. Once she was married — "

Gil sighed wearily. "I just say again, whenever you think that Compact *wouldn't* do something, think of Innis."

Josiah scrubbed his fist across the high bridge of his nose. "Well, then, I'd — "

Gil got to his feet stiffly. "Got to get on to Ketchum's. I'll look in for my bag later."

"It'll be safe here. And I'll get to work on all this stuff of yours. I'll find a way to — "

Gil reached out, rumpled the dark hair. "Know you would if you could, Jos. But forget it. The worry's mine. Leave it to me."

Josiah rose, put an arm over Gil's shoulder. "Leave it to you? Damned if I will. I'm telling *you,* leave it to me."

Gil grinned sheepishly. "You're an old fool, Jos. Thanks. I'll come in again sometime and — " He glanced at the clock that hung by a grim portrait of Andrew Jackson and stamped out of the office, nearly upsetting the anxious Mr. Ketchipaw, who, elbows aquiver, was waiting by the door.

The May air was soft and fresh as Gil turned up Yonge Street. His long shadow danced along a picket fence, played over an apple tree whose tight buds gave promise of a future glory of white and pink, skated up the brick wall of a house. Heedless of the opening world, he strode on, heedless too of the grind and stamp that filled Yonge Street as drays, carts, chaises, shuttled over it. From a doorway near King Street, a black ball of fur raced after his feet, then bounced away on stiff legs, tail erect. Gil started, then picked up the kitten, dropped it back into its sheltering yard with a stern admonition, and lost himself in his thoughts again.

Wheels ground close to him, a low voice called, "Mr. Stensrood! Mr. Stensrood."

His head jerked up and he saw a plain-faced girl, pale hair showing beneath her deep brown bonnet, leaning from a carriage. Beside her a stout maid, black-cloaked, knitted in silence. Gil lifted his beaver. "Oh — Miss McDonald. Stupid of me not — "

Her rather prominent eyes were gentle in a blushing face. "I — I shouldn't have spoken. I've never really met you but — "

Gil smiled. "But I've met you — through hearing Sandra talk so much about Alice McDonald."

"I'll never have another friend like her," she said simply. "I — I was just wondering if you'd heard from her lately."

Gil forced a smile. "Oh — of course. Why, she — "

Alice McDonald's receding chin tightened. "I know all about her — well, what her father's done and — I don't see her much either. I thought you might like to — well, talk about her. She told me of your plans."

"I'd like to — with you," said Gil.

"Could you come in for tea — about four or half-past? Mother'd be there and she's so fond of Sandra she'd love to see you. This afternoon, then? I'm so glad." She motioned to the silent coachman and the carriage rattled off toward the Markets.

He started on. Then his tread was muffled by tanbark that formed a soft sidewalk along Ketchum's solid tannery. He turned into Adelaide Street where the white house with the railed tower squatted.

As he ran up the steps, the door swung open and Jesse Ketchum's gray, benevolent head appeared. "Just on the dot. You know these others?" He stepped aside and Gil saw Francis Hincks and John Rolph behind him. "That's good. I thought we'd walk over, but John Rolph insists on a carriage. You'll ride with me." He nodded to two shiny rigs that waited by the sharp-scented walls of the tannery.

In the leading carriage, Ketchum wagged his big head. "The reason I wanted you especially today, Gil, is this. We're showing up with a petition. It's about Canada. Now Rolph and Hincks are English-born. I'm Yankee. I wanted someone, not too old, that was real old Canada." He smiled. "Who fills the bill better than you?"

Gil flushed. "Oh — you could have found a lot — "

"Maybe. But we didn't." He looked back to the other carriage. "Rolph was telling me — His Imbecile Excellency is getting people all over the Province to petition for dissolution of Parliament and a new election. Don't see what he wants *that* for. We'll build our majority still higher. Anyway, that's what he's doing. And he makes great, booming answers to each petition."

"Can't see what he's after," frowned Gil.

"I can't either. His last reply was superb. He talked about invasion — in*va*sion of Canada. Didn't say by whom, but he ended up: 'I say, in the name of all the militia regiments of Canada, let them come!'"

Gil snorted. "Invasion!" He gave to the sway of the carriage as it turned down Simcoe Street, then rattled up the long drive to the plain yellow building that was Government House. Gil scrambled out, waited while Rolph and Hincks argued with Ketchum about who should present the petition. Suddenly Ketchum turned. "I've got it. Gil's the man."

"I!" said Gil, aghast.

"Excellent," said Rolph. "The youngest member but the oldest Canadian."

Somberly Gil thought, "This is just like what Doc said about Reform. Wait till we're on the threshold and then squabble about who's going to do what. Why didn't they settle it at Ketchum's?" He shook his head at Rolph. "I won't know what to say. I — "

Ketchum chuckled. "Never saw a Stensrood who couldn't carry things off." Hincks nodded in quick approval.

Gil fumed, maddeningly aware of a uniformed butler behind the high door who eyed the group coldly through a glass panel. "I've got no standing. Just a student medico and — "

Ketchum pushed him forward. "Go on."

Gil hesitated, then spun about, stamped up the steps. The door opened slightly, showed an impassive face, inquiringly raised eyebrows. Gil paused, then, goaded by the silent stare, seized the doorhandle and flung the door wide open. The butler staggered back.

"Please announce to His Excellency — a deputation of citizens of Toronto. To present a petition."

The plush breeches stood solidly. "Have you an audience with His Excellency?"

Gil stepped into the wide hall. "Of course we have."

Outraged eyes played over Jesse Ketchum's plain clothes, then turned back to the blue and fawn and leather that covered Gil's big frame. Slightly mollified by Gil's tailor, he bowed the four into an anteroom with a shade less stiffness, slipped discreetly through sliding doors.

Gil sat squarely on a fragile chair, fanned himself with his beaver. Ketchum began to chuckle. "Picked the right man, didn't we? See that flunkey start when Gil jammed the door at him?" He slapped his fat knee gently. "And the audience!"

"What about it?" asked Gil.

"We haven't got one." Rolph laughed silently into the crown of his hat.

Gil stared, then began to grin. "Well—we have now. We—"

A crisp tread echoed outside, a tall young ensign looked doubtfully into the room. "I—ah—must ask you to state your business with His—Why, hello, *Gil!* Didn't know it was you."

Gil rose. "Hello, Weston. I didn't either, until just now. Is Sir Francis waiting?"

Weston looked dubious. "I think he'll see you." He dropped his voice. "Know what these others are after?"

"They're with me," said Gil. "We're the audience."

"But—they're just Town, aren't they? Trader fellers? I can't see how—"

Gil turned. "This is Ensign Weston, gentlemen. Weston, this is Mr. Ketchum, retired; he's given more land to the Church than any other person in Upper Canada. Dr. Rolph is a member of the Medical Board of Upper Canada. Mr. Hincks is Secretary of—you know—" He left the sentence unfinished.

Weston at once became deferential. "Come with me, gentlemen. I'm sure that Sir Francis will see you at once." Trailing in the rear with Gil, he whispered, "You pulled me out of that. The Church! Of course, I didn't know, but if Dr. Strachan ever thought that I'd turned away a C. of E. donor! And Hincks!"

Gil smothered a grin. It wasn't necessary to explain to Weston that Ketchum gave to the Methodists and that Hincks's secretarial activities were anti-Compact. Then Weston skipped ahead of them, scratched on a double door, slipped through, closed it gently after him.

There was a pause. The doors flew open. "Gentlemen—this way!" said Weston.

The big room, hung with maps and engravings, was bright with spring sunshine. Gil threw back his head, marched toward the long table where Sir Francis Bond Head rose to meet the deputation. The pleasant, high-colored face under its crown of long wavy hair inclined slightly, the small, prim mouth smiled, then snapped back into place.

"Your Excellency," Gil began, somewhat disconcerted by the figures in uniform beyond the table who either yawned or looked superciliously at the group. "Your Excellency — " Then, as he turned his eyes to the handsome shallow face before him, confidence began to flow warm in his veins. "I have the honor to present, for Your Excellency's consideration, a petition from the loyal citizens of Toronto." He turned slightly, took the roll of paper from Ketchum. "The loyal citizens — " he stressed the adjective slightly — "knowing that their well-being is the first concern of Your Excellency, have ventured to set forth certain facts for Your Excellency's consideration. In doing so, they wish to take this opportunity of assuring Your Excellency of their devotion to Your Excellency and to the Crown."

The small mouth widened in a smile, a well-tended hand stopped its incessant toying with an Order that dangled over the flowered waistcoat, took the roll and opened it. "I can assure the loyal citizens of Toronto," began Sir Francis, "I can assure them in return that — " his hand swept up in a gesture, then fell weakly to his wide lapel — "that their well-being is — ah — my unceasing — ah — care and — concern. That's it — concern." He inclined his head graciously, then stared at the last sheet of the roll through an eyeglass. "This — ah — petition appears to — ah — come — or shall we say — " he dropped his chin, looked archly at Gil — "shall we say emanates from the — ah — industrial classes of the — ah — city, rather than from the gentlemen."

He carefully placed the roll on the table, fingered his Order. "But you may rest assured that it will have — " his hand shot up again, fluttered down to his lapel in the same weak gesture — "it will have the same, the very same — ah — attention from me that I should bestow on a communication from my — ah — Executive Council." He smiled benignly. "But of course, I shall couch my reply to it" — he raised an arch finger — "in, of course, somewhat plainer and — ah — more homely language." He inclined his head, then stood with raised eyebrows. The officers about the table shuffled their feet. Weston discreetly opened the double doors.

Jesse Ketchum purred in his throat, eyes placid. "Your Excellency—" Sir Francis's eyebrows jumped still higher, mouth compressed into a knot. He tapped his eyeglass against his thumbnail, every line of his body disapproving Ketchum's clothes. "Your Excellency, if you feel that the loyal citizens of Toronto must be reached by humble language, let me say that their ignorance of gentler forms—if they are ignorant—lies in the maladministration of your predecessors. Where are the endowments of King's College? Why aren't the Clergy Reserves sold and the money used for schools?"

"That's a hard question to answer, Your Excellency," put in Rolph grimly. "We look to you—"

Sir Francis craned his neck. "Ah—Weston—is the door open? Then—" again he inclined his head coldly—"then I am ready for the next claim on my time."

Gil eyed the petulant angry face. "May I put one more question to Your Excellency?"

The Lieutenant Governor glared, seemed mollified by the cut of Gil's lapel. "Well?" he said.

"Every Canadian," said Gil solemnly, "is concerned with the sanctity of our soil."

"Eh? Yes, yes. Of course. Very right." Sir Francis's rabbity mouth twitched.

"In replying to a petition of Home District electors about a dissolution, Your Excellency spoke of invasion, appealed to the militia, and said, 'Let them come.' If there *is* danger of invasion, I take the liberty of begging to learn from just what country Your Excellency expects it."

Sir Francis flushed a deep red. "Gentlemen, I have no further observations to make! Good day!" He turned his back on the group, muttering under his breath.

In the outer air, under the green waves of the elms that spread overhead, Hincks shook Gil's shoulder. "By God, why didn't *I* think of that?"

Rolph chuckled. "That was worth the trip. Did you see his face, Jesse? Stensrood so damned deferential and mild—just wanting to know!"

Ketchum shook his big head, climbed into the carriage. "I was so near to throwing something at that giggling simpleton that I—

Come on, Gil. Oh—just going to the Hospital? All right. Well—that couching his reply in humble language that *we'd* understand. That damned, blasted, blatant, babbling brook. That serene sieve! *We'd* understand!"

The two carriages rattled off. Gil, elation fading, walked slowly down the drive, his boots crunching in the gravel. "He's worse than Father said." A chill began to creep over him. "And we'll have him probably for six years. Good God, what'll Canada be like after six years of *that!*"

He turned through the low gate of the Hospital grounds, made his reluctant way to the main door. Nurse Hartley fluttered up from the low desk. "Oh, Mr. Stensrood! The Doctor said you wouldn't be here until late afternoon."

"Did he?" said Gil absently. "Well, maybe you'd better write Sir Francis about it."

Her dull eyes widened. Then she began to laugh. "You're *so* comical, Mr. Stensrood!" Then a rapt look came over her plain, rather tired face. "You know—when he rides out in the afternoon—and he *does*—every single day—why, I can *see* him right from this door. Just think of that!"

"He's a great man," said Gil, struggling out of his blue coat. He hung it up, the buttons on the long tails clinking against the whitewashed wall.

Nurse Hartley clasped her hands. "*Isn't* he!"

"No doubt about it. He made Jesse Ketchum swear. No one else has ever been able to do that."

"Oh, haven't they?" She thought this over dubiously. "And he's *such* a fine gentleman—Sir Francis."

Fumbling about among the pegs, Gil found his vizored cap. He looked at it respectfully. Then he glared at his beaver, snatched it up, placed it in the open door, and sent it spinning out onto the grounds with a savage kick. The hat, its rich nap glossy in the sun, rolled over and over, came to a spinning halt by the gate. Gil clapped on his cap, tugged at the vizor.

"Mr. *Sten*srood!" The protest was scarcely audible. "That *beauti*ful hat! It must have cost—cost—"

"Fifteen shillings at Jared Banks's. It's a *gentleman's* hat." He jerked at his cap again, stamped off down the corridor.

Sunlight filtering through the branches of a budding lilac filled the whitewashed pharmacy with a soft, greenish light that made Gil squint as he came in. Ritter, the old pharmacist, raised his hard, lined face from a small crucible, grunted a greeting, turned back to his work. Gil flung open a closet, snatched a short, tailless jacket from a hook, crowded his shoulders into it and sat down at the scarred bench.

"What you after?" growled Ritter, face puckering as he carefully dripped greenish liquid into his crucible.

"Making something. For Mrs. Beane. Camphorated julep."

Ritter's thin hair, that waved over his head like a bird's crest, nodded. Gil began getting down jars, boxes, a small mortar and pestle. The pungent air of the little room seemed to soothe him, to form a wall between him and the world outside. He squinted, muttered to himself: "Camphor — one drachm. Rub with ten drops of rectified spirits of wine; double refined sugar, half ounce. Then — "

The pharmacy was still save for an occasional gentle drip or clink. Gil finished his compounding, looked along the shelves. "Where's the horse-radish?"

"What you want it for?" asked Ritter without looking up.

"Palsy infusion. The old man they brought in last night."

A gaunt finger pointed to an unlabeled jar close by him. Gil reached across, bent to his work again, oblivious of the slow slant of the sun through the lilac. The door flew open. An anxious voice panted: "Who's here?"

Neither of the two heads lifted. Ritter jerked his thumb at Gil. "He's here. So'm I. Don't slam the door when you shut it."

"But — "

Gil looked around, annoyed, saw the flushed face of Nurse Lamb at the door, narrow forehead beaded and long nose aquiver. "What is it?"

The nurse gasped with relief. "Oh — it's you, Mr. Stensrood. It's that Barry girl. She's — and there's no other doctor here and — "

"Barry girl? What about her?"

"She's in a fit I think. Nurse Clement doesn't know what to do."

Gil snapped. "I could have told you that. She never does. How about you?"

Tears stood in the close-set eyes. "I'm new. I've never seen — I've — "

Gil kicked his high stool to one side. "I'll go up. Barry? What's she in for? She the pregnant girl who blames the gunner corporal?" He hurried toward the staircase that climbed the west end of the building, the nurse running by his side.

"It's not that one. I don't think, anyway. This one's too young. She's only four or five."

"Not too young if she lives near the Garrison. What is it?"

"Putrid throat, Mr. Stensrood."

Gil reached the top of the stairs, flung open the door of a big room where neat beds lined the walls. Eyes fretful, patient, hopeful, curious, turned toward him as he crossed the room to a bed where a fat, fluttery woman alternately wrung her hands and dabbed at the pillow with a damp cloth.

"What is it, Clement?" asked Gil shortly.

Heedless of the voluble rambling reply, he bent over the little head that turned and twisted on the pillow. The long dark hair was damp with sweat, matted. The eyes were swollen, feverish, and the unformed childish lips caked. Under heavy blankets the slight body writhed and turned. Gil stooped lower, sniffed. The breath that struggled from the dry lips was heavy, foul. He smiled at her, passed his hand gently over her forehead. The cracked lips tried to answer, then a bright drop slid from under the lids.

Gil turned to Clement. "Pulse?" he asked shortly.

"Oh — I took it — I think I did — it was all right anyway and — "

He snatched out his watch, laid his finger on the shrunken wrist whose skin seemed to burn through his. Then he slid the hand carefully back under the covers. "Clement — go down to Ritter. Tell him to make me up an ounce of Peruvian bark with two drachms of Virginia snakeroot. Got that? Bark — snakeroot. He'll know."

Clement's fat haunches quivered as she bustled importantly out of the room. Gil turned to the other nurse. "That'll take her at least a half hour." He eyed her keenly, saw that her eyes were intelligent, her big mouth firm. "You look as if you had sense. Got upset by Clement? Forget about her. You and I'll fix this." She answered his smile tremulously. "Now — what's the first name? Josie?" He turned back to the bed. "Well, Josie, Nurse Lamb and I are going to fix you right up. Aren't we, Lamb? How long since she's been fed?"

The nurse looked worried. "I came on this morning. Clement tried to make her eat, but she couldn't swallow. Clement said she'd hardly eaten since day before yesterday."

Gil looked down at the flushed face that contracted spasmodically with the effort of swallowing. "Hurts, does it?" asked Gil.

The head tossed, the body was shaken with hiccuping sobs. "Get a basin for her. Make her spit out all that stuff. Her throat'll still contract, but it'll be a little easier. Why wasn't she given one before?"

Nurse Lamb hurried off, came back with a basin, a cloth. "Clement said she ought to be made to swallow. It'd break the tumor."

"Did she?" said Gil. "That's it. Sponge off her lips. When I go down I'll have ice sent up to you. Let her hold a piece in her mouth. Rub it across her lips." He gently touched the bandage across the thin throat. "Poulticed all right. Who did that?"

"Dr. Telfer. He had her brought in. He— "

"What'd he call it? Malignant quinsy? Right. When's he coming back?"

"I—I don't know."

"She's got to eat," said Gil, staring at the twitching face, at the hot hands whose fingers opened and closed convulsively with each contraction of the throat.

"But she can't swallow. I—I tried to give her some water when Clement was out of the room. It just ran out of her mouth."

Gil pulled at his square chin. "She's got to, though. She's starving and she's all full of poison from that tumor." He walked slowly to the window, looked out into the spring sunshine, unseeing. "Damn it, why isn't Doc here today? He'd figure *some* way." He felt his head tightening with the effort of thought, tried to visualize the festering swelling inside the young throat, blocking the passage to the stomach. Somehow, food *must* be slipped past it. He shut his eyes, saw something soft, thin, passed down over the swelling—something. Unconsciously he sniffed, cocked his head on one side, sniffed again as though he were calling in his sense of smell to aid him. Only the heavy air of the ward flowed in through his nostrils. It was very still. Over by the door, an old woman coughed, turned in her sleep. An amputation case beyond her sighed deeply, muttered.

Suddenly Gil raised his head. "Lamb! What have they got in the kitchen?"

She looked up from her gentle stroking. "It was an eel pie this noon. For tonight — "

Gil straightened, one hand raised. He seemed to lift up on his toes, poised, then ran from the ward. "Got it! Be right back."

Nurse Lamb gaped after him, heard his boots clatter on the stone stairs, die away. The ward was still again. Then she heard the boots slap over level flooring, pound up the steps.

"Got it! Got it!" said Gil exultantly. "They hadn't thrown 'em out." He dangled something in the air. "Sending up soup right away."

"What — what — " Nurse Lamb stared at the eelskin that waved triumphantly.

Gil pulled a chair up to the bed. "Now, Josie, we're going to make you feel better — right away. Lamb — a flexible probe from the cabinet there. That's it. Ah!"

A walking patient shuffled through the door, a steaming bowl in her worn hands. Gil made a cautioning gesture, took the probe from Lamb. "How'd you like some nice hot soup, Josie?" he asked, smiling at her.

The damp hair tossed on the pillow, a shoulder turned in shrinking protest.

"Just a little? Well, never mind. Let's have a look at the throat. That curtain, Lamb. Up a little. There. Now, Josie, just a look for a second. Open up — that's it."

Nurse Lamb, startled, saw him lay the eelskin on the hot, coated tongue, saw the probe move swiftly, but delicately, the guiding fingers poised and sensitive. The girl writhed, tore at his hands, head and neck straining away.

Gil, his face set, fought gently against her, watched the end of the eelskin gradually vanish. The muscles across the back of his hand swelled as he guided the probe, his face now tense and anxious. He rose slightly from his chair, whispered: "Wipe off my forehead, Lamb."

Then slowly he withdrew the probe, holding the outer end of the eelskin in his other hand. "Done it," he whispered.

A light approaching reverence spread over Nurse Lamb's face. The walking patient looked on, uncomprehending. Eyes still on the face that tossed and turned, Gil held out the probe to the nurse. "Now — that funnel from the kitchen — " He inserted its point into the eelskin tube. "Now — the broth. Pour it slowly — slowly — that's it."

The child stopped the incessant tossing of its head. Her eyes opened. Then the cracked lips curved in a broken smile. Gil leaned closer, whispered, "My forehead, Lamb." His eyes widened. "It's getting there. It's getting there. Slow — slow. Now a little more. See — the flush is going down — getting a tinge of proper color. That's — "

The child suddenly sat up, clutching at the slimy skin that trailed from her lips. Gil's hand moved like a striking snake, seized the end and slowly drew it out as she rocked back and forth in a paroxysm of coughing and retching. "Basin, Lamb! Quick!"

The nurse moved deftly, muttering, "Clement said food was poison to her. She'll — "

The coughing continued in shrill, choking spasms. Gil, white-faced, held the thin shoulders erect.

Abruptly the coughing ceased. The child sank back on the pillow, breathing heavily. Unbelieving, Gil stared at her. He whispered: "How is it, Josie?"

Slowly her head rolled toward him. "Can — swallow." The words crept painfully out.

"Sore?"

"A little."

There was awe in Gil's voice. "I don't dare — I don't dare believe it." A thin hot hand crept out, curled itself about his.

He choked back an overwhelming surge of joy, of relief. "It did it. It did it. Everything! I found it!" Then he looked down at the pillow, felt suddenly grave, almost solemn. "You can go home in two days now, Josie. How does that seem?"

The smile deepened, the reddened lids lifted toward him. "Go sleep — now." The eyes closed, the matted head sank deeper into the pillow.

Slowly Gil got up, found the nurse staring at him, her eyes moist. "See what that did, Lamb? The soup got into her stomach. That was one thing. Then the heat of the soup brought the tumor to a head, broke it." He drew a deep breath. "She'll be all right now." He bent down, smoothed the damp hair. The child was breathing easily, smiling in her sleep.

"That—that was wonderful," whispered Nurse Lamb. "How did you—"

There was a brisk clatter at the door. Nurse Clement bustled in, every inch of her fat form shaking to the importance of her tread. "Here's the bark solution. I told that Ritter just what to do and stood right over him while he did it."

"That'll put him in a good humor," said Gil tersely.

"Oh, *I* know what to do. Now where's my little patient and—" She gave a little scream. "She's—she's *dead!* She's—"

"She's asleep and she'll stay asleep if you stop screeching." Gil suddenly felt very tired, sapless. "Nurse Lamb'll know what to do. She'll look after her. Lamb—tell the night nurse—broth every three hours or so. But let her get her sleep out first."

Clement's double chins quivered. "*My* patient—and what'll I do with this?" She held up the bottle of bark.

"Have it for supper. Lamb, you did a good piece of work. I'll put it in the record." He nodded, walked heavily back to the pharmacy, where he found Ritter eying him coldly.

"Know only a regular doctor can send to the pharmacy? If it hadn't been you, I'd have sent Clement back without anything." He scowled at a dark brew that bubbled slowly over a small lamp, absorbed.

"Had to get her out from under foot," said Gil.

"Why send her *here?*" The birdlike crest shook with indignation.

"Why didn't *you* send her to Peru for the bark?"

"Will. Next time." He bent over his brew again.

Gil rested his head in his hands, lived over the scene by the Barry child's bed. Slowly his elation ebbed. He shook his head. "Why'd I *take* so long? Doc'd have thought of that as soon as he saw her. Guess he's right. I'm kind of stupid." He sighed; sat up. "Where's the Socotrine aloes, Ritter?"

Silence fell, broken only by the hiss of Ritter's brew and the occasional clink of a pestle.

There was a discreet tap on the door, a woolly head peeped cautiously around the corner. "Horse from Barnard's, Mist' Stensrood!"

Gil started. "Huh? Horse?"

"Done ordered it this morning, suh."

Gil pushed back his stool. "Course I did. Thanks, Tobey." He rapidly cleaned and put away his utensils. "Just fasten him to the hitching rail. I'll be out."

The black head bobbed, disappeared.

Gil looked at his watch. "What was I going to do? Oh, yes! Alice McDonald's. Just about make it." He thought of tea with half pleasure, half apprehension. "Maybe she'll know *some*thing about Sandra. Wish I could tell Sandra about the Barry girl. She'd be interested. She'd—" Slowly his high elation crept back over him. "Anyway, I did it all by myself. I found out something."

XII

Tryst — 1836

From the graveled sweep of Government House a cavalcade jingled out onto King Street, a tall figure riding in front, a handful of scarlet coats following respectfully. Gil stared, then grinned. He snatched off his cap, made a sweeping bow to the Lieutenant Governor of Upper Canada.

Sir Francis's empty, handsome face flushed. He raised his glass, stared haughtily at Gil, mouth compressed and eyebrows high.

Gil kicked out suddenly, caught the flying stirrup iron and through its metal hoop stared with equal hauteur, his head turning majestically as the two horses passed. Sir Francis flushed brick-red, spurred his horse. Gil caught a smothered snort from one of the aides.

The gray clattered on. Gil nodded to himself. "Not such a bad day as it started out to be." He slid his foot back into the stirrup, threaded his way toward Queen Street and the McDonald house.

As he crossed Yonge Street, he noticed knots of well-dressed men heading east, each carrying a short rifle. He narrowed his eyes, recognized Strachan's eldest son, one of the younger Robinsons, a Boulton or two. Someone shouted to him, waved a rifle, but he shook the gray into a trot, skirted the rear of a keg-piled dray from Helliwell's, brushed past the horns of slow-moving oxen, and slid out of the saddle in front of a low, neatly fenced house. As he knotted the halter to the hitching post, a single shot spatted flatly from the open fields to the north. Gil's head snapped back, eyes wide and ears alert. The shot was repeated, followed by a ragged burst. He jumped onto the stone mounting-block, craned his neck. The sweep of lawn, meadow, and woodland was peaceful, empty. Then, by the entrance to Mossfield, the Allan estate, he saw the glint of steel, saw shouldered rifles, in twos and threes, trickling past the gates. His eyes hardened, lines formed about the corners of his mouth. "What the devil are *they* up to?" he muttered. He shook himself, completed the hitch about the ring of the post, and hurried through the little garden where early flowers showed green along the flagged path.

In the drawing room, whose broad windows looked south to bay and lake, Alice McDonald rose to meet him, brown hair stringy, thin shoulders and arms fluttering.

"What have you heard?" he asked eagerly.

She laughed excitedly. "Oh — I've got a *lot* for you — such a lot. Sit down here. I'll ring for tea in a minute. Mother'll be down soon. And then — "

"When did you see her last? Is she all right? Does her father — "

Alice shook her lank ringlets at him. "One thing at a time, please." She grew serious. "I just wanted to tell you, first of all, Sandra has been my friend all my life. I want her to be happy. I saw you two driving by the day Sir Francis came. I'd do anything to make her as happy again as she looked then."

"Then you must be my friend too," said Gil.

"I want to be," she said simply.

Gil laughed. "Well then, that's settled. You are. Now — about Sandra — "

She smiled. "That's easy. Just let me show you — " Her hands fluttered about the wide seat of the chair. "I had it right here — oh — no, that's not it — " She jumped up, lifted books from a long table, shifted a cushion. "I *had* it here. I know I did — Who could have — I must have left it upstairs." Her prominent eyes turned to him. "Do you mind waiting? I'm sure I can lay my hands right on it. I'll be back in a second. There's a copy of *Zanoni* you could look at."

She ran out of the room. Gil heard her shoes click on the stairs as he turned to the broad windows and looked down to the bay. Two or three sailboats were working their way past Gibraltar Point and the Kingston steamer, whose clouds of smoke were rose-tinged by the sun, was just pulling out from Tinning's Wharf. Halfway to the peninsula, the ferry showed clear, its horses tramping their endless route, round and round the deck as they turned the heavy paddles. From the north, an occasional *spat-spat* of rifle fire sounded dimly in the still room.

Then hurrying feet drowned it out, racing down the stairs. Gil started back toward the fireplace, but stopped short as a cloud of light hair, a billow of blue, sped through the wide door, eyes eager and arms outstretched.

He swept her up, bright hair soft against his cheek. Feet clear of the floor, she clung to him, murmuring over and over: "Oh, Gil! Oh, Gil!"

Gently he set her down, bewilderment slowly struggling with the joy that lit up his face. "But — but — how — why — "

She clung closer. "Never mind now. Never mind. We're here." Her cheek rubbed gently against his shoulder. "I've missed you so." She looked up. "Been missing me?"

"Have I! Well — " Suddenly he released her, eyes on the door. "Might Alice — "

She shook her head. "Alice mightn't." She spread out her wide skirts, curled up in a corner of the sofa.

"How do you know?" He leaned over, tickled her nose with a blonde ringlet. "And another thing — why weren't you here when I came in? Why — " His voice rose. "Why didn't I know you were going to be here anyway?"

She caught his hand, held it against her cheek. "How do I know about Alice? Oh, don't be stupid. And I wasn't here because Alice wanted to be in on a surprise and I let her. And you didn't know I was going to be here because I didn't know either. Only hoped." She leaned back against his shoulder, drew his head down to her.

"Happy?" he whispered.

Eyes closed, she nodded. "Now. But — oh!" She suddenly hid her face against him, trembling. "It's so *aw*ful! Gil, that note Father sent you! And he told me I could never see you again. Never. And — "

Gently he stroked her head, held her close. "Then how did you — "

Her shoulders shook, her breath came convulsively. "I hate — hate — this. But I told him I *wouldn't* stop seeing you. I'd see you as often as I could." She fumbled for a handkerchief, held it against her buried face. "I was so furious. I told him I'd leave the house. I'd come in with Alice." She shuddered again. "Oh, Gil, suppose he locks me up. Staff told him to. Staff — "

Gil started. "He couldn't. The law — "

"He could. I'm not twenty-one. I won't be for years and years. And there's that de Sales girl. Her father locked her up in her room and she didn't come out for years. It almost killed her. The only reason I got in today was that Staff's with that idiot Rifle Corps of Fitzgibbon's. They're drilling and shooting up near Rosedale." She shook her head. "You can't stay long, Gil. As soon as the shooting stops, you'll have to go. He'll see your horse and tell Father. I've got to drive back with him."

Gil patted her shoulder, mind in a whirl. "We'll find a way. We'll—"

"But how? How? If he finds out you come here, he won't let me see Alice—or hear from her. I don't know what we'll do then." She sobbed quietly, hopelessly.

Gil set his chin. "Damn it, Sandra, he *can't* do this. After all, this is the nineteenth century. I've—been trying to think of things ever since I got his note. There are plenty of ways. We could—"

Her head moved slightly. "We can't."

"We can," he snapped. "Now—sit up. That's better. Do you know *why* he won't let me see you? Is it *all* politics?"

She nodded, woebegone eyes on his. "But *he* doesn't care that much. I *know* he doesn't. It's Staff. And then—then I found out what the Compact was frightening him about. It's his ships and—"

"But he *sold* his ships. Everyone knows that."

"He sold them, but a company was formed or something like that. He stayed in the company. And the Compact's threatening to take their licenses and things away. And then the paper mills on the Don! They told him they'd put such a tax on the Don water used that they'd have to close. It's about all Father's got. And they keep writing him and telling him that the Compact *is* the Crown. It's treason to fight it. He believes it. And Staff, of course, is—"

Gil took her handkerchief from her, carefully dried her eyes. "There! That's better, isn't it? Now, settle back here and listen to me. As long as we're careful we can always meet here, can't we?"

She nodded, trying to answer his smile.

"That's one thing. Here's another. There's going to be an election. Next month, I guess. Head made a lot of people petition for one, and when it comes off there won't be a single Compacter elected. And Robert Baldwin's really going to England. Wouldn't surprise me at all if he got Head recalled. *Then* the Compact'll be done—absolutely. See?"

She shook her head miserably. "No."

He began again, patiently. "There'll be the biggest Reform majority ever. They'll know in England that Rob's speaking for everyone except the Compact and—"

She didn't look up. "That's what everyone said when Head came. The Compact wouldn't dare this and dare that. Just elections! We've had 'em before. Gil, I'm *so* unhappy. You can't think what it's like at home. Father tries to have a lot of Staff's friends out there—hoping I'll forget you. Staff's always leering at me; he—he tries to tell me the most awful things about you. He says your meetings are held down in the Devil's Quarter-Acre. That there's lots of drinking at them. That there are awful women at them. And he keeps trying to leave me alone with a perfectly slimy thing from Hamilton—a cousin of that Alan MacNab's. He—"

Gil jumped to his feet. "Damn him! I'll have it out with that brother of yours. I'll—I'll—I know I'm bigger than he is, but I'll—"

She shook her head wearily. "That wouldn't help, Gil. He's been made a deputy something. And you'd be assaulting a King's officer. And anyway—he's my brother."

He paced about the room, scowling. Then he suddenly sat down again, took her gently in his arms. "Love me, Sandra?"

"You know I do," she said quietly. "So much that I wouldn't care if what Staff said *was* true—about the women, I mean." She cocked her chin, a hint of a smile about her lips. "I've so much confidence in you." Her arms suddenly tightened about his neck.

His eyes narrowed. "I've got a plan."

She threw back her head. "What?"

He smiled down at her. "Get ready to listen again." He gently moved her head to his shoulder. "There. Now here's what we'll do—what we're going to do."

She caught one of his hands. "Don't wave about so. I'm listening."

"First—we wait."

"Wait! But that's—"

"Shhh! I'm not through. We'll wait and see what happens about Head and the elections. If I'm right, your father'll be able to forget about the Compact."

She sighed. "You've said that before. Suppose you're wrong?"

"Then—we do this. I was talking to Jos this morning. I've heard I can't take my exams for the license and—"

"Gil! How dreadful! You never told me!"

"Never mind that now. That's just for me to think about. Well, Jos said: 'Why not go to Albany and get a New York license?'"

Her eyes widened. "New *York?* Gil—you'd be gone—"

"Course I would. And so would you. Don't you see?"

She sat forward, lips slightly parted. "New York!" She jumped up, arms wide. "Gil! I'll do it! Then we'll—"

"Then we'll either come back, if they'll let us, or we'll start our own practice in Albany. We've got Uncle Stensrood to go to there. See!" His spirits rose as he talked. "If we have to, you'll come in one day to see Alice—only you'll keep right on going down to Tinning's Wharf. That's one way. Or we might—never mind how just now. Jos'll help. He'll know the best ways of getting places. He'll—and you see, your father really won't care, because the Compact can't blame him or say that *he*'s mixed up in Reform."

She was silent for a moment. Then she said, "That's the only thing—Father."

"But don't you see? After we've gone—he can say to them: 'My daughter went away because I won't let her marry into Reform.' And once we're in Albany—"

She slowly twisted her handkerchief. "Supposing you can't get a license at Albany?"

He laughed shortly. "I'm not afraid of any exam that's fair. Now—that's what we're going to do—aren't we?"

She drew a deep breath, then nodded slowly. "It's not the way I thought it would be."

He smiled grimly. "Do you think it's what *I* was counting on? It's the hard way—but it's the only way that I can see."

"I don't care how it is, Gil dear. Just so long as we're together. That's everything, isn't it?"

He held out his hand. "That's the way I feel or else I wouldn't think up a scheme that most people'd call harebrained. It just comes down to this—nothing's worth while if we can't be together. Everything is if we are." A long finger tilted back her chin. "Be easier now?"

She nodded. "Much easier. How—how long—"

"Elections in June, probably. By the first week in July we'll know. Then — well, say about the first part of September we ought to know if things *are* going to change."

"If they only would. I can't — "

A distant burst of fire crackled across the fields. She raised her head, then let it fall to Gil's shoulder. "Still at it. We've — "

He cocked his ear. "Is it — " A shadow crossed his face. In the last echoes of the salvo a bugle sang, thin and clear. He sat up, mouth grim.

"What is it?"

"I know that call. It's — it's Assembly. That means — "

She was tense. "It means you've got to go. Gil — hurry!"

He covered her ears with his hands. "Not yet. They're way off — "

"Gil, dear! We *can't* take a chance. If Staff should see your horse here! I tell you, he's perfectly mad and Father's frantic! This is the only place I can see you." She pushed him toward the door. "Don't you want to see me? Do you want me to be locked up like the de Sales girl?"

Reluctantly Gil moved out into the hall. Alice McDonald ran down the stairs, holding up her hands. "Just in time. I saw them from the upper windows. They're standing in a line in the north meadow beyond the lawns and Colonel Fitzgibbon is talking to them."

Sandra looked worried. "They're not on their way down?"

"Not yet. It ought to be four or five minutes before they reach Queen Street."

Gil took her hand. "You're a real friend, Alice. May I look in from time to time? Even when Sandra isn't here? You said we were friends, you know."

"Any time, Gil," she said, eyes on Sandra.

Sandra leaned against him. "I hope you will, Gil." She smiled up at him. Then care drew a veil over her face. "You'd better go — and Alice won't mind." For a second she was very close to him, then he found himself on the steps, stumbling blindly toward the gray. Eyes grim, he swung into the saddle, whirled west toward Yonge Street, turned sharply north. Through the ravine that cut away toward Mossfield he caught a glint of metal, saw the Rifle Corps marching across the meadows, the late sunlight harsh on the slanted muzzles that pointed toward him.

XIII

Doc Richland — 1836

The Stensroods, in common with many Reformers, faced the elections of June 1836 with calm confidence. The Reform majority in the Assembly would be swelled to impressive proportions. England would at last know, through the very presence of so many elected Reformers, that the Compact did not speak for Upper Canada. Gradually and peacefully the old, old abuses would be corrected.

Just before the elections, the Compact struck. Sir Francis Bond Head, instead of maintaining proper neutrality, actually took the stump for the Compact, addressed crowds of voters. A vote for Reform, he assured them, was a vote for separation, for republicanism, for absorption by the United States. The issue was clear — a vote for the Compact was a vote for the Crown. So said Sir Francis. Many Reformers, alarmed, voted Compact for the first time in their lives.

Deeds backed up Compact words. Voters going to the polls were intimidated, sometimes beaten by Compact gangs. Reformers were disqualified wholesale on one technicality or another. And to assure a victory beyond all doubt, land warrants were issued to swarms of propertyless, drifting men in exchange for Compact votes.

So the mock balloting went on in towns where banners flaunted. "Vote to stay British" — "Hurrah for Head and the Crown" — "Britons! Stamp out that hydra-headed viper, Democracy."

The Compact swept through on an avalanche of votes. Even William Lyon Mackenzie was beaten in a district that had returned him year after year.

GIL skillfully eased the chaise over the ruts where Spadina Avenue crossed Queen Street West, urged the hired horse into a gentle trot. Josiah, beside him, winced to the rocking, rubbed his ankle. "You didn't tell me we had to cross the Alps to get to Doc's."

"Wait till Doc gets through with you," said Gil grimly. "You'll think you've had all the Alps piled on top of you."

"Couldn't be worse than it is now." He set his teeth. "Funny to think of Doc having a house. I always thought he and Bessie crawled up on the seat of that old chaise to sleep."

"They do," said Gil. "He rented this house just to impress you." He curved the horse over to the south side of the street. "Here we are." He got out, helped Josiah to the ground. Josiah swore, pegged on slowly, leaning on a heavy stick.

A bright moon shone on the waters of the lake that glimmered through the full-leafed branches of the elms of Queen Street. It touched the shingles of the cottage-like house, gilded its dark windows, paled the glow from the small panes in the ell that jutted east.

"This way," said Gil. "No—that's the front door. For distinguished patients only. You go in this way." With an arm under his cousin's, he tramped up a short walk, hammered on a scaly door.

Doc's voice trumpeted: "Come in."

The rickety panels swung back, showed an immaculate room where stiff chairs, worn with scrubbing, stood along a whitewashed wall. Gil half pulled, half lifted Josiah across the threshold. "Where are you, Doc?"

The old voice rumbled: "Where'd you expect to find me?"

Gil opened a second door, saw Richland sitting on his examining table carefully brushing a small gray kitten that purred ecstatically, eyes tight shut. Two more, one black and one buff, raced and tumbled about his feet in mimic warfare. Gil grinned. "Going over the stock?"

Doc nodded, then peered across Gil's shoulder. "Who you got there? Oh, Josiah?" He saluted absently with the kitten, resumed his brushing.

"Hurt his ankle, Doc."

Richland set down the kitten, which sidled across the floor, teeth bared and ears flat in mock fury. "How'd you do it, Jos? Jumping out a bedroom window?"

Josiah hobbled into the spotless office, blinking in the lamplight that gleamed back from a hundred bottles. "Line of duty, Doc. Found a burglar in the warehouse."

Gil perched on a stool, tossed his cap on the glistening head of a skull. "Tell the truth, Jos. Honest, Doc, he sprained it at the Union Jack down in the Devil's Quarter-Acre."

"So I supposed," grumbled Doc. "Get in a mess over some wench, get hurt, and then come here to break up the finest brushing a kitten ever got. Take off your shoe and sock."

Josiah bent painfully. "True about the burglar. I found him in the warehouse and had to chase him clear to the Union Jack."

"Get him?" asked Doc.

Josiah nodded. "Couldn't run very fast. Aaaah!" He drew off his shoe with a grimace.

"Where is he now?"

"At the Hospital," said Gil grinning. "And one more with him. A man that the constables were looking for. Same one that robbed Cawthra's place."

Richland took the sinewy ankle in delicate fingers. "So it wasn't a wench. Guess I'm getting cynical. Hurt?"

"Uh!" grunted Josiah.

The fingers played about joint and tendon, flexing gently. "Nothing wrong here — not much anyway."

Josiah looked outraged. "*Isn't!* Wish it was your ankle! You'd be wondering about amputation. I stepped on a rock when I was running and the damn thing just rolled with me."

"I know," said Doc. "They'll do it, won't they?"

"Won't they? Won't they? Think I do this every time things get dull?"

"Wouldn't surprise me a mite," said Richland equably, the lamplight flicking across his polished bald spot. "Stensroods are all alike. Do the God-damnedest things. Bend it a little. That's good. We-e-ell." He straightened up, rubbed the knees of his baggy trousers. "Nothing to it."

Josiah stared. "Aren't you going to *do* anything about it?"

Richland peered at him over the tops of his glasses. "Oh yes. I'll put a bandage on it. I'll give you a lot of directions that you'll be too bullheaded to follow. Then I'll tell you to come back and have a new bandage, which wouldn't be necessary if you had the sense to follow orders. Gil—get me some bandage. You know where." He bent over the ankle again. "Little sprain, that's all."

Gil fumbled in a deep drawer, pulled out a hard roll of gauze. "To hear him yell, you'd think it was a fracture."

Richland looked tolerantly about. "Oh—sure it hurts. But it ain't anything." He unrolled the gauze, snipped it expertly with his scissors. "Keep the cats away from the end of this, Gil." He began to wind the white stuff with deft sureness about Josiah's instep. "Only reason I want an assistant. Keep the patients from bothering the cats. True you're shutting down, Jos?"

Josiah nodded. "About the only thing to do, since the elections."

"You're a fool. Hold your foot straighter."

"I am not. Be a fool to stay."

"Now bend it. I say you better stay."

He gently stroked the finished bandage, cocked his eye at it. "Now that's pretty, if I do say so. When you get home, give it a long soak in hot water. See how the bandage goes and put it on the same way. Keep it up as much as you can. No, sir, I say you're a fool to quit."

Gil slid from the stool. "I'm going over to the Hospital."

Richland looked at him, frowning. "What time did you get there this morning?"

"About six."

"And we started at eight. You were with me all day. Now you want to go back there?"

Gil nodded.

Dr. Richland picked up the lamp. "You're a worse fool than Josiah—if that's possible." He held the lamp high, snatched up a small mirror. "Look at yourself. Look at your eyes! They're the color of liver. Look at your face. Could pour a quart of water into the hollows in your cheeks, and they've got the color of rotten sheepskin."

Josiah hooted, slapped his knee, then winced. "Ouch! But that's what I've been telling him, Doc. Looks as if he was going to play the ghost in *Hamlet*."

Richland waved him away. "Hold out your hand. Shakes like a birch leaf, don't it? S'pose you'd been like that when you fixed up that little Barry girl? That was the best piece of work that's ever been done in the Hospital. But—you couldn't do it now. Don't think you could even give an enema." He laid the mirror carefully on the high secretary that held his books and bottles. "I'm closing up. You two come into the house with me."

Gil looked sullen. "I'm going to—"

"And work till midnight? And then lie awake 'cause you're too tired to sleep? And not be able to eat, or if you do eat, puke it all up? Quit yawping and get into the house."

He led the way through the shining waiting room, unlocked a door, and tramped on, lamp held high. "Find a seat somewhere. I'm going to get a horn of rye whiskey all around. Maybe two. Maybe three." He fumbled about a half-seen bulk of wood and glass across the room.

Gil, bending a little under Josiah's weight, blinked. A small table in the center of the room was heaped with books, a couple of old shirts, scissors, a jug, a pair of ear muffs, newspapers, and an unexplained axe handle. He walked cautiously around it. "Here, Jos, ease down here."

Josiah sat down carefully, then wrenched aside as a dozen turnips bumped down to the floor, followed by a stack of papers. Richland, intent by the shadowy sideboard, mumbled, "Just brush off what you can't sit on. Look out for the cats." He turned, set the lamp on the table by the simple process of pushing hard on its base until wood rang under the metal. "There. H'm." He looked about mildly. "Guess the place ain't as tidy as it might be. Old woman's supposed to come in here and clean, but it don't look as if she'd been round today." He carefully took a long bottle from under his arm, fished glasses out of his pockets, pushed them vaguely toward the cousins. "Water in here," he said, picking up a heavy pitcher.

Then he frowned. "No, there ain't. How'd *that* come to get there? Been looking for it." He fished out a mouse trap, frowned again, upended the pitcher. A length of fishing line, an apple core, and a frayed collar slithered out onto the table. He looked philosophically over his glasses. "Well, things do move about, don't they?" He disappeared in the unseen regions, came back with a fresh pitcher. "Good spring water. Now—fill up." He tilted his glass, rapped it down on a cleared space on the table. "Now, Jos, what's this lunacy about your quitting?"

Josiah cocked his foot across an upset basket. "Not quitting. Just not going on."

"Why not?"

"No chance to do business that I can see. The Compact's in so strong and that means greasing every palm from here to Holland Landing."

"Any worse than it was when you first came here?"

"N-no."

"You were going to open up then." He snatched up his glass. "I tell you, Jos, I've been watching American firms up here for a long time. I got just one criticism. They're smart — always. But — " he wagged a long finger — "the least sign of trouble — what do they do? Crawl into their holes like snails and shoot the holes back across the border."

"What do you expect 'em to do? Stay and lose money?"

Richland carefully filled a pipe, lit it. "There's good times and bad. Not good all the time or bad all the time. Yankee firms want 'em always good." He pointed the reeking pipestem at Josiah. "You close up now. Maybe next year, maybe two or three years, you'll see better times here. Back you'll come. You'll have all your work to do over again, all your money to spend again, getting started. That's why these British firms outlast ours. They look ten, twenty, fifty years ahead. Eighteen thirty-six is a bad year? So was 1814, but they're still going on. Still making money. That's what Yankee firms can't get through their heads."

Josiah waved his hand. "I can't recommend to my father and the partners to put more money in here when none's coming out, can I?"

Richland wagged his head. "Money to be made here, ain't there? If you tell 'em to pull out now, and then see other fellers coining it in two-three years, the partners'll think a lot of you, won't they?"

Josiah shifted his foot, winced. "That's easy enough to say. But you're not a businessman."

"Ain't I?" said Richland. He shifted his lean haunches uneasily, reached into the seat of the chair and pulled out a small heap of loose silver, stared at it in gentle surprise and slipped it into his pocket. "Well, I'm not a note shaver and I ain't a merchant, but I *do* know that where there's folks living, there's money to be made. And there's a heap of folks living in Upper Canada. Some years you'll make a little, some years you'll make a lot. But you'll only do it by sticking right here and not going scooting off like a jack rabbit when you're scared you won't make quite as much as you thought you were going to. And a firm like yours being here's good for both countries. Or it is just as long as you keep out of fights and out of politics. And what makes you think things are so bad?"

"Head and the elections. I saw what happened at Streetsville. It happened every other place in U.C."

"That was bad," said Richland, nodding. "Compact's got a majority of twenty-five out of a house of sixty-three. You lost Bidwell, Mackenzie, and the rest. But Gibson, Morrison, Mackintosh, got back. Best of all, so'd Rolph." He jabbed a finger at Josiah. "You hold on. Write your father what I've said. If he doesn't say 'Stay,' I'll—I'll bow to Bond Head the next time I see him. That fixes *you* up." He drained his glass triumphantly, poured fresh drinks all around, spun about in his chair. "Now Gil—what's the matter with you?"

"You know," said Gil, somberly.

"No I don't," said Richland, irritably. "Politics? Well, you've seen everything you believed was right and decent chucked out like a diseased spleen, haven't you? Well, what I said to Jos goes for you. Now—about that other matter? Afraid she'll change her mind?"

Gil shook his head.

Richland threw up his hands. "It's just like I said to Jos. There're good years and bad years. If you can't stand a bad one, you don't deserve a good. Afraid of waiting? Hell, Kingscote can't hold out for*ever,* can he?"

"Seems to be making a good try," muttered Josiah.

"You set your mind on your ankle and keep out of this," said Richland. "Now—she'll be back here, you told me—when?"

Gil, chin in hand, shook his head. "Don't know. That's the worst of it. She—she was going to write from Kingston and from Quebec. Then she'd say just when she'd be back—either here or at her aunt's. But—I haven't had a word. Not one line."

Richland smacked out the ashes from his pipe, refilled a second. "What of that? The end of July was mighty rainy. Roads have been bad. Been storms, and boats have been late. What's to worry about in that?"

Gil sprang to his feet, paced nervously about. "Damn it, it's not roads and it isn't ships. I don't know what it is. But she's been gone weeks, I tell you. I haven't heard a word. I get to figuring *what* the trouble may be and—" He threw up his hands, then banged his palms together. "*She* isn't to blame. I *know* that, but—"

"Then why worry? If she's all right, you're all right. Pretty soon you'll get a letter and then you'll be laughing at yourself for being a damn fool. And let me tell you that you don't help yourself and you don't help her one bit by trying to kill yourself with work. The rate you've been going, a man could worry himself to death over a spot on his waistcoat. You worry because you're tired and you're tired because you're worried. It goes on just like one of my cats chasing its tail. It's—" A sharp rapping on the dispensary door smothered his words. He got up, stumped out of the room. " 'Nother patient. I'll get rid of 'em quick. I ain't through with you yet."

Gil heard the door click, heard Richland's growl, then a woman's voice. The door banged. The doctor's face reappeared, smugly triumphant. "Didn't I tell you?" He waved a thick white square. "Sent to the Hospital. Lamb brought it over." He scaled it at Gil, picked up his glass with a wink at Josiah.

Gil ripped open the cover with feverish haste. Then his eyes narrowed, his hands shook. He steadied them on his knees, read on while his face grew paler. At last he passed one of the sheets over to Richland with a hopeless gesture, buried his head in his hands.

Surprised, the doctor took the paper, pushed his spectacles up on the bridge of his nose, pursed his lips. He started, motioned to Josiah to look over his shoulder.

Josiah leaned far from his chair, read the clear script with growing incredulity—"and of course I went on board at Quebec to say good-bye. The ship was out in the stream. They told me that I'd go back with the pilot boat, but suddenly I knew that we were moving. Gil, dear, it was *all* arranged. Things of mine from Trafalgar in the cabin and—but this is as much as I can write. We're stopping at a place called Tadoussac and I've bribed a sailor with my gold brooch to take it ashore for me. I can't write any more. I can't think. England's so far. *When* shall I see you and—"

Richland creased the sheet carefully, laid it on the table and folded his arms, puffing hard at his pipe. His face was curiously gentle as he looked at Gil over the tops of his spectacles. Josiah cleared his throat. Richland's hand fell across his knee in warning.

He coughed, stretched out his feet, pulled furiously at his pipe. "You know, I've been thinking about that Barry girl. Now—seems to me that's something that happens pretty often and you can't always count on getting eelskins." His elbow nudged Josiah, prompting.

"Pretty hard, pretty hard," Josiah agreed quickly.

"Now I was looking at the *Correspondent* the other day and I noticed that Fancost, over in Rochester, advertising shoes of this stuff they call rubber."

Josiah nodded. "They're good. Keep out water."

"And," said the doctor, "there's a lot of things you can do with rubber. You can roll it out mighty thin. It stretches." He turned to Josiah. "Could make tubes out of it, couldn't you?"

"Uh—why—sure. Don't see why not."

"Well—" Richland threw up his hands—"*there's* your eelskin." He hitched his chair forward. "Now—here's what we'll do. Jos, you can get rubber for us, can't you?"

He nodded vigorously. "Easy. Any amount."

"That's it. We'll get to work on it. We'll get that rubber just as thin as we can. See, Gil? Won't be near as slippery as that damned skin, if we can do it. Less danger of tearing and—see? If that skin had torn when you were pouring soup down Josie's throat you'd a drowned her." He rubbed his hands. "We'll do it. We'll call it the 'Stensrood Tube,' 'cause the first idea was Gil's. And we can use it for—"

Slowly Gil raised his head, eyes clearing. Richland talked on. Suddenly Gil jumped to his feet. "Let's get to work on it."

"That's it. That's it." Richland clapped the bowl of his pipe to his lips, swore, picked up his glass.

Josiah stirred in his chair. "Give me a hand up. Gil, let's go to the office and get some letters out. That rubber—"

Richland shoved a crumpled newspaper into his hand. "You'll find the address in here. Fancost—Rochester."

"Damn Fancost," said Josiah. "He's just a booter. We'll deal with New York. I know just the firm."

Gil jammed his cap over his eyes. "Come on then."

The two clumped painfully out of the cluttered room. Richland looked after them, eyes grave. Then he sighed. "Well, maybe that rubber'll cure more things than putrid throats." He reached down, picked up a convenient kitten, began stroking it.

XIV

Return — 1837

As the year 1837 dawned and started rolling darkly along its trough of months, the fruits of the Compact sweep at the previous summer elections became more and more apparent. Thousands of men who had voted for Compact candidates in the sincere belief that such a vote supported the Crown became aware that they had been trapped. The Compact, riding high, tightened its grip on the country more firmly than ever. For alleged participation in Reform societies, prominent Moderates were stripped of office, covertly accused of treason.

At Government House, Sir Francis Bond Head, dizzy with success, disregarded injunctions from London. At times he even acted independently of his Compact advisers, to their alarm and consternation. Not that the Compact disapproved of his acts; they disapproved his acting without consulting the powers back of the throne.

In his flouting of orders and advice from London, however, Head had the full support of the Compact. The Colonial Office finally directed him to reinstate several Moderates ousted on frivolous pretexts. And more, it ordered him flatly to elevate Marshall Spring Bidwell to the bench. The Compact chuckled in satisfaction as Head quite flatly refused.

Robert Baldwin, in desperation, went to England to plead personally the cause of Reform. Alarmed, the Compact, through official and unofficial channels, shouted to the Colonial Office that Baldwin was a traitor, a republican, and unworthy of any credence.

Men who had hoped for a new era saw a complaisant Assembly, their only mouthpiece, filled with Compact creatures, knew that it would never be dissolved, that Head would keep it intact during his six years of officeholding. In growing numbers, solid men began to sell out their holdings, move south across the border. Those who remained began to consider steps that might be taken.

There was a sudden cloud of smoke far across the peninsula that shut in Toronto Bay. A distant cannon thudded, a hoarse whistle blurring its last echoes. Gil sprang to one of the bollards of the Yonge Street Pier, rested a hand on Josiah's shoulder. "It's the *William IV*."

Josiah jumped to a packing case marked "Fragile." "The devil it is. It's the *Britannia*. I can see the stacks. Look—through the gap in the trees. Now—"

Far off on the outer edge of the peninsula a midget bowsprit stabbed into view, a slanting bow, then four tall stacks set in a hollow square. Gil leaped from the bollard, climbed up again. "I tell you, it's the *William IV!*"

A long deck, awning-covered, slipped by, then a blunt stern with the red ensign snapping at the slanting flagstaff. Gil swayed perilously, swung his arms to keep his balance. "Be here soon. How long'll it take to dock, now? How long d'you think?"

Josiah shaded his eyes, shrugged. "Too long for some, too soon for others. I remember once going from Oswego to Buffalo. I met a damned pretty girl. Seems as though I'd hardly said hello to her when that damned Buffalo wharf came right into my stateroom through the porthole."

Gil laughed. "What was she doing in your stateroom?"

"I didn't say she was there, did I? I was just sitting there, thinking about her." He got down from his case, lit a cigar. "She'll be hidden now until she rounds Gilbraltar." He sat on the edge of the wharf, dangling his long legs over the water. Above him, Gil strained his eyes, tracing the belt of smoke in the sunlight as the steamer worked its hidden way west. Suddenly the long, low hull, the roaring stacks, stood clear of the land, hung silhouetted against the horizon, then nosed cautiously through the narrow harbor mouth.

Gil ran to the very edge of the wharf and leaned far out, clinging to a thick pile. At first the faces that lined the long rail aft were blurs, impersonal, meaningless. The bowsprit stabbed on, and features began to appear. An old man with a black skullcap on the back of his head; two soldiers whose shakos glinted in the sun; an anxious mother who held an excited child close to the rail; a tall man in severe black, a — Then a cloud of blue began to dance up and down, a hand waved, a blur of white fluttering from it. He snatched off his cap, swept it in mad circles, shouting: "Sandra! Sandra!"

A coil of rope hissed in a graceful arc to the wharf, was snatched up in calloused hands. The stern swung slowly in and Gil swung his cap again. "Sandra! Here I am."

Josiah's hand fell on his shoulder. "Who d'you suppose she'd think it was? Look here, I'm going back. See you later."

Without looking around, Gil said, "Don't go. I — you said you didn't have anything to do." He cupped his hands, shouted. "Sandra, did you have a good trip?" Then to Josiah, "You better stay and — "

"And listen to you shout landing-inanities? I'm busy. I've just thought of a scheme for electing Ogle Ketchipaw Mayor of Toronto. Going to get it going." His feet drummed off down the wharf.

Gil's head half turned. "Eh? What? Ogle?" Then the side of the steamer thundered against the wharf, shivered, settled back again, grated slowly with the wash of the bay. Gil ran along, then stretched to his full height, caught Sandra's hands. Her fingers were tight about his. She laughed down at him, kept crying, "Oh, Gil! Oh, Gil!" over and over. He danced about, long arms stretched to the utmost. Then he was suddenly aware of Kingscote's broad figure, not much taller than Sandra, looming up to the rail. Gil set his jaw. He smiled suddenly. "Glad to see you home again, Mr. Kingscote."

Something of the older man's natural geniality flashed across his clean-shaven face. "Ah — thank you, Gil. Thank you. Good to be home."

The gangplank thudded to the hollow boards. A shadow fell across Kingscote's eyes as a liveried man shouldered his way through the crowd shouting: "The Attorney General's carriage for Mr. George Kingscote!"

He touched Sandra's elbow. "They're waiting for us, my dear."

She shook her head impatiently. "I can't get through all this crowd." She bent over the rail again. "Gil, what *has* been happening to you? You look so thin! And *no* stock?" She brushed at her eyes, then smiled down at him. "It's time I came back."

"I think so too," said Gil, unsmiling. His eyes played over the curve of her throat, her cheeks, the clear blue of her eyes and the dark slant of her eyebrows. "It's — it's been — "

She laid a finger on her lips as her father's voice boomed out, "Come along, Sandra. They're waiting." She leaned still farther over. "Go see Alice tomorrow." Her voice was low, eager. Then her fingers brushed against his and she was gone in the crowd.

He wedged and jostled his way through in time to see Hagerman, surlily courteous, hand Sandra into his carriage. His voice came thickly as he shook hands with her father. "That was well done, Kingscote. We hear no one saw Baldwin. Not even a damned clerk. The Archdeacon's pleased. Now — "

The carriage rattled off along Front Street.

Gil drew a deep breath, then ran to Barnard's where the gray waited patiently. He mounted, rode rapidly north. He thought, "What'll it be like now? He seemed almost glad to see me until that damned flunkey started howling about the Attorney General's carriage. Anyway — she'll be here. That'll be better than having her halfway around the world. God, she looked pretty. Hasn't changed. I was afraid — all that time in — No, I wasn't. Sandra is Sandra. Wonder if she saw Jos. He was right in the doorway. I'll see Alice. Of course I will. Didn't need to tell me to do that."

Wrapped in his thought, he rode on past Bloor Street and the great brewery, past more woods, then turned sharply off to the right, the gray following a narrow ribbon of path with sure-footed precision. Gil saw occasional figures making their way across fields, through woods, headlong in the same direction as the gray. He crossed a pine grove, dismounted before a low brick house where men sprawled in the grass or rested their backs against the red sides. "Mr. Mackenzie been here?"

Heads lifted, men scrambled to their feet. "Left half an hour ago, I guess," said a hatchet-faced man in mechanic's clothes.

"Any word for me?"

Heads shook. A voice not long from England said: "He just wanted to know if you'd be here. We said yes and he went away."

Gil looked about the grassy stretch, eyes narrowed. "Let's see—twenty-five—six—just thirty."

A well-dressed man with a round, boyish face laughed. "Aren't you forgetting to count yourself, Gil?"

"Guess I am, Charley," said Gil. "Now—where's Mr. Wilkins?"

"Can't come," said a heavy-faced farmer. "Told me to tell you. His wife's bad."

Gil frowned. "Can't be helped, I suppose. Come on. Let's get into the meadow east of the barn." He walked across the slippery green grasses that whipped and slashed about his ankles. The others trailed on after him.

In the east meadow, screened on three sides by pines, Gil faced about. "Jake says Wilkins can't come, so I'll have to take over. Get into line. Sergeant Cutter—call the roll."

From the long, natural esplanade that was Front Street to the thick belts of forest trees that lay north beyond Queen, the narrow grid of Toronto baked in the sun of the late July afternoon. The waters of the bay heaved and lurched about, sluggish, oily, tepid, under the slimy piles of the wharves. Through the dusty streets horses thumped mechanically along, coats streaked dark where sweat-smeared harness rubbed. Men and women, forcing themselves along through the heavy air, stared hopelessly out toward the lake which the endless sun turned to a brazen shimmer. Even the birds had crept away to the shelter of the great green tents of the elms whose leaves dangled dusty and inert, throwing off deep patches of shade, heavy and oppressive as circles of thick black cloth.

In the dim drawing room of the McDonald house waves of hot air rolled lazily through the open windows, settled along rugs and furniture, spilled cheerlessly out into the parched garden. Alice McDonald, her eyes blinking rapidly, dabbed at her forehead with a handkerchief, stared at Sandra and Gil, who sat on the long sofa by the empty hearth. "I think you're both of you perfectly crazy." Her hands worked in her lap. "That's all I can say. Just crazy."

Sandra, fresh in blue-sprigged white, nodded approvingly over her lemonade. "Of course we are."

Alice threw back her head. "I should think *you'd* have enough sense, even if Gil hasn't." She rocked slowly back and forth, face troubled.

Gil carefully smoothed a crimson dab of jelly across a tea tart. "Perhaps we are crazy, Alice. But what else can we do?"

"Do? Do? Why—uh—I don't know. It all seems so—And *what* will people say?"

Sandra smiled. "They'll say that Gil's a damned rebel—don't look shocked, Alice. I'm just quoting our dear Archdeacon Strachan."

"That's it." Gil's heavy shoulders swayed as he reached for his glass. "And they'll say that I've corrupted Sandra's feeble mind. They'll say I'm trying to bring Yankee troops into Strachan's palace." He sipped, set down his glass. "Now that I think of it, that's not such a bad idea. Don't let me forget it."

Moisture gathered under Alice's pale lashes. "Gil, please don't be funny. This is serious."

"I know it is. I'd like to see Strachan washing the Yankees' carriages. I'd like—"

"I'll never see Sandra any more."

"Yes you will. And anyway, you just said you couldn't bear to see her the way she is now. Said she was pining or wasting or something like that."

Sandra's smile faded. "If you really knew what it's been like—being carted off to England, being smuggled back, living at Trafalgar the way things are now, hardly ever seeing Gil."

"If you knew," put in Gil, "you'd call us crazy for not planning it before. Look here, Alice, you don't even know *how* we've planned. It's like this. She'll go to Niagara. I'll follow in a day or two. Then—" He threw out his hands. "We'll be married in Buffalo. I'll get a Yankee license and then we'll come back. We'll practise up north where the people don't care so much what kind of a license you have. All they want's a doctor." He got up, began to pace up and down before the cold hearth. "See how easy it is? Slip across, get married, get my license. The Compact can't touch—"

Alice, alarm on her face, held up her hand. "Not so loud, Gil. They can hear you out in the street. They can—"

A slow, heavy step creaked on the stairs, across the hall. A wheezy voice announced, "Gil, I don't like that Mackenzie, but I'm going to tell him what a clumsy plotter you are." Immense in billowy black, gray hair gathered in a tight knot on the top of her head, Mrs. McDonald waddled into the room, hands clasped across her ample girth. A fat white dog, snuffling and mumbling, lurched resignedly after her.

Gil, red-faced, stammered: "I'm—I'm sorry, Mrs. McDonald. I didn't know I was disturbing—"

"You weren't." She sank by degrees to the sofa that creaked to her bulk. "When you get excited about anything, your voice climbs right up to your eyebrows. I was trying to creep downstairs when I heard you booming. Couldn't help hearing and thought it was about time to come in." The dog sprawled at her feet, tongue lolling and eyes rolling toward the tea table.

Alice nervously crumpled her handkerchief. "Gil didn't mean what he was saying, Mother. We were just—you know—just talking along."

Gil's jaw snapped. "I meant just what I was saying."

"So did I," said Sandra firmly, smoothing her wide skirts.

Mrs. McDonald carefully removed her small foot from under the dog's chin. "Well, *I* never heard of such a thing in my life." She sighed deeply. "I never did. When *I* was a girl, I'm sure no one would ever have thought of it." Her eyes darted from Gil to Sandra. She wheezed slightly. At her feet, the dog snuffled in bewildered sympathy. "Do you know what you're doing?" she asked suddenly.

Sandra patted her hair. "If Gil's voice carried all the way to the stairs you must know we do."

There was a snort. "You ought to be ashamed of yourselves, both of you. Someone ought to tell George Kingscote."

Sandra's eyes flicked in anger and alarm. Alice gasped, "Mother!"

The thick voice went on. "Yes, someone ought to. Somebody probably will." She drew in her circle of chins. "Gil Stensrood, you've just lost your head. For one thing—the idea of even thinking of letting a girl who's been brought up like Sandra go all the way to Niagara—*alone!*"

"Alone!" Gil sat forward. "Of course I wouldn't think of that."

"I wouldn't mind," said Sandra quickly. "But Gil's cousin, Josiah, is going to find someone to go with me."

Mrs. McDonald's small mouth puckered. "His cousin? I know whom you mean. The last time I saw him he was throwing someone off Feehan's Wharf into the bay. Gil! You'd let a man like *that*—Well, the whole thing's beyond me, just beyond me." She reared up. The dog, startled, lifted himself on thick forelegs. "Do you know what I think of it? Do you *want* to know?"

Gil, his mouth set in an obstinate arc, bowed politely. "But of course, we're going ahead with it, just the same."

"You are, are you? Well, no one ever listens to advice. But I want to tell you right now—and if no one has the spunk to tell George Kingscote—I want to tell you that *I* think it's perfectly beautiful." She bobbed her head to the ripple of surprise that followed. "It's just beautiful!"

Sandra stared at her with parted lips as Gil said: "You think—I don't just see—"

"It's just what I said—except—" She paused solemnly. "Except for one thing." She rocked heavily toward Gil. "I will *not* sit by and see the daughter of one of my friends tended by some female chosen by that Josiah. I—will—not—have—it. That's final."

"But Mrs. McDonald—I'll be quite all right. He's going to get the wife of one of the partners to come over here. Then when she goes back, I'll go with her."

"I can just *see* that female. She'll brawl with the coachmen. She'll make scenes on the boat. She'll make you so conspicuous that you'll be glad to run back to Trafalgar."

"But she *can't* go alone," protested Gil. "You're in favor of what we're doing and then say that we can't do it. I'd trust anyone Jos picked. So'd Sandra."

The chins quivered with emphasis. "If that man and any female he knows have a thing to do with it, I'll go straight to George Kingscote. I'll do it this very day."

Sandra looked at her quietly. "All right. I'll go alone."

"No. You won't."

"But where *can* we find anyone else to go?"

Mrs. McDonald folded her hands firmly. "*I* shall go with you."

"You?"

"I hope, Sandra, that you're not implying that I'm too old to travel. And don't look so startled, Alice." Fat-padded fingers worried a scone from the tea tray. "I shall inform Mr. McDonald that I feel it's necessary for Alice to have a trip." She crumped away at the scone. "Alice'll have more fun if there's someone of her own age along and I shall invite Sandra. George Kingscote'll be glad to get her out from under foot for a while where he *thinks* he won't have to worry about her or the Compact." She bent over painfully, stroked the wheezing dog. "Now you two, let us know when you want to start. The three of us'll go ahead. Then Gil'll come and join us."

"You—you'd do all this for us?" stammered Gil.

"About time someone did. I'll get some earth from the garden and sprinkle it in my shoes because I swore years ago I'd never set foot on Yankee soil." She rose slowly, held out a pudgy hand. "Alice! I was on my way out to water the flowers when I heard Gil booming. You and I will water them now. And don't forget our parasols." She padded slowly out of the room, her daughter trotting obediently by her side.

Gil sprang to his feet, held out his arms. Sandra ran to him. "Gil! Everything'll be all right." She clutched his lapels. "When shall we go? When?"

He rubbed his cheek against her hair. "When do you say?"

"I'd say right now. Only—"

"Only what?"

"We don't want anything to go wrong with this, do we?"

He laughed shortly. "Not a chance. What are you thinking about?"

"Home."

He frowned. "What about it?"

"Father and Staff are so suspicious. I think I'd better pretend to knuckle under—just a little—for a while." Her chin set. "It won't be easy, because I can't do it all at once. You see, I've been fighting them every way I could think of. And I've developed an agile mind. I'll have to taper off."

He sat down slowly, eyes troubled. "That means you'll just have to stay locked up there."

She knelt beside him, smoothed his low stock. "I'll be very nice to them—in public. I'm going to turn gradually into a model daughter."

"You're letting yourself in for a bad summer." He looked gravely into her eyes, gently stroked her brows with his finger. "I can guess what it'll be like. How long do you think it'll take?"

She smiled wryly. "I'd say it'd take the rest of the summer. Perhaps a bit on into the fall." She rested her forehead against his shoulder. "At least, it won't be as bad as when I was in England."

"Won't it? At least, you were seeing new things then. You even saw the Queen."

She puckered up her mouth. "All I could think of was—well, I wanted to shout at her: 'Why don't you *do* something about *us?* We're British too!'" She closed her eyes. "No—England was dreadful. This is better."

"Better? Yes, we're waiting for something now, aren't we? But I'll have things to *do*. There's the Hospital and—but you, what *can* you do?"

"I can be very busy being an actress. I'll have to be one all the time—except when I can manage to get in here. Then when we get to the States, you'll take me to New York and I'll go on the stage and be very famous and you can wait for me outside the theater and hold my cloak. What are you going to be doing while I'm acting?"

He laughed. "If you mean New York, I'll be setting fire to the theater. If you mean Trafalgar, there's the Hospital, as I said. And then Mac wants me to take some trips for him."

"Mr. Mackenzie? Trips for *him?*"

"Up north. Then perhaps out into the Huron Tract."

She stroked his sleeve. "He's come to count on you a lot, hasn't he? I'm awfully proud. What's it about? The Declaration?"

Gil nodded. "There's really more to it than I told you. It's—it's rather like the Declaration the Yankees had in the Revolution. I told you about it's saying that—what was it?—oh yes—'after fifty years of misrule,' you remember—and things getting worse all the time."

"I remember." Her head went back. "And the Declaration said it was time to do something. Why didn't the Reformers say it before?"

"Well, they've said it now. And what I didn't tell you was that we're going to throw in our lot with the people in Lower Canada. And we're forming committees all over U.C. There's going to be a big convention here later on—a sort of Congress with delegates from all over—they'll have full power to *act*."

She clutched his sleeve. "Gil! Has this got anything to do with your drilling? With the companies you raised?"

He started. "Don't even *think* about it!" He dropped his voice

"Yes—it has. And they're starting more companies up north and in Gore—all over. Graves has a company around Holland Landing. And there's a man in the Huron Tract—a soldier, one of Napoleon's colonels. He's going to be Commander in Chief."

"A French soldier! Commanding Canadians? Has he agreed?"

Gil laughed shortly. "No. But he will. Mac wants him. That's all there is to it. And he isn't French. He's Dutch."

Her eyes were wide. "Gil—there's going to be fighting!"

"H'm—I don't think so. It—it'll just be a sort of demonstration. That's all. It'll frighten the Compact."

She shook her head, mouth tight. "There *will* be fighting."

He struck his clenched fist on his knee. "What if there is? It'll be bad business. But if it comes to that, we'll have to go through with it. Canada's worth it. If Canada isn't worth fighting for, it isn't worth living in." He drew a long breath. "But it won't come to that. We'll keep in the Empire, get the same rights the Yankees did without fighting and without separating."

She leaned her chin in her hand. "You're fooling yourself, Gil. They'll fight." She stared gravely into the empty fireplace, at the great tufts of dried grasses that flanked it. "It makes me feel—feel perfectly sick."

His arm slipped about her. "You're wrong. But anyway, nothing'd happen to *me!*"

She turned almost fiercely. "That's not it. It's—it's that I can't *do* anything." She shook her small fists. "If I were a man! I'd—I'd fight and fight and fight. They'd have to kill me to make me stop. I'd set fire to Government House. I'd shock all these field mice who are afraid of Reform until they marched down Front Street and ripped down Strachan's palace. I'd shame every farmer in Upper Canada until they all came down and pulled the Fort to pieces." She seized his lapel, shook it. "There's no fire in any of you except Mackenzie. Gil—you just sit there and say perhaps there'll be fighting and perhaps there won't. Perhaps it'll rain tonight and perhaps it won't. If you ever marched your company down Yonge Street, a constable'd tell you to go away and you would! All of you!"

He laughed. "Don't go hopping about like that! You'll have Strachan and Hagerman climbing in the windows." He grew serious. "I feel like that—all the time. But it never gets above here."

He touched his muscular throat. "I had all my excitement in the days when I was learning what was happening to Canada. When I'd learned, it was only a question of what to do and when to do it. We're on the right track now. And whatever's to be done — I'm ready for it."

She leaned against him, suddenly quiet. "There's something nice and solid about you, Gil. I know you're ready. I guess I can be, too. There's us and there's Canada. We can be ready both ways." She lifted her face. "August's nearly here. Then just September, October. Then what?"

"Then?" He settled his shoulder under her head. "Why, then I guess a couple of wanderers'll stop wandering. Then — " He looked up quickly. "Oh Lord, here come Mrs. McDonald and Alice up the garden path."

Sandra sighed. "They're our guardian angels — but I wish they'd stayed a little longer. Still — how they dared roam about in this heat — just to leave us alone for a bit. Where are you going now, Gil?"

"To the Hospital to see Doc. Then I'm riding out to Nipigon." He turned, smiled at Mrs. McDonald and Alice. "We'd never lose a patient at the Hospital if we tended them the way you tend your garden."

Red-faced and puffing, Mrs. McDonald thudded across the room, the white dog staggering in her wake. "I didn't do much tending. Alice and I sat in the summerhouse until I thought you two had been alone about long enough." She sank to a high-backed chair, fanning herself. "Alice is telling Linda to bring up more lemonade. We'll all have some. Gil, sit down and stop fidgeting."

"He's fidgeting to get back to his spleens and livers," said Sandra. Then she caught sight of her profile in a mirror, furtively arranged her long curls.

Mrs. McDonald ignored the gesture. "He won't have any of his own if he races about in the sun."

"Much rather stay here," said Gil. "But I promised Doc." He looked at his watch. "I'll be a little late as it is."

Mrs. McDonald raised a fat arm. "Go to the door with him, Sandra. It's a good habit to form. I see Mr. McDonald off every morning of the year and if he forgets to kiss me good-bye, he hears about it. Get along with you now."

XV

William Lyon Mackenzie — 1837

GIL clattered down the broad staircase of Nipigon Lodge, slung his bulging saddlebags over the sleek banister, and burst into the living room where his mother and grandfather sat in the flood of morning sunshine. Janet, her usually serene face worn and troubled, forced a smile. "Ready at last, Gil?"

Barnabas snorted. "Ready? He ought to be. Gil, you were thumping and bumping over my head before sunrise. Made more noise than if a wendigo were after you." He shook his white mane. "Did I tell you that I wrote Kingscote?"

Gil started. "You—you *wrote* him? What about?"

"What do you think? And he's not had the courtesy even to acknowledge it. Yes, I wrote him a perfectly friendly letter. I just said, 'Dear Kingscote: Don't be a fool. I have the honor to be, sir, your obedient servant, Barnabas Stensrood.' Not a line have I had in reply."

Gil shrugged. "I didn't know you'd written. I could have told you what the answer'd be. My horse here yet?" He leaned out of the open window, stared through a vivid screen of hollyhocks that tossed and nodded in the summer breeze. Out on the drive a small Negro was leading the gray about in slow circles, talking to it in a crooning monotone. "There she is. Well— " He hesitated.

Janet laid her hand on his arm. "Gil—you're really going?"

He laughed. "Don't worry. It won't be for long."

Her face clouded. "Of course you'll be all right, but—So many things could happen. Otherwise, why does Mr. Mackenzie want you?"

Gil waved airily. "Oh—just to make a show. We'll ride into these towns and people'll come flocking and then Mac'll talk to 'em. Then we go on to the next town."

"Your father doesn't think it'll be as easy as that, Gil. *Must* you go?"

Gil frowned. "I talked to Father until midnight. He — he just doesn't seem to get the idea. And he shouldn't have said anything to scare you."

The gray head shook. "He didn't. He didn't have to say anything. I could tell from the way he acted. And *I* know that the Compact and the Orangemen are working together against Mackenzie. Mary told me. Gil, you know *how* the Compact works."

Gil laughed shortly. "Hope they'll have a go at *me*. I'd enjoy it. But they won't."

She sighed. "I'd been looking forward to this month and having you here. Since you've moved in with Dr. Richland, it seems that we hardly ever see you." Her eyes sought his. "Do stay here with us. One man more or less won't make any difference to Mr. Mackenzie. Stay with us. Can't you?"

From the great chair Barnabas spoke gently. "Janet, my dear, he'd better go."

She turned on him, eyes wide. "Father! Can't you see that this may turn into — well, almost *anything?* So much could happen."

Barnabas nodded slowly. "Almost anything probably will happen. But Gil's long past twenty-one. He's doing what *he* thinks he ought to. It'd be a lot easier for him to lie up here with us. No, he's got his mind made up. Gil, I don't know about Mackenzie. But *you're* doing right. Janet, I'd hate to see Gil twiddling his thumbs around here when he felt that he ought to be with that little Scotch madman. Give him a particularly fine blessing and let him go."

She smiled up at her tall son. "I know he'll go, if he thinks he ought to, whatever happens. And he'll have my blessing whatever he does. Gil, you really feel that you ought?"

He slipped an arm about her. "Think I'd leave you and Grandfather and Nipigon in a perfect August if I didn't think so? And I tell you, it'll be quite safe."

"Quite safe," echoed Barnabas, his eyes on an odd bulge in the tails of Gil's green coat. "Quite."

Gil patted his mother's shoulder. "See? Grandfather knows it'll be all right."

She laughed suddenly. "Of course it will. And I wouldn't keep you back for anything. But mothers just have to do a certain amount of fretting, I suppose. You're going to see Graves and Flora tonight?"

Gil nodded. "I'll have supper with them."

Barnabas got up slowly from the chair, held out his hand. "Be sure and remember everything Flora says so you can tell me when you get back. And ask her why she and John and Graves haven't ridden down to see me. Good-bye, Gil. You'll be all right. Just remember that a lot of people under this roof'll be thinking about you." He jerked his thumb toward the portrait of old Gilbert. "He will, too. There'll be no trouble, but if there is and I hear that you let some Compact pup get in the first blow—" he shook his stick—"you'll have *me* to deal with. Now get along with you. Janet, you'll see him to the door."

It was hot on the gravel of the drive and the myriad small stones threw back a radiation that made Janet shield her eyes as she watched Gil swing into the saddle. She stood with one hand resting on the thick roll strapped to the cantle and chatted gaily, repeating messages to John and his family, asking about the clothes in the roll, about the food in the saddlebags. And after Gil had bent to her, she still shaded her eyes, watching him as he cantered down the great curve. Then she turned suddenly, ran through the door. Barnabas, musing gravely by the cold fireplace, heard her feet on the stairs, heard a door slam.

The heavy trees beyond Nipigon threw cool black bars across Yonge Street as Gil headed north, his mind busy counting the miles that lay between him and John Stensrood's laborious acres. Then something rustled in the bushes by the side of the road. A woolly gray head bobbed over the top of a clump of sumac. A voice called cautiously, "Mist' Gilbert?"

Startled, Gil reined in. "Thomas! What in God's name are you doing out here? Grandfather was calling for you."

Thomas, rubbing his seamed hands anxiously, moved jerkily out into the road. "I'd just tooken an idea to ask you something, Mist' Gilbert. 'Tain't much—but I'd sure like to ask it."

Gil smiled down at him. "What's troubling you, Thomas?"

The woolly head shook. "'Tain't only me. It's—it's Primula. Guess it's all us colored folks."

Gil stared. "Something troubling all of you? What is it?"

Thomas edged closer. "It's this Mist' Mackenzie."

"Mr. Mackenzie." Gil's voice rose in surprise. "Good God, you ought to be praying for him."

"I heard different." The dark eyes rolled anxiously. "I heard Mist' Mackenzie's fixin' to do something bad to us. I told that fool nigger that works for Mist' Cameron that you wouldn't have nothin' to do with fixin's that'd hurt anybody. But folks keeps on talkin'."

"Talking? What do they say?"

"They say as how Mist' Mackenzie's aimin' to give the country to the Yankees." The black face was a mask of alarm. "Give it to the Yankees. Then all us colored folks'll be slaves again." He drew a long, quivering breath. "Me, I been a slave once. That's enough for me. Ain't aimin' to be one again, Mist' Gilbert. Trouble I had findin' folks to pass me along through the States till I got here—" He shook his head. "'Nough to turn a crow's feathers white, that it was."

Gil scowled. "H'm—so they're saying *that,* are they? Smells of the Compact a mile off. Look here, Thomas, I know Mr. Mackenzie. I know him well."

The thick lips protruded. "'At's what I tell Mist' Cameron's nigger. But he say—"

"Never mind what he says," broke in Gil. "Mr. Mackenzie's the greatest man in Canada. When he gets what he wants, we'll all be better off. I will. You will. Primula will."

"And Mist' Barnabas? Him too?"

"Of course. Now you forget about that damned nonsense and get back to the house or Grandfather'll be bellowing for you so loud they'll be able to hear him clear down at Montgomery's farm."

Thomas murmured, "Sure make me feel better, hearin' that. No one can't take us from Mist' Barnabas." He ducked his crown of gray wool, sidled jerkily off across the fields.

Stars hung high as Gil rode on through the forest late that night, John's hospitable roof far behind him. His eyes, accustomed to the darkness, peered at the wall of black that rose between the great boles. From time to time he dismounted, examined the mouth of some lost trail or wretched cart path that led into the great highway, climbed into the saddle again.

Suddenly he saw it close by the edge of the road, saw the great sea anchor that lay forgotten, one fluke buried in the thick dirt. How the anchor had come there no one in Upper Canada could say. But there it lay, far bigger than any lake boat could carry or would need, its free fluke high above Gil's head, its rusting shank stretching into a bed of ferns.

He tethered his horse to a strong sapling and sat down on the rough, flaking iron to wait. In the unbroken forest hush he could hear the steady ticking of his watch, the slow stir of his horse behind him in the shadows. Far away an owl hooted, was answered by another across some tree-choked valley. A faint crackling of old twigs and branches, a sharp, rank smell, told of the passage of a fox close by.

Suddenly Gil lifted his head. Somewhere in the gloom of Yonge Street, hoofs beat, leather creaked. He scrambled to his feet, stepped back of a tree as a vague shape loomed. The half-seen rider halted, slid to the ground, began feeling his way toward the high lift of the anchor arm. A low voice said, "Stensrood! You here?"

"Who's asking?" said Gil.

"Bob Heath. Holland Landing. Here's the mark." He held out the lapel of his coat.

Gil's fingers closed about it, found an extra notch in the edge that formed a crude "M." "That's all right. Got any word for me?"

Heath moved closer. "I've got twenty-five of the boys followin' me. You're to lead, but they don't know it yet. I saw Mac. He wants us to hit across country and pick him up at Lloydtown. He says—" The hoarse voice muttered on. Gil listened closely. "And that's all," concluded Heath at last.

"All?" Gil hesitated, then suddenly laughed. "That's easy. We've got a free hand."

There was a growing mutter in the night that swelled and thickened, and a steady-moving column of men flowed into sight, the riders' heads showing clear where a gap in the branches framed a star-flecked span of sky.

Heath whistled shrilly. The leading horseman threw up his

hand and the column came to a jerky halt. Heath ran among them, waving his arms. "Get into some kind of a line. Get 'em headed this way."

The horses stamped and churned, men swore and jostled, and at last the west edge of Yonge Street was fringed with a shifting line of riders who muttered and grumbled in the dark. Gil untethered the gray, rode out and faced them. He threw back his head.

"I've had word from Mac. He wants us to keep the Compacters and the Orangers in order. I'm responsible for getting it done. I'm giving the orders."

"We c'd a done it ourselves," growled a voice near the end of the line.

Another snarled, "Don't need no one from the city to show *us*."

Gil swung about in the saddle. "Then why haven't you done it? They've raised plenty of hell around here and you had your chance. Mac knows that ten men working together are worth a hundred looping around by themselves. Now—anyone that won't take orders from me'd better go home. Got that?"

There was an uneasy silence.

Gil raised himself in his stirrups. "Anyone going had better go now. Because anyone that disobeys is going to have a fight on his hands—with me." He swung his heavy shoulders forward. "Got anything to say to that?"

A voice muttered, "Guess it'll be all right."

Gil breathed a sigh of relief. "Then that's settled. We're going to start in a few minutes. Here's what we're going to do. We're going to hit west toward Lloydtown along the old Indian trail. Anyone who doesn't know it? That's good. We'll halt in the woods east of the town, where the trail curves around the big spring. Then we'll start drifting in in twos and threes. I'll give the word for each group to start. Mac'll be there about noon and we'll just be a bunch of people who've come to see what's happening."

"That all?" asked a stupid voice in the dark.

Gil laughed. "That depends on the Compact and their hired Orangers. But—" His voice hardened. "Remember this. They tried to murder Mac in '32. They may try again. They'll probably try to break up our meetings, lawful meetings. We've got to stop that, even if they've got all the magistrates and sheriffs backing 'em in breaking the law. They'll try to get spies in among us. They'll try—"

"How they get spies into *us?*" a man growled indignantly.

"We'll be doing most of our riding in the dark and it'll be hard to tell who's who. If you suspect anyone near you, grab his lapel and be sure it's notched."

"How if they be armed?" There was a nervous quaver to the question.

"Aren't you?"

A few glints of metal flicked along the line, short clubs lifted.

"Then why ask? Hit first, then ask questions." He turned to Heath. "Who are the two best mounted men here?"

Heath called, "Shepley! Parish!"

Two riders edged awkwardly out of line, reined in close to Gil. Gil pulled out his watch, slanted it to catch the faint glow of the sky. "You're Shepley? All right. I'm giving you five minutes' start. Then Parish'll take off. Five minutes more and we'll start. If either of you run into anything that looks funny, double back. Ready, Shepley?"

There was a grunt in the dark as Shepley swung his mount clear, bobbed off into the night, the hoofbeats dying and dying.

Gil dropped to the ground. "The rest of you, dismount and loosen your girths." He bent to the gray's saddle, then, bridle over his arm, paced slowly up and down the line. Later he looked at his watch again, signaled to Parish. For answer, Parish mounted in silence and the forest road took him away.

Suddenly Gil called, "All right! Tighten girths!" His voice rattled surprisingly in the silence.

Feet scuffed, leather creaked. Gil vaulted to the gray's back. "Mount!"

The line swayed and shifted to an incessant jangle of bits. Gil looked over his shoulder at a swaying sea of heads behind him, then rode off down the trail, the guard clattering along in his wake.

For hours they threaded the old trail which the feet of centuries had pounded into a deep, smooth funnel. The air was damp and rich about them, scented with the breath of fern-hung brooks, and the wind from the northwest brought a hint of the vast, empty lands far beyond Georgian Bay and the great sweep of Lake Huron. Slowly the dark tracery above the track paled, and, as Gil rode up a rocky shoulder, a sudden glow of reflected light painted the graceful hills where the village of Lloydtown nestled.

He held up his hand. Weary men slid gratefully to the ground. From nowhere, Shepley and Parish slouched up, reported uneventful rides. One by one the guard hobbled their horses, sprawled out on beds of soft leaves, and slept heavily. Alone, Gil strode to the edge of the woods, perched on a flat rock and, chin on knees, watched the awakening of the distant chimneys that, in calm succession, began to breathe soft, curling spirals into the brightening air.

The glow on the hills deepened. Shafts of sunlight began to sift through the trees. The shrill scream of an ungreased axle knifed through the wool of drowsiness that had closed about Gil's ears. Startled, he saw a single wagon trundling painfully over a corduroy road on a ridge to the north.

He sprang up, routed out Heath. "Get 'em on their feet. The town's waking up. Get after that lot around the spring. I'll take the ones in the little clearing."

Man after man grunted, protested, was dragged from his heavy sleep. Gil's voice was low, persistent. "Time to move. Time to move. Get out your rations if you want something to eat. Time to move. No. No. If you want to light a fire, go back over that rise where the smoke can't be seen from the town. On your feet. Time to move."

While spluttering fires glowed out of sight and sleep-numbed men stamped stiffly about, Gil gnawed at a slab of cold meat and bread, drank deeply from the clear spring. Then he resumed his seat at the edge of the woods, eyes on the roofs of Lloydtown. Heath, his long, bony face ghostly in the weird light, squatted by him.

"Anything stirrin' over yonder?" he asked.

Gil shook his head. "Looks quiet now. The boys about through eating?"

Heath nodded. "Done eatin' and gettin' restless."

Gil laughed shortly. "We'll cure that," he grunted. "Come on." He led the way back where the guard was idling about, looking at hoofs, refolding saddle blankets. He counted rapidly. "All here."

He whistled piercingly through his fingers. Men drifted slowly toward him and Heath, an odd mixture in the daylight. There were obvious laborers, an unmistakable shopkeeper or two, well-set farmers whose sleek horses spoke of solid lands and productive fields, a country lawyer, more farmers.

Gil rested one foot on a rock, elbow slung across his knee. "We're ready to go. We'll send four in the first lot. I want you to circle around and come into town from the north. You—you—you—you. If you can join up with another lot coming into town, so much the better. Keep quiet and try to get near any people you see with the Mackenzie lapel. And watch for the others coming in. If you've got arms, keep 'em hidden—but be sure your pistols, if you've got any, are primed. All right—off you go."

The four men mounted, rode off to the north. Gil turned to the others. "The rest of you saddle up. I'll start the next lot in a few minutes. You'll come in from the south and Bob Heath'll give you the word."

Little by little the woods spilled out broken knots of riders who hit out in wide, sweeping arcs to converge on the sleepy streets of Lloydtown.

The hands of his watch pointed to eleven when Gil, alone in the silent woods, saddled and rode down into the valley. The sun was hot between his shoulders as the mare swished steadily on through tall grass with thin-stemmed purple flowers nodding gravely in the breeze. Then the northern ridge was ahead of him and he watched the slow surge of men and horses along the ringing corduroy road that led to the town.

A final scramble, a thrust of powerful haunches, shot him out close by a broad cart on whose splintery boards five men sprawled. Gil eyed them covertly, caught a snatch or two of conversation, and began to whistle "Croppies Lie Down." Five heads lifted, took up the air, feet drumming on the hollow wood. A tall, fresh-faced man laughed up at Gil. "Where are *you* from?"

Gil frowned mysteriously, jerked his head toward the south.

There was a murmur of surprise from the cart. "Gowan send you? How'd you come?"

Gil bent from the saddle, said in a low tone: "Fewer names the better." He hitched his shoulder toward a knot of up-country men who rode stolidly along on rough farm horses.

The four others turned on the fresh-faced man, a bubble of muttered warnings and curses rising into the hot air. Gil nodded shortly. "It'll be safer. We've got work to do."

There was a grunt from the cart. "We have, that. And how'd you say you come here? We met to Holland Landing. Ain't seen you."

Gil shrugged. "I came the old way. You know."

Mystification spread over the five faces, was blotted out in awed respect. Gil waved, set the gray into a careful trot, stifling an excited chuckle as he wondered just what that "old way" might be. Then he caught sight of a heavy-faced man bobbing along on a lean blue roan, overtook him with elaborate casualness, saw a notched lapel on the faded coat.

"Morning," said Gil.

The man turned cautiously in his saddle, saw Gil's "M." "Mornin'." His suspicion melted. "Suppose Mac's here yet?"

"Don't know," said Gil. "But the Orangers are coming."

The man laughed scornfully. "They won't dare. We'll have every Reformer in the township there. We'll — "

"Won't they dare?" Gil raised his eyebrows. "Don't turn just yet, but there's a cartload of 'em about a hundred yards back."

The man stared. "How'd you know?"

"I talked to 'em," said Gil. "And listen." He held up his hand. Above the rattle and din of wheel and hoof on the wooden roadway, a ghost of melody blew toward them, quivered, smoothed out into "Protestant Boys."

The man's eyes widened. Gil smiled grimly. "That's not all. You'll have the Orangers from around here. But there'll be a lot more. They rendezvous'd at Holland Landing last night."

The man swore under his breath, cleared the end of a short club that jutted from the tails of his faded coat. Then the straggling town swallowed them up, parted them in the dense crowd that poured in over three roads. Pot hats, caps, Scotch bonnets, were sucked into the swaying mass that wavered and milled in the broad square, were swept slowly up side streets, against trim white fences, into the reeking stableyard of the little inn, only to be pressed back into the trampled earth of the square.

Gil stood in his stirrups, let his eye sweep slowly from the red brick of a solid house at the left to the stumpy spire of the Methodist

Church on the right. On the steps of the general store in the mid-distance, he saw Heath lounging. Beyond the store, men were hammering at a rude platform and close by the near corner, where the last nail had been driven, two or three of the men whom he had met by the old anchor stood idly.

Gil reined in, beckoned covertly to Heath, who slouched along through the crowd, hands in his pockets and a wavering straw dangling from his teeth. The press grew thicker, crowded more closely. Gil looked quickly about, then rocked in the saddle as the mare shied violently, danced sidewise into an empty angle between a vast elm and a picket fence. A hoarse voice snarled, "God damn you, why don't you look where you're headin' that camel?"

Gil recovered himself, saw Heath close by, hopping about clinging to one foot. He snapped back. "Keep your eyes open. This is a public street."

Heedless of the angry voices, people flowed slowly on past the pair. Gil leaned low. "Get 'em into their saddles as soon as Mac's signaled. Stay where they can see you."

Heath, still rubbing his foot, whispered, "Where'll you be?"

"Don't know yet. But it'll be where you can see me. Tell 'em to keep an eye out. And send someone to me."

There was a grunt from Heath. Then the hoarse voice raised again. "And by God, the next time you run into me, I'll haul you out of your God-damned saddle and—"

Gil sneered down. "Try it. Now get the hell out of here before I—"

Cursing, Heath scuttled away between two jolting carts. Gil looked after him, respect in his eyes. Then he saw a small house whose rough-cast walls were silvery in the summer sun, a house that set back from a side street, wide porch facing the square. He noted the steep rise that led to the front door and suddenly made up his mind.

The weathered door opened a crack to his knock and an anxious wrinkled face peered cautiously out. Gil smiled down at the old woman, neat in her rusty black. Her eyes shifted. "Nobody home but me and I don't want anything," she quavered.

Gil twirled his cap in his hands, looked embarrassed. "Oh—I don't want anything—I mean—I wondered—you see I hurt my knee and I don't dare go into that press—" He waved toward the swell and stir of the square. "I thought perhaps you'd let me stand here and watch." Absently his hand lifted to his lapel.

The old eyes blinked, uncomprehending. "If you be an Oranger, I'll thank you to march yourself right down those stairs." The wrinkled mouth shut with a snap. "And I warn you that I've a dog here." Back of her wide skirts, a small yellow head and beady eyes showed, a series of muttered "Whuffs" sounded above the nervous clicking of claws.

Gil sighed. "I came a long way to hear Mr. Mackenzie," he said. Then he looked wistfully at the broad porch.

The old woman hesitated. "Well, I guess it'll be all right," she said grudgingly. "But if you're an Oranger, off you go." The door slammed, there was a scraping inside the house, then it opened again, just wide enough for the chair that blue-veined hands pushed cautiously out. Then the latch clicked.

Gil grinned to himself as he slid the chair to a point of vantage. "I guess that includes all of us," he thought, and, swinging down from the porch, he tethered the gray to the worn post below the slope, taking care to limp with each step.

Suddenly the square erupted to a burst of cheering—frantic, spontaneous. Horses shied, wheels clacked and rattled. Gil's long strides swept him up the slope. By the steps, he recovered himself, shuffled painfully to the corner post, and faced the square where a thick spray of tossing arms beat and whipped. In the background the platform loomed, bare and desolate. Then there was a flash of blue, the faint gleam of a tall hat, and a little man, brown wig slightly askew, sprang to the boards, hands held high.

A fresh roar burst from the crowd, rattled along the house fronts. Mackenzie's hands waved and waved, imploring silence. Gradually the din subsided, then ceased with a startling suddenness. Far across the square, Gil could hear a restless horse champing at a bit, the squeak and slam of a door in some hidden house. Then Mackenzie's voice sailed out over the packed heads, thin and clear: "Fellow Reformers of Upper Canada—"

Subdued jeering rumbled off by the church, was caught up and echoed in a dozen places. The ringing voice went on. Gil tried to shut out the clear tones, set himself to locate the sources of the jeering, to identify his men in the tight-woven mass before him.

"And this Declaration is presented to you for ratification. We've

had enough of being governed from four thousand miles. We— "
The solid wall of shoulders beyond the neat paling stirred, gave, and a lean man in solid homespun wriggled clear, circled up to Gil. " 'Member me?" he panted. "The anchor. Rode with you and— "

Gil nodded. "You're the lawyer from Richmond Hill, aren't you? Eames? No—Ames. That it?"

"Right. Heath's seen you. The rest'll know where you are. What do you want me to do?"

"Sit here with me and help watch. Tell me anything you see." He craned his neck. "That some of our lot—there by the watering trough?"

Ames nodded. "And another group—ten yards beyond. See that man with the wide hat? Mercer, from Oak Ridges. He's watching you."

They settled back, eyes skimming the sunlit expanse. Mackenzie stormed on: "They send out their red-coated fools to govern us and that's the end so far as England's concerned. What was Colborne but a crueler Gage? Head than a stupider Howe?"

Suddenly Gil saw a wedge of men, arms locked, surging forward toward the mouth of an alley that led into the square. He raised his hand. Heath shaded his eyes, caught Gil's gesture. From beyond the church, five men rode out, wheeled their horses about in the throat of the alley, choking it completely. The locked wedge behind them, nervous at sight of the iron-shod hoofs thrashing in the cramped space, hesitated, then fell back sullenly. The five riders, backs to the alley, leaned on their pommels, apparently absorbed in the speech.

Gil grunted. "That did it. Watch where they go. Hi! Look there! By the yellow house."

More men edged along a wide strip of grass toward the platform. Again Gil signaled and more horsemen rode slowly down the narrow space between the yellow walls and the crowd, heads bent toward Mackenzie. The shuffling men tried to work back toward the mouth of a lane that ran behind some sheds to meander out into the square again. As they neared it, a heavy cart rolled lazily up, halted, blocking the entrance. The driver knotted the reins about the whipstock and leaned forward, eyes on Mackenzie.

Ames laughed shortly. "Bottled 'em up there. Can't get to the platform and they can't join any other gang — not until that crowd breaks up. How about my joining Mercer now?"

Gil nodded impatiently, eyes playing ceaselessly about as Ames slipped away. The Scotchman's voice cracked and rattled against his ears. "I want to tell those in power that if they follow the example of 1775, they'll live to see the day when there won't be a single British Colony in North America for them to hide in . . ."

Again Gil signaled and another press of men was neatly shepherded into a pocket.

". . . and this Declaration which I now submit to you — " Mackenzie's voice soared up. "The time has arrived, after a half century's forbearance . . ."

In the hot sun, men nodded grimly as the old landmarks of abuse floated by. Gil found himself nodding mechanically as the phrases crashed out from the platform.

Suddenly feet rang on the porch. A hard voice rasped: "Who you signaling to?"

Gil felt the blood pound in his temples, turned. "Who's asking?"

The three men who walked slowly toward him, low beavers tilted over their eyes, had short clubs jutting from their pockets. The leading man, short and barrel-chested, barked, "Who you signaling to?"

Gil set his feet apart to control his knees, jammed his hands hard into his pockets. "Will you get out of here?" His voice, to his surprise, was level, cold.

"Somebody's going to get out," snapped the short man. "Something funny's going on. If it's you — " His eyes glinted hard.

Gil swung about, waved his arm in a short arc, stared out toward the square while he counted ten to himself. Then he made a gesture of disgust and turned back to the three, who began to shift their feet uncertainly. He flung his cap down. "Mucked it," he snarled. "I'm supposed to be here *alone*. Look at that!" He pointed vaguely. "They — they were supposed to rush it. So, because you were here, they missed my signal." He thickened his voice in feigned anger. "When Mr. Gowan sent me up here, I was supposed to have a free hand. What the hell are you doing here? You ought to be out there taking orders! Get out! Get those men moving! Spill over the platform! Break a few heads! Get out!"

The leader made an odd, jerky gesture, then repeated it. He

turned to the others. "He's out of no Lodge. Don't even know the signs." He faced Gil again. "You're not Orange. I don't know you. Nobody does. Now by God — "

"You answer to Mr. Gowan for this," snapped Gil. "Do you suppose you damned Orangers are the only loyal men in U.C.? Just because Mr. Gowan heads the Lodges is no sign he won't use anyone that's sound. Of course you don't know me. But — " he paused, meaningly — "neither does that scab lot out there. That's why I was sent." His voice raced on, he began to gain confidence. "Someone'll have to explain *why* no one rushed the platform when Mackenzie first came. There were a dozen men down there that knew me, saw the signal. What happened? Nothing. God damn it, a dozen Toronto men could have broken up this meeting before it ever started."

The men shuffled uneasily. One of them growled, "We did what we were told. There's the men that ride with Mackenzie. They're blocked off. But every time the rest of us tried to move — well, uh — someone got in the way."

"Someone got in the way," mimicked Gil. "Mr. Gowan'll be glad to hear that. So'll Mr. Hagerman, so'll Archdeacon Strachan."

"Done the best we could," growled the third man.

Gil nodded wearily. "Yes, I guess you did. I'll write that to Gowan and tell him to send up some men from around Niagara. *They'll* do it, if you — er, can't."

The short man nervously rubbed his hand across his thick chest. "Not too late to do something now," he mumbled.

Gil swung on him. "Right! And I'll tell you what to do. Get as many men as you can and hit out east." He held up his hand. "Oh, I know Mackenzie *says* he's swinging west down toward Esquesing, but *we* — " He paused, staring haughtily down. "But we know he's heading back toward Holland Landing. I guess if Mr. Gowan hears that Mackenzie's carriage was wrecked — or something like that — he'd feel better about today."

The three looked anxiously at Gil. "Think it might help?"

Gil shrugged. "Only one way to find out. Get that crowd off there by the stables. Those over by the trough. Tell 'em Mr. Gowan wants it. Tell 'em — " His words were drowned in the clatter of boots pounding off the porch and away to the square.

Gil wiped his forehead. A sudden elation made him want to

shout, to whoop and stamp about as he watched the three men butt their way into the tense crowd. Danger had been turned into farce with unbelievable ease.

Out in the square, Mackenzie's voice rattled on. "And when those rights are denied him, it is the right, it is the *duty* of the free man to arm himself in their defense. It is the right—"

Distant patches of the crowd seemed to shift and waver like sheets of ice on thawing Ontario. Clumps and trickles of men began to ebb away toward the road to Holland Landing. Gil nodded to himself. The speech must be nearly over and then he would ride along back of the houses to join Heath and the rest on the road to Boltontown. He could see Jesse Lloyd and the others on the platform behind the speaker begin to shuffle their feet, reach for their hats. Across the square, he caught Heath's answering signal, raced down the slope to the gray.

The ground on the eastern slope of Lloydtown was rough and broken. Gil nursed the mare along a steep ravine, galloped over a short, level stretch and then swung up a grassy lane that led back into town. The vista was blotted out by a twist of the path. Then the square was before him and over the packed heads there fluttered a blue banner across whose dark folds the words "Liberty or Death" marched in compact lines, framed by sheaves of white pikes and muskets. The cheering boomed deeper and louder. Suddenly Gil leaned sharply from the saddle, caught an upraised arm. The man staggered, the round stone rolled from his tortured fingers as Gil slung him hard against the flaking paint of a low fence. Running feet surged toward him. There was a shout of, "Who's that? Drag him down! Drag him down!"

Gil reined the gray back on her haunches, waved his arm. "Out of my way. There's a woman hurt back there. Where's Dr. Nevers? I've got to find him! She's hurt, I tell you. Where's—"

The group fell back, uncertain. The stone thrower struggled to his feet, eyes wild. "He near broke my arm, he did! Get him—"

The gray reared to the touch of the bridle, pawed the air. Gil swung his arm. "Time for that later. Get that damned flag out of there when you get a chance. But I've got to get Nevers first. Seen him? The woman's hurt and—"

The mare shot forward, circled the edge of the crowd, cantered smoothly along behind the platform and down the Boltontown road. Steadily the hoofs drummed on, beating an accompaniment to the muttering surge of voices that still thundered from the sleepy square of Lloydtown.

The sun was low in the west when Gil, lounging in the shelter of a great sandstone parapet, heard the steady shuffle of hoofs and peered out past a clump of sumach. Then he hailed.

"Pull in, Bob. Here's headquarters. How'd it go?"

Heath's face lightened as he swung his mount off the road, slid from the saddle. "Well, it was pretty quiet. Guess you could see that for yourself."

"Pretty well, but not all. Any rows?"

Heath grinned. "Well, some of the Orangers talked pretty hard, but what could they do? They'd try to get up an alley and find four or five people who'd come to listen were there just a bit before 'em. Ought to have seen Jake Green. He's that big feller from Simcoe way. He'd damn near take off his hat to 'em, apologizing for being in the way, and all the time his horse'd be sawing and weaving and stepping on toes." His face grew serious. "Saw three men talking to you up on that porch. Who were they?"

"Orangers," said Gil.

"No! How'd you get rid of 'em?"

"Luck. Pretended I was too. Talked a lot about Gowan and chased 'em back."

Heath nodded slowly. "That was smart, damned smart."

"And dangerous," said Gil.

"Huh? Dangerous?"

"Look here, Bob. If I can do that to Orangers, they can do it to us. I've been thinking a lot, waiting for you here. We can't have a man that isn't known to his local secretary. We're going to have men dropping out and they've got to be replaced by people we know."

Heath squatted on a ragged stump, bridle loose in his hands. "Seven dropped out. Twelve came in their places. All known."

"You told 'em where to gather?"

"Just like you said. Ride till they see me."

"They won't start too soon?"

"They've scattered. They won't hit this road till after dark."

Gil nodded shortly. "Good. Now better get some sleep, Bob.

We'll be riding a long time. And I want to hit some place where we'll be out of sight and where we'll have room to drill a bit. If our group had moved together, the job'd have been much easier. Anyway, we'll go over that later. Now roll up for a while."

"Not me," said Heath. "I slept some last night. You didn't."

"Don't need to."

"The hell you don't. You're in charge. Where'll we be if you start rolling out of your saddle?"

Gil suddenly felt desperately tired. His eyelids flickered and a tight band seemed to settle about the back of his neck. There was a deep bed of dry moss at the foot of the cliff, softer than the big four-poster back in faraway Nipigon. With a saddle blanket across him—He shook himself violently. "I'm better off awake. We'll sit up together."

Silent, Gil and Heath watched night sink down over the forest ridges. Far over the treetops, stars twinkled soft and bright, seeming to flicker to the cool breeze that poured damply down over the piny ridge. The woods beyond the road stirred with invisible life.

One by one, shadowy figures drifted down the road, were halted by a low whistle from Heath, were identified and told to wait in the arching gloom behind. Little by little the rustle of fox and thud of rabbit were replaced by the slow lurch of cropping horses, the muffled voices of men.

Then off in the night wheels clanked, hoofs slapped dully, and a long, weaving column wound slowly west—ragged knots of horsemen, then three light carriages, then more horsemen.

"It's Mac," whispered Heath.

"I know," said Gil. "Where's he staying tonight?"

Heath shrugged. "Some house—Hull's, Elliot's, somewhere."

Gil yawned. "Doesn't concern us." He sat up suddenly. "Hey! How d'you know some of our lot aren't riding along there? They've got no way of telling—"

Heath edged closer toward the road, whistled twice. Two riders swung out from the closing files of the column, staring over their horses' ears. "Who's there?" snapped Gil.

The men slid to the ground. "Jake Green. And this feller's Ab Clary. He's all right." Green hooked his bridle over his arm, walked cautiously on through the dark. "What you hidin' here for?"

"No need to shout at Mac," said Gil. "We're no concern of his. Any more of our lot there?"

Green shook his head. "Just me and Ab. The rest is fellers that ride regular with Mac."

"Just you? What's Mac got such a crowd riding with him for?"

"Guess it's 'cause they heard all the Orangers and the Compacters is goin' down to Boltontown. Just had a few at the meetin' today." He tilted a wide straw hat over his forehead. "That's what they say. Most of 'em are waitin' near Boltontown for tomorrow's speechin'."

"You're sure? About Boltontown?"

"What I heard. Someone told Jesse Lloyd. Someone that used to be an Oranger."

Gil paced up and down the road, head bowed. Suddenly he said, "Bob, count 'em."

Heath rustled off and Gil could hear his hoarse voice crackling away in the night. At last he called, "Thirty-one, Gil."

"Damn it! We'll never do it with that. Needed all we had just for a few at Lloydtown." He paced on while the men lolled, half disinterested, half expectant, under the black trees. The picture formed slowly in his mind. Compact and Orangemen would have heard of the fiasco at Lloydtown. They'd be in an ugly mood. Whoever was back of this movement to smash the Mackenzie meetings would redouble, treble his efforts. Men would be armed, would be under specific orders. He stopped suddenly, raised his voice. "Anyone here who knows the Reformers in this district?"

A shape detached itself from the bank of shadows. "I do."

"Who's that? Ames? How— "

"Used to live here. I know 'em all."

"Good. Anyone else?"

Two or three voices rumbled. Gil sprang up onto a rock, where he stood silhouetted. "We'll split up into three parties. We'll start now. Ames, you stay with me. Who's that? Gordon? You go with Bob Heath. Where's that third man? Evans? You go with Jake Green. Nine men'll go with each group. My crowd'll hit west. Bob, you go north and Jake Green'll go south and west."

"What'll we do?" growled a surly voice.

"Do? You'll rout out every Reformer. Pound on the doors, get 'em, head 'em off for Boltontown. They better be armed. And tell 'em to pass the word. We'll scatter, cover the country, and let me tell you this—if we don't have close to nine hundred men at Boltontown, there's a good chance Mac'll never speak again. Now the guides'll take the groups where they ought to go, show 'em the houses, the towns. Wake up every Reformer, drag 'em out of bed if you have to, but get 'em there. We'll meet by sunrise on the bald hill back of Boltontown."

XVI

Reform — 1837

So they rode in the great sweep to the west. Men of the guard dropped out, were replaced again and again. Sometimes Gil had fifteen men pounding at his heels, sometimes fifty. Little by little the band grew into something like a legend. Along the silent reaches of the Humber, people muttered of the quiet, timely appearance of mounted men when trouble seemed about to crash forth, of sudden, deadly rushes at platform or carriage that were stopped, rolled back by a seemingly accidental wall of horseflesh.

Echoes of this drifted far across the Province. They reached a solid farmhouse near the shores of Lake Simcoe where two men nodded in grave understanding and a sunburned woman cried out in fierce joy that was blurred with the tang of the Highlands. They came to the ears of an old man who gripped his gold-headed stick and slowly shook his mane of white hair. They were even heard across the Don where a blue-eyed girl clenched her small fists, then forced a smile and suggested to her father that it was time to start for Government House and Sir Francis's reception.

Through Caledon, Chinguacousy, Scotch Block, Churchville, the cavalcade swept. Sometimes the little man with the ice-blue eyes shouted and stormed to cheering mobs. Sometimes the Compact, getting wind of the next stop, choked the town with its men, toughest hangers-on of the Orange Lodges. Twice pistols snapped, twice there was a blind rush to bear away the little Scot. And with each attempt, the tone of the speeches soared wilder and wilder. The old hesitation of the crowds began to melt away. More and more flags appeared, flags embroidered with pikes, muskets, death's-heads. And as each town was left behind, there formed in its streets, in the outlying towns, a hard core of men who had finally cast off the old fears, muttering Mackenzie's words: "This is what *must* happen when the name of Briton is so debased that no man may bear it without branding himself a slave."

As he rode, Gil lost all reckoning of time and distance. He often dozed in the saddle, Heath or Ames by his side, the guard following in close ranks. And always through the night and through the rare, sun-drenched hours when he slept in some grove or hidden valley, his ears rang to the voice of Mackenzie, the voice that snapped and cracked in his mind.

On a pine ridge, beyond the Gore of Toronto, Gil was roused from fathomless sleep by a steady tugging at his shoulder. Alarmed, he shot from his blankets, then rubbed his eyes, staring. "For God's sake, Jos, where did you come from?"

Squatting beside him, Josiah Stensrood laughed. "What kind of a nightmare were you riding, Gil? I tried to wake you and you nearly tore my head off."

Gil yawned again, then suddenly began to study his cousin with a new interest. "By God, I've got an idea. Jos, you're going to ride with us." His red-rimmed eyes began to narrow. "We'll drive the Compact crazy, looking so much alike. The people up here don't know us. They'll report my gang in a dozen different places at once. You can take — here, I'll get Heath, Ames — " He struggled up.

Josiah pushed him back. "No good. Mac wouldn't want it."

Gil stared. "Mac wouldn't — but *I'm* running this. I can — "

"No, it won't go." Josiah shook his head. "Nothing I'd like better but every time I open my mouth around here, people begin yelling 'Yankee.' It'd get 'em thinking that Mac had help from below the border. He'd lose a thousand people right away if *that* got around."

Gil looked disgruntled. "Hell, I thought you'd help."

Josiah leaned against the pitchy trunk of a pine, tossed a cone at a squirrel that started to skate down the tree, eyes bright and tail aquiver. "I am helping, Gil."

Gil stared. "What the devil are you up to now?"

Josiah dropped his voice. "Lower Canada. Montreal — Quebec."

There was a long whistle. "Down there? Doing what?"

"Picking up a little business," said Josiah, grinning. "Got some, too. Old Ketchipaw's been busy, burrowing into the warehouse, I can tell you. But mostly I've been listening."

"How did you like it — for a change?"

"Not bad at all," said Josiah solemnly. "Maybe I'll try it again, someday. But I've been talking since I got back—talking to Dr. Rolph and Dr. Baldwin. That's why I came up here. Had to see Mac."

"What's going on?"

"Well—" Josiah stretched out his long legs. "If you think things are bad here, you ought to go down into L.C. for a change. That Papineau—he's one of the greatest speakers I ever heard. He just twists those Frenchies up into clove hitches. And he's got plenty to talk about, too. For every dirty trick the Compact's ever done up here, the Château Clique's thought up a hundred. And plenty of English in with Papineau, too. Brown and Wolfred Nelson out in the parishes, yelling to the people to melt down their spoons into bullets. They've even set up Liberty Poles, just the way books say they did in Boston and New York in the old days." His eyes began to shine. "And there've been some great fights. Doric Club against the Sons of Liberty. I got thrown into the river, one night."

Gil nodded loftily. "I always said you ought not to go out without a bodyguard. Just can't take care of yourself."

Surprisingly, Josiah jerked his head in agreement. "Guess you're right. You see, I chucked an ensign of the Thirty-fourth off a dock. And the Frenchies were so pleased they tried to kiss me, and fighting 'em off I slipped and went right in with the ensign." He sighed. "It's bad, though. Gil, if things could only blow up here at the same time L.C. goes up in smoke—and I tell you it's going—you could make your own terms with the Crown."

"Trust to Mac," said Gil shortly. "Uh—did you stop off in Toronto?"

"Course I did. Had to get Master Ogle Ketchipaw stirring." He frowned. "Funny thing—hardly like to mention it—but I saw Sandra, looking pretty as the devil. I waved and she just looked right through me. I tell you, she did. No farther from me than I am from that pine." He smacked a pebble off its rough bark. "She was in a carriage with an old hatchet-face, turning up the drive of that big house off Queen Street—the Grange, I guess."

Gil's mouth tightened. "Don't mind that, Jos. She's acting Compact as hard as she can." His weary brain deadened at the thought of Sandra, toiling patiently on through the hot August days. But soon their life and work would be together.

Josiah showed his surprise. "It's that way, is it? What for?"

"Tell you later," said Gil. "Did you get out to Nipigon?"

"Oh yes," said Josiah airily. "I'd never miss a chance to pay my respects to my Great-uncle Barnabas and to Uncle Forsyth and Aunt Janet."

"Everything all right there?"

"Right as it can be with their youngest sprig racing about the country with low characters. I gather my aunt hasn't heard much about you except that you're riding sedately about and patting out polite applause when Mac speaks. But my great-uncle got me aside and told me that from what he could learn you were as much of a fool as his hotheaded brother, my grandfather. Your father — I mean my uncle — is pretty worried. You see, he gets about more. He wanted me to tell you something that I'd heard already in town. That's why I came up as soon as Mac told me where you'd be."

Gil laughed. "What is it? Has Strachan put a price on my head?"

"About that," said Josiah with unaccustomed gravity.

"Huh! He wouldn't part with sixpence to save his own mother's soul — unless it was someone else's sixpence."

"It must be someone else's then. The Compact counted on blacking Mac's eye when he first started out — riots and so on. All the magistrates are Compact of course, and they were supposed to read the riot act, break up all meetings and throw the blame on Mac. But it seems it hasn't happened that way, except in one or two places. They expected riots at Lloydtown, at Boltontown and Scotch Block. For some reason they haven't happened. I don't think they know for sure what — or rather who — the reason is. But they're doing a lot of guessing and I don't think they're wide of the mark." He shook his head, concern on his face. "I wish to God I could come with you. You're just fool enough to go sticking your neck where someone can swing a nice sharp axe on it — or bounce a pistol shot off it."

Gil reached out, rolled him in the pine needles. "So I need someone cool and cautious like you in tow, do I? They won't touch us." He spoke lightly, pushing into the back of his mind the ball that had whizzed over his head as the troop crossed into Esquesing, the trip wire across the dark lane by the forks of the Credit.

"Something might happen," said Josiah quietly, brushing pitch from his shoulders.

Gil laughed. "Don't believe all the tales you hear. All I've been doing is seeing that the right people got from here to there at the right time. When this is over, I'll give up the Hospital and work for Weller's stage lines. I've had beautiful training for that."

"Looks like it," said Josiah, watching the shady ridge where men began to stir about, dropping down to the north side to light little smokeless fires, splashing stiffly in a brook that dropped down a series of limestone steps across the narrow valley. "God, I'd like to be with you, Gil." His eyes were wistful. "But I'm going off toward London for Mac. Know Dr. Duncombe? Well, he's the leader there and I've got to tell him about Papineau and Brown and Nelson, plus a few messages from Mac."

"What then?"

"Back to Toronto. Oh—meant to tell you. Had a note signed by someone named Alice McDonald, asking me to have tea. Know anything about it?"

"So much that you're going to wait and take a letter to her for me." He bent over his saddlebags, rustled paper about. "She'll give you a lot of news." He wrote busily while Josiah squatted, patient, by a pine.

As Gil rode on through the day, alone, Josiah's warnings kept flashing through his mind. At an arm of the Credit, the bridge was down and the ferry below had its bottom stove in. Once he saw three riders on a distant ridge who halted while one of them raked the countryside with a glass. Towards sunset, he heard a sudden crackling in the bushes, snatched out his unused pistols, then slid them back as Briggs and two men from Scotch Block trotted from a side path to meet him. Little by little the party swelled as it headed for the tree-hidden cliff that was the meeting place. Twelve men rode in his wake as he swung into a grass-grown lane that wound slowly south. A roof or two showed through the trees and Gil held up his hand in warning, broke into a trot. Then he shouted as he saw a long, narrow farm cart drawn across the lane, put the gray at it. The mare gathered herself, cleared it neatly, thudded to soft ground beyond. He could hear the break in cadence as other mounts rose to the obstacle or were swerved around through crackling underbrush. There were sudden angry shouts from the half-seen houses back of the cart, a wild yell: "God damn you, Cope, you let 'em get past." A rifle cracked, another, a third, and bullets hummed and snarled, smacked into living wood.

Gil shouted, "Ride for it!" gave the mare her head, clods of soft earth spatting out into the bushes on either side. A brook spilled gently along in front of him. He swung south along its pebbly bottom, bending low to avoid overhanging branches. In the rear he could hear the others pounding and splashing as they left the road.

For a mile he followed the watercourse, then forced his way up a steep bank where bees hummed and darted among yellow blossoms. At the top, he reined in, counting his troop as they took the slope one by one, halted their blowing horses beside him.

"All sound?" he asked.

"Peatfield got hit," panted Briggs.

Peatfield, a squat, red-faced man, shook his head. "Just furrowed my shoulder. Ain't even bleedin' now."

"I'll have a look at it later," said Gil. "Did they follow?"

There was a labored laugh. "All too drunk," said one of the men.

Gil nodded somberly. "We were lucky. Anyone know where we are?"

A hand lifted. "I do. The brook swung us about two mile from where we're going."

"Know how to get there?"

There was a nod.

"All right. Take the lead. I'll bring up the rear. Peatfield, if you begin to rock in the saddle, I'll haul you down and get that bullet out if I have to probe with my teeth."

The little column wound through the woods, spilled down into a tree-choked valley where riding was a torture from the boughs that lashed at hand and face. Then there was another ridge, a rocky gully. Suddenly the guide halted, held up his hand. Steel glinted among the rocks, muffled footsteps padded across beds of dead leaves.

Gil shouted, "Wheel to the rear!" and wrenched the gray's head about.

Then a laugh rattled among the birches. "What you scared of?" Bob Heath, heavy musket trailing behind him, slipped out from a clump of trees. Farther along, other figures edged down toward him. Heath called again. "Head in this way. The cliff's off to your right."

Tension relaxed in Gil like a taut string severed. He trotted carefully up through the trees. "All right here, Bob?"

Heath nodded. "All here except a few that went back home. That always happens. We'll get more to take their places."

Gil looked at the dull sheen of the barrel that slanted out from under Heath's arm. "How long have you been carrying that in your pocket?"

"Got it off a cousin of mine up the Credit. Hate to be shot at without shooting back."

"So?" said Gil. "We got dusted a little back there ourselves. Where are the boys?"

He followed Heath's lead, the others clopping on behind, and brought up at last by the foot of a gray cliff where twenty-odd men lounged behind a screening curtain of trees. There were more muskets, an old cavalry carbine or two, and one man had lashed a broken scythe blade to the end of a long pole.

Gil quickly unsaddled the mare, gave her oats from his bulging saddlebags, then bandaged Peatfield's shoulder. Heads turned toward him as he stumped wearily to the base of the cliff. "We'll sleep tonight. We'll sleep as late tomorrow morning as we want. Mac knows where we are and he'll give us word for the next move. Guards out as usual and be sure the horses can't break loose. Nearest guard to wake me at each relief." He scuffed his foot in the heap of old leaves that had drifted in a soft mass along a fault in the rocks.

Heath strolled up. "You bedding down here, Gil? Looks good, guess I'll join you." Before Heath's knees had touched the ground, Gil was fathoms deep in sleep.

Shafts of morning light slanted down through the lancet windows of the high branches, fell across the icy pool where Gil knelt, his face screwed up to the bite of his razor. Stroke by stroke the mass of lather fled before the keen blade, revealed the grayish pallor of fatigue under the deep tan, showed the skin drawn tight across hard cheekbones and the high-bridged nose more prominent than ever. Unconscious of the reflection in the clear pool, Gil finished his shaving, tightened his jaws to the sting of the cold water that he splashed over his face.

As he rose to his feet, a rough towel rasping his cheeks, he heard a sudden stir among the trees that masked the near-by cliff, was aware of the sound of steady hoofs to the east. Cheering welled up somewhere out of sight, was abruptly choked off. Then Heath's voice, high and strident, slashed through the quiet. "Gil! Gil! Get up here — quick!"

Gil snatched up his shaving tackle, ran toward the cliff where men were staring down the slope, staring and pointing at three horses that shifted and turned in the grass-grown ruts. And up through the beeches that straggled along the slope there ran nimbly a small man, ducking under branches and twigs.

Again a murmur broke out to rustle along the stone face of the cliff. A single hushed voice muttered: "It's Mac!"

Gil hastily struggled into his worn coat with its notched lapel, heard a quick voice call, "Where's that Stensrood? I want to see him. Where is he?"

Straight through the groups of staring men Mackenzie strode. Gil saw him brush past Ames, past Heath, found a hand suddenly clutching his. The nervous lips worked. "You've done good work, Gil," said Mackenzie abruptly. Then he swung on his heel, waved his arm. "You others, form a circle. That's it." Heavy boots shuffled among leaves and dry sticks. Mackenzie faced them, hands locked behind his back. "I haven't got much to say — yet. But I want every man here to know that he's done a big job for Reform. I've been watching. I've been listening. I know what the Compact's been trying to do and I know what they haven't been able to do. If they'd succeeded, there'd have been no meetings after Lloydtown. But they didn't and now Reform — *real* Reform's rolling up strength that's going to explode in the Compact's face. Reform's in your debt and that means that all U.C.'s in your debt."

He swung about to Gil. "You've kept track of the men that have been with you? Fine! I want you, as soon as you get back to Toronto, to send me a list of every single soul who's ridden with you. Write it out. Take it to my house. Give it to Mrs. Mackenzie yourself. Don't slip. The Compact'd pay a thousand pounds for that list." He whirled toward the waiting men again. "That's all. I thank you. Now — Gil!" He slipped his arm through Gil's, walked off toward a great slab of rock that some unrecorded frost, generations ago, had split from the face of the cliff to thunder down into the timeless calm of the forest.

Mackenzie perched himself on the slab, short legs dangling clear of the ground. "How d'you think it's gone—so far?" he asked abruptly.

Gil rested his foot on a low stump, forearm over his knee. "Couldn't you tell?"

There was an impatient gesture. "I know how it looked to me. What have *you* been thinking?"

Gil's eyes narrowed. "The crowds were jumpy at first. But as you went on, the hotter you talked the better they seemed to like it. I'd say after—well, Boltontown, they'd have followed you anywhere."

Mackenzie played nervously with a twig. "They may have to." He raised his keen eyes. "You've been all over the Declaration? What do you think it means?"

"Doesn't what it means depend on the Compact?"

Mackenzie started. "Why do you say that?"

"The Declaration's fine—so far as what's printed. But I've been studying over what's between the lines." He raised his head. "Every Reform meeting so far's ratified it." He paused.

"Of course they have. It's only sense."

Gil shrugged. "I don't say it isn't. *But*—if the Compact keeps on going and we *act* on the Declaration—"

"Well—what?" snapped Mackenzie.

"It means that we've set up a Provisional Government with you as President and we're in alliance with Papineau in Quebec—right up to the hilt."

The Scotchman's hands fluttered to the brown wig, tilted it askew, fell to the wide lapels, plunged into the coat pockets, flew out again. "We're in alliance with Papineau and all French Canada anyway." His jaws worked. "But about the rest—you're right. What do you think about it? What—" His hands moved quickly as Gil started to speak. "Wait a minute. Put yourself out of it. Forget about the Compact and your license. Oh yes, I know all about that. Forget about Kingscote. I know about that too." He clawed at his wig again. "Just try to think that you're all Canadians rolled into one. I don't want people who start shouting because the Compact's done something to *them*. The people I want are those who'll go anywhere because of what the Compact's done to *all* Canada." He sprang up from the slab, took a few quick steps, scrambled back to his perch.

"So — forgetting your own case — how far do *you* think we ought to go?"

Gil's jaw set. "We've got to go as far as we're forced to, until things are settled. I told you that before. I still think so."

"What do you think about the old Colonies in '75?"

Gil slowly rubbed his palms together. "I used to think they were wrong — criminally wrong."

"And now?"

"They did the only thing they could do and keep their self-respect."

"Then — we're justified in doing what they did — *if* we have to?"

"If we have to. I only hope we don't."

Mackenzie's hands beat the air. "We all hope so. *I* think we've got every chance in the world of not having to — just so long as we show the Compact and the Crown that we're not afraid of the last step if they drive us to it. You see it. I want everyone to see it. I want you to slip around, just from day to day, and make every soul you meet feel like that. When you get back to Toronto in a couple of days — "

Gil started. "What! In a couple of days?"

The other nodded. "You're going home. So are the others. You've done your work."

Gil frowned. "You're not speaking any more?"

Mackenzie laughed. "Of course I am. But I shan't need you and your moss troopers." His face glowed. "Gil, the rest of my speaking'll be done around Streetsville." His eyes became gentle. "Streetsville. They turned me down badly in '36. But they've learned their lesson. Now they want me. As soon as I cross into that township I'll be among my own people, I'll be going home." His voice fell, softened.

There was a pause. Then Mackenzie bounded up, hand burrowing among crackling papers in his pocket. "Got to get on. Got to get on. Write Morrison. Write Bidwell. Write Rolph." Without another glance he scurried off through the trees, heedless of the staring men whose eyes followed him down to the waiting horses.

Gil walked slowly toward the base of the cliff where his men clustered, whispering. Heath came toward him, chewing a splinter. "What's up, Gil? We got to saddle right away?"

Gil looked at the long arc of faces. Some he scarcely knew by name. Others had stayed on, riding hard, from that first night by the forgotten anchor in the forest close by Holland Landing. He shook his head. "Boys, we're through — for now. Mac's going where he'll be safe. We're going home."

There was an incredulous gasp. "Home!"

Gil nodded. "Our job's over."

A hushed voice whispered: "We ain't goin' to ride no more?"

Gil shifted his feet. It had been so easy before to talk to this random group, to rasp out his orders. He cleared his throat. "Well — I guess that's about all. When Mac needs us again, we'll be ready. You — you've all done a great job. Guess I'll be kind of sorry that we won't be saddling up again and — "

A ragged cheer snapped out into the warm air. There was a sudden rush and Gil felt his hands gripped in hard palms, felt knotty fists thumping his back.

In the late afternoon of the next day, Gil rode out of a belt of dense pine. Before him was Dundas Street. A mile or two to the south spread the great blue sheet of Ontario where sailboats and schooners moved like bright, cautious moths, tacking in to the narrow mouth of Toronto Bay. On the horizon, a chunky steamer splashed a cloud of soft black against the breaking clouds.

He felt a sudden wave of emotion as the familiar scene unrolled before him. Sail and smoke beckoned a welcome. The distant roofs of Toronto seemed to peer through the screen of trees, and windows, like open mouths, called wordlessly. It was his city. It had known the blight of war and the curse of fire, but always it grew, slowly and steadily. And it came to him that in the past weeks he had been playing his own small part in its destiny. He felt humble and yet somehow exalted as he rode in by the Dundas Street tollgate and past the well-remembered houses of Queen.

There were few people about in this upper part of the city, but now and then a passer-by waved to Gil, and once he caught an awed mutter: "Been ridin' with Mac. Why, they say — "

His elation grew. He'd ride straight to the McDonald house, hoping for a word or message. Then he'd stable the gray at Barnard's and spend the night talking with Doc Richland, who'd make sardonic comments that his eyes would deny. His work was over, for the moment, and he could draw in deep gusts of unhampered leisure, recruit himself for whatever the next months might bring.

The gray clopped steadily along. Then a trim carriage, immaculate coachman on the box, swung down the drive that led to the Boulton house. Gil's eyes hardened as he saw, erect and dignified in the back seat, John Beverley Robinson, Chief Justice of Upper Canada, and, rigid beside him, the Honorable and Venerable Archdeacon of York, John Strachan.

Unexpectedly, Robinson called to the coachman, then raised his hand to Gil. Gil, mouth set, pulled over by the halted carriage.

The Chief Justice's handsome face was interested, not unkindly; his voice was almost friendly. "Saw your father the other day, Stensrood. I took the liberty of suggesting to *him* that he suggest to you that summer nights are not the most beneficial or healthy times to ride. Surely *you,* who hope to practise medicine here some day, must realize that, eh? Your training'd tell you, eh?"

Gil, hands crossed on his pommel, smiled grimly down. "My training let me recognize some very unhealthy symptoms, Mr. Robinson. In the day and in the night. But I think that they can be remedied."

Robinson nodded gravely. "That's interesting, to be sure."

"I've an idea it may be a matter of diet," went on Gil.

The Chief Justice looked mildly surprised. Beside him, the Archdeacon sat rigid as ever, jaws biting tightly and face reddening. "Diet?" repeated Robinson.

"Fruits, chiefly," said Gil. "Some can be used injudiciously. Oranges, for example."

The black shovel hat beside Robinson quivered. "You're making us late," snapped the Archdeacon of York.

Robinson turned to him. "I'm very thoughtless." Then he looked up at Gil. "Remember, Stensrood, that the cure can sometimes be worse than the disease." His hand lifted gravely to his sleek gray beaver. "I wish you a very good afternoon." Strachan barked out an impatient order to the driver.

Traffic was thicker as he rode deeper into the heart of the city. From the iron-grille gates of Osgoode Hall, well-dressed people sauntered in cool leisure to waiting carriages. Probably the Law Society had been giving a tea or a reception, Gil thought as he idly looked up at the stone walls that rose sheer from the surrounding green. Deadly dull affairs, he'd always found them, and there was usually trouble when the women, in their wide skirts, tried to get through the gates that slanted narrowly to keep roving cows off the judicial sward.

As he came closer, weaving past the carriages that one by one swung out into the street, he caught a glimpse of his cousin Ruth, laughing up from under a wide hat at a gaping ensign in scarlet; saw Edward Sperry and Kate strolling importantly down the gravel, Edward trying to keep pace with D'Arcy Boulton, to give the impression that the three were leaving together. Then he started, stared at a carriage that was just passing the gate, his heart pounding and a warm flush spreading over his drawn, tanned face.

In the back seat he saw a hint of bright hair in the shade of a wide straw hat close by the shoulder of George Kingscote.

Gil hesitated. Kingscote's short nod was lost on Gil as he tried to catch Sandra's eye. He saw her father touch her arm gently, nod toward Gil. The blue eyes looked up, calm, uninterested. The round chin sank in a ghost of a bow.

Slowly the hot stab of Sandra's bare recognition died away, faded to a dull ache. He tried to banish it altogether by forcing back into his mind the long part that she had had to play—and still must play. He swore under his breath, tried to recapture that ease of mind that had been his as he had first ridden into Dundas Street, that freedom from tension. But now there was no ease. He had been wrong. His work was not over. Day and night the fight must go on. He must do his share.

XVII

Eve of Storm — 1837

HEEDLESS of the spreading elm outside that welled up in a golden cloud against the October sky, Gil paced nervously up and down the McDonalds' long drawing room, head low and hands behind his back. From time to time he cocked his head, listening to the hushed sounds of the solid house, trying to interpret each rustle and creak. Then light heels tapped on the stairs. He turned, caught up the slim figure that whirled through the wide door into his arms.

Breathless, she laughed up at him. "Gil, Gil! Isn't this luck? Twice — and in ten days! Isn't it — "

He swept her from her feet again, perched her on the high back of the sofa. "Luck! When I got word, I just couldn't believe it! Remember when I came back last summer, we had to wait nearly two weeks before you could get in here? Remember?"

His hands held her steady on her high perch; she drew a ringlet across his nose. "Was it that long? Really, I don't remember." She raised her eyebrows languidly, then ran her fingers through his thick hair, laughing. "Don't look so sulky. *I* thought it was a month, not just two weeks. And now today and — oh, Gil!" Her arms were suddenly about him. "I've got the most wonderful news. I'd made up my mind to tease you about it a little, but I just can't. It's — "

His gray eyes glinted to her joy and excitement. "I thought there was *some*thing special, the way you came sailing down those stairs. What is it? Coming in again soon?"

She shook her head, her eyes dancing. "Better than that. Guess again?"

"Your father changing his mind?"

She was suddenly grave. "Not that, Gil. If it only were. But — it's next best to that."

"Next best!" Gil started, color flooding under his hard cheek-bones. "That means — "

"Just that." Her eyes began to sparkle again. She slipped from the back of the sofa. "Sit here beside me. That's right." She settled herself against his shoulder. "Now listen. Sometime in November Father's going to Montreal."

Gil shook his head glumly. "He did that before — and the next time I heard about you, you were in England."

She stroked his cheek. "Not this time, though. Gil — he's going alone and — " she paused — "Staff's going to meet him there. It's something about politics. I don't know just what."

Gil sat up quickly. "They're — they're going to — to leave you — at Trafalgar?"

She nodded slowly. "It's the first time I've been out of their sight since they tried to lock me up." Her voice grew sober. "Gil, it's been dreadful. I've been so close to both of them all my life. It's as though they'd been wearing masks. They look the same — but they aren't the same. Sometimes, when just the three of us have been alone, I've been almost happy. Staff's been like his old self. Father's grown years younger. Then the masks come back on again. And I know I've been wearing one too, and hate myself for wearing it."

"I've thought of that," said Gil. "Thought of it often. I said your end was the harder. You've made Strachan unbend. The Boultons say you're the cleverest girl in U.C. on account of that poem you wrote about Mac and — "

"And I've pretended to be friends with people who make fun of everything that I think's decent. And I've made fun, in public, of a young man I seem to be very much in love with." She smiled sadly up at him. "Did you know you're called the Heedless Horseman of Hogg's Hollow?"

Gil nodded, grinning. "After that story that Yankee — Erwin, Irving — wrote? One of the Compact sheets used it — the Heedless part, I mean." He grew serious again. "Now — let's get back to your father. What then?"

Her smooth forehead wrinkled. "I hate this so. But it's the only way. Now — the day after he leaves, Mrs. McDonald and Alice and I'll go on the *Transit* to Buffalo. If they're not ready — I'll go alone."

He made a protesting gesture. "You can't."

"I know it. But I will. And you've got to be in Buffalo to meet me."

He nodded. "At the pier. Jos showed me where it is on a map.

I'll have a minister all ready, licenses, papers, and everything." He drew a deep breath. "I've thought of this so often that I swear I know every step we have to take. I know just what part of the deck you'll be standing on when the *Transit* docks."

"So do I," she said softly. "You'll be leaning against a bollard and you'll start waving. And just as soon as the ship touches, you'll jump on board and I'll look at you like this — " she lifted her eyebrows haughtily — "and I'll say, 'Mr. Stensrood, isn't it?' and — "

"And I'll say, 'Why, I do believe it's Mrs. Stensrood to be!' "

She laughed happily. "It'll be soon, now, Gil." They talked on in low, broken whispers. The clock beyond the tall mirror struck four. She jumped to her feet. "Now I've got to chase you away. Yes — it's time." She rested her hand on his arm, eyes troubled. "What is the trip this time? Can't you stay in town until you go to Buffalo?"

He shook his head. "I promised."

Her frown deepened. "But what is there to *do?* It's not like last summer, with meetings and things."

He dropped his voice. "I've got to see that wagons get up-country. I'll have Heath and some of the boys from last summer with me."

Her eyes darkened. "Wagons?"

He whispered, "Powder. Muskets. Cases of bayonets, I hope. They've got to get there."

Fear set a mask over her face. Her fingers dug into his arm. "But it doesn't *have* to be you, does it? Gil, I heard so much about last summer. I knew you were riding and when I went to bed I could see people waiting in ambush for you. And there were all sorts of stories. People said that soldiers had been sent out; they said a lot of anti-Compact men had been hanged." She looked up at him, pleading. "Gil — must I go through all that again? I know it has to be done. But you've done so much already. And you see — I happen to love you."

He laughed. "The worst part of last summer was those rumors. This'll be safe as choir practice at St. James's. Who's going to worry about a few country carts going north? And besides — I promised Mac I'd see them through."

Her lips quivered a little. Then she smiled. "Of course you'll be all right. Only — remember, Gil dear, don't let the Horseman be too Heedless." She caught his lapels, stretched high on tiptoe. "Now you'd better run."

He slipped out into Queen Street. "One more trip, maybe. Then Buffalo. I'll be waiting for her. I'll—" He frowned. "Hope Bob Heath's got enough men for me. Compact's got wind of this powder somehow, I'll bet. Two men a mile ahead, two a half mile. Same order behind. Flankers out. I'll let Bob—"

October had turned unusually cold and Forsyth, chilled with his ride out from the city, came quickly into the broad living room of Nipigon, rubbing his hands briskly. By the tea table, drawn close to the fire, Janet looked up as she handed a cup to a little, gnomelike man who was huddled in a deep chair opposite Barnabas's oaken throne.

Forsyth stroked his wife's hair, shook hands with the little man, smiled acknowledgment to Barnabas's bark of greeting. Then his eyes sought Janet's in unspoken question. The glance went unanswered as she said: "Mr. Post was just hoping that you'd come before he had to leave. We were—"

Barnabas rapped his stick on the floor. "We were being accused of conspiracy, of high treason against Her Majesty, just because you've got too much sense to lock Gil up." He glared at the wizened little man. "Confound you, March, you seem to think Gil's riding about the country on broomsticks! Bah! Riding on fiddlesticks!"

March Post turned faded eyes on Forsyth. "My point was, Fors, that *some*one ought to speak to him. He'll get himself—and you—misunderstood."

Forsyth took a cup from Janet, sat comfortably on the sofa. "It seems to me, Mr. Post, that a lifetime Reformer like yourself ought to understand him very well."

"March can't understand anything," snapped Barnabas. "He retired to his chimney corner far too young and the fire's cooked his brains. Ha! Look at me. *I* didn't hear my last case until I was eighty-five. Overruled three other judges and when they objected I sent them all a challenge. Pistols. Clubs. Fists. I didn't care."

"My brains are all right, Barney. They're good Reform brains and they tell me that there are lots of kinds of reform." Post rose jerkily. "Some kinds of reform lead to revolt and revolt leads to separation from the Crown." He turned his lined face toward Forsyth. "I'd rather see a hundred Compacts and a million Strachans than even think of separation. It'd mean changing from a dirty mess to a dirtier. Mackenzie's heading straight for annexation by the Yankees. You ought to keep your son out of it. I'm taking a great liberty in talking to you like this, but I'm older than you, older by—"

"Rubbish!" Barnabas's voice rattled the windows. "You're not a day over seventy-eight. As an older man, *I* take the liberty of telling you that what Gil does meets with our full approval. And if he didn't have our approval and held back from what he thought was right because of that, I'd take a stick to him myself."

Janet spoke gently. "You'll agree, Mr. Post, that Gil must work out his own salvation in his own way. He wants the same things we do. Perhaps, if we were all younger, we'd have been right with him."

"Younger!" spluttered Barnabas. "We're young enough." He wheeled on Post. "Know what I did last night? Raided the larder after midnight and ate a whole plate of cold roast pork and downed two bottles of beer." Post shuddered slightly. "Then I went back and slept like a baby. Younger! Damned if I don't think I'll go riding with Gil."

Post shook his head. "Well, I've had my say. I still think it's outrageous." He made his adieux hastily, padded out of the room, muttering: "Cold roast pork! At midnight."

When the heavy door of Nipigon had slammed Forsyth turned to Janet. "Gone?"

She nodded. "Just the way he did on the tenth. And he packed a lot of winter things to be sent down to his room at Dr. Richland's." She sighed. "I wish I didn't worry. Do many Reformers feel the way Mr. Post does?"

"I'm afraid so. They say to be anti-Mackenzie isn't being pro-Compact. What they don't see is that that feeling strengthens Strachan and the rest."

"It's a damnable situation," growled Barnabas. "Two extremes and the Compact won't allow a middle ground." He looked up as Primula waddled gravely into the room to take away the tea tray. "Primula! My brandy."

"And for me," said Forsyth. "Janet—Gil say anything about when he'd be back?"

Primula broke household discipline to murmur reassuringly, "Mist' Gil, he all right. I done put a rabbit's foot in his saddlebag."

Tactfully ignoring the breach, Janet said, "As usual, he said nothing and I didn't ask questions. Fors, he's getting terribly bitter and sullen."

"Don't blame him," barked Barnabas. "They've kept him away from the Hospital." He threw back his white mane. "And how about the Kingscote girl?"

"Again—I don't know," said Janet. "He just says they'll be all right. Says it's their problem and they'll see to it." She rose gracefully, gray silk rustling. "I'm going to leave you now and run through the larder. Primula, just set the glasses there and come with me."

Soft gray hair and kinky black wool vanished behind the portieres.

Barnabas sipped his brandy. "Might as well face it, Fors. Things look bad."

His son nodded gravely. "I do wish I'd seen Gil before he went away. I wanted to talk to him. And I hoped *he'd* talk a little."

Barnabas stirred in his big chair. "Ever think of a reason why he doesn't? It may be because you and the rest of us'll be safer—*safer,* I say—if we don't know what he's doing."

"Hadn't thought of that. It's—well, yes. I suppose I had." Forsyth stared out the window into the dying light. Far away on the next ridge, a red sunset played about the steep roof of Montgomery's farm.

XVIII

Pikes of Rebellion — 1837

Sir Francis Bond Head, ordered again by the Colonial Office to promote Marshall Spring Bidwell to a vacant judgeship and to reinstate certain other officers removed for politics or spite, informed London that he would resign rather than obey such orders. His resignation was accepted.

In the meantime, the old cadres of the Canadian Alliance expanded, took in thousands of waverers of other days. Mackenzie, lashing himself to fever heat, kept in touch with the movement in Lower Canada, consulted with leaders in his own Province, planned a mass demonstration, talked, worked, wrote, to draw into the movement the prominent Reformers of every district.

The Compact, fully aware of Mackenzie's actions and plans, organized against him, even succeeded in bringing about the fantastic union of the Orangemen and Catholics — in the name of loyalty to the Crown. Every day Head was warned of the boiling unrest. All the Government arms in the Province were collected, stored in Toronto's City Hall. Sir Francis smiled blandly — and sent the entire Toronto garrison to reinforce Sir John Colborne, who, his orders for England canceled, had been placed in command of all troops in Lower Canada.

Then the autumn nights in the long reaches to the north were lit up by the flare of countless forges where country blacksmiths slammed and hammered iron into long, pointed blades — the Pikes of Rebellion.

THROUGH the last nights of November, Gil anu his men threaded their way through narrow tracks, roused sleeping farmhouses or innocent-looking inns at crossroad towns, unloaded sacks that clanked strangely. Sometimes he took on rattling sheaves of poles, neatly trimmed and tapered, to be cautiously dropped at some hidden smithy, lost in the bush. And as he rode on through sleep-cloaked villages, forgotten hamlets by some confluent of the Humber or the Holland, unseen forges threw out their subdued glow, spoke to him as sledge fell on hot metal. Clink-clink, clink. Clink-clink, clink. The musical sound sang in his ears as he dozed in the saddle, hummed to him as he woke in a remote farmhouse, stretched out through his memory like links in a ringing chain, vibrated the length of Gwillimbury West, Tecumseth, King, to tell of the forging of the pikes.

The first night of December found him delivering his last sack of pike heads at a small farmhouse far to the north of Lloydtown, where an anxious-faced man threw a small bundle of shafts into the cart.

"That all, Gil?" asked Heath, yawning.

Gil nodded. "Now here's what I want you to do. Take the cart back to Holland Landing and get more heads from Sam Lount's smithy. Pick up all the shafts you can on the way, because Sam needs 'em. Then get back here as quick as you can."

"You ain't coming with us?" asked Heath dubiously.

Gil shook his head. "I'll stay right here at Joe Williams's house. You've got room, haven't you, Joe?"

The anxious Williams rubbed his chin. "Guess I'll have to put you in the barn, Gil. That all right?"

"Anywhere but the pigpen," laughed Gil. "Now Bob — remember — get back here as soon as you can. I want to get back to Toronto by the fifth."

"Whyn't you come with us?" objected Heath.

"Told you last night," said Gil. "If Mac wants to get word to me, this'll be the place. We arranged that before we set out. Get the boys moving. And be sure and tell Lount he'll find me here."

The cart creaked off into the night. Williams heaved up the sack of pike heads. "I'll see the boys get these before tomorrow night, Gil."

"That's good, Joe. Mac says it's important." He caught the gray's bridle. "What's the best corner of your loft? Southeast? Well, call if anything comes in while I'm asleep." The horse clopping after him through the chill night, he led the way to the stable.

As he rolled up in his blankets in the prickly hay, he thought: "Get back by the fifth. Sandra'll leave on the seventh and I'll be waiting for her in Buffalo. Damn Kingscote. What did he change his plans for? If he'd left when he said he would, we'd be married right now. Well—it's all right this time. Her note said so. I'll pick up Jos and—" A black wave of sleep rolled over him.

Joe Williams's placid wife poured acorn coffee into a cracked cup, pushed it cautiously past Gil's elbow. "Don't do good to fret. You're worse'n Joe and that's something mighty bad."

Gil shook his head, looked about the clean, bare kitchen. "This is something to fret about." He got up, stared out the window at the ragged fields that the sudden thaw had turned into a bog, then spun about eagerly as Williams slammed into the kitchen, clods of mud flying from his boots. "What luck, Joe?"

"Ain't a sign of anything. Stopped by at Glaze's farm, but he ain't seen no one."

Gil dropped into a chair. "Damn it, I *can't* wait. Heath should have been back yesterday." He stared angrily at his fists. "How are the roads?"

"Thaw's knocked 'em all to hell."

Gil sprang to his feet. "I'm going. Joe, if anyone comes for me, tell 'em I'll leave word at Hitchens's place on the way in. I'll leave word at Montgomery's Tavern, too. Good-bye, Mrs. Williams. You've taken great care of me. Good-bye, Joe." He ran out of the house, saddled, and rode off toward the track that wound away east.

The thaw had turned the wretched road into a motionless river of mud through which the horse splashed heavily, geysers of liquid mire squirting into the undergrowth. The sodden trees hitched slowly past, and he thought of the miles of country he'd have to cover. As soon as he reached Toronto, he'd send word to the McDonalds and catch the first Buffalo boat.

It was nearly dark when he finally skirted the edge of a swamp and turned into the long reaches of Yonge Street. The mare, snuffing the air from the south, quickened her gait as Gil tried to think of the nearest farm or settlement where he could get news of Mackenzie and his doings safely. He felt that, waiting at the Williams house even for two days, he had somehow slipped out of time, that the world, spinning by, had left him far behind.

At last he saw the ragged mouth of the forest gap that straggled west to Lloydtown. The gray began to blow, then puffed gratefully as Gil dismounted a few yards beyond the entrance to the road. He let her forage at will among the dead leaves as he lolled on a fallen log, back against the thick bole of a spreading elm. Gradually his chin sank forward and he dozed fitfully.

He woke with a jerk, eyes staring. There was a strange sound in the air, a thick, soft mutter. "Storm coming," he thought, then hopelessly vizualized the distance to the nearest friendly roof. Joints aching, he got to his feet, stared at the treetops to gauge the direction of the coming blast. He blinked. The high branches against the black sky barely stirred. He held up a moistened finger, but felt no cool current about it.

The noise grew heavier. Then from the black funnel of the Lloydtown road a new sound joined in the confused murmur—the ring of metal. Eyes alert, Gil glided back into the shadows. Suddenly, out of the night-filled road, a slow straggle of men spilled, a ragged column, faces drawn and eyes sunken, lurching south toward Hogg's Hollow and Toronto. Over their heads danced and flickered a forest of long pikes, sharp points glinting dully in the vague light.

Gil stared incredulously, heart pounding and breath coming quick. Unheeding, the weary, irregular files squelched past him in the mud that gripped at aching feet, tugged back at every step, turned treacherous as glare ice under the soles that slopped and plashed in its depths. There was no talking, no singing, nothing but a blind, tortured urge to wrench one foot from its bed of slime, plant it in gluey slop just ahead.

Gil crouched low, trying to silhouette the heads against the belt of sky that hung low over the treetops. But he saw only the slant of pikes, the awkward loom of shapeless hats. From time to time, the high reach of the pikes was broken and heavy muskets, stumpy rifles, bobbed along, seemingly by themselves, as their blunt muzzles sailed into a patch of sky before being swallowed up in the relentless tangle of trunk and branch.

The mud-smeared men were unrecognizable. They were timeless. They were a Tatar horde, intent on a merciless desert raid. They were men of the *Jacquerie,* of the Peasant Uprising. They were hurrying to Edge Hill, to Culloden, to the hot roads about Lexington, to the south portals of Paris and nameless barricades.

On edge with anxiety, Gil clenched his fists, poised between concealment and a rush into the road. The pikes looked familiar, but Orangemen and Compacters could forge pikes as well as any Holland Landing Reformer.

Almost before he knew it, the muddy rope of road was under his feet. He held up a hand, shouted: "Who's there?"

As though a hidden cord had been pulled, the plodding straggle froze, and the faces that turned toward him were shapeless blurs in the night. Then, one by one, bent forms staggered to the edge of the street, sprawled on the wet litter. Pikes fell to the ground with a solid smack, muskets were leaned against trees by shaky hands, thudded unwatched to crash against rock or rattle among briars. Those who remained on their feet crowded about Gil, peering anxiously, leaning on pikestaff or barrel. Then a creaky voice croaked, "It's him. It's Gil Stensrood."

The men pressed closer, as Gil, swept with relief, asked crisply, "Who's in command here?"

There was an uncertain pause. Then a short, bowlegged man said, hesitating, "Well, guess I am. 'Member me? George Charles. Farm around Tecumseth. Railey's company is following, I guess." His voice took on more assurance. "What's happening? What are we going to do? Where's Mac? When do we eat?"

Gil felt a cold wave of fear settle over him. His eyes clouded, his forehead wrinkled. *They* were asking *him*. A head taller than the biggest pikeman or rifleman, he stood there, bewildered. He was the man from the Outside. *He* would know everything, everything that was hidden from the anxious ruck of marchers, from distracted leaders. Again Charles asked, "What are we going to do?"

It was appalling, the blindness of these men, armed and blundering on through the dark. Gil's breath hissed through his teeth in apprehension and exasperation. "I don't know anything," he said shortly. "What started you out?"

Then wild flurries of words swept past him like dead leaves stirred by a sudden blast. "Got news we was to march. Be there December seventh. I was just— " . . . "Ain't told us. So then orders came we were to turn out today instead of the seventh. Just like that. No warnin'." . . . "And they say Mac's at Government House and the Compact's all in jail waiting trial. They're going—" . . . "And down in L.C., Brown's beat the army. At St. Denis. Colborne's killed. Papineau's marching on Quebec." . . . "Ain't so. Head's caught Mac and we're goin' to break into the jail. He's hanged Rolph and Baldwin and Bidwell." . . . "Yes, and he's sending Indians against us, 'cause the Frenchies in L.C.'ve killed every British soldier in the Province." . . . "Me, I walked twenty mile afore I ever got to Lloydtown. My feet's afire. When do we eat?"

Gil held up his hands, shouting, "One at a time. Charles, you say you guess you're in command. Don't you know? Well, you must be if Kirk isn't here. Now get your breath and tell me what happened."

Still panting as he leaned on a short carbine, Charles shook his head. "Honest, Gil, I don't know. We got word to be ready to march on the seventh. That's right. So's we'd be at some inn on Yonge Street. Morrison's — Madison's — "

"At Montgomery's Tavern?" asked Gil quickly.

"That's it. Then we heard about St. Denis and Colonel Gore getting beaten. That's true, I guess. Then orders came in to march tonight, to be at Montgomery's on the third. So we — "

"Who sent the change in orders?"

Charles scratched his head. "Well, Mac sent the first, all right. Don't rightly know about the others. Some say Rolph, some say Sam Lount."

A heavy-faced man, squatting on his heels in the mud, growled, " 'T warn't that. Rolph sent word to Sam Lount. He warn't to home. Mrs. Lount tried to find him. Then she told Fletcher, I guess it was, or maybe Jesse Lloyd or maybe — "

"Were the orders in writing?" asked Gil, his bewildered brain trying to sort out the maelstrom of hearsay and fact.

"First was. Guess we just heard about the second. Crawford had an idea the date was changed on account of St. Denis. I don't know."

"Well, you'll know what it's all about when you get to Montgomery's," said Gil. "Better start 'em along, Charles." He watched the column take crude shape, slouch on through the mud. He mounted, rode on past it. Mile after slow mile the streak of slime that led to Toronto rolled past under the mare's hoofs. Then the dank, warmish air was filled again with the now familiar stir and murmur. The darkness ahead of him seemed liquid, flowing, and he rode up to the tail of another disorganized band. Heads barely lifted as he passed them, lifeless eyes turned away from his sharp question: "Where are you from?"

The gloom of the road was an opaque curtain through which faces showed shapeless, inhuman. Drooping heads were oddly disfigured by low beavers, broad-brimmed hats, round-vizored coonskins. Shoulders sagged under muskets, pikes, more pikes. Some men, lacking better weapons, had whittled clubs. Here and there weary figures straggled along, empty-handed, trusting to the thought of others, to luck, to fate.

He hailed the column again, saw muddy hands pointing toward a limping gray-haired man as the captain. Hollow-eyed and dry-mouthed, the leader had little to add to Charles's story. His men were drawn from the tract south of Holland Landing. They had had orders and counter orders, rumors as wild as those that racked the Lloydtown men. They were to attack Toronto at once. They were merely to stay drawn up close to Montgomery's farm while Mackenzie parleyed with Head. They were to march peacefully into the city, surround Government House while certain resignations were demanded. After that they were to go home. They were to embark at Toronto, sail for some New York port — Oswego, probably — march through the States and join Papineau from the south, to help in the final destruction of Colborne's army.

Gil listened wearily to a dozen voices that muttered out of the night to add to the captain's store of fact and rumor. Then the inevitable shower of questions descended on Gil, the one man who had not been caught up in the blind, deaf march, the one man who *must* know.

He shook his head violently. "I tell you, I don't know anything. No. I don't know when you'll eat. But I do know — and so do you — that Mac'd never forget."

He rode on, leaving the struggling trickle of men in his wake. He tried to remember all the things that Doc had told him about men in the field — how, in the Yankee army in '12, forty rumors would spring from nowhere, sweep through regiments, companies, platoons — how undisciplined men would grumble, snarl, melt away, unless they were fed and housed, unless they were kept busy. Then he recalled the endless energy of the little, bewigged Scot, saw how, with food and sleep, with sure knowledge of what they would be called upon to do, those same sullen muddy clusters of men might change in a few hours to steady, reliable entities. Mac'd see to it. And if he had anything really big afoot, there was Napoleon's old Colonel Van Egmond from the Huron Tract who would mold these raw masses overnight. There was Anthony Anderson, a soldier of '12 who held the rank of captain under Lount's colonelcy. There were unknown men who, with such a task ahead of them, would appear from nowhere, take their sure places as guides and leaders.

Slowly, hope began to form in his mind. They were men coming at Mackenzie's call. They were resolute, else they would have long since scattered in the face of the appalling mud roads, night marching, and no rations. Once at the rendezvous they'd be seen to, cared for. Then—all that was needed was time. His spirits rose further as he thought of the solid Reform bodies in the city itself, of the first company that he himself had raised, that had swelled to three—four. They'd be at the farm now—or if they weren't, they'd still be in Toronto, ready to join with any march on the city from the rolling ridges by Hogg's Hollow. More valuable there, perhaps, as they could keep in check any Compact move. He'd see Mackenzie, then push on to the city and the Buffalo boat.

Then he recognized a clump of trees off to the left, knew that they masked a farm where he could find shelter, where no questions would be asked, and where a few might even be answered. The mare curved gratefully off the deep, clinging mud of the road, scenting the reek of a warm barn and equine companionship.

Early in the following afternoon, Gil felt a sudden pang that was partly joy as he saw the rambling roof of Nipigon shouldering up through a cloud of bare branches, far off to the right. He whistled excitedly to the mare, started to swing up the curve of the drive. In a distant window he could see a patch of pale gray that must be his mother, bent over a book or a bit of embroidery. Faint voices drifted to him in the still air and he saw two figures, one tall and capped with a mane of white, the other, bent and woolly, attentive.

He checked the mare suddenly, stared longingly toward the graceful spread and sweep of the old house. Then he shook his head. The rendezvous was at Montgomery's and that was where he belonged. He tried to tell himself that a half hour at Nipigon was highly excusable. More—stepping through its door, hearing his mother's gentle tones, the peppery explosiveness of his grandfather, would renew him, send him on his way strengthened, keener. Under this reasoning another thought, ominous, sinister, slipped like a stealthy rattlesnake. There was no telling what might be brewing under a distant inn roof, or under a huge pot hat. Whatever there might be, he was pledged to it, and that very pledge might bring flaming disaster to the old timbers of Nipigon—if things went askew. No one must be able to say that he, Gilbert Stensrood, had talked with a single member of his family before pushing on to Montgomery's. Face grim and eyes hardened, he turned back.

The slopes of Hogg's Hollow were twisting ropes of mud that pitched headlong into the deep-scooped valley to heave painfully up the other side. Fetlocks hidden in the shaking mire, the gray picked her way to the bottom, hoofs lifting high with a catlike daintiness. Then the heartbreaking south grade was behind them and Gil, pulse beating faster, stared away at the roof of Montgomery's Tavern, at the tight huddle of the Paul Pry across the road. There was smoke from the chimneys of the Price house away to the northwest, from David Gibson's at the left. But the fields of Montgomery's farm were empty. No orderly lines of stacked arms, no smoldering cooks' fires, no stir and bustle of men moving about.

Gil turned pale. It was false, what he had heard at the little farm the night before. The mud-smeared men from Holland Landing, from Lloydtown, from a hundred scattered homes, would find no solid gathering from the lakeshore to bolster up their exhausted bodies and nerves. Perhaps—perhaps there was even no store of arms to equip weaponless men, no food for them. He cursed himself for every second he had delayed in pushing on, spurred toward Montgomery's.

A shrill voice raved and stormed as Gil vaulted from the saddle in the dooryard. "But it's *got* to be done. Food! Food! Food! They'll be coming here any minute. Food! I—I *order* you. I—" Gil darted into the common room where Mackenzie, clothes in disorder, hat on the back of his head, hands flying in the air, danced before a sullen aproned man. In a corner, David Gibson and Joseph Shepard looked on grimly.

Mackenzie screamed on. "Linfoot! I order it. I—"

Linfoot shook his head slowly, eyes on Mackenzie's. "Show me your money and I'll do what I can. But I can't feed five hundred men—not without a week's notice."

"You—you—" Mackenzie spluttered with exasperation. "You're in the pay of the Compact."

Linfoot shrugged. "I ain't in anyone's pay. Look here, mister. I ain't a politician. I'm an innkeeper. I rented this place from Montgomery to make a living. And I won't make no living giving credit to a lot of men that'll likely be dead the next day. I don't give a damn about you. I don't give a damn about the Compact. Show me your money and I'll do what I can. That's flat and—"

Mackenzie sprang at him, shook him. Linfoot looked down at him tolerantly, grinned. "I said money."

Mackenzie whirled about, then caught sight of Gil, frozen in the door. He ran to him. "Here's a man that'll *do* something! Gil, this fool won't feed our men. He won't—"

Gibson spoke quietly. "After all, Mac, we don't know if *any* men are coming, after all this change of orders."

Gil laid his hand on Mackenzie's shoulder, steadied him as he might have steadied the startled gray. "They're coming, Mac. Some of 'em are, anyway. Now will you tell me what's happened?"

"Happened? Happened? *I* sent word for all Reformers to meet here, armed, on the seventh. That idiot, John Rolph, changed the orders. He didn't tell me. He didn't tell Lount until it was too late. Nothing's ready. No food! No arms! In four more days, I could have equipped an army. No one knows anything. Someone told Lount not to come after all. Someone told him to start last night. Someone—"

"What's happening in Toronto? What does Head know?" cut in Gil.

"Nothing's happening. Nothing. I could take the city and jail Head with fifty men. They're asleep. I've just been talking with Rolph. He's gone back. I know everything that's happening there. Head's asleep most of the time. Strachan swears we won't dare try anything. There it lies and nothing's ready. Where's Lount, where's Matthews, where's Anderson? And Van Egmond? He can't get here till the sixth at the earliest! We've got to—"

Gil drew up a chair. "Take it easy, Mac. Let's see what's got to be done." He glanced at Linfoot, who shrugged again, vanished into some hidden den in the back of the inn. "Now look here. I've just come from beyond Lloydtown. I've seen at least two companies on the march. They tell me that there are more. That Lount and the rest are coming too."

"Are they armed?" asked Gibson crisply.

Gil sighed. "Some have got pikes. A few have muskets. Most of 'em have clubs or fists and that's all. They think they're going to find about a thousand men here and a thousand stand of arms extra."

Mackenzie jumped onto the short bar, slid down again. "Fools! Fools! They would have found that—almost. *Who* changed orders? Why did Rolph—" He pounded the smooth surface. "*I*'m giving orders. *I* am. No one else—"

"Give some, then," said Gil shortly, fearing another outburst. "Here's what you're going to find. About sundown they'll come straggling in. The roads have been wicked and the men'll be about beat. They've had damn little to eat. They'll—" He raised his hand. "Forget about it, Mac. Orders were changed. That's all there is to it. But—we've got to see about these men. That's our job."

"Linfoot's got enough to feed about four people," said Shepard dryly. "How are you going to see about *that?*"

Gil looked at him sarcastically. "And this is the *only* place in U.C. where there's food?" He sprang to his feet. "Get wagons! Go to every Reform house you can find. Take what they'll give you or sell you. Eggs! Bread! Doughnuts! Carrots! Meat! Doesn't matter much. And let's get started *now*."

"Huh," grunted Shepard, lolling against the bar. "How many'll you feed that way?"

"Doesn't matter!" shouted Gil. "The thing to do is to let 'em see when they get here that *some*thing's been done about 'em, someone's remembered 'em. One piece of ship's biscuit'll turn a beaten man into one that's worth something. Just the thought that *something*'s waiting for him."

Shepard stirred, slouched to the door. "You've got sense," he said unexpectedly. He turned to Gibson. "Come on, Dave."

All that afternoon Gil scoured the countryside, ranging as far west and as close to town as the Peacock Inn on Dundas Street. The results were meager. Salt beef at this house, a few loaves at another. A small cask of biscuit from a bent old man near Bloor Street, a crock of doughnuts from an anxious-eyed woman out Davenport Road.

As he rode back to Montgomery's through the gathering dusk, he shook his head at an idea that came to him. "We'll let Nipigon alone. I'm the only one of the family in this and if there's trouble, I'll keep them clear. I'll — "

He lifted his head. From the half-seen bulk of Montgomery's, an angry hum sang threateningly in the air. He cantered up to see a growling crowd swarming about the porch. He caught hoarse shouts of "Where's our rations?" . . . "Yes, and where's the others? We got to do this alone?" Then a higher, strident yell. "We been sold out! That Scotch bastard's in Head's pay. We'll — "

Under the hanging lamp on the porch, a small figure darted, arms waving. Gil, springing to the ground, could catch only tattered phrases. ". . . And I'm with you . . . plans had to be changed . . . knew *you'd* take it the right way . . . doing what we can for food . . . the city's ours for the taking . . . not a guard around Head . . . the city Reformers are just waiting for you to march in . . . arms at City Hall . . . glorious triumph for Reform . . . credit is yours . . . after a march down-country that'd put Bonaparte's infantry to shame . . . proud to be with . . ."

The shouts changed from derision to sympathy to enthusiasm as Gil elbowed his way through the press, waved to the following wagon. By the time he had gained the rear of the inn, he heard calls of "On to Toronto! March now! Lead us, Mac! Yeaaaah! We'll put little Mac in Government House by midnight. Mac! Mac! Mac!"

Rations distributed, Gil tramped inside, found Lount and Matthews muttering with Mackenzie. The Scotchman looked up. "They eating, Gil?"

"What there is. It'll help. But we'll have to have more tomorrow — either more food or more trouble."

Mackenzie jumped to his feet. "We'll march now."

Lount and Matthews stared. "March?"

Mackenzie's eyes snapped. "Right into the city. We'll — "

Gil threw open the door, jerked his head at the sprawling forms that littered the floor of the common room, filled passage and corridor. "There are more of 'em just slumped down in the fields. Mac, they've got to rest."

Lount nodded. "March in the morning. And don't forget, Mac — there are more companies on the road. If they get here and find the place empty, they'll go back. We'll have no reserves."

Mackenzie jumped to his feet, scurried up and down the room. "Got to do something. Got to *do* something." His hands flipped into his pockets, out again. Then he spun about on his toes like a top, arm pointing. "I've got it! I'll go to Toronto myself! Now!"

The shock of his words could almost be felt in the room. Gil exclaimed, "To Toronto! In God's name, what for, Mac?"

"We've—we've got to be doing something. And we can see for ourselves how the city is. That's it. We'll reconnoiter, get information!"

Gil looked at him hopelessly. "Listen, Mac. You saw Rolph this afternoon. He told you what was going on. It can't have changed. And what could we find out, riding through the streets in the dark?"

"Find out one thing," said Lount dryly. "You'll find that Head's got a warrant out for you, Mac. That's no rumor."

Mackenzie shook his head obstinately. "He can't touch me. And I'm going. If none of you gentlemen have a taste for night air—or are afraid of Head—I'll go alone. I'll—here! Gil! Where are you going?"

"For my horse," said Gil over his shoulder.

A little cavalcade assembled outside the tavern. Across the dark road, some hundred yards north, a line of armed men closed Yonge Street to all passers. The same distance to the south, a similar belt of clumsy steel had been placed. Through the southern guard rode Gil, close behind Mackenzie. In the rear, Anthony Anderson, alert and keen-faced, muttered to his companion, Shepard. Two others trailed along, not far behind. Gil tried to question Mackenzie, but the working mouth chewed silently on hidden thoughts, heedless of interruption. So Gil shrugged, pulled back beside Captain Anderson.

"Any more news from L.C.?" he asked.

Anderson shook his head. "Nothing more than the last batch."

Gil frowned. "Make things a lot easier if we knew. Do you suppose it's common knowledge in town? With the Compact?"

Anderson's firm mouth set. "Good God, I hope not."

"*Hope* not? For God's sake why?" Surprise wrenched the question from him.

Anderson turned. "Why? Why? Because they'd just heard of St. Denis and it had shaken 'em. Now with the St. Charles action—"

Gil interrupted. "St. Charles? What's that?"

"Hadn't you heard? The *patriotes* were about as thoroughly smashed as a force could be. Papineau's in flight. Brown's in flight. So's Nelson. Unless, of course, they've been taken. And Colborne's men are gutting the country. Burning all the French homes where the head of the house can't prove he wasn't in arms. Turning people out into the winter — "

Gil slumped in the saddle, eyes sober in the darkness. "That cancels St. Denis, then. Do many of our people know about St. Charles? Then we'd better keep it close."

"Can't — forever," said Anderson. "We'll have to — "

A sudden shout from Mackenzie brought the escort clattering up beside him where he had reined in on the crest of Gallow's Hill.

"Listen!" he snapped.

Somewhere off to the left a barn door creaked, a cow lowed plaintively — homely sounds that jarred against the dark tenseness of the road. Then the damp wind that crept up from the lake and the sleeping city trembled to the beat of cautious hoofs. Gil swung sharply to the side of the road, drew his pistols as Anderson unslung his short rifle.

The hoofs thudded nearer. Two dark shapes loomed, faces blurred white. Gil tried to snatch Mackenzie's bridle, but the Scot shook his horse into a jouncing trot, lurched toward the newcomers, his escort closing in behind him. Quick words whipped out from the oncoming riders. "Who's there?"

Mackenzie shook with excitement — his phrases tumbled out jerkily. "You're my prisoners. My men have got you covered. You — you — you're John Powell." He peered through the gloom. "Who's with you? I don't know him. Who is he? It doesn't matter. He's a prisoner. Put up your hands. Higher, Powell." He waved a long-barreled pistol. "My men'll take you to headquarters. Hopeless to resist. By tomorrow I'll be in Toronto. I've got a thousand men. I've — "

Powell's voice was heavy, vibrant. "Damn you," he said slowly. "Damn you for a traitor."

Gil pushed his horse up by Mackenzie's. "Shall I frisk 'em, Mac?"

Mackenzie shook his head. "Powell, you're a gentleman. Will you give me your word that you're not armed?"

Powell, ignoring the question, stared at Gil. "What the devil are *you* doing here? A Stensrood, with a Scotch mountebank!"

Gil stirred in his saddle, a sudden surge of uncertainty, of uneasiness, sweeping over him. Then slowly the man in the dark changed from the handsome alderman who held so much power in the city, who belonged to the great Powell family, who had sometimes dined at Nipigon — changed into a mere symbol of the Compact, impersonal, ominous. Gil shrugged. "There's a bulge in his pocket, Mac," he said shortly.

Mackenzie shook his head violently. "No — no — no. He's given me his word. He's not armed. He said so. He — "

Anderson's voice soared up in protest. "Mac, he never answered you."

"That's right," cried Gil. "Did you say you were unarmed, Mr. Powell?"

Powell sat his horse in grim silence. Mackenzie waved his arm. "Anderson, Shepard — you others. Take him and this man back to the tavern. You're responsible for him. Take him along."

Powell and his shivering companion set their horses grudgingly in motion as the men fell in on either side. Mackenzie clucked to his horse. "Come on, Gil. We're going to push on a little farther."

Gil started. "Just the two of us? Look here, Mac, Powell may have been sent out by the Compact to find out what was going on. They must have had *some* word about us in town. Suppose they — "

Mackenzie shoved his pistol into his pocket. "Keep closer to me. Can't have you straying off like that. No. They won't move in town. Powell was — well, I guess he was just going somewhere. He'd have been armed, otherwise. We'll push on. We'll push on. Want to see — "

"What *can* you see?" protested Gil. "The town's quiet. If they do know about us, they haven't done anything yet. You'd hear the bells ringing. So nothing big's afoot yet. But suppose they had other people out — just to see. What'd happen back at the tavern if you got picked up? What — "

"I know what I'm doing," snapped Mackenzie. "Look down Yonge Street. Hardly a light. Fifty men — twenty men could take the city. Oh God! Why the devil wouldn't they march! Why — "

His voice was choked off as he and Gil swung in their saddles, staring up the long sweep of the hill. Somewhere in the belt of black to the north the shot still echoed, the flat smack of a pistol. Then a rifle cracked, another, and the distant beat of hoofs rustled like leaves racing before a gale.

Mackenzie clutched at Gil's wrist. "What was that?"

Gil strained his eyes through the dark. "It was right up the road. Not more than a mile. I'd— Look! Another shot. See the flash? Along the slope?" He cocked his pistols. "Get ready, Mac! It's coming this way."

The hoofs drummed on, now sharp and clear, now blurred as the rider apparently swung off into a field. Gil stood in his stirrups. "Here he comes. Mac! Mac! Watch out!"

Mackenzie's horse backed awkwardly to the side of the road as, pistol raised, he swayed to the crescendo of the oncoming rider. A swift shape flickered past a tumble-down shed and Gil caught a glint of steel, a twinkle of white pasterns. He shouted: "Stay where you are, Mac!" and spurred to meet the bulk that flew over the fields. The pasterns were sharper now. Gil tried to swing his horse between the rider and the dark city, tried to head him off from the road that led back to Front Street and Government House. He knew the white pasterns now, knew the rider hunched low in the saddle. "Pull up! Pull up, Mr. Powell!"

Powell's mount swerved sharply, broke from the road where Mackenzie waited. Gil's horse jumped a low fence, thudded to the road. Then yards ahead of him there was a sudden crash, a stab of red, and Gil, whirling past, saw Mackenzie slumped over the neck of his horse.

Again Gil shouted. "Pull up!" But the racing hoofs rushed away to the south. Gil's hand and arm stunned to the kick of his pistol. He fired again, but the distance between the two horses widened and widened, Powell's stocky figure untouched by either ball.

"Missed him, God damn it!" fumed Gil. Reluctantly he reined in as he saw the shed of the Bloor Street tollgate, saw the dull loom of the roof of Dr. Horne's house and the showier bulk of the Jarvis Mansion beyond. Then he remembered the slumped figure by the side of the road and hurried the laboring gray back north, a cold fear clutching at his heart. Relief flooded warmly through him as he saw Mackenzie, dismounted, fussing with girth and stirrup leather. Gil swung to the ground beside him. "All right, Mac?" he panted.

Mackenzie grunted. "No thanks to him, the murdering devil. The ball went right through my hat. Damn it, I'd have had him only my pistol flashed in the pan. Where'd you leave him?"

Gil stared. "Leave him?"

"I heard you fire. Where's his body?"

Gil laughed shortly. "Getting close to Government House by this time, I guess."

Mackenzie whirled. "You let him get away? You let him get away?" He seized Gil by the lapels, shook him.

Gently Gil freed himself. "Take it easy, Mac. What can he tell 'em that they don't know already? Just that he was held up on Yonge Street by a half-dozen men."

Mackenzie rubbed his chin. "And he gave me his word he wasn't armed. He— "

"No he didn't, Mac. He kept his mouth shut and wouldn't answer."

"I thought he did. I thought he did." Mackenzie looked vaguely about. Suddenly he drew himself up, a trace of his old animation flaring out. "We'll have to see how he got away. We'll have to go back to the tavern. Come on."

The two rode steadily through the dark, the ancient trees slipping jerkily past. Gil, frowning, tried to piece together Powell's escape from four armed men, wondered where those same four had vanished to, why— The gray shied, throwing Gil forward in the saddle. He recovered himself, saw Mackenzie staring down at a huddled heap by the side of the road, heard choked tones: "Look— Gil! Look!"

Horror-struck, Gil dismounted, bent over the hunched shoulders and drawn-up legs among the dead leaves. Waves of nausea swept over him as he saw a dark clot oozing in a slow trickle over the collar. He steadied himself, tried to see the motionless figure as though the white walls of the Hospital were about him instead of the timeless lift of the dark trunks. He struggled to change this man who had ridden down from Montgomery's Tavern with him into some nameless shape brought into the wards on a shutter. An accident from the docks—a stabbing in the Devil's Quarter-Acre. He drew a deep breath, knelt among the branches. Skill flowed back to his fingers, knowledge to his numbed brain. He struck a light that flared briefly in the tinderbox, showed him a gunshot wound in the nape of the neck. Gently he turned the man on his back.

From the dark Mackenzie's tense voice asked: "Who is it?"

"Anderson," said Gil tersely, then, almost to himself, "H'm—broke his neck in falling, too. Never knew what hit him. Can't—"

He became aware of Mackenzie's voice, high-pitched. "No. It can't be Anderson. Can't be. I tell you, he's the only man we've got that knows anything about soldiering. It's not Anderson. I tell you it isn't."

Gil rose slowly. "It is," he said.

Mackenzie's nervous hands whipped up. "Our only soldier. And he's dead. The only one the men'll follow." He broke off suddenly, wheeled about, pistol raised. "They're coming, they're coming! By God, they won't take me—"

Gil sprang behind a tree, loaded his pistols with nervous care as fresh hoofbeats sounded. Then a deep voice bellowed: "Mac! Oh, my God, Mac!"

A single rider materialized, a heavy-set man whose face glimmered pale as he clawed at Mackenzie's bridle, panting. "Oh my God, Mac!"

Mackenzie shook with impatience. "Well—what is it? What is it? Here's Anderson and—"

The man's voice quavered with alarm. "Mac! It's Colonel Moodie! I lived on his land. It's Colonel Moodie!"

"Moodie! Moodie! What about him? I don't want anything from him. He's Compact. He's—I've got to get back to the tavern. Here, Gil, see what this man wants. I'm—"

Gil, remounted, stared at the breathless man. "What about the Colonel? I know him. I—"

"He's dead!" The tones rang flat.

Gil started, echoed "Dead?" He couldn't be dead. Gil could remember him so clearly, could recall a far-off day when the jovial ex-soldier had sat before the fire at Nipigon, drinking port with old Barnabas and tapping an inexhaustible mine of stories about fighting against Napoleon in Spain and Portugal, while a very small Gil, perched on a cricket, listened with wide eyes. He jerked himself back to the present, tried to follow the broken tragedy unrolled in the night hush of the road.

"—and he'd heard about us, Mac. He was going to ride to town to tell Strachan. We had guards out above and below the tavern. The colonel, he rode right through the first line. There were a lot of us trying to sleep on the porch and the noise woke us up. He wouldn't stop and someone — I don't know who — fired. He fell off his horse and — "

Slowly the three rode back toward Montgomery's, Mackenzie alternately storming and sullenly silent. The south picket line let them through and, their horses stabled, they clumped wearily up the steps of the tavern past snoring rows of men who stirred and muttered in their sleep.

Mackenzie immediately raced upstairs to hold an interminable conference with Lount, Matthews, and Gibson. Gil, stepping high over sleeping forms, tried to find a corner where he could lie down, gave up the search as hopeless, stumbled on a group of men who, awake, were standing, simply because, barring the open field, there was no inch of space available.

By a flickering candle he saw Shepard's drawn face, seized his arm eagerly. "How did it happen?"

Shepard's shoulder sagged. "I've told it so damned often I begin to wish it'd been me that Powell shot. Hear the bastard didn't get far, though. They say Mac shot him down by the Bloor Street gate."

Gil shook him. "Powell came past us. How did he get away?"

Shepard looked at him sourly. "Just pulled in his horse in a hurry and shot Anderson in the neck. We couldn't fire for fear of hitting each other. Then Powell's horse jumped the bank and took off through the fields. We fired but I guess we didn't hit him. So we came back here for orders. Wasn't no one here to give any, so — " He shrugged expressively. "Glad Mac got him, anyway."

Gil started to speak, then snapped his jaws shut. They'd learn soon enough what had happened. In the meantime, it might tide them over a bad stretch if they thought the city was still unsuspecting. And it would restore their faith in Mackenzie to think of him as the avenger of Anderson, the one trusted soldier. Let them —

From a shadowy corner a rough voice spoke. "Mac didn't get him. Heard him tell Lount on the stairs he'd got away. Guess everyone knows about us now."

There was a startled murmur of disbelief that deepened into alarm. Voices rose and fell, discouraged, angry, hopeless, as each mind, in its own fashion, visualized Powell thundering through the sleeping streets, clacking up the drive to Government House.

Gil forced a laugh. "Why the gloom? Good Lord, what can Head do? He's got no troops. Fitzgibbon'll try to get out the militia, but he'll find that plenty of 'em are for us." He yawned elaborately, stretched. "Well, I'm going to roll up out in the fields. We'll be going into the city tomorrow. Better get some sleep, all of you."

He shuffled off down a dark corridor, fumbling for a side door that would lead into the open. His fingers bumped against a heavy latch and a door swung easily to his touch. Warm air crept about his face instead of the damp wind of the fields. Surprised, he peered into the blackness. "Anyone here?" he called.

The blackness gave back only the flat echoes of his own voice. He grinned. "First piece of luck today. I'll get a corner for myself and then call the others in. Where's a light?"

He tiptoed down the corridor, snatched a candle from a high bracket, then cautiously entered the room.

He stopped short. On a heap of blankets by an empty hearth lay Colonel Moodie, staring eyes glazed and strong features contorted. His weary brain numb, Gil found himself wondering why the old veteran had set out on a night ride in such light clothes, noted that he had shaved carefully not long before. A glint of metal caught his eye. At least there had been no plundering of the body, for the gold coin with Napoleon's head still dangled from the fob that Gil remembered from his childhood. A silver cigar case showed in the pocket of the flowered waistcoat whose pattern had never varied from year to year. The candle, in Gil's unsteady hand, threw wavering shadows over the face, seemed to bring a flickering life back to it as though the colonel were still struggling against the fate that had brought him unharmed through French sabers and bullets to fall in the dark before a Canadian rifle outside a country tavern.

Gently Gil closed the door, set the candle carefully on its bracket, and at last made his way out to the dank fields where men now slept heavily. Beyond a group of outbuildings, sentries slumped over pikes or muskets, guarding a sullen group of men—prisoners, picked up on the march or trapped on the road by the cordons of pickets.

Gil spread his horse blanket in the lee of a shed and at once plunged into sleep. The stars swung slowly across the sky, their faint radiance outlining the roof of the tavern and touching the wide fields with silver. In the second story a single light burned, throwing a golden patch down onto the trampled, muddy grass.

The breeze from the south freshened. The sore, hungry men asleep in field and shed stirred restlessly. There was a dull vibrance in the air that half roused them, the vibrance of the alarm bells booming and slamming in the dark city by the lake.

XIX

First Blood — 1837

Josiah Stensrood, a greatcoat huddled about him, bent over the fire place in the early morning chill of his office and carefully fed sheets of thin paper to the flames. One by one they flared up, blackened, crumbled, were mashed into a fine powder with the end of the poker. From time to time Josiah smiled grimly as white letters showed staringly against the charred black, letters that formed such words as "Montreal," "rifles," "St. Eustache," "Papineau," before they were ground into oblivion.

One rustling stack had vanished and Josiah was about to begin on a second when a cautious tapping pattered against the locked door. He jammed the papers into a drawer, called: "Who's there?"

The flutelike tones of Ogle Ketchipaw quavered through the panels. "It's a — a young lady."

"Tell her I'm busy," said Josiah, fingers closing about the papers again.

There was a discreet cough. "It ain't that kind of a young lady. Says she's Miss Alexandra Kingscote. 'Pears she wants to see you, like."

Josiah flung open the door. Ketchipaw backed away, rubbing his elbows. "Where is she, Ogle?"

"In kind of a carriage outside. She said — "

Josiah scowled. "Why the devil didn't you ask her in? Have the boy bring in some more wood for the fireplace."

"The boy ain't been in today. Guess he's to City Hall, listenin' to Fitzgibbon damnin' and blastin'. Guess — "

"Get the wood yourself," snapped Josiah. He flung open the outer door to find Sandra, eyes troubled and face white, looking out of the window of the Kingscote carriage. She caught his hand, her eyes troubled. "Jos, *where* is Gil?"

Josiah raised his eyebrows. "I could give a guess."

Her small fist drummed on the window frame. "Jos, don't be funny. Please! Where is he? And *what's* happening?"

He shook his head. "I'm not being funny. I think I know where he is. As to what's happening — "

She swung the coach door open. "I'll come inside. I want — "

He held up his hand. "What will Toronto say? A stealthy Yankee luring an unprotected girl to his lair! Better — "

She sprang to the ground. "I don't care what they say. I want to know about Gil. Jos! He was to have come back to town yesterday afternoon. I waited and waited at Alice's. And anyway, Toronto's too busy to notice me. It's a bedlam."

Josiah stepped aside, then followed her into his office where Ketchipaw fussed and mumbled over the growing fire. The old clerk bobbed his head to Sandra, scuttled out. Sandra sat down, drew her coat tighter about her, buried her hands in her sealskin muff. "Jos. It's freezing in here. Have you just started the fire?"

He shook his head. "Had a little one of my own. Getting rid of a few souvenirs of Lower Canada." He ruffled the papers at her. "Well — about Gil. I'd say he was probably out at Montgomery's Tavern."

"At Montgomery's! But what for?"

Josiah looked unexpectedly grave. "Things have broken out at last. You can guess the rest."

"But I tell you I don't know anything. All those bells ringing last night and people riding down the valley. What's happening? And today — not a shop open and all those people shouting around City Hall and men galloping off to Government House. Jos, what *is* it?"

He looked surprised. "You haven't heard?"

"Not a thing. Staff and Father wouldn't tell me anything. I just heard the bells last night and saw the crowds today."

Josiah whistled. "Well, this is what's happened. Mackenzie's got some kind of an army out at Montgomery's. That's why the bells were ringing. And as for the town, that's the Tired Reformer's doing. Or rather — not doing. He was at City Hall this morning, where all the arms are, and I *heard* him tell old Fitzgibbon — " he pursed up his lips, spoke with mincing precision — "'Colonel, I do not apprehend a rebellion.' The old colonel's about crazy. He's getting out the militia as fast as he can, but Head won't let him make a move. Now, I'm certain that little Mac hasn't got many men out there. I'm certain he hasn't got much in the way of deadly weapons. If old Fitz'll only move — "

Sandra held up her hands. "Jos, do wait a minute. You're going too fast. Now — you say Mr. Mackenzie's got an army out Yonge Street."

"That's it," said Josiah, nodding.

Her face grew even paler. "Then — then *that*'s where Gil is." Her voice was low, hushed. "I know it. He was coming down from the north and met someone. He stayed there." Her hands twisted in the soft depths of the muff. "Why did he have to? Why didn't he come to me?"

Josiah stretched out his long legs. "You know that cousin of mine about as well as I do. All this that Mackenzie's trying to do means an awful lot to him. I don't say that it means more to him than you do. But it means enough." He looked at her keenly. "You know pretty much how deep he's been in all this. Would you want him to back out when things begin to happen?"

Her chin set. "I was nearly sick yesterday when he didn't come and didn't come. But if he had, it wouldn't have been Gil." Her blue eyes narrowed in thought. Then she looked up suddenly. "Jos — you're sure he's at Montgomery's?"

He shrugged. "Sure as I can be about anything."

"Then let's go to him."

"Huh?" Josiah's head jerked forward in surprise. "*Go* to him?"

"Yes. You and I. I don't care what happens. I'm not going to be kept away from him any longer."

Josiah drew a long breath, eyed her keenly. Then he laughed. "Some Stensroods have all the luck. H'm — now, let me see. Yes — I guess we could do it. The city's open to the four winds. Head's doing nothing. Last night, after the bells began ringing, I went out as far as Bloor without seeing a soul." He shook his head. "Mac could have marched in and taken Head's nightcap if he'd wanted to." He raised his eyebrows inquiringly. "Well — when do you want to start?"

Eyes alight, she jumped to her feet. "Jos! You will? We — "

There was a rap at the door. A rather husky voice asked: "May I come in?"

Josiah opened it a little. A rusty beaver above a heavily lined face showed in the gap. "Kind of guessed I'd find you two here," said Dr. Richland. "Where's that young fool?"

Sandra ran to the untidy man as he pushed his way past Josiah. "You don't know either? I hoped you might. I hoped you'd come to tell us."

Dr. Richland's eyes were suddenly gentle. "I wish I could tell you that he was messing up my dispensary with his devil's brews. But I can't." He turned to Josiah. "Where do you think he may be?"

Josiah smiled. "We're pretty sure he's at Montgomery's farm. What do you think of that?"

Richland rubbed his stubbly, obstinate chin. "You might be right."

"And we're going out there to find him!" cried Sandra. "What do you think of *that?*"

Richland sat down suddenly, bony hands cupped over his knees. Then he chuckled. "Most times I'd say Godforsaken foolishness. But there's so many fools in the township today, you'll most likely not be noticed." He coughed, ruffled the deplorable nap of his beaver. "Guess I'll go with you."

"Fine!" said Josiah, rising. "Sandra, you better send your carriage home or wherever it's going. We'll ride with Doc and Bessie."

"Bessie'll take us if Sandra don't mind getting a mite crumpled," said Doc. "Guess we better wait a bit before we start, though."

Sandra shook her head impatiently. "Why? Why? Let's go now and—"

Richland held up a gnarled hand. "Pretty soon we'll know what'll happen. We don't want to be slipping out when Gil and his maniacs are trying to slip in, do we?"

Sandra's small hands clenched. "But—"

"I've been around the town a bit today. No one's doing anything —yet. There's Mac with a whole army out Yonge Street. He's not doing anything. There's His Excellency Francis Fool Head, with all the resources of the Province to hand, and *he*'s not doing anything. If nothing's happening by afternoon, we can be pretty sure nothing'll happen the rest of the day."

"What makes you think that?" asked Josiah.

Richland looked at him tolerantly. "I'm an old soldier. I can sniff the wind and tell a whole lot of things."

"What'll you do if Head does get chased out—and there's every chance of it?" said Josiah.

"I've told you before, medicine and politics don't mix," said Richland firmly. "Now you better slip out and send Sandra's Roman chariot home."

Josiah went to the door and sent the carriage rattling off. Then he looked toward the brick bulk of the Market, on whose second floor the city government functioned in a heavy reek of meats and produce. The open space in front was black with people, milling and shuttling about, faces raised to the silent windows where Fitzgibbon wrangled respectfully with Head. There was a stir, a ruffle, as a mounted orderly galloped off toward Government House. Then the crowd swayed back, silent and watchful. Josiah shook his head, started to close the door, when running feet, a shout, checked him. A hatless man ran toward him, waving. "Is Dr. Richland there?"

Josiah looked down on the panting man. "Sure. What is it? A broken leg or only childbirth?"

The man shoved a scrap of grimy paper at Josiah. "Ain't either. It's this. Give it to him."

Josiah stared at the folded sheet, then tramped back to the office where Richland and Sandra looked up expectantly. "Here's a little billet-doux for you, Doc," said Josiah.

Richland seized the paper, which unfolded in a stiff crackle. Then he sprang to his feet, snapping his fingers. "They're coming! By the eternal, they're coming!"

Sandra and Josiah broke out into a gust of questions. Richland, eyes on the paper, waved them away. Slowly he sank back into his chair, face incredulous. His voice was hushed, awe-struck. "I wouldn't have believed it. Never."

Sandra clutched at his arm. "They're coming? That means Gil's with them. He'll be here! He'll be here! Dr. Richland! Let's go out and meet him. He's — "

Richland shook his head. "I spoke too soon. I read the first line and frothed over. There's more to it." He studied the sheet again. "Here's what's happening. Mac *is* marching on the city. He's got about as far as Bloor Street and — "

Sandra shook his shoulder in her impatience. "Then let's go. Bloor Street! We'll be there in a half hour. Jos! Come on."

Josiah, keen eyes on Richland, shook his head. "Just a second. Doc, what else have you got there?"

Richland carefully folded the paper. "It was what followed that knocked me out. Mac's coming. And Head — God, what a man. The only head he's got's in his name. He's — "

Josiah shook his fist at him. "Stop gibbering. What's Head done?"

Richland's voice dropped. "He's sending out — not the militia, but a flag of truce! It's true! A flag of truce!"

Josiah stared at him open-mouthed. Sandra, bewildered, looked from one to the other.

Richland went on. "A flag of truce, sent by the representative of Her Majesty to a rebel army. And guess who's taking the flag?"

Josiah brightened. "Maybe it's Hagerman and they'll shoot him."

Richland shook his head. "No such luck. Rob Baldwin and Doc Rolph. No less. Two Reformers." He scratched his grizzled head. "Well, maybe it's all right. Everyone trusts Rob."

Josiah took the paper from Richland, examined it curiously. "How'd you get this?"

Richland grunted. "I've got patients all over town. One of 'em's keeping me posted on what's going on. I've left word where I'd be."

Sandra smiled. "I thought medicine and politics didn't mix."

"They don't. But if those fools are going to start squalling and brawling all over King Street, I want to know about it. Got to have bandages, got to — Well, just like to be ready, that's all."

In the slowly warming office the three waited. At noon Josiah sent Ogle Ketchipaw to near-by Ontario House for food, which was tasted absently, forgotten. Huddled by the fire, Richland carried on a long monologue about medical practice in Canada, about the difficulty of getting students of the right type. Then he swung off onto the subject of Gil, who, though he'd never even hint it to his face, was the type of pupil that a real teacher dreams about. "And Gil could teach, too," he mourned. "Knows how to tell someone else what he's learned, and puts a lot of himself into the telling. Now he's tangled himself up in politics and when Mac comes into the city he'll make Gil some kind of a fool admiral or something instead of letting him go on in medicine. And medicine's the only reason, so far's I can see, why the good Lord ever turned that six-foot fool loose in the world."

The others listened mechanically, Josiah restless and fidgeting, Sandra quiet but tight-lipped. The afternoon wore on. Once a riot of smashing bells brought Josiah to the door, but there was nothing for him to see beyond the eternal confusion off by the

Market. Later, Richland fell into an uneasy doze by the fire while Sandra, glad of something to do, helped Josiah burn the last of the Montreal papers.

Something scratched at the door. Josiah flung it open on the bobbing head of Mr. Ketchipaw, who held out a crumpled paper. "For the doctor," he piped. "A feller just brought it."

Josiah snatched the sheet from him, banged the door. "Doc! Doc! Wake up. Your patient wants more calomel or something!"

"Eh? What?" Richland started, eyes blinking. He held out his hand. Sandra and Josiah bent over his shoulder as he read, trying in vain to decipher the muddy script.

Then the doctor sighed, folded the paper. "Too bad. Too bad."

Sandra shook him. "What's too bad? What's happened?"

Richland rubbed his hands together slowly. "That fool Head promised everyone a pardon if they'd go home quietly. Mac wouldn't take the terms unless they were in writing. Said he didn't trust Head. Now Head's got a fit of the sulks and says he won't give it in writing, so everything's off, I guess." He sighed again. "Another bit of news. Mac's burned Horne's house."

Sandra started. "Old Dr. Horne's? He can't have. Why—why Dr. Horne's always been—"

"Always been as strong Compact as Strachan," said Richland tersely.

"That means Mac's come into town?" asked Josiah.

Sandra shook her head. "Dr. Horne's house is just beyond the Bloor Street gate." She sat down slowly. "Burned! But I *know* that house. I've been there. It's horrible. Burned! Why didn't someone stop him? Why didn't—"

"Why didn't someone call a constable?" said Richland grimly. "It's not pretty. But then, what they're fighting ain't pretty either."

"Never mind that," said Josiah. "What'll we do now? I'm for starting."

"Of course," echoed Sandra, rising quickly. "Let's go to Gil as fast as we can. Let's—"

Richland held up a scarred finger. "Let's do a mite of thinking. It'll be dark in less than an hour. Then we'll start and no one'll bother us. If we go now—well, they might take Bessie as a cavalry horse or something."

"Must we wait?" asked Sandra impatiently.

"Don't see it," said Josiah. "I'm for heading right out Yonge Street now."

"And run into pickets? I heard that Jarvis has got some men nearly out to Bloor, without Head's knowing."

Josiah hunched quickly into his coat. "That's all right. I'll ride ahead and if anyone gets in my way — "

Richland snorted. "Stensroods are Stensroods, no matter what side of the border grows 'em. I suppose you'd rather go right to City Hall and break Head's jaw and chuck Strachan into the bay. Now listen, you two. Here's the way Bessie and I are going. Come or not, just as you like. We'll go up Yonge as far as Queen. Then we'll swing west to University Avenue and go north to College. At College, we'll take that little road that cuts across the Elmsley grounds onto Yonge. Then I'll give Bessie her head until we meet some of Mac's men."

"But why wait until dark?" asked Sandra.

"Because I'm an old soldier," said Richland. "No one'd be fool enough to try to attack in the dark with men that haven't fought before. Good Lord, they'd be shooting each other or jabbing each other in the rump with bayonets and pikes." He spread out his hands. "Well, that's my plan. Anyone that wants to come with Bessie and me's welcome."

"I still think my plan's best," growled Josiah.

"No you don't," snapped Richland. "Sandra and I aren't letting you drag us into any gutter fights. Are you waiting or aren't you? Good."

Time crept slowly on. The little office blurred away into a soft gloom, lit up by sudden flares of the dying fire. Josiah sent Mr. Ketchipaw to the Ontario House for coffee, then to Barnard's for Bessie and the ancient chaise. At last, in the gathering darkness, they set off out a Yonge Street that was strangely hushed, a ghostly street where people walked furtively, eyes shifting as footfalls echoed against the shuttered fronts of shops.

As they turned into Queen, Richland gestured with his frayed willow switch to the knots of men grouped about Elliot's Tavern, alert men who seemed poised, expectant. "Reinforcements for Mac," said Richland tersely. "They'll move as soon as they know he's on his way."

"What's against them?" asked Josiah.

Richland waved the switch again. "Well, my patient told me that not more'n a couple of hundred had signed up to defend the city against Mac." He shook his head. "Mac's wasting time. You all right, Sandra?"

Huddled between the two men, she nodded shortly. "I will be as soon as I find Gil." She settled deeper into the seat, watching the trees of University Avenue flick past, as though she were pulling herself along by each weathered trunk. Then the shaggy head of the horse turned east, leaving the deserted cricket ground behind, and bobbed its cautious way through the rough track that circled behind the great house of the Elmsleys. Sandra could see the squat bulk looming on the high ground to her right. The windows were dark blotches against the gray walls. Or — or — had it suffered the same fate as Dr. Horne's? She strained her eyes, thought she saw a ragged gap in the roof. But it was only a trick of light, a faint glimmer cast by the rising moon that was beginning to touch hill and valley with silver fingers. The big house was deserted, not ruined. The Elmsley men were probably at City Hall with Head and Fitzgibbon, the women sheltered at the Robinsons' or the Grange.

Then the land fell away to the north and the cold moon lit up tree-masked hills and valleys and the long slope that swept evenly away. The mansion and its fate were erased from her mind. Somewhere in the darkness off there was Gil. Slow-creeping fear moved into her heart, as she sat there between the silent men. The night was fathomless, distances were immeasurable, and one man was a tiny pin point cast by the hand of chance into one of a thousand dark-choked hollows. She drew a deep breath. Gil was there somewhere. She would find him.

As they topped a curving rise, Richland suddenly checked the old horse, climbed creakily to the ground. "Think Jos and I'll take a look around here first," he muttered. "You better stay under that robe. Getting cold."

Without answering, she swung herself down between the high wheels and trotted on with the doctor and Josiah, small feet clicking over the slaty ground. Then Richland held up his hand and they halted.

They stood on a conical knob of ground that looked down onto the eternal climb of Yonge Street. On their right loomed the Elmsley house. The street itself showed in a lighter streak against field and garden. The few houses that straggled along the road were cold, lifeless. Sandra hunted for landmarks, then said: "That's the Sharpes' house there with the fence. Their garden's — "

Suddenly Richland laid his hand over her mouth, held up a warning finger. Josiah started, staring. On the very edge of the Elmsley grounds, a few figures moved cautiously. Metal caught the touch of the moon and shone back to the high skies. Then, across the road by the Sharpe house, there were more glints. Somewhere under the trees a man coughed rackingly, a horse stamped.

Richland tapped Josiah on the shoulder, drew Sandra into the shelter of a clump of bushes. "What is it?" she asked.

"Must be Jarvis's picket I heard about. We'll hit farther north and avoid 'em."

Josiah stirred angrily. "What good's that? Any reason why we can't use the Queen's Highway? They've got no right to stop us."

Richland pointed to the glint of metal in the fields below. "There's one reason."

Josiah bristled. "Think they can stop *me?* By God, I'd like to see 'em try. Here, you wait for me and I'll tramp right on through their damned lines. I'll — "

Richland nudged Sandra, who laid a hand on Josiah's sleeve. "I wish you'd stay here with us." He looked wistfully at the distant moving shapes. She went on, "After all, Jos, we're trying to find Gil, aren't we? It won't help him any if the Compact ties you up."

Josiah, grumbling, stepped back behind the bushes. Richland shook himself. "Let's get back in the chaise. There's another track that'll take us out farther up the road."

"Yes, yes. Let's go," said Sandra quickly. "Jos! Jos! Come on. Don't you — why, what's the matter?"

Josiah, half crouched behind the bushes, was staring beyond the Sharpe house, chin jutting and hand raised. She touched his elbow. "Come on!"

He slowly straightened up, drew a deep breath. Without looking back he said crisply, "Get her out of here, Doc."

Richland, uncomprehending, shuffled in the dark. "What? What?"

"I said get her out of here. And make it quick."

Sandra slipped nimbly past the staring doctor, crouched by Josiah. "What do you see, Jos?"

He swung her to her feet. "Didn't you hear me? Get back into the chaise. You're going back to town."

She ran a few steps in the dark. "I'm staying, if you are. And if you try to catch me, I'll run right down toward the picket."

Josiah swore softly. "All right, but keep low. See 'em, Doc?"

"See what?" Richland craned his long neck, eyes following Josiah's outstretched arm.

About a hundred yards up Yonge Street, something heavy and black flowed jerkily over the lighter surface of the road, a sluggish black serpent whose head vanished in a grove to reappear in the faint moonlight beyond, its thick body trailing along after it. High in the air, points of light twinkled dimly, vanished, reappeared.

Sandra breathed in shaky spasms. "They've come," she whispered.

Richland nodded silently, pointed to the slant of pikes that showed close behind the head of the column. Then he squirmed in pain as Josiah's fingers bit into his arm, stared as a long hand pointed to the sudden stir at the edge of the Elmsley grounds, in the Sharpe garden.

"Going to be bad," muttered Josiah through clenched teeth. "Look — lining the fence with riflemen."

Sandra tried to close her eyes, but the lids seemed to snap open against her will. She could see knots of men moving stealthily on both sides of the road, could see the steady surge. They were closer now, and what had been a slow-moving rope gradually changed into recognizable marching men, those near the head of the column carrying short rifles. Behind them, long muskets jutted toward the sky, and farther to the rear pikes towered, their steel points gleaming.

She clenched her fists. She wanted to shout, to run out on the road to warn these men of the shapes in field and garden, of the dull-glinted barrels that slowly swung north. Dimly she was aware of Richland muttering over and over between set teeth: "No scouts out. No scouts out. Why in hell don't they send scouts? Why — "

Then the hush of the night was torn by a ripping explosion that flared red along the white fence by Sharpe's, stabbed in short, plunging flames in the trim fields of the Elmsleys. Sandra felt the ringing world spin about her, saw the high stars whirl down the sky. There was another crash, this time from the road. She pressed her hands to her throbbing temples as the rifle flashes down below left lurid bars across her eyeballs.

Then she was nearly jolted off her feet as Josiah, his deep voice crashing out, sprang up, arms waving. "Yeeeaaaah! Come on! Come on! Hit 'em again! Hit 'em again. They're running. Doc, Sandra. The whole damned Compact crew's running. They've—Come on, you rebels! Give it to 'em, give it to 'em."

She tried to rub the blur of the flashes from her eyes, stared at the moonlit stretch where armed men had crept just a moment ago. Field and garden were empty. There was no sign of Sheriff Jarvis's picket, save for a confused drumming of boots that died away to the south.

She clutched Josiah's arm. "We've won? Is that it? Gil'll come into the city now? We've won?"

Josiah, jumping frantically up and down, threw his arm about her shoulder, whacked Richland's stooped back. "Won? Of course we have. Now if they'll just keep on going, they'll sail right into City Hall and nobble off Head and Strachan and—Oh, by God! Didn't they run? Took the fire and—Come! Let's join 'em. Doc! Sandra! We'll march right into the city with 'em. Leave Bessie here! Come on!"

Sandra linked her arm with his and started skipping lightly over the rough ground. Then Richland's voice snapped in their ears. "Don't go kiting off like a pair of ninny-hammers! Want to get shot? How'll they know you're not Compact? Wait a minute and—" He peered through the gloom. "Wait a minute—" His voice trailed away. Then he sat heavily on a stone. "Missed it. Damned if they ain't missed it."

"What? What?" Josiah's voice was querulous. "Missed what?"

"Missed Head. Missed Strachan. Missed anything you like." He waved a vague arm toward the road where the acrid smell of powder still hung heavily. "Where are they?"

Sandra went forward a few hesitant steps, eyes trying to break the unreal veil of moonlight that, in revealing, distorted. Road, field, and garden were empty. Off to the north she could hear a confused murmur, faint, angry shouts. "They're gone," she said mechanically. Her own voice rang dull and flat in her ears. "They're gone."

Richland's hat bobbed. "Seen it happen before. Both sides fire and both sides run away."

"Just a pack of mice," fumed Josiah.

"Don't be a fool," snapped Richland. "Raw troops'll always act that way. And these ain't even troops. Give 'em a month or two and they'll rip into wildcats with their bare hands." He shook his head. "Funny, though. Doesn't seem to have been anyone hit."

"Hit!" snorted Josiah. "You could hear the bullets rapping way up in the trees. They aimed — Here — Sandra! Where are you going?"

Sandra, her eyes fixed on the white fence, was moving slowly toward it. Josiah caught up with her. "Don't go wambling off like that. Might — "

Her arm pointed stiffly to a vague blur, a formless huddle against the white pickets. "I've got to see," she said. "I've got to see." Josiah caught at her arm, but she broke away, ran stumbling across the moon-soaked grass, the two men racing after her. Then she suddenly stopped, one hand at her throat, the other clutching a sapling that swayed gently to her touch. Her breath came fast, broken. She turned to Josiah. "No. No. It isn't." Suddenly she began to laugh, shrill and high-pitched. "It's funny. I thought it was Gil. But it isn't." Her voice soared higher. "It's a little man. He's — " Her fingers loosened about the sapling. She stumbled away from the tree, found Richland's arm supporting her, heard his voice, the rasp quite gone out of it. "Take it easy, Sandra. Easy does it. It's a shock. Know it's a shock. Been hard times for you. Today's been hard." He patted her shoulder. "Just get a deep breath. Nothing's happened."

Waves of fire seemed to ebb from her, leaving her shaken but collected. "I'm sorry. I'm a fool. I didn't — "

Richland shook his head. "Rubbish. Not your fault. You thought that might be Gil. It wasn't. I could draw you a picture of just what happened to you. Could happen to anyone. Extreme fear, sudden relief. Felt a bit that way myself lots of times. Uh — Jos — any work for me to do around here?"

Josiah, returning from a tour of the field, squinted up the road that now showed sharp and hard in the moonlight, shook his head. "He's the only one."

"Well — better have a look at him, I guess. Take Sandra back to the chaise and — here — what the devil have you got there?"

Josiah balanced a short rifle in his broad palm. "No one else seemed to want this, so I thought I — "

"And you were going to drive back to Toronto with *that!*" Richland barked in disgust. "If anyone saw a pair of Yankees like us coming back from the fight, armed, they'd have us in Innis's old cell in about three seconds." He snatched at the barrel, sent the weapon crashing among dried branches and rocks. "Get along now. I'll join you."

"Come on, Jos," urged Sandra. "Then we'll go to Gil."

Richland wheeled about. "That's just what you won't do."

She threw back her head, eyes flashing in the shade of her deep bonnet. "We most certainly are going— "

"We most certainly are not. Two reasons. In the first place, that crowd out Yonge Street'll be in such a state that they'll be shooting their own shadows for the next twenty-four hours. Second, I'm going to give you a powder and send you home or you'll be in for a bad time. Now—march!"

She looked appealingly at Josiah. He shook his head. "Better do what Doc says." She frowned, bit her full lower lip. "Come on," he urged. "Gil'll be coming in most any time now. If he doesn't we'll go to him. Tomorrow. Next day. Come on."

Resigned, she trudged along beside him, eyes still turned toward the north and the infinite mystery of the night.

XX

Montgomery's Farm (I) — 1837

THE unseasonable weather held and the early sun of December 7, 1837, was almost warm on Gil's back as he stared at the tall, white-bearded old man who tramped up the steps of Montgomery's Tavern, high boots caked with mud. Deep-set, piercing eyes fell on Gil, the only soul stirring about the building. "Vere iss Mac?" The voice was harsh, guttural.

Gil, unshaven and red-eyed, bristled at the abrupt question. "He's asleep. Orders are not to wake him."

The white beard jutted. "He vill vake for Colonel Van Egmond. Now run. Tell him."

Gil gasped, recovered himself. This farmer, innkeeper, trader from the Huron Tract, shaggy in homespun, clumping in cowhide boots, couldn't, just couldn't be the man who had seen the French eagles through the mists of Austerlitz and Jena, who had sniffed the smoke of burning Moscow. There was some mistake. There was—

A long arm shot out, caught Gil's shoulder. "Ven you are tolt to run, run. So ve haf discipline."

Gil blinked. The rasping voice seemed to change the colorless homespun into blue broadcloth, gold-braided. "Sorry, Colonel Van Egmond," he stammered. "You weren't expected—"

The deep-set eyes were hard. "A field officer iss *alvays* expected. Get Mac." Gil started into the inn. Again the long arm checked him. "Vait. You haf been here long? So! Tell me. Vot iss *dat?*" A clawlike finger pointed to an untidy straggle of men that moved out from the shelter of a shed, noses pointing toward a smoldering fire.

Gil squinted. "Hard to tell from here. I think they belong to the Sharon Company."

Van Egmond snorted. "Ha! And dot iss Mac's army?" The sharp

eyes puckered, the beard shook. "Dere iss vork here to be done. No one hass seen to it, no?"

"Done what we could," said Gil shortly. He suddenly felt protective toward the footsore, hungry men out in the frosty fields.

Van Egmond's lined face softened. "Ah—de poor boys. Dey are so young and dey know so leetle. I haf seen it before. I—"

There was a clatter behind the closed door, a slamming of feet on a staircase. The door flew open and Mackenzie bounded out, wig awry. He seized the old Dutchman's gnarled fists. "Here we are. We can go. Gil, why didn't you bring him right up? I've been waiting and waiting. You're slack. You're losing us time." Still clinging to Van Egmond's hand, he shouted over his shoulder: "Lount! Gibson! I've got him! We'll march! We'll—here's a *real* soldier." He hurried the reluctant old man through the door. Gil heard Mackenzie's voice rising higher and higher. "We'll have to move at once. Van Egmond'll be Commander in Chief. Hurry, hurry, hurry. Want Head and the rest to get away? Hurry, hurry!" The slam of the door drowned out his words.

Gil drew a deep breath, stepped down onto the trampled earth of the yard, frowning. "Mac's no better for his sleep. Can't think what was wrong with him yesterday. Screeching like a peacock. And we can't march yet. Van Egmond ought to have about a week or more for training—if the men'll follow him."

Absorbed, he walked north through the fields where frowzy men crept out of rude shelters, yawning and scratching. Here and there the low huts were neatly aligned, trim-looking, with firearms stacked, their locks covered against the damp, or pikes lashed into uniform bundles. But for the most part uncleanly lairs were dotted about, haphazard, with wasteful fires where scant food was being prepared in a slovenly way. In one tangle of branches an old musket rusted. In another a pike lay, its shaft snapped by a clumsy foot, its blade dulled and fire-blackened. Gil shook his head and the concern about his eyes deepened as he saw that the field south of Gibson's house, where some fifty men had bedded down the night before, was empty, the muddy boots that had trampled down the grass already miles away, no doubt, homeward bound.

By a swift brook he set his teeth, shaved in the waters where random bits of glasslike ice spun and whirled. Refreshed, he stowed his kit away, stepped out onto Yonge Street. Then he stopped suddenly, his eyes narrowing. Something moved up over the crest by Hogg's Hollow, crept along the great level stretch to the tavern and the ragged fields.

The sound of feet came to him against the wind and he saw a short column of men marching briskly along, heading south. He stepped back to the edge of the road, watched the steady progress, judged the strength to be about twenty men, a tall figure at their head. Gil stared, then gave a shout and ran toward them calling: "Graves, by God!"

Graves Stensrood, rifle slung over his shoulder, waved a grimy hand. "Morning, Gil. Where do we go?"

Gil eyed the halted men. They seemed more alert, more confident, than most of the groups that straggled about the tavern. "Got rations?" he asked.

"Some," said Graves. "We slept in the woods and cooked our bacon about an hour ago. We're ready for anything."

"Hope there'll be something ready for you," thought Gil. Then he slapped Graves on the shoulder. "Good to see you. Just go to the tavern and see Silas Fletcher. Tell him who you are and how many. Come on. I'll show you where."

The little column stepped out again, Gil walking beside Graves, some ten paces in front. He dropped his voice. "Keep your lot where you can see them. And another thing. Keep 'em as far away from the rest as you can. Don't let 'em talk to the others if you can help it."

"So?" Graves raised his eyebrows. "That's how Father thought it would be—if you were still here. It was like that in '12, he says, until they got under way. Flora didn't agree with him."

"What kept you?" asked Gil. "Thought I'd be seeing you the first night."

Graves shrugged. "Things at the farm that had to be done. Then I had trouble in getting the men together. Only about half of 'em came, and they're the ones that did the least talking before things broke out."

"Been the same with us," sighed Gil. "Er—did you take a look at Nipigon when you came by? How was it there?"

"Looked all right," said Graves. "Thought I'd drop in, but then I thought better not. If things go bad—eh? Just as well not have the story of armed men running in and out of the place."

Gil nodded. "That's what I figured. I'm worried about 'em, though. I haven't dared send word for fear Grandfather'd come storming out and tell the whole lot to go home. Or else join 'em. Here's the tavern. Take your crowd in and I'll wait for you under the oak there."

Gil stretched out on the cold grass under the bare branches, waited until Graves clumped across to him. "Well, Gil, what's it been like, so far?" He leaned his back against the trunk.

Gil shrugged. "All right." Then he suddenly burst out: "Graves, it's been a madhouse. Waiting and waiting. Men coming in, men going home. And there's Toronto—" He launched into a heated description of the first encounter by the Sharpe house, of his own walk clear into Queen Street unopposed. Graves nodded from time to time, frowning.

"And next day—that would be Wednesday—" Gil went on, "the men were ready to try again. Or most of 'em were, and Mac went off to the west with a few men. *I* don't know what his idea was. He captured the mail coach at the Peacock Inn and brought the stuff back here. The rest of us hung about and slept or did pike drill. More of 'em went home. Then Mac lined everyone up and raged for an hour. I tell you, Graves, I'm worried about him. He's cracking. He's had too much on his shoulders. The whole plan was big enough. And then the orders were changed without his knowing and that threw everything out. And things have been going wrong ever since. Mac can't sit still, and when he moves, he can't make up his mind where to go or what to do."

Graves shook his head. "Guess Mac knows what he's doing. I'm not worrying."

"I am," said Gil shortly. He rubbed the back of his hand across his chin nervously. "Why the devil did he burn Horne's house? And you ought to have seen him at Howard's house on Gallows Hill the day the flag of truce came out! Ripped down Howard's fence with his own hands. Yelled at Mrs. Howard to get food ready for three hundred men! She couldn't do that anyway. Howard's postmaster here. And I thought Mac was going to hit her with his whip. Think he would have if Sam Lount hadn't smoothed things over. Everyone saw it. That's why I told you to keep your men away from the others. They'll hear enough rumors and half-truths to send 'em back to Holland Landing."

Graves frowned, then hummed softly to himself. "Well, Lount's here. Van Egmond's come. They'll take command. Mac's no soldier and he knows it. We'll be all right."

Gil hammered his fist on the hard ground. "But look at the time we've wasted! And we don't know what's going on in town. Head may have recalled Colborne and the troops and when we try to go in we'll find two or three regiments of regulars waiting—if they don't come out after us. I tell you, the town's been helpless. We could have marched in and taken all those arms at City Hall. The people in town would have joined us. Look at yesterday! Went clear out to Dundas Street and captured the mail! Just a lot of letters! With the same men he could have captured Government House! And that flag of truce. Rolph and Rob Baldwin brought it out. Why? And I saw Rolph hang behind and say something to Lount. What did he say? Is Rolph selling us out? Is—"

Graves patted him on the back. "Cool down, Gil. You're getting worse than you say Mac is. Course, he's under a strain. But he'll be all right as soon as we can get under way. Good Lord, what was he waiting for? Why, for Van Egmond, of course. Now the old Dutchman's here and we'll swing right into town. He'll know *how*—He'll—"

A voice from the tavern shouted: "Gil! Gil!"

Gil sprang to his feet, saw Lount waving to him. "Come on, Graves. Something's going to happen. Something—" Graves at his heels, he raced to the broad porch. Lount stepped down on the ground, nodded to Graves, and pulled Gil roughly aside.

"What's happening?" asked Gil.

"Devil to pay," growled Lount. "Look here, Gil, we want you to do something. Now—Mac trusts you and we want—" His eyes flickered away uncertainly. "That is, if you're close to Mac you'll be able—Oh, damn it! Look here. Mac's simply gone mad! Mad, I tell you! It's—"

"I saw him at Howard's and Horne's," said Gil.

"This is worse. We've been up there talking. He and Fletcher and Gibson and Van Egmond. Mac can't even talk straight. He wanted Van Egmond to start the men right off to the city. Van Egmond said the idea was crazy. He'd put out scouts and move tomorrow and Mac—" Lount's voice broke— "Mac pulled a pistol on him. I tell you, he tried to shoot him, just because he wouldn't agree. Dave Gibson and I took the pistol away from him. From Mac! And he turned against us—" Lount broke off short.

A deep wave of hopelessness that had been mounting since he had first blundered onto the exhausted muddy men up Yonge Street swept over Gil in full force. For a fraction of time the picture of Nipigon flashed through his mind. He could disassociate himself from Mackenzie's tottering structure, escape the certain doom that seemed to be gathering, the sure disaster, as possibility faded into improbability, darkened to impossibility. Then he set his chin. "What do you want me to do?"

Lount clutched his arm. "Stay by Mac when things begin to happen. He won't mind. He was talking about you up there. If he tries to do anything—anything—well, dangerous—you see, eh? You can keep him from it, eh?"

Gil nodded shortly. "I'll try."

Lount looked slightly relieved, started to speak, and then turned abruptly and went back into the tavern. Gil, standing in the warm sun, felt as though a tight band were about his forehead, as though his arms and legs had suddenly become inert, useless. An air of unreality settled over the fields that were now swarming with men, armed and unarmed, over the soggy road that stretched away to Toronto. Even Graves, in earnest talk with some of his men a few yards away, seemed a crazy puppet.

Then he tried to shake himself back into real life, found the sunlit world clearing a little. The building behind him was silent, save for a steady, even buzz of voices from the second floor. His mind began to play over the various problems that had absorbed him earlier. That eastern picket, for example. He'd ordered it placed the night before, but it might not have been relieved, the men might have become bored or frightened and wandered back to the tavern and the companionship of field or shed.

He started over the rough ground toward the hollow among the slaty outcropping which he had selected. There was no sign of the picket as he stumbled along, but he realized that, hidden away in folds of the ground, the men might still be there.

Suddenly there was a distant shout. "Stop, there! Pull in!" Gil nodded grimly. The picket was there and alert, probably challenging some new arrivals that had slipped up from the lake-front townships. He broke into a trot. The voices echoed again, angrily; there was a clash of metal, a whinny. Gil pounded over the uneven ground. Bushes rustled beyond a slight hollow and a man, musket at trail, ran heavily toward him.

Gil stopped short, shouted, "What is it?"

The man jerked back his head, quickened his pace. "Someone askin' 'bout you. The boys have — "

"How many?" snapped Gil.

"Just one. Keeps hollerin' for you."

"Come on," said Gil and started off at a trot again, crashing through the bushes. Then he stumbled, caught himself by a low branch. Down the slope the ragged men of the picket, pikes and muskets wavering, stood about a small bay horse, hedged in a flutter of blue. There was a high cry: "There he is! I *told* you!" and Sandra, bonnet pushed back from her bright hair, struggled up the slope toward him.

Gil stared in horror, started to shout, "Go back!" but found that heedless of the gaping men he had her in his arms, that her cheek was against his and her eyes closed in her thrown-back head. Over and over she told him: "I tried to come to you before, Gil. I tried to."

Wordless, he stroked her hair. She murmured on: "Why didn't you let me know? Why didn't you tell me how to come? Gil, I'd have been here long ago. Couldn't you — "

He started to answer. Then a thin, muffled sound, the snick of a musket lock being eased off, recalled him abruptly to the present. He straightened up, held her at arm's length. "Sandra. You've got to go back. Now!"

She shook her head. "I've come to you," she said simply.

For a moment they stared at each other. Then her eyes flashed, her slim hand caught at his frayed cuff. "Gil! You've got to take me to Mr. Mackenzie. I've got news from town. They're going — "

Gil silenced her with a gesture, raised his voice. "I'll send you right on to Nipigon. They'll see to you there." He caught the bay's bridle, turned to the still-astonished men. "When did you come on duty? At eight? I'll see that you're relieved by noon. Come along, Sandra." He took her arm, the bridle trailing from his free hand.

Out of earshot at the crest of the slope he said quickly: "What's happening in town? Why do you want to see Mac?"

She passed a hand over her forehead. "Gil, the militia's coming out today—against you. Staff came home early this morning and told me. Then he went back into town. Gil, you've got to make Mr. Mackenzie go away. They're really coming. They've got cannon."

Gil wrinkled his forehead. "Maybe. But Sandra, we've had rumors ever since sunrise that they were coming. We've sent scouts nearly to Bloor Street and nothing's happened."

She beat on his arm. "But *I know* this. Staff's got command of a company. Mr. de Grassi's got another. Father's on a committee with Strachan and Mr. Robinson. They're really *doing* something. I could hear bands playing over in the town when I started."

Gil whistled. "Looks like it, doesn't it? But I doubt if they can get the militia to march."

"Gil, Gil! Don't be so blind. And more people are coming into town all the time. And that awful Alan MacNab's brought boatloads and boatloads of men from Gore, from Hamilton. They say Mackenzie's got the Yankees helping him, that Yankee gunboats are coming across the lake. They've made people forget about Reform. They think they're fighting the Yankees again." She stopped, held up her hand. "Listen."

The soft wind brought a faint vibrance, urgent, incessant. The bells of St. James's were tolling.

Quickly Gil handed her the bridle, pointed toward the tavern. "See those men by the oak? Graves is with 'em. Go right to him. Wait until I come back."

She caught his arm as he started to run. "There's something else, Gil. Head knows everything about the people here. That nasty little de Grassi girl rode out here yesterday." Gil stared. "I mean it. It was Cornelia. She told Father and he told Colonel Fitzgibbon. Head knows that you haven't had much to eat. He knows how many men are here and how many have run away."

Still incredulous, Gil tried to visualize the shapeless adolescent face of Cornelia de Grassi. Grotesquely the picture came into his mind of a squalling, pigtailed girl being soundly spanked for putting tar in Alice McDonald's hair, years ago. It couldn't be. "How could she know?" he stammered. "How could she tell how many—"

She pushed him gently. "Get along to Mr. Mackenzie. Cornelia's seen her father's company often enough. She said you had about five hundred men here and that they were all hungry. She — "

No longer doubting, Gil raced off to the tavern porch, thundered through the door and up the stairs. The little room that faced east was shut tight. Heedless of discipline, Gil burst in. Four angry heads looked up: Mackenzie, calmer and cooler than Gil had seen him since his arrival; Van Egmond, every hair in his white beard bristling; Lount, scowling and puzzled; Gibson ruffled and alarmed.

Van Egmond's strongly accented voice rolled out. "So! Dis iss discipline?"

Mackenzie spoke quickly. "He's been with me a long time, Colonel. Gil, I'm afraid this is a bad time."

"I know it's bad," said Gil. "But I've got news. Head's marching."

Van Egmond scowled. Mackenzie said wearily, "Gil, we've heard that ever since sunrise. I thought you had more — "

"My — ah — Sandra Kingscote just came in with the news. She's from town. MacNab's brought a lot of men from the head of the lake. They're — "

Lount flapped an impatient hand. "Do you put the word of a girl over *ours?* The colonel has assured us that there's no sign of life down there. He's a soldier. He knows."

"But I tell you — " Gil began. Then, seeing nothing but disbelief about the table, he flung open a window. Faint but unmistakable, the bells of St. James's sang through the still air.

Mackenzie's calm vanished. Again he was the wild-eyed, feverish man who had stopped the mails, who had burned Dr. Horne's house. "Bells! Bells! Damn it, bells can't march. Bells can't fight." He sprang to his feet. "Gil! Get back to your men. Don't come back here unless you're sent for. We're — we're — "

Slowly Van Egmond rose. "Der young man iss right," he said. "Haf you heard bells today? Yesterday? Dey aren't ringing to amuse dat devil Strachan."

Mackenzie pounded the table. "Of course! Of course. I told you we ought to have marched. We'll march now. We'll — "

"Ve'll not," snapped Van Egmond. "Put der best men in voods, in bushes. Dey come and ve fire. Dey go avay."

Mackenzie flung his hands in the air. "But they're coming. We can hit them on Gallows Hill. We can — "

The white beard shook. "I vill not let raw men march. Dey vould scatter like sheepses. Here vill ve meet dem. So!"

The little room was very still. Gibson gnawed at the shaft of a quill, Lount drummed soundlessly on the table. Mackenzie made a sudden gesture. "What are we waiting for? I want to lead my men into Toronto. Gil! Have my horse ready! My pistols. Where's the portable press? I'll write a proclamation. I'll — "

Lount's level voice broke in. "Gil, better pass word to the company commanders to stand by. And be where we can find you."

Gil went slowly down the stairs, more and more disturbed. If Van Egmond could only have a free hand! He knew what to do with men, raw or trained. But with Mackenzie veering about like a weathervane, first applauding, then interfering — Suddenly he thought of Sandra, flung open the door, and stepped out into the sun.

At the end of the porch, a group of haggard-faced men clustered about a slim girl. Graves stood close by her elbow while a shaggy giant of a man, from some nameless clearing on the shores of Simcoe, scraped mud from the edge of her skirt with a kind of rough gentleness. She heard Gil's step, turned.

He made a cautioning gesture, then said, "Mac thinks it'll be all right for you to go on."

She nodded noncommittally while the shaggy man rumbled, "How's Mac today?"

Gil looked surprised. "Mac? Same's he's always been. He's been pretty tired, but he and the Dutchman are going over plans." He winked confidentially. "We'll have something to surprise Head with pretty soon."

A reassured murmur broke out from the little group. Gil went on, "Just slip around and tell the other boys to be ready." The men moved away, talking excitedly.

Graves raised his eyebrows. "Well?"

"If they come, Van Egmond's going to meet 'em here. Now Sandra, you stay with Graves. I've got to find Matthews and some others."

For a half hour he went from hut to hut, from shed to shed, to the Gibson house, to the Price house, returning at last with his roll complete. On the porch, Sandra smiled up at him. "Where are we going now?"

Gil studied her. "You're going back — the way you came."

She shook her head gravely. "But I'm not going back."

Gil's mouth tightened. "Listen, Sandra. You know Head's coming with all the militia. It — well, it may get rather hot around here. You're going back."

Her bonnet dangling in her slim hand, she shook her head. "I said — I'm staying."

Gil caught his breath, looked south over the empty, rolling country. Empty now. How would it be in an hour? Two hours? When would the crest of Gallows Hill be swarming with a sudden rush of men?

The inn door slammed open, Lount's flushed face looked out. "Where's Matthews?" Then he started, ducked his head to Sandra, repeated his question. Silently Gil pointed to a solid group of men coming into sight around a cluster of sheds. Lount nodded, dashed off.

"What's all that?" asked Graves. There was a brief conference, papers fluttered. Matthews shouted and several more men joined his group, alert and eager. Suddenly the ragged knot thinned out, fell into two ranks, wheeled smartly and moved off across the fields, heading south and east.

Graves stared. "Who's that lot?"

"Matthews's men," said Gil shortly. "They're about the best trained we've got here. They've all got rifles, too. Wonder why Mac's sending them off."

Lount clumped heavily back, panting. "What's up?" asked Gil quickly.

"We're moving." Lount spoke crisply and excitedly. "Those men're going to burn the Don bridge and go west along Queen Street as far as they can. Hit Head in the flank. It's Van Egmond's idea."

Sandra looked after the swift-moving men, lips parted. "They — they're going!" Her voice was almost a whisper.

Graves suddenly shifted his short rifle. "Never saw a bridge burned before," he said. "Guess I'll go with 'em."

"Wait a minute," said Gil. "How about your men?"

"They've joined the rest of the Holland Landing lot," said Graves, stepping off the porch. " 'Bye, Sandra. Take care of yourself, Gil. See you at Strachan's palace."

Gil looked after him, half enviously, half fearfully. Then a small voice spoke at his elbow. "Gil — "

He turned slowly. "What?"

"They're going down the Don. There'll be fighting there, too."

Gil groaned. "Oh, Lord! Now what on earth'll I — " He caught sight of Lount, eying them curiously, and presented him. Lount looked at her wonderingly. "So you're the one that brought the news!"

"But what are we going to do with her?" urged Gil. "She can't go home. Matthews has gone that way. She can't stay here."

"Of course she can't," said Lount quickly.

Gil turned to Sandra. "You see?"

She sat down on an upturned box. "If I can't go home, I've got to stay here. And it's where I wanted to be. That's why I came." Pale, but perfectly calm, she folded her hands, looked up at the two big men. "I'll tell you another thing," she said. "They're letting little Cornelia de Grassi carry messages along the Kingston Road. They're — "

Gil frowned, but Lount's face brightened. He snapped his fingers. "I've got it. Look here, Gil, you agree she'd better not be here?"

"Of course," said Gil.

"Then how about the reinforcements?"

Gil slapped his knee. "That's it. Look here, Sandra — do you want to help?"

She looked at him suspiciously. "Is this just to get me out of the way? Or will it really help?"

"Both," said Gil. "Here's what you can do. We know that there are more men coming down from the north. They ought to have been here long ago. You mount up and ride along Yonge Street. These people will just be shambling along. I know. I've seen enough of 'em. You've got to tell 'em to hurry. Tell 'em they're needed badly."

She frowned, dubiously. "How'll they know I'm telling them the right thing?"

Lount rubbed his heavy chin. "Most of the boys are tying something white around their left arms. Take Gil's handkerchief and — "

"It isn't very white," she objected.

"It'll look like a snowdrift compared to most of 'em," said Gil.

She rose slowly. "Oh — all right. I'll do it. But — "

"Fine! Fine!" said Lount. "And any you meet, put it as strong as you like. They're needed all right." He bobbed his head, clumped off up the stairs.

Alone, Sandra looked up at Gil. "Do I really have to?"

He nodded. "We don't know what's going to happen. Possibly nothing. But a lot *can*. If it does — "

"But Gil, don't you see? This is where I want to be. I told you. I don't care what happens. So much has happened. It's always kept us apart."

He shook his head. "You better go. And there's another thing you can do."

"Something that'll take me away again?" Her mouth quivered.

He lifted her chin. "And keep you away — where I can find you afterwards. I want you to go to Nipigon." She made an impatient gesture. "No — wait a minute. They don't even know where I am. You can tell them. You can tell them that I'm all right, that I'll come back there as soon as things are over. And they'll know I'll come back because you're there." He took her arm gently. "And it really is important about the new men. From Nipigon you'll be able to see a long way north."

They walked slowly toward the tethered bay, Gil stern-faced and Sandra with head bowed and eyes on the ground. She rested a hand on the brown neck, looked up at him. "I'll do just what you say," she said in a low tone. For a second her arms were about him. Then she mounted deftly, gathered the reins. Her eyes turned back to the porch, suddenly alive with men. "That's where we drank our first toast — do you remember? The day Head came and — " Her mouth worked a little, her hand touched his upraised cheek. "Oh, my dear, be careful." Then she was gone, a lone blue figure bobbing off along Yonge Street.

XXI

Montgomery's Farm (II) — 1837

GIL watched until the trees hid her. Then he turned back, tried to lose himself in the sudden new stir about the tavern. An odd feeling that was part unreality and part fear numbed him. The aimless rush about the porch would go on forever. He'd spend the rest of his life wandering about Montgomery's fields, watching the crest of Gallows Hill over which nothing would ever come, listening for orders that would never be issued. Sandra had faded off up the road to Nipigon, had vanished as eternally as Graves and the men of Matthews's column.

A shout from an upper window roused him, sent him on an endless pursuit of various unknown leaders who, when found, were either vaguely curious or resentful and usually in possession of orders just received by another messenger, in direct conflict with those that Gil brought. One lean, tanned man at the head of a small group from west of Lloydtown scratched his head. "Now how in hell can I send half my men off to Dundas Street looking for horses, another half to Gallows Hill as a picket, another to bring up water, and another to roll cartridges? You go back and tell Mac and that damned Dutchman that they ain't but two halves to nothin'." Gil shrugged hopelessly and went on.

Then, as he was crossing to see to the relief of the eastern post, he stopped short, staring at the hunched shoulder of Gallows Hill. A single rider was silhouetted for an instant, then plunged down the northern slope. About a hundred yards down Yonge Street men moved out of the belt of trees into the road, then stood aside to let the horseman pass. A few of them ran heavily after him, their distant shouts thin in the soft air.

Gil sprang into the road, held up his hand. The rider saw him, reined in sharply. Gil recognized him, a man named Asher who'd been missing at early rollcall. "What is it, Bill?" he snapped.

Asher tumbled from his bony mount. "Been out on a scout. Been — "

"Who told you to go?" asked Gil sharply.

"Didn't anyone tell me not to," said Asher, aggrieved. "Look, I been clear in to College Street. Spent the whole mornin' there. I seen 'em. They're comin'."

"Sure?" said Gil.

"Sure. Bands! Flags. Strachan's marchin' with 'em. So's Hagerman. So's Robinson — only they made 'em go back. But the rest's comin' and no mistake."

Gil spun on his heel. Most of the men were swarming about the stableyard in anticipation of their next scant meal. He cupped his hands. "Pass the word to Mr. Mackenzie that — "

A sudden ripping shout from the yard drowned his words. Another rider dashed across the fields shouting: "Here they come. This is the real thing. I saw 'em. I saw 'em."

Gil turned back toward the town, staring until his eyes ached. He tried to shut out the yelling and stamping that drowned all other sounds. He clapped his hands over his ears, then dropped them as an unexplained hush fell momentarily. The breeze from the lake was gentle, and hummed through the trees in lost melody. Then the humming grew slowly louder, throbbed and beat rhythmically, swelling in deep, muted undertones. Gil leaned toward the sound in the effort of listening. The tones swelled, thickened, took form as some hidden band blared out "The British Grenadiers." Then brass flashed and twinkled on the crest, the music grew louder, clearer, and in the heavy column the militia of Toronto began to spill slowly over the hill, to flow sullenly on toward Montgomery's farm.

Gil drew a deep breath. The sense of unreality fell away. Sandra was safely on her way to Nipigon. Soon there would be a clash, the Compact would be swept away. Of that he had no doubt. Hadn't Van Egmond, tried old soldier, said so? And raw as the Reform forces were, the militia was little better. As he ran back to the tavern he thought of other farmers and lawyers and doctors and mechanics who had blasted away the King's best troops outside Boston more than sixty years before. Regular troops, not farcical militia like those now marching raggedly to the sound of tinny bands.

He was suddenly caught up in a shouting mass of men who stormed toward the porch. Here and there unit leaders waved their arms, screaming frantically, trying to shepherd their men into some sort of order. Unheeded, they were elbowed away, were shunted into quiet backwaters like logs in a freshet.

The door flew open and Mackenzie shot out, his diminutive figure broadened unbelievably by layer upon layer of overcoats, sleeves dangling over his hands, tails flapping about his heels. Behind him loomed Van Egmond. Mackenzie's voice was high and shrill. "Now we're ready! Now we're ready. We can — "

Van Egmond shook his head impatiently. Lount, close by, caught Gil's eye, jerked his head toward the gesticulating Scot. Wedging his way through the press, Gil slipped up onto the porch. Mackenzie broke off in the midst of a phrase, wheeled on Gil. "What are you doing here? Why aren't you with your men? Why — "

Gil spoke soothingly. "I'll be with 'em as soon as we get to town. They're waiting for us there. I just wanted to tell you that the boys hope you won't give the Compact the chance to pick you off. We need you."

He caught an approving gleam in Van Egmond's eyes as the flush faded from Mackenzie's face, his expression became calmer. The old soldier stepped forward. "Ve haf persuaded Mac dot he cannot be rash. Me, I am jost old fool. It not matter vere I go."

"That's right. That's right." Mackenzie's voice was more level; something of his old decision crept back into his tones. "The colonel's in command. Soldiering's no business of mine." He suddenly looked about him, bewildered. "*You* ought to be talking to them. Not I." He stepped back from the railing, pushed the old man forward.

Van Egmond's beard shook. "Dere is no time to talk. Ve issue bulletin ven ve shall beat dem, yes." Then his voice blared out, harsh and guttural, crisp orders snapped into the air, terse, concise. Chaos began to fade and the men, eyes on the tall figure, slipped awkwardly into line behind their leaders.

There were more orders. A large body swung clumsily about, began to trail off toward a belt of woods about half a mile away on the west side of Yonge Street. Then a smaller force crossed the road, headed for a stretch of pine and brush nearly opposite the position of the west flank.

The sound of feet swishing through dried grass grew fainter. Gil, watching the masses of men on Gallows Hill, saw that they had halted, were deploying unskillfully to the right and left. Van Egmond nodded. "Dey are as vorse as ve. Ve haf only to stand firm. Now — der horses!"

Hoofs thudded and a wizened man led two white mares around the corner of the building, a black clumping close behind. Mackenzie turned to Gil. "Now — what was I going to do with you? What — "

Van Egmond frowned. "I vill borrow him." He turned to Gil. "You are not soldier? No? But you haf eyes. You can t'ink. You will go to der voods. Ven you see somet'ing not right, you send a man running to me. And remember, de man you send, he vill not haf your eyes, your brains. Make vat you tell him simple like child-talk. So — he vill not stumble der feet over big vords. You haf rifle?"

"Hidden in the barn," said Gil.

"Get it and go to der voods. Mac and I, ve shall be on der v'ite horses. You can see us easy. So run."

Gil caught a slight nod from Lount and ran off to the barn, where he found his short rifle hidden under a stack of useless iron. He looked longingly at the gray, who whinnied gently as he came into the stall. Then he shook his head. He'd be as well off on foot and the gray might shy — might even be hit. Regretfully he patted the dappled neck, then hurried into the sunlight. The two parties had nearly reached their positions and Van Egmond, Lount, and Mackenzie were riding slowly south.

The whole force was gone, waiting for the Compact onslaught. The whole force — He stopped, amazed. Crowds of men still loitered about in front of the tavern, some huddled in whispering groups, others stretched out contentedly in the sun. In the hush, he heard the riffle of cards, a muttered exclamation of triumph as a bit of pasteboard snapped to the ground.

He saw a familiar face, ran to the nearest knot. "Hi! Parsons! Haven't you boys got your orders?"

There was an awkward pause. Gil caught a mutter from a near-by pair in deep consultation. "But I *got* to get home tomorrow night. She's more'n eight months along, near's I can reckon. It'll come any time and — "

Parsons cleared his throat. "We got our orders all right. But — "

he held out his empty hands—"but that's all. Ain't got anything to fight with. Even the pikes is gone. Tried to steal an axe from the Sharon fellers but—" He spat. "Just ain't anything for us to do."

Gil racked his brains. More than one hundred able and willing men! Their presence might make the victory easier, less bloody. Arms for them? Where? Only in the City Hall at Toronto, the City Hall that might have been taken without loss a dozen times.

"Like to do *some*thing," growled Parsons.

Gil caught his arm. "You can! Are you a good runner?"

"Best this side the Ottawa River," said Parsons.

"Know two others who are good?"

"H'm—Jake Woods, he's most as good as I am. So's Clem Hodder."

Gil suddenly grinned. "Well, I can't give you arms but I can use your legs. Come on."

The three started off south past the sheds. Then a hidden raspy voice twanged. "And if I catch any of you fooling with that black bag, I'll stuff you so full of calomel you'll be spitting till the Day of Judgment. I'll—"

The end of a rusty musket bobbed into sight, followed by a familiar shabby beaver.

Gil nearly dropped his rifle. "Doc! What the hell are you doing here?"

Richland's watery eyes tried to glare, then dropped sheepishly to the ground. "Oh, well." Then he began to bluster. "I heard about goings-on here and I knew Head was coming out. Can't shove that many fools together in one pasture without *some*one's getting hurt. Who's going to look after 'em? Need someone older'n a cub like you. I—"

Gil looked at him solemnly. "What did I use to hear you say about medicine and politics being a bad mixture?"

Richland grunted, showed a battered case of lancets that jutted from a frayed pocket. "Never heard me say anything about surgery and politics, did you?" He flipped back the end of a long woolen muffler. "Now—where's this battle of yours?"

It was damp and chilly in the woods. The men who crouched or knelt behind thick trunks, or screened themselves in masses of brushwood, looked pale and shrunken in the shifting light that filtered down through the interlaced branches. Some of them fiddled nervously with the trigger guards of rifles or muskets. Others mechanically dug pike points into soft earth or crumbling bark.

Gil worked through to the edge of the woods, Dr. Richland close behind him. The ground to the southwest was partially masked by a gentle fold. To the south and east, he could see the shifting masses of the militia, motionless along the crest of the hill.

"What do you think they're doing, Doc? Waiting for us to come on?" asked Gil.

Richland blinked. "If they didn't have a real soldier leading 'em, I'd say so. But Fitzgibbon's a mighty sound man."

"Doesn't look much like moving now," objected Gil.

Richland shook his head impatiently. "That's because you can't see everything. Likewise, 'cause you don't understand what you do see. Fitzgibbon knows he's got militia that's most as bad as what you've got. He knows you won't run away, so he's putting every man's feet in just the right place, heading him in just the right direction and then most likely wiping his nose for him."

Gil cocked his head. "Can't hear the bands any more."

" 'Nother sign he's probably coming on. He's sent 'em back. Ain't nothing that'll take the heart out of a band like a nice bullet smack through the bass drum."

Gil, stretched out flat among dead leaves and pine needles, studied the motionless lines. Here and there metal glinted from the dark mass. Rare bits of red, of light green, showed against the prosaic, peaceful shades of civilian clothes — some devoted militia officer who had bought the prescribed uniform out of his own pocket, some half-pay officer who had dug a treasured, creased souvenir of active days out of a hair trunk. The distant scene suggested nothing so much as a crowd at the edge of the cricket grounds, along the race track, waiting for some spectacle, after which they would all straggle off home. Suddenly they became personal. Each glint of metal seemed to flash directly into the woods. Gil felt his heart beating faster. A strange, empty feeling sprang up in the very center of his being, spread slowly over his entire body.

"Lot of people there," said Doc amiably.

Gil stirred uneasily. "Why don't we do something?"

"Are doing something," said Doc. "Waiting — and not losing our heads."

Gil looked back over his shoulder. In the bright sunlight of the open fields to the rear he could see two white horses, a black, where Mackenzie, Van Egmond, and Lount were stationed. About him in the woods men shifted, grumbled, talked in broken phrases: "And I thought we were just going to march into town and let Head see us. Didn't know Mac—" . . . "And hell, all we been waitin' for's to get the Dutchman here. If Anderson hadn't got killed the first day, I'd be back in Lloydtown now and Mac'd be at Gov'ment House—" . . . "And I tell you, it was at that farmhouse near where we stopped the first night. 'Member the girl? Well, she come out to talk to me when you was asleep. Went off to that grove with her. She was—" . . . "All I ask is that schools is taken out of Strachan's hands and give to the people. That's why I'm here." . . . "That ain't it. We got a right to know how our money's spent. We got a right to say how it's spent. Now, take Colborne—"

Doc yawned. "Listen at 'em, Gil. That's the way folks have been talking before fights since Cain killed Abel. I remember when Brock came to Detroit with all his Indians, two fellers near me was arguing whether a hen had kidneys. Got pretty mad about it, too."

Gil grinned mechanically, then burst out, "Wish something'd happen." His hand closed about the butt of his rifle. "There's nothing to *do*."

Richland squinted up at the trees. "Well, now, if I was Van Egmond, I guess I'd like to see what was happening in that dead space just in front of us. Guess I really would—"

Gil sprang to his feet. "Parsons! Can you get up that pine so you can see over that rise? Well—high as you can. Shout down if you see anything."

Parsons scrambled expertly up in a shower of bark and dead twigs. "What can you see?" called Gil.

"Nothing much. Still up there on Gallows. Don't seem to be as many as they was." Then he yelped in excitement. "Hi! They got cannon! Two of 'em! They're wheelin' west of Yonge!"

Gil swung himself into a lower branch. Two brass barrels shone clean and clear, a cluster of men wrenching at their wheels. He was about to send Woods to tell Van Egmond, then realized that the old man could see that section of the field as well as he could.

He slipped down, bark pattering to the ground. "All clear in front of us, Doc."

Richland rubbed his chin, gnarled fingers scraping over the stubble. "Well, now, seems to me Van Egmond'd like to know that."

Gil beckoned to Woods, gave him the message. Richland held up his hand. "One thing more. Tell him nothing happening—*so far*."

Woods nodded, zigzagged off through the trunks. The waiting men eyed Gil curiously, clucked to themselves. Somehow, the sending of the messenger seemed to tie them in closer with Mackenzie and the Dutchman, it linked them up with a world that lay outside the dank woods.

Then, high in the tree, Parsons whistled shrilly. "They're movin'. They're movin'!"

Gil ran to the edge of the woods. The right wing of the militia had begun a slouching march north across rolling fields, heading straight toward the body that Van Egmond had posted to the east of the road. Pieces cocked with sharp clicks, snapping like many feet walking over dried branches.

By Gil's elbow, Doc snarled over his shoulder. "Don't fire yet. You can't afford to waste powder until you've got City Hall and you're a hell of a long way from it."

Gil, fascinated, watched the slow surge of the militia. It was like being a spectator at some deadly kind of game, a game which he could watch, detached, untouched. He could—

Then something twinkled just over the fold in the ground in front, figures moved rapidly. There was a stunning crash and something yelled wailingly through the air, high above the trees. The echoes of the shot died away as pale faces looked skyward. Branches crackled and Parsons slithered to the ground, palms raw and clothes ripped. "The guns! The guns!"

Gil gulped, nodded. "I—I could see 'em. On the high ground beyond that fold. How many?"

"Same two!" gasped Parsons. "They've—"

Then heads spun round as broken fire crashed out from the advancing right wing. All over the woods men sprang to their feet, blazing senselessly and filling the grove with acrid smoke and a shattering din. Richland raved among them, knocking up muzzles, waving his arms. "You God-damn fools! You can't hit anything from there. Watch your own front! Watch your own front!"

Gil jammed his hands in his pockets to control their incessant shaking, tried to break through the feeling of tightness about his throat. The few men in command looked helplessly about or joined in the wild, indiscriminate firing. Gil seized the nearest man. "Get up that tree a little way. Pick off the gunners. They're in range!"

Men hesitated. One started slowly up a pine trunk. The rest, their attention seized, stopped to watch him, forgetful of the crashing of musketry to the east.

Another flashing roar, another weird scream in the air that ended in an abrupt smash. Trees quivered and a heavy branch thundered to the ground. The man who had started up the pine dropped quickly to earth, began to back away toward the far edge of the woods, glassy eyes on the soft blue of the sky above.

Gil started with the general drift, then caught himself. "Hold on! That can't do you any harm. They're aiming high. Stay in the front edge. Stay — "

There was another stunning roar. Light branches and twigs pattered down, drummed on the heads below. Someone shouted, "Let's get out of here!" Gil reached out, caught the nearest man by the collar. "Stay where you are! Afraid of a few dead sticks? Get back to — "

A strong hand wrenched at his arm. He whirled angrily about, found himself face to face with Richland, who, grim-mouthed, was pointing. At first Gil could see nothing. Just the drift of smoke from the last discharge. Then something blurred over the slight rise in front, blurred and took shape in a line of heads that rose and rose as unseen feet climbed the easy slope — pot hats, caps, a single shako in front, its brass plate winking in the sun.

"That's it," snapped Richland. "That other move was a feint. We're catching the brunt."

The pieces slammed again and far in the rear boards crashed as hot iron balls ripped into the walls of Montgomery's Tavern.

Gil looked quickly about. Men were weaving and shuttling aimlessly among the trunks. He unslung his rifle, knelt at the edge of the woods, shouting: "Give it to 'em!" The target was perfect and their own cover good. The men must see that. No need to bother about them. They'd — Slowly his finger tightened on the trigger. The rifle bucked, its report unheard in the slamming roar that tore out from the oncoming line that had halted to fire. Gil saw the shako pitched into the air, saw its owner, a slim man in a red jacket and ordinary trousers, look about—annoyed more than startled. He began to reload hurriedly, eyes on the straggling line that was beginning to advance uncertainly. The shako still lay on the ground. Ramming home a charge, Gil felt the rammer slip from his fingers. The man in the red coat was Carleton Sperry, a flushed, excited Carleton, who turned to shout something to the men behind him.

Gil set his teeth, recovered the rammer. He felt suddenly glad that his shot had gone high. He'd pass up the red coat as his next mark. He swung the muzzle toward a sober black coat, felt his hand tremble as he recognized a plodding good-natured lawyer whose struggling practice Forsyth Stensrood had tried to help.

The lines were nearer now, their step more assured. Gil leveled his muzzle, shut his eyes. Let fate direct the course of the ball. Let—

He staggered back, Richland's hand on his shoulder. "Get out of here, you damned young fool! D'you think I wasted all those years on you so's some damned Compacter could stuff your head and hang it over his mantel? Get out of here."

Gil started, saw that the woods were empty. The field beyond was covered with a mass of men who tore over the dried grasses toward the tavern. Across Yonge Street, a white horse reared and thrashed as a shapeless man in a welter of coats raved and screamed at the fugitives who butted on unheeding, rifles, muskets, and pikes flung blindly into the air.

Gil bellowed. "Come back! Come back! They haven't beaten you! We'll—"

Then Richland seized his arms, hurried him protesting out of the woods in whose farther edge men were moving cautiously, prodding piles of brushwood with long bayonets.

Gil began to run. "Come on, Doc. We'll rally 'em by the tavern. Still time!" He pointed to the first wave of fugitives, who, winded by their half-mile run over rough ground, had begun to slacken their gait, to look back over their shoulders.

"Might do it," puffed Richland.

"Might? We've damn well got to," panted Gil. He saw another white horse circling about the field. "Colonel! Colonel Van Egmond! Hold 'em there. There—by the porch. We'll—"

The field pieces, far behind them, slammed again. Again there was a wail of torment high in the air. The walls of the tavern shook, bulged, blasted out a cloud of dust and splinters. The fugitives, spurred by the near-by crash, ran the harder, while from every door and window men scrambled, jostled, fought, to get out of the flimsy trap.

There was more rifle fire off to the east, a fresh scurry of fleeing men. Richland began to lag behind. Gil caught his arm. "Got a horse, Doc?"

"Think I'd turn Bessie loose in a lot of damned fools like this? She's home where she belongs," wheezed Richland.

Gil hesitated. "Look, Doc. I'll get my beast. You can mount up behind me. We'll go on up Yonge and head 'em off, chase 'em back. Wait by that elm. I'll pick you up."

Richland nodded, swerved toward the elm. Gil sprinted toward the sheds which were now clear of the last of the fugitives. Mackenzie, Lount, and Van Egmond were nowhere to be seen. At least, he'd be able to help them, as they must have had the same idea and pushed on north ahead of the broken wrack. He'd—

There was a sudden shout. "There he is. It's Gil Stensrood!"

Two riders, one in a hunting coat, the other in dark blue, suddenly turned from the road and raced toward him, pistols raised. "Give up, Gil! Give up or I'll shoot."

Gil dug his heel in the ground, reversed his course, and ducked between two outbuildings. No Parry Campbell was going to catch him. The hoofs came on. Gil remembered that a pen, where horses were turned loose, opened beyond a low shed. He tore into it, across the trodden, soggy ground, caught the rails on the other side, and swung himself over just as Campbell, eyes eager, tore through the gate. There was a flat crack and a ball sang over Gil's head. Quickly he ducked back of the shed, slammed the heavy gate of the pen shut before Campbell could recover himself, and ran across the fields, smiling grimly as he heard Campbell's mount racing about the pen as its master tried to find an exit.

Then he thought of Doc, but the ground about the lone tree was empty. He started to shout, but spluttering fire from the south drowned his words.

He looked back hastily, saw the lines advancing slowly, obviously fearing an ambush, while ahead of them a few mounted men raced and scurried.

It was all over. At least for the moment. There was nothing he could do. The gray was lost beyond all recovery. The nearest fugitive was a hundred yards away and the militia lines were creeping nearer and nearer all the time. He drew a deep breath, then hit off across country toward the dark western woods at a steady trot. There was no fear of pursuit at the moment, for the foot soldiers were now far behind and any horseman who took after him could be easily lost in the woods into whose shelter he was about to plunge. He'd keep west, then circle around to the north. Perhaps he'd meet some of the belated reinforcements, perhaps he could rally them. One solid body thrown at the tavern now could change the whole picture, for, he reasoned, the Compact forces would have lost what little organization they ever had in the flush of victory. The reinforcements! Sandra! Either she'd missed them or there had been none on the main road. At any rate, she was safe at Nipigon. A sudden chill swept over him as he thought of what might have happened had she come back to report at the moment of contact. No. She was safe at Nipigon. He heard a faint shouting behind him, saw more riders moving toward him across the fields. He lowered his head, lengthened his stride, and soon felt the dry branches of the woods crackle beneath his feet. He'd find Doc and . . .

XXII

Nipigon Lodge—1837

JANET, outwardly calm, bent over her embroidery. "And he—he was all right?"

Sandra, huddled in a big chair by the east window, nodded quickly, her lips tight.

"I still can't see why he didn't at least stop in here," said Janet.

Barnabas, seated by the fireplace, glared at Forsyth, who, eyes on the floor, paced up and down the long living room. The gold-headed stick rapped on the floor. "Fors! If you really want to mount sentry, get my old musket and run down to Mackenzie. Tramp, tramp, tramp! Tramp, tramp, tramp! Damn it, you're wearing a path right through my brain."

Surprised, Forsyth looked up. "Sorry, Father. Just don't seem to be able to sit still." He dropped to the long sofa, then jumped up again and stood behind Sandra's chair, staring out the window toward Yonge Street.

Barnabas snorted. "Well, try to stand still, at least. As to Gil not coming here—why, that shows he's got some glimmerings of sense. Makes me almost hopeful. He was afraid I'd have tied him up for one thing. For another, he didn't want Head's men ransacking Nipigon."

Sandra, chin in hand, said absently, "That's what Graves said, too."

Barnabas's head snapped back. Janet gasped. "Graves!"

Barnabas scuffed his feet. "Damnation! Graves! He there too?" He shook his mane. "What a fine lot of imbeciles I've sired!"

Eyes still on the road, Sandra said quietly, "Gil's not an imbecile—except that he wouldn't let me stay."

Barnabas jerked around in his chair. "And you're the worst imbecile of the lot. Must have Stensrood blood in you somewhere.

Galloping out just because you'd been reading too much Scott and thought Gil had changed into Ivanhoe or something. You make me —you make me—" He rose stiffly, crossed the floor, and laid a hand on Sandra's shoulder. "You make me very proud of you, my dear."

She smiled up at him. "It was the only thing for me to do—and besides, I wasn't going to let that de Grassi girl beat me." Her smile faded. Her eyes swung back to the end of the drive where a little Negro was watching Yonge Street, a white cloth in his hands. "Have you heard from Cameron and Mary?"

"Cam's been arrested," said Janet, head lower over her work.

Sandra gasped. "Cam? Arrested? Why?"

"I should be, too, if I went into town," said Forsyth. "We've always fought the Compact. We defended Innis." He read an unspoken question in Sandra's suddenly upturned eyes. "You wonder why I'm not with Mackenzie? In the first place he wouldn't have me. He thinks I'm too moderate. In the second place, I don't think this is the way to fight the Compact. Those people step aside and you find that you're attacking the Crown." His face grew even graver. "But—but—I don't know. Perhaps Gil's right. We've tried everything else—and nothing has happened. Perhaps everything we've wanted'll come out of this. And we're just standing by. We're—"

Sandra jumped to her feet. "I can't just sit here. I'm going out to the road to watch. Gil said they needed more men badly. He said—" She stopped, one hand lifted, head turned toward the south. The others looked at her wonderingly.

Then, faintly in the hush of the room, a new sound was born, a sound like old, dried logs burning briskly in a deep fireplace, like distant footsteps crunching over dead twigs. She ran to the window. The ridgepole of Montgomery's Tavern showed far off, rising above a tangle of naked branches. To its right, patches of open fields lay empty and desolate in the sun. The phantom crackling rolled on, spread.

"It's come," said Barnabas softly. "It's come."

Sandra, forgetful of the waiting Negro down the drive, quickly turned the high-backed chair so the old man faced the window that framed that distant ridgepole, now darkly sinister in her eyes. Janet quietly slipped her arm about Sandra's shoulders, drew her close. Forsyth, tragedy in his eyes, rested his hand on the back of his father's chair.

The crackling ebbed away, swelled, ebbed, in irregular waves. Barnabas fumbled with the head of his stick. "It's ragged. It's ragged. Both sides. Aaah! Look!" His old finger pointed south through the clear panes. The ridgepole seemed to have moved nearer, was silhouetted against a whitish cloud, thin but distinct, that rose sluggishly somewhere beyond it.

"Rain coming," whispered Janet. "The locks will get wet. They won't be able to fight."

Forsyth laughed shortly. "Rain? My dear, you saw the same thing, years ago, when Pike landed his Yankees beyond the old Fort. Smoke, powder smoke."

"Gil's there! Gil's there," said Sandra, half to herself. "They can't hurt him. They can't touch him. They can't." She felt a sudden pressure on her shoulder, caught the older woman's hand reassuringly.

"Bah!" said Barnabas. "I'm never afraid of Gil getting hurt. It's the others, the Compacters. They're the ones to worry about." He scraped the floor with his stick. "Remember the night they burned the effigies here? That Yankee scamp Josiah told me Gil nearly broke a man in two and then tried to turn him inside out." He turned slightly in his chair. "You say that foreigner, Van — Van — what's his name? — is there? *He*'ll show 'em what to do! He'll — "

The deep-throated booming slam, far off, but menacing seemed to force his half-spoken words back into his throat. Pale, he muttered: "Ours?"

Sandra shook her head, hand to her mouth. "No. No. It can't be. Gil said they didn't have any. He said — "

Again the room vibrated almost furtively to the distant brazen voice. Forsyth winced. "And just rifles against cannon!" He swung away from the window, then whirled back as though moved by an invisible hand.

"Some didn't even have rifles — even have pikes," said Sandra. "I saw men cutting clubs in the woods across the road. Just clubs." Her voice broke.

Suddenly Barnabas started. "Listen." The small-arms fire had died away, burst out again feebly, died.

Sandra shut her eyes, tried to recall the fields about the tavern as she'd seen them not long ago, saw the hungry, ragged men who were there because it was where they felt they ought to be. Nothing held them, nothing forced them except their own deep feeling that what they did was right. Poor farmers and rich, men from towns, men from lonely clearings, blacksmiths, grooms, lawyers, bakers, doctors — She opened her eyes at a fresh booming that was louder and without the old undertone of snarling rifles and muskets. She craned her neck to see the open fields, but they were still lifeless, unpeopled — belonged to a different world than that which echoed and smoked out of sight to the east.

She heard a question from Janet, then Barnabas's short reply. "Can't tell. May mean anything — everything. Mackenzie may have fallen back. He may have chased the militia away — may have captured the guns. May have — "

Forsyth cleared his throat. "One thing. We haven't heard anything about that lot that went off toward the Don. They may be working back toward Head's flank. They may be — "

Then the slowly creeping wreaths of thin white that had been coiling up from the hidden ground were blotted out. A black, angry cloud began to rise about the tavern roof. The four by the window leaned forward, breathless. The cloud thickened, spread, grew ruddy, livid about its lower edges.

"The tavern. It's burning." Janet's voice was unsteady.

The white head beside her shook. "Doesn't *mean* anything, I tell you. Stray cannon ball — embers jarred from a fireplace — untended fire — anything — nothing — "

Janet's eyes saw the mounting, swelling cloud. But her mind paraded tauntingly before her an old, old memory of a bigger, blacker cloud over Toronto, with Yankee ships pouring men ashore and all the garrison fleeing east under the timorous Sheaffe. Sheaffe's regulars had burned the Don bridge. At this very moment it might be burning a second time.

Sandra's low voice brought her back through the years. "More smoke. Oh — it's spreading east; it's — "

"It's Montgomery's own house — the farmhouse," whispered Forsyth.

"And the cannon have stopped," said Janet. She suddenly became aware that her hand was limp on the chair back, close to her husband's, that Sandra's arm was about her shoulder protectively.

Barnabas rose slowly. His strong old face was singularly gentle. "I'm afraid, my dears, that we must be ready for bad news — bad news."

Janet suddenly threw back her head. "People may be coming by here. They'll need things." Calmly, as though ringing for tea, she pulled a bell cord. Primula, ashy-faced, shuffled into the room.

"Yankees come to fotch me?" she asked quaveringly. Behind her, half-hidden by the portieres, Thomas's wrinkled face showed, fear-masked.

Barnabas shook his stick. "No Yankees coming here. If they did — well, I'm here. Stop that sniveling. Now — Janet, my dear — "

Janet spoke quietly. "Primula, get together all the food you can. Have the boys carry it out to the woods back of the stables."

Primula's face lost its ashy tint, began to glow with drama. "What we do with it? Bury it?"

"Give every man we send there what he wants."

Barnabas drew closer to her. "Have you thought that she might be giving to people who — ah — don't need it? Have you thought that some people might object?"

Janet paused, forehead wrinkled. Her husband cut in quietly. "If anyone asks you *why* you're doing it, tell them it's at my order. Mine. Understand? Good. And Thomas — get out all my warm things. Have them ready for anyone who needs them — out in the woods."

"And that by *my* order, Thomas!" barked Barnabas. "And put all my things where you can get at them."

Thomas stared. "That new overcoat? With the fur to it?"

"Damn it, yes!" snapped Barnabas. "*I* don't need it. I'm getting soft. Pampering myself like an old man. Overcoats are made for old men and fools! What did I want one for?"

"Yes, *sir!*" said Thomas, wonderingly.

Sandra touched Barnabas's arm. "You really think it's all over?"

He bent to her gently. "My dear, I'm afraid so — for the moment anyway."

She leaned against the arm of a chair. "And — and what are we going to do?"

He touched her shoulder gently. "Keep our heads."

She clenched her fists. "But Gil! How can I — "

"Anything you want to do you can do best, just as I said, with a cool head. And — don't think I'm harsh — after all he's my grandson — there are bigger things on the wind today than just one man. Far bigger."

"Nothing's bigger to me than Gil," she said, young eyes on his.

"There's the world that you and he are going to live in. And that world's melting and reshaping at this very minute. How it reshapes will depend on everyone keeping his head — or hers."

Sandra bit her lip, turned away to the east windows. Then she felt her heart leap with apprehension. The little Negro stationed at the edge of the drive had dropped his white cloth and was running frantically across the dry lawn. She clutched at the strip of white that she'd discarded on coming into the house, bound it about her left arm, and started for the door. The heavy latch balked her efforts to open it. She strained again, found Forsyth at her elbow. The door swung open. She ran out, called, "What is it? Where are they?"

The little Negro, tongue lolling, panted, "Lot of folks. Comin' this-a-way."

Sandra caught him by the collar. "*Which* way?"

Pop eyes bulged. "I told you, miss. *This* way."

"But where from? Why didn't you wave the way I told you? I was watching."

"Don't wave less'n folks come from the north. These is comin' from town."

"What is it, Sandra?" Forsyth's voice sounded close by her side.

She turned, white-faced. "There are people coming this way. From town."

The Negro nodded emphatically. "Comin' up Hogg's Holler thicker'n fleas on a dog's back."

Forsyth nodded. "Go in and help Primula. She'll tell you what to do. Sandra, I'd be glad if you'd go stay with Janet. I'll go down to the end of the drive and see what's happening."

She looked at him, pleadingly. "Gil might be — "

He hesitated, then said: "All right. Come along."

She ran along by his side, trying to keep up with his long strides, the dry grass whipping about her ankles. "What can you see? What can you see?"

He halted at the edge of the road, threw back his head. She

hopped onto a flat stone, balanced delicately. "Why — why, there's nothing at all! The road's — "

"Look!" said Forsyth, pointing.

A straggle of men, hatless, empty-handed, suddenly topped the north slope of the hollow, paused, tense, staring back over their shoulders. The bottom of the hollow was hidden from them, but the opposite slope swarmed with running men.

She saw Forsyth's face set, saw the muscles about his firm mouth tighten. "It's a rout," he muttered. "Just a rout."

The bushes at the edge of the lawn crackled. A single figure, bareheaded, burst into the open, stopped short as though terrified at finding himself without cover, looked about, white-faced and wild-eyed. Forsyth ran toward him shouting: "Wait a minute! Wait a minute!"

The man froze for a second, then shot off across the lawn, head low and knees pumping. Forsyth called again but the man only ran harder, lost himself in a patch of woods to the north.

Sandra got down from her rock shakily, clung to one of the stone gateposts. Her eyes, haunted, stared at Forsyth. "I saw that man. When I got to the tavern. My dress was muddy and he tried to scrape off the mud. He was clumsy, like a child trying to help." She looked back at the road. The foremost fugitives were abreast of her now, legs driving wearily, heads rolling on aching shoulders. She put out a hand, called huskily, but the broken boots drummed the harder on the rough surface. She called again: "Have you seen — "

Forsyth pushed past her, ran out into the road, arms held high. The men looked at him from glassy eyes, swerved almost in unison, tore on. A single cracked voice bleated, "I ain't goin' to get took! I ain't goin' to get took!"

Forsyth cried: "Turn off the road. Make for the woods behind the stables. We've got food for you. We've — "

He was left standing in the road. One wave of panic-stricken men had passed him. Another was pouring up over the edge of the hollow.

Sandra looked back toward the house. Hatless and coatless, Barnabas stood by the edge of the stables, head erect and stick waving. A few half-crouching men gathered about him, then followed his gesture and ran off toward the hidden woods. She heard louder footsteps, saw more men beating their way toward her. Some of them were in the last stages of exhaustion and ran mechanically, arms sawing the air, feet dragging in wasteful effort. A man on a black horse suddenly loomed into sight, rode swiftly along the far edge of Yonge Street, waving his arm and shouting to the running men.

Sandra ran a few steps toward him. "Colonel Lount! Colonel Lount!"

But his shouts and the beat of hoofs and boots drowned her voice. Forsyth ran toward her. "Sandra! You *must* stay — "

She only shook her head. "He would have known. He would have known. He thought a lot of Gil. He — "

Then something white blurred at the crest and a tall old man with a flowing beard came into view, shaking his reins as he reeled in the saddle. Again Sandra called. "Colonel Van Egmond! Colonel — "

The old man reined in, leaned courteously from the saddle. The hand that he raised to his broad hat shook with fatigue. "Ah! It is our messenger. Diss iss a bad day!"

She caught at his bridle. "Where — where's Gil? I want to know." Out of the corner of her eye she saw Forsyth edging closer. "This is his father. We want — "

The white head shook wearily. "I only know vere iss Antony Van Egmond. Dot iss all. Mac? Vletcher? De odders?" He shrugged.

Forsyth's grave voice broke in. "Is it very bad, Colonel? You see — my son — "

"I know. I know. Yes. It iss bad. Dey run like de French after Vaterloo. *Sauve qui peut.*" He swayed in the saddle.

"Colonel — " began Sandra. "Were — was there — "

He touched her hair gently. "You vould ask about der men. So. Ve lose few. Me, I haf seen just von man fall. No more. Him I do not know." He sighed. "But dey run like devil, just der same."

"Come into the house and rest," urged Forsyth, alarmed by the parchment-like pallor of the old man's face.

The white head shook. "I most go on. Maybe der iss vork to be done."

"Trying to rally them?" asked Forsyth.

Through his blanket of exhaustion the old man laughed. "If so I sharpen dem de teeth, maybe dey can bite old Strachan. But dot iss all. Guns, lances, dey t'row over like childrens."

He suddenly wrenched himself about in the saddle, stared south. On the far crest of Hogg's Hollow a single rider reined in, whooped, snatched off his hat, gestured north with it.

Van Egmond muttered wearily under his breath, straightened himself with an effort. "Dere dey come. Leetle Compact pups vat t'ink dey are Murat." He laughed mirthlessly. "Head's hussars, riding down der poor boys vat try to fight." He raised his hand to his hat, swayed again as the horse lurched off.

Sandra felt a touch on her arm. "We can't do any good here," said Forsyth gently. "Better come back to the house."

She shook her head obstinately. "Gil may come by."

Forsyth pointed to the opposite crest of Hogg's Hollow. The horseman had been joined by others. The group hung against the sky for a moment, then swept down the steep, crazy slope at a mad gallop. "See that?" he asked.

She nodded, uncomprehending.

"Well, if Gil can't see them, he knows that they'll be there. He's got a good level head. If he's caught up in all this, he'll take to the woods. He won't tramp along the roads like those poor, bewildered men, just asking to be taken. No, Gil'll take to the woods where they can't follow. And remember, he's shot over this country since he was big enough to hold a fowling piece."

She took one last look at the road, then turned and walked blindly up the drive, hand on Forsyth's arm.

The warm rooms of Nipigon seemed curiously remote, detached. Janet sat close by the east windows, her work untouched in her lap. Barnabas, mouth a tight line, sat rigid in his chair by the fire. He looked up inquiringly at Forsyth and Sandra as they came in.

Forsyth nodded. "It's a rout, Father. No doubt about that."

Barnabas stirred uneasily. "Had some wild stories from the men who came through the yard out there."

Sandra sat on a cricket by his feet. "We saw Colonel Van Egmond. He says the men are just scared. He says no one — almost — was hurt."

Barnabas brightened. "He said that? He wasn't just being soothing, was he?"

"I don't think so," said Forsyth.

"Well, well, well." Barnabas stroked his stick. "Maybe this'll be all right after all. No one's hurt. Head, if he's got any sense, which he may have, will issue amnesties. The row'll force the Crown to see what's going on here. Then London'll have to take steps to fix things." He rubbed his chin slowly. "Suppose that little Scotchman was shrewd enough to have thought all that through?"

Forsyth sighed. "I hope so. And I pray that Head'll do what you say. Or his successor. They'll be sending one out any time now on account of that old resignation. I'd like to think that's how it'll be. I'd like to." Then before his eyes came the vision of Strachan's flushed, angry face, Hagerman's unpitying swarthiness, Robinson's sincere acceptance of his own position: someone of finer clay who must regretfully discipline the lower orders. "Did any go to the woods, Father?"

"A few. Most were too scared." He started. "Eh? Sandra? What's the matter?"

Sandra had run suddenly to the window, was staring out toward Yonge Street, terror on her face. She pointed. "Look! Those men!"

The others crowded about her, wondering. Then they were silent. Along the road, guarded by a few horsemen, a line of men stumbled slowly. Their heads were bowed and their shoulders sagged pitiably. Their arms were bound behind them and lengths of frayed rope linked each man to the plodding figure ahead. Barnabas flung open the window. Shouts, scraps of excited laughter, burst from the riders.

The stick rapped sharply. "Cattle! Cattle! They can't do that! Roping free-born Canadians together and driving 'em to town like beeves. Damn it, I say they can't—" His voice rose to a high bark. "And what the devil's *this* indignity?"

A group of riders had turned into the drive, were trotting up toward the house. The leader wore a well-fitting red coat, a cocked hat whose points hung down toward his shoulders. There were other uniforms in the group with him. In the rear men in plainer dress rode compactly.

Barnabas drew the window tight shut. "I shall meet them at the door. Janet, you and Sandra will be good enough to occupy the sofa. Fors, I'd be glad to have you with me."

There was a scuffle of hoofs outside. The knocker jarred. Barnabas stood by the wide doors, nodded to Thomas, who glanced at his master, then drew himself up in impeccable dignity and grasped the latch. Sandra, tense on the sofa, heard his soft voice: "And who shall I announce?"

Several voices answered, then one, sharp and firm, snapped, "Your places, gentlemen!" Then, courteously, "Colonel Fitzgibbon. I'd like to see Mr. Barnabas Stensrood."

Barnabas stepped into the open. "I'm honored, Colonel. What may I do for you?"

Other uniformed men crowded in on Fitzgibbon's heels. The hangings framed the group like a stage. The Colonel's honest, Irish face was grave. "Her Majesty's service, Mr. Stensrood." He paused. Then, lower, "I'm sorry. Devilish sorry."

Barnabas's head went back. "What does Her Majesty's service require from *me,* may I ask?"

Fitzgibbon looked troubled. "That my men search the house. Your grandson, you know. I — I'm — oh, dash it. May I come in?"

Barnabas stepped aside. The elderly colonel edged past the portieres, glared at his staff, who hung reluctantly by the door. "Your grandson. He's always been with Mackenzie. This is awkward, but he was seen today."

"Is that against the law?" asked Barnabas. "I'm frequently seen myself."

Fitzgibbon looked almost pleadingly at him. "Don't make it harder for me than you must. I've got to search the house."

Barnabas bowed slightly. "I should presume that my word that he was not here would be sufficient."

"For me. Not, unfortunately, for Sir Francis. He is particularly anxious — ah — to know where your grandson is. In fact, he sent me — most unusual — I'm in command of the militia."

Barnabas flared. "That snipe! That simpering Foreign Office mistake! Since when has he begun to question the word of a Stensrood?"

The Irishman looked uncomfortable. "Sir Francis is — well, I guess he thinks that he might be here without your knowing it, so — " He stepped farther into the room, bowed courteously to Janet, started with surprise as he saw Sandra, nodded gravely to Forsyth. "Well — I've got to have the place searched."

Forsyth shook his head. "Jim, how can a decent chap like yourself play lackey to Head?"

Fitzgibbon flushed, swallowed hard. "It's not Head. It's the

Crown. I'd lackey the devil himself—for the Crown." He paused. "I hope you're not in this, Fors."

"You know where I've always stood. I don't change. Look here. Suppose you go back and tell Sir Francis that two loyal subjects, who look upon him and those who pull his strings as black offenses, refuse to allow the search?"

Fitzgibbon's hand shot out. "Don't, Fors, don't." He hesitated, dropped his voice. "He burned all the Montgomery houses. He burned Dave Gibson's. But—" he looked about the room—"Nipigon's been here a long time. I'd hate—"

"Search," said Barnabas.

"That's wise," said Fitzgibbon.

"Then you'll take your men away?" asked Forsyth.

Fitzgibbon coughed. "That's another thing. Not my orders, of course. Head gave 'em to Captain Donne of the Hamilton militia. He's out there." He coughed again. "He's got to leave a lieutenant, a sergeant, and five men here—until further notice. You're to ration them, billet them." His face grew redder. "I'm afraid—I'm afraid that none of you'll be able to leave the house without permission or without a—an escort."

"Do you mean to say that *I'm* going to feed a lot of men to please that unadulterated jackanapes? By God, sir, they won't get fat. They won't keep very warm in that old shed. They'll—"

"Excuse me, sir," said Fitzgibbon. "Martial law, you know. They'll pick their own quarters. They'll draw what rations—" His uncomfortable flush turned to a deep purple. "Oh, damn it, just give me some sort of a paper saying that you're with Head and cursing Mackenzie a bit." His eyes were pleading again. "It's for the Crown, after all. Then we can take the men and go—leave you in peace."

Barnabas stiffened. "Damn the Compact and all its works. And I'll write *that* to Head and add a few particulars." He bowed. "I'm afraid, Colonel, that your men will be tired waiting."

Fitzgibbon drew himself up, saluted stiffly, and clumped out, sighing. Then they heard his voice. "Take your men, Captain. You've got your orders. But for God's sake, use your head." There was a muttered response, then the old Irishman's strangled voice. "What a *hell* of a day!"

The door slammed. Boots clumped about on the second floor,

cupboards and closets echoed to thumpings and proddings. Sandra, eyes bright, clutched Janet's hands. "He's safe! He's safe! They'll *never* catch Gil. Never!"

Janet looked straight ahead of her. "I nearly screamed out when he asked about Gil. I knew he was all right. I knew it." She spoke in a low, rapid voice. "He'll hide away—just for a time. There'll be an amnesty. He'll come back to us. He'll never leave us again. They can't *catch* him. They—" She suddenly leaned back against the sofa, eyes closed, hand firm in Sandra's. Then she sat up, free hand searching for her work. "Do you know, Fors, I'd quite forgotten that we hadn't served a thing since breakfast. I'm turning into a very bad housekeeper."

Barnabas beamed on her. "Confound it, I wish Head could have heard you say that. Fors, I think the boys can bring back what they took out into the woods. If our gallant sentinels are curious, tell 'em that it's a family custom to dine in the woods until mid-December."

Overhead the boots clumped on. Men shouted and called to each other. Sandra rose slowly, walked to the west window and looked out onto the darkening world. Janet joined her, stroked her hair. "I never had a daughter, my dear. But I've got one now—and one that we're all very proud of."

Sandra leaned her head against Janet's shoulder. "He's out there, somewhere. They're after him. I can't stop thinking—"

A mist spread over Janet's eyes. She controlled the twitching of her throat. Then softly she sang:—

> "Who watcheth over all, whose eye is never sleeping,
> God make the dark night bright to the wanderer."

It was nearly dark as Gil threaded his way through thick woods that masked a low ridge. He reckoned that he had put a good ten miles between himself and Yonge Street, although distances were hard to judge in such broken country. He watched bars of sunlight slanting red between the trunks, decided that he'd better get his bearings, so he slipped to the edge of the woods, looked cautiously out. The west was a glory of gold and purple and apple-green, one bar of dense black cloud slashing across the top of the setting sun like a scar. Beyond the ridge, a mere crease of earth, the land rolled away flat, desolate, ragged trees sprinkled over it like the nap of a worn carpet. Occasional clearings glowed somberly, cold, forsaken. A single wretched road trailed away, diving behind screens of trees, slipping out like a lazy snake across the flats.

He shut his eyes, tried to picture the whole sweep of country, decided that he was well to the north and west of Weston. He nodded to himself, swung on north through the woods. He reasoned that the flight would carry the wreck of Mackenzie's men on and on out Yonge Street, or nearly parallel to it. The pursuit would be hot at first, but would soon lose its force. Doc had told him that raw troops, hot with their first victory, were harder to handle than beaten ones. They'd straggle off, go home, loot a little, thinking their work over. And such a breathing space would let Mackenzie and Van Egmond rally the scattered men, perhaps as far north as Holland Landing, well beyond the Compact reach. Then they'd try again.

He stopped by a cold spring, drank thirstily, kept on. Then a movement on the trail-like road caught his eye. He saw a dull glint of metal, a hint of white. From a clump of bushes he studied the road, then nodded, satisfied. There could be no doubt about it. A company, perhaps fifty strong, and at least partly armed, was swinging east. Their white arm bands told of their allegiance. He ducked his head, broke into an easy trot. He'd give them the news gently, then head them north. They'd be a fine nucleus for some swift raid to test out the Compact forces.

He kept well within the trees, judging the distance carefully. If he hit the road behind them, he'd have a tiring stern chase. Then his eyes widened. Another man was running west along the road, something white on his arm. He must have seen the column, for he was waving. Then the running man was nearer. The head of the column had caught sight of him and quickened its pace. The space between them closed and Gil could see the runner, sagging with exhaustion, talking to the leader.

Gil ran on. He wanted to shout, but that would have taken too much breath. Speed was better. He could, perhaps, do something to counteract the tale of disaster that the man might spread.

Then he saw something that sent him scurrying for cover. The leading men of the column had seized the newcomer, bound him.

A few men broke away, ran for the near-by woods, or plunged heavily back west. The others, stripping their white arm bands from their jackets, started after them, then gave up the chase, content with their one prisoner.

Gil, beneath a low spruce, raised his rifle, then dropped it wearily. What was the use? God-damned turncoats! Whirling about at the first sign of reverse! Nearly blind with helpless anger he watched the now shrunken column trudge on east, heard them shouting and laughing. They'd pose as loyal men, come to rescue Her Majesty.

He cursed mechanically, rolled over on his back. What was the best thing to do? If people were acting that way, Mac and the Dutchman would never rally a force. He crossed his arms back of his head, studied the stars that were beginning to spatter the blue of the sky. A train of agonized thought started in his mind. Sharp pictures of the red walls of Montgomery's Tavern, ragged lines of men coming across the fields — Almost viciously he blocked out the whole afternoon. There was still work to do and he couldn't let past regrets blur his mind.

He'd run across Doc somewhere. But it wouldn't be by going north. Stronger and stronger the conviction came to him that, for the moment, there was little profit in that quarter. But there was more to Upper Canada than the north. He snapped his fingers. That was it. Dr. Duncombe was operating — or should be — in the west, driving on from the border region or somewhere about it. Duncombe was said to have done very well in the matter of equipment, to have a strong force following him.

He scrambled to his feet, brushing pine needles from hands and knees. He'd swing down that way, traveling by night and calling for aid at the various Reform houses which he knew. The rebellion wasn't over. It was just beginning. He slapped at the haversack that swung by his side and, reassured by its tight bulge, struck out west. Later he'd turn south, find Duncombe, and join in the final lunge that would sweep the Compact out of Upper Canada forever.

XXIII

Flight — 1837

THE startling touch of mild fall weather that had ushered in the month of December had fled before gusts of cold, sullen winds that swept down from Georgian Bay and the mysterious plains beyond. Gil, peering out at the fading light over the hilly country back of Hamilton, cautiously parted the mask of straw that shielded him. The wind had freshened again and random flakes of snow were darting erratically about, pitching down from a sky that had the dull sheen of tarnished silver. He whistled soundlessly between his teeth. Snow would mean tracks and he would no longer be able to take to the comparative anonymity of bare ground. The trackers who had so nearly cornered him beyond Streetsville must not find his sign manual across white ridge and drifted valley.

He edged closer to the outer air, looked down at the tight farmhouse at the foot of the hill, then shot his body deep into the straw. There were half-a-dozen horses at the side of the house, a group of men about the kitchen door, a glint of metal, a slant of slung rifles. He had no fear of detection. The straw rick in which he had hidden was too common a place to search. Besides, it was honeycombed with tunnels grubbed out by exploratory pigs, tunnels that gave him a wide choice of well-screened exits. But if the riders stayed too long, he'd be delayed in getting away. Or if they took up quarters at the farm, he might have to lie by for an indefinite time.

He watched the horses, like little black toys, tossing their heads and stamping in the thin film of snow. Suddenly men appeared about the horses, several of which swung their heads toward the distant rick. Gil stiffened, ready for instant flight, then puffed in relief as the cavalcade trotted away to the east, obviously heading for the road to Toronto. The muffled hoofbeats died away and Gil saw a single dark figure, a sack slung over its shoulder, leave the house and begin a slow climb, circling well to the west but curving gradually toward the hiding place. It was lost for a moment, then reappeared beyond some stunted apple trees, clumping on through the snow. There was a cautious hail: "You there, Gil?"

Gil pushed aside the heap of straw. "Who were your friends, Jake?"

Jake, muffled in a long caped coat, carefully eased his sack to the ground, pushed back his sealskin cap. "Thought they were friends of yours. They sure were anxious to talk to you." His hands fumbled in the sack, drew out slabs of bread and meat, three bottles that frosted in the keen air. "You been all right?"

"Stiff as the devil," said Gil. "What have you got there?" He took the bread and meat greedily, eyes on the bottles.

"Hot tea in this one. Hot water in the others. Put 'em at your feet so's you'll be thawed when you start."

Gil, twisting in his narrow tunnel, worked the bottles down to his feet, felt the warmth creep through his heavy boots. He gulped the hot tea, eyes watering. "What news, Jake?"

Jake's square face puckered. "Got plenty. They caught Van Egmond. They caught Matthews. Don't know who else."

Gil's eyes darkened. The tea bottle remained unnoticed in his hand. "Caught 'em? But — "

The man's head wagged. "That's what they said. Head swears he's going to hang 'em all."

Gil scowled. "Let him try. Damn it, we've got hundreds of men in Toronto that didn't even get into the fight. They'll break into the jail. They'll — "

"Maybe," said Jake tersely.

"Van Egmond. Matthews. And — " He started. "How about Mac?"

For answer, the man dug into his coat, drew out a folded paper. "Take a look at that. Those fellers left it with me. Want me to nail it up on my door."

Gil reached for the sheet eagerly. The glaring type flared through the fading light. "Reward! By command of His Excellency, the Lieutenant Governor. A reward is hereby offered . . . One Thousand Pounds . . . apprehend and deliver up to Justice, William Lyon Mackenzie. . . . Further reward . . . five hundred pounds . . . David Gibson . . . Jesse Lloyd . . . Samuel Lount . . . Silas

Fletcher . . . Gilbert Stensrood . . . known to have been traitorously in arms against their Sovereign . . . God Save the Queen."

Gil grinned stiffly. "There's five hundred easy pounds for you, Jake."

"Shut up," said Jake. "Anyway, it shows most of 'em got away. Those bastards said they were all heading for the States."

Gil's eyes narrowed. "Mac's going to the States? Well, he must have known that there was no chance of rallying anything just now. I wonder. How about Duncombe? Can't see that I can help much there. Jake, I think I'll go on Mac's trail. He'll make for Buffalo, I guess. I'll run into him somehow."

Jake nodded. "Guess that's best." He dropped his voice. "I don't think Duncombe's going to do any better than Mac. You see, the doctor's a mighty fine man but—well, he just isn't a leader. And he can't seem to do any more about arms than Mac did. A whole lot'd join him if they thought he'd get anywhere. As it is— here! What d'you think I heated that tea for? Drink it."

Gil drained the rapidly cooling bottle, handed it back. "Well, I owe you a lot, Jake." He wriggled out into the thickening dusk, stowed most of the bread and meat into his haversack. "Guess I'll be getting along."

"Need money?"

Gil slapped his flat waist. "Got some gold in a belt."

"Know where to go?"

"Got that list you gave me. Didn't think I could use it, but it'll save me a lot, now that I'm going to Buffalo." He sniffed the crisp air, looked about. "Guess I'll trail up through that beechwood and start curving west." He held out his hand. "Well, thanks, Jake."

"Good luck, Gil."

Picking his course where the snow lay thinnest, Gil slipped up the hill while his host gathered up sack and bottles and trudged back to the lonely farmhouse.

The beech grove was hushed, mysterious. So far, little snow had filtered down through the branches and Gil's boots left few marks behind them. He plotted his course in a great arc that would curve west and then south. The bearing would be simple for a while, as through the trees he could catch the distant glimmer and sheen of Ontario.

The night grew darker as he swung along at an easy pace. The wood ended and he had to strike out across open fields, his moving figure a black point against the sharpening white. Then there were more woods, a country road to be crossed, a stretch of ancient forest beyond. From time to time he rested, his eyes seeking the icelike glow of the lake or resting wistfully on a point of light that marked a snug, warm farmhouse.

Toward midnight he judged that he had crossed over into Glanford and headed his course farther inland, for Jake had told him that the shore road was especially well-patrolled here and that parties were known to be circling into the back country. The snow was falling heavily now, hissing across fields or pattering against tree trunks. The wind, which was now in his face, stung his cheeks almost unendurably, dashed hard white particles into his eyes, sifted down his muffled neck. He set his teeth. "I'll be all right just as soon as I get to the border. Won't be walking like this forever," he thought. "Be all right when I get to the border." He rapped his boots against a bare rock to help circulation, ducked to the storm and kept on.

A sudden roaring of water thundered through the air. Gil, surprised, halted. Through a sharp hollow ahead he caught a hint of a dull ruffle of tossing waters, the sour smell of wet rocks. Then he moved cautiously down to the creek's edge.

The current, its swiftness mottled with flecks of creamy white, shot on in tossing swirls. Through the curtain of flakes, the opposite bank looked a good twenty yards away. Reasoning that such a stream must have a bridge, he worked up the bank, skidding on snowy rocks, catching himself by overhanging branches, the interminable slip and rush of the black stream at his elbow. At last he saw a dark patch spanning the water, a patch on which a thin crusting of white was slowly gathering. He circled away from the river to hit the country road that must connect with the bridge, found its rough surface under his feet, headed west and south again. Then he saw the flimsy handrails, white-capped, the roughness of the logs that reached from bank to bank. He'd be across and —

He brought up suddenly, heart beating wildly. Crouched by the white bank beyond the farther end, two figures waited, muskets in mittened hands. A third, rifle slung over a thick shoulder, was clumping up toward them. Gil blessed the padding of snow that had muffled his tread, and slipped behind a tree. Perhaps they'd go away now, leave him to the white night.

Then, in the unreal stillness of the storm, a voice sounded flatly. "What kep' you?"

There was an answering growl. "Got here soon's I could."

Peering cautiously out, Gil saw one of the crouching figures rise stiffly, stamping in the snow. "Ain't no one been by. God-damn foolishness, squattin' in the snow."

"No, it ain't," growled the newcomer. "Caught two fellers tryin' to get 'cross Twenty-mile Creek."

"They can have 'em." The man shouldered his musket, started heavily off. The third called to him. "Tell 'em to wake Powers when you get back. He relieves me and I'm near froze."

The woods were silent again, save for the eternal rush and splash of the creek. The two men across the bridge settled down with an air of finality.

Gil swore bitterly to himself. The bridge was barred irrevocably. What should he do next? There was no point in trying to work back downstream. The very presence of the picket at this place argued that there would be more toward the lake, possibly some upstream. But the latter course would be the safer. He broke from the cover of his tree, darted across the road.

There was no movement on the other side. Cold, boredom, and the flying flakes must have blinded the eyes of the shivering picket. Relieved, Gil worked back toward the creek, hoping that it might grow narrower before the next bridge was reached. But the churning waters raced on toward the flat lands that edged the lake far away, through a flumelike channel that seemed to widen rather than shrink.

He paused, irresolute. The stream must turn some millwheel lower down on its course, for the channel and banks looked well-tended. No tangle of debris offered a chance to cross, no fallen tree spanned the steep banks. He stared at the swirling waters and set his teeth.

He unslung his rifle, carefully drew the charge. Then he sent it in a long arc across the creek, heard it crash into yielding bushes on the other side. His haversack followed, its long straps trailing through the driving flakes. Swiftly he stripped, teeth chattering and fingers stiff, rolled his clothes into tight bundles, weighted them with small rocks, and sent them hurtling to join the rest of his equipment. His boots, landing with a soft thud, rolled back toward the water. Horrified, he watched them bounce from rock to rock until they stopped, settled in an unseen hollow.

Gingerly he stuck one foot in the water, wrenched it out quickly. The icy flood had seized it in pitiless jaws. For a moment he cursed himself for having burned his bridges by heaving his clothes to the other side. He shook his head, drew a deep breath, and plunged in.

For a second there was no sensation. Then the air was driven from his lungs. Red-hot blades of ice slashed and tore at him, numbed his thrashing arms, seemed to force his eyeballs from their sockets. The pain was unendurable, it was sheer agony. Something whacked at his knee under the water. His feet shot out from under him. He struggled, gasped as a swift ripple dashed across his face.

Suddenly there was ground under his feet. His hands were clutching, clawlike, among the roots of the bank. A desperate lunge carried him out of the water, rolling in the snow that sifted from the pines above.

The change was magical. The flaky air seemed balmy, tropical. He closed his eyes, and in the moment of closing he sprang to his feet, began to race up and down as he had seen an old Indian do, years ago, when he was shooting at Manitoulin Island. His mind began to clear. Action became reasoned instead of automatic. Running, he told himself that he was just an exposure case that he himself was treating. The warm wards of the Hospital were far away, but the principles of treatment were close.

Shivering violently, he bent over his haversack, drew out a flask, and drank deeply—drank again. His fingers fumbled with the cork, but at last it was firmly seated. He stowed the flask away and snatched at the towel, carefully dried, that was wrapped about his shaving things. It was small but thick and he rasped at chest, arms, and legs until the sluggish blood began to stir under his skin like a river of hot needles. He scrubbed, swung his arms, scrubbed again.

At last, creaking, he huddled into his clothes. He wished that he could start a fire. That would make everything much safer. But the thought of the picket downstream drove the idea from his mind. He managed with difficulty to sling his haversack over his shoulder, to pick up the rifle that lay unharmed in the brush. His legs still burned as he took his first steps but slowly pain ebbed away and he started out at a slow, uneven lope.

He was out in the open again. The snow bit at his face and neck and seemed to blur the horizon, make it circle slowly about him. His feet seemed to slip with every step. He found himself laughing, stifled the laughter with low curses, looked up at the stars to set his course surely. He laughed again. Of course there weren't any stars. It was snowing. But still, little points of light danced and swung against the endless gray-black of the heavens. His feet went out from under him. He lay in the snow, still laughing.

Something stuck into Gil's cheek. Something small and sharp. He brushed at it with a vague hand. His eyelids quivered open and he blinked. He saw a yellowish mass about him, thought he was back in the straw rick at Jake Willet's. Then his vision cleared. He sat up with a start, throwing back the heavy blankets that swathed him. He was in the hayloft of a barn—a small barn, he decided, for there was no opulent spread to the sharp slant of the roof above him. He felt something hard under his elbow, burrowed in the hay, and found his boots, dried and well greased. "Well, I'll be damned," he thought. "How'd I get here? And where's here? Did I take too much of the flask last night?" He reflected. His course was perfectly clear. The agony of the icy creek, the semi-paralysis on emerging. His run through the snow—what had happened then? But there his memory trailed off into an unfathomable blank, soft and woolly as the snow itself.

He heard footsteps somewhere below him, crept cautiously to the edge of the loft and looked down. A man in a ragged coat, uncut hair sprouting from a battered fur cap, was slowly climbing the ladder from the floor.

"Hi!" called Gil.

The man crawled on. "Stirrin', are you? 'Bout time." He stepped knee-deep in fragrant hay.

"How'd I get here?" asked Gil.

"Me," said the man.

"You?"

"Sure. Heifer got loose. I went to look for her. Found you in my field. Nigh friz."

Gil stared at him. "Well—you saved my life. No doubt about that."

"Guess they ain't. And they come lookin' for you."

Gil steadied himself against a post. "Head's still spinning. Know what happened to me?"

"No. And I ain't askin'. Keep your secrets."

"All right." Gil laughed uncertainly. "Lucky a Reformer picked me up."

The man glowered. "I ain't no Reformer."

"You're not?" He started in alarm.

"No."

Gil gathered himself for a spring, but found the sharp tines of a pitchfork gleaming in his eyes. He backed away, eyes darting about for a weapon. "All right. Bring your damn men in. But they've got to take me first. I'm not surrendering."

"They've gone," said the man, lowering the pitchfork. "Think I'd sell blood for a damned five hundred pounds?" He spat. "Not for five thousand."

Gil looked at him curiously. "They're gone? They didn't know I was here?"

"Not 'less you told 'em. I ain't. Now look here. I ain't a Reformer. I got no use for Mackenzie. But when I sees a feller in trouble I don't give a damn what his politics is. See? I just got to help him."

Gil's hand went instinctively to his belt. There was an exclamation of disgust. "Put your damn money away. I took you in like I'd take a neighbor's cow."

Gil still stared at him, almost unbelieving. Then he nodded. "You can't stop me from being grateful, at least. I'll get out as soon as I can. And I'll keep my mouth shut. What time is it?"

"You better be askin' what day it is. Well, it's Sunday. And it's three in the afternoon."

Gil thought. Sunday would be the tenth. He'd lost a day somewhere, because the tragic day of Montgomery's had been the seventh, a Thursday.

The man watched him, smiled wryly. "You slep' right through, 'cep' when I fed you. I got took like that once, comin' back in that blizzard in '31." He started down the ladder. "Get to the house. It'll be safe. We'll feed you again."

With uncertain knees, Gil followed. He told himself he was a fool to trust the man, that his best move was to break for the south as soon as he got clear of the barn. Yet he found himself following close on his surly host's heels, into a small house that sagged under the brand of poverty.

In the wide room that was used for living, eating, and sleeping, a worn-looking woman bent over a cradle. Gil's eyes brightened as he heard an odd sound. The kitchen underwent a sudden transformation. He was no longer a refugee, stumbling in the house of a man who had sheltered him simply out of decency and not out of any fellow feeling. He had tramped into a hundred such rooms, alone or with Doc, shabby farmhouses out on the Don or the Humber. He strode across the room, looked down on the flushed face of the child. Then he grinned at his host. "Got you this time. I can pay you back something, at least." He found the mother's anxious eyes on him. "How long's he had this?"

The answer was weak, quavering. "Just today—sir."

"Fine. Fine," said Gil absently. Croup, beyond a doubt, but in the first stages. He turned to the man. "Got any vinegar? Get me some. And a basin of hot water."

While the parents looked on anxiously he poured vinegar into the boiling water, propped the child up. "Now—fold the blanket to make a sort of tent. That's good." The baby made a face as the aromatic steam began to tingle in its nostrils. It choked. Then suddenly its breathing became easier, the slight rattling wheeze grew fainter, died away. Gil nodded. "Keep him at it. It'll help."

The woman looked at him with wondering eyes. "Is he all right now? I lost three through the croup—or something like it. Choked right here in the kitchen."

Gil shook his head. "This'll help him." He faced the man. "Give him a bowl like that every time he starts to choke up. It may do the trick. But anyway, you'd better get some of this as soon as you can." He sat at the scrubbed table that was pushed close to the low bed and drew out his notebook. He flipped over the leaves. The notation "Be sr. rl. gd. st. rv." seemed part of another world. The guard at the south ravine had been relieved long ago. God knew where the men were now. He wrote rapidly, muttering to himself. "Pennyroyal water, three ounces, oil of althea—" He ripped out the sheet, gave it to the man. "Where's the nearest chemist? Well, he'll fill this for you and tell you how to use it."

The man started to speak, then folded the paper quietly and thrust it into his pocket. "Got some stew for you. Then I'll take you into Gainsborough Township. Takin' some hides."

Gil looked doubtful. "In the daylight?"

"You'll be under the hides. Won't no one stop me. I'm knowed."

Gil reflected, then said abruptly, "Thanks. Be glad to go with you."

"That'll be all right," said the man.

While her husband held a fresh basin of water and vinegar under the child's nose, the woman ladled hot stew almost reverently for Gil. She was as monosyllabic and tight-lipped as the man, but her eyes were eloquent.

Well fed and with strength fast returning, Gil took a last look at the child in the cradle, now peacefully asleep, then joined the man in the trampled barnyard. The clumsy cart was stacked with hides which rested on a layer of wool bags. He crawled in among the rank strips of leather, heard his rescuer shuffling and poking them into a solid mass. The stack lay heavily on Gil's shoulders, but by wriggling down among the soft sacks he managed to achieve at least passable comfort.

There was a grind, a lurch, and the cart started off through the crisp air. The niche among the hides was a world apart, a world that had no being outside the boards of the vehicle. Gil sensed rough roads, hills, long level stretches, guessed that he was being rolled away from the great Niagara Escarpment that loomed over the flat plains to the east. Time had vanished with space. When the team halted briefly, it might have been at the end of an hour or two hours. It was all the same under the stacked hides.

The jolting started again and Gil was trailed away into some great space that had no bounds. He tried to doze but the incessant jarring overcame fatigue. He closed his eyes, tried to plot the course he would follow when he reached the States. First he'd—

The hides shifted as the cart rattled to an abrupt halt. He was about to call out when he heard voices.

"What you got there?"

"Hides and wool. Can't you see?"

Another voice, hoarse and weary, rasped, "Hell. We know that feller. Let him go."

There was an uncertain pause. Gil grew tense with fear as something rustled among the skins at the foot of the cart. The driver shouted. "Get your damned bagnet out'n my hides. Hell, I'll throw 'em off if you really want to look. I'll — "

Gil was aware of a muttered consultation. A new voice broke in, brisk and authoritative. "Never mind. You say he's all right. Let him go." Gil drew a long breath of relief.

Then the wagon creaked, the brisk voice said, "Guess I'll just take a look — matter of form."

Light flooded in on him as a stack was slid to one side. Gil, staring in horror, saw a shako'd head filling the gap. Amazed eyes looked down and Gil recognized a man from Hamilton who'd often gone shooting around Simcoe with his brother, Cameron.

Darkness, quicker than the light, shut down on his niche. Feet thudded to the trampled snow. "All right. Nothing in that load. Sorry to have troubled you."

Incredulous, Gil felt the wheels start bumping. He drew a long, quivering breath. "Nothing can stop me now," he thought. "Nothing."

The sun was setting when light sifted down to him again. The farmer grunted. "Safe here. Better get down."

Stiffly, Gil worked his way out from under the hides, slid to the ground, feet tingling with the shock. He looked about him. The cart had stopped in a shallow valley, heavily wooded. No house, no clearing showed. "Well, here you are, I guess," said the man.

Gil studied the cold landscape. "Never been in this part of the country before. What's my best route?"

"That's up to you. I housed you 'cause you was in trouble. I hid you in the cart 'cause you done something for the boy. But I ain't doin' nothing more to help a rebel escape." He climbed back onto the seat. "Figure it out for yourself." The cart swung in a wide circle, started its slow roll.

Bewildered, Gil looked after it. "Well, I'll be damned. Either the country's gone crazy or I have. Takes me this far and turns me loose. Then that friend of Cam's who looked into the cart. He saw me. He knew me." He shrugged. "Well — what to do now?"

Hands in his pockets, he thought regretfully of his nearly empty haversack, of the priceless rifle lying somewhere in the snow on the hills, far away. Everything seemed to balance against him. Everything. Then he laughed suddenly. The one big balance was in his favor. He was still free. More than that, he was near the border. Gainsborough Township was nearly in the middle of the strip of land that separated Ontario from the foot of Erie, a strip not more than twenty-five miles at its widest place. Thus he couldn't be more than ten miles or so from the Niagara River or Erie. Which should be his goal?

He squatted in the snow, tracing vague lines with a bit of bark. The Niagara frontier would be the more closely guarded. The safest course would be to hit for Erie, crowd onto some boat by hook or by crook. He knew no one in the district, but counted on the reported Reform sentiment.

He nodded. His choice was made. The lake won against the river. The road seemed deserted, with few tracks in the snow, but he decided against it. Woods and fields were safer. So he scrambled over a low wall and started up a gentle slope toward the sunset glow that still lingered.

The shadows deepened, the light slowly faded out, leaving only the faint glow of the stars and the sheen of the snowy fields. Gil pressed steadily on, husbanding his strength which had suffered perceptibly as a result of his ducking and exposure, keeping under the trees when he could, hugging the edges of fields when his route forced him into the open. The whole countryside seemed deserted. Rarely did he see the twinkling lights of a house, and the roads which he cautiously surveyed from the cover of rocks and trees were empty.

Then he was out of the hills and he found himself skirting a half-frozen bog that quaked treacherously to his one attempt at crossing it. The footing, even at the edge of the morass, was wretched and he debated the idea of finding a sheltered hollow where he could roll up for the rest of the night. The country seemed such a waste that he felt it might be safe to move about by day. Suddenly he stopped, sat down on a rock, his breath escaping in a great sigh of relief as he wiped his damp forehead.

Far away toward the horizon a single spark of light glowed, glowed as it moved slowly but unmistakably over a level black plain that was broken by neither hill nor tree. He stared harder.

It could be one thing and one thing only. The black, unbroken plain was Lake Erie and the moving light shone in the bows of some vessel, small schooner or sailboat.

Joy in his heart, he jumped to his feet, ran on toward the phantom spark that slid steadily along in the night.

After an hour's hard going, he felt the strong, cold breath of the lake on his face, heard the small waves lapping among the pebbles at his feet. Somewhere in the impenetrable night to the south lay the New York shoreline. And the tossing waste between was bare of searchers, of traps. Once he had solid wood beneath his feet he could scud across, throw himself into the interrupted work that the fiasco on the plains above Toronto had halted.

With methodical care he began working west along the shore. At last he saw it—a short wharf that jutted out into the lake, the flare of lanterns, the stark masts of a schooner. He dropped inland for a hundred yards, still moving west, and finally looked down on the rickety pier, the grotesque shadows that danced to the lanterns' light.

Stealthily he came nearer, saw that lumber was being stowed by a grumbling gang of men. There was no sign of guard or weapon—simple lake-front folk busy with an untimely stowing of cargo. He slipped a gold piece out of his belt, tramped resolutely down to the echoing boards of the wharf, hailed the nearest man. "Where's the master?"

A thin, angular figure shambled forward, staring suspiciously. "What d'you want?"

"Crossing soon?"

"Soon's these clowns get the boards stowed."

"Will you take me?"

The man, lanternlight flickering on his long nose and receding chin, stared. "Ain't they reg'lar boats runnin'? What you want to stow with us for?"

"I want to get over as soon as I can," said Gil.

"How much you pay?" A ragged-nailed hand scraped over the stubbled chin.

"I'll pay a pound—in gold."

"You will, will you? H'm." The master studied him. "Must be kind of anxious to get across. 'Tain't 'count of politics?"

Gil shook his head. "I've got business."

The master nodded. "Funny business to chase you down to a lumber pier at night. Well, guess we'll say five pound — gold."

Gil hesitated. The master, seemingly disinterested, spat into the water. "Five pounds it is," said Gil suddenly. "Payable as soon as you weigh anchor."

"Right! But you'll land where I say. I ain't runnin' out my course — not for ten pound."

"I don't care where you land," said Gil. "Just so long's it's the other shore."

There was a curious, calculating stare. "Well, your business is your business, I guess." He jerked his head. "Come on."

Gil stepped onto the deck, wedged his way between piles of lumber, was shown a dark, noisome sort of hutch, well to the bow. "Better keep out of sight," said the master. "I ain't licensed to carry passengers. Where's my five pounds?"

"I said when you weighed anchor," said Gil.

"Guess you did," said the man. "I'll be round to collect." He tramped off. Gil settled in a corner of the hutch, waited.

At last the slamming and bumping on deck ceased. Feet clumped toward Gil's hiding place and he was conscious of a gentle rocking and rolling. A lantern flared. "Where's my money?" said the master.

Gil slid a small heap of coins into the scaly palm. "What time will we get across?"

" 'Bout dawn, most likely. Got some food for you." He stepped aside and an unseen hand pushed forward a plate of cold meat, a steaming mug that sent a tang of coffee through the close, chill air.

Gil ate and drank greedily. "Needed that, ain't you?" said the master. "Well, your business is your business. Lie up where you are and no one'll bother you. I'll call you when we sight land." He stamped off, shouting orders to his small crew.

Gil found an old, dirty blanket in a corner of the hutch, rolled up in it. The close air and the motion of the vessel disturbed him at first, but he finally slept.

The hutch was still dark when he was awakened by a hand shaking his shoulder. "Gettin' there," said a hoarse voice. Gil got stiffly to his feet, followed the master out on deck.

There was a faint glow that shone up through the shifting water as though sunken treasure were touched by mysterious light. A thin haze veiled the shore, but Gil could make out a few treetops. A sudden elation swept over him. He grinned at the lean master. "Made it in good time, didn't we?" he chuckled.

"Ain't so good as it looks. Got blowed off my course." His eye flicked toward Gil, then to the silvery waters that were glowing in the false dawn. "Aimed to put in at Silver Creek." His eyes flicked again. "Kind of east of it, I guess."

Gil laughed. "I don't care. Another hour or so won't trouble me any."

"M'm. They's folks to Silver Creek as might ask questions. You was just wantin' to get across?"

"One place is good as another to me."

"I guessed." The master gnawed at his roughened thumb. "Now I ain't wantin' questions asked. I got a canoe towin' astern. You'd better take it and paddle it ashore."

"Here?" said Gil, surprised.

"Here's as good as any place. And you can beach the canoe. It ain't mine, found it driftin'."

The trees on the shore were clearer now and Gil could see patches of snow between the trunks, patches that seemed to beckon him on into the interior. He struck his hands together. "I'll do it. Well, Mr. — " He paused.

"I ain't asked your name, have I?"

"All right," said Gil, good-humoredly, his eyes on a trail that led inland. "Anyway, you've kept your word. Where's the canoe?"

"Astern, I said. Pull up the painter and drop in."

Gil held out his hand. The master took it limply. "Good-bye and good luck," said Gil.

The master nodded vacantly. Gil ran aft, found a small canoe bobbing in the schooner's wake, pulled up the painter. The flimsy craft danced and tipped on the waves but Gil finally managed to swing into it from the low hull. A splintery paddle lay in the bottom. Gil seized it, pushed away from the schooner, and started toward the shore with swift, driving strokes. Soon hard sand grated under the flat bottom of the canoe and Gil, with a wild whoop, sprang ashore, waved to the fading outline of the ship and dug his heels deep into the ground.

"Safe! By God, safe! Now I can get to Buffalo and find out

what's happening. Mac'll be starting something and he ought to get plenty of help. I'll get word to Nipigon. By God! Sandra can come and join me. She can—" Elation swept over him as plan after plan raced, half-formed, through his mind. And he'd get word over somehow to others that Erie was the place to cross. He'd try to start a regular chain for bringing Reformers safely into the States. All fatigue, all depression, had fled from him. He chuckled. "Knew I'd be all right, just as soon as I got here. Knew—"

He followed the trail that soon curved away, paralleling the lake front. He'd find a house soon. He'd—He suddenly stumbled, recovered himself, staring. Alarm struck through him like a cold sword blade.

Jutting into the lake was a rough pier. Hypnotized, he stumbled mechanically toward it. Suspicion thickened into hideous certainty. It was the identical wharf where he had found the schooner the night before!

Sick with rage and helpless frustration he stood staring at it. Then he broke out into dull, hopeless cursing. "The bastard! The cheating bastard! He just stood offshore all night and then turned me loose. How the hell could I know in the mist which shore it was? How—"

His shoulders sagged as the ground seemed to rock beneath him. The nerve-racking, indecisive days at Montgomery's, the final tragedy of smashed hope, the bitterness and fatigue of flight, seemed to pile up over him.

Then something stirred by the water's edge beyond the pier. Habit drove him behind a tree, sharpened his eyes in an alertness that had become mechanical. A horse stretched its long neck, drank deeply from the cold waters, while on the rocky shore a man in a plumed helmet and green jacket, travel-stained, clung precariously to the bridle.

Gil started to back away, stepped on a dried branch that cracked like a pistol shot. The trooper looked up, startled, then shouted over his shoulder, dragging the unwilling horse from the water. There was a stir somewhere among the trees, more hoofs sounded, the clank and jingle of arms.

For a moment Gil's spirits crumbled. Why not give up the unending flight, the splitting strain on mind and body? Then he raced back down the trail, sprang into the canoe, his desperate drive shooting it well out onto the waters of the lake. He picked up the drive with his flimsy paddle, shoulders and arms working like pistons. Behind him he could hear a great din on the shore, hoofs pounding on rocks, wild shouts, then a flat smack and a tearing whine as a bullet sang over his head to spat sharply into the water well beyond the bow.

He snatched a look shoreward. About six of the dragoons had ridden their horses fetlock-deep into the water. The leading horseman had fired a pistol at him and the others were hurriedly unslinging carbines, taking aim. He started to swerve away, then realized that he must present the narrowest possible target and tried to keep the curved stern pointing directly at the shouting group in the water.

A carbine cracked—another—a third. Spouts of water shot into the air to his left. Then the canoe bucked and a neat hole showed in the bark, close by the gunnel. Frantically he straightened his course, heard another report. This time the ball dropped astern. He was pulling out of range, rapidly vanishing into the mist that hung in snaky wreaths over the lake.

At last he dared slacken his pace. He looked back. The shore was hidden, and only faint, muffled shouts told of the baffled dragoons. He thought rapidly. He might circle back, try to find a boat that he could trust. He reasoned that the dragoons would have split up, would be patrolling east and west to stave off a possible landing. They might even commandeer a boat to continue the pursuit. He made up his mind. He would keep on. The lake at this point was about twenty miles wide. It would be a difficult paddle at the most favorable season. Now, with sudden gusts, with the tricky currents, it was a formidable undertaking. Formidable—but the only possible course.

He paddled cautiously. Then he saw with alarm that the mist was slowly lifting, would leave him naked and glaring on the broad waters, an easy prey for paddle or sail. "Damn it, will this ever end?" he thought savagely. He stared through the thinning haze, and his eyes met relief.

A small island, rocky and well wooded, loomed to the east. He drove the canoe toward it, saw it was uninhabited, hurriedly beached his canoe, drew it up into the shelter of low bushes, and sought the highest point of the crumb of land.

His refuge was no more than one hundred feet across, rising to a slaty cone in the center. There, screened by trees, he could watch in all directions as the mist lifted. If it didn't, his security was that much greater. He settled himself by the base of a tall pine and kept his eyes on the northern shore.

The peace of the little island was almost overwhelming after the agonizing tempo of the last few days. The mist lifted. A cold, hard sun climbed slowly up a deep blue sky, brought out tints of purple, of gold, of pale green, in the waters that lapped and whispered about the rocky shores. A single crow, winging its way south, lit on the tall pine, shot cawing away. Gil watched it enviously, then took up his study of the Canadian shore.

The peace was unbroken there, too, save for a small group of men who came down to a distant point and raked the waters through a single glass. Then they went away and the coast became primeval, lifeless again.

Noon came and he slept, twitching and muttering. A hawk swooped low, stared at him, then soared high into the blue. Toward sunset, Gil began to shiver, woke with a start, and looked about wildly. Far to the west, a single steamer left a trailing feather of blue-black smoke against the gold of the sky. Closer, a small sailboat tacked on its sober course, bound perhaps for Sherbrooke and the mouth of the Grand River.

He got to his feet, rubbing his stiffened knees, scrambled down to the hidden canoe and examined it carefully. Barring the single hole, well above the water line, it was intact. Satisfied, he turned his attention to the paddle, which was frayed but sound. Then he sat down to wait.

When the last bars of gold had driven bright furrows through the lift and toss of the waters, he launched his boat, began to paddle with slow, careful strokes, keeping the bow pointing well to the south. Darkness fell, intensified by the high shine of the stars, and still he paddled, eyes straining and ears alert.

Suddenly he backed water, froze. Somewhere off in the blackness he heard the sharp slap of waves, a dull humming. A light flickered, lit up the low hull of a schooner bearing down on him. With feverish haste he paddled, reversing his course, but the rays of the lantern picked him out of the crisping waves.

A voice shouted: "Hallo! The canoe! Hallo, there!"

Gil sat motionless. The hail was repeated. Another voice roared. "Come aboard, sir! Come aboard!"

The schooner, huge in the dark, shot past him. A boathook swept out, caught the gunnel, smacked the canoe against the low hull. There was a crack. Water gushed about Gil's knees. He made a wild clutch, caught the rope that sang through the air, and pulled himself aboard, defiant.

Then hands thumped his back, a gale of shouts welled up about him. "Here's another. By God, we got him!" The dazzle of a lantern cut into Gil's eyes. "Another! And Mac's safe across. We'll see him in Buffalo by morning."

Gil clutched the low thwarts. "What? What's that?"

"He's safe, I tell you! And I know you. I saw you when you went through Lloydtown with Mac. We're away. We're all away." The voice was high, excited. "You don't know me, but I'm the one that kept the Orangers from getting at Mac's platform."

Gil's arms fell limply by his side. "Well—I'll be damned!"

Later, he sat in the bows, listening dully to stories of rescue, escape. He sighed, turned his eyes toward the cold black belt, blacker than the night, where, strange and comfortless, the towering lift of the trees of the south loomed menacingly. Over their ragged crests a single bright star danced and wavered.

XXIV

Buffalo — 1837

Gil, crowded into a pitch-black space below decks, waked with a start as a series of muffled thuds jarred against the heavy woodwork behind him. He tried to move, but found himself strangely weighted down. For a stunning second the thought of recapture, of treachery, swept over him. Then something stirred beneath him, across him, and he recalled the headlong flight below decks in the face of the sudden gusts of sleet that a rising wind had driven on them. He hunched his shoulder, found that a tousled head was resting on it, felt a pair of rough boots digging into his knees, an outflung arm across his ankles. The air was cold but stifling, and the breaths that Gil drew set his head and neck throbbing.

Then a voice above bellowed, "Everybody out!"

The darkness writhed, stirred. Men began scrambling to their feet, jostling, stumbling, pushing. Gil stepped on a hidden foot as a blind elbow dug into his head, sent him staggering against a man who was trying to rise from the boards. Light flooded down through a thrown-back hatch, a gray, shifting light that struck on close-packed heads, on bobbing shoulders. Nearest the rough companionway, he pulled himself up on deck, the fresh air of the morning flooding into his lungs.

He saw first the trim deck, stumpy masts, then — he sprang back. It was well past dawn and the schooner lay close to a snowy wooded shore. Behind every tree eyes might be peering. Down that rutted track that curved away inland, green-jacketed dragoons might clatter, carbines unslung. Suddenly he knew that he was safe, that he was at the south shore of the lake. Something snapped and fluttered high in air and he looked up to see a striped flag, streaming from a staff back of a low wharf, its blue canton white-starred.

Relief made him weak, dizzy, for a moment. Then he shouted in sheer exultation, joined the pushing mass that sprang over the low bulwarks. Behind him on deck a voice boomed, "Everybody off. Hurry it up. Everybody off! Got to go back and pick up more. Hurry it up!"

Gil looked over his shoulder to see the master of the ship waving his arm in wide sweeps, herding the refugees onto the dock, then walked ahead uncertainly toward the shore. A hand fell on his elbow. He turned to see a long face under a fur cap. He seized the man by the shoulders. "Bob Heath! Where were you hiding? Where — "

"I was aft!" shouted Heath. "Knew we picked up someone but didn't know who. Gil, what the hell happened to you?"

"Got away after Montgomery's. Didn't see you there, Bob."

"Didn't get there," said Heath shortly. "Started. Then a bunch of men chased me. Hit for the lake and found a ship that took me and some others way below Hamilton. Then we walked across to Erie and this one picked us up." He pointed up the track that swept inland. "Right enough. Here's the wagons." Two low-wheeled carts were rolling carefully toward the wharf, the drivers waving their whips and shouting.

"Wagons?" Gil stared. "How'd you know about 'em?"

Heath jerked a thumb toward the schooner. "Master's partner. He's a Yankee. Had it all planned."

Gil watched the oncoming carts in amazement. "Well, *some*body did some thinking. If there'd been as much done around Montgomery's, maybe Head and Hagerman'd be hitting for the border now."

The wagons swept up with a flourish. Gil and Heath ran to the second, scrambled in. The driver grinned at them. "Takin' you right into Buffalo. Eagle Tavern. That's where your fellers is all headin' for." He wagged his head. "Yes *sir*. So full of patriots you can't hardly turn around."

Men poured on over the board sides until the cart was packed, squatted red-eyed and unshaven. Gil crouched in a corner, listened to tales of what had happened since the first mustering at the tavern. Morrison arrested; Van Egmond taken; Rolph in flight across the border; hundreds of people seized, the action dictated by suspicion, panic, or spite; militia billeted in known or suspected

Reform houses, quartered on people who had merely incurred the enmity of the Compact in some way. One man had been taken for owning some old, old copies of Mackenzie's paper. Another for owning lead, which he had been slowly accumulating for a roof.

Narrow-eyed, Gil listened. He had expected that those actually under arms would be hunted down ruthlessly. But the sudden burst of Compact spleen against people merely suspected or disliked—he tried to picture Toronto, the whole back country stretching up to Lake Simcoe. Suddenly his jaws snapped. "They're helping us. They don't know it, but they are."

The wagon had swung down toward the lake, then climbed slightly inland again. A great expanse of snowy roofs showed over the shoulder of a hill and Gil, interested, propped himself up to watch the strange city roll into sight.

There were few buildings, so far as he could see, to match the splendor of the Grange, of Strachan's palace, of rebuilt Spadina House. But the simpler buildings looked somehow trimmer, better tended, than their Toronto equivalents, and away to the east he could see huge, solid structures, public buildings perhaps, that dwarfed Osgoode Hall and the Market. More houses, trim white fences edging a decent street.

Suddenly a small boy, fur-capped, threw mittened hands in air, whistled shrilly. Doors flew open, people ran out of alleys. There was a shout: "Patriots! More of 'em! Come on!"

The driver bellowed, waved his whip. "Sure, I got 'em! I got 'em!"

Yelling, stamping, whistling, the crowd pelted on in the wake of the wagons, cheering, waving their hands. Women smiled from snug doorways and a pretty dark-eyed girl flourished a brilliant scarf from an upper window.

The wagons crunched to a halt in front of a square brick building, whose white door shone against the red walls. The driver whooped. "Here you are! The old Eagle!"

Gil got stiffly to his feet, watched Heath slide to the ground, leaped after him. Heath vanished in a swarm of sailors, blacksmiths in leather aprons, grave, well-dressed men, shawled women. A man in a white cap seized Gil with flour-smeared hands, thumped his back. "You'll be all right here. You'll be—"

Then the crowd shook and boiled. There was a rush and vast

hands smacked on Gil's shoulders. He tore loose from the baker, swung about. "Jos! By God! How'd you get here?"

Palms thumping Gil's back, Josiah shouted. "Where the hell else would I be? I knew you'd get away. I knew you'd come here. They all do. Now get inside. May be some other folks you know." He pushed Gil ahead of him past solid stables, hurried him up some short stairs to a side door.

The sudden warmth of the little half bar, half parlor, struck Gil's weather-worn face in a gentle slap, blurred his vision. Then he saw a bent man rise quickly from a table by a window, was aware of tired eyes and a mangy beaver. Richland's hands were on his arm, the sardonic lines gone from his face and the rasp from his voice. "Gil! Gil! You're all right? You're all right?"

Gil sat slowly down, staring from the grinning Josiah to the worn face of the old doctor. "Well," he said, and felt his voice weak, uncertain. "Well — I'll be damned."

Richland grunted, sat down. "Guess you're all right." He looked keenly at Gil. "Ain't had a very easy time, have you?" He swung about in his chair, glared at the man behind the short bar. "Ain't you got the sense God gave a goose? Get something hot. Get something strong. No — one hot and three strong."

Gil drew a long breath, eyes moving over the white wainscoting, the landscape paper hung with bright prints; watched the barman slide a plate of smoking chops before him; heard the smack of three glasses of hot rum on the table. He began to eat, slowly, as the unaccustomed hot food seemed to choke him.

Josiah pulled a creaky chair to the table. "Now Doc and I want to know what happened to you. How'd you get here?"

"Walked some. Rode some. Sailed some," said Gil between careful bites.

Richland sighed. "I reckoned you'd keep going ahead, butting into anything that got in your way. Seems the Lord protects my pupils as well as drunkards."

Gil nodded equably. "Seems to take care of the teacher, too." His eyes grew graver. "Worried a lot about you, Doc."

Richland snorted. "Think I don't know how to take care of myself?"

"But where'd you go? I told you to wait there by that tree and — "

"So you thought I'd just wait there until someone came for me with a rope! Bah! I saw that Campbell pup chasing you by the stables. I saw you get away and head for the woods, so I knew you were all right—or right as you could be without me to tell you how to pick up your feet and breathe and things like that. Well, I just went back to the shed and got my bag. No one bothered me. Then I found a militia boy with a bullet burn in his shoulder and tied him up. Just then that blistering idiot of a Head came by and made a speech about both of us. Then I rode back to Toronto on a horse I'd borrowed." He rubbed the bottom of his glass on his worn black sleeve.

"How'd you get away, Gil?" asked Josiah.

Gil rapidly sketched out his course, Josiah listening eagerly, while Richland, hat pushed on the back of his head, grunted sarcastic comment. At last the doctor puffed out his cheeks. "Well, Gil, you're doing better. Seems to me that once or twice on your trip you came mighty near to sitting down and thinking."

"Maybe I did," said Gil. "Jos, I'm damned glad to see you, but I wish you'd stayed in Toronto."

"Couldn't!" barked the doctor. "Damned fool was getting into too many fights."

Josiah grinned. "I was having a swell time until they began marching companies of militia around. Until then, all I had to do was whistle 'Yankee Doodle' to have at least three men come running with their fists out." He drank sadly. "But after they got organized, it all changed. A brigade or a platoon or a file or something stopped me on King Street. They were mighty anxious for me to give a cheer for the Queen. I did that all right. I'm sorry for the poor girl. Then they wanted one for Head."

Gil laughed. "What did you do? Tell 'em to go to hell?"

"No," said Josiah mildly. "I cheered, all right. But they didn't seem to like the sound of it. So we argued awhile and then I went down to the waterfront and found a boat that was crossing." He drank his hot rum appreciatively. "Well, Gil, what are you going to do now?"

"Work—if there is any," said Gil shortly.

Josiah and the doctor exchanged glances. "Guess you might find some," said Richland.

Gil leaned forward eagerly. "Where?"

"We-e-ell, a lot's been happening. I'd let Jos tell you, but he gets too excited. Now—Mac's here all right. Soon's he got in, a lot of people here had a big meeting at the Opera House down the street. Next night they had another. Voted sympathy for the patriots. Mac was there and they near took the roof off. The people said they'd give money. A man named Sutherland said he'd raise an army. Looks as if he'd do it. Gil, you ain't got an idea how many people have come over. Lots that ain't had a thing to do with Mac. One of 'em told me he didn't like Mac, but that the Compact'd run hog-wild now. No place for a man unless he wanted to lick boots at Government House."

Gil nodded slowly. "Who's Sutherland? A Yankee?"

"Says so," said Richland. "But the Lord left out Yankee sense when He put him together."

"Wait a minute," said Gil. "You mean it's not sense to get an army together? To help us?"

Josiah held up his hand. "Listen to that." Somewhere off in the street, brasses blared discordantly, an ill-strung drum thumped. "That's Sutherland, marching through the streets trying to pick up recruits. No—hold on a minute. Recruits are all right. But he's getting 'em publicly off the streets of an American city. London won't like that. Washington won't. We haven't heard yet, but I guess Washington'll want to be neutral as hell."

"What business is that of Washington?" flared Gil. "It's our own fight and—"

"Look here." Richland leaned across the table. "We ain't at war with England. But we could be if we start fitting out armies here to hit British territory."

"And another thing." Josiah frowned at his empty glass. "There's plenty of feeling here for Mac and his people. All along the border, I guess. You see, a lot of men figure that you're trying to do about what we did in '75. Not kick loose, necessarily. But you've had a bad deal, so bad that you've had to fight it. Some pretty big Americans are backing you—on that count. But—" he cocked his head toward the distant blaring—"if Mac loads himself down with a lot of clowns, people that count'll begin to drop away. You and Mac might just as well figure on settling in Buffalo."

Richland nodded gravely. "There are some folks with money and nothing to do. They'll be glad to have a uniform and a title. There's others that got no money and nothing to do. They'll be glad of a dollar and a meal. Mac's got to keep slapping at folks like that same's he would at mosquitoes."

"Of course, we'll have to watch that," said Gil. His mouth set. "Makes me feel good to hear that things are going on. What's Mac's plan?"

Josiah shrugged. "It's all over town. If Head's got spies here, he'll know pretty soon. Mac figured first on getting a lot of men together and joining Duncombe in Canada West. Now he says he's going to open headquarters on Navy Island. Know it? It's about four miles above Niagara Falls."

"And it's British," put in Doc. "He can do what he wants from there without its being any of Washington's business."

Gil pushed back his chair. "Is Mac there now? How can I get there?"

Richland eyed him. "Sure you want to go, Gil? Maybe Mac'll have an awful scratch lot with him. Some Canadians and a lot of rat-faces off the Buffalo waterfront."

"All the more reason to go," said Gil.

"What makes you think it'll do any good?" Richland raised shaggy eyebrows.

Gil sat down, frowning. "Look here, Doc. The things we were fighting are still there, aren't they? And aren't there thousands of Reformers who never got near Montgomery's? Look at the hundreds in Toronto that were waiting for us to come in." He made an impatient gesture. "You know how near we came to bringing that off, as it was. We could have taken the town a dozen times. What beat us? Changed plans. No organization. Paralyzed because no one knew what to do."

Richland nodded somberly. "Guess you could have come in."

"Of course," said Josiah. "Why, Ogle Ketchipaw wanted to lay in a whole stock of Mackenzie banners."

"Hope you let him," said Gil quickly. "This isn't over. The Compact's coming down so hard on everyone remotely suspected of revolt, they're getting so damned harsh, they've scrapped what little law there was so utterly, that the Reformers'll see that they've *got* to fight on. We'll go across. They'll rally and we'll kick the Compact out. Good God, don't you see that everything the Compact does now gives us men, waiting over there for us? And now we'll have plenty of time. We'll have arms. I can tell Mac—"

"M'm, now there's another thing," broke in Richland. "You've got a profession. You've got a mighty fine girl waiting for you. Just think of this. Things'll change over there. The rage'll die down. Then, you can go back and—"

Gil burst out, "What makes you think they'd let me go back—ever? The Compact knows—"

"What does it know?" asked Richland. "A lot of people think it was Jos who rode with Mac last summer. A lot think that Jos was at Montgomery's. I'll bet in six months' time they'll be sure it was Jos—especially the way a lot of good people are quitting the Province now. They'll *want* you back. They'll—"

"I'm keeping on," said Gil shortly. "I didn't go out with Mac just because the Compact's interfered with me, personally. I went because the whole lot's rotten. And they're still rotten and they're still there. I'll keep on even if the whole Compact swears I was in Strachan's study all through the fight. Even if they give me my license and make me head of the Medical Board."

Josiah nodded to himself. "So you feel that way, do you?"

Richland sighed. "Just what we figured, Jos. Gil just ain't got sense. Well—I heard there was a wagon heading for Fort Schlosser pretty soon. Schlosser's just across from Navy Island, on our side."

Gil rose again, slammed his chair back against the wall. "I'll go with it. And I don't give a damn what you say or think."

"We were pretty sure what you'd think," said Doc. "Jos and I, we just wanted to be sure you knew all there was to know—that you saw all around things."

"Sure," grinned Josiah. "I'll go out and get three places in the wagon."

"*Three?*" said Gil.

"Why the devil not?" spluttered Richland testily. "Ain't we told you there's a lot to be done? And God knows how many messes you'd get into if we ain't there to pull you out."

XXV

Navy Island — 1837

GIL leaned from the creaky carriage that Josiah had hired at the farmhouse where they had passed the night. "Doc! Doc! Is that it?"

A heap of buffalo robes stirred. Richland's nose, red-tipped, poked cautiously out. "If you and that damned gangling cousin of yours keep routing me out before sunrise, I'm apt to tell you it's Manhattan." His eyes blinked. "No! That's Grand Island. Navy's clear to the north tip of it—if it ain't drifted over the Falls."

Gil, disappointed, stared at the great mass of land that stretched for several miles along the river. "Where are we going to cross?"

Josiah, huddled beyond Richland, stirred, pointed to a small tavern, a wharf. "That's all that's left of Schlosser. We'll get a boat there." He sank among his skins again.

At last the carriage jounced and rolled on past the tavern, down onto the wharf, where Josiah argued fiercely with several boatmen, threw up his hands, and pushed Richland and Gil into a small scow that lay just beyond the thick ice that rimmed the shore. The current was swift, but the scow snuffled and butted its way through the swift-moving ice cakes, grated its bow onto the frozen shore. The boatman, blowing on numbed fingers, snatched at Josiah's money. "Walk 'bout a half mile. You'll see Navy. Plumb ahead of you," he said.

The three started over the snowy fields, thinly wooded. "Why wouldn't he take us all the way?" asked Gil.

"Wait till you see the current at Navy," grunted Josiah. "Course, if you *want* to have a closer look at that— " He waved to the east.

Gil slowly became aware of a muffled, muttering roar, of a thicker mist that hung over the distant reaches of the river where the great Falls tossed and battered against the timeless rocks. Years ago he had seen the short river pitching headlong from the vast cliffs, had wandered close by the edge to watch the eerie rainbows in the spray, a spectacle that had then seemed wildly joyous, almost friendly. But that had been in summer, near the cool hotel. Now, on the frozen meadows, the shifting mists seemed to scowl furiously, the eternal voice of the Falls to thunder a murderous threat.

He shivered, tramped along after Josiah and Richland, stumbling and sliding over the wretched path. There were more woods, a meadow, woods again, and he stood on the river's edge, staring across at a small island, tree-shrouded.

There was a crazy landing, a hint of a path sketched out, and from a half-seen clearing a blue flag fluttered, twin stars sharp on its folds. Richland hitched his frayed shawl tighter about his throat. "Well — there you are, Gil. What do you figure on doing? Swimming?"

Gil did not answer. There, on that crumb of land that seemed to toss in the swift-slipping current, lay the beginnings of the sledge that soon would be swung and swung surely, that would shatter the last vestiges of the Family Compact, would reshape Canada into a fit land for free men.

Richland jogged his elbow. "Well — we're waiting for your lead."

Gil started. "What? Oh — " He stared at the rough landing where a broad-beamed scow rocked and dipped. Then he shouted. "Hello, the island! Navy Island!"

His voice echoed, was lost in the faraway grumble of the Falls. He shouted again. There was a movement on the path and a man came uncertainly to the end of the wharf, a tall man who peered across the narrow gap.

Gil cupped his hands. "Mac there? Tell him Gil Stensrood wants to get across. Tell him — "

The man tumbled into the scow, began poling with cautious skillful strokes. Gil eyed him, then recognized the face under the misshapen bulk of a fur cap. "Ralph Dening! How'd you get here?"

The scow worked nearer, grated on rocks and ice. Dening grinned. "Hello, Gil! Heard they'd took you." He stared at Jos and Richland. "They with you? They all right?"

Gil explained them to Dening, hurried them onto the scow,

which shot into the stream again. "Haven't seen you since Lloydtown, Gil. Have trouble getting here?"

"Some," said Gil. "Got many on the island?"

" 'Bout thirty-forty men. More comin'."

"Anyone I know?"

"Don't think. Mostly men from Hamilton way. Some Yankees." He swung expertly alongside the pier.

"Where's Mac?" asked Gil.

"Going round the island with General van Rensselaer."

"Who?" said Gil.

"Yankee general." Dening began to grin. "Name's Rensselaer van Rensselaer. The fellers say he's twins."

Richland moaned softly to himself. "*That* feller!" He nudged Gil. "What did I tell you about loading up with clowns? Mac's got a whole boatload in that feller. General!" He snorted in disgust, then stiffly climbed onto the wharf, Gil and Josiah following.

Gil drew a deep breath. "Now—let's find Mac." He started on up the trail, came into a clearing where the twin stars floated over a few board shacks, some of them completed. The cheery slam of hammers echoed from the others, rang sharp in the still air.

Then Gil saw movement among the trees by the west bank of the river, heard a thud of axes. Two men walked swiftly along toward the clearing. The first was a big, full-blown man in a semimilitary coat, a flat cocked hat on his head. The other, small and quick-stepping, hurried by his side, head bent in earnest talk.

Gil broke into a trot. "Mac! Mac! Just got here! I'm—"

Mackenzie stopped short, stared. Then he put out both hands, ran toward Gil. "You've come! You've come! Knew I could count on you." His hands flew about in familiar gestures, but the hectic bursts that had seized him at Montgomery's farm were gone. "You came all the way to join me. You could have stayed. You could have—" He whirled about, presented Gil to Van Rensselaer. "He'll be invaluable, General. Invaluable. Young, but—I tell you, we'll need him." He pushed his hat down over his forehead, knocked it back with a thin wrist. "He'll do everything. He'll—who's that?" He darted off toward the others. "Who's that? Josiah! Might have known it. And Dr. Richland! General! General! Two of your fellow countrymen. Josiah, he did a lot for us in Lower

Canada. Maybe he will again. Papineau's not done for yet. And Richland — "

Van Rensselaer flicked the ash from a cigar. "Good boys. Good boys. Need more of 'em, don't we?" His flushed, rather handsome face puckered in a mechanical smile. Gil caught a strong reek of brandy that seemed to push out each word, noted grease stains on the frogged, brass-buttoned blue coat.

"More of 'em? We won't need many of your people, General. I'll have this island jammed with Reformers in a week. Now Gil, you three better come around the island with us. We're — " A sudden boyish smile lit up his face. "Know where you are? Hah! You think you're on Navy Island, but you're not. You're in the temporary capital of the Provisional Government of Upper Canada! You are. We've got our flag. We're issuing notes and the Buffalo merchants are accepting them."

"How about guns?" asked Josiah.

"Guns? Guns? All we want. We've got two cannon now. More coming. Now I want to show you what we're doing along the west shore. I'll — "

Van Rensselaer coughed. "I think, Mr. Mackenzie, that our counsels — eh? Better kept close — eh? Can't let 'em all know what we're up to — eh?"

Mackenzie waved. "All right with these fellows. I know 'em. They've worked for me — "

"And we want to keep on," said Gil. "Where'll I start, Mac?" He looked through the trees where the axes rang, saw panting men dragging logs into a rude abatis facing the Canadian shore. "Give me an axe. I'll start in with that."

Mackenzie shook his head. "Got all the axe men I want. Letters! Letters! Coming in so fast I can't read 'em. You'll be busy enough." He seized Gil's arm, dropped it, spun around to Josiah. "You want to work for us? All right. Go back to Schlosser. We've got provisions coming in. Hurry 'em up. Find barges that'll be heavy enough to come right to Navy. We lose too much time hauling across Grand Island, and then reshipping." He waved his hands again. "That's all. You've got my authority." His quick eye fell on Richland. "Got some sick men. In the north huts. Fever. One man's got a poisoned splinter in his hand. Got to get 'em on their feet. Sick men mean wasted men. Now Gil — " He hurried off toward the largest shack, Van Rensselaer striding behind him, frowning. Gil watched Josiah and Richland vanish into the woods, then followed Mackenzie.

The big hut was chill and dark. Mackenzie ripped sacking from a window, lit a thick candle that shone on a rude table, two beds of pine boughs on the dirt floor. "Rough quarters, Gil, rough quarters. But it's a palace compared to what Washington had sometimes, isn't it?" He snatched up a thick heap of paper, thrust it at Gil. "Go through these. Use your head and draft answers. I'll sign 'em when the general and I come back."

Van Rensselaer made an impatient gesture, then burst out, "Look here, Mr. Mackenzie, those are confidential papers. And how about that doctor? I know a very good man in Rochester who'll come. Old friend of mine. I *know* about him. This man—"

Mackenzie ran out of the hut. "Yes, yes. Of course. Richland's a good man. See to all that. Now I want your advice on siting that brass six-pounder that's coming from Watertown. Have the letters ready when I—" His voice trailed away under the trees. The general threw down his cigar with an exclamation of disgust, stamped out after him.

Gil frowned, then shrugged and turned to the letters. He bent over them, impatiently at first, then with growing interest that deepened into intense concentration. They bore full witness to what Josiah and Richland had told him about the sympathy already current in the States. A society, which wished to be nameless for the moment, had actual cash to contribute. To whom should it be remitted? And further, it could send one hundred men if some way could be found around the law. Gil nodded over the letter, added two or three others to it, scrawled "Active Help" on a scrap of paper, laid it on the growing pile.

A man wrote that, having suffered severely at the hands of the Compact, he had one hundred acres of land in Canada to give to the cause. He suggested it might be used to pay troops. A baker near Buffalo announced that he was sending two wagonloads of bread which he hoped would be useful. A woman at Fort Schlosser would have several large baskets of cakes at the wharf at sundown. If the baskets could be sent back, she'd refill them.

Slowly the piles grew, each letter bearing a notation for the tone of the answer. Several he set aside for Mackenzie to see personally. On the top of this heap lay a letter which he read and re-read, a letter from a group of Germans in faraway Philadelphia. They had all fled their country to escape political persecution, and offered their service to Mackenzie. One of the members had been a major in the Prussian army and suggested that he might be instrumental in getting help from Europe.

The papers rustled on. Fourteen kegs of powder were coming. Military men in New York, Ohio, Vermont, were anxious to know what rank would be assigned them.

Gil finally stretched his long arms, blew on his fingers, and picking up a rough quill began to write.

In the midst of a careful reply to an itinerant preacher who offered to send word from Toronto of doings there, a shadow fell across the paper. Gil looked up, saw Richland's hat scraping the top of the low door. He threw down his pen. "Doc, you and Jos were right!" He riffled through the papers. "Why, even without this, we've got more arms and powder than we ever thought of having at Montgomery's! And look at this! Trained officers from the States! They want to join us. They want—"

Richland sat down on an upended box, ruffled his thin hair. "They want to be generals or something, don't they? Ain't any of 'em come in to say: 'Here I am'?"

"Uh—why, no. I—I don't—"

Richland rubbed his hat on his sleeve. "Lot to learn from the mistakes other folks have made. Read much 'bout our Revolution? Well, we had one bad thing to fight besides the British. That was that every man in Europe that had ever watched two soldiers getting drunk thought he was a military genius. Wanted to come and be one of Washington's generals—or take his place. Gil, they was all just burning with love of freedom—plus general's rank and 'bout a million dollars bounty." He calmly reached out, took a few letters from the the heap, eyes blinking as the lines stared out from the paper. Then he grunted. "What you doing with these?"

"Saving 'em for Mac to see."

Richland raised his eyebrows. "I wouldn't, Gil. I wouldn't. They've got a nice fire going over beyond the huts. If I was you, I'd dump all these right in there. They might help to cook some food. But that's all they'll help."

Gil laughed shortly. "Don't be a fool, Doc. We might get another Van Rensselaer this way."

Richland nodded gravely. "That's what I'm afraid of."

"Afraid?" said Gil staring. "A full general?"

"Listen, Gil." Richland edged his box closer to the table. "Remember what Jos and I told you about loading down with clowns? Well, I've been looking after some of the boys and I've heard a lot."

"You mean you've heard a lot of camp rumors," said Gil scornfully.

"Been in a lot more camps than you have. I can sniff out a rumor 'most as quick as I can a flux. Here's what I heard. Rensselaer graduated from West Point. He served in the army. He went to South America and soldiered a lot with this Bolivar down there."

"What's wrong with that?"

"Just that it ain't so. Now, I could pop up in, say, Cuba, and say I'd fought with Wellington. Nobody'd know me. But Van Rensselaer's family's too well known. I know—and most York Staters know—what every one of the family's been doing since old Kilian van Rensselaer settled in the sixteen-hundreds. And going to West Point and fighting with Bolivar's two things this Rensselaer van Rensselaer ain't done. And one thing he *is* doing is sopping up a quart or two of brandy every day."

Gil took the papers with a sinking heart. The offers had encouraged him enormously. He'd been looking forward to the joy of presenting an impressive list of trained soldiers to Mackenzie. He sighed. "Guess you're right, Doc."

"Course I am," snapped Richland. "And you just keep this in mind. No one that says 'What do I get for joining?' is going to be worth a jug of spoiled cider to you." He eyed Gil keenly. "Damn it, don't look like a calf that's got into the wrong pasture! Ain't I told you you got work to do? Weeding and pruning like that's part of it. And if you can get near enough to the general to push him over the Falls, you'll be doing Mac a big favor. Get back to your work now. When you're finished, come and look for me over by the shack they're putting up at the west end of the island. Got a fever case I want to show you. Kind of like to get your ear on his breathing."

Gil dropped his pen. "Breathing? How's it sound?"

Richland smiled to himself. "Get your work done and I'll show you." He stumped out of the hut.

Gil sighed, then began to write:—

SIR:—

Mr. Mackenzie directs me to inform you that he will accept with deep gratitude your generous proffer of twenty muskets. He will arrange to have your wagon met at . . .

Gil stood by a twisted pine that hung over the swift arrow of the east channel, whose waters were leaden under a dead sky. The roar of the Falls thudded against his head, punctuated by the sharp slam of hammers as fresh boards were spiked to the wharf. Across on the American shore, beyond the tip of Grand Island, black specks moved briskly against the background of snow, swarmed over the distant pier, thin voices echoing against the hull of a small steamer, frozen in the sluggish inshore water.

The afternoon barges were late in leaving the Schlosser pier, Gil thought. He turned to the camp that spread out behind him. In a few days, the atmosphere of the island had changed. In a level stretch in the center, men were drilling under the eye and barking voice of a man whom even Richland approved—Matthew Hayes, High Bailiff of Toronto and an ex-sergeant of Her Majesty's Fifteenth Foot. The men of Captain Harper's "A" Company stepped briskly to the sure, ringing commands while "B" and "C" watched critically.

Beyond the drill ground, new huts were being run up, and along the west bank branches crashed and thudded as a new abatis slowly took shape. Gil thought of the hungry, footsore mob that had swarmed about Montgomery's Tavern, unfed and unled, willing to go anywhere in answer to a firm command that never came. Things would be different this time. Rations poured onto the island; weapons, miscellaneous but useful, were ample. In a few more days there'd be a fine chance of hurling a compact, well-trained force over the narrow strip of water between Navy Island and the mainland. A few more days, a few more recruits.

A distant hail from the river, a cessation of pounding, turned him back to the pier. Three broad-beamed scows were working out from

Fort Schlosser, edging cautiously along the tip of Grand Island. Then a fourth and heavier craft crept out, followed in the wake of the others. The little flotilla came on, the blunt bows nosing away from the swift water, until Gil could see the blur of faces in the two leading scows, as close-packed men stared over their shoulders at wharf and island.

The first scow thudded against the pierhead, swung broadside. Gil ran down to the edge. "Everyone that's joining us report to Captain Osborn at the main building. Craft, you take 'em up." An oxlike man shoved his hammer into his belt, led a shuffling, uneven file up the path. The second and third scows eased in. Gil sent the added volunteers to Osborn, set the wharf crew to unloading great sides of beef, barrels of flour, sacks of bread.

A shout echoed over the water. Gil looked up to see Josiah standing in the stern of the last boat, waving his arms. "Gil! Hi, Gil! Wait till you see what I've got here!" His laugh boomed out. "Nice presents for Head. Wow! Wait till Mac sees 'em!"

The sculls churned the water, the scow worked into the last vacant space between shore and wharf. Josiah leaped ashore in a wild flourish. Gil caught him by the shoulders, spun him about. "What the devil's riding you now? Want to get chucked into the river?"

"Don't care what happens to me!" Josiah roared down toward the grinning men in the barge. "Rip off those covers!"

The men dragged stiff canvas from a muffled heap that lay in the bottom. Gil stared. Four brass cannon lay snugly on poles, two shorter iron pieces beyond them. "We—we've got a regular battery now. Five—that means eighteen pieces in all." He whistled through his teeth. "Just one of those—just *one*—at Montgomery's and we'd—"

Josiah caught his arm. "And that's not all. Look in the stern. Carriages for 'em! Wheels! When we go across, we can take 'em with us—not just leave 'em squatting in an abatis."

Gil slammed his hands together. "By God! What a haul! Where'd they come from?"

Josiah dropped his voice. "State arsenal. Someone forged the general's name—you know, Winfield Scott. The arsenal people let 'em right out. We'll get more. We'll—"

Gil caught the nearest man. "Go to Hut One. Get Consider Button down here with his crew right away. Tell him to bring tackle." The man raced off.

Josiah, eyes shining, went on excitedly. "And even that's not all. Look. You see those recruits that came ashore? I found 'em all trying to get across to Whitechapel on Grand Island. Said they were supposed to go there, but I bayed at their heels until I'd run them right up to Schlosser. Save a lot of time that way. Oh—and I've got—"

A rush of feet pelted down the path, pulleys clanked and ropes trailed on the ground as Button's crew, whooping with joy, set to work to hoist the guns. Then slower steps sounded, and Mackenzie, hands behind his back, picked his careful way down to the water. His eyes lit up as he saw the first brass tube swing in air, come to rest on a rough cradle on the shore.

"How's that, Mac?" cried Gil.

Mackenzie ran to the cousins. "Who got those? Who got those? You? You, Jos?" He clutched Josiah's sleeve, dropped it, snatched out a handkerchief and mopped his forehead, eyes darting back to the cannon. "This is big. This is important. I tell you—why, we can blow anything out of the water that tries to get across." Then he flung up his arms. "Wheels! Wheels! They'll march with us! The general knows all about fieldpieces. He'll—"

Josiah touched Mackenzie's shoulder. "I've got something else. I've found we can cut out the *Caroline*. We—"

Mackenzie stared across at the ice-bound steamer, a wry smile on his face. "You want to steal it? Well, go ahead, but don't get caught."

"Steal be damned," shouted Josiah. "I've found out all about it. It was built for Cornelius Vanderbilt. It's built for sea work. Copper-sheathed and all. But he sold it. And I've got a list of men in Buffalo that'll lease it. And if it happens to touch at Navy—well, what of it? Mac, it'll carry a month's supplies for you. It'll do as a transport. It'll—"

Mackenzie still kept his eyes on the distant hull. "How'll it clear port? How about its papers?"

Josiah grinned. "That'll be all right too. We've found a customs officer who's got two blind eyes—and a Canadian wife."

Mackenzie drew a long, slow breath. "We'll look better. We'll look a lot better. Our own island—our own ship." He began to speak rapidly. "We'll look like a going concern. We are a going concern. But so few see it. So few. They'll begin to look up to us now. They'll have to." He whirled about. "Jos! Keep these men going. Gil, come with me."

He walked rapidly away toward the main building, tramped into his bedroom office, Gil following, puzzled. Mackenzie slammed the door, snatched up a pile of letters, stared at them, flung them down. Then he turned to Gil. "You're no use to me."

Gil started as though struck. Mackenzie had been completely his old self all the time on the island. None of the sudden, blinding rages, the bursts of senseless oratory, erratic actions, that had marked him at Montgomery's. Was he—

The crisp voice went on. "Not a bit of use to me here. That's not because you aren't valuable. You are. But you can be doing something a lot more important for all of us. Gil, I've got a job for you."

Gil breathed a sigh of relief. "What is it?" he asked.

Mackenzie fussed nervously with the papers, picked up a pen, dropped it. "Back before Montgomery's, I laid plans—just in case anything happened. I've got a patrol of men, real Reformers, covering a belt from the border clear to Toronto and beyond. They have ten-mile beats and they keep moving. They pass word along. So I know what's happening back there. The Reformers know what's happening to me." He spoke more slowly. "I know they got Lount. I know they got Matthews. Gibson's still in hiding, waiting for a chance to get across. I know all that. But here's where you come in. The people that send me word haven't been here. They haven't *seen* how strong we are. And none of us have been back there. Gil—I want you to run the patrol from end to end. I want you to tell people about us. I want you to tell me about them when you come back."

Gil stared, his heart heavy. "Then—you don't want me when you cross the river? I won't be with you?"

Mackenzie shook his head. "Don't be a fool. You'll be back long before we can move. We've got to get more men. A week ago I was worried about that. Now, I'm not. They're coming slow, but they're coming steady. That's one thing that you've got to tell 'em." He paused. "You'll go?"

Gil thought a moment, then said, "Of course."

The other sprang to his feet. "I knew you would. Knew it. Now take these papers. Read 'em. You'll know most of what's in 'em, but get it in your mind. Then burn 'em before you start. Then here's a list of people along the way that you can trust. And where you'll find the patrols. It's all made out in jargon. You'll understand it but no one else will." He unfolded some papers. "See —on billheads. Thomas Crane, Glanford. Three bolts white cotton. George Wray, Pelham, two and one-half bullock hides. See how it goes? The township always means the next one north till you pass Hamilton, then east. The name of the man is the first word after the quantity. So in Glanford, which means Ancaster, you'll find a man named White, three miles out of town. In Pelham, which means Gainsborough, there's a man named Bullock two and a half miles out, and so on."

Gil frowned at the papers, working out the clumsy code in his head. "Suppose there are two Whites three miles out of Ancaster?"

"There aren't. That's been checked. And, of course, the measure is along the main road so you'll never be in trouble. Each man'll pass you on."

"Guess I can do it," said Gil.

Mackenzie sprang up. "I want you to start right away. Start at dark."

Gil nodded slowly. "I can do it."

"Then start right in on those papers. I won't see you before you go. The general's coming. Colonel Sutherland and—" He suddenly bent over the table.

"Nothing else?" asked Gil.

The big head shook. "You've got all I can tell you."

Gil hesitated, then swung abruptly out of the office. Mackenzie's voice snapped suddenly after him. "And—oh, Gil!" Gil stopped. "I just—well—I mean you've got everything?"

Gil looked surprised. "You said so."

"Oh, well. Guess you have. It occurred to me that—you'll tell 'em everything, won't you?"

"Of course," said Gil, irritated.

Mackenzie bent to his table again. Gil stamped off into the gathering dusk. "Damned cool about it. Does he think I'm going to a picnic? Ever occur to him that—that things might go wrong?

That—" Then it suddenly dawned on him that the little Scotchman, fully aware of the journey that lay ahead, found himself, for once, lacking words.

The voice of the Falls was thick in his ears as Gil stepped into a frail canoe at the south end of the island, just out of reach of the gathering swiftness of the stream. Josiah balanced a light paddle, pushed off. "Wish Mac'd let me go with you," he growled.

"No good, Jos. You're doing more right here. And you don't know the country the way I do."

Josiah gave a few vigorous strokes. "Got an idea I'll go just the same. When are you coming back?"

"In a few days. Before we move, anyway."

"God knows when that'll be. Since Mac gave Van Rensselaer full command, he won't give out a single plan. They say even Mac doesn't know."

"It'll be all right," said Gil. "How'd you get rid of Doc?"

"Left him with that broken leg. He'll be busy."

"Glad of that. He'd have squawked so you could have heard him below the Falls. He will anyway, when he finds I'm gone, but it'll be too late to do any good."

The canoe grated on the frozen shore under the sparse trees of the Canadian mainland. Far to the right, the lights of Chippewa twinkled. Gil sprang out, slung his haversack about his shoulders. "Well—take care of yourself, Jos."

"You too, boy," said Josiah. "I'll be looking for you."

There was a quick grip in the dark. Gil slipped out of sight beyond some stunted trees. Josiah blew out a long breath, leaned on his paddle. "Shouldn't have let him go. Bad if they get him. Hell, Mac had a dozen men he could have sent instead. Never miss 'em." He cocked his head, listening for Gil's sure footfalls that were already lost in the misty night.

He turned over and over in his mind the thought of leaving the canoe, running after his cousin. Then he blinked, stared. Inland, a strange procession moved slowly toward him, a broken string of balls of red that glowed, eerie, through the mist. He leaned forward, trying to melt the haze. Suddenly the darkness crackled. He put one foot into the canoe, ready to push off. A voice called softly. "Jos! Jos! You still there?"

Josiah sprang out. "You damned fool. Haven't you gone yet?"

Gil hopped down onto the little beach. "I saw something. Tell Mac." He pointed to the drifting red balls. "Jos! That's the militia! I nearly ran into one of the columns. They're coming this way."

"This way! What the hell for?"

"I think they're lost from what I heard. They're heading for Navy all right, though. Get back and tell Mac."

"Here! You come with me!"

"No chance," said Gil. "I can skip by 'em in the dark. It's easy. No guards, no flankers. Just those torches. Get back and tell Mac."

Then he was gone. Josiah, eyes still on the lights, saw them lose the shrouding globes of mist, reveal themselves as torches. He pushed out into the current, his paddle driving.

Half an hour later, Gil paused on a slight rise that overlooked the distant Welland Canal, looked back toward the dark-hooded east. As he stared, a dull flash lit up the woolly horizon, a heavy thud, another, beat in waves against his ears. He smiled grimly, started on again. The guns of Navy Island were speaking. There would be no Montgomery's farm on the shores of Niagara.

XXVI

Toronto — 1837

FORSYTH STENSROOD swung the carriage about in front of the square white house on Bloor Street. The green door swung open and Mary, drawn and white-faced, ran down the steps, the wind whipping the cascade of capes that fell from her green coat. She forced a smile as he helped her in and took the reins again. "You think they'll really let me see Cameron?" Her fingers worked in her little seal muff.

Forsyth's grave mouth set as he turned the horse. "Just as I said in my note. There may be a chance. I thought it was worth taking."

She watched the broad sweep of the Elmsley estate roll past, the neat fence of the Sharpe house. "I'm glad you let me know. I—I really don't expect to see him. But if I do—" Her head in its deep bonnet drooped. "What *can* they do to him? What?" She clenched her hidden hands. "But I'm not going into that again. Have you still got a guard at Nipigon?"

"Relieved yesterday," said Forsyth. "Contingent, of course, on our good behavior." He smiled. "I think the real reason's Father. He deviled those guards until they were glad to go. He used to get up in the middle of the night and wake the men that were off duty. Said as long as he was paying for their keeping watch, he was going to see to it that they did a good job." Then his face was grave again. "You've not had any?"

She shook her head. "No. We've been spared that. But Uncle Sperry has been around twice. He keeps telling me that if I say where Gil is, they might let Cam go. He says they wouldn't do anything to Gil, of course."

"Don't even think about him," said Forsyth. "I don't know where he is either, but I'm so afraid I might let fall a hint without realizing it, a clue that they could pick up." His face set in an impassive mask. "You know that Van Egmond's very ill? Well, they've got him in the lowest and dampest cell of all—in December."

At the corner of King Street he had to pull up as a line of carts rumbled past, crowded with haggard, anxious men. Double files of un-uniformed cavalry, rude lances aslant, hemmed in the rolling wheels. "Poor devils," said Forsyth. "From Duncombe's lot, I imagine. Though I doubt if Alan MacNab's militia'll make much distinction between Duncombe's men and ordinary Reformers. The force is smashed and the militia's just running wild."

The carts trailed off to the east and Forsyth followed at a careful distance, somber eyes on the uneasy streets. Down by the waterfront a mounted patrol under command of a green-jacketed officer rode off toward the west. Up from the Market, a detail of men with fixed bayonets clumped off toward the Bank of Upper Canada, where the men waiting to be relieved stood in a wavering line by the distant façade. Before occasional boarded-up shops, militiamen lounged, muskets cradled in idle arms or resting against the doors that Reform owners had opened in the past.

Mary raised her muff to her pale cheeks as Forsyth pulled up before the brick front of the jail, stared across the open stretch where a sea of faces, stern, smug, worried, frantic, wove an endless, moving pattern. Forsyth tucked the robes about her. "Wait here, Mary. I'll go in and see what I can do."

She nodded quickly, pleading eyes on his. "And do let me know as soon as you can. Just waiting here— "

He patted her hand. "If we don't see him, at least we'll be able to send word."

Eyes on the cold red of the brick, she murmured, "At least, he'll know we've been here— "

Forsyth smiled reassuringly, crossed the open space, and climbed the stairs. A good-natured-looking countryman swung his musket awkwardly across the door. Forsyth inclined his head. "To see Mr. Gray. Tell him it's Mr. Stensrood."

The man grinned. "See Mr. Gray? Sure." He pushed open the door. "Tommy. Gent to see Mr. Gray." Forsyth strode into the chill, dank interior, followed a powerfully built guide down an echoing corridor, was shown into a small office where a fire burned briskly.

"Mr. Gray?" said Forsyth.

The face that looked up from the littered desk was affable, ruddy. "Oh — Mr. Stensrood. To be sure. I was half expecting you."

"So I presumed," said Forsyth. "No — thank you. I'll not sit down, if you please."

Gray's smile was almost paternal. "Been riding a long way, eh? I always like to stretch out when I've been on the road. Cold, isn't it?"

"I had your note," said Forsyth.

"To be sure you did. To be sure you did." Gray's face exuded kindliness. "Ah — that door's closed, isn't it? Good. Now, you must have gathered from my note that there was some error in your son's arrest."

"I knew that anyway."

Gray tapped a quill against his teeth. "As to that — a mere matter of opinion, eh? What I meant was — well, you see, there's no *record* of his arrest. No charge."

"Then he should be released at once."

"Absence of charge doesn't mean innocence, Mr. Stensrood. Your son's opinions were well known. What I meant was that the absence — a mistake — you see?"

Forsyth inclined his head. "I believe that I see. But a mistake that perhaps fifty pounds might correct."

Gray's hands clutched his blue lapels gently, the firelight playing on the brass buttons of his cuffs. He looked pained. "My dear Mr. Stensrood. Fifty pounds? For Mr. Cameron Stensrood? Why, Mr. Brodie out Yonge Street paid forty to get *his* son off. Just a plowboy."

"I'm not in a mood to bargain, Gray. It's my son. What do you want?"

Gray beamed. "I'm glad to see you look at it in a reasonable light. Suppose we say one hundred and ten pounds. If it's in gold, of course — " Then his eyes narrowed. Forsyth had drawn a bag from his greatcoat, began to count out neat piles of gold pieces, being very precise that each stack should be trim, symmetrical.

"There," said Forsyth. "One hundred and ten pounds — in gold. I'll thank you to send for my son."

Gray tugged at a bellpull, shouted, "Send for Mulqueen." Then he folded his hands over his slight paunch. "I'm really glad that we were able to see eye to eye in this matter."

Forsyth looked coldly out the window. Gray went on, "Of course, it's not strictly regular. But you mustn't think that I'm — "

"I don't think about you at all, Gray," said Forsyth shortly.

Gray flushed, then hastily flung a handkerchief over the heaps of gold. The door creaked to his shout and a bright-eyed Irishman, long upper lip twitching in a grin, peered in.

"Bring out Mr. Stensrood."

The grin broadened. "It's today he's goin', then?"

Gray nodded. Mulqueen looked shrewdly at Forsyth. "It'll be Your Honor that's takin' him? Then there's a little matter Your Honor'd like to be seein' to. I been feedin' Mr. Stensrood like me own son, that I have, and — "

"How much?" asked Forsyth quickly.

"Well, now, you'll be after thinkin' I ain't treated him like the gentleman he is if I'm tellin' you less'n a pound, now will you?"

Forsyth reached under the handkerchief, picked out a coin, and flipped it to the Irishman. "Bring him here."

Mulqueen caught the coin, deft as a monkey, scraped a bow to Forsyth, and clattered off. Gray, eyes bulging, stammered: "That was *my* money. That was — "

"You've got palms to grease. You can cross that Paddy off your list. Aah!" He whirled about. The door swung open and Cameron, pale, thin, but neat as though he were in his own trim office, stood on the threshold.

"Father!" he gasped.

Forsyth put his arm over his shoulder. "Come on, Cam. You're going with me." He swung him out into the corridor, arm still about his shoulder and eyes searching his son's face as though he feared that he might melt away into the shades of the prison.

Cameron, blinking in the hard light, asked, "How did it happen? Where am I going?"

"With me," said Forsyth.

"They're moving me? We're so crowded that a lot of people are being taken to Osgoode Hall and to the Parliament Buildings. That'll be a lot better than this. Glad you could come with me. How's Mary? Is she all right? How's Mother? How's — "

"Let's not talk till we get outside," said Forsyth. He pushed Cameron through the door, watched him stumble ahead of him, feet still uncertain. Then he saw him stop, saw a sudden flurry of green from the waiting carriage. There was a half-choked cry of "Mary!" and Cameron began to run.

Forsyth drew a deep breath, stopped to talk with the grinning guard, then slowly descended the broad stairs. When he reached the street, Cameron and Mary, oblivious of the stir of the city, were clinging to each other wordlessly.

Forsyth made his boots ring on the frozen ground, fussed with the horses' bits, then climbed in on the other side of the carriage. Cameron reached across Mary, gripped his hand. "Father—I didn't know what was up until I saw Mary."

She shook her head, eyes unnaturally bright. "Why didn't you tell me?"

Forsyth picked up the reins. "I didn't know what would happen until I talked to Gray. Then—" He sketched rapidly his conversation with the ruddy, smiling man.

The bitter lines about Cameron's mouth deepened. "And I was only one of a hundred. If you knew what I know about that jail—" He looked back at the receding brick bulk. Then he said shortly, "Know where Gil is?"

Forsyth shook his head. "But we're quite sure he's with Mackenzie."

"I'm very much tempted to join him," said Cameron. His face reddened. "By God, if I'd ever realized what the Compact was capable of—"

"I thought we knew pretty well," said Forsyth dryly.

"We didn't. That Innis trial was an honorable affair compared to what we have now. And if I'd known, I say, I'd have been at Montgomery's with Gil."

"Cam," said Mary gently, "we've only just got you back. Rest a little. Then we'll talk things over. If you feel you ought to, I won't do a thing to hold you."

Forsyth, eyes on the rising sweep of Yonge Street, drew a deep breath. "Cam, we've all been thinking. After you've thought in clear air, I don't think you'll feel you ought to go. No—let me finish. Things are bad—fearfully bad. But they can be worse. We've got to stay here and fight—in our own way. If Mackenzie wins—and I think he has a good chance—those of us who don't believe in his most radical measures have got to work and work and work to keep things level. He'll want to join the States. He'll want to set up a kingdom, he'll want to go under the protection of France. The Lord knows what he'll want to do. What most of us want are an Englishman's rights and we could lose them under Mackenzie as well as under the Compact—unless he's checked."

Cameron growled, "That sounds as though you were getting ready to support Head and Strachan."

"Never that! I just told you what's got to be done if Mackenzie wins. It'll be harder if he loses—and he well may. Then our fight against the Compact'll go on and on and on. But it's got to be a Canadian fight. Right here in Canada."

"Then why not go with Mackenzie?"

"Cam, we've never distrusted his basic ideas or his sincerity. It's his judgment. If he wins and brings a lot of Yankee adventurers as well as our own exiles back with him, how'll it be then? And the Yankee adventurers won't be very much like the Yankees we've known and respected. Mackenzie is heading the same way we are. But his road's different and he's apt to pick up mud on the way. He may overshoot his mark. But a strong tempering force, staying here and fighting quietly, may win for all of us. Just keep thinking about that. Now, about Nipigon. You and Mary'll come right out there. The children are there now. You'll have—have Gil's old room. So now suppose you tell us about the jail."

The carriage climbed the long slope that was crowned by the ruins of Montgomery's farm and tavern. Cameron talked on in a low hard voice. Forsyth, eyes on the road, listened, while Mary leaned her cheek against her husband's shoulder.

Janet carefully snipped a thread, smoothed out her embroidery. "It's just as I was telling you at dinner, Cam. We haven't heard a word from Gil. We know he got away from the battle, because Dr. Richland told us. He must be with Mackenzie."

Mary, eyes always on Cameron, said, "And they say that he has the whole Yankee army with him."

"Rubbish," said Barnabas. "They'll treasure their neutrality the way Janet does that old Chinese platter. And they've got a new President coming in in March. Van Brunt, Van Brenner, Van Buren—that's it. If that damned fire-eater Jackson were going to stay, I'd expect him to go up and pitch that Scotch imbecile and all MacNab's militia over the Falls."

Cameron looked surprised. "The militia there now?"

"A lot of it," said Forsyth. "Reached the river about three days ago."

"And that Bombastes Furioso MacNab in command. He enlarges my ideas of the possible. He's even a worse clown than Head." He threw back his mane, stared up the room. "You send Thomas out for anything, Janet?"

She shook her head. "Not I. Why?"

"Heard a rattle at the door."

"Maybe it's the guard coming back," said Mary, eyes shifting toward the door, a hand on her husband's arm.

Forsyth laughed. "If you'd seen the guard fly before Father, you wouldn't say that. It's probably the wind jarring things. It's—"

A blast of cold air suddenly swept through the room, stirred the portieres. Then there was a heavy tread in the hall. "Hello," said Gil. "Guess you'd better draw the curtains. All the way."

Janet uttered a low cry, then flew down the length of the room where Gil, shabby in travel-stained clothes, held out his arms. Forsyth, close behind, heard her low cry: "Safe! Safe!"

"Bring him here!" trumpeted Barnabas as Mary and Cameron rose, staring in amazement.

His father and mother clinging to his arms, Gil, grinning sheepishly, stood before the great chair.

"Well, sir," said Barnabas. "Is this your idea of a joke?"

Gil laughed, then grew grave. "You don't think I'd have come here if I hadn't known everything was all right, do you? I knew when your guards were sent away. I know they won't be back. I know just where all the patrols are now. I—"

"Gad!" said Barnabas. Then he glared at Forsyth and Janet. "What do you mean, letting him stand like that? Make him sit down. Push him into a chair. Now sir, what have you been up to?" His tone was sharp, but his old eyes were proud.

Gil drew a deep breath. "First thing I want to know is, where's Sandra?"

Janet touched his hand. "Gil dear, we don't know. She was here and told us about you. But then her father sent an escort for her and took her away. She's probably at Trafalgar."

Gil's face darkened. "I can't go there. Not this time. I'd hoped she was here, because I was going to take her back with me."

Janet stiffened, then said in a quiet voice, "You're going back?"

"Of course I am," said Gil, surprised. "The job's not done yet. And I could have taken Sandra, easily." He set his jaw. "Well—next time, then. Just let her know, if you can, that you've seen me." He looked at Forsyth. "How about Graves, Father?"

"The Compact think he's in hiding," said Forsyth. "But we have reason to believe that he's safe in the States—ah—in fact your Uncle John and Flora have gone to join him."

"Good," said Gil. "Now don't forget to let Sandra know about me."

Cameron leaned forward. "We'll help all we can, Gil. Now, how about Grandfather's question? What's been happening?"

Gil stretched out his long legs, launched into an account of his trip. In a farmhouse near Niagara he'd been sheltered, then sent on his way. Each district, each town, had yielded up its store of news. Near Twenty-mile Creek a lawyer had given him a whispered list of forty sure men, waiting to rise. Farther on, he'd heard of sixty, then twenty-two. He had waited on a windy hill at midnight and a horseman had slipped from a pine grove to tell him of three militia companies that would go over to Mackenzie in a body. Again, Gil had actually marched as a private in a militia company, Hamilton-bound, had seen ruthless confiscation of Reform property. His teeth set as he told of a woman whom he had seen threatened, struck, in an attempt to make her give information about her fugitive husband. The woman had been pregnant, a miscarriage had resulted, and Gil had called on his painfully acquired skill to save her life, saying he'd once had to help a doctor. Ten men of the company deserted, enraged at the brutality. He had, he thought, an interesting packet of news to take back to Navy Island.

Barnabas stretched out his blue-veined hand. "Gil, I'm proud of you. God bless you." Then he blew his nose fiercely. "Brandy! Thomas shall bring us brandy."

Worshiping eyes on Gil, the old Negro, knees high, set out a decanter, glasses. Barnabas held up his glass. "We're drinking to a real Stensrood—to a man who's found what he knows is right and is giving himself to it."

"Amen," mumbled Thomas, head bowed.

Forsyth replaced his glass on the low table. "Gil, just what do you make of everything you've heard?"

"Just this." Gil spoke crisply. "All Mac has to do is show himself solidly across the border with a steady force back of him — not just a raid. Really show himself — and he'll have nothing to fight. The people who held back before because they thought that violence was wrong will come to him in thousands. He can march into Toronto and the thing will be over."

"And then?" said Forsyth, eyes on Cameron.

"Then we'll set up the government that everyone wants. It may mean separation. I hope not. But the Crown doesn't seem to care about us, doesn't care how we're governed. If that keeps up, we're better off by ourselves."

Forsyth shook his head. "I hate to think of it. I hate to think of it."

Gil turned to Cameron. "How'd you like to think that your children would grow up under a succession of Heads, Strachans, Colbornes?"

His brother sighed. "I can't argue against that, Gil."

"Can't argue?" snapped Barnabas. "Of course you can. You can say that the new order might be even worse than the old. That's what you'll have to keep on fighting if Gil's Dundee-Bonaparte wins." His eyes rested longingly on Gil. "What I'd give to be your age!" He rapped on the floor. "Damn it, you're *doing* what the rest of us have just talked about. Not sure your way's the right one, but you're doing it, anyway."

Gil rose slowly. "Well — guess it's time for me to start."

Janet, lips tight, caught at his arm. "Gil — going back — you won't — will it — "

He laughed down at her, stroked her hair. "Easy. I know just where to go and whom to see. I'll get news all along the way, too. If MacNab's moved as much as a company during the day, I'll know about it by midnight. Why, this noon I heard that Mac's got the *Caroline* running regularly from Schlosser to Navy. And I'll find some way of getting word to you from time to time." He looked searchingly about the little group as though he were trying to stamp the picture in his memory. He straightened himself. "Better not come to the door with me. I'll slip out back." For an instant he was among them. Then he was gone.

XXVII

Reunion — 1838

Gil sprang from the jolting country cart at the foot of the Fort Schlosser pier, saw a heavy-shouldered figure shouting directions through the dusk to a slow-moving scow. "Jos!" shouted Gil. "Got your cigars."

Josiah whooped, raced up the pier, thumped Gil's shoulder. "God, I'm glad to see you back! How'd it go? Where are the cigars?"

Gil shoved a packet at him. "That's nice! I've been grooming horses for MacNab and the first thing you ask about's the cigars. Got 'em at Rawson's in Buffalo. You owe me three-fifty."

"Damn the cigars," said Josiah. "Have a bad time?"

"No. Pretty easy. Hoped I'd get to Nipigon on this trip, but there wasn't time. Can't count on it always, I suppose."

"Er—anything about Sandra?" asked Josiah anxiously.

Gil shook his head. "She knows where I am. I hear she'll be all ready if I can manage to get up the Don."

Josiah whistled. "Damned dangerous work, Gil. Why don't you wait? If anything happened— "

Gil shook his head obstinately. "Been waiting too long. We've— " There was a distant flash that flickered like sullen lightning over the water, a crashing roar. He smiled grimly. "Doing some damage over there, I hear. They've had to give up at least three posts. Too exposed. They haven't hurt us yet, have they?"

"Not they. Their shots are wild. The trees are a fine screen for us, too. Well, want to cross over? I'll have another barge in about a half hour."

"Not for me," said Gil. "I saw Mac in Buffalo and gave him all the news." Another flash and roar split the darkness. "That's it. Give it to 'em. Why—I think I'll grab that cabin on the *Caroline*. She won't put out again tonight, will she? Well—I'll be there.

Tell Doc I'll see him in the morning. And tell him they're sending more bandages and calomel for him tomorrow."

"Come on and have a drink first," urged Josiah.

"Couldn't keep my eyes open that long," said Gil. "See you on the island." He tramped on, sprang across the narrow gap that separated ship and wharf. " 'Hoy! Captain Appleby!"

A long, goatlike face peered down from the lighted pilothouse. "Who's that?"

"Stensrood. Got a cabin for me?"

"Sure. Take the same one you used last time. Give you the big one, except there's five fellers from Albany and Rochester sleepin' there."

"Thanks," said Gil and, eyes blinking with sleep, stumbled down the long corridor to the little cabin. He kicked off his boots, rolled into the narrow berth, and a Niagara of sleep swept over him.

The hours slipped by on the steady current of the river, crashed to some dark oblivion of their own as the waters smashed over the distant lip of the Falls. Once Gil stirred in his sleep, turned, sank back into infinite depths of slumber. Gradually he floated upward to consciousness, slowly at first, then with a rush. Overhead, along the decks, there were shouts, pounding feet, the sharp bark of a pistol. He staggered to his feet, the mists of sleep still thick about his brain. The shouts grew louder. A voice roared: "Everyone ashore! Turn out! Get ashore!"

Gil struggled with his boots in the dark. The *Caroline* was sinking? It was attacked? It couldn't be the latter. Even MacNab would have sense enough not to storm a ship in American waters. The steamer must be sinking. It must—

Then the panels of the door splintered to a kick, the latch ripped, and three men, bright cutlasses drawn, rushed into the cabin. Gil reached for a chair, swung it high, but a sharp point stung against his ribs. The leading man shouted, "We won't hurt you. Get ashore. Get moving!"

Helpless, Gil let the chair crash to the floor. "Who the devil are you?" he snapped.

"Never mind. Get ashore. And keep your hands high." The three stood aside, blades gleaming in the light that streamed in from the corridor. Gil made a helpless gesture, walked sullenly through the door. From other cabins, blinking, disheveled men poured, while at the head of the short companionway more cutlasses glinted, rifle barrels shone.

Gil was prodded up onto the deck where he joined the slow shuffle that moved toward the pier. Among the fugitives were two street girls from Buffalo, their hard eyes, even in panic, looking appraisingly at the armed men. In a corner by the short gangway, a man in a red coat leaned weakly, two others supporting him, and there was blood on the decks.

Gil suddenly began to push at the men ahead of him. "Get ashore quick," he muttered. "Get to the tavern. Arms there. Get ashore."

The men stared helplessly, continued their dazed shuffle. Gil shoved roughly past them, sprang to the wharf where a group of men hacked furiously at the *Caroline's* cable. Then the wharf echoed to his flying feet, light snow crunched under his boots.

About the tavern, frightened men clustered, staring at the glow of the steamer's ports. Gil hurled himself among them. "Get rifles! Pistols! Anything! My God, they're trying to steal the boat. Get along the bank and pick 'em off! Stave in their boats!"

A few men looked at him uncertainly. A quavering voice said, "They've got swords. I seen 'em. They've— "

Gil pushed into the tavern, burst into the room where neat cases of muskets lay, ready for shipment. He snatched a weapon, ripped open a box of cartridges, ready rolled, found bullets fresh from the molds, and stuffed his pockets.

Loading as he ran, he jammed his way into the chill of the night, dropped to one knee and fired. A black figure by the deckhouse jumped, then ran for cover. A musket roared close by Gil's elbow, another. The crowd had begun to lose its inertia of panic and a few men knelt beside him, firing at the bright bulk of the steamer. The darkness spat red and the black waters mirrored fleeting tongues of fire as the raiders answered. Down by the wharf, a man pitched forward, sprawled in the snow, kicking. Then he was still, a dark pool welling out from his head.

The steamer began to move slowly away from the wharf, a long string of boats trailing behind it. Gil sprang to his feet, ran along the bank. A half-seen figure crashed past him, flung itself on the snow, fired, reloaded with frantic haste. A voice snarled, "Never mind the damned steamer. Shoot for the little boats. By God, this is United States territory." His musket slammed in unison with

Gil's and two distant rapping thuds told them that lead had pitched against the sides of a low barge.

The *Caroline* began to swing slowly, broadside to the current, bow pointing toward Navy Island. Gil's companion rose to his knees, snow clinging wetly to his long coat. "Look at that. Bow's fast on that bar. They can't — "

Gil's hand on his shoulder cut off his words. "Look!" shouted Gil.

The barges were pulling away from the *Caroline*. "They're giving up. We'll be able to float her off. We can — " His voice died away in his throat.

The lights of the steamer that raced and flickered to the dull ruffle of the river seemed to harden, then to glow red. A crimson sword blade slashed dazzling from an open port, a great scarlet tongue swooped upward, leaping high above the deckhouse. A bristle of flame, like frantic, waving arms, burst from every opening, tore along the railing, flooded over the stern. The *Caroline* shivered, swung to the current, began to drift toward the Falls.

The flames shot higher and higher, their shifting light turning the tall parade of trees on the American shore into a weird witch's saraband. The tall smokestack began to glow sullenly, to brighten into a scarlet finger that stretched toward the polished black sky. The current was swifter now, and the blazing pyre shot on along the rough floor of red gold. Then suddenly all was black and the tossing waters were dark, empty. They had always been so. No spark had ever shone on them. No raging cargo of red-white hell had ever hissed and crackled down the swift track to the Falls.

The man in the snow drew a deep breath. "Gone."

Gil nodded, shakily. "Over the Falls."

"Couldn't a done that. She'd a hit the bridge by Goat Island. Guess her innards just dropped through the bottom." He turned to Gil. "You're one of these patriots? Well, never thought much of you. But, by God, no river rats can cross over and take an American ship at an American wharf."

Gil, eyes still fixed on the black expanse where the *Caroline* had flared so brightly, shrugged. "Well — what are you going to do about it?"

The man jerked his head toward the western gloom. "Going over and join that Mackenzie." He hunched his musket under his arm, slouched off through the night.

Gil, depressed, walked slowly back toward the tavern. The raid had come with such stunning surprise, had been crowned with such success, that its shadow seemed to hang in the sky like a lowering cloud. He found a chattering swarm of people at the tavern, where the body of the man from the wharf had been carried, but there was nothing to be learned from the bubbles of excited rumor and report that welled up. Twenty men had gone over the Falls in the *Caroline*. The raiders had tied the captain and crew in the boiler room before firing the ship. A hundred men had been killed in the exchange of fire. All the raiding boats had been captured and the survivors were being marched to Buffalo, where they would be executed by order of General Winfield Scott.

Gil turned away in disgust, stopped as a sudden ripping fire from Navy Island tore open the night. He began to run toward the wharf. "Drew's barges! They've tried to go back between Navy and Grand! We'll get 'em there. We—" Then the night was quiet, the last echoes of the explosions muttering away along the chill, dark shores. Gil kept on, saw a single figure puttering about a broad scow. "That you, Clay? Take me to Navy?"

The man straightened up. "Who's that? You? All right. Get in."

"Not afraid of running into the barges?"

Clay spat in the water, picked up his scull. "Bastards. Like to get my hands on 'em."

The scow worked skillfully over the river, its prow edging along in the quieter waters, keeping clear of the swift ruffle that might send it toward the Falls. At last its side scraped against the pier of Navy Island. Gil sprang ashore. "Thanks, Clay. Going to lie over here? All right."

He left Clay busy with the painter of the scow and walked cautiously along the unseen path to the main building, where a dull light glowed. He started to shout, then checked himself, staring. The door opened and a woman's figure was silhouetted against the background. "That's a damned fine example to set the camp," thought Gil, disgust flooding over him. "Van Rensselaer might at least keep his wench ashore if—" He stared at the figure. There was something familiar, something— She lifted her hand to her throat in a graceful gesture. Gil laughed. "Well! Mrs. Mackenzie! Now we'll get along better. How did you get here?"

Her gentle voice answered, "Gil! Is that you? I managed to get away. I came across by boat tonight."

"You're a heroine. Is Mac asleep?"

"He ought to be. It's past two. But he and the general are talking. Or rather, the general is." She turned, called to an inner room. "Will, here's Gil Stensrood."

Quick feet thumped on the dirt floor and Mackenzie loomed in the dim light. "Gil! Glad you came. I was just going to send for you. I need—"

"Did we get any of the barges?" broke in Gil.

The thin wig shook. "No luck. We had all our heavy guns on the other bank. They kept out of range. Did you see it all ashore?"

"See it!" Gil laughed shortly. "I was on board. They herded us off like sheep."

Mackenzie seized his arm. "Any damage? Who were they? When—"

"One man—a peddler, I think—killed by a stray shot. That's all, except the loss of the boat. And they were led by Andy Drew. You know him. Royal Navy, retired. And a man named McCormick was badly hurt. I saw him on deck. He was lieutenant in one of the militia companies, I think."

Mackenzie shook his head. "It wouldn't have helped if we'd got 'em all. The *Caroline's* gone. At least, we got some good loads across in her first. It'll just mean—"

Van Rensselaer's heavy voice echoed from the inner room. "Mr. Mackenzie. There are several other points I want to discuss with you."

Mackenzie looked impatiently toward the half-open door. Gil drew him outside. "Just a minute, Mac. A lot of the boys think he has too much to say around here—and won't stand it. I want to give you a plan for a raid by us. Slip twenty men ashore—"

Mackenzie looked wistfully at Gil. "He's in control. And then that Committee of Thirteen in Buffalo. They do all the planning. They—they don't consult me very much."

Mrs. Mackenzie's hand touched his shoulder. "You can't waste yourself on soldiering, Will. They know that."

Again Van Rensselaer shouted, angrily. Mackenzie's lips set. "Come with me, Gil."

Gil followed him into the little room where the general frowned over a mass of papers, a brandy bottle by his elbow. He raised his eyebrows as he saw Gil. "Really, Mr. Mackenzie. I don't see the need — "

Mackenzie sat down, pushed up a chair for Gil. "He's got an idea I want you to hear."

Van Rensselaer smiled tolerantly. "Perhaps, perhaps. Later on. Since he's here, I want to ask him about the figures he brought back the last time." He drew out a soiled sheet. "How much of this is guesswork?" He pointed to a neat column of names and figures.

"I wouldn't waste your time with guesses," said Gil quietly. "I talked with a lot of those men. I talked with all the leaders. And — " he tapped the paper — "Mr. Mackenzie'll tell you how important this list is. Hastings County has always been heavily anti-Reform. Look at this — " He held the sheet up. "Number of men sworn to rise as soon as we come in: Belleville, forty-two; Thurlow, ninety-three; Sidney, one hundred sixty-five, and so on. That gives us a known total of four hundred eighty-two men in Hastings alone."

"That true? About Hastings being usually loyal?"

"You don't need to question anything that Stensrood says," answered Mackenzie shortly. He sprang to his feet, the fire of old days in his eyes. "Can't you see? If we move *now,* the whole country'll rise to us. We can — "

Van Rensselaer shook his head. "The Committee doesn't think that now is the time. MacNab's got five times the number of men around Chippewa that we have here. And besides — don't forget that we're doing a lot in the Detroit area. We're going to move there. Our actions must be harmonized." He repeated the phrase with deep relish, poured himself more brandy.

"But the longer we wait, the better organized they'll be on the other side. They're in a bad way now. Why give 'em time?" urged Gil. "And our own people'll get tired of waiting."

"Time is with us," said Van Rensselaer pompously. "And what can they do, except move more shaky militia here?"

"They've got plenty that's not shaky," said Gil. "And another thing. They're raising Negro companies. They've got them believing that the Americans are coming over to take them back to slavery. They'll make the solidest troops the Compact's got — given time. And then look at Colborne. He smashed the French for good and all at St. Eustache. He'll be able to spare men to use here. We'll have the Fifteenth, the Eighty-third, marching in."

Van Rensselaer snorted. "He'll be too busy there for another six months to think of Upper Canada. We know that."

"But let's *do* something, besides bombard the other shore. The men are getting restless and — "

"Tell him your plan, Gil," said Mackenzie quickly.

Van Rensselaer sighed. Gil, unheeding, went on. "Send fifty good men — you can spare 'em — up-river a few miles — land 'em. Let 'em make a show of attack. It'll draw MacNab's force upstream for one thing. For another, it'll be good for the men. For a third, it'll have a tremendous effect on the Reformers over there. Then, while that's — "

The general waved impatiently. "Just send men across the river to — "

"There are a hundred safe places to land. I know 'em. I use 'em. But there's more than that. We've got more arms here than we have men — a lot more. While the demonstration's being made, another group, still farther upstream, will land with cases of muskets, powder. I know places where they can be hidden, where they'll get into the right hands over there."

Mackenzie looked up quickly. "Through George Wilson?"

"For one," said Gil. "The biggest trouble, you see, is that so few of our people are armed. We can do that out of surplus. They'll all know where to go. Then, when we finally move from here, MacNab'll be attacked by us in front *and* in the *rear* by the men we'll have armed."

Mackenzie smacked his hand on the table. "General! We've *got* to do it. I — I urge it, urge it strongly. Those muskets at Schlosser — "

"Not Schlosser!" Van Rensselaer looked alarmed. "I tell you, Win Scott's not going to stand for any forces setting out from the American side. No. No. Not the Schlosser arms."

"They can be brought here," explained Gil patiently. "Our boats'll push off at night from the upper end of the island. The arms boats'll start first, because they've farther to go. Then the attacking party."

"And we can use the men that Silas Fletcher's sent down from Oswego — Canadians and Americans," put in Mackenzie eagerly.

Van Rensselaer blew out his cheeks, rubbed the end of his nose. "Well — well. I'll think about it."

"Can't you say yes now?" Gil leaned across the table. "We've got to move the arms here, get the boats ready. Time's important. We've sat here doing nothing so long that people are beginning to say we're afraid of MacNab's men." He paused, eyed the flushed face before him. "They say you're afraid to attack — to move."

The American started. "What? What's that?" He thumped a mottled fist on the table. "I'll issue orders now. This instant."

Weary and heavy-footed, Gil sought out the hut where he kept his scant belongings, lit a carefully hoarded candle end. The flame wavered, then shone on a white square that lay on the heap of straw and leaves that served as bed. Wonderingly he picked it up, saw Richland's gnarled script. He focused aching eyes. "What the devil's Doc got on his mind?" His jaw dropped. He sat down slowly.

Dear Gil: —

That brandy-drinking baboon sent for me. I told him his only trouble was liquor. I further added that I did not recommend his abstaining on the grounds that did he continue his present course, he would undoubtedly die and thus Mackenzie would have a fair chance of success. As a result, I'm barred forever from the island. Poor Mac tried to protest, but to no avail. A letter to the Eagle will always reach me until I find some way of getting back to you again. I've left you a list of my cases. Please look to the dressing of McCarthy's arm and see that Lefferts keeps his bowels open. I've made a packet of medicines and left them with Captain Burnham of the Rifle Company. And try to crowd a little sense into that thick head of yours. You're the only doctor left on the island and if you go wambling off to see what MacNab's having for breakfast, you'll be doing a bad turn to some pretty sick man. They need you and . . .

Dully, Gil folded the letter. "Doesn't anything *ever* go right in this damned world?"

The fires across the river began to die down as MacNab's shivering pickets rolled themselves in their blankets, exhausted with their celebration of New Year's Eve. From the south tip of Navy Island, Gil watched the distant pools of light fade and shrink. The air was clear, sharp, and occasionally he could hear a muffled shout, a distant whinny, over the black waters. Behind him, the stir of the camp hummed and muttered in preparation for the expedition. It was a pity that Van Rensselaer had cut the original plan in two, eliminating the raiding party and allowing a scant thirty men to carry the cases of arms inland to the Wilson house, lost in a wooded tangle of rocks. Gil had hoped for that number as a covering force alone. Still, the job could be done, and he glowed to think of its effect on the waiting, unarmed Reformers in the Niagara district. And news would spread. Perhaps Wilson's place could be used as a depot from which arms could be smuggled by sure routes to the hills back of Hamilton, to the wild tangle of the Huron Tract, to—

He started as a twelve-pounder slammed from the southern abatis, the ball whining into the thick darkness that now shrouded the militia camp. There was an answering crash from the other side and a heavy ball ripped into the tangle of trees that hid a well-covered casemate on the island.

Gil blinked, the flash still dazzling his eyes. Something had moved on the current. He crouched in the bushes, pistol drawn. There could be no doubt about it. Something long and narrow was working out into the stream, skillfully avoiding the rushing water that might sweep it in spinning helplessness past the island and on to the Falls. He drew his breath, ready to shout an alarm, then checked. The object was nearer now—a single canoe. He could handle that himself, if it came too close. No need to rouse the guard, or delay the loading of the scows. He crouched lower, staring incredulously. The canoe was actually working in, close to the south point, the paddler in the stern apparently heading for a deep-scooped cove just at Gil's left.

He looked to his priming, moved silently back of a screen of trees just as the bow grated softly on the little beach. He cocked his pistol, dropped behind a low rock. "Up with your hands!" he snapped.

The paddler's arms went up with a swoop. Then something stirred in the bow. A vizored cap showed against the skyline and a slim figure sprang to the beach. Gil's pistol fell from his hand as a voice cried: "Gil! Gil! Where are you? Gil!"

He swung himself over the rock, dropped to the beach, and caught the waiflike trousered figure in his arms. "Sandra! What—what—" But she stifled his words, clinging close. The absurd cap fell to the beach.

Then a voice spoke from the canoe. "Well, miss, you said you was anxious to get across and I guess you wasn't lyin' none."

Sandra's arms slipped from Gil's neck. "Oh — I'd forgotten. I — "

"Who's that?" asked Gil sharply.

"You Gil Stensrood? I talked to you the night you come to Scotch Block. George Semple."

Gil, his arm still about Sandra, stammered in bewilderment. "But how — how — "

She caught his hand. "Don't talk now, Gil. Mr. McDonald sent Alice and her mother to stay in Hamilton. Father made me go with them. Then I heard about your being here. I decided to come. It was so easy. I went to all the places you'd been. I've even got papers for Mr. Mackenzie. From Mr. Stone."

"And I reckoned folk wouldn't stare if she dressed like a boy. She and me, we come down together on a load of meal. Found George Wilson and he gave us a canoe." The paddle waved again. "Here we are. Now where's Mac?"

"Are you staying?" said Gil.

"Got to. They took my farm. Guess I would have anyway. Where'll I find him?"

"Follow that path till someone stops you. Tell him you're from me." Semple climbed out of the canoe, clumped off through the woods.

Sandra turned, felt herself caught up again. "We're together now. There's no parting us," he whispered.

She shook her head contentedly. "Nothing can. I couldn't go back now, even if I wanted to. It was bad enough when they found I'd been to Montgomery's. They — "

"Been a hard time?" asked Gil gently.

She lifted her chin. "Not as bad as you've had." Her fingers caught one of the buttons of his coat. "Gil — we can get married now? Right away?"

His arm tightened about her. "Just as soon as we can get to Buffalo."

"Tonight! We'll go now. Let's begin our 1838 together!"

He laughed. "Tomorrow. Buffalo's a long way. It's — " Suddenly the joy of the moment slipped from him. "No — not tomorrow — I don't know — there's — "

She seized his arm. "Gil — what is it? What's the matter?"

He shook his head. "We've got to wait. Just a little while, though, You see, I was just starting out—I was waiting for the men to come up when I saw you. I've got to start."

She gave a low cry. "Gil! Not now! Not just as we're together again."

"I've got to," he said simply.

"But why? Another time! Not now!" Her upturned face was drawn with anxiety.

In a few broken sentences he told of his plan. "And if we don't do it now, we'll never do it. Van Rensselaer has changed his orders twice already. If I go back and say we'll do it another day, he'll cancel the whole thing for good. And we've let people know—they're waiting for us across there. They'll get discouraged if we don't come."

She was crying quietly against his shoulder. "It's been so hard to come to you. And you're leaving. I'll be alone again. On the island." She held him tighter.

He stroked her hair. "I'll be back in twenty-four hours. That's all. And it is important. Think I'd go if it weren't? And it's just as safe as walking across King Street."

She drew a long, quivering breath. "Twenty-four hours? Then you'll be back?" Her voice was low, unsteady.

He forced a laugh. "This time I'll make the quickest trip ever. There! Now I'd better take you to Mrs. Mac. She just came. She'll look after you—she and Jos. Catch hold of my hand. I'll go ahead up the path."

He strode off through the dark, her fingers twined about his and the soft patter of her feet in his ears, toward the main building. Gil could hear the thud and bump as the barges for the night's expedition were being loaded. He hailed: "Mrs. Mackenzie! Mrs. Mackenzie!"

The flimsy door flew open and the inner light shone down on Van Rensselaer and Mackenzie in heated talk. Gil hailed again and the general's full face thrust out into the darkness. "What's that? Who's there? Stensrood? Eh? What you got there? A spy? Mr. Mackenzie! He's got a spy, by God. Order out a firing squad! We'll teach 'em a lesson. We'll—"

Gil scowled as excited footsteps scurried through the dark, heading for the oblong of light. He pushed Sandra through the door ahead of him. "Shut the door, quick. Send the men away. She's no spy."

The door banged. There was a gasp as the light fell on Sandra, her cropped hair tucked under her cap retrieved from the beach, her slim shoulders swallowed up in a vast blanket coat, patched trousers falling in billows about ankles and broken, country shoes.

Mackenzie stared at her, unbelieving. Then he muttered: "It *is!* It's Sandra Kingscote. She came to warn us at Montgomery's."

Sandra's pale face turned appealingly to him, the down slant of her eyebrows even more marked by fatigue. "You'll let me stay." Her blue eyes looked from him to the flushed face of the general.

The cloud of brandy and pomposity fell away from Van Rensselaer. He whipped off his frogged overcoat, gently muffled it about Sandra, bowed. "You may have whatever the camp offers. Mr. Mackenzie, my quarters will be at the disposal of Miss—ah—Kingscote and Mrs. Mackenzie. Perhaps you'll call her—" He smiled gravely at Sandra. "You'll excuse our rough quarters, I hope. I'll have the men cut fresh hemlock boughs for your bed."

"Eh—oh, yes." Mackenzie raced to an inner door, called, "Isabel! Isabel!"

There was a hidden stir and Mrs. Mackenzie, enveloped in a vast cloak, bare feet scuffed into shoes, peered into the room. Then she saw Sandra, went quickly to her without questioning word or look, took her hand gently. "You'll stay with me, my dear. Those clothes! Mine'll be too big for you, but we'll fix them up somehow."

Mackenzie sidled to Gil's elbow. "This won't—uh—change *your* plans?"

Gil, eyes on Sandra, shook his head. "She'll wait here till I get back."

"Then—you better be starting."

"She knows," said Gil shortly. "Sandra—"

She rose, put out her hands. Mrs. Mackenzie spoke quickly. "Will—we don't want any other men in here. You and the general better help me move my things into his quarters."

"But Gil's got to—"

She stamped her foot lightly. "Come along."

Sandra turned her back, fumbled in the folds of her blanket coat. "I've got something for Mr. Mackenzie." She held out a scrap of crumpled paper.

He ripped it open eagerly. "From Hatcher. St. Catherine's. Twenty-two more names. Militia getting out of hand. Looting. Time's ripe for — " His voice trailed away as his wife's hand seized his shoulder, hurried him out of sight on the heels of the retiring general.

Gil drew Sandra out into the dark, the tails of the general's coat dragging over the dirt sill, the sleeves masking her hands. "You'll tell Mrs. Mac," he whispered. "Right to Buffalo as soon as I get back. She'll find some kind of a preacher."

She laughed softly. "I don't care if it's a medicine man." Then her arms grew tense about him. "Gil, Gil. Don't let anything happen this time. Be careful. Because anything that happens to you happens to me." She looked up at him, her delicate profile oddly set off by the flat cap.

He shook his head. "I'll be walking on eggs." His voice grew graver, deeper. "This'll be the last time. Then Buffalo. Then — "

"I know. I know. You've got to go. We can't do anything about that. But Gil, do remember that half of you's right here on the island."

There were dull shouts from the landing. He started. "They're waiting for me." He caught her up, lifted her over the threshold. Gently he brushed the tears from her upturned eyes. "You poor, tired little scrap! Mrs. Mac'll look after you. You just sleep till I come back — "

She hid her face against his coat. "I'm not tired and I'm not a scrap. And I've got a good mind to stow away with you." She smiled up at him shakily.

There were more shouts from the pier. Gil bent over her quickly, then ran out into the dark. By the pier he found three scows low in the water while the last boxes were being thudded into a fourth. "Bob Heath there? Bob, go to Hut Four and tell Jos that — "

"He's gone," said Heath. "He and two others started ahead. Said they weren't going to miss any fun."

"Damned fool!" fumed Gil. "I wanted him to stay here." Then he reflected that Jos couldn't do much for Sandra, that she knew Doc could be found at the Eagle Tavern in case of need. He shrugged, clambered into the leading scow. "Everyone here?" He looked at the other three. "Now — I'm the only one who knows the way after the landing place. If any groups fall behind, send one man ahead to let me know. I'll wait till they catch up. No straggling. Now—all lanterns out? Talk as little as you can. Ready?"

The scows pushed out against the current. Gil looked back over his shoulder at a steady light that glowed from the main building in the heart of Navy Island.

XXVIII

Capture — 1838

SPADES hissed in soft dirt, rocks rattled as the last heavy case slowly disappeared from view. Gil watched the working crew — men from the high slopes above Toronto, from the flatlands that swept away from the Niagara Escarpment, from the hilly, tangled country west of Hamilton. But with them strained and sweated boatmen from Ogdensburg, strange drifters from Oswego, a man or two from the shores of Lac St. Clair and the growing bustle of Detroit. There was even one gaunt, fever-wasted man who had drifted north from some lost valley in Kentucky, who rippled on in soft, meaningless oaths and held England in burning hatred from long-past Indian raids on the settlements of his childhood.

The last of the earth was turned back in the hidden, rocky hollow. Gil nodded to the short, stout man beside him, a prosperous merchant from the mouth of the Welland Canal. "Think that'll do, Mr. Story?"

"Fine! Fine!" Story's red face glowed with fierce satisfaction. "I'll start men coming through from the lake shore right away. Tell Mackenzie we can use every musket, every pistol he can send us."

"That your only source?" asked Gil.

"Around here, yes. It's better across from Detroit. I hear that all the arsenals of the Michigan militia are going to be emptied for us. On the quiet." He narrowed his eyes. "Of course, the States'll declare war, after the *Caroline* affair. Hope they won't stop sending us arms."

"I wouldn't worry about that," said Gil. But he frowned. There had been a growing tendency on the part of the American volunteers to take matters into their own hands, to treat the Canadians as well-meaning but not very useful allies, and he'd found it best to keep nationalities in separate groups. Then he smiled as Josiah, panting and muddy, scrambled up the rocky ledge, nodded to Story.

"Dirt didn't fly fast enough," he explained, holding out his grimy hands. "Had to take a shovel and show 'em how. Say, this is a good storage place. Gil, after I've taken you and Sandra to Buffalo, I'm going to see what I can do about a militia arsenal or so. The arms are rotting. Never get taken out until the Fourth of July muster. A change of air'd do 'em good."

"Don't get in trouble with the authorities," cautioned Story.

"Why not?" said Josiah. "I'm a taxpayer. I figure I bought at least two muskets and a cross belt. If the state won't use 'em, I can." He stretched. "How about going back, Gil?"

Gil glanced up at the gray sky through a network of bare branches. "Guess you'd better. Take your Americans. I'll give you a half-hour start and follow. You wait by the boats."

Josiah grunted. "Why the devil not stick together?"

Story broke in. "Stensrood's right. Don't want to have large armed parties moving about in daylight."

Josiah looked uneasy. "But twenty-five men are better than ten in case—"

"There's more apt to be an 'in case' if we crowd together," said Gil. With satisfaction he watched Josiah's men pick up their muskets and carbines and file off to the east. Carefully he timed the half hour, thinking that, having the current with him, he'd be back at Navy in the early evening. Then—the short jump across to the American side with Sandra and Mrs. Mackenzie—quick passage to Buffalo. They'd meet Doc at the Eagle and—He picked up his short carbine, shoved his watch back into his pocket. The waiting men sprang to their feet, eager to be off, and reached for their muskets. Story waved a grave farewell and the little column trailed away, being careful not to follow in Josiah's course.

The way lay through a broken tract of hummocky hills, ragged patches of woodland through which the men picked their way deftly. By the foot of a sharp rise, Gil gave the signal for the men to scatter as they always did in open country, circling wide to assemble again in the next dense woods.

Then the gray trees at the other edge of the field snapped and crackled. Red fire flicked among the trunks and the air was full of whining noises. Close by Gil's side, Bob Heath pitched to the snow. Gil, heart pounding, dashed to the cover of a rock, sighted on a distant figure, fired. All about him, his men were answering the fire from the woods, crouched behind stump or snowy rock. Gil shouted: "Work to the right. Take 'em in the flank!" He saw another man fall, cried: "Never mind the wounded! Get 'em later!" A trickle of men in dull red coats began to ooze from the edge of the woods. Gil aimed, saw the leading figure leap to the flash of his carbine. He raced toward a high stump, waving his men on. If he could work his force over the next crest, he'd be safe, for he judged that the men in the woods were a small patrol, not strong enough to bar his passage. He looked back over his shoulder. The men were slipping after him, firing slowly as they went. Only Heath's inert figure marked the scene of the surprise.

The woods lay well to their left now and the patrol was keeping up a desultory fire from cover, wild and ill-directed. A few yards more and Gil's men would be able to fire down through the thin branches. The patrol would give ground and perhaps they'd be able to recover Heath's body. The patrol—

There was a wild whooping from the left, a mutter of hoofs, and a ragged body of men, lances aslant, thundered down across the face of the woods. Gil fired at the oncoming mass, roared: "Keep together! Don't scatter!" But the men, panic-stricken, wavered irresolutely, ran uncertainly, veering like frightened sheep. Gil shouted again: "Make for the west woods! Make—" But the swooping rush of a fresh body of lancers shot into view, pounded away in a wide curve, closed in toward their fellows. Two of Gil's men went down under stabbing lances and smashing hoofs. He loaded, aimed hurriedly at an oncoming horseman.

The carbine was knocked from his hands. He felt a blinding wave of fire, tried to stagger up, the crowded white field spinning about him. Something got between his feet, a heavy weight dropped on his back, and, struggling frantically, he felt tight cords lash down about his arms.

Gradually his vision cleared. A dozen men, dismounted, stood about him, while other horsemen milled around. From the cover of the woods, a thin file of men in red jackets trotted, muskets at trail. Four figures lay dark and still in the snow. The rest of Gil's men, looking strangely thin and tall with their arms bound behind their backs, stood in a ring of lances.

The commander of the lancers, a fat, ruddy-faced man in an old hussar jacket, hallooed to the oncoming infantry. "By gad, Blakeney, it worked, eh?"

Blakeney, obviously a retired sergeant, touched his old shako. "That it did, Cap'n Ewart, sir!"

"Ha!" Ewart barked in angry laughter. "Got 'em! Old trick Boney's cavalry taught us. Dashed near caught me that way once." His full, prominent eyes stared at the prisoners. "Who's the leader? I suppose you got some sort of a leader. Who is it? Speak up!"

Blakeney tilted his worn shako. "A big chap was shoutin' orders, sir. Looks like—looks like—*him!*" A scarred finger pointed at Gil, who'd been shoved to a kneeling position.

"You, eh? You, eh?" barked Ewart, his fur busby quivering with excitement. "Get him to his feet, you men. Now—any more of you?"

Gil, head throbbing, tried to focus on the captain. "I don't know."

"You don't, eh? Where you from?"

"I don't know," said Gil sullenly.

"Don't know? Don't know? Perhaps you know this, though. I've got the power to have you shot right here in the snow. Know *that,* eh?"

"No," said Gil. "Neither do you."

Several of the lancers, decent-looking countrymen on farm horses, began to snicker. Ewart snarled: "Silence! Sergeant—take their names!"

A long-shanked man, lolling on his horse, drawled, "He ain't our sergeant. And if he starts takin' names—well, MacNab's in command here. Guess he knows we've voted for him often enough."

Ewart wheeled about furiously. "I made you a corporal yesterday. I'll unmake you as soon as we get back to camp."

The man laughed. "See what MacNab says to that. Now listen, mister. We need you 'cause you know more about soldierin' than we do. But there it ends. We ain't no Dragoon Guards for you to wipe your boots on. We're Canadian militia and if you yell too much you'll be goin' back tryin' to explain where your troop is." He slowly raised himself in the saddle. "Come on. Let's get them rebel bastards on their way."

Gil found himself roughly shoved with lance butts into a huddle of his fellows. He tried to mumble a question to the man next him, but his words were cut off by a stinging slap across the face from a lancer's reins.

Head throbbing, he walked on in silence, his heart sinking as he thought of Sandra, waiting on the dark island. It would only be for a while, of course. He knew every inch of the country through his solitary expeditions, knew a hundred men who'd be waiting to help, some of them ostensibly militiamen, two of them officers. He'd manage an escape. Of that he had no doubt. They'd head via Grimsby to Hamilton where the people were sullen and restless, where the Compact officials moved nervously and fearfully. Well—wait she must. In the meantime—the arms were well hidden. Josiah and his lot were clear away. That their existence was not suspected was obvious from the questioning of the irate Ewart.

Slowly the throbbing of his head lessened, leaving only a feeling of soreness where the lance butt had hit. He trudged along, eyes and ears alert.

Late that night the column slid down the brow of the Niagara Escarpment. The prisoners had had difficulty in keeping up, so each man's arm was bound with a thong passed through the saddle ring of a lancer, a thong that produced first a tingling numbness, then swift-darting flames of pain that licked from wrist to shoulder.

The white streets of Grimsby were silent as the dark line crunched over the snow. Then lanterns flared by a squat brick building and the thongs were loosened as the prisoners were herded into a narrow, dank room. The inner air quickly became heavy, fetid, as the crowded men tried to settle themselves as best they could, their arms free but their legs securely ironed by the sleepy jailer. Gil, his back against an oozing wall, waited grimly for sunrise and the next lap of the journey. He felt oddly encouraged, for tattered fragments of speech that had drifted through the thick door told him that the lancers would be relieved by other troops in the morning. He counted on seeing a few known and trusted faces in the new escort. It might even be that guard and prisoners would vanish in the snowy waste, to reappear along the Niagara River or before Buffalo.

But in the livid glow of dawn, as hard bread and cold water were hastily doled out to the prisoners, the guard that fell in by the door of the jail presented an unbroken row of black faces—Negro militia in hastily cobbled red jackets and tattered overcoats and breeches. Gil's heart sank. In the liquid eyes he read a certain respect and a deep fear—a fear lest these shivering prisoners were the advance guard of a horde of men who would round up every dark skin in Upper Canada for the slave markets far to the south. A string of wagons rolled out. To barking commands Gil and his men scrambled in, huddled against the keen wind. Ahead of them were more wagons, packed with hollow-eyed captives herded out of some other foul den in the town. Gil watched a slow crowd gather in the early streets. Something of his despair lightened as he heard jeers for the guards, a shout of: "Heads up, lads. And damn the Compact." His mind turned with the wheels, rolling along the road to escape.

The road from Hamilton to Toronto was a ribbon of brownish-gray slush in which the horses splashed as the wagons lurched along, now climbing a low hill, now skirting the fringe of rotting ice that edged the lake. A steady, sullen drip pattered from the eaves of the villages that lined the sodden road.

Gil, knees drawn up to his chin, huddled a damp blanket about his shoulders in the crowded cart and coughed hollowly. The weeks of dank inactivity in the Hamilton jail had weakened him, sapped his hard muscles. His face had a curious, grayish pallor, but the lines about his mouth were taut, firm, and his restless eyes watched every motion of the Negro guard, every fold of the countryside, every knot of people gathered to stare in the towns and villages.

There had been no chance of escape from the heavily guarded jail and, partially resigned to captivity for the moment, he had devoted all his energy and all his wits to keeping in touch with the world outside. From hints unwittingly dropped by wardens, guards, from the very atmosphere of the captors, much could be learned. There had been activity in the west, raids heading out from Detroit and aimed at the country about Amherstburg. He had been first aware of something in the wind through a sudden softening of the rigid jail discipline. He and his fellows had been allowed to exercise in the small, high-walled yard. Fresh meat had been furnished in place of the scant rations of salt pork, old bread, and cold water.

These small favors had been abruptly withdrawn, but Gil was too stunned to resent the cessation. For hard on the heels of the return to severity had come news of the abandonment of Navy Island, of Mackenzie's flight to New York, of the ousting of most of the Canadian leaders in favor of unknown Americans with glittering military titles. The racing thoughts that followed this news had nearly choked off all hope. Where could Sandra have gone, following the evacuation? A fever, brought on by hardship and intense worry, had been jeered at by the guards. They had kicked him, helpless, and called him a rebel bastard. The rage into which this had thrown him seemed, oddly enough, to aid in his recovery.

Then, miraculously, a doctor called, fresh straw was spread for him, special food allowed. Gil, weak but rallying, smiled grimly and was not surprised by the news that fresh activities on the part of the American-Canadian forces had been reported.

So the barometer of prison life had told him of faraway events. He watched the faces of the guards, noted their tones, and could assure himself that the rebellion was not over, that it had hardly begun. Sometimes he heard from freshly arrived prisoners of Dr. Rolph, of thousands of refugees who, catching their breaths after headlong flight, began to look about for means of return. Americans along the border, he was told, still burned with a cold fury over the destruction of the *Caroline*. The militia of Ohio and Michigan were ready to enroll in a body. The great arsenals in Michigan had been opened to the patriots, as the Yankees termed them, and only a freak of chance had closed them. The opportunity would come again, men thought.

Toward the end of February Donald McLeod, a retired British soldier, had essayed an invasion from Fighting Island below Detroit. Again jail life became softer, despite the fact that the raid had been a failure. There were mutters about the jail that the rebel force had behaved well, although it had been opposed by the Thirty-second and Eighty-third, regulars whom Colborne had rushed from Lower Canada. It was even said that had not United States troops, jealously guarding the neutrality of the border, broken up bodies of reinforcements on their way to the island, there might have been a real success to celebrate. As it was, the uneasiness of the local authorities opened the gates for news and a ray of light that no gray walls or damp air could dim. For a visitor had been allowed to see Gil, had told him in muttered talk that rebellion seethed on both sides of the border, that it was gathering strength. But overshadowing all else, the unknown man whispered that Sandra was safe in Buffalo under the care of a sister of Richland, that Josiah had tried to send her to his parents in Albany, but that she refused to leave the frontier. As a result, Josiah spent most of his time in Buffalo, watching over her, raging at not being able to join with Sutherland or McLeod but unwilling to stray far.

Now the transfer had come. Prisoners were being sent on to the overcrowded Toronto jails for trial and—so said the head jailer—speedy sentence.

So Gil, the sideboards of the wagon jarring his shoulders, watched the impassive Negro faces that plodded along by the slow-moving wheels, noted every roof, every path or road, that led back into the country he had patrolled. A jingle of metal, a fresh, hearty voice, broke into his tight-knit thoughts. Annoyed, he looked up, saw the lieutenant in charge of the wagons pacing his horse alongside, a smiling, ruddy-faced young man of the Brantford militia, a fur cap, gold-braided, set rakishly on his head, a white blanket coat open over a dark red jacket. The lieutenant grinned at him. "Damned bad going, this thaw, eh?"

Gil muttered an answer, tried to pick up his broken thoughts. The young officer went on. "Wish I could let you chaps walk—or take turns on my beast, here. Damned mess, the whole thing, isn't it?"

Gil smiled. "Turn the convoy around, hit for the border, and help clean it up. The mess is getting worse each day."

The lieutenant frowned, then laughed heartily. "You've got good pluck, you know, joking like that. But this mess—what'd you start it for? Still—I guess it'll be all for the best. Look at that house there." He pointed to a distant mansion, cold and solitary in the midst of well-tended fields. "Know who owned that? Old Blodgett. Always deviling Strachan about schools for the farmers. What's a farmer want to know how to read and write for? And he was cold-water temperance, like a Yankee. He's had to run for it and his estate's been confiscated. I know the man that's buying it in. He'll keep a pack of hounds, have a good cellar, a wench or two, and a good stable. Good thing for the country."

Gil started to answer, then swallowed his words, discouraged by the good-natured, laughing, thoughtless face under the fur cap.

The officer went on. "My name's Colton. You're Stensrood, aren't you? Well, someone got five hundred pounds for taking you. Filthy way to earn money, isn't it? I'd chuck it in their damned faces if it was me." He sighed. "Wish I could let you make a break for it but — " His face grew solemn. "Look, when you come to trial, I'll be glad to swear you were — you know, model prisoner and so on. Think that'd help? Like to do anything I can — "

He rambled on. Gil, watching the landscape slide by, wondered if McManus still lived in the little house that showed over the next rise, if he had his men at hand. Then he looked at the Negro faces, shook his head. If they'd only had white guards, from the same district, McManus and his crew could easily have effected a surprise.

There was a rumble of wheels from the east and another line of carts came into view, a straggle of shako'd men marching beside them, an ensign in a long blue overcoat riding in the rear.

Colton waved cheerily to the other rider, then confided to Gil, "Detail of the Thirty-second. Escorting arms west. They'll double the guard at Hamilton and triple it at London. Have to, you know."

"Why?" asked Gil absently.

Colton winked. "Damn rebels nobbled two convoys last week. Fact. Hear they're using our own arms against us."

Gil pricked up his ears. "Where'd that happen?"

"Near Brantford. They — Ho! But I shouldn't be telling *you* this. Keep forgetting." He shook himself, then said cheerily, "Well, one nice thing about this guard work is that you see a lot of country. Back in January I was on the patrol at the Hospital guarding the old rebel Van Egmond."

Gil looked up quickly. "How is he?"

Colton shook his head. "Oh — he got awful sick in the jail. They had to move him to the Hospital and he died — about the fifth, I think."

Gil's heart sank. So the testy old man with the white beard was dead. They said he was consumptive so the Compact had thrown him into the lowest cells of the jail. He closed his eyes, heard the guttural rasp of the old voice, saw the care-worn stoop of the broad shoulders. Was the Compact afraid of the disclosures he might make of the Huron Tract, the Canada Company, and the malfeasance of Strachan's son-in-law, at a trial? Did they know they couldn't stop his mouth with gold, so chose cold, damp air instead?

A new jarring vibrated through the wagon. Gil looked up, surprised, and saw the first houses of Toronto ahead, the Peacock Inn and the Dundas Street tollgate. Beyond the gate, the wagons rolled on into Queen Street. People began to collect at the edge of the belt of slush, staring.

Then a voice shouted, "It's Gil! My God, they got Gil!"

Gil looked up quickly, saw men pointing at him, recognized two or three faces — men who had muttered at the smoky meetings of Doel's Brewery or had cheered Mackenzie as he rode through the streets, long ago.

The shouts increased, the other men in the wagon, strangers to the district, staring in wonder. Someone by the Robinson house shouted: "To hell with Head! Three cheers for Mac!" A snowball whistled through the air, smacked against the neck of one of the Negroes. There was a dull surge forward.

Colton drew his sword. "Stand back! Stand back! My men have orders to fire. These are state prisoners. Stand clear!"

Then a column of mounted men rode up from Simcoe Street. Below the faded pennon of the lances Gil recognized a face or two, knew them for Orangemen, possibly from Ogle Gowan's troop. The crowd fell back, muttering, then followed along in the wake of the last cart.

One by one familiar sights slipped past Gil. Osgoode Hall! The last time he'd seen it, there'd been a tea in progress and he'd seen Sandra, aloof in the Kingscote carriage. Now the broad lawn swarmed with men and horses. Orderlies dashed up to the gates with self-conscious flourishes. Sentries paced solemnly in front of the gray walls, prompt to present arms to the knots of officers who shuttled in and out of the wide doors, blue or red jackets sharp against the monotone of the building.

Down York Street was Mackenzie's house, and a block farther east the sprawling bulk of Doel's Brewery. The column swung down Yonge Street and Gil looked back, mouth tight, at the stretch that led to Montgomery's farm and Nipigon.

Then King Street and the dull red bulk of the jail, where the wagons swung in through a heavily guarded gate, halted by a small door. The lancer captain, a bony-faced North of Irelander, shouted an order. Stiffly the prisoners rose, were helped roughly from the wagons as their roped feet tripped them. The small door opened and they were shoved through into a dim stone anteroom where a small fire burned.

Gil joined the general sidling toward the flames, was pulled roughly back. A fat man with small, pig eyes cut the ropes from his feet. Gil started to thank him. There was an amused chuckle and heavy irons were snapped about his ankles, handcuffs connected by a jointed iron bar were locked about his wrists. A voice bawled, "I got his name! Take him away."

Hard hands fell on his shoulders, hustled him along a dark corridor, down slippery steps, another corridor, more steps. Then a key grated in a protesting lock and he stumbled into a black, airless hole that echoed to the slam of an iron door.

Blinking in the intense dark, Gil shuffled cautiously about, found a wall with his elbow, followed it around the narrow limits of the cell, pacing carefully. It was about six feet by nine, with no trace of furniture, although under his feet he felt something like sodden straw, heaped in a corner.

It was like being blind — blind and half-crippled, standing there in the dark where every scrape of his worn boots echoed hollow, where he could even hear the beat of his pulses. He tried to find the heap of straw again, shouldered his way round and round the walls in vain. Where had it gone? He felt a sudden panic of utter helplessness, began to doubt his senses. Had he really felt it under his feet, the pulpy straw?

He drew a long breath, cursed himself sharply. If he went to pieces, he'd be serving the Compact, making their task easier. He caught his whirling mind, told himself that there *had* been straw, that — Then he felt it under his feet, eased himself down. What next? Should he shout, demand light, food? He decided against it, stretched out full length on the sour-smelling straw. He'd sleep first. But his body twitched, his mind raced. He shook himself, thought that present concern could best be faced with a clear head, refreshed by sleep. He flooded his mind with past scenes, stripped them of any connection with the present — skating on the bay, shooting on Manitoulin Island, his first ride on his first pony, the time —

A light glowed in his eyes. He stirred, tried to sit up, felt his irons slam against his body. He stared, unbelieving. A lantern, held high, glared down on him and lit up the grave features of Powell Courtney, a lawyer who in bygone years had often worked on cases with his father — had worked until political views parted them.

Gil wrestled himself upright. "What do you want, Mr. Courtney? I was just getting to sleep."

For answer, Courtney waved the lantern. "Guard! Send for Mr. Kidd! I want Mr. Kidd at once!"

Gil rubbed his eyes, stared at the trim bottle-green-and-snuff suit that paced up and down the cell, the head above it lost in shadow. "I wish you'd let me finish out my sleep," he protested.

Courtney waved a hand. "Just a minute, Gil." His voice was low, kindly. "I've a word to say to Kidd. Several words. Ha! Here he is!" The jailer's footsteps halted in the corridor, his voice rumbled almost inaudibly. Courtney threw back his head. "Kidd!" His tones snapped into the chill dankness. "What the devil does this mean?"

The unseen Kidd protested. "I got my orders from — "

"You've got higher orders than that. By Jove, sir, you'd answer to the Board for throwing a man already convicted into a place like this! But Mr. Stensrood! He's not even been charged yet. We don't even know that he's guilty. Kidd! You'll have him removed to better quarters at once! Has he dined? No? By Gad, Kidd, you've gone too far. As soon as I leave, see that he's moved and well fed. Damn it, you're not Torquemada!"

"Yes, Mr. Courtney! At once! At once!" Kidd's bow could almost be heard in the dark, then his footsteps jarred away. Courtney shouted. "Guard! My stool, my writing board, the rest of the things."

A stool rattled on the stone floor and Mr. Courtney, board propped on knees, sat down in the lanternlight. "Now, Gil, first of all I want to tell you that you've been abominably treated. That will change."

Gil looked at him. "This is a funny time to change it — not for me but for most of Canada. Why didn't you start ten years ago?"

Courtney shook his trim gray head. "I'm sorry you feel that way. Perhaps there's something in what you say. But about the present — I'm here to help you. For your own sake as well as that of your father, my old friend."

Gil leaned forward, fetters clanking. "Now wait a minute. About twenty men came in with me. I'm not having anything they can't have, just because my father used to win your cases for you."

"Don't be so bitter, Gil." Courtney's voice was earnest. "It'll make it just that much harder to help you. Now — about your case. I find it very hard not to sympathize with you. I think most feel as I do." He sighed. "Of course, you'll come to trial—"

"I've seen Compact trials before," said Gil. "At least, Father'll defend me."

"I'm afraid not. But I'm sure Robert Baldwin will, so—"

"Damn it!" cried Gil. "If Baldwin can act, so can Father. One's as much a Reformer as the other. He—"

Powell shook his head. "You see, Gil, Baldwin hasn't any sons charged with treason—or about to be. Then your brother was arrested. Your cousin Graves is hiding somewhere. You see? Your father really couldn't—"

"All right," said Gil. "I'm content with Baldwin."

"But it may not come to that," went on Powell. "Sir Francis is disposed to be lenient." He drew out a sheet of paper. "Now, if you'll sign this confession and apology, I'm sure you'll be released—"

Gil shook his head. "I'm not saying I don't trust you, but if a signed confession ever got into that shyster lot, I know how I'd be released—it would be a permanent one."

Courtney looked sadly at him. "I'd hoped you'd sign. I assure you you'd go free." He ran the plume of his pen through his shaven lips. "There's another way perhaps. Will you write out—of course *we* all know you didn't just realize what you were doing—the names of the men who led you into this and the arguments they used? It'd produce a splendid effect on the Government." He dipped his pen in the ink, held it and a sheet out to Gil. "As unofficial counsel to you, I strongly urge it."

Gil stared, then grinned. "Sure. Let me have it." He edged nearer the lamp and began to write as well as his shackled wrists allowed. Eagerly, Courtney leaned forward. Then he frowned, snatched the paper from Gil. "What the devil's this? John Strachan, Kit Hagerman, John Beverley Robinson—"

"That's only part of the list," said Gil. "They—and a lot more—are the men that led me into whatever I've been in."

Courtney slapped his knee. "Gil! Can't you see? I'm trying to save you from hanging. *Hanging!* I mean it! It may come to that. Just give us the names of the leaders, where they are, what men are still active here, and—the gates open."

Gil edged back along the floor to his straw, yawned. "I'm going to finish my sleep. You'll excuse me, I hope."

Courtney rose slowly. "You're tired, Gil. I'll see you again soon. Think over what I said." He kicked the stool outside, picked up the lantern, and slipped quietly out. The great door clanged behind him.

Later that night Gil was roused by Kidd, the jailer, who with many apologies led him up to the very top of the jail, unlocked a door. "They're all asleep, I guess," he whispered. "Just a dozen or so. It's a fine, sunny room and the beds are good. I'll send up a chop and some coffee for you."

"Never mind," said Gil. "I'll wait until morning." In the light of Kidd's lantern, he picked his way over a wide board floor, edging cautiously past the rows of low cots that jutted from the wall, conscious of an uneasy muttering and stirring from the huddled forms. In a far corner he found an empty cot, spread out some folded blankets, and painfully stretched out his shackled limbs. In the clear, warm air of the room, sleep swooped down on him. Once he was vaguely conscious of a shaded light on his face, two forms that bent over him, sliding the irons from ankles and wrists. He tried to murmur his thanks, but before he could shape the words, the figures had gone.

XXIX

Justice — 1838

THE smell of wood smoke, the clatter of furniture, roused Gil; a shaft of sunlight from a high window fell across his eyes. He started up. In the big, square room, men were stacking the light bunks neatly along the walls, dragging tables and chairs to the center of the room. On a black stove, pots and pans hissed, sending out fragrant steam that rose into the nostrils of anxious-faced men. Voices clattered against the high ceiling.

Then heavy steps came toward Gil's cot, a broad, ruddy face stared down at him. Gil gasped. "My God! John Montgomery! How'd you get here?"

Montgomery shrugged. "They burned my house and my tavern, so they had to let me sleep here until I could build new ones." He sat down on Gil's cot. "Sorry they got you. Heard you were away, away clear."

Gil spoke briefly of Navy Island, the expedition ashore and his capture. Men began to gather around his cot, grave, worried-looking men, eager to snatch possible hope from his story, to learn of lost friends.

At last the questions died away. Montgomery rose. "We've got a kind of discipline going here, Gil. We're up at seven. All beds against the wall. Chairs and tables out. Stove started. Breakfast started. We take turns at cooking, though most of our stuff comes in from the outside."

Gil whistled. "This isn't like Hamilton. You mean people can send you things?"

"If they don't you starve," said Montgomery grimly. "Of course, you pay for it. Her Majesty's Government can't be bothered giving more than bread and water to rebels. They been around for a confession from you yet?"

Gil nodded. "Powell Courtney. Promised the world for my signature."

Montgomery blew out his cheeks. "Hope you didn't sign. Good. You see — they may release you. But if they do, you don't go home. You either go to Van Diemen's Land or across the border. *And* all your property's confiscated. Happened to Joe Nash last week."

"Nash?" said Gil, staring. "He was never a Reformer."

"Course he wasn't," said Montgomery. "But some people that owed him money informed against him. He was brought here, was talked into a damned confession. Sure, he was innocent, but there's the confession, and he'll be leaving for Van Diemen's before long and the man who owed him the most's bought in his land and his business for a quarter of the debt."

Gil nodded gravely. "It's the same in other districts. But look here — what I can't see is how they managed to herd in so many — well, so many men that we know."

Montgomery frowned. "That was a bad bit of work. You see, when Mac had to leave the tavern, he forgot all his papers. Head got 'em. There they were. Every soul who'd ever worked with Mac or — what was almost worse — every soul Mac had ever hoped would work with him." He laughed shortly. "Why — they'll be arresting men for the next ten years on the strength of it."

"Any trials yet?" asked Gil, dropping his voice.

Montgomery looked worried. "No big ones. Don't talk about it. It's something we've all got to face. Lount and Matthews'll be the first, I guess."

"They're here?"

"Floor below. Head swears he'll — " He sprang to his feet. "Better have some breakfast."

Gil stacked his cot on top of another against the wall, joined the twenty-odd men who crowded about the long table. There was a stir as he sat down. Familiar faces, strange faces, stared at him. Beyond Montgomery was Dr. Morrison, then James Lesslie, John Doel, John Price from beyond the fatal tavern, Brammer, an English farmer, young Edmundson from Newmarket, Milburn from Thornhill, Charles Durand, a Hamilton lawyer.

Morrison caught his eye, nodded. "All we need is to have Mac here," he said dryly. He looked about the table. "Where are those rolls that came in for me last night? Pass 'em up, Price." He carefully examined the plate, then selected a crisp roll. "Your turn to go to the door, Durand."

The lawyer rose, went quietly to the door, stood there listening as Gil looked on in wonder. Morrison carefully broke open the biscuit, drew out a tight-rolled scrap of paper, spread it out, frowning. Then he folded it carefully, dropped it into the stove.

"Well?" Lesslie's question was impatient.

Morrison started. "Sorry. Lount and Matthews to stand trial next month — say about mid-April." He turned slowly to Montgomery. "And you and I with them, John."

Montgomery drew in his breath. "It'll be better than this damned waiting. Rob Baldwin going to act for us? Well, we've a chance then." He turned to Gil. "Your family probably knows now that you're here. They'll send things in to you. Look at everything. There'll be messages. We've people outside who'll tell how to do it — and how to mark things so you'll know."

"How about Theller?" asked Lesslie, drumming on the table.

"He ought to have something for us," said Doel. He rose, went to a corner of the room, hands running over the brickwork. "Got it," he muttered, fumbled again, then came back with another paper roll.

"What is it?" asked Brammer, sharply.

"About the new Lieutenant Governor. He'll be here soon." He sat down, staring at the paper. "What a man to send us!"

"Another Head?" asked Gil.

"I'm afraid even Head'd be better. Sir George Arthur. Governor of British Honduras — a slave colony. Governor of Van Diemen's Land — a convict colony."

Muttered comment rippled heavily down the table. Doel said dully: "Might just as well send out the common hangman. Anything else, Jem?"

Lesslie whistled. "Hi! This *is* something." He sprang to his feet. "They're — they're sending out a commission from England — to see what's wrong! Investigate everything!"

Sullen gloom lifted from the room. Morrison murmured, "If we can just hold out!"

"If they only send the right people," snapped Gil. "If they send out Strachan's double — or Hagerman's — "

Lesslie raised his head. "Anyone know anything about the Earl of Durham?"

Montgomery's hand banged on the table. "If they're sending *him!*"

"Well?"

"He's old aristocracy. But his family's always gone liberal. He's — he's — well, he's something like an English Rob Baldwin."

"We heard that about Head," said Gil dryly. "Let's wait and see." He watched Lesslie drop the second paper into the stove. "Who's Theller? How'd you get that?"

Morrison jerked his head toward the wall. "Dr. Theller's in the next room. Calls himself 'General.' They caught him at Bois Blanc. As for the paper — that's his idea. We've punched through all the walls and we poke papers through the holes. We can even get to Lount and Matthews downstairs. We know a lot of things before Head does."

"How does Theller get his news?" asked Gil.

"He's Irish. So are a lot of the guards." He turned to Montgomery. "You know, I think that Head wishes he hadn't caught Theller — or Sutherland either."

"What? They got Sutherland? They've done us a service."

"Well, anyway, Head's in a stew," said Doel. "You see, the Irish guards here swear they'll mutiny if Theller is hanged. Sutherland's a Yankee and Head's afraid of what Washington'll do."

"And they were captured in armed invasion of Canada," put in Morrison. "Head can't let 'em go and still prosecute people like Durand, here, who had as much to do with things as the jailer's cat." He pushed back from the table. "Did Morrison collect sixpence from you for the girls?"

"The *girls?*" echoed Gil.

"They come in each day and sweep up for us. There's sixpence a week from each of us."

Gil spun a coin across the table to him. "We'd better open the lower shutters if there's going to be sweeping here — get some air stirring."

Durand, munching a bit of bacon, laughed. "They're permanent, Stensrood. One of Head's improvements. You see, our families used to come and stand outside and wave to us." He sighed. "It did help, you know — just to see them. But Sir Francis thought he'd be called too lenient if he let that go on." He tilted his head toward the windows. "So they boarded up the whole row halfway, just high enough so we can't see out. It's — well — here are the girls."

There was a clatter of brooms and pails in the corridor. A grinning guard threw open the door and into the room tramped a dozen draggled women, picked up from the Devil's Quarter-Acre or seized for illicit liquor vending.

"Our chambermaids," said Doel with a shrug.

Gil watched them splashing water about, raising clouds of dust with worn brooms. There were bent, red-nosed hags with straggling gray hair; thin, consumptive-looking women, hard-eyed; a blonde girl, nearly six feet tall, whose loose clothes more than hinted at a superb figure. They were, thought Gil, about what one would expect from the Quarter-Acre. Then he saw a shy-looking gray-eyed girl, slim, almost childlike, who moved timidly among her harsh-voiced fellows. How the devil, he wondered, had she been caught up in the police net? A convent — a drawing room — she was suited to settings like — Gil's wonder vanished as he saw her hack at another girl's ankles with her broom, heard her snarl: "Damn you for a clumsy slut! Keep out of my way!"

He felt a touch at his elbow. A fresh-looking young man in countrified elegance, eyes glowing, whispered in Gil's ear: "Say! I just found out! Know where they are?"

"Who?" asked Gil.

"The girls! By God, they're in the next room." He seemed to derive excited satisfaction at the thought. "In the very next room. By *God!* Right there. I'm going to find out — "

The women shuffled out in a clattering drove and the prisoners settled down to the interminable business of watching the hours roll by. Gradually the strangers in the cell took form in Gil's eyes. The three silent Americans, Lewis and the Parker brothers, whose one offense seemed to be their nationality and their misfortune in having debtors with Compact affiliations; Joseph Gould from Uxbridge, a Quaker's son; Dr. McCormick, a scholarly young Irishman with a roaring wit and a quick temper; Adam Graham, son of a retired British colonel; Curtis, the country dandy who had been so excited by his discovery of the women's quarters.

There was nothing to do except pace up and down the room, a scant twenty-five feet square, for the authorities forbade exercise in the prison yard. Gil spent most of the day in deep conversation with Morrison and Montgomery, stood guard at the door while messages that came with the noon meal were read, wrote notes of encouragement to be poked along through the screened holes until they fell into the narrow cell where Lount and Matthews were confined.

At last, yawning, Gil saw with relief the last light snuffed out, tumbled into his cot. A half hour later he was roused by a touch on his shoulder. Curtis, the countryman, was grinning down at him.

"What do you want?" asked Gil.

"Listen. I bribed the guard. Come on."

Gil sat up. "You're getting out? How do you go? Who—"

"No, no! It's the girls. He's going to lock me in there for the night!" He slapped his thigh softly. "For the whole night. Come on. He'll let you by, too."

"In *there?*" Gil stared. "With that lot? Don't be a fool!"

"All right!" said Curtis. "I gave you your chance." He settled his coat, tried to combine a jaunty swagger with intense caution as he made his way to the door.

Gil rolled over, began to review what he had learned since coming to Toronto, trying to see the loophole through which he might escape. Then he turned his mind to immediate problems. Tomorrow he would be allowed to see Robert Baldwin, to plan his defense.

The two armed militiamen behind Gil halted, thumped their musket butts on the floor. The guard threw open the door and Gil, ice about his heart, walked mechanically back into the dimly lit room. Montgomery heaved his bulk from a chair by the stove, lumbered over, threw an arm about Gil's shoulders. "Knew you'd be late, so we saved something hot for you."

One of the Parker brothers threw open the oven, carefully drew out a steaming pan. The third American, Lewis, pushed a chair to the table.

Gil shook his head. "Thanks. Don't feel much like eating. Guess I'll just turn in."

From all sides of the room, sympathetic eyes watched him. Morrison lit his pipe. "Gil, you've trained for a doctor. Do you tell a patient he hasn't got anything wrong with him? Course you don't. You tell him he's sick. But just because he's sick, you don't give up trying to cure him, do you? Well, that's like Rob. A lot of us here are pretty sick men. But Rob's the best doctor there is for what ails us."

Gil forced a smile. "Well, I seem to have some pretty grave symptoms." He sat down. Durand raised his eyebrows, edged the loaded plate closer. Gil tried to eat, sensed with surprise that the others seemed to take comfort in his action, to lift their heads with more assurance. Dry of mouth, he forced down a few morsels.

Then he pushed back his chair. "It's no go. I'll get some sleep and we'll all have a talk in the morning." Wearily, he walked to his bed, stretched out, tried to bring into order the black welter of thoughts that arose from his long talk with Baldwin. The case was very grave and the young lawyer made no attempt to hide it from him. Gil's name had been on the list taken among Mackenzie's papers. Several people had sworn to his presence at Montgomery's on the fatal seventh of December. Spies had reported on his doings across the border and, worse, he had been taken in arms, fighting against the militia. Then, skillfully, Baldwin had let Gil talk, had listened, keen mind alert, to the long succession of steps that had brought him into active participation. Through Gil's intense worry, lying there, face to the wall, he was amazed at the logical sequences which Baldwin's shrewd questioning had brought into being. When the trial came, he knew that he could count on his advocate to present a picture of a loyal man, driven to desperation by the malfeasances of those in office and of their satellites.

A solid core of hope hardened in Gil's mind as he turned back to the inevitable question of escape. Already he'd found three of the militia guards who were openly sympathetic, another who was approachable by bribery. Every day some little fact, some new bit of knowledge, chipped away flakes from the wall of captivity. A strong body, combined with an alert mind, *could* not be held against the owner's will. Give him time.

The last light flickered out. Gil wrenched his thoughts from the sober words of Baldwin, sternly set himself to the mental compounding of some of Richland's favorite remedies. Then he considered the state of his fellow prisoners. The cruel order against exercise was telling on them, most of all on those whose lives had been spent in the open — Brammer, the English farmer, for instance. Gil felt sure that he could detect symptoms of jail fever in the big, inarticulate man. Durand, too, was —

Lights flared suddenly close by. He started, saw two guards bending over Curtis's cot. Dully, Gil wondered what they could want. Curtis had crept back into the cell that morning, white and rather shaken after his expedition, had slept most of the day. Could they be releasing him? Sending him on to another jail? Or—

He heard a frenzied whisper from Curtis. "No! No! By God, I'm *not* going back!" His voice rose higher. "You can't make me! Oh, God! *Don't* send me back again. No! No! No!"

"Get up!" said one of the guards.

Curtis huddled under the blankets. "I won't go back! I won't go back!"

The two men suddenly lifted him to his feet. "They're a callin' for you."

Curtis struggled. "I only paid you to go there last night. This is— Here—I'll pay you again. Anything. Only *don't* put me in there again."

The guards caught him under the arms, started dragging him across the floor. "When we gets paid for doin' something, we does it. Now, them gals in there, they pooled all their sixpences, they've give 'em to us, so in you go!" Curtis's feet trailed across the floor. The heavy door slammed. Down the corridor came a wave of shrill giggles, a scream of laughter. Another door slammed.

In spite of himself, Gil began to laugh, heard a ripple of chuckles sweep around the room. Then his mind whirled back to Baldwin's serious counsel. He closed his eyes. Now what was that remedy of Doc's for a light flux?

Gil's hands were tense on the rail of the prisoner's box. By a strange quirk of memory he suddenly thought of Innis's hands resting on that same rail, their owner smiling vaguely at a fleck of sunlight that played across them. The Innis trial—then his father and his brother had taken their places for the defense—But now, his whole family had been denied admission to the court as they had been forbidden to visit him during his imprisonment in Toronto. He recalled himself to the present and listened to Robert Baldwin's appeal to the jury. It was hard to tell what effect it was having. At least, Gil thought, he had done much to offset the savage battering attack with which Hagerman had opened the case, dark face flushed with anger, broken nose butting toward the twelve men.

With an ordinary panel, there would have been grounds for strong hope, but Gil was convinced that each impassive face had been carefully chosen in view of the desired verdict.

Baldwin's rich, mellow voice rolled on: "... And to have dreamed of a free land, a land of free men in full enjoyment of the rights of Britons—gentlemen of the jury, can you find treason in such a dream? In his eyes, law and due process of law were flouted, free speech and a free press strangled. In his eyes, the schools were under the selfish domination of a Church whose members he knew to be few. In his eyes, the vast lands of Upper Canada were held by this Church, by speculative companies whose profits flowed to a handful of individuals in England." The voice deepened. "In his eyes, the wish and mandate of the Crown were set aside by a few in favor of their own wishes and ambitions, wishes and ambitions which he held to be selfish and narrow. To safeguard the true rights granted by the Crown, to safeguard the rights which he holds the Almighty gave to man before there were crowns, he followed the course which he had chosen. This is the question which you must consider in arriving at your verdict. Did the defendant commit acts of treason against the Crown or did he, in defiance of local authority—and for such defiance there is ample precedent—move to defend that Crown against that usurped authority? Gentlemen of the jury ..."

At last he rested his case. Gil drew a long breath, leaned back against the rear railing, listened while the icy voice of Judge Blaine summed up the case, directed the jury to withdraw. Gil recalled that that selfsame judge, in presenting the charge against George Innis, had stressed the case for the Crown, slighting the defense. And now the chill, precise voice piled up a structure for their consideration as though Baldwin had not spoken. Gil nodded slightly. In the other case, the jury had announced its verdict without retiring and he expected the same procedure to be followed now. To his surprise, the men rose, trooped away to the jury room, disregarding Hagerman's furious glare.

Gil relaxed, found Baldwin at his side. "You were fine on the stand, Gil," said the lawyer.

"What do you think?" asked Gil in a whisper.

"Ah—that answer to Hagerman's question about aims—that couldn't have been better. And I thought—"

Gil smiled slightly. "Thanks. But I'd really like your opinion."

Baldwin shook his head. "I haven't one. You never can tell until the jury — "

A door flew open, the jury shuffled back to their seats. Gil tightened his mouth, felt Baldwin's hand on his arm. The foreman arose. "My Lord, the verdict is guilty."

Gil stiffened, caught a whisper: "Steady, Gil, steady. We've other things we can try, you know, if — "

Then it suddenly occurred to him that he'd known it all along, known what verdict such a court would return in his case. The defense, the elaborate preparations, had been useless. Numbly he stared at the crowded courtroom, feeling an odd relief that his family had been forbidden admission. So long as he could keep his mind on the court, and the court alone, as the embodiment of what he had been fighting, would continue to fight, then everything was —

He was suddenly aware that the expressionless eyes of Judge Blaine were on him, that the bench was addressing him. "— And, Gilbert Stensrood, you were offered opportunity to make reparation to the country for the injury which you have done it, to make reparation by disclosing to those in power the infamous plots that are still laid against it. For your obstinacy in refusing such amends, you shall feel the full weight of that power you affect to despise. Yes, should the Province rise en masse and beg for clemency, you shall receive none." Blaine rose in a rustle of black gown.

"You, Gilbert Stensrood, shall be taken from the court to the place from whence you last came and there remain until such day as the court may direct. And on that day, between the hours of eleven and one, you shall be drawn on a hurdle to the place of execution and there hanged by the neck until you are dead, and your body shall be quartered." The corpselike voice paused, then added, "The Lord have mercy on your soul."

Gil suddenly threw back his head, met the judge's unwinking gaze. In the whirl of his mind, two solid facts tossed and pitched about, spun like logs caught in the swift currents about Navy Island. "I'm still alive. There's a way out." As the guard marched him back through the closed-in prison yard he clung to those thoughts as he would have clung to the logs in the last whirling levels of the Niagara River.

He was aware of climbing stairs, of the cell door being thrown open. The room rose to meet him. A chair was pushed forward, a glass of rum poured out. Reuben Parker, grave-faced, patted his shoulder. "This isn't the end. It's the beginning. Your counsel—"

Gil sipped from the glass, then tilted the rum quickly down his throat. "Right. But anything that's going to be done, I've got to do myself." He turned to Montgomery. "When you were tried, the jury recommended mercy. Well—look what happened. And with me, I had a quick verdict—guilty and no recommendations." He rapped the glass on the table. "Just the same, I'll be rid of them yet."

Morrison smiled wryly. "Do you remember Arthur's first speech when he relieved Head? All clemency and forgiveness." He nodded to himself. "Those qualities must have been pretty well diluted by the time the recommendations reached him."

Gil leaned his elbows on the table. "I don't know. It's not Arthur's fault. He's new here. And who tells him what's what? Strachan, Hagerman, Powell, Boulton, Sherwood. No, I don't think Arthur's so bad. Remember that letter I gave one of the girls to smuggle out? Well, Arthur got hold of it somehow. And the next time he inspected us, he gave it back to me, with the seals unbroken. Just said quietly: 'I think you'd better keep this.'"

John Parker, his lean New Hampshire face drawn and worried, shook his head. "I'd feel better about him if I knew what had happened to all the petitions for Lount. They've got nearly thirty thousand names, Dr. Theller said. Plenty of Compact ones, too. They all know Lount was a good man."

"No news on that?" asked Gil, eager to turn his mind to another's problems.

Brammer frowned. "One thing Theller can't seem to find out. It ought to be well enough known. And we got a note this afternoon from Bigelow on the next floor. He says the same—no news."

Montgomery jumped to his feet. "Well, keep hale, eat when you can and sleep when you can. That's my motto. I let Gil prescribe for me and he's right. If you toss half the night and miss your meals, you're only half a man. Is it about dinnertime?"

Dr. McCormick rubbed his hands, cocked his head. "Hear that?"

Through the boarded windows, a long mournful hail quavered into the room—"Six o'clock and all's well." The Irishman chuckled. "And it's my dinner tonight and if I don't set before you the finest geese that ever grew outside of Donegal, you can call me an Orangeman, God damn 'em."

"And a bowl of punch from me," said Montgomery. "Gil, I'll let you be the tapster tonight. Reuben Parker'll see to the glasses. Charley Durand, you'll keep an eye on the stove. Damned if we won't be as snug here as Sir George at Government House."

A rap at the door ushered in six geese, golden and steaming, covered dishes of vegetables, a pudding, and a clanking array of bottles. A sudden, high-pitched gaiety swept into the room, as the prisoners forced their throbbing minds away from their problems.

At the head of the long table McCormick carved expertly, sent heaping plates down a line of reaching hands. Suddenly he dropped knife and fork, uttered a shout of joy, drew from the goose a long roll of paper, buried in the stuffing. He read it eagerly, slapped his knee. "Bless the girl!" he cried. "It's yes she says."

Lewis ran quickly to the door, listening for the step of the guard. "What girl says yes to what?" asked Brammer, his mouth full of goose.

" 'Tis my own Ellen!" crowed the doctor. "And she'll be Mrs. McCormick two minutes after I'm leaving this jail." He leaned forward, eyes bright. " 'Twas in Hamilton I knew her and never a smile she had for me. Then Head's men, hell roast 'em, took me and brought me here. First, 'twas a pudding with a note in it. Then a bit of cake, and warmer and warmer did she write. Then, by Saint Barnabas, and he's the patron of doctors, what does she do but run away from her family and hide with a rich aunt out Queen Street in this very town." He grinned boyishly. "And it's for me she's doing all that. So what could a good Irishman do but ask will she trip to the priest's with him and here — " he waved the paper — "here's the answer and that she will."

Gil thought suddenly of a lost, frightened figure in ill-fitting coat and trousers on a narrow beach at Navy Island. He pushed his way back to the present. For the moment, the world could hold only this night, this group, this room.

The doctor chuckled away, his soft brogue rolling like a swift brook down the table. "The punch, man, the punch," he shouted to Gil. "And we'll have a bit of a song, we will. And we'll start off with a good Scots tune for the sake of little Mac, God bless him." He pushed back his chair, roared out into the opening bars: —

"Scots wha' hae wi' Wallace bled,
Scots wham Bruce has often led."

He waved a knife in time and the whole table joined in as Gil uncorked bottles, poured into the great bowl that Kidd had sent up. The bowl began to empty. The doctor went on to "Sweet Vale of Avoca," his rich voice vibrating along the dusty rafters. Glasses were filled. The level of the bowl sank slowly down, was raised, raised again.

As the last chords of "In the Sweet By-and-by" died away, Montgomery called to John Parker. "You must have sung when you taught Sunday school at Hamilton. Haven't you got a Yankee song for us? Can't let McCormick keep on with his everlasting emerald hills and vales."

Parker slowly rose. "Yes. I used to sing there. And for a Yankee song—well, I guess the Yankee that wrote it wrote for the whole world." Eyes on the high ceiling, his voice swept out with surprising resonance.

"'Mid pleasures and palaces though we may roam,
Be it ever so humble, there's no place like home."

The laughing gaiety of the room died. Men leaned forward, lips parted, eyes far away. The voice soared up:—

"A charm from the skies seems to hallow us there—"

Gil glanced nervously along the table. Montgomery was biting his lips, while Durand, his face a mask, drummed noiselessly on the plate before him. The doctor turned his face away, a bright trickle unheeded. Suddenly Morrison sprang to his feet, hand upraised. Parker checked himself in the midst of a bar, the last notes fading into the heavy hush that had fallen over the room.

Outside in the April night a new sound was born. Slam-slam-slam. Slam-slam-slam. There was a heavier crash. The regular slamming began again.

"What is it?" whispered Gil.

"The answer to the petition for Lount and Matthews," said Durand in a low voice.

Lewis nodded, eyes haunted. "The scaffold. They're putting it up. They're putting it up now."

Slowly the prisoners pushed their chairs back from the table, began to pace up and down, wordless. Slam-slam-slam went the hammers and mauls outside. Slam-slam-slam.

Gil, caught up in the aimless pacing, suddenly paused by the door. Down the corridor he heard the steady clank of iron, faint at first but growing clearer. He listened, almost fearfully, then said, "Someone's coming."

With his words, every foot was still and men turned to face the sound. The clanking drew nearer. There was a rasp in the lock and the guard flung open the door, and Samuel Lount, irons at wrist and ankle, stood on the threshold, his head nearly touching the top of the frame. His strong, rugged face was gentle, his voice low but steady. "Boys, I've come to say good-bye."

Morrison flung an arm over his shoulder. "No. No, Sam, no. The petition. They can't — "

Lount smiled gravely. "I know how you feel. Perhaps I'd have done better to stay away." He shook his head. "My old friends, saying good-bye to all of you was the one luxury I couldn't deny myself." He held out his shackled hand. "Good-bye, Doctor. I know now that we were right. And I know that none of us counts — it's what we fought for. Gil, you did good work. You'll never regret it. And it'll go on. And you, John — "

Montgomery tried to answer, but his voice failed him. He turned away, bumping blindly into a chair that he couldn't see.

Lount, his irons clanking, went from man to man, then shuffled slowly to the door. There he turned. "Keep fighting — my old friends." There was a clang and he was gone.

The room was silent. Gil, throat working, sat on the edge of the bed. Little by little his broken breath steadied. He set his teeth. Yes, they'd keep fighting.

Gray morning light flowed sluggishly into the room where the men paced up and down, heedless of the unwonted disorder of unmade and unstacked cots, unswept floors. Eyes on the floor, they brushed against each other, mumbled apologies, caught up the unthinking rhythm of their broken steps. Gil, pausing by the boarded windows, looked at a sullen sky that seemed to be dropping slowly down on the budding tops of the elms. Durand jostled him, excused himself in a flat voice. "Didn't see you. Uh — have they come out — is it — "

Gil shook his head impatiently. "You can hear as much as I can."

"You're tall," said Brammer nervously. "Take a look."

Gil felt hot anger flow over him. "D'you think this is a country fair? Do your own gaping!"

Brammer's jaw fell. "Didn't mean—didn't know." He sprang to his feet. "God damn this waiting! I can't sit here! I can't—"

Gil's anger and disgust changed to swift pity. He took Brammer's arm, walked him slowly up and down. "Sorry I barked at you. We're all jumpy this morning. You know, I was thinking last night about what you told me. You know—crossing Shetlands with the wild ponies out Huron way. I'll bet it would be worth trying."

The white-faced farmer stared, then seemed to find a sudden link with a peaceful day, talked heavily and ponderously about the durability of the Huron animals, their hardihood. Morrison, folding his blankets with meticulous care, gave Gil a short approving nod.

The slow tramp of feet in the room stopped abruptly. The sound seemed to float out through the windows and echo, thicker and heavier, in the gray world outside. Pale faces turned in mute inquiry. Drums crashed, rattled, throbbed, the brisk spatter of sound rolling away against the brick walls. Then they were still. A single hoarse voice shouted, staccato. A dull crash followed.

Gil thought, "They've grounded arms." He was suddenly aware that he was sitting in the chair beside the stove, that the other prisoners, heads bent forward, were moving almost automatically toward the windows, drawn without their knowledge or will.

A voice croaked: "By God, I can't stand it—just listening. It's—" A single figure sprang to the window ledge, clung to the thick iron bars and stared out over the top of the boarding. As though chained to him, others swarmed to the sills until the grayish squares were choked. Those unable to find foothold stood below, hands half raised and necks tense. There was a hush that fell apart to McCormick's choked tones: "God help me! Here they come."

All outer sounds were buried in wild shouts, a confused roar that sifted in broken waves into the room. The drums snarled again. A voice bellowed: "Silence."

Gil found himself halfway to the windows, wrenched himself back to his chair, sat down heavily. Then a new sound drummed against his ears—the sound of slow footfalls on hollow steps. He counted them almost unconsciously. "One — two — three — four — five — "

From the window Brammer cried thinly, "God bless 'em, they're walking steady."

Curtis, hands working about the bars, nodded. "There goes Lount. Sheriff Jarvis after him. Matthews, Deputy Baird. Here come Reverend Richardson and Beatty."

Gil started angrily, wanted to shout to the clinging men to drop from the window. Then he realized that it was not morbidity but taut nerves that drew them there. He choked back his words, tried to drive out of his mind the tragedy that was taking place below. He tried to think out a problem in obstetrics, but the very word reminded him that both Lount and Matthews had large families. What would Doc do to keep the men in that room quiet, efficient? Doc would have known. Doc was the friend of any man in trouble. And down below there, Sheriff Jarvis would have to fit cap and noose about the throat of his old friend Samuel Lount — Gil sprang up, paced rapidly about, forcing himself to keep away from the crowded windows.

Fascinated, he stared at the clinging men. Then a sudden tremor ran over the straining backs, the hands frozen to the bars stiffened. The silence was absolute. Gil halted. Outside, a heavy voice intoned in a rolling mutter. Silence fell again.

There was a faint slam, like a door being forced open — another slam. With a sound that was almost a moan, the men fell away from the windows, some staring blindly, others with arms thrown across their eyes. Brammer took a few steps, staggered, and pitched to the floor.

Gil bent quickly over him, shouted to Lewis: "Get his feet. That's it. Lift him onto his cot. Durand, get some water — cold water from the bucket. Parker, set some heating on the stove. Ready, Lewis? Heave!"

They carried Brammer's heavy frame to his cot while the others splashed water about, stoked the fire. Gil, seeing others standing around, dazed, their faces white or feathery red, set them to warming blankets, breaking up more wood. Curtis brought a steaming bucket into which Brammer's feet were plunged. McCormick loosened the neckcloth from the thick throat. Brammer's eyelids fluttered. He stared, groaned, then struggled to his feet, sheepish and flushing with embarrassment. One or two of the men laughed nervously. There was even a lame attempt at banter.

Morrison eyed Gil. "That was good work."

"That? Simple case of fainting. Can't see—"

"It's not *that* he's meaning," said McCormick. "You've revived the whole room." He jerked his elbow toward Durand, who was carefully straightening out his cot, stacking it on Lewis's. "The shock's broke. 'Twill come back, of course, but they're the better for the jobs you've given 'em."

"Right," said Montgomery. Then he sighed and sat down on his cot, hands working. The artificial bustle of the room died away and men stood with drooping heads and haunted eyes. At last Brammer shook his head. "So that's what it'll be like."

Gil looked up quickly. "No—it won't be. There's a way. I tell you, there's a way."

Heads lifted slowly. Eyes cleared, narrowed. There was silence again. But it was the silence of planning, not of despair.

XXX

Quebec — 1838

John George Lambton, Earl of Durham, strange but gifted radical aristocrat, arrived in Quebec in May of 1838, as virtual dictator of the two Canadas. At once an order was sent to Sir George Arthur, successor to Sir Francis Bond Head, that the death penalty was to be invoked only in the utter absence of mitigating circumstances. It was whispered in Toronto that, forewarned, the Compact had hurried on the execution of Lount and Matthews.

All other death sentences were changed, some to life imprisonment in Van Diemen's Land, others to banishment. The Compact raged. Sir George Arthur, now aware of the real nature of Compact pressure on him, welcomed the turn of the tide toward leniency.

Across the border, the Rebellion still flickered on. Some of the raids narrowly missed blossoming into major successes. But the character of the invaders was slowly changing. Many Reform refugees preferred to settle down in their new homes, while American adventurers, ne'er-do-wells, nondescript trash, mingled with sincere men who sought to free — according to their own lights — their fellows across the border. A strange organization, the Hunters' Lodges, sprang up in the States. Its aim, it was said, was sport — and sportsmen need rifles and powder. But in the Lodges, men talked of the liberation of Canada.

While armed bodies gathered, fumbled along the Lakes, men reprieved from the noose by Durham's order were passed slowly along, under guard of Her Majesty's troops, to Kingston, to Montreal, to the Citadel in Quebec, waiting the transports that would take them to a convict's life in Van Diemen's Land, below Australia.

GIL leaned his elbows on the sill of the barred embrasure and looked down on the broad blue avenue of the St. Lawrence, far below. The same soft, steady breeze that ruffled his hair was gently rocking the great man-of-war that lay at anchor out in the stream, its bare masts bold against the yellowish cliffs of the opposite shore. Smaller craft drifted with the current or skillfully tacked in to the steep town of Lévis across the flood or worked cautiously into the docks that jutted from the towering, fantastic mountain of rock that was Quebec.

Just before him lay a smooth green parade ground, ending in a gray stone curtain that dropped swiftly to meet the upthrust of the living rock. From behind a square stone building, red and blue glittered. A sentry, musket aslant, marched stiffly into view, the sun glinting on the brass plate of a high fur busby. Directly below the embrasure he met a second red figure, halted, swung about, and marched back toward the square gray bulk.

Gil shook his head, leaned farther into the gap in the thick stone walls to avoid the dreadful din behind him, where a fife squealed and brayed and heavy boots thumped on the echoing floor in a wild jig. He jammed his fingers into his ears as the fife shrieked up into "The British Grenadiers" while clattery voices whooped and shouted. Face pressed against the bars, he saw the sentries meet again, look up at the embrasure, exchange winks.

The tumult died down slightly. There was a touch on his elbow and Dr. Theller's broad, flushed face panted in his ear. "Sentries all right?"

Gil nodded. "*They*'re all right. But my reputation as a sober man's ruined forever."

"What good did it ever do you?" laughed Theller.

Gil shrugged, looked over his shoulder at the next embrasure. "How's Culross coming?"

"Slow does it," said Theller. He turned back to the long narrow room, waved his arms. "That's not enough! Dodge! Culver! Damn it, shake the Citadel down. What's the matter? Afraid of breaking into Colborne's nap?" He snapped his fingers, thumped his boots on the floor with a wild whoop.

Gil watched the tight-lipped man at the next embrasure, a man who carefully worked at a chink in the heavy masonry, a short, edged bar of iron easy in skilled fingers. The gap was noticeably wider.

Gil nodded in satisfaction, resumed his study of the sentries, the river, and the great wave of gray-brown rock that rose from the water. By craning his neck, he could catch a distant glimpse of the Île d'Orléans, far to the east, its white villages sleeping in the green fields under the summer sun.

The man Culross turned from the embrasure. "That's enough for now. Arms get tired."

At once the fife's high squeal died away, the shouting and thumping stopped, and the men threw themselves on cots and benches, panting. Dodge, a rawboned American who had been captured with Theller at Bois Blanc, mopped his face. "All right for you to grin, Stensrood," he scowled. "But it'll be your turn to howl and stamp tomorrow while I watch the guards. They seem to notice anything?"

Gil poured two bottles of brandy into a small bucket, shoved it out of sight. "You could have blown up the Citadel. God, what a row you were kicking up." He rolled the empty bottles out onto the floor. "How's your lampblack, Culross?"

"Got plenty," said the lean man, careful fingers smearing soot about the crevice. "Got in so deep I've hid the iron in there. General, when do I get a longer bar? Going to need it soon."

Theller purred in his throat. "Our good friend Monsieur Drolet down in the town is seeing to that." Wheezing, he got to his feet. "Come on, boys, got to have your medicine." He dipped a cupful of brandy from the bucket. Short and fat, he stumped from man to man. "Slosh it around in your mouths. Splash some on your neckcloths. When the inspector comes, we want to stink like a boozing ken. That's it, Gil. Get it up your nose. Never mind if you snort a bit—" He cocked his head, hid the cup hurriedly as a knock jarred on the iron-bound door. The men lolled stupidly on the benches or sprawled, jaws sagging, on their cots. Gil flung the door open, staggered, caught himself by the heavy handle and bowed foolishly to the busby'd ensign and his squad who stood outside.

The ensign grinned sympathetically. "Here we are. Sergeant—the usual." The sergeant, his men at his heels, clumped into the room, examined the stonework, prodded the cots.

The ensign drew a paper from his red jacket. "Just to comply with orders," he muttered, then cleared his throat: "British subjects:

Theller — Stensrood; American citizens: Dodge — Culver — Pew — Partridge — Reuben Parker — Hull — Culross . . . all present and accounted for."

Gil laughed shrilly. "Present or unconscious."

The ensign guffawed. "I'll report that to Sir John." He sniffed. "Damned if you chaps aren't running up my mess bill. I get the smell of your diggings in my nose and then I have to go back to quarters and open a bottle."

The sergeant saluted. "All in order, sir." At the ensign's nod, he kicked the bottles out from under his feet, tramped away with his men.

Theller threw an arm about the ensign's shoulders, swayed. "Don't want to look any more? Gil, show him your tongue."

"Damn his tongue," laughed the officer. "His breath's all I want to know about and I can catch that at ten paces. Oh — look here. Had a message for you. Sir John says you can have all the medical stores and things that you want — so long as you pay for 'em. Of course, we'll look over anything that comes in at the guardhouse, so don't be up to any tricks."

Dodge raised himself on his elbow. "Why'd we be playing tricks? I always wanted to live in a bar and now I'm doing it." He swung his feet to the floor. "Have a drink with us?"

A fresh bottle was brought from a cupboard, glasses were raised. The ensign smacked his lips gratefully, raised his hand to his busby, and stepped out into the sunshine. Then the door closed, a key grated.

The men, sprawling on bench and bunk, sat up abruptly. All eyes swung toward the embrasure where Culross had been working. "Didn't see it," muttered Parker.

"They won't," growled Dodge. "God damn that Sutherland. We'd be out now if he hadn't peached. By God, I'd have killed him if the guard hadn't pulled me off him."

"Poor devil," said Theller. "He's just going to pieces. You see, he argued that if we couldn't escape from Toronto with a militia guard, how could we escape from the Citadel of Quebec with the Coldstream Guards as a watch. So he thought *he*'d get out at least, by informing on us." He wiped his forehead. "Saints be praised, they didn't find anything."

Gil went back to his embrasure, watched the play of sun on the high cliffs at Lévis. "I always feel as if the whole Citadel had been lifted off my neck when that squad goes out."

Theller rubbed his hands. "Well — there'll be no ships for us for a long time. I heard that from Drolet." He yawned, stretched. "I'm for a nap. Culross, you better get one too. We need your arm to-night."

"Let someone else do it," said Culross. "My hands is worn through."

Theller smiled blandly. "Oh no. That was the bargain. You're the only mason here. We'd botch the job. Come on. Get some rest."

Silence fell over the room. Gil, restless, strolled to Culross's embrasure. The designers of the Citadel had pierced the wall at this place to catch a storming party from the flank and it looked out onto a narrow strip of grass, a blank curtain of wall. No loophole, no turret, looked down on it, no sentry stared up from the grass below.

He looked admiringly at Culross's work. Even to the touch, the filled-up crevice showed no signs of tampering. Then he began to pace about, weighing over and over the chances of escape. He thought they were fair — no better, no worse. The men with him were all intelligent, resourceful, and of undoubted courage. Theller, through past residence in Lower Canada, had valuable connections in Quebec, connections that were working steadily outside the walls of the Citadel and reached up into the officers' messes, the guardhouse, and into the very cell. And in the hollow room, Theller had formally made him a Hunter, had passed him through the four degrees — Snowshoe, Beaver, Master-Hunter, Patriot-Hunter. This status might be valuable once he was across the border, knowing the signs and watchwords.

He turned back to the loosened stone. Moving that would be only the first step. Then they must get out of the Citadel itself, solve the terrific drops of the stone curtains, the staggering pitches of the living rock that hung over the Lower Town. Each stage was carefully planned. Yes, he thought, the chance was fair. He stretched out on his cot, mind leaping across the border. Sandra, safe with Josiah's family at Albany, must have known for some days that a letter addressed to Drolet would reach him. Perhaps there'd be word from her before long. He settled to the sleep which he had rigorously schooled himself to snatch at any hour. After dinner, Dodge would watch the sentries and he himself would join in the whooping and singing.

When he awoke, a grinning guard was bringing in lanterns which shone on a bottle-covered table, a vast roast of beef. As the last light was hung, the man pushed back his busby, looked wistfully at the table. "I'd be a prisoner myself to sit down to them bottles," he murmured.

Gil sprang from his cot, snatched up a brandy bottle, a glass. "We're just going to drink the Queen's health," he announced jovially. "We can't let a man wearing her coat get away without joining us."

The others shouted approval, rushed to the table. The grenadier took the glass, looked cautiously toward the door, then tipped back his head. His eyes watered as he set the glass on the table. "If the gentlemen need something in the town—something that'll not get me into trouble bringin' it—the name's Dawkins. Third Company."

Gil slapped him on the back. "We'll remember. And there'll be something left in the bottom of the bottle for the man that brings it to us."

The soldier grinned, tramped out whistling at the top of his lungs.

Pew wagged his long head. "Stensrood, you've treated about everyone in the garrison."

"Except Colborne," laughed Parker. "They'll make us take out a license if we keep on."

Theller nodded gravely as he sat down to carve. "Gil and I are going to brew up some powders that'll make one or two of you look as if you were on the edge of the grave from drink. We'll call in the garrison surgeon, too."

"That'll help our reputation," said Gil. "Don't you think it's about time we had another fight?"

Culver, gobbling beef, mumbled, "You've got to keep out of it, though. The last time we put one on you nearly threw Partridge through the wall."

Theller frowned judicially. "About next Wednesday we'll get ugly. Gil, you and Culross better be under the table. You looked too damn sober when the guards came in last time."

"I'll remember," said Gil. "Hi—there's the door again." He got up, slid the small panel. "From the guardhouse. All right. I'll take it." The door swung open and a red-cuffed hand pushed a big parcel into the room. Gil took it, peered at the level ground outside. "Anyone there, besides you?"

A voice answered, "Sentries to other end of the beat."

Gil caught up a glass, which was snatched eagerly, shoved back empty. The door banged and Gil plumped the heavy bundle on the table.

Theller smoothed back his thin hair. "Stand by the panel, Hull." His strong hands broke the cord. "H'm, been opened as usual. Now —aren't they beauties?"

The heavy mortars and pestles shone bright and new on the table. The others stared. "What the devil—"

Theller winked. "Gil and I may have to brew up medicines for you when you get too alcoholic, eh, Gil?"

Gil took one of the pestles, frowning. "These aren't any good, Theller. Look at the length of the handle—look at the thickness."

Theller's smile deepened. "It's Drolet's own pattern. Trust him to keep up with the times." He took one of the pestles from Gil, twisted it in his hands.

There was a gasp around the table. The bell-like base had unscrewed, leaving a glittering steel end protruding. The doctor slipped out the steel, opened the other pestle, thick fingers pointing to the threads that shone bright at the lower end. "Screw those together, Culross, and there's your longer bar." He reached for one of the mortars, slid his hand across the bottom. The base came away in his palm. "There." Theller beamed at the whitish powder, sniffed delicately. "Gil, you and I'll take care of this—later."

Gil nodded, then turned to Culross. "Better try out your new toy. Hull, let's get the fife going."

The table was pushed back to the wall, bottles set out. The fife wailed and screeched. The floor shook to the stamp of feet. From time to time Culross stepped away from his embrasure as Gil dipped brandy from the bucket, passed cupfuls through the panel to the guard outside. Then the new bar chipped on, slowly but surely, its clink muffled by the din that grew thicker and wilder.

XXXI

Escape — 1838

Autumn rain splashed and gurgled on the weathered Citadel, whipped about the gun ports and dashed against the shuttered embrasures of the prisoners' room, where the nightly debauch echoed and banged. Theller and Pew flung their arms about, banging through an Irish jig, while the others clapped and stamped in unison. Hull, his face purple, blasted through the fife as though he wanted to blow out the closed end.

Gil, bellowing "Sweet Vale of Avoca" off key, slid back the panel, looked out into the streaming yard beyond. Lights glowed through the slanting rain, glinted on cascades of white water that muttered and gurgled along to the dreadful plunge over the mountain of rock. A single sentry, greatcoat muffled about him, huddled in the shelter of a deep door a dozen yards away. Gil looked at his watch, turned to Theller, who paused in the midst of a wild caper.

"Past eleven. He'll be coming soon."

Theller waved his arms to the others. "On your feet. Stamp, shout, sing." He turned to Culross, who leaned against the wall far from his usual embrasure. "Down on the floor. The way we showed you. Gil — " He raised a warning hand. "I'll see to the guard this time."

Gil nodded, moved toward a deep cupboard. Theller, head tilted, stood close by the door. Then he pounded on it, gently. The panel slid back and a dripping face peered through. "Officer's abed?" asked Theller.

There was a nod.

"Better come in and warm yourself. We'll keep watch for the relief."

The eyes outside in the storm looked doubtful, then cleared. "That's kind of ye, sir. I'd be — "

The door swung open and the dripping man stamped in, slamming the heavy frame behind him. Theller slapped him on the shoulder. "Pull up by the fire." He eyed the man closely. "You'll be from Donegal?"

The face under the sodden busby lightened. "From Meath, and a weary way it is from this divil of a rock." A glass was shoved into his hand. "Yer Honor's good health." He drank, bayoneted musket between damp knees, then watched the whirling, shouting prisoners wistfully. His feet tapped to the tempo of the fife. Pew sat beside him, arm across his shoulder, swearing that when he was a free man, damned if he wouldn't take the Queen's shilling and serve along with — what was the grenadier's name? O'Malley? By God, he'd serve with his friend O'Malley. And where was another drink for his friend?

At this, Theller's face assumed owlish, drunken wisdom. "I'll not send a Meath man into trouble. Give him beer. That damned brandy'll have him reeling when the relief comes." He waved his arm, shouted, "Who's got beer for our friend O'Malley?"

The brass mortar grated on the cupboard shelf, the sound half muffled by the rush of foaming beer. O'Malley grinned. "It's wise Yer Honor is. I'd a liked the brandy but — " He buried his nose in the frothing glass.

The dance went on. Hull tootled till his cheeks cracked. O'Malley began to rock his head in time to the wailing. Back and forth, back and forth. Suddenly the wet bearskin busby tilted heavily. The musket clattered to the floor and the grenadier slumped in the narrow chair.

Gil and Theller sprang to the sagging man, caught him under the arms, bound and gagged him expertly. "Sheets!" snapped Gil, busy with a knot. Three men stopped dancing, ripped open the beds, and, working with furious haste, began knotting the sheets into a solid rope.

Gil listened to the heavy breathing. "That powder works quickly. Dead for hours, Theller."

The little doctor nodded. "The stone!" he shouted. "The rest of you keep up your racket."

Gil, Pew, Partridge, and Culross ran to the embrasure. There was a moment of straining. The heavy stone slid out, was eased painfully to the floor. Gusts of rain battered in through the gap, slapped against Gil's face as he wrenched out one loosened bar, another.

"Door!" he shouted, and began to slam his feet on the floor. Culross fumbled under his bed, drew out two heavy cramp irons, a maul, drove the irons deep into the frame of the door and slid O'Malley's musket through the loops. The door was barred effectually.

Theller grunted approval. "Keep up your screeching, Hull. Now — the bars."

Strong hands knotted the sheet ropes to the bars. "Out with 'em," said Gil.

The sheet rope trailed into the drenching night, one end anchored by a bar wedged horizontally across the window. Gil drew a deep breath. "Ready!" he said.

Theller's broad face was set, his eyes glinted. "Alphabetical order — barring me and Gil. I go first as we arranged. He comes last. And keep up that howling till the last man's out." He squared his shoulders, brought up a chair, thrust his legs through the gap, and began slowly to let himself down. Gil saw his bald head glimmer in the wet darkness, vanish.

Gil danced a wild reel on the floor. "Culross, then Culver, Dodge — " One by one the men eased themselves cautiously out into the night, slid slowly into the blackness. When Hull's turn came, Gil snatched the fife from him, blew wild discordant notes, tipped over a chair.

At last it was his turn. The rain pattered hard against his worn trousers as his legs swung into the void. There was a horrible moment when his thrashing feet lost the sodden rope. Then it was between his ankles. Slowly he let himself down. Ten feet, fifteen feet, and the rough stones scraped at his boots, burned his knuckles.

High in air, there was a sharp ripping sound. The rope was suddenly limp in his hands. His body rocketed on through the dark, through the dark that was stabbed with fire as he tumbled in a heap, half stunned, at the foot of the wall. He rolled to cover, then realized that the flashes had been back of his eyelids.

Strong hands pulled him to his feet. Theller's voice was anxious. "All right, Gil? You all right?"

"Just dizzy," panted Gil.

Theller shook his head. "Thought that rope was strong enough to hold a regiment. Ready? Single file and follow me."

They crept along in the shadow of the wall, slid down a forty-foot ditch, its earthen sides mercifully softened by the rain, scaled the other face. On the crest, Theller held up his hand. "Guard post near here. Careful. Twenty feet away around the corner. We'll — "

Gil, close behind him, suddenly froze as something clattered in the dark. Parker had fallen over a woodpile, sent some logs thundering down the ditch. There was an instant of dead silence. Then a voice barked: "Halt! Who's there?"

Parker, trembling, huddled close to Gil at the foot of the wall. Gil held his breath, ready to break back for the ditch. The challenge snapped again, the words hissing in the rain.

Then through the night another voice shouted: "Relief. Post number seven."

Gil drew a deep breath, slumped against the wall as he heard the invisible squad tramp up to the sentrybox, caught a mutter as it tramped away. "You made enough noise coming. Had to challenge twice. That's — "

Gil caught Theller's arm, felt an answering grip. It was about time luck changed, said the Irishman's clutch. There was a whispered "Ready?" The little party filed on in the shelter of the wall. Gil took the lead, feeling his way along. He led them safely across an open space, looped them around an old powder magazine. Then he flattened himself against the rounded wall. A single lighted building showed at the left front. In its doorway huddled a cloaked sentry. Gil turned suddenly. "Pew — your cape." He snatched it from the man's shoulders, slung it about his own.

"What the devil are you going to do?" whispered Theller.

"Never mind. You keep in the shadow of that wall. Meet me beyond by the path that goes into the Upper Town."

Theller caught his arm. "What in God's name — "

"Let me alone. Start 'em off." He watched the little group vanish along the foot of a high wall, then, cocking his vizored cap, marched straight toward the sentry in the lighted doorway.

The man stiffened as Gil came near, then became a motionless statue, musket at present. Gil, swinging along at an easy stride, returned the salute. "Bad night, m'lad. See that you keep sheltered."

The Coldstreamer became human. "That I will, sir. Good night, sir."

"Good night," said Gil cheerily and swung along into the shadows.

By the steps that led into the Upper Town, he found Theller, who rushed at him, seized him by the shoulders. "God, Gil, don't do that again! God! Went right past him! He saluted you!" The hands on Gil's shoulders were trembling. "Don't, for God's sake — "

Gil unslung the cloak, gave it back to Pew. "Risk be damned," he said shortly. "Can you see color tonight? No. And isn't this cap just like an artillery cap in the dark? And would that damned fat-faced guard be expecting to see a State prisoner come right past his post? It was safe as — Well — let's get going. All here?"

Theller looked around. "Yes — we're — no! Where's Parker?"

Somewhere in the dark something crashed. A dog began to bark. There were running steps, then a wild shout. "The American prisoners! The American prisoners! They've got loose!" The shout was taken up. In the Citadel a bell began to toll ominously. Across the deep ditch, torches flared. A hidden drum beat savagely. In a bright flare, Gil could see a man struggling in a knot of redcoats. "Parker. He trailed behind. They've caught him. Come on!" Gil started back toward the ditch.

Theller clawed at him. "Remember. Every man for himself. We agreed!"

With a curse, Gil turned around. Theller went on: "They'll be closing the gates into the Lower Town. We've got to hurry. Listen!"

The great bell of the Citadel boomed on, was caught up, echoed by other bells in the city beyond the walls. Gil took a last look at the flame-spattered darkness, then set his foot on the slippery staircase that led to the city.

They were on solid ground outside the gray *enceinte*. Theller waved his arms. "Spread out. Single file. We'll go out by the Hope Gate. No talking. Walk on the grass as far as you can."

Gil caught Theller's arm. "I've got a better idea. Form up in column of two's. That's it. Theller — keep to the outside. Now — get in step."

The little column swung on through the pouring rain, heading for the Rond des Chaînes, the drilling water muffling their footfalls. As they passed the Château St. Louis, where Colborne was quartered, the guards presented arms smartly. Gil, swinging along beside the column, returned the salute.

As soon as they were out of earshot, Gil quickened the pace and they plunged into a narrow street that sloped down from the great

Place. The bells were booming louder and along the Rue de la Fabrique shouts echoed. Thellar broke through the line, caught Gil's arm. "Better run for it now. Drolet said there'd be someone to meet us at the Place d'Armes. Something's gone wrong." There were more distant shouts. "Every man for himself," said Theller in a tense voice. "You've got your maps. You know where to go. You'll be expected. Good luck!"

He darted off down a dark alley. Gil watched the others melt away, started down a long, ramplike street that curved sharply to the St. Lawrence. Then he saw torches and men came pelting down from a fragment of the old city wall at his left. He looked around quickly. The street was bare, open, and the stone houses were built close to the sidewalk, offering no cover.

He controlled his breath with an effort, waved his arms. "I heard someone running this way," he shouted. "This way!"

A tall man raced up, caught his arm. "Who are you? What are you doing here?"

Gil braced himself, thought desperately of an imaginary past. "Ensign Cox of the *Endeavor*." He forced a smile. "Want to see my papers?"

The men hesitated, then another called roughly, "He ain't a Yankee anyway. Don't talk like one. It's Yankees and that Irishman that's away."

Gil started eagerly. "Is that it? I thought it might be thieves. They ran like the devil off there. What's up anyway? My ship only came in last night."

"Never mind what's up. Two thousand dollars to who catches 'em. State prisoners. They— "

The group pounded off down the steep street, Gil running with them. At the bottom the leader paused, looked around. The night, barring the steady pitch of the rain, was still. He looked suspiciously at Gil. "Sure you heard 'em?"

Gil nodded in violent agreement. "Five or six. Running like the devil. I— "

The man turned to his followers. "Break up. Go through the alleys."

"Can I help?" asked Gil.

"Know the city?"

"Just landed. I'd be glad— "

"Go along with him. Seamen ain't much on runnin' but you might help."

Gil joined a small group that raced back up the steep hill, brushing past the very rock on which the city stood. The man in charge of his group sent a runner down one alley, another into a parklike space in the shadow of the rock. Suddenly Gil saw a steep flight of steps leading down to an old, old street where dim lamps flared in the rain. He shouted, "I'll take this one. All right?"

There was a rough shout of "Don't break your God-damn neck."

Gil clattered down interminable slimy steps, found himself in a narrow stone street. He paused for breath, listening. High above he could hear more shouts, the booming bells. He looked up toward the black bulk of the Citadel, vaguely outlined against the streaming sky. This must have been the street whose entrance he had stared at so often from the high rock, where he had seen antlike men and horses crawling far below. A mile beyond the end of it— He shook the water from his cap, walked rapidly on.

Then from the side came a sudden shout: "There he is! I seen him to the barracks." Gil, a cold hand at his throat, darted away as three men rushed out of a narrow alley.

He had a good start and his long legs carried him on in great leaps. He looked over his shoulder. Two of the men were trailing behind. The third, a short, stout man, was surprisingly holding his own. He was even gaining. Gil remembered the stride and the voice —a sergeant of the Coldstreams whom he had often seen at inspections. He looked again. The sergeant, a famous runner, had gained still more.

Gil lengthened his stride, dodged down an alley, found a narrow street at right angles, a high wall. He caught the combing with his hands, swung himself over, and fell onto soft earth.

Cautiously he rose to his knees, looked about. He was in a wide garden—a vegetable garden, from the frames. At the far end a squat building loomed, a huge cross stark against the dripping night—a sisters' hospital, perhaps, or a small convent. Then a ribbon of light showed close by. The door of an outhouse opened and an old nun, lantern in hand, came out. Within the shed, a faint bleating sounded. The nun clucked encouragingly, shuffled up the path. Then she saw Gil, dropped her lantern with a scream.

Gil tried desperately to summon broken phrases of French, stammered: "*Pas mal! Pas mal.*"

The nun, hand to her fat throat, wheezed, "*Qu'est-ce que c'est que s'agit, quoi?*"

Gil repeated, "*Pas mal.*" Then, on inspiration, he patted his stomach, slapped his sodden clothes.

The nun's fears seemed to melt. "*Ah! Le pauvre gars! Viens au guichet. On vous donnera —*"

At the far end of the garden, light slashed through the rain. A hoarse voice shouted: "I seen him. And Theller'll be with him. I — "

The nun scuttled off toward the building, lantern waving. There was a sudden yell. "There he is! It's Theller. Never mind the big bugger. Get Theller! Hidin' in a nun's dress, by God!"

Gil shouted, hurled a rock, but the men darted after the nun. Gil swung to the wall. "They won't hurt her. No one'll hurt a nun — " Then the three figures closed on the short, fat woman, who, in terror, fell on her face. Rough hands seized her. There was a disgusted yell. "It's a woman, all right. I say it is. God damn it, can't I *feel?* Where's that long-legged — "

Gil showed himself on the top of the wall, slung his legs over, dropped toward the street, caught himself by his hands, and hung there for a moment. He heard a bellow: "He's off again." The pursuers pounded through the building.

With an effort, he swung himself back, dropped to the garden, and ran toward the nun, who, weeping, was struggling to her feet. He gently caught her by the elbow, helped her up. But she shrank from his touch, tottered to the building.

Gil watched her close the heavy door with shaky hands, then, cursing the sergeant, moved quietly back toward the wall. The street was dead, lifeless, save for the patter of rain. In the distance he heard feet thudding up the long staircase to the Upper Town.

He set his chin. "They think I've doubled back. Hope the bastards break their necks!" He scaled the wall, looked over cautiously, then dropped to the pavement.

The house that he sought was about a mile from the west end of the street. He'd seen it time and again from the embrasure, high above. White it was, and narrow, with a scanty garden toward the rock and a flimsy pier jutting into the stream. He kept close to the wall, glided on as quickly as he could.

The clump of elms, close in the shelter of the rock, dripped heavily on him as he passed under. Then a shape moved quickly. Something sharp prodded his back. A voice snarled: " 'Ands op!"

A sudden wave of helpless despair swept over Gil as he stood in his damp clothes. He started to spring aside, but the keen blade dug deeper. "*Marche!*" snapped the voice.

Sodden shoes slopping through the puddles, Gil shuffled on, was guided to a small house where the unseen man with the knife whistled shrilly. A door opened stealthily and Gil was pushed roughly into a dark room. The door slammed, a bolt rasped. The man shouted: "*Holà! La lampe, 'cré nom de dieu!*"

Another door opened, a flood of light poured in, and a wrinkled old woman set a lamp on the bare table, peering at Gil. The boring point of the knife dropped, and a slight, swarthy man, white teeth flashing in a smile, patted Gil's shoulder. "*Ça!*" he said, pushing forward a chair. "And 'ow is my frien', *le docteur* T'eller?"

Gil dropped down, arms hanging limp, the sudden shock of relief choking off the words that formed in his throat.

The dark man whirled about. " '*Faut manger, quoi! Faites porter de la soupe, hein!*" The old woman scuttled off. "Now—*attend!*" said the Frenchman. "First we mak' dry ze clothes. So!" He stripped Gil's wringing jacket from his shoulders, ripped at the collar of his shirt. "You are ze *canadien,* eh? Me, I am Angus McLachlan, *gaspésien.*"

Through his daze, Gil stared again. "Angus—Angus—"

"*B'en oui! Mon père*—'e French, Hamish McLachlan. *Ma mère,* she Scotch—Claudine des Rosiers. Now—*ze pantalons.*"

His clothes in a wet heap on the floor, Gil scrubbed at himself with a thick towel while McLachlan, armed with another, rasped his back. The blood began to flow under his clear skin, his teeth stopped chattering. "And T'eller?" suggested McLachlan.

In sentences broken by fierce towelings, Gil told of the escape, the dispersion. His host nodded, threw him a vast, warm cape. "Zere is somet'ing wrong. Bilodeau was told to meet you in *la haute ville.* An' ze 'ouse w'ere you were waited, zat is full of *gendarmes.* Zat is why I bring you here. Zat is why I poke knife at you. If someone see, zey say: 'Godam! Jost a Frenchy who cut purse!' Zey forget."

Gil stretched his slippered feet toward the low hearth. "What do I do now?"

McLachlan shook his head. "Mos' difficult! I tell you, somet'ing go wrong. I 'ave no word from Monsieur Drolet, from 'Unter, from Grace. You eat our soup, you sleep. Maybe I make little promenade, eh?"

The old woman shuffled in with a bowl of thick pea soup, stared at Gil, and mumbled something to McLachlan. He took the bowl, gave it to Gil. "She ask, are you *bastonnais*. She remember old days w'en we 'ave lilies in the Place d'Armes, not lions; w'en we 'ave w'ite coats, not red, in the Rond des Chaînes. Zen one call all from down dere *bastonnais,* since from the *ville de* Boston came all our fears."

Gil began eating greedily, the heavy, steaming soup scalding his throat. At last he laid down his ladlelike spoon. "About your going out—what if people come here—looking for me, you know?"

McLachlan held up his hand. "I 'ave sent for Hercule Belliveau. 'E know T'eller well. 'E will stay here. Now you mos' sleep." He led the way to a small, cupboard-like room where a wide feather bed stretched nearly from wall to wall. The Frenchman bowed. "I will send Belliveau to see you. Zen I make my promenade."

Gil burrowed into the softness of the feathers, eyelids sagging. But he tossed and turned, his body for so many months accustomed to hard beds and scant covers. He stripped the blankets, spread them on the floor, and rolled up in them.

A hand on his shoulder ripped him back into consciousness. He blinked, then started in alarm as his eyes focused on a huge raw-boned man in kilts, gingery hair flying out from a Glengarry bonnet. A vast hand pushed him back. "I am Hercule Belliveau. My *sacré* cousin, Angus, he make *reconnaissance*. Now I watch, *hein?*" The high-boned Scotch face softened. "*Ah, le pauvre gars. Fatigué, hein?*" He muffled his light, closed the door softly.

Gil lay back, bewildered. What sort of world was he in? Swarthy McLachlan; huge, kilted Belliveau. He gave up the problem as sudden sleep stunned him into unconsciousness.

There was bright, hard sunlight in the room when he awoke and McLachlan stood over him, a great bowl of coffee in his hands. "Ah! Better, eh?" He sat on the edge of the bed, looked down at Gil, who gulped the coffee eagerly. "Now I mos' tell you—" In broken English, spattered with French phrases, he told of a town in tumult. Theller had hidden in a stable. Culver and Hull, along with Parker, had been retaken. Of the others he had no word, except that he thought Dodge was with Theller. During the night convents had been invaded (largely by anti-Catholics, thought McLachlan), men, women, and children stopped and searched. At one place, a coffin had been opened. Sir John Colborne had offered a reward of two thousand dollars for the recapture of the fugitives. The Coldstreams, jealous of their name as a crack corps, had added another thousand from the regimental chest.

Gil smiled wryly. "So I'm worth three thousand, am I?"

"Zey say so," said McLachlan noncommittally. Then he shook his head. "I am mos' fearful. You are here. *Bon!* But — " He held out eloquent hands. "But ze rest? Zey are buried in ze wors' places. St. Roche, Ste. Geneviève. 'Ow to get zem out."

Gil frowned. "It's going to be hard?"

McLachlan shrugged. "If zey were here — maybe not so hard. But in St. Roche, Ste. Geneviève."

Gil sat up. "I better go and find Theller."

McLachlan stared in alarm. "No! No! You mos' do what we say or — make visit on Colborne. Look, m'sieur," said he, leaning forward as he saw protest in Gil's eyes, "zere are many here who work for you, for T'eller. Zey 'ave zere own plans for zat work. If zey fail — if someone catch — it would not be *gentil* for zem. Colborne does not love ze *habitant*. Me, I can show you t'ousand houses w'ere is no roof, no flame in ze *foyer*. Zat is Colborne's work. You mos' trust us an' — "

Gil sat up quickly. "All right. All right. But I must say I don't like to lie here while Theller and the rest — Well, what do I do?"

McLachlan got up. "We make dry your clothes. Put zem on. Zen — you wait. You will do nossing but wait."

Gil nodded and the little man scurried out of the room.

Through the rest of the day, Gil fidgeted, fumed, ate a vast meal that the old woman brought in, napped from time to time. Through the one window he could see nothing but a stretch of water, the base of the high cliffs of the opposite shore, a hard, bright light shining on them from a hidden sun. Occasional boats drifted by or worked upstream against tide and current.

The shadows along the Lévis shore had gone far on their eastward slant when the door flew open and McLachlan stormed in. Gil looked up from his blankets. "Well — what's the word?"

"For T'eller, for Dodge — zey 'ave long wait. Days. Maybe weeks — onless zat *sacré* Colborne find 'em. But you — " He stared out the window. "Maybe you wait, too." He shook his fist at the bright glow of the river. "Jost one little piece fog, mist. Jost for two hour! I 'ave boat. I 'ave men! But — " He pointed out the window. Along the blue of the water, a gig rowed slowly, the sailors keeping a sharp eye on flood and shore, two red-coated figures alert in the stern. " 'Ow we get by zat?" He leaned his chin on his fist. "Tomorrow, more boats, more soldiers. On ze river, in ze streets. I 'ave spread word zat you and T'eller 'ave gone to Montreal. Maybe it 'elp."

Gil joined him at the window, watched the stir of river life. The sun sank lower. Suddenly Gil narrowed his eyes, blinked. The cliffs west of Lévis — were they a little blurred, vaguer? Was there a whitish tinge to the sunset riot of gold and blue on the St. Lawrence? Then McLachlan jumped to his feet. "It come! It come!" He danced about the room, waving his arms, crowing with delight as the long deep funnel outside slowly filled with circling wraiths of mist.

In a half hour it was dark, a last deceptive flicker clinging to the distant highlands of the south shore. McLachlan threw a cape to Gil, then gave a tremendous heave to the bed, which slid with a thud against the opposite wall. In the narrow strip of floor the outlines of a trapdoor showed sharp. The swarthy man flung it up and slimy steps showed in the chasm below.

"What's that?" asked Gil, staring.

"Ze boat. Ze river, she come right under 'ouse. Now you go, eh? Zey wait down zere."

"You're not coming?"

The dark head shook. "I 'ave work in ze town."

"Here — wait a minute. Who's taking me?" asked Gil, suspiciously.

"Again a cousin. 'Is name — Georges-Marie Onésime McDougall. 'E'll descend you to Lévis." A small hand was thrust out. "Now — *au 'voir et bonne chance*."

Gil stammered his thanks, was waved hastily down the steps. At the bottom he saw black water, a small skiff, and a muffled man who rested on long oars. There was a grunt from the skiff. "We not talk, eh?" said a low voice. "Better zat way."

Somewhere in the darkness above a pulley whined, a wooden

panel lifted cautiously. The rower dipped his oars, sculled carefully out into the stream. Then the panel sank slowly back into position.

The mist hung well over the water and the ships anchored near the foot of Cape Diamond were shapeless hulks hanging in a world that had no limits, no horizons. McDougall pulled steadily at his oars, skillfully nursing the sharp bow against the push of the river. Gil looked back over his shoulder. Far above him, looming from the woolly masses below, the hard brow of the Citadel stared down, seemed to move toward him in slow, inexorable progress.

He shuddered, turned his back on the great rock. Ahead, only the crest of the Lévis cliffs showed, a white crawling mass clinging to the swift slopes. McDougall, eyes seemingly on the floorboards of the skiff, held a steady course, now slanting far west, now heading more directly toward the hidden land. Once Gil started, braced himself, as another skiff, ghostly in the fog, shot into view. But the armed men in the stern only waved, called "*Bonne chance*" in low tones. McDougall nodded gruffly, muttered, "Zey are of ours."

At last the bow grated on the rocky beach that stretched along the great sweep of the cliffs. McDougall drew his craft out of the water. Gil sprang ashore, swung his arms, shouted.

McDougall scowled. "*Tais-toi!* You have not yet begun."

Gil, suddenly sobered, thought of the long stretch of country that lay between him and the American border. Then he stared up at the gullied face of the great earthen scarp.

The dour McDougall grinned suddenly. "Not easy, eh? But I show you." He led the way along the little beach, skirting narrow inlets and leaping over rocks. Then he stopped, pointed to a stunted bush about twenty feet up the slope. "You can see, eh? From zat bush, zere begin little path. Follow to top and—"

"Where does it come out?" asked Gil.

"On ze top," said the Frenchman. "*Naturellement.* By it we smuggle tea from ze Yankees. It is safe. I tell you so, I. Now, *bonne chance.*" He ran back to the skiff, pushed off, and began rowing with quick, choppy strokes.

Gil looked at the dim mass before him, then began to scramble up the slope toward the scrub. It was hard going and at times he had to swing himself along by clutching at the tussocks of grass that jutted in the scarred face. Then he was at the foot of the bush and a deep, sheltered path slanted upwards.

Slipping, stumbling, but always keeping on, Gil finally clutched the very edge and pulled himself onto solid land. There was a stir in the darkness. A voice called, "That you, Stensrood?"

Gil flattened against the ground. The voice called again. "It's all right. You're from McLachlan and McDougall brought you over." A wavering shape appeared, materialized into a stocky man who held out his hand. "I'm Carey. Got a horse for you. Better get going."

Gil stared as other shapes moved, hoofs padded on the soft earth. A half-seen rider tossed reins to Gil, who swung into the saddle, found a carbine snug in the boot. He curved the horse over to Carey. "Things have been happening so fast I can't quite take them in. But I want to say—I mean, these horses and everything—"

"All right," said Carey shortly. "We're organized for this. When you get to the States, perhaps you'll be able to help someone. Come on." He waved his arm and the horses padded off into the night, four men riding behind Gil.

Carey settled his pistols in his holsters. "We're going to keep right on till sunrise. No stops, if we can help it. We're going to stick to the back roads and at times we'll want to ride fast. If we meet any patrols, we're a squad of militia from Beauceville, down there on the Chaudière. I've got papers for all of us. If anyone doesn't like our papers, we shoot. Your carbine's loaded and primed. Saw to it myself. And if we run into too many, we'll scatter—everyone for himself. You don't know the country but if you keep straight south you'll have a fair chance of getting through. Remember—when you're across the border it won't mean you're safe. There's plenty that'd sell you for the reward. I'll give you a map and a list of people you can probably trust. Now—no talking. And stick close to me."

All through the misty night the little troop rode, sweeping over the bare plains that stretched from the St. Lawrence to the hills of Maine and New Hampshire. Once, swinging up from a deep gulley that fed west to the Chaudière, Gil saw campfires burning, heard distant shouts that set the six horses rocketing off to the east again, circling back.

Just before dawn they made camp in the hills to the east of Beauceville, taking turns at watching the country below. While on guard, Gil saw armed men ride out of the little town that straggled along the broad Chaudière, saw others swinging in a wide arc on the west bank.

The stars came out and they rode again. In the first light of false dawn, Carey reined in on the top of a wooded rise and pointed to a road that lurched north unevenly over a wide plain. "See that frame sticking up there? Well, that says 'Lower Canada' on one side. The other says 'State of Maine.' Ride ahead till you're abreast of it — only don't go too close. Keep a good mile to the east — and you're across the border. We filled your saddlebags. You've got money. Good luck!"

He waved. The four others closed in behind him, filed off through the sparse pines.

Gil, hands on the pommel of his saddle, stared, almost unbelieving. A short gallop and he'd be across the border, safe in the State of Maine that seemed to spread out its pine-covered hills, its broad lakes, holding them out to him, proffering refuge. Then he remembered Carey's words about caution even across the line, chose a dry watercourse, and let his horse pick its way over the rough stones, his own eyes sharp on the horizon.

By sunset he calculated that he was twenty miles within the American side. Twenty miles. The thought seemed to lift a heavy stone from his chest. The deeper he went the safer he was. He swung his horse's head down toward the great road that ran over the border, north to Beauceville and on to Lévis.

The long straight stretch ahead of him was houseless. Then he caught a twinkle of light beyond a pine grove, saw a rambling house close by the edge of a still, deep pool. He spurred up a rutted path and banged the knocker on the broad door.

There was a pause. Then he heard muffled footsteps. The door swung slowly open and a thin, lined face, unshaven, looked out. "What you want?" said the man shortly.

"I've been caught on the road," said Gil. "There don't seem to be any inns about."

The door opened wider. Gil saw small, close-set eyes staring at him. Thin lips parted and the man said, "No — they don't seem to be."

Gil settled impatiently in the saddle. "Well—it's getting late. I wondered if you could put me and my horse up. I'd pay, of course."

Lines on the thin face deepened. "Where you from?"

"Riding over from the east," said Gil.

"What town?" asked the man, rubbing his unshaven chin.

Gil burst out, "Damn it, does that matter?"

The man shoved his hands in his pockets. "So it's that, is it?" He squinted up at the sky. "Gettin' late in the year, ain't it? If you was a mite later, you might have to go on snowshoes. Ever use 'em?"

Gil leaned forward, eyes alert. "Often."

"Don't say. Now, what kind d'you use? I'm kinda partial to them Indian ones—flat-like."

"Shoes with a spur are better."

Straggly eyebrows lifted. "Spurs? Don't just know what you mean, and I've been on snowshoes all my life. Now, I'd kinda like to see what a spur shoe looks like. Mebbe you'd scratch a picture of one in the dirt."

Gil shook his head. "Guess I'm talking tall. I've never seen one with a spur. So—I couldn't draw one."

The door opened wide. The man stepped out. "So. But you look like a Hunter to me. Couldn't hunt 'thout snowshoes."

Gil nodded. "I hunt some, generally Thursdays."

There was a tight smile. "This bein' Wednesday, eh? I most usually go for beaver. Do you know the beaver to be an industrious animal?"

Gil raised his left hand to the level of his mouth. The man stepped farther out. "Trouble?" he asked.

"Calm," said Gil.

"Well, that's good. Do you snuff and chew?"

Gil nodded solemnly. "I do," he answered.

"Have you any news for me?"

"Some."

The man stepped back into the house. "Get off that horse. I'll have a boy take it round to the barn." He held the door open for Gil, then slammed it behind him and led the way into a broad, whitewashed room where a low fire blazed. "Sit down. Have you mealed? Well, I'll set out something hot."

He opened a cupboard, set a kettle on the hob. "Now, I didn't think much of you when I laid eyes to you. You see, there've been fellers tryin' funny things around here. Two night ago, a pair of 'em come, claimin' to be Hunters. Had some of the words, too." He laughed shortly. "But I tripped 'em. One of 'em drew a snowshoe for me so I knowed they wasn't proper." He scooped stew out of a deep pot, set hot tea on the table. "Now—what can I do for you?"

Gil stretched out his long legs. Sudden exultation swelled almost unbearably in his chest. He slapped his hand on the table. "You can let me have paper and ink—you can—" His laughter was thick, heavy. "You can—"

The unkempt man nodded wisely. "It always hits 'em like that. First time they think they're safe. Try to talk—try to laugh, try to sing. I had one feller here that wanted to open all the windows, build fires out on the grass. Well—eat up. I'll see what I can do for you."

The hot stew seemed to glow through to Gil's very finger tips, the hot tea reinforcing it. Between mouthfuls he glanced at his host, who, as he pottered about the room, said that his name was Madison Bemis and that he hunted only when smuggling wasn't doing well. And he talked at length about the Hunters' Lodges, how they were going to bring liberty to Canada, Upper and Lower. Gil only half listened, remembering what rigmarole he had thought the solemn ritual that went with the hastily constituted Lodge in the Citadel. He had felt that he was almost humoring Theller in going through the intricate steps that led from Snowshoe to Beaver and on to the higher degrees. Now he found that he had a sure key to safety, to help when needed.

Bemis rambled on. "Course, they ain't many Hunters in Maine. Just 'long the border. Ain't many to Vermont, neither. But in New York and Ohio, they're thick as fleas in an Indian's blanket. Had 'nough stew? Well, then you might tell me where you're goin' next."

Gil pushed back his chair. "Straight to Albany. What's my best road?"

Bemis raised his eyebrows. "You ain't goin' to join up with Von Scholtz?" He looked disgruntled. "Hell—that's one reason I was helpin' you."

"Von Scholtz?" asked Gil. "Who's he? I haven't heard of him."

Bemis brightened. "Well, you'd better. He's a Proossian. Real soldier. He ain't like some of the others that ain't never seen a gun. He's fit. Yes sir. Major in the Proossian army. Well, he's got a lot of men up Ogdensburg way in New York. Got plenty arms, money, anything you want. And he's got Bill Johnstone with him, workin' out the Thousand Islands. You heard of Bill, ain't you?"

Gil nodded. The river pirate had been notorious since the War of 1812, preying chiefly on the Canadian side, from which he had been evicted by the Compact of those days, it was said. His eyes narrowed. Von Scholtz—a trained soldier. Plenty of men. Bill Johnstone's boats would give him command of the river long enough to get big forces across.

Bemis's voice went on. "And they's lots of fellers—from here and from Canada in the militia regiments over the border. They'll throw in with the German, arms and all, as soon as he moves." He chuckled, slapped his knee. "Old Johnstone. The King's been trying to catch him for near twenty years. He's the feller that burned the *Robert Peel* to make up for the *Caroline*. I tell you, you'll see the Stars and Stripes floating over Toronto and Quebec before the year's out. We'll—"

Gil, chin sunk in his stock, listened. This did look like the best chance of all. People working on both sides of the border; skillfully handled troops, that would be joined by at least some of the force that was sent against them. It might be—

Then he remembered Richland's earnest words in the little parlor of the Eagle in Buffalo. "If Mac loads himself down with a lot of clowns, people that count'll begin to drop away. You and Mac might just as well figure on settling in Buffalo." Well—Mackenzie was a drifting waif somewhere in New York, had even been arrested once for breach of neutrality laws. The fighting had gone on, sporadically—but under whom? Under people that counted?

His chin sank lower. Doc had been right. The clowns had taken over the Upper Canada Rebellion. Van Rensselaer, Sutherland, Brophy—yes, and even Theller. Clowns, in Doc's reasoning. Mechanics, lawyers, doctors, drifters, masquerading as soldiers. And why? For glory, like Van Rensselaer and Sutherland. For hatred of England, like the flaming Irish Theller, who was willing, untrained, to take command of men for the sole purpose of damaging the Crown. What did the earnest frightened men who had massed about Montgomery's mean to such people? Just convenient rungs by which to climb to titles, money, revenge. He knew nothing of Von Scholtz. But he could visualize the men who would follow him. Murderous Irishmen, desperate drifters from the waterfronts of Ontario and Erie, starving men rounded up with a loaf of bread and a pint of whiskey to take their places in ragged platoons and companies. And Von Scholtz's allies — Johnstone and his family. This would be for them merely a grandiose chance to practise their marauding on a wide scale, flimsily sheltered under military law. What would the success of such an invasion mean to the little shopkeeper on King Street, to the farmer in Stormont or Durham, to the schoolteacher in Wentworth?

His chin jerked up suddenly. Bemis, hand slapping on the table, was urging. "Now, if I was you, I'd go right south to Skowhegan. Then I'd light out east clear 'cross New Hampshire and Vermont — say Wells River to Montpelier. Then you'd strike Champlain, ferry 'cross it and make for Plattsburg — "

Gil put out his hand. "You said you'd let me have ink and paper. I want to write a letter. And what's the best route to Albany? Of course, I'm paying for all this."

XXXII

Doc Richland — 1838

THE western sky caught a last cold band of orange-red, held it for an instant, and the bare branches of the trees across the Hudson were stark against the dying glory. Then the color faded, glowed dimly like massed embers. Gil jumped from the country cart, stared at the long, thin blade of frozen water that tapered away to the north. "Sure this is the place?"

The Vermonter, bony shoulders huddled in a shapeless coat, grunted: "Ain't I said I'd take you there?" He pointed to a narrow bridge, a snowy roof beyond. "That's Ferris's. Albany coaches all stop there. You ain't got six mile to go on the other bank."

Gil still looked at the narrowing stream. "Thought it'd be wider than this."

The man gathered the reins. "Well, dig it wider, if you're so minded. I ain't sayin' you can't. G'dup." The cart creaked away over the road that, snow-powdered, vanished into piny hills.

Gil picked up his satchel. "Must be right." He tramped across the bridge, eyes on the sides of the inn that night was turning into black velvet, orange-dotted. "Get some dinner here. If there's a night coach I'll get it. Must be one first thing in the morning anyhow. Maybe I can sleep in the stable. Money's most gone."

The bridge was behind him and he struck out across a winding path that led to the great highway along the dwindling river. Then rutted snow crunched under his feet and he turned south, wondering if Ferris might, by chance, be a Hunter. If he were, it would help. He strode up the short walk to the inn, gave the Hunters' knock. The blows echoed hollowly, were swallowed in a deep silence. He rapped again. A curtain at a side window was pushed cautiously back. "Hello — the house!" shouted Gil.

Quick footsteps beat on the floor. The lock jarred and clashed.

The heavy door banged open and a slim girl flung herself into his arms. "Gil! Gil! I knew you'd come! You're not going away again. You're not, are you?"

Dumb with surprise and joy, Gil could only hold her close, shaking his head. Her voice raced on. "We heard about that German. Gil, I was so afraid that you'd go with him after all."

Gil rubbed his cheek against hers. "I'm here. Sandra, we're staying. It's over. We — "

There was a sudden roar from inside the great room. A big man plunged through the door. One of Gil's hands was torn from about Sandra, crushed in a tight grip. "By God, we knew you'd get here. We knew it." Josiah stamped in the snow, banged his palms together, caught Gil's free hand again. "Look at him, Sandra! By God, jail agrees with him! We'll put him in jail here. Put both of you in."

He parted them, threw his arms about their shoulders, and marched them into the big common room of the inn, crowing, "We've got him, Father. We've got him."

A short stocky man, neat in a dark blue coat, turned from the fire, held out his hand. "Gil, we're glad to see you, mighty glad." His gray eyes, bright under shaggy brows, looked at Gil keenly. "Been a bad time, eh? Well, it's over now and we've got very fond of the daughter you've let us keep while you were away."

She looked up at Gil. "They've done everything for me."

The older man snorted with something of old Barnabas's violence. "She wouldn't let us do anything for her. She's been — she's been — " He swung suddenly toward his son. "How about the horses? How about the carriage? We've got to get back to town." He took him by the arm, shoved him out of the room. Over his shoulder he said: "I tried to keep the idiot from bursting out the door, but it'd have taken an ox chain to hold him." A door banged behind the two.

Gil dropped to a wide settle by the fire, Sandra's hands in his. "Got that medicine man all ready? Remember? We talked about him at Navy."

She smiled. "Just as soon as that letter came, Uncle Schuyler — that's what I call him — saw to everything." She reached up, gently stroked his cheek. "Gil — you're so thin. And we thought you might come yesterday, so we all drove out here." She clutched his hand tighter. "I began to be so scared, when it got dark. I thought it might mean another day. I thought you might have gone off with that German. I thought—"

"And I thought I might have to spend the night here and come into town tomorrow. I had to get new boots somewhere in Vermont—Brattleboro, I guess it was—but it was Sunday and I had to wait over another day. I was going to come right to the house and—"

She threw back her head. "Think we'd have let you do that? As soon as you mentioned Ferris's in your letter, we decided to come here and meet you." She settled against his shoulder. "Happy, Gil?"

He nodded ecstatically. "*Am* I? But what are you frowning about?"

She shook her head, then turned to him. "I'm not frowning. It's just—"

There was a discreet rap. An aproned pot boy bobbed his head. "Mr. Schuyler Stensrood's carriage. It's to the door."

Gil sprang to his feet, caught Sandra's hands again. "Come on. No pickets to dodge."

She hesitated. "I was just going to say—"

"That you're in a hurry to get started," laughed Gil, spinning her about. The pot boy, grinning, flung open the door. The lamplight shone on glossy bay flanks, a trim, well-slung carriage. Josiah held out his hands, swung Sandra inside, while his father, smiling, motioned to Gil. The lock clacked, the coachman flourished his whip, and the carriage started off on the road to Albany.

As they cleared the inn, Schuyler Stensrood touched Sandra's arm lightly. "Have you told him?" he whispered.

She shook her head, eyes troubled. "I tried to—at the inn. Then you and Jos came."

Gil pressed her hand. "What are you conspiring about?"

She bit her lip, then stroked his arm. "Gil—I was trying to tell you there at the inn. It's—it's Dr. Richland. He wants to see you."

Gil shouted with delight. "Doc here? Why didn't he come along with you? Course I'll see him. See him the first thing in the morning. Go right away and—"

Schuyler Stensrood, so like an older Cameron with his broad

chin and stocky body, shook his head. "I — I think he'd like it if you looked in as soon as we get to town."

Josiah nodded emphatically. "We'll roll right past there."

"But it'll be late," protested Gil.

Sandra looked quickly away. "It may be. But Gil — he's counting on seeing you. It — it'll mean so much to him. You don't know."

Gil thought of the old, lined face, the sharp, rasping voice, the veined hands that were so skilled and so sure. See Doc? Of course he would. Why, Doc — Doc meant more to him — perhaps they'd practise together.

Sandra leaned against him as the carriage swayed ahead. Josiah rambled on about doings in New York State. Marshall Bidwell was going to settle in either New York or Albany. John Rolph was, he thought, near Rochester. Mackenzie had been in New York, but there was talk of his moving to Rochester. There was still activity along the border despite Von Scholtz's desperate, hopeless stand across the river. The spring would bring more raids, but — He shrugged.

Gil sighed. "That's all gone as far as I'm concerned. The people running things now aren't going to do anyone but themselves good — if they even manage to do that. I looked in at a lodge in Vermont. They were talking of getting Indians in Michigan or Illinois, turning them loose on the border settlements. That's not what we were fighting for."

"You don't want to go with Mr. Mackenzie?" asked Sandra softly.

Gil shook his head. "Mac's just grabbing at straws — the way I was until I had a chance to think, to get things in proportion." He sank back against the seat. He felt very tired, content just to sit quietly and watch Sandra's profile against the carriage window, to listen to Josiah's rumbling comment, Schuyler Stensrood's pungent interpolations.

At last the lights of Albany shone before them. A steep hill, sprinkled with glowing windows, swept up from the river to the right and Gil could see the spread and lift of fine roof lines, the dim bulk of great buildings.

Then the carriage veered sharply, turned off along a narrow street that skirted the base of the hill. Gil, peering through the windows, could see rather shabby houses, sparsely lighted, doors from which the paint was flaking, an occasional broken window. To his surprise, the carriage stopped.

"What's this?" asked Gil, staring.

"This is where Dr. Richland lives," said Sandra, eyes on Gil. "I think he'd like it better if you went up — without the rest of us."

"But — but this house!" protested Gil. "Doc can't be — "

Schuyler Stensrood spoke quietly. "He wouldn't hear of anything else when he came down here." His voice grew suddenly tense. "Damn it, he could have had the best room in our house, but he — " He broke off. "Better go along, Gil."

Gil stepped out into thin snow, climbed a shaky flight of steps. The knocker gave out a splintery sound and someone in flapping slippers shuffled down a corridor. The shabby house melted away in the sudden surge of joy that swept over Gil. Those steps — sounded a bit like Doc. The door would open and Doc would peer at him and shower him with rasping questions.

The latch clicked. An old woman in a soiled wrapper gaped at him. "What's the matter?"

Gil's heart sank, then rose again as he saw, hung on a peg, a gnawed-looking beaver. "Dr. Richland," he whispered. "I want to see him. Don't tell him I'm here. I want to — "

A shaky thumb jerked toward carpetless stairs. "First door on the right. You'll know it. Two panels is split."

Gil edged past her, ran lightly up the stairs. Doc would storm at him and he'd play penitent, then tell him about the grenadier's ulcer that he'd cured at the Citadel after Theller had given it up. He began to grin, then carefully composed his features and pushed the door open.

His hand fell from the latch. On a narrow bed an old, old man lay, blue-veined hands on a tattered counterpane. The wrinkled lids were closed and the big nose seemed to jut more than ever from the bony cheeks. Gil took a cautious step nearer. "Doc!" he whispered.

The old eyelids flickered, the weary eyes blinked. Then the thin hands moved, lifted, reached out. "Gil!" said Richland. "You got back. You got back." His voice was low, unsteady. He moistened his lips. "Where — where is she?"

"Who?" asked Gil. Then, forgetting the question, he sat by the bed, Richland's cold hands in his. "Doc — what's the matter with you?" In growing alarm, he noted the heavy breathing, the bluish tinge about the lips, the tremor in the worn hands that held his feebly.

Something of the old rasp came back into Richland's voice. "Now who the hell would I mean? Sandra! Where is she?"

"Outside," said Gil. "She's all right." He leaned forward, touched Richland's forehead. "Doc — who's been looking after you? By God, you've got a fever that'd — "

A limp hand waved. "Never mind 'bout me. I got better care'n a young cub *I* raised could give me. Get her up here. Want to see her. Want to see her with you." He coughed, waved Gil away angrily. "Go get her."

Gil raced down the stairs, flung open the carriage door. "Come on. Doc wants you." As they ran up the steps and into the house he whispered hoarsely, "Why didn't you tell me? Sandra, Doc's awful sick. He's — "

"Sh! He knows it. But he pretends he's all right." She paused on the last step, laid a hand on his arm. "He's been worrying so about you. And when he heard you were coming — " Her eyes filled. "Gil — he got up. The landlady found him on the stairs. We tried to take him home but he wouldn't come. Now — don't fuss over him." She opened the door softly, peered in. Then her laugh rippled through the house. "Hello, Doctor. We caught him after all." She stepped over the sill, Gil close behind.

Richland had made some attempt at smoothing his counterpane. He had even rubbed his hands over his scant gray hair and there was a ring to his voice. " 'Bout time someone hog-tied the young fool. Climbing down stone walls and gnawing through iron bars when he ought to be looking after someone's liver! Sit down, Sandra. Gil, you get right alongside of her." He drew a deep breath. "Well — there you are." His eyes rolled toward Gil. "Now — what are you going to do? Be a fool or stay here?"

Sandra slipped her arm through Gil's. "He'll stay here. At least, until your cold's better."

Richland grunted. "It'll get better long's *he* don't mess around me. Gil, all I can say is you don't deserve to be here. But Sandra don't deserve not to have you, I guess. There's a sight to be done. There just ain't time in one man's life to do it. And there's some things one man can do and another can't." He raised himself slightly.

"Far's I've been able to see, there ain't very much that *you* can do — barring looking after sick folk. That and teaching. Sandra, you been talking to him?"

Gil caught a slight tremor of her lower lip, but she masked it in a light laugh. "I left that for you."

The old eyes turned back toward Gil. "We been talking a lot about you — the way folks do when there ain't much else to talk about. Now — " The uncertain voice trailed on. Gil's trained eye watched the old man closely and at every word, every gesture, the weight of misery that was gathering about his heart thickened. The eyes were clearer, the voice stronger, but Gil knew that some strong stimulant, taken while he went downstairs, was responsible.

" — and that's what he's got to do and if he ain't willing, you got to make him! Canada needs doctors. The day'll come when he can go back and then he's got to go. He's got to go back there to be a doctor, and more than that, he's got to make doctors. Make 'em by the dozen, make 'em by the gross. Hear that, Gil?"

Gil saw the stringy throat quiver, knew that lungs and heart were straining with every word. "Sure I will, Doc. I had an idea that we'd go back together. Take that little stone house on Adelaide Street and — "

Richland glared at him. "Hell! You don't think I'd be hollering for you to go back unless I was there looking after you, do you? What I want's for you to take the teaching off me. Sandra and I'll be there to keep you out of trouble the rest of the time."

She set her chin. "When we're through with him, he'll wish he was back in the Citadel."

"He'll wish he'd got sent to Van Diemen's Land if he starts messing about in politics again," said Richland. Then his eyes grew serious. "Gil, I trained up a lot of young fellers, first and last. But you're the only one I ever had that was fit to go on training others." He snorted, glared. "God knows why it had to be you. But it was. There's some folks that think I knew a bit about healing. Well, all I had I packed into that thick skull of yours, and if you let it go to waste, I'll come back and strangle you if I've been fifty years in the grave. It ain't given many folks to teach, Gil, and Sandra and I are going to see that you don't spill the load I gave you." He sank back on the pillows. "When you going to get married?"

Sandra pulled the coverlet higher about his wrinkled neck. "Tomorrow. And you keep covered up or you'll have a sore throat and won't be able to come."

Richland's mouth tightened. "I'm coming. See that?" He pointed to a small package on the battered dresser. "I sent the landlady out yesterday to get it. It's a white tie. I'm going to wear one for the first time in my life."

Sandra tried to speak, then turned her head away. Gil forced a smile. "Doc, I had a case at the Citadel I wish you could have seen. It was — " He spun out the story, elaborating technical details while Richland, his eyes closed, nodded from time to time. His breathing became even, regular. Sandra looked at Gil, raised her eyebrows. He stared into space, listening, a faint hope growing in his heart. Then he found Sandra's hand as his quick ear caught a new note.

Quickly he turned back the covers, listened to the thin beat of the heart, felt the threadlike flutter of the pulse. The hands that still lay outside were cold, the joints slow to move to the pressure of his fingers. The stimulant was wearing off. Gil replaced the covers, lifted Sandra to her feet. "Don't you want to wait for me in the carriage?"

She shook her head, voice uneven. "He's been like a father and mother to me while you were away. Gil — please — I want to stay."

"Better go down," he said gently. "There's — there's nothing to do." Then he saw the mute pleading in her eyes.

Suddenly a voice spoke, strong and clear. "God damn it! Where's my black bag?"

They stared down at Richland. His face was flushed, his eyes tightly closed. The old voice rasped on. ". . . then we go see old Mrs. Bemis. Nothing wrong with her but a long, hot summer and weak bowels. . . . Hi Gregg . . . team bolted with him . . . Karl Lester with his busted leg out of falling from a loft, the clumsy fool . . ."

Sandra dropped to the chair, face in her hands. Gil stood staring, helpless, in a room that filled with a sudden mist. He crouched by the bed, caught one of the veined hands. But the long fingers lay limp in his.

The tones grew weaker, then soared up. "Wish I could get out and see that Kelley girl. Just ain't got time. Hell — what am I worrying about? Gil'll see her. *He'll* know . . . Can't sometimes see why I bother 'bout bringing more people into the world. Take the Mannings, now. What their young ones got to live for? Still — they got their place out the valley of the Don. Mighty pretty country. Don't know much nicer. Ain't never going to forget it . . . And if you start giving too much calomel, Gil, you're going to get your patient in trouble. Course, you'll be in trouble too, but that ain't nothing new for you . . . Damned young fool. Gone tracking off to Montgomery's with the rest of 'em. Guess I got to tie Bessie up and see he don't get into mischief . . ."

Sandra's hand fell across Gil's. She suddenly leaned her head against his arm. "Gil, can't you do *some*thing?"

He shook his head, spoke through the bands of misery that were tight across his chest. "Nothing. If I could — but he's just running down — just flickering out like a light that a lot of people have steered by."

Suddenly Richland stirred. His eyes opened, looked about unseeing. "Who's there?"

She caught his hand. "It's Sandra."

A vague smile flicked at the corners of his mouth. "Kind of dark here. You and I, we got something to do. Just as soon as Gil comes — " He paused. "No. Forgot. Gil's here. We're going to keep him working. You and I. I'm going to put on that white tie tomorrow." There was a long breath. "You're both here. Guess — guess I can go to sleep." His head fell back on the pillow.

Gil looked at the lined face, so still and quiet. He felt a tremor sweep over him, forced it back. Then he drew the patched sheet over the pillow.

He set his chin, gently lifted Sandra to her feet. She leaned against him, crying quietly. "He was good to me and — he loved you so much," she whispered.

Gil stroked her hair. "The carriage — " she began.

Gil nodded. "You — you tell 'em. They'll know what to do. People to notify." His voice broke. "I've done this before — with Doc. I've — "

Sandra turned from Gil. Small hands rested lightly on the patched sheet, smoothed it gently. Then she was gone.

Gil sat down by the bed, listening for a raspy voice that was stilled forever.

XXXIII

Albany — 1840

Gil tramped up the steps to the narrow verandah, battered black bag dangling from a moist hand. There was a stir behind the thick trumpet-flower vines and Sandra, cool in flowered muslin, ran to him, reached high to flip off his tall hat, pushed him into a cane chair. "I found some lemons in the market and I've made a big pitcher of lemonade," she said, dabbing at his forehead with a handkerchief. "Don't you dare stir until I bring it out."

He sighed, stretched out his legs, and watched the shadows creeping across the baking meadows on the east bank of the Hudson. Somewhere in the pearly mist that was gathering to the south, a steamer hooted. A long string of carts bumped and jolted past the little house, horses sweat-streaked and unkempt drivers sprawling on shaky seats.

The door clicked. A ball of orange wool raced madly onto the verandah, swarmed up Gil's legs, perched purring on his shoulder. There was subdued clinking and Sandra, in frowning concentration, edged cautiously out, in her slim hands a tray holding a vast glass pitcher and tall glasses.

"There! And a whole lot of claret to help out the lemons," she announced, filling the tumblers. Her face puckered with pleasure. "Oooh! That's good. It's been awful here today. Was it bad in town?"

Gil set his glass down, rubbed the kitten's purring throat. "Bad enough, when I had time to think about it."

She looked at him, hesitant. "I suppose — he was pretty bad, wasn't he?"

Gil blew out his cheeks. "Yes — but we pulled him through. The crisis was over about three."

Her eyes glowed with pleasure. "No! Oh, Gil! I'm so proud! And that New York doctor said it was impossible, didn't he?"

"He did," said Gil emphatically. "But he was under a handicap. He hadn't been trained by Doc." He studied his glass. "Know where this ice comes from?"

She took the kitten and tossed it an empty spool, which it banged and slammed about. "Why—I know that answer. Ice, my good man, comes from water that's been frozen."

He shook his head. "But what water? This ice I mean. Ever know it was probably cut about a mile out from the Yonge Street pier?"

She sighed, hands in her lap. "The Yonge Street pier. I hear they're building another one at the foot of York Street. Gil—will we ever—"

He cleared his throat. "I was talking with Canning—you know him—used to be Governor Marcy's secretary. I think—I think maybe I'll take out citizenship papers."

She stared. "Gil! And—and stay here—always?"

He looked surprised. "Why—don't you like it?"

"Oh—it isn't that." She looked across the hot meadows. "Everyone's nice to us here. Uncle Schuyler and the others want to do so much for us—but—after all—we're Canadians. We're British subjects."

Gil pointed to a low hill that swelled from the plain to the north. "See that? That used to be Stensrood land. And a mile north of it I found the traces of the house that Great-grandfather Gilbert built. Some day I want to go down into Connecticut and see where your great-greats came from. You see, Sandra, I've come to feel that lines on maps don't really mean very much. We're the same stock, both sides of the border. As long as there is a border, though, you have to follow the differences—and a lot of them are surface—that have been set up on your particular side. But north or south of the line, we're North Americans. And time's going to do an awful lot to those differences. At present, I feel more at home here—more at home inside—than I would if I went back—if I could go back. The Compact is still there. Strachan's still raging, so's Hagerman. And when they go there'll be a lot of younger editions to take their places."

"But it was our home, Gil. We could still fight," she said quietly.

"And what happens if we do?" asked Gil. He took her hand. "Honestly, Sandra, would you like to go back — now?"

"You *could* go back. Your father said so when he was here last spring."

Gil made an impatient gesture. "At the pleasure of the Compact. They've had a scare over the report that the Earl of Durham made. But what did that amount to? They won't act on it in England."

"But the Compact's still scared. Now's the time to — "

Gil shook his head. "Yes — they have pardoned a lot of people. A lot have never come to trial. Some that were actually at Montgomery's have been turned loose. But I'm suspicious. The Colonial Office told them to go easy. There's nothing written. Just a Compact promise and we know enough about them."

"But the pardons — " Sandra persisted.

"Verbal," said Gil. "Look here. When Head came up to Montgomery's, he had a sudden wave of magnanimity to his fool brain. He shouted to the men who had been captured that they were all pardoned, everyone pardoned, told them to go home. Then, of course, he changed, burned all Montgomery's houses, burned David Gibson's. Now Head's gone and the Compact's using that verbal amnesty that Head later canceled as a pretext for showing mercy. Suppose we apply — go back. In another month, Hagerman'll rule that a verbal pardon has no weight and begin making a lot more arrests — particularly those who've come back under it."

Sandra's eyes were wide. "They couldn't do that."

He laughed. "If you'll show me anything dirty that the Compact can't do — why, I heard they learned in advance that the Colonial Office was going to tell them to go easy. So what did they do? Set ahead the date of hanging for Lount and Matthews so they couldn't possibly be saved. It's just by luck that it didn't hit me and Montgomery and a lot more."

She caught his hand. "Sh, Gil! I don't even want to think about it. I — I guess you're right about staying."

"I think so. We might stay right here in Albany. Or we might go to New York. Dr. Slagle thinks he could get me an appointment at the New York Hospital. Or we might — " he sat up — "have you ever thought of this? We might go out into Michigan and join Uncle John and Flora and Graves. Graves wrote that things were booming out there." He suddenly snatched up the old black bag. "Speaking of booming — some collections came in today. And I had fees from both the state and the city." From the depths of the bag he pulled out a small canvas sack, an old wallet.

Sandra swung her chair close by his, drew up a little table. "Let's see! Oh, Gil! What a lot!" Her bright head bent close to his. Notes rustled and coins clinked under her slim fingers. At last she pushed back her chair, stared at the neat piles and stacks.

Gil smiled at her. "Now — how much do you need — for the house and yourself?"

She puckered up her mouth. "Oh — not much." She pushed a stack of bills aside. "I know I don't need this. It's fifty dollars."

He nodded. "That'll go to Uncle Schuyler," he announced with satisfaction. "Only two hundred left to go." He frowned. "I wish he'd charge interest. When we talked to him last year, we told him it was all business and no family."

"And he said he had no interest in his family." She gathered up the notes, thrust them into the black bag. "You can leave them at his office when you go by tomorrow."

They both looked up as hoofs clattered in the quiet, shaded street. Gil leaned over the rail. "It's Jos. Look at him. Shouting about something. He's — "

Josiah tumbled from the saddle, tossed his reins over the hitching post, ran up the steps waving a paper. "Sandra! Gil! I got a paper for you!"

Sandra laughed. "When did you turn newsboy, Jos? Give him tuppence, Gil."

Josiah waved the smeared sheet. "Look! Look! Don't sit there like zanies! Get up and yell!" He shook his fist at them, crumpled the paper. "I told you it would happen. Didn't I? Didn't I?" His arms waved. "How the devil can you sit there just gaping at me?" He pulled Sandra to her feet, threw an arm about her, slapped Gil on the back, dropped the paper, picked it up.

Sandra, laughing, fell back into her chair. "It's just the heat, isn't it, Gil? He'll be better soon?"

"I tell you I'm serious," shouted Josiah. "It's the Act of Union. It passed Parliament. Passed by a big majority. Passed in July and word's just in from London!"

Gil sprang up, tore the paper from Josiah's hands, opened it. Sandra slipped under his elbow and caught an edge. Gil muttered, "They did it. They did it." He and Sandra read on in silence. At last the paper fluttered to the floor. They sat down slowly, staring at the triumphant Josiah, who trumpeted: "Didn't I tell you? Didn't I tell you?"

"I—I can't quite take it in," stammered Gil.

"It's easy," said Josiah. "First—Upper and Lower Canada are joined. That's one thing you always wanted, isn't it? Second, you're to have full control of your own affairs. There's going to be a Council with all parties represented."

Gil nodded slowly. "That's something. It's—"

"It's the beginning," said Josiah. "Now it'll be up to you to see whether the Compact stays in or whether you chuck it into the lake. And you won't have to forge pikes up at Holland Landing to chuck it, either."

Sandra slipped her arm through Gil's. "We can go back."

Josiah's face fell suddenly. "Damn it! I hadn't thought of that." Then he brightened. "But you won't have to. In a year or so Gil'll have a nice house up on the hill and be head of all the hospitals and—"

"I agree," said Gil. "About staying here, I mean. Hagerman's still there. Strachan's still there. Look at this. The legislature at Toronto passed a bill breaking up the Clergy Reserves. Strachan went to England. He got the bill killed." He snorted with indignation. "It's the old story."

"But they aren't the whole Compact," said Sandra. "And they aren't all Upper Canada. They—"

Gil snatched up the paper again. "Look at this, then. Who went to England to fight the Act? Why, John Beverley Robinson. He got to the Duke of Wellington and told him that the rest of U.C. was just a lot of mutinous peasants. Didn't do him any good, though. The Act passed."

"Well, isn't that everything?" said Sandra.

"Not at all. Robinson'll be back. He'll join with the rest of 'em and in a year's time you'll never know the Act went through. It'll be forgotten and we'll go on living as we did in '35. Or rather—we won't, but people in U.C. will."

"Of course." Sandra nodded. "They'll do just that—if there aren't people to fight them. Gil, I think you belong there."

Josiah frowned. "Oh—look here, Sandra," he protested, "I know a swell house you can get up on the hill." He got up, shoved his hands into his pockets. Suddenly he turned on Gil. "Damn it, Sandra's right. You ought to go back. You can — and you've got something to go back to now. You'll have Baldwin, your father — my uncle, that is — all that lot. They've got something to fight with, now. And they've got something to keep, something that's been won. They've — "

Gil raised his hand. "I've been through all that. And what's the use?"

Sandra put her arm around Gil's neck. "There's another thing."

"What's that?" asked Gil, absently.

"Doc," she said. Josiah nodded energetically.

"Doc? What's he got to do with this? And didn't he always say that medicine and politics didn't mix? He'd say stay here."

She shook her head. "Gil — you're forgetting. Remember what he said about teaching? About people who had the gift and people who hadn't? Remember, that last night, he said over and over that you had to go back to Canada — carry on what he'd started. Gil — he wanted it so, wanted you to take up his work. He told me so often what you could do and what you could mean up there."

"I'm not Doc," said Gil.

Josiah waved his arms. "You're right — you're not. Doc'd be on his way there now, if he was around. He was only hanging around here until he knew that you were all right. And don't be so damned modest. One night — it was when we hadn't heard from you for a long time — he told me that you were twice the teacher that he was. He said you could do more in five years than he could in fifty. Then he called you a fool and told me he'd poison me with calomel if I ever told you what he said."

"He said more than that," said Sandra. "He used to talk about his patients. People in little farms out the Don or the Humber. People down by the waterfront. You had a way with them, he said. He used to worry about what would happen to them now." Then she smoothed down her skirts, smiled. "But of course, he died over a year ago. Probably his patients are all right now." She nodded to herself. "I put some flowers on his grave yesterday. I couldn't help hoping that somehow he'd know that all those people were being looked after — the way he'd want them looked after."

Gil raised his head slowly. "I'll go back."

Josiah whooped, slapped him on the back. "I knew we could batter him round if we went after him."

Sandra smiled. "I knew he was going, anyway. I knew he'd go, just the way I knew he'd go to Montgomery's."

Josiah eyed Gil. "Sure you won't change?"

Gil laughed. "Change be damned. I'll be in to see your father in the morning." He looked at Sandra. "I guess we'll want to start about as soon as we can, won't we?"

Josiah swung down off the porch. "Or sooner. I know you two. I'll ride home and tell Father. He'll want to know." He lunged into the saddle, headed his horse north. Suddenly he made the animal spin about, forced it up the short bank, its long head hanging inquiringly over the low railing where the orange kitten fluffed out its tail and spat. Josiah held out his hand. "Forgot the paper. Want to show it to Father."

Sandra picked it up. "Can't you just tell him about it?"

"He'll want to see for himself." He backed the horse away. Over his shoulder he called, "You see, I want him to convince me that we ought to open up again in Toronto. Had a letter from Ogle Ketchipaw, about things up there."

Gil sprang to his feet. "You'll be up there with us?"

Josiah checked his horse, which danced nervously in the soft road. "Think I'd let you go off without me? And I'm not going up there alone, either. Got to see about that right away." He waved his arm, galloped off, his coattails flying.

Sandra stared at Gil. "Not alone? Has Josiah got a girl?"

Gil slipped his arm about her. "I guess it's the Newberry girl—you know, that little red-headed spitfire who lives near Kinderhock."

Sandra settled back, a contented smile on her soft lips. "I knew you'd go, Gil. But if you'd wanted to stay, I wouldn't have said a word." Then she folded her hands with pleased anticipation. "The Newberry girl. Well, I'll take her to all the shops on King Street. I wonder if Parsons is still there. He had the nicest hats." She clasped her hands about a rounded knee. "Gil—'member the time when we were driving out to Nipigon, the day I made you propose to me? You talked about a little house on Bathurst Street near Dr. Richland's. Do you suppose we could still get it? I saw some stuff for curtains yesterday, and if we take that one, I'll know just how much to get, because I went and measured the windows one day—and oh, Gil, we're going home."

Gil smiled. "Two wanderers," he said gently.

XXXIV

Nipigon Lodge — 1840

Old Barnabas raised his glass. "Marriages. I like 'em. So does Thomas." He looked up at the black face that hovered behind his chair. "Don't we, Thomas?"

"Yes *sir!*" Thomas showed his teeth in a wide grin. Then his eyes turned, worshiping, to Gil and Sandra, who sat on either side of Barnabas.

Barnabas scowled down the table at Josiah, between Janet and Mary. "What's she like?"

Josiah grinned. "You'll see her tomorrow. I've promised Aunt Janet that I'll bring her right out here from the boat."

"Confound it, she better be pretty. Stensroods always marry pretty women." He turned to Sandra. "Is she pretty? No! Won't have a word from you, Josiah. In your state you'd swear a cockatoo was pretty."

Sandra, white shoulders rising from a cloud of lace, laughed. "*I* think she is."

"Damn it, she must be," snapped Barnabas. He looked about the table. "Well, here it is — my ninety-fifth. Haven't got all the people we had when Josiah came for my ninetieth, back in '35. Had a letter from John today. Had one from Flora and Graves." He sighed. "I'd have been glad to have had Kate come — but — " He tossed back his white mane. "As long as I live, no Sperry'll cross the threshold of Nipigon. They acted abominably. They're acting worse now, because they're scared."

Forsyth lifted tolerant eyebrows. "It may be they thought they were doing the right thing."

Barnabas spluttered. "The right thing! Confound it, do you call lodging complaints against Cam the right thing? Do you call getting their hands on John's lands the right thing?"

Cameron shrugged. "Uncle Sperry really thought I *was* working with Mackenzie." He smiled. "But then, he thought everyone who didn't fight for cards to a Government House levée was with Mac."

Janet spoke quietly. "I'll always be glad to see Kate — alone."

"I shan't," said Mary. "She cut me dead on King Street. And I'm sure it was Ruth who sent those men to search our house after Cam was released."

Forsyth shook his head. "I wish we didn't have to harbor grudges. We'll never get anywhere that way. Not that I don't feel about the Sperrys the way you do. I just wish I didn't."

"Wish you *didn't?*" said Gil. He shook his head. "Know one thing that Uncle Sperry did? He was on that Jail Commission. He'd come to a perfectly innocent man and tell him while *he* was sure he was innocent, he happened to know there was a lot of written evidence against him that would look very bad at a trial. That would scare the prisoner. Then Uncle Sperry'd suggest that if he signed a confession, he'd go free. He would — across the border — and Uncle Sperry'd bid in his property."

Sandra looked reproachfully across the table. "Gil, every time you talk about that you get red around the nose."

He laughed. "Sorry. But — well — I can't say I wish I didn't feel that way about 'em. I just wish they hadn't done it."

Forsyth nodded, then smiled at Sandra. "Just look at your father, my dear. He was against us, but he played fair. And now he admits that he was wrong. Did it handsomely, too."

"I wish he could have been here tonight," said Janet.

"He'll be out to call as soon as he's back from Montreal," said Sandra. She smiled happily. "I'm going to show him the house on Bathurst Street."

Barnabas patted her hand. "I wish I could tell you, my dear, how I feel when I hear you and Gil talking about your plans." He sighed. "It reminds me of the way Gil's grandmother and I used to talk, way back there in the Hudson Valley." He blew his nose, stared down at Josiah. "And now I suppose I've got to listen to you and that girl of yours babble when she gets here."

Josiah grinned. "You haven't heard anything yet. Wait till you listen to a Yankee girl's ideas."

Barnabas compressed his lips, then began to smile. "Sandra just whispered to me that she's red-headed. *You* won't have any planning to do. I tell you, you'll take refuge with — with — what's that confounded clerk's name? Ketchipaw." He chuckled. "Yes, sir. That's my advice to you. Stick close to Ketchipaw until the storm's over. She and I'll manage it. I'll tell her — " He caught Janet's eye, that was trying to signal to the women. He thumped on the floor with his stick. "Blast convention. I say confound it. I know dessert's been taken up, but you're all going to sit right here with us." His glance played along the table. "We've had too many lonely nights here at Nipigon, and I'm not going to be left alone with just these — these rattle-pated boys on my ninety-fifth. Janet, my dear, you'll humor me? You and the others? Good."

The fat decanters circled the table. Barnabas thumped again. "I'm not going to apologize. Ordinarily I should, but on my ninety-fifth, I'm a — a chartered libertine and — what are you smiling about, Sandra? Out with it."

"I was just thinking about the rest of the quotation — 'a chartered libertine is *still*.' "

Barnabas scowled. "Quotation be blasted. *I* shan't be still." He leaned forward, frail old hands on the white cloth. "I've been thinking — not that that's unusual — I often do. I've been thinking about the years we've just seen — the years that you've lived and that I've had to watch, confound it! We always start the port with a toast and I'm going to give it, though none of you young people can join me, because the toast is to all of you." He lifted his glass in a steady hand. "I'm drinking to the men and women who won the Rebellion of 1837."

There was a murmur of surprise about the table. Barnabas leaned back. "I say — who *won* the Rebellion. Maybe some history books will say the Compact won it. But they didn't. You did. Every soul in this room fought, each in his or her own way. Because you fought, you're winning rights that you knew you ought to have. And not a soul here took the easy way."

He turned to his son. "Fors, you and Cam have held to your convictions. I know what's been done to try to shake them. But you kept the boat steady. You were there as ballast when young hotheads like Gil began splashing water over the sides. Yes — hotheads — you and Josiah. Don't deny it, Jos, you were in it every bit as much as Gil." His face became suddenly grave. "I wish that Sam Lount, dead,

Mackenzie, in exile, could know that *in losing they won.* They did! So did you all. Because things mattered enough for you to fight and keep fighting, those fools in England finally realized that something was wrong." He studied the faces along the table. "It makes me proud of you—every one of you." He nodded, set down his glass.

Gil looked across at Sandra, then said, "Aren't you forgetting one? Or, rather, two?"

"Forget?" said Barnabas. "I don't forget."

"Well," said Gil, "it seems to me that we've just been carrying on, as well as we could, the work of the two men I'm going to drink to now. And you can drink to one of them. Yourself and Great-grandfather Gilbert."

"I'll add another," said Barnabas quickly. "And that's my brother Josiah. Just like his confounded grandson."

"And I'll add something else," said Josiah. "You haven't spoken of Aunt Janet or Mary or Sandra." His eyes grew grave. "If you could have seen Sandra on Navy Island—her hair cut short—wearing a pair of—"

"Jos! Please," cried Sandra.

"I know all about that too," said Barnabas. "And I'll tell you this. A man may think he does this or does that. But it's been my experience that if what he does is any good, he's only done half of it. We've all stuck to hard roads. And never have any of our wives tried to change us from those roads. No! They said: 'If you feel you're right, go ahead. The cost doesn't count.' Janet, your lot in Toronto would have been a lot easier if Fors had stayed on the bench. But I know what a row you kicked up when you thought he was staying on for your sake. The same goes for Mary. It goes for Flora." He paused, looked affectionately at Sandra. "And you took the hardest road of all. I—I—when I heard that you'd run away to join Gil, I said: 'She's mad. She's a fluttery little fool, galloping off like that.' And I said to myself, 'By George, I'm proud to have a grandson that's got a girl with that spirit.'" He sighed. "Well, you've won. You haven't won all you were after. But you've got a grip on it. You'll keep it."

Gil shook his head dubiously. "The Compact's still strong."

His father smiled. "When you've been back here a little longer, I think you'll see how they're losing strength. It's going to be a long fight, but they're on the defensive. They've been so ever since the Earl of Durham sent in his report."

"And where did he get those ideas?" cried Cameron. "A lot of them from the letters that Rob Baldwin wrote to the Colonial Office in Head's time. Durham read them on the trip out. And who helped write those letters?" He gestured toward his father.

Josiah laughed. "And maybe some day you'll celebrate the Seventh of December the way we celebrate the Fourth of July at home."

"Gil and I will, anyway, if no one else does," said Sandra. She looked across at her husband. "But you'll have to look more cheerful than that if you're going to make anyone believe in your celebrating."

Gil looked up, startled. "Sorry — I was thinking."

Barnabas snorted. "Knew you could, if you ever put your mind to it."

"All right," said Gil. "Laugh if you like. But here's what I was thinking. We heard a lot about the American Revolution when we were with Mac. We heard more about it, living in Albany."

"Remarkable," said Barnabas. "It seems to me that I've heard of it, too."

"I shouldn't be surprised," said Gil blandly. "As I say, I heard a lot about it. And I thought a lot about it. And I came to this conclusion — that there was no such thing as the American Revolution."

Josiah stared. Barnabas shouted, "Idiotic nonsense. Your mind must be turning."

Gil shook his head. "I still say — there was no such thing — as the American Revolution. There was an uprising there — free men rising in defense of their rights. It *happened* to result in political separation. But what was it?"

"I can tell you that," snapped Barnabas. "It was a damned, pinched, bloody uncomfortable time. That's what it was."

"I don't mean that," said Gil. "At bottom, it was a lot of men, bred up in the idea of what a Briton's rights are, fighting when they were denied those rights."

Forsyth nodded slowly. "Something in that," he said.

"Wait a minute," said Gil. "I'm not through yet. There's nothing unique about it. It's a process that goes back to Runnymede. It may go even farther than that. I don't know. But it runs through all history. It was the same urge that set the Colonies against the Crown. *After* that came separation. Isn't that so, Grandfather?"

"Confoundedly right," said Barnabas.

Cameron nodded. "Just a sort of chain — "

"And we're links in it," said Sandra.

Barnabas twirled his glass in his fragile hands. "I think it's got something to do with an Englishman's liver. Take a Frenchman — he'll submit to things an Englishman'll fight. Not through lack of courage on the Frenchman's part. But a sort of lack of the cantankerousness that belongs to all — well — call 'em what you like — British — Anglo-Saxon — it doesn't matter. But get enough of 'em together under the wrong conditions and you get a revolution."

Janet said: "Father used to worry when Simcoe talked about an aristocracy here, he told me. He said the people wouldn't have it."

"And he was right," said Barnabas. "You see, what you call democracy is a sort of benign disease. Once you let it in, the disease has to run its course. And it's always with you."

He looked down the table again, met Janet's eyes, which filled with happiness. He thought: "The night is always bright to the wanderer — the *free* wanderer. Gil and Sandra — Forsyth and Janet — Cameron and Mary — " He smiled to himself. It was the same old stock. The old, free stock.

Suddenly the heavy fatigue that had been troubling him lately slipped away, as though his own old blood had been freshened by the stirring life about him. He chuckled. "I'm beginning to feel mighty sorry for those Compact fools." He sipped, nodded, chuckled again. "And *I'm* going to watch the next twenty-five or fifty years with a great deal of pleasure." He turned to his right. "Sandra, my dear, if you'll give me your arm, we'll all move along, and I'll start watching them now from my chair by the fire."

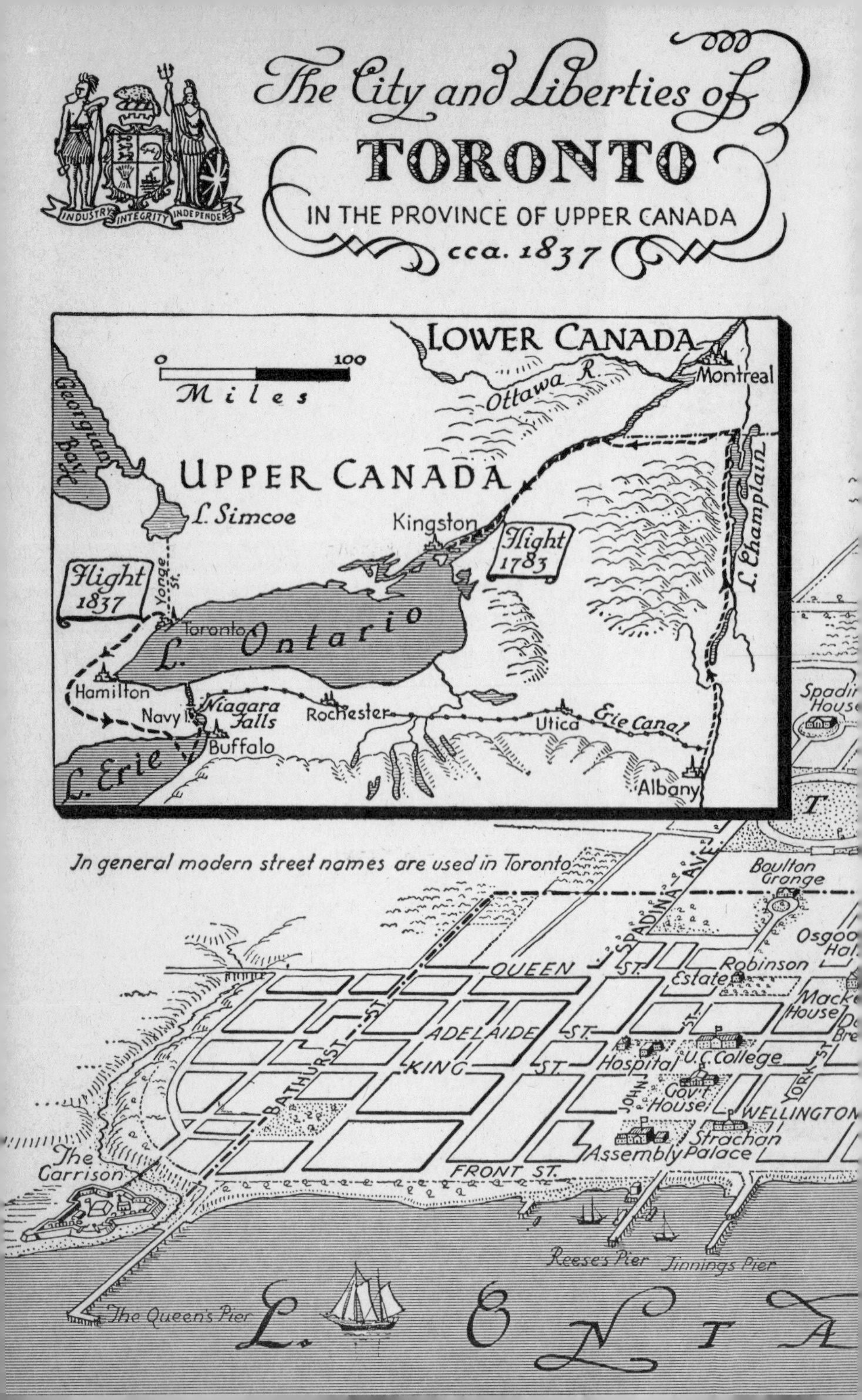
The City and Liberties of
TORONTO
IN THE PROVINCE OF UPPER CANADA
cca. 1837
INDUSTRY INTEGRITY INDEPENDENCE
LOWER CANADA
0 100
Miles
Montreal
Ottawa R.
Georgian Bay
UPPER CANADA
L. Simcoe
Kingston
Flight 1783
L. Champlain
Flight 1837
Yonge St.
Toronto
L. Ontario
Hamilton
Navy I.
Niagara Falls
Rochester
Utica
Erie Canal
Buffalo
L. Erie
Albany
In general modern street names are used in Toronto
Boulton Grange
SPADINA AVE.
QUEEN ST.
Robinson Estate
ADELAIDE ST.
KING ST.
BATHURST ST.
Hospital
U.C. College
JOHN
Gov't House
WELLINGTON
YORK ST.
Assembly
Strachan Palace
FRONT ST.
The Garrison
Reese's Pier
Jinnings Pier
The Queen's Pier
L. ONTA